# PRAISE FOR M. L. BUCHMAN

Buchman has catapulted his way to the top tier of my favorite authors.

— FRESH FICTION

One of our favorite authors.

— RT BOOK REVIEWS

Buchman has catapulted his way to the top tier of my favorite authors.

— FRESH FICTION

A favorite author of mine. I'll read anything that carries his name, no questions asked. Meet your new favorite author!

— THE SASSY BOOKSTER, FLASH OF FIRE

M.L. Buchman is guaranteed to get me lost in a good story.

— THE READING CAFE, WAY OF THE WARRIOR: NSDQ

I love Buchman's writing. His vivid descriptions bring everything to life in an unforgettable way.

— PURE JONEL, HOT POINT

Nonstop action that will keep readers on the edge of their seats.

— TAKE OVER AT MIDNIGHT, LIBRARY JOURNAL

M L. Buchman's ability to keep the reader right in the middle of the action is amazing.

— LONG AND SHORT REVIEWS

The only thing you'll ask yourself is, "When does the next one come out?"

— WAIT UNTIL MIDNIGHT, RT REVIEWS, 4 STARS

The first...of (a) stellar, long-running (military) romantic suspense series.

— THE NIGHT IS MINE, BOOKLIST, "THE 20 BEST<br>ROMANTIC SUSPENSE NOVELS: MODERN<br>MASTERPIECES"

I knew the books would be good, but I didn't realize how good.

— NIGHT STALKERS SERIES, KIRKUS REVIEWS

Buchman mixes adrenalin-spiking battles and brusque military jargon with a sensitive approach.

— PUBLISHERS WEEKLY

13 times "Top Pick of the Month"

— NIGHT OWL REVIEWS

Tom Clancy fans open to a strong female lead will clamor for more.

— DRONE, PUBLISHERS WEEKLY

(Miranda Chase is) one of the most compelling, addicting, fascinating characters in any genre since the *Monk* television series.

— DRONE, ERNEST DEMPSEY, AUTHOR OF THE SEAN WYATT THRILLERS

(*Drone* is) the best military thriller I've read in a very long time. Love the female characters.

— SHELDON MCARTHUR, FOUNDER OF THE MYSTERY BOOKSTORE, LA

Superb!

— DRONE, BOOKLIST, STARRED REVIEW

A fabulous soaring thriller.

— *TAKE OVER AT MIDNIGHT,* MIDWEST BOOK REVIEW

Meticulously researched, hard-hitting, and suspenseful.

— *PURE HEAT,* PUBLISHERS WEEKLY, STARRED REVIEW

Expert technical details abound, as do realistic military missions with superb imagery that will have readers feeling as if they are right there in the midst and on the edges of their seats.

# THE COMPLETE NIGHT STALKERS 5E

## A MILITARY ROMANTIC SUSPENSE COLLECTION

## M. L. BUCHMAN

# Other works by M. L. Buchman: *(* - also in audio)*

## Thrillers

### Dead Chef
*One Chef!*
*Two Chef!*

### Miranda Chase
*Drone**
*Thunderbolt**
*Condor**
*Ghostrider**

## Romantic Suspense

### Delta Force
*Target Engaged**
*Heart Strike**
*Wild Justice**
*Midnight Trust**

### Firehawks
**MAIN FLIGHT**
*Pure Heat*
*Full Blaze*
*Hot Point**
*Flash of Fire**
*Wild Fire*

**SMOKEJUMPERS**
*Wildfire at Dawn**
*Wildfire at Larch Creek**
*Wildfire on the Skagit**

### The Night Stalkers
**MAIN FLIGHT**
*The Night Is Mine*
*I Own the Dawn*
*Wait Until Dark*
*Take Over at Midnight*
*Light Up the Night*
*Bring On the Dusk*
*By Break of Day*

**AND THE NAVY**
*Christmas at Steel Beach*
*Christmas at Peleliu Cove*
**WHITE HOUSE HOLIDAY**
*Daniel's Christmas**
*Frank's Independence Day**
*Peter's Christmas**
*Zachary's Christmas**
*Roy's Independence Day**
*Damien's Christmas**
5E
*Target of the Heart*
*Target Lock on Love*
*Target of Mine*
*Target of One's Own*

### Shadow Force: Psi
*At the Slightest Sound**
*At the Quietest Word**

### White House Protection Force
*Off the Leash**
*On Your Mark**
*In the Weeds**

## Contemporary Romance

### Eagle Cove
*Return to Eagle Cove*
*Recipe for Eagle Cove*
*Longing for Eagle Cove*
*Keepsake for Eagle Cove*

### Henderson's Ranch
*Nathan's Big Sky**
*Big Sky, Loyal Heart**
*Big Sky Dog Whisperer**

### Love Abroad
*Heart of the Cotswolds: England*
*Path of Love: Cinque Terre, Italy*

# Other works by M. L. Buchman:

### Contemporary Romance (cont)

**Where Dreams**
*Where Dreams are Born*
*Where Dreams Reside*
*Where Dreams Are of Christmas*
*Where Dreams Unfold*
*Where Dreams Are Written*

### Science Fiction / Fantasy

**Deities Anonymous**
*Cookbook from Hell: Reheated*
*Saviors 101*

**Single Titles**
*The Nara Reaction*
*Monk's Maze*
*the Me and Elsie Chronicles*

### Non-Fiction

**Strategies for Success**
*Managing Your Inner Artist/Writer*
*Estate Planning for Authors*
*Character Voice*

# Short Story Series by M. L. Buchman:

### Romantic Suspense

**Delta Force**
*Delta Force*

**Firehawks**
*The Firehawks Lookouts*
*The Firehawks Hotshots*
*The Firebirds*

**The Night Stalkers**
*The Night Stalkers*
*The Night Stalkers 5E*
*The Night Stalkers CSAR*
*The Night Stalkers Wedding Stories*

**US Coast Guard**
*US Coast Guard*

**White House Protection Force**
*White House Protection Force*

### Contemporary Romance

**Eagle Cove**
*Eagle Cove*

**Henderson's Ranch**
*Henderson's Ranch*

**Where Dreams**
*Where Dreams*

### Thrillers

**Dead Chef**
*Dead Chef*

### Science Fiction / Fantasy

**Deities Anonymous**
*Deities Anonymous*

**Other**
*The Future Night Stalkers*
*Single Titles*

# CONTENTS


*About This Series*     xiii

Target of the Heart     1
Target Lock on Love     175
Target of Mine     371
Target of One's Own     611
Enjoyed this? You'll love the Night Stalkers and the Navy!     882
Christmas at Steel Beach (excerpt)     883

*About the Author*     889
*Titles Exclusively Available at Buchman Bookworks Emporium*     891
*Also by M. L. Buchman*     893

# ABOUT THIS SERIES

*First there was the 160th Night Stalkers 5th Battalion D Company.*

*Then they formed the 5E. The few who knew about them called them "E for Extreme." Equipped with stealth helicopters, they take on only the most dangerous of Black Ops missions.*

*Small, lean, paired with an equally elite squad from SEAL Team 6, their careers send them into dangers of both the body and the heart.*

***Target of the Heart** launches the team...and sends them into China in the dead of night.*

***Target Lock on Love** throws two pilots into the fray when a secret Russian drone factory threatens the future of international military balance.*

***Target of Mine** puts the team directly in the sights when they must abandon their helos and plunge into the lethal Honduran jungle to take down a conspiracy.*

***Target of One's Own** drops a feisty drone pilot into an elite race car as she and the SEAL team's leader go after an arms smuggler hiding in the ultimate driving event, the Dakar Rally.*

*Turn the page to discover the laughter, tears, and love as adventure flies their way.*

# TARGET OF THE HEART

**MISSION:** *China's newest Coast Guard ship is a monster that threatens to change the balance of power in the West Pacific. Now the only ones who can stop them are the Night Stalkers' newest company—the 5E—when they unite with SEAL Team 6.*

*TEAM:*

**Captain Danielle Delacroix**

*— Strives to build a team stronger than any single pilot.*

**Major Pete Napier**

*— Flies for one goal: to be better than everyone else.*

*Launching a new Special Operations helicopter company may be the hardest assignment a commander could draw. Forming it with a bunch of rookie helo pilots then slamming them into a Black Ops crisis mission infiltrating China—well that's just uncalled for.*

*And what is Pete to do with the soft-spoken woman who can outfly him on his best day? Maybe China isn't his biggest challenge.*

CHAPTER 1

ajor Pete Napier hovered his MH-47G Chinook helicopter ten kilometers outside of Lhasa, Tibet and a mere two inches off the tundra. A mixed action team of Delta Force and The Activity—the slipperiest intel group on the planet—flung themselves aboard.

The additional load sent an infinitesimal shift in the cyclic control in his right hand. The hydraulics to close the rear loading ramp hummed through the entire frame of the massive helicopter. By the time his crew chief could reach forward to slap an "all secure" signal against his shoulder, they were already ten feet up and fifty out. That was enough altitude. He kept the nose down as he clawed for speed in the thin air at eleven thousand feet.

"Totally worth it," one of the D-boys announced as soon as he was on the Chinook's internal intercom.

He'd have to remember to tell that to the two Black Hawks flying guard for him...when they were in a friendly country and could risk a radio transmission. This deep inside China—or rather Chinese-held territory as the CIA's mission-briefing spook had insisted on calling it —radios attracted attention and were only used to avoid imminent death and destruction.

"Great, now I just need to get us out of this alive."

"Do that, Pete. We'd appreciate it."

He wished to hell he had a stealth bird like the one that had gone into bin Laden's compound. But the one that had crashed during that raid had been blown up. Where there was one, there were always two, but the second had gone back into hiding as thoroughly as if it had never existed. He hadn't heard a word about it since.

The Tibetan terrain was amazing, even if all he could see of it was the monochromatic green of night vision. And blackness. The largest city in Tibet lay a mere ten kilometers away and they were flying over barren wilderness. He could crash out here and no one would know for decades unless some yak herder stumbled upon them. Or were yaks in Mongolia? He was a corn-fed, white boy from Colorado, what did he know about Tibet? Most of the countries he'd flown into on Black Ops missions he'd only seen at night anyway.

While moving very, very fast.

Like now.

The inside of his visor was painted with overlapping readouts. A pre-defined terrain map, the best that modern satellite imaging could build made the first layer. This wasn't some crappy, on-line, look-at-a-picture-of-your-house display. Someone had a pile of dung outside their goat pen? He could see it, tell you how high it was, and probably say if they were pygmy goats or full-size LaManchas by the size of their shit-pellets if he zoomed in.

On top of that were projected the forward-looking infrared camera images. The FLIR imaging gave him a real-time overlay, in case someone had put an addition onto their goat shed since the last satellite pass or parked their tractor across his intended flight path.

His nervous system was paying autonomic attention to that combined landscape. He also compensated for the thin air at altitude as he instinctively chose when to start his climb over said goat shed or his swerve around it.

It was the third layer, the tactical display that had most of his attention. At least he and the two Black Hawks flying escort on him were finally on the move.

To insert this deep into Tibet, without passing over Bhutan or Nepal, they'd had to add wingtanks on the Black Hawks' hardpoints where he'd much rather have a couple banks of Hellfire missiles. Still, they had 20 mm chain guns and the crew chiefs had miniguns which was some comfort. His twin-rotor Chinook might be the biggest helicopter that the Night Stalkers flew, but it was the cargo van of Special Operations and only had two miniguns and a machine gun of its own. Though he'd put his three crew chiefs up against the best Black Hawk shooter any day.

While the action team was busy infiltrating the capital city and gathering intelligence on the particularly brutal Chinese assistant administrator, Pete and his crews had been squatting out in the wilderness under a camouflage net designed to make his helo look like just another god-forsaken Himalayan lump of granite.

Command had determined that it was better for the helos to wait on site through the day than risk flying out and back in. He and his crew had stood shifts on guard duty, but none of them had slept. They'd been flying together too long to have any new jokes, so they'd played a lot of cribbage. He'd long ago ruled no gambling on a mission, after a fistfight had broken out about a bluff hand that cost a Marine three hundred and forty-seven dollars. Marines hated losing to Army no matter how many times it happened. They'd had to sit on him for a long time before he calmed down.

Tonight's mission was part of an on-going campaign to discredit the Chinese "presence" in Tibet on the international stage—as if occupying the country the last sixty-plus years didn't count toward ruling, whether invited or not. As usual, there was a crucial vote coming up at the U.N.—that, as usual, the Chinese could be guaranteed to ignore. However, the ever-hopeful CIA was in a hurry to make sure that any damaging information that they could validate was disseminated as thoroughly as possible prior to the vote.

Not his concern.

His concern was, were they going to pass over some Chinese sentry post at their top speed of a hundred and ninety-six miles an hour? The sentries would then call down a couple Shenyang J-16 jet fighters that could hustle along at Mach 2—over fifteen *hundred* mph —to fry his sorry ass. He knew there was a pair of them parked at Lhasa along with some older gear that would be just as effective against his three helos.

"Don't suppose you could get a move on, Pete?"

"Eat shit, Nicolai!" He was a good man to have as a copilot. Pete knew he was holding on too tight, and Nicolai knew that a joke was the right way to ease the moment.

He, Nicolai, and the four pilots in the two Black Hawks had a long way to go tonight and he'd never make it if he stayed so tight on the controls that he could barely maneuver. Pete eased off and felt his fingers tingle with the rush of returning blood. They dove down into gorges and followed them as long as they dared. They hugged cliff walls at every opportunity to decrease their radar profile. And they climbed.

That was the true danger—they would be up near the helos' limits when they crossed over the backbone of the Himalayas in their rush for India. The air was so rarefied that they burned fuel at a prodigious rate. Their reserve didn't allow for any extended battles while crossing the border…not for any battle at all really.

---

It was pitch dark outside her helicopter when Captain Danielle Delacroix stamped on the left rudder pedal while giving the big Chinook right-directed control on the cyclic. It tipped her most of the way onto her side but let her continue in a straight line. A Chinook's rotors were sixty feet across—front to back they overlapped to make the spread a hundred feet long. By cross-controlling her bird to tip it, she managed to execute a straight line between two mock pylons only thirty feet apart. They were made of thin cloth so they wouldn't down the helo if you sliced one—she was the only trainee to not have cut one yet.

At her current angle of attack, she took up less than a half-rotor of width, just twenty-four feet. That left her nearly three feet to either side, sufficient as she was moving at under a hundred knots.

The training instructor sitting beside her in the copilot's seat didn't react as she swooped through the training course at Fort Campbell, Kentucky. Only child of a single mother, she was used to providing her own feedback loops, so she didn't expect anything else. Those who expected outside validation rarely survived the SOAR induction testing, never mind the two years of training that followed.

As a loner kid, Danielle had learned that self-motivated congratulations and fun were much easier to come by than external ones. She'd spent innumerable hours deep in her mind as a pre-teen super-heroine. At twenty-nine she was well on her way to becoming a real life one, though Helo-girl had never been a character she'd thought of in her youth.

External validation or not, after two years of training with the U.S. Army's 160th Special Operations Aviation Regiment she was ready for some action. At least *she* was convinced that she was. But the trainers of Fort Campbell, Kentucky had not signed off on anyone in her trainee class yet. Nor had they given any hint of when they might.

She ducked ten tons of racing Chinook under a bridge and bounced into a near vertical climb to clear the power line on the far side. Like a ride on the toboggan at Terrassee Dufferin during *Le Carnaval de Québec,* only with ten thousand horsepower at her fingertips. Using her Army signing bonus—the first money in her life that was truly hers— to attend *Le Carnaval* had been her one trip back to her birthplace since her mother took them to America when she was ten.

To even apply to SOAR required five years of prior military rotor-craft experience. She had applied after seven years because of a chance encounter—or rather what she'd thought was a chance encounter at the time.

Captain Justin Roberts had been a top Chinook pilot, the one who had convinced her to switch from her beloved Black Hawk and try out the massive twin-rotor craft. One flight and she'd been a goner, begging her commander until he gave in and let her cross over to the new platform. Justin had made the jump from the 10th Mountain Division to the 160th SOAR not long after that.

Then one night she'd been having pizza in Watertown, New York a couple miles off the 10th's base at Fort Drum.

"Danielle?" Justin had greeted her with the surprise of finding a good friend in an unexpected place. Danielle had always liked Justin—even if he was a too-tall, too-handsome cowboy and completely knew it. But "good friend" was unusual for Danielle, with anyone, and Justin came close.

"Captain Roberts," as a dry greeting over the top edge of her Suzanne Brockmann novel didn't faze him in the slightest.

"Mind if I join ya?" A question he then answered for himself by sliding into the opposite seat and taking a slice of her pizza. She been thinking of taking the leftovers back to base, but that was now an idle thought.

"Are you enjoying life in SOAR?" she did her best to appear a normal, social human, a skill she'd learned by rote. *Greeting someone you knew after a time apart? Ask a question about them.* "They treating you well?"

"Whoo-ee, you have no idea, Danielle," his voice was smooth as... well, always...so she wouldn't think about it also sounding like a pickup line. He was beautiful but didn't interest her; the outgoing ones never did.

"Tell me." *Men love to talk about themselves, so let them.*

And he did. But she'd soon forgotten about her novel and would have forgotten the pizza if he hadn't reminded her to eat.

His stories shifted from intriguing to fascinating. There was a world out there that she'd been only peripherally aware of. The Night Stalkers of the 160th SOAR weren't simply better helicopter pilots, they were the most highly-trained and best-equipped ones anywhere. Their missions were pure razor's edge and Black Op dark.

He'd left her with a hundred questions and enough interest to fill out an application to the 160th Special Operations Aviation Regiment (airborne). Being a decent guy, Justin even paid for the pizza after eating half.

The speed at which she was rushed into testing told her that her meeting with Justin hadn't been by chance and that she owed him more than half a pizza next time they met. She'd asked after him a couple of times since she'd made it past the qualification exams—and the examiners' brutal interviews that had left her questioning her sanity, never mind her ability.

"Justin Roberts is presently deployed, ma'am," was the only response she'd ever gotten.

Now that she was through training—almost, had to be soon, didn't it?—Danielle realized that was probably less of an evasion and more likely to do with the brutal op tempo the Night Stalkers maintained. The SOAR 1st Battalion had just won the coveted Lt. General Ellis D. Parker awards for Outstanding Combat Aviation Battalion *and* Aviation Battalion of the Year. They'd been on deployment every single day of the last year, actually of the last decade-plus since 9/11.

The very first Special Forces boots on the ground in Afghanistan were delivered that October by the Night Stalkers and nothing had slacked off since. Justin might be in the 5th battalion D company, but they were just as heavily assigned as the 1st.

Part of the recruits' training had included tours in Afghanistan. But unlike their prior deployments, these were brief, intense, and then they'd be back in the States pushing to integrate their new skills.

SOAR needed her training to end and so did she.

Danielle was ready for the job, in her own, inestimable opinion. But she wasn't going to get there until the trainers signed off that she'd reached fully mission-qualified proficiency. FMQ was the gold star of the Night Stalkers pipeline.

The Fort Campbell training course was never set up the same from one flight to the next, but it always had a time limit. The time would be short and they didn't tell you what it was. So she drove the Chinook for all it was worth like Regina Jaquess waterskiing her way to U.S. Ski Team Female Athlete of the Year.

The Night Stalkers were a damned secretive lot, and after two years of training, she understood why. With seven years flying for the 10th, she'd thought she was good.

She'd been repeatedly lauded as one of the top pilots at Fort Drum.

The Night Stalkers had offered an education in what it really meant to fly. In the two years of training, she'd flown more hours than in the seven years prior, despite two deployments to Iraq. And spent more time in the classroom than her life-to-date accumulated flight hours.

But she was ready now. It was *très viscérale,* right down in her bones she could feel it. The Chinook was as much a part of her nervous system as breathing.

Too bad they didn't build men the way they built the big Chinooks —especially the MH-47G which were built specifically to SOAR's requirements. The aircraft were steady, trustworthy, and the most immensely powerful helicopters deployed in the U.S. Army—what more could a girl ask for? But finding a superhero man to go with her superhero helicopter was just a fantasy for a lonely girl who'd once had dreams of more.

She dove down into a canyon and slid to a hover mere inches over the reservoir inside the thirty-second window laid out on the flight plan.

Danielle resisted a sigh. She was ready for something to happen and to happen soon.

PETE'S CHINOOK and his two escort Black Hawks crossed into the mountainous province of Sikkim, India ten feet over the glaciers and still moving fast. It was an hour before dawn, they'd made it out of China while it was still dark.

"Thirty minutes of fuel remaining," Nicolai said it like a personal challenge when they hit the border.

"Thanks, I never would have noticed."

It had been a nail-biting tradeoff: the more fuel he burned, the more easily he climbed due to the lighter load. The more he climbed, the faster he burned what little fuel remained.

Safe in Indian airspace he climbed hard as Nicolai counted down the minutes remaining, burning fuel even faster than he had been while crossing the mountains of southern Tibet. They caught up with the U.S. Air Force HC-130P Combat King refueling tanker with only ten minutes of fuel left.

"Ram that bitch," Nicolai called out.

Pete extended the refueling probe which reached only a few feet beyond the forward edge of the rotor blade and drove at the basket trailing behind the tanker on its long hose.

He nailed it on the first try despite the fluky winds. Striking the valve in the basket with over four hundred pounds of pressure, a clamp snapped over the refueling probe and Jet A fuel shot into his tanks.

His helo had the least fuel due to having the most men aboard, so he was first in line. His Number Two picked up the second refueling basket trailing off the other wing of the Combat King. Thirty seconds and three hundred gallons later and he was breathing much more easily.

"Ah," Nicolai sighed. "It is better than the sex," his thick Russian accent only ever surfaced in this moment or in a bar while picking up women.

"Hey, Nicolai," Nicky the Greek called over the intercom from his crew chief position seated behind Pete. "Do you make love in Russian?"

A question Pete had always been careful to avoid.

"For you, I make special exception." That got a laugh over the system.

Which explained why Pete always kept his mouth shut at this moment.

"The ladies, Nicolai? What about the ladies?" Alfie the portside gunner asked.

"Ah," he sighed happily as he signaled that the other helos had finished their refueling and formed up to either side, "the ladies love the Russian. They don't need to know I grew up in Maryland and I learn my great-great-grandfather's native tongue at the University called Virginia."

He sounded so pleased that Pete wished he'd done the same rather than study Japanese and Mandarin.

Another two hours of—Thank God—straight-and-level flight at altitude through the breaking dawn and they landed on the aircraft carrier awaiting them in the Bay of Bengal. India had agreed to turn a blind eye as long as the Americans never actually touched their soil.

Once standing on the deck—and the worst of the kinks had been worked out—he pulled his team together: six pilots and seven crew chiefs.

"Honor to serve!" He saluted them sharply.

"Hell yeah!" They shouted in unison and saluted in turn. It was their version of spiking the football in the end zone.

A petty officer in a bright green vest appeared at his elbow, "Follow me please, sir." He pointed toward the Navy-gray command structure that towered above the carrier's deck. The rear admiral of the entire carrier strike group was waiting for him just outside the entrance. Not a good idea to keep a one-star waiting, so he waved at the team.

"See you in the mess for dinner," he shouted to the crew over the noise of an F-18 Hornet fighter jet trapping on the #2 wire. After two days of surviving on MREs while squatting on the Tibetan tundra, he was ready for a steak, a burger, a mountain of pasta, whatever. Or maybe all three.

The green escorted him across the hazards of the busy flight deck. Pete had kept his helmet on to buffer the noise, but even at that he winced as another Hornet fired up and was flung aloft by the catapult.

"Orders, Major Napier," the Rear Admiral handed him a folded sheet the moment he arrived. "Hate to lose you." He saluted, which Pete automatically returned before looking down at the sheet of paper in his hands. The man was gone before the import of Pete's orders slammed in.

A different green-clad deckhand showed up with Pete's duffle bag and began guiding him toward a loading C-2 Greyhound twin-prop airplane. It was parked Number Two for the launch catapult, close behind the raised jet-blast deflector.

His crew, being led across in the opposite direction to return to the berthing decks below, looked at him aghast.

"Stateside," was all he managed to gasp out as they passed.

A stream of foul cursing followed him from behind. Their crew was tight. Why the hell was Command breaking it up?

And what in the name of fuck-all had he done to deserve this?

He glanced at the orders again as he stumbled up the Greyhound's rear ramp and crash landed into a seat.

Training rookies?

It was worse than a demotion.

This was punishment.

By the time the C-130 transport jet he'd hitched a ride in across the country smacked down at Fort Campbell, Kentucky, Major Pete Napier still didn't know what to make of his orders. Command had clearly lost their marbles. And sending him out looking for them was just pissing him off—especially after a straight-through from the carrier to the Philippines and on around.

But, when the orders had pulled him off of forward deployment and sent him Stateside to test trainees, it had probably been a good career move *not* to call the Rear Admiral who delivered the orders an ignorant ass. Navy one-stars didn't take any more kindly to such things than Army Brigadier Generals—no matter how richly the epithet might be deserved in both cases.

He hit the main desk at Fort Campbell with a severe dose of jet leg and a lethal dose of foul mood.

The desk orderly gave him a room key for the transient quarters in the Richardson Complex, informing him that it was for a maximum three-day occupancy so alternate arrangements should be made rapidly. As if base transient quarters were such a luxury. He managed not to execute the man on the spot, mostly because his sidearm was stowed in his duffle.

Pete didn't plan on being here longer than it took to track down his commander and talk his way back up to forward deployment. The trick was to do it without earning a court-martial for punching out a superior officer.

The guard also gave him a pass for the gate to the Night Stalkers compound and instructions to report immediately upon arrival to Colonel Cassius McDermott, the commander of the entire U.S. Army 160th Special Operations Aviation Regiment. Perfect. Exactly the man he needed to tackle.

Pete found a corporal to give him a lift, but was dumped unceremoniously outside the 160th's front gate with his gear. "Sorry, sir. I'm not authorized inside the compound."

The midday heat had baked into the pavement and was re-radiating with a vengeance as evening threatened to exceed a hundred-percent humidity even if it had to make up numbers to do it.

His body and his clothes were still oriented for the summer chill of Tibet and the not much warmer temperature of Air Force transports at altitude. He'd only been so much cargo to them: pressurized air was provided begrudgingly, heat barely crossed sub-Arctic.

Pete thought wistfully of flying over the cool Himalayas as he slung on his pack and trudged through the heat, the blazing idiocy of security, and the long dusty stretch to the Colonel's on-base office—a bolthole for when he wasn't at the Pentagon doing whatever useless crap they performed there.

At least when Pete reported he was ushered straight into "the presence."

Colonel Cassius McDermott answered his salute with, "Pete, sit your sorry ass down. You look whipped, boy." He would have remained standing, but his legs didn't think that was really advisable at the moment and he collapsed into a chair.

"What the hell am I doing mingling with the recruits, Cass? And what's a One-Star doing messing with Night Stalker assignments?"

Cass McDermott had always been there for him: when Pete was a fresh-faced idiot Army National Guard pilot, when climbing the career ladder, even through an ugly marriage that led to an uglier divorce—all of it.

McDermott's field office was so plain that it might have belonged to a clerk, except for the photos of the Colonel shaking hands with each of the last three Presidents. The three photos and the American flag were the only relief to the colorlessness of the room; beige and khaki.

Cass leaned back in his chair and studied Pete through narrowed eyes like he was looking at a bug. Friend or not, the Colonel was like that. He wasn't just the commander of SOAR, he *was* SOAR. The man had flown every ugly mission there was for thirty years. But he didn't flaunt it. The only evidence of who this man really was appeared in the ever-expanding array of medals in the three progressive photos.

Rumor was they'd tried to promote him to JSOC half a dozen times and he'd refused. Well, Joint Special Operations Command's loss was definitely SOAR's gain. Pete respected few people beyond the cockpit, but McDermott was one of them.

"The Rear Admiral was handy. They're actually my orders, but I figured I needed a bit of rank to deliver them so that you didn't spit in the messenger's face."

"Thought about doing more than spitting, but he'd already ducked and run."

"You don't rise to command an entire aircraft carrier strike group by being stupid."

Pete grimaced. He knew his reputation was bad, but *that bad?* He preferred being in the field, that was all. That and he didn't suffer fools lightly—a skill that a good trainer needed and he totally lacked.

McDermott looked at his watch and then back at Pete.

Pete had a sudden bad feeling about what was going to happen next, but the look on McDermott's face shifted as if he'd thought better of something.

"Tell you what. You go look the crew over and then we'll talk. I even provided you with a pair of ringers."

Pete waited, but the colonel wasn't doing any explaining. Instead he rose to his feet, forcing Pete to struggle to his own.

"Here are the night's orders," McDermott handed over a single sheet of paper. He didn't give Pete time to look at them, instead offering a sharp salute. "I'll see you in eight hours. Dismissed."

Once in the outer office, Pete looked at the sheet. It would have been cryptography to anyone other than a Night Stalker.

To his trained eye, it read like only one thing.

He decided that Cass McDermott wasn't the only man who was wise enough to know when to duck. Cass had done it by making sure that Pete had been neatly ushered out of the Colonel's office before Pete had had a chance to look at the orders and heave them back in the Colonel's face.

He'd been awake for three days now and in ten minutes he was scheduled to face rookies.

Rookies!

Shit!

CAPTAIN DANIELLE DELACROIX brushed a bang of dark hair out of her eyes and surveyed her classmates gathered in predictable clusters in front of the barracks that housed the Special Operations Aviation Training Battalion. The hangar had been their semi-permanent home these last two years, when they weren't further afield training in the worst terrain the SOATB could find.

They had started with over a hundred and twenty men and six women. They now stood at eight and two, one of the highest graduation rates in history…if they graduated. None of them were sure, and that was presently the sole topic of conversation, which frankly bored her to death at this point.

The 160th's trainers gave you information when you needed it and not a single second before. Second-guessing was a waste of effort, something she wasn't a big fan of to begin with.

Predictably, they were winging around a couple of Frisbees; so gob-smack frustrated that most of them had joined in rather than continue discussing their unknown future. They used glow-in-the-dark discs which, in the falling dusk, made their pale-green color almost impossible to see.

One whistled sharply when thrown due to a 7.62 millimeter hole some Al-Qaeda fanatic had shot through it. It belonged to the Mighty Quinn—a big Alaskan native. The Whistler was a real favorite among the crew, practically a mascot. It always sounded like a little cry to her when it flew. It was covered with signatures: some fresh and clear, others faded, some of the living, others who were no longer. Most of the trainees had signed it, perhaps all except her.

Stray throws came her way once or twice and she shot it back, but she remained separate, outside their game.

Their group still had a Sergeant and two Sergeants First Class who flew as crew chiefs and gunners in the back of the Chinook and Black Hawk helicopters.

The class had become small enough that a rotating group of instructor pilots were often sent to fill in the gaps—they needed two extra crew chiefs and one pilot whenever they all flew together.

Tonight's crew chiefs were a pair she'd never seen before: a big, powerful black man who it was hard to imagine fitting in a helo, and a woman who barely came to his shoulder. They stood easily together off to the side with none of the foot-shifting and constant looking over their shoulders that marked the trainees.

The players winged a disc at them a couple of times as a test. Each time the big guy stretched out a long arm, snagged it out of the air, and then sent it pounding back so hard that a missed catch sent someone running a long way after it.

The pilots and copilots, if they were anywhere else, would have been divided by aircraft type: Little Birds, Black Hawks, and Chinooks. But this was the U.S. Army's 160th SOAR and the Night Stalkers—as they were known—were so far outside the curve that they tended to gather together regardless of the platform they flew. Or perhaps it was that if the pilots divided by platform they'd each be standing alone; there weren't many of them left after two years of training. Eighty-five percent hadn't made it out of the first three weeks.

A pair of Chief Warrants, one Second Lieutenant who had made the jump from being a backseater shortly before applying for SOAR, three Lieutenants, and herself—The Lone Captain. Didn't quite have the ring of *The Lone Ranger,* and she didn't even have a Tonto. As the sole remaining Chinook pilot, her copilot was always a trainer. And whoever he was, he was late.

It was odd how different the world was between those who flew in the backs of America's military helicopters and those who piloted the craft. She had tried to blend, but the line had been drawn deeply in prior service and even here few crossed between them—the Frisbee game making one of the few social bridges between the front and backseaters.

Danielle hadn't intended to turn "outsider" into a science any more than she'd meant to turn "gifted" into a reason to be isolated throughout her school years. She'd decided she had two choices, get angry every time they sat her close beside the teacher's desk so that she could be given advanced work that all of the other kids would resent, or become little Miss Perfect. Somewhere along about third grade, yet again the teacher's pet because she knew all of the answers, her brain discovered a third option.

She watched and she laughed—silently of course.

People were about the funniest things on the planet. And, because she was such an outsider, no one ever dared ask what made her smile at the oddest of times. Danielle reached up a hand to check. Yes, she was smiling at the predictability of the groupings, right down to her own hermitic self.

To an outsider, there was very little to distinguish the candidates. It would appear that you could rearrange the pieces on this chessboard with no effect. All wore flightsuits and Army boots. They each had survival vests, FN-SCAR rifles strapped across their chests— though the ammunition was issued wrapped in plastic and you'd better have a damn good reason to have broken the security wrapper on U.S. soil—and helmets stacked off to the side of the game.

To an insider, it was only in knowing the individuals' habits and quirks that separated them, but that separation was obvious. Most of the crew chiefs had a free hand on one or another of their weapons when they weren't chasing the Frisbee. The pair of instructors also displayed this habit. Whereas pilots never knew what to do with their hands on the ground. They looked lost without a helicopter's cyclic and collective to hold onto, like a gamer looked when you suddenly unplugged his computer.

Other than the two new crew chiefs, she was the only one standing off to the side; disconnected, her hands in a studied neutral position. Originally she'd done it so that she could fit in with either group—and it worked for that. But she now understood that it also made her *not* fit in with either group.

Danielle had been called many things over her seven years in the U.S. Army before SOAR…actually for her entire life before applying to the 160th: aloof, distant, stuck up, men had called her lesbian, and lesbians had called her bitch.

She'd tried to leave that behind when she left the 10th Mountain Division to apply for SOAR, and mostly succeeded. Oh, she'd over-heard conjectures that she didn't hit the town bars because she was a Mormon or had a lover back home who had made her promise never to enter a bar. In some tales her lover was male, other times a woman, and a few other typically Army suggestions involving both higher numbers and lower life forms that she chose to ignore.

She actually had no one waiting at home, but by not commenting on the rumor of a hidden lover, it had grown and kept most of the unwanted attention away.

Danielle didn't go into bars because they were loud, smelly, and her mother was an alcoholic. She'd asked Danielle to lean close for what she knew were her mother's last words—she'd asked for a gin and tonic. It used to make Danielle physically ill just to watch someone drink.

It was one of the things she liked about SOAR. They were on constant alert and the rules said twenty-four hours between a drink and a flight. Regular crews could count on a week off here and there, but not the trainees. There seemed to be a gleeful sadism among the trainers' cadre in promising vacation time and then blowing it up with a call-to-mission alert only after you were in transit.

Danielle had learned to work with the people of SOAR more smoothly because she completely owned the only currency that truly counted to the Night Stalkers—she flew better than almost anyone. It had been built into her DNA or blown into her bloodstream by a radioactive spider bite or something. She liked the idea of the spider. *Spidey rules!* If she ever met a man named Peter Parker she was going to marry him on the spot and they'd have superior radioactive children.

Danielle's secret identity wasn't her everyday self, it was her super-hero occupation. When she was stuck in airports, restaurants, whenever out in public and the men came around—they always did—she'd use it. She learned quickly that she had to set the rules or they'd never go away.

Danielle invented the simplest of challenges to turn away the unwelcome attention.

"Guess what I do for a living. Three guesses and then you're gone. Guess right and I'll let you stay." Men understood bounded rules, even when the deck was stacked against them.

"Model."

"Actress."

"Singer/performer."

Those always took top spots. Especially country-western singer, which was odd since her bloodline and her accent were Québécois French and her musical preferences were primarily medieval, through renaissance and baroque to the classical period. She danced to modern music—when absolutely no one was watching—but for listening Mozart was recent enough for her tastes. Handel was better.

No one had yet guessed military or even any kind of flying, other than—

"Stewardess."

—which she always corrected with...

"Flight attendant, but no."

Their general lack of creativity was astonishing. She eventually had tried announcing that she was none of the standard three right up front just to see what they came up with, but that stupefied most men into silence. Those who recovered invariably went to:

"Dental hygienist."

Someone had guessed:

"Language teacher."

Which she'd almost given him partial credit for. Like most Night Stalkers, she spoke several languages other than her native French and English. But then he'd followed up with:

"Porn star."

And she'd booted his ass.

Danielle belonged in the Night Stalkers, yet here she stood off to the side observing both herself and her classmates. She belonged, but didn't. Which meant...

Her idle speculations were dragged beyond the gathering of trainees by the man stamping into view around the hangar from the direction of Regimental Command. Her missing Chinook copilot?

He moved like no Night Stalker she'd ever met, trainee or instructor. He moved with power and grace...and like a German Shepherd war dog ready to bite someone's head off.

---

PETE TRAMPED past the rookies as if they weren't there, not even looking directly at them.

A few reacted, most didn't.

Someone sent a Frisbee winging by just feet in front of his nose. He considered pulling out his sidearm and shooting it out of the air. Instead he slapped it and left it where it rattled to a stop against the concrete pavement of the landing apron. The field was suddenly silent except for the distant roar of a C-130 taking off down the main Fort Campbell runway.

One of them, the one standing off to the side, had spotted him even as he rounded the hangar as if he'd been waiting for Pete's arrival.

Pete assessed the situation as he moved past them. One Black Hawk helicopter, squat and heavily armed with training rounds. One massive twin-rotor Chinook heavy-transport assault helo. Two Little Birds, both mission-enhanced as attack craft rather than for delivery or extraction. It was an odd mix, as were the puppy-panting hopefuls.

Pete continued to the Black Hawk, jerked open the massive side door. As it slid toward the rear of the helo, an oven-blast of trapped solar heat rolled over him. The remote Himalayas that he'd escaped just twenty-seven hours ago kept looking better and better.

While they waited or worried or whatever, he stripped down to his skivvies then dug out and donned his flightsuit that still reeked of too many hours spent squatting on the Tibetan soil with its foreign smells and dangerous feel. He grabbed his helmet and chucked the rest of the mess behind the rear cargo net.

When he turned back he noticed that the loner still watched him. Cool behind dark shades despite the failing light, narrow face, well-defined features...and dark brunette hair down to his shoulders.

*Shit!*

Her shoulders.

And it fell in one of those slightly disarrayed cascades women never understood was a hundred times sexier than the fanciest hairdo. Or maybe they did.

He scanned the others. The redhead, also clearly female, also watched him closely, though she had a wide and saucy grin. He must be even more exhausted than he'd thought, to miss them.

Women. Two.

He knew the 160th's 5th Battalion D Company had women, both crew chiefs and pilots, and he wouldn't wish that hell on anyone. He'd lost good fliers, ones he thought were good men, to rape charges because they couldn't keep their dick in their pants, fraternization courts-martial, or simply falling in goddamn love and losing their edge as they worried more about "home and family" than the person trying to shoot them out of the sky. Good men turned into "lovesick bull calves" like whatever that old movie was.

Now he was probably going to get his ass hauled in by one of them because he'd changed clothes right out in the open. Well, to hell with them. And he'd kept his underwear on, hadn't he? He was too tired to be sure. Or to care.

Thank god this assignment was only temporary.

"You! Specialty?" he snapped out as he moved over to the loner. There was always one in every group.

"Civility, sir," she answered with a light French accent and a deadpan tone that almost made him smile. That was pretty unexpected given his current frame of mind. But it wasn't your average soldier who could tell a superior officer he was being an ass so graciously.

"Civil Sybil? Woman of many personalities?"

---

DANIELLE COULD FEEL the cusp before her. She'd earned a hundred "tags" over the last nine years, but none had stuck, though they sometime took months to shed. She could feel "Sybil" hovering in the air, but she had no interest in being tagged with a nickname implying multiple personality disorder. Very *not* superhero.

Specialty? She'd flown in all three birds. The Little Bird as a copilot just so she could viscerally know what they could do. She liked the tactile knowledge, had ultimately run it through the obstacle course without killing herself or her pilot. She was technically still qualified to Readiness Level 1 on the Black Hawk, but not to SOAR standards. She done the yearly requisite basics to still be qualified to fly one around—more out of stubbornness than need—but she'd never be dumb enough to take one into battle again.

Her training and reflexes had been honed to a single craft.

She pointed at the big Chinook. That was the monster helicopter of the Army, and SOAR's MH-47Gs were equipped like no others in the entire American fleet. Much to her own surprise, SOAR had taught her that the big beast was more than her favorite craft, it was her baby.

The man eyed her skeptically. He wore no rank, had offered no salute. He looked haggard and frustrated and she considered offering him a moment of sympathy. Then his piercing brown eyes focused on her.

"What was the hesitation?"

"Sybil aside," she did her best to drive that tag off the map, "I have a specialty, I am Basic Mission Qualified in the Chinook. But I am also still rated RL1 and served as a pilot-in-command in the Black Hawk with the 10th Mountain. I also have thirty hours in the Little Bird in which I'd rank myself as a Readiness Level 3 at best." RL3 was flight school-level skilled, nothing practical for the real world.

He squinted at her in disbelief; she couldn't tell if it was of the mock or macho-chauvinist variety. It felt as if she was back at the three questions stage of fending off unwanted men.

"Nobody flies all three. Hell, I don't fly all three."

She held up three fingers for emphasis and resisted the urge to lower all but the middle one. Granted it was pretty damn unusual—pilots spent their entire career in just one platform—but she was as she'd said, and to hell with him whoever he was.

"Wait, you said you were Basic Mission Qualified?"

"We all were. Eighteen months ago."

The guy slapped at his pockets looking for something. She finally pointed at the sheet of paper clutched in his hand.

He sighed then read it carefully.

"Not rookies."

"We've all had two years of every hell the Instructor Pilots could put us through and six one-month tours overseas."

"One-month tours? That's whacked." He shook his head, like a wet dog trying to clear his ears.

How was she supposed to judge what was whacked and what was normal for SOAR?

"Three platforms, huh?" he eyed her more carefully, head to foot and back. "Cerberus perhaps?"

She had to duck her head for a moment to not laugh in his face. Probably not a good move if he was her training pilot for the night. And image of the guy as the three-headed puppy dog guarding the gates of Hell felt totally appropriate; especially for calling her the Hell Hound.

"This is not the Three Dog Night. I prefer the three sister-Fates." Danielle lowered her tone and added some volume, "Beware mortal for I am Atropos and I shall sever thy thread ere it is fully spun."

"Caution, for I am Clotho," he replied without so much as an eyeblink. "Without me there is no spun thread for you to cut nor your sister to measure." He moved off toward the others without further comment.

She'd had strange discussions before with different commanders. Never had she spouted Ancient Greek myths at one, and he didn't look like the sort to reply in kind as easily as most guys did with football scores. Danielle followed in his wake.

"Who else here has flown in all three platforms?"

No one responded.

"Two?"

Rafe's hand went up—at least some familiarity was a standard part of SOAR training and Rafe had done well enough in the Little Bird—but the taciturn commander could read the tentativeness as clearly as Danielle could. Had he asked "Basic Mission Qualified in two platforms" Rafe's hand would still be down as would hers.

The two new crew chiefs also raised their hands—with decidedly more confidence than Rafe's—which was almost more unusual than a pilot who had flown all three.

"Well, you know your birds, go to them."

Rafe and Julian headed for the Black Hawk.

The Mighty Quinn and M&M headed for the two Little Birds with Patty and Kenny following in close formation.

The man looked at her, "You called it, Atropos. Get thee to thy Chinook."

She heard the Shakespearean line of Hamlet to his Ophelia of "Get thee to a nunnery"—a nunnery in Elizabethan times being a whorehouse.

"With the God Zeus *himself* as my copilot?" She wanted to stuff his arrogance back down his throat.

The smile didn't touch his lips, but it might have lurked briefly near his eyes. "What misbegotten idea makes you think that I'm not the pilot in command?"

"Because, despite what the others think, my Spidey sense says that our training is not yet complete."

"You're Spiderman?"

"Spiderwoman." Spiderman had rocking superpowers; there had already been a Supergirl and a Catwoman, it was about time for a new heroine. She offered him a curt nod and her best smile before heading over to the Chinook.

PETE WATCHED the slight woman head for the massive helicopter. Even the bulk of the flightsuit couldn't beef her up. She stood several inches shorter than his six feet. Call it five-eight. Her boot size was small and her hands had looked fine and delicate as she held up the three fingers. But he'd also been able to easily see the one-finger salute she'd been considering. He liked spunk, especially when he was being an asshole and deserved it. She also had an education, though it remained to be seen if she had brains to go with it.

Then she had dug up that laser bright smile. He'd figured her as over-educated and dour. Getting a smile for a comic book reference was the last thing he'd expected. And one that shifted her face from merely beautiful to...

He sure as hell wasn't going to follow that thought no matter how exhausted he was.

Pete let the crew chiefs sort themselves out. McDermott's two "ringers" were easy to spot even if they hadn't raised their hands. Since they both claimed multiple platforms, he sent the big guy to the Chinook and the other—crap, another woman—to keep an eye on the rookies aboard the Black Hawk. He wanted to assess the group's strengths and weaknesses.

SOAR crews flew out at the edge. Special Operations depended on them for extreme results, whether flying undetected into the heart of

Tibet or racing the Pakistani jets to the border after landing in bin Laden's compound. The isolation of training was about to be broken for these folks.

"Move it out," he ordered.

"Yes sir, oh mighty laird of the clans," the redhead offered in a bright Irish brogue that rang distinctly of one of those New England cities.

He let it go, let them get a head start, then strolled among the aircraft as they went over them. There wouldn't be anything to find, SOAR had the best mechanics in the business, but no crew flew an aircraft they hadn't preflighted themselves no matter a ground mechanic's signature on an airworthiness certificate.

They soon had their flashlights out as the sunset had finished turning blue sky into red. The occasional transport jet flashed into the sky along one of the runways, but otherwise the area was quiet. Only the Night Stalkers were based on this side of Fort Campbell.

Without asking names, he began mentally tagging them.

He'd be joining Spiderwoman, two of the crew chiefs, and the big guy ringer on the MH-47G Chinook.

The pair of pilots in the Black Hawk could have been twins if one wasn't six inches taller and the other one black. He considered "Pete" and "Repete" but didn't want the confusion with his own name, so he went with "3PO" and "R2." Another crew chief and the female ringer landed there.

That left two MH-6M Little Birds with a pilot and copilot each.

One of the Little Bird pilots practically vibrated with energy, a good match for the fast and agile craft. "Bunny." The copilot attracted no name in particular, a tall gawky nerd. Pete tagged him with "Geek" for now.

The second Little Bird pilot was the one he'd expected to head for the heavy Chinook; Pete dubbed him "Dozer" for his powerful build. The redheaded woman was his copilot.

"Got a name, Mister?" she asked when she spotted him watching her preflight her helo.

"I do, Boston."

"I'm from Gloucester."

"Right," he moved on, leaving "Boston" cursing his back. At least she had the good sense from her years in the service to do so silently.

When he reached the Chinook, the feel was different. The two trainee crew chiefs were moving sharp and silent over the craft chasing after the circles of light cast by their flashlights. The ringer showed all the signs of extreme competence, but it wasn't the big guy the trainees were reacting to. The crew chiefs moved as if in fear of something.

He couldn't put his finger on it until Spiderwoman, the loner brunette pilot, circled around the nose of the craft. She wasn't up in her cockpit; she was doing her own walk-around, a habit that he wholly approved of. The crew chiefs were afraid of…her? No. Of not being up to her standard? Actually, yeah. He could see by the way she was inspecting the craft that she missed nothing and every man-jack of her crew knew it.

Unexpected in a newly trained SOAR pilot; he liked it. Despite his preferences for male-only combat crews, he liked her.

The Chinook MH-47G was a monster. It could lift fifteen tons of gear or a platoon of troops and deliver them fifteen thousand feet up. The rear cargo ramp was wide enough for a Humvee to load aboard and the main bay could hold two of them at once. It flew with two pilots and three crew chiefs who manned the cargo bay gun positions.

The helicopter should have dwarfed this woman, but instead it made her seem larger.

Pete moved up into the cockpit and settled into the copilot's seat, for she had been absolutely right. The training might be done, but the final test wasn't.

That was tonight's mission. Find their limits and then push past them.

# CHAPTER 3

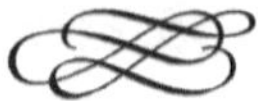

*B*y the time the aircraft were all spun up and ready to go, the sunset had wound down and the four helos were nothing but green, white, and red running lights on the concrete apron in front of the Fort Campbell hangars.

"Everyone sleep well today?" Pete wished he had, but he'd never been one for snoozing off on a transport plane. Even with earplugs they were too bloody loud. Of course, he'd taken two hundred and fifty bucks off the other grunts stuck aboard the flight in a quick round of poker, so he wasn't complaining. He didn't release the mike switch for them to answer.

"We have a flight tonight. If your altitude crosses above two hundred feet, you will automatically fail and be returned to your unit." Not true, but it didn't hurt to scare them a bit. "If you cross over one-fifty you will want to pass every other aspect of this test *perfectly*—none of the criteria for that will be explained beforehand."

He could feel the indrawn breath around him. *That's right, people. Graduation exam time.* That's what had been on the orders from Colonel McDermott; though he'd still have to corner Cass as to why he'd dragged Pete half-around the planet to run the test.

"The planned flight level for this test is fifty feet. The Chinook is taller and gets an allowance to sixty feet."

He paused, expected a huff of complaint from the woman beside him. The Chinook wasn't merely ten feet taller. It was also long, wide, and heavy. That much craft needed space to maneuver and he wasn't giving it to her.

But she sat immobile behind her helmet's closed visor, left hand resting on the thrust control beside her seat—called a collective on any other rotorcraft—and the right on the cyclic between her knees as if she was a machine merely ready to be turned on.

*And there was a dumb image.* He was *not* turned on by beautiful women who flew massive helicopters. It simply wouldn't do.

…as if she was a machine ready to start.

"Anyone who wanders more than three rotor diameters from the Chinook, do us all a favor and simply quit now." The Chinook's rotor was sixty feet across; the front and rear rotors overlapping for a total diameter of a hundred feet. He'd give them that much. Three hundred feet sounded like a lot, until you were following the terrain at a hundred and fifty miles an hour in a ten-ton chunk of steel.

Pete knew that when all combined, these were stricter requirements than any mission they'd flown in the last two years—stricter than what was in the orders as well, but they didn't need to know that. It had been five years and he could still feel the fear in his gut from that last day of training, not that he'd showed it any more than the woman sitting next to him was. See how she was doing by the end of the flight.

"First stop is," he read off a set of coordinates quickly and by his tone made it clear he wouldn't be repeating them. "Little Birds will have seven minutes to refuel." The Little Birds could travel only half the distance of their two big brothers. They were short strike craft that were going to be pushing their limits tonight.

The Sister-Fate Spiderman—Spiderwoman, crap!—had punched the coordinates into the navigation console as he read them. He stared at the terrain map she pulled up and managed not to laugh.

"Which is a swamp in central Mississippi." It was not going to be a pleasant refueling site. The Little Birds would have to hover in place for the entire seven minutes, shifting their controls to compensate for the growing fuel load as their tanks were refilled. And do it without ticking off or killing the waiting ground crew.

"Now, move it!"

He had to give them credit. If anyone hesitated, he couldn't see it.

---

DANIELLE HAD SEEN his type before. Arrogant and, only through the courtesy of modern military command training, not quite displaying what an asshole he was. Clearly the Equal Opportunity training of Army Regulation 600-20 and Command Training Guidance course on Sensitivity had been even more of a burden on him than it had on her.

For her, she'd been pissed at having to take all the classes that certified her as being human and having rights. As a trained and armed Special Operations Forces soldier she could damn well enforce her own rights.

For him...that's why they'd written those *imbécile* courses in the first place. The attempt to evolve him from Neanderthal to Early Cro-Magnon had clearly been a gamble that had only marginally paid off. That he was a nice-looking asshole with a quirky sense of humor and the education to use it well didn't change the base noun despite the assorted adjectives.

He hadn't even set the intercom to automatically include the crew. She preferred to run an open channel throughout the craft, but *Monsieur Imbécile* hadn't set it that way when he was done with the radio. No, it wasn't his doing. It already had been set to isolate the cockpit and she hadn't changed that during preflight. And since he wasn't helping her, she couldn't free up a hand to change the setting.

She crossed the two-lane security road of Nightstalker Way, edged over the Fort Campbell back fence, and rolled up the hills to the tree line. She chose a path that kept her rotors above the trees but slalomed her aircraft's body down among the treetops. Special ten-foot dispensation for her Chinook? To hell with that.

He did nothing to assist her flight, which made the Chinook a huge challenge. It was a complex craft that required two experienced pilots, especially if she was planning to survive a long-distance Nap of Earth flight. NOEs required perfect concentration and fast reflexes… and on a Chinook MH-47G moving at a hundred and fifty knots, *it required two goddamn people.*

"Did you say something?" His Imperial Namelessness asked over the intercom.

"Not a word," at least she didn't think she had. But now that he mentioned it, "How about you start doing your goddamn copilot's job, sir?" She led the flight of four helos west until she picked up Kentucky Lake. Ten feet above the water she turned south and crossed into Tennessee.

"All you had to do was ask," suddenly he was all *le chevalier,* Sir Sweetness-and-Light. In moments he'd cleaned up a half-dozen settings, adjusted the throttle sync on the two Honeywell T55 turboshaft engines so that the irritating beat frequency of their slightly different speeds became far less annoying, and rested his hands on the controls as a backup to her own motions.

"Damned lucky I need both hands to fly this thing," she muttered to herself.

"Or you'd be snipping my thread?" he returned jovially.

She really needed to learn to keep her mutters to herself. Or first make sure that no one was there to hear. "I thought I was Spider-woman. If that was truth, you'd be lucky that I need both hands to fly or I'd plaster your face with the stickiest web I could come up with."

"She both spins threads and cuts them. Half Spidey and half Atropos. You got a name, pilot?"

"Only if you do."

He laughed.

Who knew the taciturn bastard could laugh. It was a good laugh and she liked it despite being fairly convinced that she hated him thoroughly.

"Pete."

"Not Peter?"

"Not even on my birth certificate. Parents named me Pete."

"That's a relief."

"Why?"

"Because if your name was Peter Parker then—" she cut herself off before she could sound even more stupid about how she'd have to marry him.

"Major Pete Napier at your service."

Danielle almost bobbled the controls at that. She'd been teasing Pete "The Rapier" Napier? He was notorious throughout the five battalions of SOAR and beyond, right into her former Falcons—10th Mountain Division, Combat Aviation Brigade, 3rd Battalion, 10th Regiment. She'd worked to get assigned to the 10th of the 10th because they flew the same three birds as the Night Stalkers, less advanced versions, but still it had let her learn what all three types were truly capable of.

But The Rapier?

"Captain Danielle Delacroix at your service, Major," she managed to keep her voice neutral.

She'd studied his techniques almost as much as those of the legendary Majors Beale and Henderson. Major Napier was one of the top pilots in all SOAR—perhaps the top now that the other two had retired to fight forest fires. He sent back techniques to be added into training that were nearly irreproducible...and he'd come up with them while flying combat which made them downright miraculous.

Unlike Beale and Henderson, who were *famous* within the SOAR community, *notorious* was the proper adjective for Major Napier. Notorious for being a total hard ass. No one flew farther out on the edge than Pete Napier.

He was also the reason she'd ultimately given in to Justin Roberts' attempts to get her to switch to the Chinook; Major Napier was generally acknowledged as the master of the MH-47 throughout SOAR. *Keep it light, Danielle. Keep it light.*

"Napier?" she managed to say his name as if maybe it was French or, if not, perhaps it should be. Though if she'd been a teenaged boy, her voice would have cracked horridly in a total fan-girl moment.

Kentucky Lake had led to the Tennessee River. She rode through the sharp oxbow bend at Waverly and watched how the others were keeping formation on her. Rafe's Black Hawk held tight as did Quinn's Little Bird. "Tighten up, M&M." The second Little Bird pulled in closer until they were a flying wedge of death.

"M&M? I thought of him as Energizer, like the bunny because of how he moves."

"Lieutenant Manfred Malcolm. M&M."

"He'll be in trouble if he ever makes my rank," Major Napier's voice remained deadpan.

"Napier?" mangling it with an Italian accent this time. "Jack or the butler?" Let's see if he was half as sharp as he thought he was. Jack Napier had been The Joker's name in the Michael Keaton *Batman* movie. Alan Napier had been the actor who played Alfred the Butler in the original TV series.

"Oh, I dare say, madam," Pete made his voice butler-pompous, but no Michael Caine-English accent which would have been inappropriate for Alan Napier. "I am not cruel."

Unlike his reputation.

Well, The Rapier wasn't known for cruelty, not exactly. It was more a combination of vicious and lethal. His battle-plan attacks consistently struck at the very core of the enemy with an overwhelming force, even when the core was deceptively hidden. He had a strategic sense that made his attacks master strokes that the enemy could not evade.

Danielle kept low to the water, made sure everyone was well inside the training envelope of three rotor diameters. But mostly she watched the terrain map inside her visor for stray bridges and water-crossing power lines…and potential enemy surprises. This was a training flight, perhaps their final one, and there were bound to be at least one or two engagements to test their mettle.

Napier yawned loudly into the intercom and she remembered the exhausted look as he'd arrived from Command.

"When was the last time you slept, sir?"

"Before Tibet. Shit! I did not just say that," he scrabbled at the communication system and then huffed out a sigh of relief when his finger tapped against the switch set to isolate the cockpit's intercom. "You, Captain, are not authorized for that information. Are we clear?"

"I can only assume you were hunting for a blue flower at the base of a mountain topped by a league of evil assassins." And now that she'd evoked the image, she wished she hadn't. Christian Bale had been seriously hot in *Batman Begins.* And only now did it register quite how much Napier looked like Bale. She'd certainly gotten an eyeful when he'd stripped down to change into his flightsuit back at Fort Campbell. Bale had worked out for the role, whereas Pete the Rapier had done soldiering for a career and the difference showed. He was remarkably fit; that was a safe word for a commanding officer wasn't it? Very remarkably—

*Keep your mind on your flying, girl!*

Knowing he had his hands on the controls, she released the thrust control for a moment and set the intercom to the whole aircraft. The sounds inside her helmet expanded to include the crew chatting quietly on the other circuit, making sure they were staying sharp. It also served to inform Pete the Rapier that she wouldn't be pursuing his unintended comment.

Didn't mean she couldn't think about it though.

Tibet, huh? A politically impossible mission, because even a whiff of American military on Chinese soil would have created a major international incident. Things certainly weren't going to be dull once she'd passed into the Night Stalkers. If this was the graduation exercise, it meant that her real missions were about to begin. Finally!

While it was easy to file away thoughts of Tibet, the image of flying with Pete the Rapier dressed only in his briefs as her personal butler wasn't going to go away anytime soon.

---

PETE KEPT an eye on the pair of Little Birds as they were refueling in a swamp along the Black Warrior River watershed of northern Alabama. The ground team would report on just how well they did, but they looked good from where he sat forty feet up and a hundred yards to the side in the Chinook. SOAR training had made sure these people were good or they would have long since been washed out.

But were they good enough?

The attack came a quarter mile after they left the refuel point. He knew it was inevitable even if he didn't know when.

The trainees hadn't a clue.

Two AH-64 Apache gunships waited side by side around a bend in the river. At the far edge of the tactical display he also spotted an F/A-18E Super Hornet jet coming down from fifty thousand feet, at least it wasn't moving at supersonic speeds. Still, a nasty scenario. Personally, he might have added another helo coming from behind.

Danielle burped the radio, "Craft please identify."

What came back from the Apaches in response were a pair of missiles, at least simulated ones.

"Flares and up," she called on the encrypted frequency.

"Up" was not a choice he would have made, especially with the jet descending from above. Clearly she hadn't spotted the jet out at the very edge of the display.

Of course with "Down" they were under twenty feet from hitting the soggy soil. Most students went to the sides which exposed their bellies to the Apache attackers and also counted as a kill.

All four helos rolled upward. As they hit vertical they all triggered their flares. Bright flares shot out to the sides of each helicopter which would hopefully distract a heat-seeking missile. The helos climbed in such a tight formation that the flares created a veritable wall of shining light between their four helos and the attacking Apaches.

For the moment, the Apaches' night-vision gear would be overwhelmed.

As Danielle pulled vertical she called, "Jules, two away on the jet."

So she had seen it.

The Black Hawk unleashed a pair of simulated Hellfire missiles and sent them streaking directly up at the diving F/A-18E Super

Hornet. The fake missiles fizzled after a hundred yards and would fall harmlessly to the swamp where a follow-up team would recover them. But the jet's computers decided it was dead and out of the game.

"Mighty and M&M," was her next call, with no additional instructions and Pete could only wait to see what they came up with.

The Chinook and the Black Hawk continued their loops, but rolling over sideways as they did so. Instead of flying onto their backs, they were once again upright and diving back down to the riverbed the way they'd come.

The two Little Birds had done the opposite. Hidden behind the wall of flares, they'd climbed and then nosed over until they were diving on the Apaches from above. They burst clear of the bright wall painted by the flares, firing simulated chain guns. The Apaches' sensors registered that they were destroyed just moments later.

"Maximum height during engagement?" Danielle called out.

"Shit!" one of the Little Bird pilots swore.

Pete double checked the readouts. He'd told them that the plan was fifty, they'd be on probation over one hundred and fifty feet and would fail over two hundred feet. A total lie. After two years of training, SOAR didn't discard pilots that lightly, but he wanted to see what they could do.

The swearing Little Bird pilot had hit a hundred and thirty feet as he nosed over. The other bird hadn't even crossed a hundred. Clearly Danielle had held them to a higher standard.

"Re-form. Continue mission," Pete snapped out trying his best to sound irritated.

In silence they formed up around her once more and continue to roar south along the Black Warrior River.

"Mighty?" he asked over the Chinook's intercom to avoid complimenting Danielle on the exceptional maneuver. Plus he wanted to prompt her into speaking more. He generally appreciated a closed-mouth pilot, but that French accent of hers was about the only thing keeping him sharp…he could listen to it all day.

"The big Alaskan guy, Mickey Quinn. We call him The Mighty Quinn from the Bob Dylan song *Quinn the Eskimo.*"

"I thought of him as Dozer."

"The Mighty Dozer? Bet he'd like that."

Pete didn't want to be as impressed as hell, especially not by a bunch of trainees, but he was anyway. He'd flown with new teams before and they didn't function the way this one had. Hell, he'd flown with fully qualified teams that couldn't do that last maneuver...or wouldn't even think to.

There was the difference to this group and he'd bet that he knew its source.

---

"All craft."

Danielle had already learned enough about The Rapier's tone of voice to know that bad news was incoming.

"During the last engagement, Captain Danielle Delacroix was critically injured. I am a Chief Warrant Two only RL2 on the Chinook platform."

Which meant he could fly well enough, but don't depend on him to complete the mission.

"The mission is critical, continue on profile. Out."

"I'm not—"

"I need to see how much they rely on you, Delacroix, because I'm betting that whole last piece was you're doing."

"But they need to know I'm not—"

"Shut up, Spidey."

A bark of laughter over the Chinook's internal intercom told her that she'd better like that tag because she'd just become stuck with it—at least for a while. Maybe a long while.

She wanted to argue, but it was true. The jet had been unexpected, but by chance she'd penciled out everything else about this exact scenario a few months ago and they'd made it a mental puzzle over dinner. That it had come off so seamlessly made her damn proud of the team, and more than a little surprised at herself. She hadn't really expected it to work so neatly in the real world.

Rafe "Yank" Grant, the Black Hawk's pilot, took command.

He'd been tagged the day he told how his slave ancestors had chosen their last name after Ulysses S. Grant had freed the South—despite his thick Georgia accent. Yank shifted the Chinook back into the pocket with himself in the lead and a Little Bird to either side.

"Is 'Yank' the tall white one or the little black guy?" Napier asked her.

"The little one," she replied. Yank was shorter than she was, but she'd never thought of him as little. He was solidly broad-shouldered, serious, and an exceptional pilot. They were constantly pushing at each other. "Julian flies copilot."

When Rafe asked for Pete's name—she was still the only one who knew who was flying with them—Napier simply replied, "Call me Butler."

Unintentionally, her snort of laughter went out over the air. She could feel the others relax, see it in how they flew. And if "The Butler" didn't like that she'd just revealed she was uninjured, screw him.

"Did you consider having your Black Hawk drive straight ahead through the flare wall?" Pete asked her as if they were all hers to order and command. Yank led them once more along the Black Warrior River and passed the "dead" Apaches who rocked side to side in a wave before turning for home.

She hadn't. "That seems a desperate maneuver. The Black Hawk would take severe damage."

"Think about it. There are times when enemy air traffic radar is only a hundred feet over your head and you couldn't have done your little climb."

She'd never contemplated sacrificing one of her crew. Of course, the 10th Mountain Division wasn't about being subtle, it was about being so obviously overwhelming that the enemy turned tail and ran or was destroyed in place. The 10th Mountain was likely to throw twenty or more helos at a battle—backed up by a dozen M1 Abrams tanks along with other odds and ends—to humble the enemy into submission.

SOAR was all about subtle and would send two or three. The

seven, or perhaps eight, that they sent against bin Laden had been a massive campaign by Night Stalker standards.

She continued to do the flying and Pete The Rapier continued to bring it down on their heads. But with each engagement he would ask her one or two questions that would force her to completely rethink the scenario. He was so good, and so far inside her head, that he knew exactly what she'd missed.

It wasn't just a one-way flow of information though. His voice was always sharper when the crew did something he hadn't expected. He dug after every nuance of her thinking about those situations, and always followed her last answer with a, "Huh."

At first she thought she was being accused of screwing up. Then she understood that he wasn't being aggressive, he was learning. From her and the team. He pursued each morsel of knowledge as if it truly mattered. The other trainees had appreciated—eventually—the results of her obsessive "beating the facts to death."

Pete was the first pilot who she couldn't leave behind in that mental pursuit. He was right there with her and it was...completely the wrong thought...sexual in its power—the back and forth as they both strove to be better.

Eight hours, four little Bird refuelings, a mid-air refuel for the Chinook and the Black Hawk, and seven attacks later, everyone was still alive...except for her, of course. They'd recovered a team of SEALs out on the Gulf of Mexico and redeployed them in a staged attack against a "terrorist held" oil platform. And still she was "dead." But even the attacks they hadn't discussed previously as possible scenarios had gone off smoothly enough using tactics she'd helped create.

Danielle might not know what to do with people on the ground but, God, she totally rocked it in the air. Even when she wasn't the one giving the instructions.

———

THEY SETTLED to ground in a remote corner of Fort Rucker Army

Airfield an hour before sunrise. It was the absolute center of all Army heli-aviation training.

The four helicopters of their flight clustered at the far end of the otherwise empty Ech Army Stagefield Heliport.

Pete stripped off his helmet and went blind. All of the information that had been feeding into his visor—flight data, engine status, tactical overlay, night-vision territorial view—was gone and now he was sitting in the dark.

He slumped in the seat and closed his eyes. Two days in Tibet, a day in transit, and an eight-hour graduation test flight. The exhaustion was past palpable and actually made him nauseous.

"Someone has it in for me."

"Who might that be?" Danielle asked in that lovely French ripple of hers. He could hear her finishing the shutdown checklists. He should be helping, but he was too damn tired.

"My money is on Colonel Cassius McDermott. Oh crap. You—"

"—didn't hear that, I know. You must be more careful, *Monsieur* Rapier, so that you are not snipping your own thread."

He stared out the broad windscreen of the Chinook at the blacked-out heliport, with only vague outlines of trees and a few stars showing. He'd been to Mother Rucker, as everyone called the Fort, innumerable times—for all Army pilots returned to the Mother throughout their career for everything from periodic tests with instructor pilots to advanced training. And the trainers were total motherfuckers in how hard they drove you, so it all fit.

The Fort had a dozen of these stagefields scattered about the local counties for training, but Pete had never used Ech. By the look of it, no one else had in a long time. He'd barely heard of it. In all his flights around the area, he couldn't be sure he'd even passed over this field. Were all flights routed around it? There was an interesting thought.

Hanchey, Knox, Lowe, and Shell heliports all had a hundred or more tie-down spots for individual helos. Only the main airfield at Cairns had runways for fixed-wing aircraft. They all had lights and instrument approaches. The big Stagefields like Allen, Brown, and Runkie did as well. Not Ech.

Ech had nine tie-downs and five short runways appropriate for practicing rolling and emergency landings. There was one small building that had definitely seen better days and was barely big enough for four or five offices. Close beside it was a hangar that looked brand new—at least it had through the night-vision gear as they'd descended—and was big enough for a half dozen birds.

The heliport was surrounded by a curtain of trees and was three miles of narrow dirt road from the next nearest piece of Mother Rucker.

He looked out into the darkness, but they were the only ones there. This was the last set of coordinates on the training document, so it was the right place. But it certainly didn't say what to do next.

Shit!

That's what he'd landed in, a total shithole. Right down the old crapper.

Spiderwoman clicked on a cabin light and pulled off her own helmet. He blinked at the surprising brightness, and then again at Captain Danielle Delacroix. He hadn't been this close to her without her helmet on. Or if he had, he'd been blind. Her features weren't merely fine, they were elegant. And when she dug her fingers through her hair, the helmet hair went away and the thick mane of dark brown flowed once more down to her shoulders.

He'd noticed her beauty before, he must have, but he'd seen her as a female burr upon his own existence. However, burrs upon his existence didn't fly as well as she had. And about to be graduated trainees never ever functioned so cleanly as a team.

"You are staring, Monsieur Butler."

Pete was. And he wasn't having much luck stopping. That French accent of hers only added to the fine picture she painted. Let Spidey keep Kirsten Dunst as his Mary Jane ideal, this was his idea of beauty.

She snapped her fingers right in front of his face and forced him to blink.

"Sorry," he rubbed at his face and it made no difference. "It's been three or four days since I slept and you're gorgeous. And I can't believe I just said that either." He couldn't read the reaction on her face. There was one, but he couldn't read it.

"No more than you said the other thing which I have already forgotten. I truly think you should sleep more often, Major Napier."

Just that simply she targeted and destroyed the easy mood that had settled over them during the flight. The teasing tone hadn't particularly shifted, but the message had totally changed. His rank and name now stood between them, as did six years of flying for the Night Stalkers.

By the time they had the helos shut down, log books completed, and the crews had exited their birds, the first light of day was ghosting to life somewhere over the horizon toward Georgia.

They were the last ones to exit down the long length of the Chinook's cargo hold, only the slightly pale square of the open cargo ramp guiding them forward. The heat was already oppressive and right in front of him, Danielle began peeling down the top of her flightsuit to tie the arms around her waist.

Her silhouette was clear against the backdrop of the open cargo ramp. As trim as her face implied, with curves that promised so much.

*She's a flight officer in the 160th SOAR, man. You aren't supposed to notice that kind of shit.*

She also had a heavenly scent of mountains in the fall. He'd grown up outside of Boulder, Colorado. How did a French beauty remind him so much of home?

He was tired enough that his reactions were wholly out of sync, he walked right into her when she stopped. He'd have plowed her to the deck if he hadn't grabbed her around the waist and kept them both upright.

But he'd also underestimated her reflexes for she saved herself with a step-and-turn that brought them face to face the moment before they pounded together.

---

DANIELLE'S HEAD rang with the aftermath of the hollow "clunk" that had resulted from their foreheads smacking together. The room...the Chinook's cargo bay spun for a moment. The three round windows to either side swirled and the square portals for the M134 miniguns—two forward and one aft beside the ramp—appeared to bob and swirl as she struggled to regain her equilibrium.

When she did, she became aware that she was holding tightly to the front of Major Napier's flightsuit. At least she'd tried to think of him that way; Pete made for far too intimate a sound inside her head.

Having a commanding officer tell you "you're gorgeous" was a fast flash of a path to hell. She'd learned long ago that if she didn't slam down the door, it led to unwanted gropes and casual caresses that made her want to both shower immediately—with a scrub brush and as much soap as possible—and break someone's arm. More than once she'd had to shove her M9 handgun down inside their belt and offered to caress their balls with a couple of 9mm rounds before they backed off.

So she'd slammed the door on "Monsieur Butler" and transformed him back into Major Napier. But for once she hadn't wanted to. She'd just spent eight hours sitting shoulder to shoulder with one of the best pilots in the Night Stalkers. And when they hadn't been teasing each other, they'd both been stretching their tactical minds together.

One of his hands was on her hip and the other clamped hard at the small of her back holding her hard against him with such force it took her breath away.

"I'm," he leaned forward and took a deep breath with his nose buried in her hair, "really sure I'm supposed to say I'm sorry I ran into you." He breathed her in again. "But I'm finding it difficult to feel that way."

The last man who'd held her this tightly had earned a dishonorable discharge after she'd broken one of his feet and he'd almost broken her jaw with a massive punch before he collapsed to the floor. She'd used her Army boot to un-pretty his face but good.

But this time, the man wasn't the only one holding on. Pete had left his survival vest on the copilot's seat. Even through his flightsuit she could feel the strength of him. And also, that there was not a single thing to fear.

He hadn't groped her. Or gone for a kiss. He'd simply saved her from what would have probably been a painful fall onto the steel grating of the deck and then…wrapped his arms around her.

She managed to unfist her hands until they were lying flat on his chest. A part of her, the part that had found a mind that was her match for the last eight hours, wanted to haul him in and see just what kissing The Rapier would feel like.

But her common sense intruded and she pushed lightly against his chest.

He shifted backward. She could tell that it was reluctantly, but even in parting, those big hands of his took no advantage as they slid off her. In moments they were standing as closely as they'd been when they whacked foreheads, but now their only connection was her hands resting lightly on his chest.

"Awfully forward for a butler," she managed on a dry throat.

"Awfully forward under any conditions. But your web appears to have ensnared me."

"My web?" As if this was all her fault?

He took a half-step back, enough that she could remove her hands but didn't have to.

For the moment, she didn't.

"I am unused to beautiful, intelligent, competent women in uniform. Especially Spiderwomen."

Oh. Right. Her thinking was confused, so deeply *embrouillé* for her to have missed that reference.

Then he was gone, back into Major Napier and she lowered her hands. He bowed ever so slightly, stepped around her, and once more headed down the slope of the dim cargo bay.

The whole encounter had lasted perhaps ten seconds.

So why did it feel as if they had just moved past dating and meaningless sex right into courtship?

---

Pete had not just…

He couldn't have with…a fellow officer.

No. He hadn't. He hadn't grabbed her except to keep her from a fall. Hadn't brushed a finger across her brow to check for a bump where their foreheads had hit. His still throbbed, but when he rubbed at the spot, if felt more as if he was rubbing at the confusion within.

He had resisted the urge to dig his hands deep into that thick hair and bend down to see if she tasted anywhere near as good as she smelled.

He'd held her though. He could still feel her skin, the warmth separated from his palms by only a thin layer of cotton. The shape of her waist. It was easy to imagine how it would feel to be pressed against her, into her, plunging hard into pure heav—

*Fellow female officer, goddamn it!* He'd *never* crossed that line. Not once. He didn't understand how the mixed-gender teams did it. It was cruelty when someone like Danielle Delacroix…

Not fellow *female* officer. Fellow *officer.* Period.

One who had probably busted her ass twice as hard as any male officer to fly with the Night Stalkers. And he'd wager it was a nice ass even if he hadn't groped her to find out if…

Pete sighed with some relief when he reached the pale light at the foot of the Chinook's rear ramp. He was a goddamn wreck. He needed twenty-four hours sleep and then needed to get back to where he belonged—half a planet away from Captain Danielle Delacroix.

With that plan firmly in place he took the last step off the lowered ramp and out onto the pavement.

The breaking daylight slowly resolved faces as the crew chiefs chocked the wheels and tied down the rotors so that they didn't spin unexpectedly in the wind. At the moment it was only a gentle breath carrying the thick smells of Alabama, lush foliage soon to sweat with the intense humidity under burning skies.

The only thing missing were the sharp smells of engine exhaust and the piercing overtone of the kerosene in Jet A aviation fuel that usually floated around Fort Rucker mornings. They were far enough afield that there were only their birds, silent now except for the pings of cooling metal, and nature's, now beginning to awaken and call from the trees.

Already the Frisbee was in flight between the various crew members. Check a wheel, catch and wing off the disk, check the other wheel. It appeared to work for them, so he didn't comment.

There was a bright flash and roar from above as the flight crews finished up and gathered about him on the otherwise empty airfield. A descending blast of hot air sent the Frisbee tumbling aside.

In a blinding glare of white-hot jet exhaust, an AV-8B Harrier II Jump Jet descended out of the sky and landed on one of the nearby runways. The jet—with its vertical/short takeoff and landing capability—was one of the few fixed-wing aircraft that could land at Ech Heliport. Even a little private Cessna 172 would be hard pressed to get in and out of here.

Once down, the jet turned to taxi up to them. It was a two-seat trainer version and within moments of stopping, a man climbed down from the forward cockpit. He was barely clear before the jet was once again on the roll and lifting back into the sky with an earsplitting roar.

"Eight hours," Colonel Cass McDermott looked at his watch as he strolled up to them. "You're right on time, as I'd expect from Major Napier."

There was a collected round of gasps and exclamations from the flight crews that had gathered around when they discovered they'd flown the entire night with The Rapier in command—or rather pretending he wasn't.

"Damn straight, Colonel McDermott."

The sounds of surprise were cut off as they all snapped to attention and offered salutes.

"At ease," Cass offered one of his rare, wintry smiles as left boots stomped a half-step sideways and flightsuits rustled as hands were folded behind backs. "Relax people."

Again the shuffle as they shifted to as natural a stance as could be expected in front of Pete The Rapier and the regiment's commanding officer. Pete echoed McDermott's smile, but kept it between himself and his commander.

"Your assessment?" Cass prodded. "Or would you rather step aside to discuss it?"

"No need, Colonel. While unable to perform an in-depth analysis of each individual because of the situation, based solely on tonight's flight I would be proud to fly with any of these soldiers." Especially one, because, damn, Captain Danielle Delacroix was beyond good. So good that she'd managed to drag an entire class of trainees to excellence along with her.

"Good, because that's your new assignment."

He squinted at his commander. The morning light revealed nothing that would allow Pete to interpret this as a joke: foul, cruel, or otherwise.

Finding no answers there, he glanced over at Danielle. She offered a microscopic shrug of uncertainty.

***

DANIELLE HAD no idea what was going on, but Pete Napier wasn't looking happy about it. They were trainees. No one had told them if this was it. Was there more testing? Had they graduated?

If the latter, then they would receive their assignments and be dispersed among the five battalions wherever they were needed. With only ten graduates and twenty-four companies among the five battalions, they might none of them serve together.

That sent a surprising pang of regret through her. She might still be the loner of the crowd, but she'd come to know and appreciate the skills of Rafe and Julian and the others. She started being friends with Irish Patty and Rafe the Yank.

Though she had been hoping for the 5th Battalion D Company assignment. All of the previous women, who had become legends of the SOAR community, had ended up there. Chief Warrant Lola LaRue, Captain Casperson, Kee Stevenson the sniper, Sergeant Connie Davis the wizard mechanic and her giant of a husband…

Danielle turned slowly on her heel to face the two training crew chiefs who'd been along for the flight.

"Connie and Big John," she spoke aloud in her surprise.

"What?" Pete spun to follow her gaze. "No way."

They were the mythic mechanics of the entire 160th. Over half of all design changes sent to MD, Sikorsky, and Boeing factories originated with these two. They weren't just cross-platform mechanics, they'd as good as reinvented all three platforms between them.

They nodded in unison and offered her smiles. Connie's was slight and barely graced her quiet face. Big John's smile was large and brilliant in the morning light against his dark complexion.

The other crew members, even Patty, shuffled to open up a space around the two sergeants.

"Told you I had a couple ringers for you," Colonel McDermott sounded terribly pleased with himself.

This was like Babe Ruth and Willy Mays showing up on your T-ball team.

"I did it," Danielle couldn't believe it. "I really did it."

"Did what?" Pete was looking at her strangely.

"I," *really need to not speak my thoughts aloud,* "I made it. I flew with…" she waved a hand a little helplessly at Pete and the two mechanics. "I…" she looked at the rest of her fellow trainees and struggled to stop babbling. "We. Did it. We made it through SOAR training."

"Yes, you did, little Lady," the Colonel looked down at her. "Damn fine job the lot of you. You're all cleared as Fully Mission Qualified per unanimous agreement of the Instructor Pilots who have been making your lives hell these last two years and were watching this flight from a half dozen following craft. We've never had a team pull together like this one. I'm guessing that you'll be Pete's Number Two. Congratulations," McDermott held out a hand to Danielle who took it; though at the moment she wasn't sure what to do with it. The Colonel gave her hand a good shake and she did her best to reciprocate.

"The Rapier's Number Two what, sir?"

"Didn't he mention?" the man was clearly enjoying himself immensely. "Pete's forming up a new company, 5th Battalion E Company."

"What?" Pete spun back to face his commanding officer. "The hell you say."

McDermott didn't look the least perturbed at The Rapier's blast of anger. "Oh, did I forget to tell you, too?"

# CHAPTER 4

The crews sat at a pair of picnic tables, chowing down on breakfast or whatever meal you called it when you were eating hamburgers and chips at six a.m. after working all night. They were regaling each other with last night's simulated battle in grand gestures and extravagant terms—utterly giddy with having graduated.

He, Cass, and Danielle were seated in a small group of chairs off to one side. They were seated in front of the slowly decaying Ech Heliport office building and close by the pristine hangar. A food truck along with a couple of Army cooks had pulled in alongside, fired up, and begun feeding them as daylight broke over the field.

Pete contemplated the situation. "How much trouble will I get in for murdering my commanding officer?" He ignored the sour expression on Cass' face. They'd known each other far too long for that look to scare him.

"Well," Danielle took a bite of her grilled chicken after cutting it neatly with a knife and fork despite having to balance the paper plate on her lap.

He was so tired he doubted if he'd trust himself with such dangerous implements. Figures that she'd be beautiful. Beautiful. Shit, there was another problem. In the bright morning light, her Army-beige t-shirt displayed her figure magnificently—how good she'd felt in his arms for that moment hadn't been any kind of an illusion. Trim where she should be trim and rounded in such an ideal form that… that he should be taken out and shot. But that would have to wait until after he'd killed Cass McDermott.

"I think," Danielle continued after she was done chewing—good manners too. Hard to believe she'd been in the Army for seven years plus two in training. "It would depend if you intend to murder him *un petit peu*, a little bit, or kill him dead."

"Dead dead," Pete decided.

"Not my first choice," Cass commented as he sat back as if removing himself from the range of fire.

The morning had turned into a fine one and Pete had no interest in it, no more interest than he had in forming up a new company with a batch of newbies fresh out of training. And he wasn't going to admit to learning anything from them last night, no matter how much he had.

But he couldn't get away with that. The trainees had cooked up some ideas that, quite simply, *needed* to be added to training. And it wasn't just Delacroix. She'd given credit for each idea to the one who said it first, though it was clear that she'd been the spark behind every discussion.

"Court martial, *certainment*," she informed him placidly. "Life imprisonment, perhaps the firing squad?"

"Been shot enough as it is," Pete tried not to think about it. Four times in fifteen years of service, and his little brother who'd winged him when Pete had been trying to teach him how to hunt in the Colorado wilderness. His foot had been in a cast for months.

"No," Cass corrected her. "Firing squad is French, madame, or rather was."

"*Mademoiselle, s'il vous plaît.* And I am Québécois by heritage only. I grew up in Cleveland."

"*Excusez moi, mademoiselle.*"

To hell with Nicolai and his Russian, Cass made the French sound so smooth that Pete wished he'd studied that instead. He hadn't even made a study of French women who…he was not going to complete that thought.

The Colonel turned back to him. "If you kill me, Napier, I fear that hanging would be more traditionally appropriate if anyone has a yardarm handy. But come along, man, don't you want your own company?"

Pete tried to answer that one in the negative, unsure why he was fighting the bit so hard. The 5th Battalion was only five years old, based out of Joint Base Lewis-McChord in Tacoma, Washington. A through C Company were straightforward outfits—Black Hawk, Chinook, and Little Bird respectively.

Then Mark Henderson had formed up the 5D. He'd insisted on creating the only mixed company in the entire Regiment, all three craft types combined under a single command. He'd talked with Mark about it once when they were all sitting out a sandstorm at Bagram Airbase a couple years back.

"Mixed team allows me to be flexible on the fly. I don't have to wait for mission units to be called up from other companies. No questions about command precedence. My team. My training regimen. My orders."

And soon after their talk, "my wife" as well. He'd married the first woman to ever qualify for SOAR, and just like each woman who had followed, she'd done it by being exceptional. And when Henderson's wife had gotten pregnant, they'd dumped SOAR as if it didn't mean a goddamn thing. Pete shoved his plate aside and almost knocked his lemonade into Cass' lap.

Well, to hell with that shit. Any woman he fell for was going to be stuck with a lifer for a husband. They were going to have to retire his ass into an old age home to get him out of the air.

Yet Henderson and Beale had flown together for a couple of years before that. Somehow the 5D was so far out on the edge that they allowed married couples aboard the various helos.

He glanced over at Connie and Big John seated at one of the picnic tables. They were from the 5D. Talk about an ideal match, the two best helicopter mechanics outside the factory—and better than most of those inside as well.

Maybe that's why McDermott had decided to let them serve together, because he couldn't afford to lose either one? Was that what was happening in the 5D? Was command allowing married couples serving in the same theater of operations to happen, perhaps as an isolated test? Had command learned that some pairs of people consti-tuted a synergistic pairing that created more than the sum of their—

Shit! He was so tired he was getting all poetical.

"Choice is simple, Pete," Cass leaned in now and the tension went up at their table of three.

It rose far enough to focus all of Pete's waning consciousness back on his commander.

"You say no, I put these folks on their birds and kick them back to Fort Campbell for assignment. The units are hungry, we're getting pushed hard on a dozen fronts—as you know."

"Or?" Pete considered a mixed company of craft. It offered inter-esting possibilities. Of course a Night Stalker company was typically a dozen craft each. Though he'd heard the 5D was running with only seven or eight. The people sitting at the tables around him could crew just four birds. And that was only if he was allowed to keep Connie and John.

*A couple of ringers for you,* McDermott had said. Yes, they were here long-term if he said yes. Hell of an enticement to have direct access to two such skilled crew chiefs. But what bribe had he offered them to leave the 5D?

"Or," Cass pointed at the brand-new hangar behind him, "we can go look at what's inside there. But..." then he waited.

"And here comes the other shoe," Pete hated it when the other shoe dropped.

Still McDermott waited, but Pete couldn't get his mind around it.

"He must makes his choices," Danielle made her voice sound like Gollum from *The Hobbit* as she dropped the shoe for him, "before he gets to sees."

Oh.

"Yesss, he does, Precious."

Cass simply smiled as if such Gollum-speaking captains were completely normal.

Though Gollum with a French accent was distinctly strange.

"Good choice for a second in command, Pete. I approve."

Pete studied the crumbs that were all that was left of his hamburger. He was glad to see that his body had the good sense to eat even if he'd been too tired to be aware of it.

"No choice of personnel?" Pete didn't know if he was hoping for a yea or nay on that one. If he was smart, the first thing he'd do would be to reassign Captain Danielle Delacroix to anywhere else, as long as it was far away. He knew it wasn't merely exhaustion that made him want to drag her back into his arms. But it had to be his exhaustion that made that sound like any kind of a good idea.

The last time he'd been with a woman was on leave four months ago. Sally May Ketchum, as in Ketchum, Idaho, as in wealthy, tall, skier-athlete fit, and having no use for a soldier beyond a few nights' fling. Which had made her just about perfect.

Which is what he'd thought of his ex, Lucy. Except she'd wanted marriage and he'd been young and dumb enough at the time to give it to her. Built, blond, as avaricious as a snake, and about as constant. He'd had her less than a year and it took him three to get rid of her.

Danielle Delacroix evoked none of the common logic that went with a choice like Sally Ketchum—the kind of woman best designed for a career soldier to enjoy and then move on. Nor was she a clinging, officer-hungry, conniving bitch. Danielle was made for cozy cottages and long winter nights. For whole long strings of them.

"No changes," McDermott insisted. "We haven't had a class like this one in years and I've been waiting for it. Part of that is thanks to you, missy. You may rest assured that I know that." He managed to deliver the line without sounding condescending. "That's why we held them together right through Basic Qualification and into advanced training."

Pete couldn't argue. Even after he'd "killed her off" her influence on the team's performance had been unquestionable.

"Perhaps you can change a few selected people later, but only by special petition directly to me. Also, every one of these people are security classified for the level of mission you have just returned from. Every single one."

Pete had to blink at that one. The Tibet mission had included only senior personnel with a minimum of five years in SOAR which meant at least twelve years in the service. If all of these people were cleared to that level, it meant that the 5E would not be a small shit-kicker outfit for long. They'd be capable of deployment where only the smallest, most flexible teams could go. For a bunch of rookies to have that in common, they'd have to have been…

He spun to study the faces of the crew at the other tables.

"Ah, the light goes on," Cass teased him.

"You started building this class two years ago," Pete accused him. The cooks and their food truck were gone, leaving a cooler of soft drinks and a platter of freshly grilled seconds and thirds if anyone was still hungry. Once again, the graduating crew, the two ringers, and the Colonel Cassius McDermott were the field's only occupants.

"Three years ago," the Colonel replied. "Right after you did the Myanmar mission. My whole plan for the 5E is based on the combination of you and Captain Delacroix, whose career I have been following for some time, even before I sent Captain Roberts to recruit her. Don't disappoint me, Napier."

The two of them? Cass had designed this company based on his and Danielle's skills.

Danielle was watching him carefully. Then she arched a single one of her fine eyebrows in question.

He was tired enough to stop fighting against his knee-jerk reactions and actually think. The chance at command, not merely of a single flight or mission but his own company. He had always groused at others' rules, things he'd always imagined he could do better. Now there would be the opportunity to try them out and see if he was right.

Captain Danielle Delacroix as his second in command. There was no question that she would fit perfectly into the role. She clearly respected the hierarchy of command, but also had plenty of ideas of her own. She wouldn't merely push him, she would drive him to innovate.

That she was female and far too attractive wasn't her fault, even if it was his problem.

"Hey!" One of the Chief Warrants shouted from the picnic table; the redheaded female, Boston. She'd been fooling with her cell phone for a while. "There's a Mother Rucker Disc Golf course. C'mon you lame-os. I gotta need to kick some butt."

"No sleep first."

"Sleep is for wimps," she declared dragging slow movers to their feet. "Game first. Then we can sack out in base accommodations. You know we ain't doing shit until those commander types stop jabbering."

Everyone glanced their way.

Danielle's look of surprise at being "one of the commanders" made him feel better. It was the first thing he'd seen that caught Danielle flat-footed. Nice to know she could be.

In moments, the field emptied as crew and pilots piled into waiting vehicles and headed off to play. Even Connie and Big John had tagged along for the game.

Now it was just the three of them.

"Captain Delacroix would make an exceptional second officer," he admitted to McDermott.

At that Danielle hit him with another blast of her radiant smile. He refused to go weak in the knees over a woman, but he could feel himself smiling back at her despite his best intentions.

"Let's go see what I've gotten us into, Spiderwoman." He didn't even need to nod toward the hangar to explain that he'd just accepted the command of a brand-new company.

The 5th Battalion E Company.

The first new company since Henderson's 5D formed almost six years ago.

The 5E.

He liked the sound of that.

She rose to her feet and headed for the hangar. Pete remained a moment longer at the table.

"Cass?" he said softly as soon as he was alone with the Colonel.

"What is it, Pete?"

"Remind me to beat the shit out of you some day."

"Sure thing," McDermott clambered to his feet and Pete followed suit. "Any particular reason?"

"Yeah," was all he said. Then he rose to follow Danielle Delacroix.

Pretty women were great, but they weren't exactly rare. Pretty women who turned him on had to have something special. In Sally Anne Ketchum's case it had been the competence of how she'd skied—the payoff there was that she'd flowed down that course the same way she had in bed—smooth and lithe.

Competence was a huge turn on.

And a challenge was always good. His best friend and girl-next-door Kim Waverly had challenged him throughout high school. Pushed him to always be better, to always excel. Had she been straight, he would have gladly skipped his family's tradition of military service in order to be with her. Both of them were first pick in every gym class, they'd captained several of the sports teams, co-captains in volleyball.

In the end they'd both signed on the same day...and her jet had been shot out of the sky four years later. They'd never slept together, but the woman's spirit had been a major turn on. Her personal preferences had led him to numerous cold showers and a whole string of bad choices, but he still appreciated every second of her short life.

Elegant Danielle Delacroix had the competence. And the drive. And something else that his brain, finally spent after making the decision to command, was wholly unable to process but he knew there was no way he could ever avoid.

---

DANIELLE HAD the lead toward the new hangar; perhaps a bit too overeager to see what was parked inside there.

So, she tried to slow down and look casually around. Ech Stage-field was like a dozen other practice fields, except this one was buried in trees and no other piece of Fort Rucker was close by. Only a narrow dirt road led from the sad office building toward the main fort.

And then the hangar. It could hold a half dozen helos, but she'd wager there were just four. Chinook, Black Hawk, and two Little Birds—had to be or their crew wouldn't fit.

That meant there was something extra special about these. Latest models? Some crazy tech mods—which would mean more training? Unheard of weapons? Or—

That's when the events of the last few minutes caught up with her and her foot caught on some unseen crack and sent her stumbling into the wall of the hangar. She spun around to check, but Pete and the Colonel were discussing something…and she'd bet it was her.

She'd been glad of the excuse to get away from the table, sitting that close to Pete Napier was doing strange things to her nervous system. Usually her thoughts didn't just slip out, like never. Yet every-thing seemed to around Pete. And her Gollum voice? She wasn't sure she'd ever used that aloud, never mind in public.

A little distance was a good thing.

He and Colonel McDermott had some history, long history by the sounds of it. She sure wasn't about to call the commander of the entire regiment "Cass."

It was only after the two of them were walking toward the hangar that she realized she wasn't going to get distance from The Rapier for some time to come. Had she really just gone from graduation exercise to second-in-command of SOAR's newest company?

That would be a "yes."

Was the commander Major Pete Napier?

Uh-huh.

Was she inexplicably attracted to the handsome man with: a repu-tation from hell, a calm manner in flight, and a wholly unexpected gentle smile?

Totally. She could still feel exactly where every finger had rested against her back and hip for the few instants that he'd held her.

*You're in such trouble, girl.*

His personal magnetism was making this woman's internal compass point Napier-ward. That was both disorienting and incredibly dangerous.

At the door, the Colonel keyed down the ten-digit lock code.

"Did you get it or do I have to repeat it?"

"Uh," Pete looked lost, probably too tired for his eyes to focus.

"I got it, sir." Every other digit of her personal cell number and the zip code of Fort Campbell backwards. "I'll bring The Rapier up to speed after he's slept." The Rapier. That was it. Keep some safe distance in her head.

The Colonel opened the door and led them inside.

---

PETE FUMBLED for a light switch and Danielle's gasp sounded close behind him. He himself was too shocked to make a noise.

For a moment, the room spun. Not because he had vertigo, but because what stood in front of them was so foreign that it made almost as little sense as finding alien spaceships in the hangar.

"*Merde!*" Danielle whispered so close beside him that he could feel her warm breath across his ear.

# CHAPTER 5

cDermott was long gone. And still The Rapier wandered back and forth among the four helicopters parked in the hangar.

Danielle had become even more fascinated by her new commander than by the four amazing machines.

She'd killed the big ceiling floods once the sun reached high enough to stream in the high windows. Plenty of light to navigate by; it left the hangar's interior filled with bright highlights and cool shadows.

Pete didn't *inspect* the vehicles of his new command—far too mild a term; he *prowled* them. His attention was worthy of a preflight by a post-battle mechanic's team checking every possible surface and control for damage. His eagerness was that of a ten-year old boy and a brand-new train set. His power and beauty were—messing with her brain.

Danielle came to a stop long before Pete did and sat with her back against the main hangar doors. Ranged in front of her were four very unique craft.

She'd guessed right on the airframes: a Chinook, a Black Hawk, and two Little Birds; just as they'd flown in from Fort Campbell. But that's where the similarities stopped.

The Black Hawk was a DAP. The Direct Action Penetrator was the hammer-blow version of the Black Hawk—built and designed specifically for SOAR. The DAP Hawk bristled with the weapons and sensors that made it the most lethal helicopter ever built. It was sensitive in dozens of ways that were very bad if you were the enemy...and it was stealth-rigged.

The stealth transport Black Hawk that had been lost in bin Laden's compound had not been the end of the program, but apparently the start. This craft didn't look in the least bit jury-rigged, like the tail section left behind. This was one sleek, cohesive structure.

The two Little Birds had also been *stealthed.* The hull covered in reshaped forms of leading-edge composite materials. Even the weapons were encased in radar-deceiving pods, only their snouts peeking out through darkened holes.

But even more formidable than its three companions...

Danielle wished she'd chosen to sit somewhere else but lacked the energy to move. She'd landed with her back against the hangar door directly in front of the massive Chinook. It was a wholly daunting piece of machinery that felt as if it was about to crush her.

Her Chinook...did she really get to say that? Her baby that rose so high above the smaller machines, was a work of the mechanic's art at its pinnacle. Every surface was reshaped so that radar sweeps would be reflected in unexpected directions. Unlike other Chinooks, the wheels could tuck up into wheel wells making the helo smooth-bottomed in flight. Instead of looking like the biggest street thug on the block, a little ungainly but wholly unstoppable, it looked downright nasty. She liked that in a helicopter.

Connie and John would go ape shit when they saw these helicopters. No, they'd stand aside and looked pleased with themselves. Of course, the two master mechanics of SOAR—who also had extensive forward combat experience as crew chiefs—would have been deeply involved in the designs of these craft.

No wonder they'd agreed to transfer from the 5D to the 5E. These four craft represented the very best of helicopter tech anywhere on the planet. Connie and John would want to be the ones on hand during the shakedown and first missions. Each time she looked at them, she identified another level of tech that she'd never used. ADAS cameras. Predictive terrain-following. A range of aircraft survivability equipment she'd never even known existed.

And all four aircraft were that elusive gray-black of stealth composite materials.

Stealth. That thought clearly hadn't sunk in yet.

Nor had it for Major Pete Napier. He'd done his survey in layers, she could see them building in his mind. First the walk-through noting what to study. Then the next layer to make sure he hadn't missed anything in the overwhelm of that first inspection. Then detailed systems study on the next lap…

And somewhere in there she had burned out and had to sit down to process what she'd seen.

But the man, tired beyond reason and tact, drove himself from 20 mm cannon to heat shrouds on the engine exhaust ports. From fuel tank specs to Health and Usage Management Systems. She could feel him building up the layers in his mind as he studied and absorbed each helo's capabilities. And all Danielle could manage was to admire his relentless pursuit of that knowledge.

Eventually, when he was circling the craft—make that staggering around them—to no new purpose, she called to him.

"Stop already, Pete."

And as neatly as if she had indeed snipped the thread holding him up, he came over and slumped against the closed hangar door close beside her.

"Christ! What have I done?"

"What do you mean?"

He waved a hand at the assembled birds, "Look at them."

She couldn't look at anything else. The four fabulous machines, as in straight out of a fable, and the captivating man who had prowled among them for half an hour after she'd collapsed to the floor to watch him.

"You don't see it?" he sat so close that she could feel his body heat.

She looked back at the craft and it was as if his simple words had transformed them. These were not craft for training. Her days as a trainee were done. A SOAR pilot kept training through their whole careers—whenever they weren't actively deployed—but the Colonel had said "Fully Mission Qualified."

Colonel McDermott had said more. That being the 5E was an appropriate company designation, "Evaluate. You'll be responsible for receiving and testing the very latest equipment. That's how I convinced Connie and John to come join your merry band. You will always get new tech first."

Danielle blinked at the aircraft. So, they would be *evaluating equipment* that was out on the very *edge* of the *envelope*—a whole bunch of *Es*.

But now she saw what she'd missed.

The hardware defined the missions. Three lethal helos to protect the single workhorse Chinook. All stealth. These craft were for very high security missions. *High* security? Who was she fooling. That didn't begin to cover it.

"What comes after Black Ops?"

"No idea what to call it, but now you see it. Bet you that none of the others will without being told. Damn but you're sharp, lady. That's very sexy by the way." He didn't apologize or try to take back those words. So natural that he'd missed them going by, even if she hadn't. He wasn't sexist, but he was by-God male. Looking the way he did, he'd have to be.

"These craft don't need testing," Danielle spoke in order to think about something other than the man seated so close beside her. "They're beautiful, state-of-the-art craft at the peak of development." As was the man.

Pete nodded.

"The 5E. E is for *Extreme!*"

His bark of laughter was appreciative, "Just like you. Danielle, the extreme Spiderwoman, Delacroix."

She'd hadn't just graduated into the 160th Special Operations Aviation Regiment (airborne); she'd graduated into the 5E. The 5th

Battalion Extreme Company was going to be special even by Night Stalker standards. Once their team was up to the caliber of these helos, they were going to be assigned to places no one else *could* go. Tibet would be nothing compared to where these birds could fly undetected. Even the massive Chinook would have less radar signature than a little six-foot ScanEagle drone.

Pete was still nodding, just a little dreamily. This close, his rich brown eyes were half lidded and he looked far less scary than he had before, standing in his skivvies while he'd been changing clothes. Was that only last evening? A dozen hours and forever ago. How could so much change so fast?

"You know something, Spiderwoman?"

"Many things," again she was teasing The Rapier, but it didn't feel dangerous anymore.

"I'm just tired enough to do something wholly inappropriate."

Danielle could feel all of her blood drain out of her brain. She had a very clear image of what that meant and she'd been fighting against the thought herself for some time. If he was less handsome. Or less competent. Or his reputation wasn't so sterling…

She took a deep breath and braced herself for the result of her next words.

"And what makes you think that it wouldn't be welcome?" Had she really just said that? To her new commanding officer?

*To The Rapier!*

His eyes didn't widen in surprise. A man of action, he also didn't hesitate. Pete didn't go macho and grab her, he didn't try to dominate or control—which she'd been ready for. Instead, he turned and leaned in until their shoulders brushed the moment before their lips did.

The man might have a body and a reputation of steel, but his kiss offered a lush softness of surprising contrast and heat. Neither of them moved their hands. He didn't grab her breast, she didn't clutch his chest. Instead they simply explored the electricity that had been building all through the flight and the formation of the 5E.

At that she started to smile. It was small at first, but it kept growing until she interrupted their kiss with a laugh.

"What?" he whispered from a half breath away.

She shook her head and let some of her hair partially hide her face. He brushed it back behind her ear and she'd swear she could feel every line of his fingerprint along her skin as he did so. She was sitting on the floor of the 5E's hangar, her legs stretched out on the concrete that was still so fresh she could smell the dusty newness, and had just received a lovely kiss from a man she'd known less than a dozen hours.

"What?" he insisted with a smile that wholly belied his rough reputation. "As your new commanding officer I insist that you tell me."

The changes of the last twenty-four hours were just sufficiently overwhelming for her to set that aside. Commanding officer was a problem all on its own. For this one instant, they would stay in this idealized, non-military-code moment.

This time she didn't keep her hands off him when she kissed him again, but instead felt his need for a shave against her palms. Instead of heat, this touch was warm electricity, like a welcome shock that raced up her arm and straight into her pulse, amping it up higher and higher.

He rested one hand on her thigh as if he was merely steadying himself. It was neither suggestion nor possession, it was as natural as the kiss.

Pete sighed. It was a sigh of male self-satisfaction that had her smiling again. Moments later, he'd shifted until he was lying on the floor with his head on her thigh. And between one breath and the next—he was asleep.

Danielle marveled at the feel of it, the absolute rightness of it. When she felt the inclination to run her fingers through his collar-long dark hair, she didn't resist the temptation. She brushed it into an order of semblance that it resisted.

His face quieted, but didn't wholly clear. Even in sleep there was a hint of the frown of concentration that he wore so easily when awake.

She rested her other hand lightly on his shoulder and looked back up at the Chinook which had her centered in its sights. She couldn't wait to fly it.

To the finally silent hangar, still now from their inspections and from Pete's restless energy, Danielle whispered her answer to The Rapier's question regarding her smile and laugh. It didn't begin to cover what she was feeling, but it was the best she'd been able to find.

"It's been a good day."

———

PETE WOKE with his cheek warm on a woman's leg. There was no mistaking the texture, even through a flightsuit. Definitely a female's thigh.

He opened his eyes to the dim light of his new command's hangar. That thought was immediately clear...the woman's thigh was less so.

The concrete pressed unyielding against his left side, but he'd certainly slept in worse circumstances. Inches from his nose a sand-colored cotton t-shirt stretched tight across a very flat stomach and one of the nicest breasts he'd ever seen. He looked a little further afield, make that two of the nicest—

He must have jolted in his surprise, for Danielle woke up and looked down at him.

Danielle. He'd—Shit!

Her hair slid forward and masked her face in shadow, even this close he couldn't read her expression in the failing daylight. But he could feel one hand resting lightly on his shoulder and the other tangled in his hair.

He tried to remember the last thing he'd done.

And then he did and wished he hadn't.

Please tell him that he hadn't gone and...*jackass. No games.* He'd just kissed an inferior officer under his command. That it had been mutual didn't make it any more right.

The last days had blurred together...*and that was another lame-ass excuse.*

"How long have I been asleep?" *Smooth Pete. Real damn smooth! Way to sweet talk someone who...who you really shouldn't be trying to sweet talk in the first place.*

"Long enough for my leg to be completely numb."

"Oh, sorry," he pushed upright and she hissed as blood flowed back into her leg.

She complained and twitched as he massaged it for her.

That set them both to laughing and he remembered her smile in the middle of last night's kiss.

That led him to remembering the kiss itself and the sensual pull of her lips.

And using the excuse that he wasn't really awake yet, he was kissing that smile again. This wasn't some timid little testing like last night.

This time there was a roaring flash of heat that ignited deep within him and burned engine hot.

He knelt over both her legs and leaned down to drive their mouths together. He fisted his hand in her hair. He did it again and again to relish the feel of its soft depths slipping through his fingers.

His heart pounded with his need to have this woman, to take her beneath him. Here. Now!

The pounding increased and again Danielle's kiss shifted from welcome, to smile, and finally to silent laugh.

"What?" he demanded. This time he'd get an answer about why his kiss was so damn funny to her. She should be swooning, not laughing at him.

Danielle nodded toward the entry door to the hangar.

That's when Pete understood that the need pulsing through him wasn't the only source of the pounding. The first of the crew had arrived and, not having the entry keypad code, were pounding on the door to get someone's attention.

His attention.

But his attention, and his hand, were still lost in the texture of Danielle's magnificent hair. And his other hand was well on its way to ripping loose her t-shirt all on its own.

"Shit! Sorry. I'm so sorry," he pulled his hand out from under her t-shirt and made brushing motions at her hair. It seemed to fall pretty well into place. Mostly. A little.

Double shit. The woman looked like they'd really just had a long tumble. For a moment he considered ignoring the pounding, but that was even stupider.

That's when he noticed that: a) Danielle didn't look at all upset, and b) her own hands were up under his own t-shirt.

"Okay, mutual. Still really bad idea."

She looked down as she freed her hands and tucked his t-shirt back into the waistband of his trousers. Then she shooed him toward the door.

He arrived at the door, and glanced back just in time to see her disappear into the Chinook to buy herself a moment.

Pete blew out a relieved breath that she hadn't seemed upset. Then he *swore* that what had just occurred was absolutely *not ever* going to happen again.

He opened the door to see that most of the crew was already assembled.

Pete did his best to nod sagely at their varied gasps of awe at the four stealth helicopters they discovered waiting inside the hangar.

Moments later, a vision with dark flowing hair and a luminous smile swung into view around the Chinook. Never in his life had he seen a woman look even half that delectable and delightful.

"I know! Can you believe it?" Danielle perfectly covered her still slightly disheveled appearance with her excitement. "Come see! Come see!" She waved the crew forward from where they'd stumbled to a halt just over the threshold.

Beneath the rising tide of the crew's enthusiastic chatter he just hoped to God that he'd be able to keep his promise as a commander to never again put Captain Danielle Delacroix's career at risk again.

He was never again going to touch her!

And it was going to kill him.

# CHAPTER 6

Colonel McDermott settled in the jump seat close behind the pilots' seats in the big Chinook.

"Haven't seen you in a month, Cass. What are you doing out here? Pentagon boring the shit out of you?" Pete knew he sounded more irritable than he felt. Or perhaps not. He was sick near to death with the training.

Not that it was wasted, the stealth aircraft had no operational differences from their more normal brethren, except that the wheels were retractable in flight, removing even that tiny bit of radar signature. The visual imaging systems were such an improvement over the standard that they were simplicity to adapt to.

But the helo's handling characteristics were quite different. Not enough to matter to most pilots—which was a world apart for a SOAR pilot. Reaction times had to be reworked, performance envelopes investigated and integrated into skill sets.

Even if he'd been stupid enough to break his self-promise not to touch Danielle, there wouldn't have been a chance. Over the last month, Pete and Danielle had driven themselves and their team until the behavior characteristics of the stealth-modified birds were wholly incorporated into their nervous systems.

They'd flown tortuous courses throughout the lowlands over most of the East Coast, missions at the top of the Idaho Rockies, and spent the last week fighting war games back and forth across the Nevada Testing and Training Range.

The NTTR was five thousand square miles of convoluted desert terrain broken by deep canyons and abrupt mountains. With elevations ranging from four to ten thousand feet, they attacked various targets: mountain strongholds, anti-aircraft emplacements, simulated industrial and railroad targets, even mocked up cities.

But despite being inside the heavily protected boundaries of the NTTR, their birds were flown exclusively at night and were always under wraps by daybreak, inside hangars or beneath camouflage nets.

For a whole month Pete had managed not to touch Danielle Delacroix even once. They sat two feet apart in the cockpit every night and co-led the pre-mission briefings and the post-mission debriefings. They were perfectly cordial...and it was goddamn killing him.

He was actually glad to see the Colonel so that he could insist that Delacroix be transferred to any outfit, so long as it wasn't his, because he couldn't keep his hands off her much longer. He'd thought not touching Kim Waverly in high school had been a torture. Not dragging Danielle Delacroix into the nearest dark corner was agony.

He'd clearly hurt her when he clamped down the "steel barricades," but he'd had no idea how to explain or apologize. His reasons should be obvious.

And just to make him feel like a total shit, she'd responded by doing her damnedest to be the best flier and the best Number Two a commander could ask for.

"Might a surprise for you, Pete," he'd forgotten Colonel McDermott was even aboard.

"Great, just what I need." Pete and Danielle had gone through the startup procedures for tonight's flight with the smooth synchronicity born of fifty simulated missions in thirty days. The pace had been exhausting for the crew, but it had left them with no doubt that they could handle whatever came their way.

"Typical time for a new company to hit effective-for-deployment status is—"

"Six months outside, three months inside." *Outside* being anyone who wasn't *inside* SOAR.

"And the record was seven weeks for Major Mark Henderson of the 5D."

Three more weeks. He could beat that.

"Thought I'd do a mid-training eval, see if you're even close to beating that," McDermott continued over the intercom as they finally began winding up the engines. "Can't wait to see what you folks can do."

The 5E team was so small that Pete had decided to be the Air Mission Commander from the copilot's seat of the Chinook. Danielle had proven that she was good enough to handle most of the flight tasks herself. That left him free to manage the strategic AMC role of directing the company in combat situations and still assist her as needed.

Dammit! If he pushed Delacroix off to a new assignment, he'd need two people to replace her. And that would shove him out of the copilot's seat. He didn't want to stop flying just because the woman beside him was so goddamn attractive.

*Pay attention to your commander, Napier. Worry about the woman later.*

"Engine Number One at a twenty-five percent rated compression," Danielle spoke.

"Roger. Engine Number Two start," he kept an eye on the oil pressure and thought about McDermott flying all the way to Nevada merely to "see what you folks can do." He had twenty-five companies totaling over two hundred craft and twenty-five hundred personnel. SEAL, Delta Force, The Activity, and Ranger commanders would be begging for every spare minute of his time. People like him never just "dropped in."

Pete didn't want to do it, but he glanced over at Danielle. She was watching him. Her visor was still up so Pete could see that same fine eyebrow arch upward ever so expressively, just as it had that first flight back at Fort Campbell.

McDermott wasn't here to observe a training flight, he was here for a certification test. And that meant that McDermott needed the 5E to be ready—now.

"*Hundred percent* Rotor Rotations Per Minute on One and Two," Danielle announced. Her subtle emphasis let him know that she agreed with his assessment that they were a hundred percent ready for it.

"Oil pressure stable. Generator One and Two on," he threw the switches. *Bring it on McDermott!*

"Roger, APU Gen switch off."

Pete knew one other thing he was going to have to change in his plans. If McDermott needed the 5E to be ready now—for that must be why he was here—there was no way in hell Pete could afford to lose Captain Delacroix.

It didn't matter that having her remain so close at hand was going to cause him an insane amount of frustration. It was the best choice for the company.

He wasn't ready for how pleased he was that the choice had been taken out of his hands and she'd be forced to stay.

---

DANIELLE KEPT her thoughts to herself as she'd done since that first night in the hangar.

Finished with the Engine Startup Checklist, she buzzed through the Engine Ground Operation, Before Taxi, and Taxiing Check checklists.

She taxied forward from the hangar and out beneath the Nevada sky sparkling with the first stars and the last hint of gold at the desert horizon.

Despite the warm Nevada evening, she felt a shiver run up her spine; so strong it almost drove tears from her eyes—except she'd learned long ago to never show the tears. Never let them see you were afraid or hurt, never let her mother see how much every failure wounded. Cover it with a laugh—only inside her head, but still a laugh.

She'd been planning to ask for a transfer the next time she saw Colonel McDermott. Despite sitting in her dream helicopter doing what she loved, because she could feel the pain her presence was causing Pete. A month of flying together had done nothing to relieve the unbearable tension that had arisen between them.

Except when they flew. The way that man could fly…she couldn't get enough of it. And that perfect synchronicity in the air only fed her other, non-regulation thoughts, which didn't help matters in the slightest.

Most people who flew a Chinook thought that simply because it was such a massive bird, it needed a strong hand. The anti-torque foot pedals were indeed muscle builders. Some days after particularly long and stressful flights, she wondered if she was developing leg muscles like the Hulk. They'd certainly been weary enough to feel that way.

But the thrust control wanted a merely firm hand and the cyclic wanted its guiding French heroine to possess the light touch of a Juliette Binoche in *Chocolat*, not a kick-ass Carole Bouquet in Bond's *For Your Eyes Only*.

Pete understood the Chinook. His touch was as light and perfectly controlled as that single fingertip of his that she could still feel catching her hair and tucking it back behind her ear—though the gesture was a month gone and there hadn't been so much as a tap on the shoulder since.

She couldn't blame Pete for standing back. It was his integrity that had slammed the door between them.

But it was a door she didn't want closed, even if they weren't supposed to open it. Danielle had considered approaching Connie Davis and asking how she and Sergeant John Wallace had managed to be married and to serve together.

But Connie was almost as terrifying as Pete. She lived and breathed the helicopters until Danielle wondered if the woman even *saw* her husband, though he was always beside her. And then Danielle would see the couple sitting quietly together over a meal, conversation whispered back and forth between them in a manner so intimate that it was impossible to imagine them as separate…which made them even more uncomfortable to interrupt.

That's what Danielle wanted. To feel that *merveilleux* connection.

Instead, she'd become convinced that the best thing she could do was leave the 5E and grant Pete his freedom from being so close beside her.

The Before Hover, Hover Check, and Before Takeoff checklists done, she lifted them into the night sky and turned toward the night's target range. The mission brief had been for a simple anti-tank op—

She twisted to the left and focused through the data on her visor to look at Pete.

He must have noticed her motion—or their thoughts had been so linked that he looked across at the same moment. In unison, they turned to look at McDermott and then back at each other.

The Colonel would not be aboard for a "simple anti-tank op."

Without a word, they both turned their attention back to their flight and their tactical display.

Tonight's flight was going to be about much more.

What would it be like to make love to a man with whom you were in such perfect sync? And why must she have that thought every time they were together?

Rather than risk even an encrypted transmission to the other helos in the flight—for the radio's energy output might give away their position even if their message was hidden—she performed a maneuver that she'd developed a few weeks ago.

Danielle spun the Chinook in a sharp three-sixty, like a spinning top, without slowing or veering from her flight path. It was a neat trick of maintaining speed and direction flying sideways, backwards, sideways, and finally forward again and had taken her several tries before her first success.

"What the hell?" McDermott hadn't been prepared, but she could feel Pete riding on the controls with her.

"We call it *l'étude regarde*," Danielle told him.

"*Étude?* That's Chopin or Beethoven or one of those guys."

"An *étude* is a musical composition developed specifically to practice a difficult technical skill. The purpose of this exercise is to *look* in all directions very quickly."

"But your helmet—"

"Does not," she was interrupting a Colonel, "tell everyone else in your group that tonight's flight is a trap and they must keep their eyes open."

"Did I say it was a trap?" The Colonel offered no hint of fake-innocence in his voice; he made it a cold, hard statement. As a commander of the 160th, she'd expect him to have perfect control like that.

"Get real, Cass," Pete spoke up.

The Colonel's harrumph didn't sound pleased.

"*L'étude regarde* is also useful if a rear camera is shot out and can no longer show on our helmet's display. That is why I originally developed it."

"You? Of course you. That's why I put you and Pete together. Knew you'd be a damned fine team. I want that trick submitted to the trainers by sundown tomorrow."

"Already done, sir," she informed him. And there went any chance of her transferring away from Pete.

---

THE ATTACK CAME as Pete was setting up the final tactical strike against the tank company out in the middle of the NTTR. His attention was mostly involved with the targeting information, and the occasional attack incoming from the tanks. Their shots weren't very accurate courtesy of the stealth modifications, but they knew the 5E was out there somewhere and were firing simulated rounds at even the slightest hint.

He had Danielle do a quick reveal with the Chinook by nosing briefly up out of a canyon. It drew a series of shots from the six tanks. That in turn distracted the tanks from the double-pincer of two Little Birds attacking from one side and the Black Hawk from the other, while skimming only a few feet above the thorny brush of the Nevada desert.

But Pete had kept watching for the attack that hadn't materialized yet.

"Two o'clock high," Danielle's voice was a whisper against his ear. He'd been watching for it, but she'd spotted it first.

And then it was gone.

Once their sensors had a signal, it shouldn't be able to disappear again like that. Unless…

"We're not the only stealth craft here."

Danielle slammed the controls backward on the Chinook, diving backward into the canyon that they had departed only moments before.

A slice of laser light, passing mere feet beyond their rotor tips, simulated an attack through the heart of the dust cloud they had just left behind.

"All craft," he risked the radio. "Dance."

"Dance?" McDermott asked over the intercom.

"Shut up, Cass," Pete was enjoying himself. He shouldn't be. He'd just been attacked, insulted his commanding officer, and decided that he couldn't afford to lose the woman who was driving his libido nuts. But he was feeling beyond good.

The 5E broke off their attack on the tanks, switching to their favorite dance moves. It would make them almost impossible to follow, especially as each bird's movement was different.

The two Little Birds'—now named *Leeloo* and *Linda*—pilots were fans of hip-hop and country respectively. The Black Hawk *Beatrix's* favored rock and roll. And Danielle flew the *Carrie-Anne* to Gregorian chant as far as he could tell.

They'd named all of the birds for action heroines—Pete completely suspected Danielle's hand behind it though he hadn't been able to prove anything—with the first letter matching the helo type.

Little Birds *Leeloo* and *Linda* from, respectively, *The Fifth Element* and Linda Hamilton in *Terminator Two*.

The Black Hawk was *Beatrix* after Uma Thurman in *Kill Bill,* a very hot heroine he had to admit.

And the Chinook was named for the best kick-ass helicopter-flying heroine of them all, Carrie-Anne Moss as Trinity in *The Matrix.*

"This is *Linda,*" the Mighty Dozer's Little Bird broke radio silence. "Partial hit. Sim systems state that all weapons are offline. Patty is labeled as *copilot down,* which is ticking her off no end." Pete could hear her griping in the background; the system had switched off her microphone since she was technically dead.

"Roger, *Linda.* Get sideways and high. Give me some eyes on these people."

"Roger, *Carrie-Anne.*"

"You have three birds on the attack."

Pete didn't recognize the voice, but they were on the 5E's encrypted frequency.

"Identify," he snapped back as Danielle dragged the *Carrie-Anne* sideways along a cliff face.

The voice proceeded to list their enemy's locations with no self-ID.

*Beatrix* called in, "Can confirm two of the three. One in sights."

"Take it out," Pete ordered.

"Direct hit," the unknown voice continued. Female, he finally had time to register the speaker as female.

The opposing "struck" helicopter turned on its running lights and headed out of the conflict. It was a stealth Little Bird. The other two craft turned out to be a second Little Bird and a stealth DAP Hawk just like their own.

It took twenty minutes—an impossibly long time in an aerial combat—during which they raced, dove, and dodged over the night-time, nightmare landscape of the NTTR.

The terrain was a brutal enemy as well, providing protection and hiding places to both teams.

Danielle tucked under an overhanging cliff, her rotors spinning within meters of rock, but was able to surprise one of the opposing Little Birds.

The unknown voice interposed with data when it could grab some, which had proven to be reliable info when it came.

The DAP Hawks met time after time, their sophisticated targeting and attack avoidance systems making for such an equal contest that it was only after the 5E "killed" the other Little Bird that they were able to gang up on the opposing DAP Hawk and "kill" it.

By the time they were done, Pete was wrung out with the strain of coordinating the engagement. He'd led fights innumerable times, but it had never been *his* company. *His* people. It made all the difference in the world.

It cost them the partial loss of *Linda* and the complete loss of *Leeloo* but they'd managed to defeat all three of the attacking craft.

While the final rounds of the aerial battle had been on-going, Danielle had used the distraction to work her way around behind the six M1 Abrams tanks.

The instant the last of the opponent rotorcraft was declared dead, Pete squawked, "Opening note!" over the radio. After all, their first objective in this crazy dance had been the tank company.

Danielle punched on the full landing lights that should blind the tanks' night vision even as they spun their turrets to get an angle on the Chinook. But Danielle had slipped the *Carrie-Anne* into a gap between the second and third tanks so low that if they shot the helicopter, their shell was likely to pass right through the Chinook and hit one of the other tanks in the line.

When they tried to bring their smaller top-mounted M2 Browning and M240 machine guns to bear, Danielle's crew chiefs killed them with simulated hits from their vastly more powerful M134 miniguns.

While the tank operators were trying to unravel all the hell that the *Carrie-Anne* was unleashing on their heads, the Black Hawk *Beatrix* unleashed simulated Hellfire tank-buster missiles from their other side. The non-weaponized rockets struck each tank with a loud *klonk* that he could hear on the Chinook's external pickups. It must have really rattled the tank crews.

The war game computers declared all six tanks simultaneously disabled or destroyed.

"Back to Tonopah Airport," McDermott ordered. He sounded very pleased. As he damn well should have.

Pete however was still pissed at losing one helicopter and another damaged. Losing a person upset him, even if it was just a simulation; losing three was unacceptable. If only he'd somehow been better. Been able to…but he couldn't think of what he might have done differently; and neither had Danielle or she would have suggested it.

Pete found the thought a bit surprising. He was used to being the smartest man in the flight, always a step ahead. Danielle kept him moving, on his toes. He liked that more than he'd have thought; like missing a part of himself that he'd never noticed until someone pointed it out.

Danielle was that part; their flight operations simply fit together. He couldn't even tell anymore who had an idea first in a battle—their back and forth dynamic was that tight.

Cass had found him a great ally in his Second Officer.

Cass McDermott had also found him a good foe for this test; these people had been fantastic. That the 5E had won at all should be a victory even with the simulated losses.

"You just won the Kobayashi Maru," Danielle whispered over the intercom.

"What?" Pete spoke Japanese but didn't know that phrase. Perhaps it was Mandarin, but he knew that as well.

"The unwinnable scenario," Big John spoke up over the intercom in his deep voice. "You gotta catch up on your *Star Trek,* boss. Lady's got it right though. Sometimes you can't win the whole game. But the people you just beat? Oh brother, I didn't give us a snowball's chance. I'm so gonna be rubbing this in Tim's face for years. Years!" He was practically crowing with delight.

Tim? Pete decided it was better not to ask.

By the time they had flown back to the 5E's hangar he was glad he had on his helmet with his visor down and a breather mask in place to hide his expression. He was smiling, and he shouldn't be after losing personnel.

He'd fought them, watched them disappear right in the middle of a radar sweep, but he still wasn't prepared for what he saw waiting for him at the hangar.

The DAP Hawk and two Little Birds that his team had "killed" were lined up there—all three were stealth configured. How had he not known those birds even existed? Not so much as a whisper.

Yet Sergeant John Wallace, and presumably his wife, knew about these people—*not a snowball's chance of beating them.* That meant his crew had just beaten the 5th Battalion D Company.

Now Pete was definitely smiling.

They landed and ran through the shutdown in record time.

He did his best to school his expression as he stepped off the Chinook's rear ramp, but he wasn't having much luck.

Three women and five men awaited the members of the 5E on the tarmac outside the 5E's hangar, lit only by the soft wash of worklights from inside the hangar's open doors. They were lined up as if for a formal military review. The 5E formed up just as neatly in a line of respect.

The leader by the stealth DAP Hawk was tall with a long flow of mahogany hair; he'd met Lola Maloney of the 5D a few times. He'd heard enough of the others to identify the blond as Captain Casperson and the redhead would be the notorious Lieutenant Trisha O'Malley.

He also noted that the men who flew with them did not stand casually off to the side of their pilots, but instead stood close to their...spouses?

Two of them weren't dressed like SOAR. They were dressed like... he knew Delta Force operators when he saw them, he just didn't know what to make of the strange array. At least for tonight the 5D's two Little Birds flew with Delta operators at their side.

Rather than lining up with the rest of Pete's team, Big John walked up to the man standing beside Lola, wrapped him in a quick headlock and rapped his knuckles on the man's head, hard. The other man struggled, but no one moved to help him. In moments they were both laughing.

Pete had heard the 5D was different, followed its own rules, but confronting the reality was far more confusing than contemplating it from afar. Other than John and Tim, who must be the guy in the headlock, the two lines of fliers remained facing one another.

"Assessment, Maloney?" Colonel McDermott strode into the breech before Pete could figure out how to greet them after the recent air battle and defeat.

"Shee-it, sir," Lola Maloney offered a low New Orleans-accented drawl. "You entice away the best crew chiefs in the business and you expect me to happy when they kick my ass. Grumpy, sir. That's my official assessment. Very grumpy!"

"I meant your assessment of your opponents."

"Thought that's what I just said, sir. But I can repeat it for you if you'd like."

Pete had thought he was the only one who could get away with speaking to Colonel McDermott that way.

Lola stepped past the Colonel and came over to shake Pete's hand. "Damn fine job, Napier. Knew you and yours would be tough and we thought we were ready for it. Guess not. Damned fine."

Her grip was strong and he returned it gladly, "Anyone ever manages to take one and a half of my birds again, it had better be you. That was sensational flying, Chief Maloney."

"Climbing out of Pahute Alpha, how did you—"

"None of that now," McDermott cut them off. "Let's first get these birds tucked away then I'll let the chow truck out here."

---

DANIELLE WAS TURNING for her Chinook when she spotted a change that she'd missed earlier. Tucked close beside the hangar was a white shipping container with a set of radio antennas on the roof, big ones. Two women came out the door and then carefully closed and locked it behind them.

She recognized the voice of one of them as they approached across the grass that grew thick alongside the pavement.

"Pete," Danielle called just loudly enough to get his attention, but not the other crew members who were even now tucking the helos back into the hangar.

The two women had drawn close by the time Pete reached her side. Was he aware that he was standing as close to her as Connie and Big John usually stood, as the couples of the 5D had stood? No, because if he was, he would have shied off as he'd done dozens of times this last month.

"What is it?"

She silenced him with a look and nodded to the two approaching women.

One was small with a straight fall of dark hair down her back. Her skin was olive-toned, her accent Brooklyn-Italian, and her walk like she was just daring someone to take her on. Her uniform was military, even if her hair wasn't. Danielle, like many Night Stalkers, had taken advantage of the unique rules for Special Operations Forces, letting her hair grow longer like their SEAL and Delta customers. This woman had clearly decided to use that to her full advantage.

The other, the one she recognized, was a taller version of the first, except her hair, which swirled in great curls, stopped at her shoulders like Danielle's and her voice had the round tones of Spanish...no, Portuguese. Brazilian? At least in origin.

"*Ciao* and *Olá*," Danielle interrupted their intense debate about attack angles and flight endurance.

She'd nailed it when the women greeted her in Italian and Portuguese respectively; the Italian one continued over to the hangar confer with Lola Maloney.

"What?" Pete still didn't get it.

"Listen," she told Pete then turned back to the Brazilian woman who had remained behind with a soft smile on her full lips. "Please greet Major Napier, *por favor.*"

"Napier? Marvelous! I have heard so much of you. And now I have learned even more from how you fly," she pronounced *from* with a lush, round *frohm* sound. Her Brazilian accent was softened by some-thing...Los Angeles, maybe? Definitely Southern California. "You were better than I have even expected." Her words were a mellifluous flow that cascaded over Pete. It was the kind of voice that turned men into stunned puppies and it irritated Danielle that it looked to have done precisely that to The Rapier.

"Actually, Captain Delacroix was piloting the Chino..." Then Pete finally caught onto what was happening. "The voice," he focused on Danielle and nodded rather than turning back to the beautiful woman right away. That made Danielle feel a little better in a way that she decided was entirely too petty.

"Avenger pilot, Lieutenant Sofia Gracie, sir," the woman offered him a sharp salute which he returned even as he continued to face Danielle a moment longer before facing the woman. A Remotely Piloted Aircraft, as RPA pilots preferred them to be called. They became quite testy when you called their aircraft "drones."

"That explains it," Danielle confirmed. "We were wondering who was on our private frequency."

"*Si.* I helped you and Kara Moretti, she has the MQ-1C Gray Eagle, and she helped the others," pronounced *awthers.*

"Wait, did you say Avenger? I didn't know those were even deployed yet."

Sofia's smile was radiant. "There is only the one. I make Kara," she indicated the Brooklyn-Italian woman who had been with her, "so envious she almost cried. Colonel McDermott sent me. He said it was a tryout. I hope I served you well."

Danielle had many trite images of how men might answer that statement from this tall, curvaceous beauty.

"An excellent audition, Lieutenant," Pete at least didn't appear to fall for the trap.

Sofia nodded and looked sad, "I am sorry that I do not see them sooner. It was only after you broke off the attack on the tanks that I spotted them. The stealth you all fly with, it is *so* very good. I am very happy my baby Avenger also has stealth. We must not let enemies have any."

Danielle hadn't seen a stealth drone...RPA, and couldn't wait. And the Avenger? High-flying, long-duration, and with a heavy equipment load, it was also the first jet-powered RPA in the entire

American inventory—one of the most staggering pieces of hardware aloft.

She looked around for it, but there was no unmanned aircraft pulling up the hangar.

"Oh, they are still aloft. Our copilots," she waved a negligent hand back toward the white trailer of the ground control station, "they wanted to practice more together."

"Not just *Extreme...*" Pete offered Danielle a smile of acknowledgement despite the raw sexual power being exuded from so close at hand.

"E for *Extraordinary,*" Danielle whispered.

"It wasn't him," Sofia faced Danielle squarely. "It was you that saw them first. I want to know how. How do you fly so *fantástico* and see them before I did when you are supposed to be busy watching these tanks?"

Danielle shrugged uncertainly as Pete and Sofia inspected her, both waiting for an answer. "I saw something that didn't feel right," it was the best explanation she could find. The battlespace had been a gestalt, all the pieces as clear in her mind as on the inside of her visor. Nothing should have been changing outside of her primary target area, but it had.

"Oh," the woman leaned in and wrapped her in a surprisingly strong hug against her generously curved body. "You and I, we are going to become such good friends that I will someday know all of your secrets. You see if we don't."

Danielle had never been one to collect friends.

Pete was watching her with one of his unsmiling smiles that reached only his eyes, but shone from there. The man knew by now just exactly how much of an outsider Danielle really was.

Oddly after a month sitting side-by-side with Pete Napier, Danielle felt as if he knew her better than anyone she'd ever flown with. And she knew a lot about him and his family. Not a real close family, but absolutely a functioning unit; going through life together and supporting each other. She had tried to explain the luxury he had, but he still didn't see it. It was just a part of who he was.

And now he was laughing at her in his quiet way, because he knew Danielle made friends very slowly and still kept them at a distance even when she did.

"I'd like that," she turned back to Sofia. That would put him in his place. Besides, maybe it was time to stretch a bit and test out friendship—real friendship, not fellow-soldier acquaintances. She'd never find better people than the members of the 5E to start with.

"Of course you do," Sofia linked her arm through Danielle's. "We always need more friends. Come. We will eat together and leave this Major to dream of how much he wishes it was his arm and not mine linked with yours." And Sofia had her moving along.

Half horrified and half intrigued, Danielle tried to turn to see Pete's reaction.

"*Not* with the looking," Sofia whispered sharply and tugged on their joined arms to halt Danielle's turn to see. "You must make him wonder if I am crazy or if I am right. Do you know nothing about teasing men?"

*Apparently not.* And she didn't want to tease Pete. Of course that opened up the question of what she did want to do with him and she had no answer for that either.

She and Sofia chatted amiably about the flight as they headed back into the hangar to help the crew chiefs.

Danielle did sneak a quick look back at Pete when she was sure Sofia wasn't watching. He was still rooted to the grassy spot close beside the hanger where they had left him, still looking in their direction.

"Is he still there?" Sofia asked while she appeared to be looking elsewhere.

"So much for being subtle."

"You can't fool a woman from Brazil. Not even when she comes to your country when she is about to be a teenager. It is in our blood."

"He's still there," Danielle reported dutifully.

"Good," Sofia nodded definitely and once more faced Danielle. "Then that is where you will find him tonight after all of us others are gone away. He will be on that exact spot, though he will not know it.

Now, for rest of evening you will stay near women and we will all laugh together to make him even more out of his mind."

She wouldn't go to him. She wanted to go to him. Danielle did her best to hide her internal conflict and her surprise.

But Sofia's smile said that it was pointless to try and hide such things from a woman from Brazil.

The practice engagement in the heart of the NTTR, for all its stress and ferocity had been brief. The celebration meal had once again been set out in front of the hangers except the lush heat of August in Alabama had given way to a cool September night in the arid Nevada desert.

After several hours, most of which he'd spent with Lola Maloney and Cass talking tactics, reminded Pete again that Cass had *flown* his way to his position, not politicked it, because damn the man's brain was sharp. The members of the 5D headed aloft to fly back to Joint Base Lewis-McChord in Washington state before dawn. The area emptied as his team members headed for their beds in ones and twos; no desert disc golf course here and too tired even if there was. The last of them shrugged into jackets and left as Pete went to see McDermott off.

As they walked downfield toward Cass' waiting jet, McDermott offered him an opportunity to change out personnel.

Pete bit on his tongue for a long moment before replying, "I...don't have a problem with any of them if you don't, sir."

"When was the last time you called me, sir, Pete?"

"Day you recruited me for SOAR, sir," he said it again just to mess with Cass.

The Colonel continued to move slowly toward a waiting jet.

"We need to change, Pete. In a lot of ways. I've given the 5D a lot of leeway in the past and they've performed. But Mark Henderson thought he was pulling the wool over my eyes on every operation. I don't need you to merely go out and be better than the 5D, they're already doing that—outperforming themselves every damn day. I lost Mark and Emily and assumed I'd have to rebuild the whole unit. But they trained Lola and she's added Trisha, Claudia, and others who are just as excellent in their own ways. They have two fully embedded D-boys to keep them on their toes."

Pete had forgotten to ask Lola Maloney about that. He liked the idea. Delta were some of their biggest customers. He'd need to think about the advantages of doing something like that himself. Once he'd seen what types of missions they drew, he'd figure out who to approach.

"I need you to go out and find the edge. That's why I'm glad you decided to keep Danielle. Every one of these people are very good, but she's as exceptional as a young punk 2nd Looey I hauled out of the Army National Guard a lifetime ago."

Pete kept his thoughts to himself about the lame kid he'd been back way back when. Then-Captain Cassius McDermott had told him Pete was being transferred to the 82nd Airborne and later to SOAR. Saying "no" to a fellow Coloradan hadn't been an option.

"You've never made me regret that decision."

"I won't let you down, Cass."

"I know that, you young idiot." Cass was all of six years older than he was. "You need to make sure that your people never regret signing aboard with you. You've run rough over a lot of people, Pete. There's gonna be a goddamn riot in my office when the others hear that I gave a new company to you. But I know what you can do. Don't run rough over these folks, Pete. They're yours. You're in big boy school now. Prove it."

"Yes, sir," Pete saluted.

"Not to me, you dolt. I already know what you've got in you or your sorry ass would still be parked in the Colorado Guard dinking around the sky in an aging UH-60 with a bunch of weekend warriors. Now prove it to them," he pointed back toward where the others had headed off to their barracks.

Then Cass climbed aboard his jet and was gone.

Pete wandered back toward the hangar. Stopped to look at the white control trailer for the Avenger RPA. Sofia Gracie was apparently one of his now along with her copilot Zoe DeMille who he'd barely met.

He stood alone on the grass strip beside the sealed hangar that held the 5E.

His company.

It was three a.m. and the half moon was little more than a suggestion low in the western sky. The constellation Hercules was descending toward the western mountains as Perseus the Warrior began climbing over the eastern ones.

No birds in the desert, no spring peepers, not even any passing helos. The silence was so vast that a man could become lost in it.

"Hercules descends," he told the silent evening.

"Sent to his labors for murdering his wife and children while under the goddess Hera's spell of madness."

Danielle's voice was a body shock. He thought she'd gone with the others.

Pete couldn't turn to face her, though he could hear just how close she was—her voice had been little more than a whisper.

"And Perseus ascends..." he managed.

"...flying to meet and rescue his Andromeda."

"Danielle," still he didn't turn, though it cost him. "You should leave. We can't..." He couldn't finish the sentence.

"I know," she shushed him as softly as a kiss.

He wanted.

He needed.

"How did the others...?" There was no need for him to explain what others. The couples of 5th Battalion D Company had been around them all night. As comfortable together as could be. Comfortable in front of their commanding officer who turned a blind eye. Perhaps because they were already married. The Army was changing, but not *that* fast. Not so much that he didn't recognize it or understand how—

Then she rested her fingertips ever so lightly against his back. The thin cotton of his t-shirt was warm enough for the evening, but not enough to fend off the heat of her touch. Hell, he'd feel the searing brand through full battle armor.

Her simple touch silenced all his careening thoughts.

"Tonight, we aren't here. Not the Major and the Captain, not Napier and Delacroix, not even The Rapier and Spiderwoman. There is only *tu et moi*."

THE ICY CHILL of Pete's unmoving silence made Danielle instantly regret taking Sofia's advice. But exactly as Sofia had predicted, he had returned to the same spot they had left him earlier, a mere shadow in the darkness of the night. The temptation had proved too much and she'd come to him—to be told to leave.

How could she have been stupid enough, for even a moment, to reach out for something she wanted.

There was only one thing she had ever wanted so deeply that it became a part of her: to fly. She'd been tempted to risk even that for this man, but still he didn't turn toward her. How had she read everything so wrong?

She let her hand drop. It was not for Danielle Delacroix to want things. She was the only child of an alcoholic mother and no father. Why had the gods made her want so much?

And now she had gone too far.

Would Pete even let her remain in the 5E? No. He would want her as far from him as possible, just as she had known he should.

Her fingertips were still warm with his heat as she turned toward the lonely road to base housing. There was only the one vehicle that had been left for Pete's use; she'd do her best to not give in to the tears on the long solo walk.

Danielle curled her hand into a fist to hold in the warmth at the same moment Pete grabbed her by the shoulders and spun her about. She inadvertently clipped his chin with the back of her fist; hard enough to knock back any normal man.

Pete Napier didn't react.

Didn't hesitate.

He pulled her in tight, trapping both of her arms between them, and crushed his mouth down on hers.

His voracious need surged over her.

She struggled for a breath, couldn't find it, didn't care, and leaned into the kiss.

Pete tore at her clothes and, as soon as her hands were free, she did the same to his. In moments they were mostly naked in the faint light of the sliver-thin moon. His shirt caught around one wrist and her khakis snarled on one ankle where the bootlace had knotted.

"I don't..." he gasped out as he drove her mad with his desperate grasps and grazing teeth.

She lifted the booted foot where her pants hung about one ankle, dug a foil packet out of the pocket, and shoved it into his palm. She had so hoped...

He had her down on the grass and drove into her faster than a DAP Hawk diving to the attack.

Their need let neither of them slow until the sensations rose too huge to contain and she released them into the night. Pete's moan was the bass note to her treble cry, the only sounds echoing down the dark length of the deserted airfield.

# CHAPTER 8

"I've," Pete huffed out the word and tried again. "I've never needed anyone so badly."

Danielle wrapped her legs around his hips and crossed her ankles. Her arms were locked about his neck so hard he couldn't have moved if there was an attack.

"I didn't," he'd kill himself if he had, "hurt you, did I?"

Her purr wasn't one of contentment but rather of triumphant declaration. He'd take that as a *no*. By the sounds she was making, an emphatic one.

He lay against her and only slowly became aware of other sensations around them. One of her feet crossed over his butt was still clad in pants and an Army boot, the sole of which was digging in hard. The long Nevada grass wasn't as soft as the lush Alabama grass of Fort Rucker. He'd imagined in a hundred fantasies bedding this woman outdoors on a lush soft bed of nature. This wasn't soft at all. Dry, scratchy, and embedded in hardpan soil with all the give of fifty-year old concrete. But he couldn't imagine moving just yet, not even to accommodate her comfort.

Pete noticed next how well they fit together and just how uninterested he was in moving. Her curves pressed against him and her

Chinook-flying powerful legs wrapped around him. She shifted once or twice, but it wasn't in discomfort, it was to settle their hips closer together.

He'd never just *taken* a woman like this. Not in high school, not drunk in college. He might have paid less attention to a woman's pleasure than he should have at times, but he'd never simply needed to drive himself into one and declare that was where he belonged.

Pete spotted her discarded shirt off to the side. He gave them both a judicious roll that placed his back, at least most of it, on her shirt and shifted her off the itchy grass.

Ever since that first brush of lips a month ago he'd wondered what it would be like to make love to this woman. *You still don't know, Pete.*

"What don't you know?" her voice came out on a happy sigh.

"I'd, uh," *have to be more careful about thinking aloud,* "pictured our first time together differently."

"You pictured it?" No hint of disgust in her voice.

"Yes."

"How often?" No hint of coy either. Or of letting him off the hook anytime soon.

He tried to get enough distance to look at her face. But since her arms were still crossed behind his neck and he was lying on them and then the ground, he could neither move downward nor she upward. Despite the crick her arms were putting in his neck, he wasn't ready to release her yet. So they lay there speaking mouth to each other's ear.

"Often."

She did a thing with her hips that had him hissing with the sensations scorching up his body, and grinding his butt into the sharp grass.

"Very often," he amended.

"How?"

"How what? How have I fantasized about you?"

"Um-hm."

"No way am I answering that, woman."

She did the hip thing again.

"No way," he managed on a groan. "Spiderwoman going to bite off my head now?"

"That's praying mantises…mantis*i?*"

"I'm the one on the verge of death and you're conjugating verbs?"

"Plurals as in nouns, not tenses as in verbs. Latin conjugation is always tricky. Conjugal rights? No, I didn't just say that."

He started to laugh. He was buried, uh, shaft deep in a woman and she was debating parts of speech. Well, not much debate from him really. She was *analyzing* parts of speech. And stumbling over words that meant marriage when they'd barely had sex. After what he'd just done to her, he'd let her off…this time.

And now he was thinking about word choices. *Fine job making her first time all screwed up.*

"No, you screwed *down.* Now that we've rolled over you could screw *up* though."

He tried thumping the back of his head against the ground to knock some sense into it but, with her arms still trapped there, it wasn't very effective.

Pete leaned upward enough for her to recover her arms. As soon as they were gone he missed them because he was a total fool.

"Danielle?"

"No. Don't go rational yet. There's plenty of time for that later. *Tu et moi.* We are all that exist in this moment."

"I don't speak French."

"Why not?"

"Because I speak Viet, Mandarin, Japanese, and—"

"What does that have to do with anything? A civilized man who is going to share my bed—"

"This isn't a bed."

"Never interrupt a French woman when she is lecturing you. If you had any manners you would *parles français* when you are inside her."

Damn but he really liked this woman.

She propped her forearms on his chest, rubbed her hand over it for a moment, and offered another purr of contentment despite her rant.

His hands, which he only now realized had remained firmly clamped on her butt as if it was somehow physically possible to force them closer together, traveled up from her waist and encountered her bra. He began searching for the release clasp.

"Hello. Sports bra." She reached down between them and tugged it off over her head flipping her hair across him in a soft caress of dark liquid that caught a thousand glints of the very last of the moonlight. Then she lay back down on him before he could test if her breasts' feel and shape matched the fine lines they'd made beneath her t-shirt. They did feel moderately fantastic where they pressed against his chest though, so it was hard to feel too bad about the missed opportunity.

He stroked his thumbs along the soft skin to the sides. Even against his rough hands it was remarkably soft.

"Back to those fantasies, Mr. Napier."

"That's Major to you."

"You already did *major* to me. I'm just waiting for you to recover so that you can do more."

"Recover, huh?" He pushed her up until they were both standing on the grass. They stumbled about in the starlit darkness, doing their best to find their various pieces of clothing tossed among the grass. He would come back at first light to make sure they'd found everything.

Grabbing her hand, he led her into the dimly-lit interior of the hangar. Danielle stumbled along behind him, her one still-booted foot clomping loudly on the hangar's concrete floor. She turned for the Chinook, but he had something else in mind. For one thing, the pilots' seats in the MH-47 were almost six feet off the ground.

The DAP Hawk, a machine they both flew well, suited his purposes much better. A low seat and a wide-swinging door. Better yet, a Little Bird which had no door at all.

Before she could protest, he scooped her up in his arms and dropped her into the seat.

"Cold," she tried to climb back out of the seat.

"Stay."

When she again attempted to get out of the seat, he snapped the seat belt harness across her waist and pulled the strap tight to pin her there. He left off the dual shoulder harness as that would cover her breasts. They were very nice breasts, that perfect cross between perky and fullness, and he didn't want them hidden.

She crossed her arms there to achieve the same result.

He gently unfolded her arms, admired the shadowed view for a moment, and then leaned in to kiss her.

---

IT WAS LOVELY. Danielle could do nothing but hold onto the flight controls where her hands had naturally landed as Pete kissed her.

Numb. Toast. Shorted out nervous system. She couldn't even raise her hand to investigate how incredible he felt or to trace the muscles of that truly exceptional chest of his.

Her grip tightened on the controls as his hands reached out to her. One dug into her hair offering her no escape from the lush kiss he offered, not that she wanted to miss a moment of it. Despite the almost violent heat of the possessive kiss, his other hand brushed downward more softly than a nighttime breeze.

Again she braced for him to grab and squeeze. Instead—twice as thrilling because he was so strong and his hands rough with hard work—he traced, caressed, and cradled. He gave the shape of her ribs just as much attention as he had her breast, and then—skipping the wide waist belt he'd pinned her with—her hip and thigh.

By the time he slid his hand up the inside of her thigh she was powerless to do anything but receive.

It was his fantasy. And it was so clear and so persuasive that she could make no effort to resist or assist; she could only receive. Her hands slid loosely off the controls as he drove her up until she was bucking against the restraint of the harness and his hand. Her ultimate release came on a sigh rather than a cry—a soft sigh of a woman she didn't recognize. She was always in careful control of her emotions, but around Pete she had no barriers, no internal gauge with neatly delineated areas of operation. He asked and she gave everything she had.

Danielle had never enjoyed dominance games, those power games that were so important to men.

For some reason that she couldn't identify, she knew that Pete Napier was not playing a dominance game on her. Instead, he was focused on giving all that he could to her in a place she so belonged, the cockpit of a helicopter. The pilot seat of a SOAR helicopter was a place that only a handful of women had ever sat, and she was one of them.

Pete was making love to her there out of all the possible places he could have chosen.

He acknowledged who she was and whatever trouble it would cause her—it was sure to be much trouble—and she loved him for it.

---

It was the sound of the tractor arriving outside the hangar that afternoon that had once again sent them scrambling for their respectability. Pete recognized the tractor's noise; it was a mower, a big one.

Definitely time to get moving if they didn't want to be caught. Somewhere in mid-morning Pete had finally bedded Danielle properly in the back of the Chinook upon a pile of folded-out rescue blankets, or rather she had bedded him. He had screwed *up,* and she had knelt over him and controlled his every sensation as she went *down* on him.

He liked the power of being on top, but the opportunity to caress and watch such an amazing woman as she slowly unraveled in the throes of passion and release had been incredible. The privacy of the shadowed interior of the helicopter had only added to the image.

They had then laid there together for the longest time afterward talking idly of nothing much at all. He couldn't recall a single one of the topics, far too aware of how Danielle felt lying against him. Of how protective he felt for the simple arm he kept wrapped about her waist. For the perfect contentment of her head on his shoulder and his cheek against her hair.

But the mower dragged them back to real life and they began tracking down their clothes. Some were in the Chinook with them, most were over by the Little Bird. A few other pieces were scattered about the hangar floor in places he didn't remember stopping during the night, Danielle's panties had ultimately ended up dangling from the long, phallic tip of the DAP Hawk's refueling probe for reasons neither of them could recall.

It was Danielle, not himself who identified his missing piece of apparel. No matter where they looked, he had no pants.

He sent the fully clothed Danielle out to check the grassy verge between the hangar and the flight control container for the Avenger RPA.

She made it two steps out the door and then turned back, closed the door, and fell laughing into his arms.

"What?"

"*Tes pantalons, monsieur.* They are now in teeny tiny pieces."

"He mowed them?" Pete pictured a thousand tiny bits of khaki scattered about the runway's grassy verge.

She nodded and burst out laughing again.

Thankfully, he had some gear in the small locker room at the back of the hangar, but it didn't help that Danielle's bright laughter followed him as he crossed the broad concrete floor in his underwear.

anielle had thought they were being discrete, until she saw Sofia's smile when everyone gathered at the base Mess Hall for breakfast that evening. The 5E's team suddenly felt overwhelming large. Two pilots times four aircraft, five crew chiefs, and now Sofia and her copilot, a petite blonde.

She and Pete had slept little, but she felt simultaneously wide awake and languid. And she also felt as if everyone could see writ large on her face that she'd just spent hours participating in life-changing sex.

Pete was such a powerful personality that he was constantly overwhelming her. Her nerve endings were exhausted by the unprecedented scale and quality of messages they'd had to transmit. And her emotions were wrung from the degree of pleasure and joy they'd been forced to contemplate.

"Was it filled with goodness, little sister?" Sofia asked in a moment when they were shuffling their trays down the chow line together.

"Very much goodness," Danielle agreed.

"I knew it would be. The way he looks at you, I wish someone would look at me that way."

"I think all men must look at you that way." Sofia's beauty was undeniable.

"Your Major Napier did not look at me so. This is how I knew he is in love with you. Besides, when men look at me, they look at this," she brushed a negligent hand down her body in a move so graceful that Danielle could never hope to match it. "Not this," she tapped a finger against her heart.

Danielle had a soothing reply on her lips, but couldn't seem to complete the delivery.

Sofia's words "he is in love with you" had sunk in somewhere after dishing up bacon but before the scrambled eggs. The rest was a blur and she arrived at the table with bacon, green beans instead of hash browns, and a hot dog rather than the eggs she'd been looking forward to just moments earlier.

Orange juice instead of cranberry.

Hot chocolate instead of coffee.

She needed coffee. She caught herself only moments before she began dumping sugar into the hot chocolate, but couldn't seem to halt the addition of cream. Her brain knew it was wrong, but signals to her hand were not making it through.

"I'm…he's not."

"Who's not what?" Patty asked. The redheaded Chief Warrant folded a long slice of steak into her mouth as she spoke. Her meal of steak and fries with a cup of soup made sense when Danielle looked at it. She looked at her own tray again and knew it was wrong but still couldn't quite get a handle on how. She was fairly sure that she despised hotdogs, about the only thing her mother had known how to cook, but even that thought didn't gain much traction in her whirling thoughts.

Sofia started to explain, but Danielle put up a hand.

"No. Don't you dare."

Sofia offered an elegant shrug and a teasing smile.

"I mean it. Violence will ensue," Danielle warned.

"You should not say such things to a woman from Brazil, my friend."

"Why not?" Danielle knew her voice was far too close to being a demand, but she didn't have control of it back yet.

Sofia simply looked down the table.

Danielle followed her gaze. The other three women of the 5E were seated close beside them and Danielle hadn't even noticed.

Patty was chewing her steak and watching her closely through narrowed blue eyes.

Sofia's copilot, Zoe who had emerged from the Avenger's Ground Control Station only after several hours of practice looked at Danielle in utter confusion.

Connie Davis' dark amber eyes were assessing, calculating. One thing that Danielle had learned about Connie over the last month was that there was a very sharp mind working beneath her placid exterior. She was a woman who observed and analyzed everything, even if she rarely spoke.

Connie hadn't missed what Sofia said, even if Patty had. But Connie hadn't been in line with them when Sofia had dropped the L-word. Still, somehow she's heard.

Or a worse scenario?

Like Sofia, perhaps Connie somehow just knew. Knew that Danielle was completely gone on her commanding officer Major Pete Napier. The over-serious, full-speed-ahead soldier—in addition to being the best pilot she'd ever flown with—was also the powerful lover who could not get enough of her. Or she of him.

And that they'd acted on that need. In the Army that wasn't a sin, it was a crime.

The odd thing was, the after-sex feeling was backwards. Usually there was initial attraction, getting to know each other a bit, sex, and then trying to keep it going…which had always unraveled on her.

With Pete, they'd spent a month flying side by side and she knew him better than any man in her life…and then the sex. In a funny way, it was the flight test after they'd done all the training, which made much more sense when she thought about it that way. And the test had been passed with beyond flying colors.

"I find it interesting as well," Connie began. Her meal was a perfectly normal breakfast that she was eating very neatly. None of the foods were even touching each other on her plate.

Danielle longed to be Sue "Invisible Girl" Storm of the Fantastic Four and simply disappear, but the Spidey accolade had stuck so far—not that it helped, the requisite superpowers had yet to put in an appearance. It left her powerless to halt the conversation.

"We have integrated so rapidly with our equipment," Connie twisted the topic unexpectedly.

Was she being kind or merely exhibiting more of her typical mechanic's tunnel vision? Danielle couldn't tell by the expression on Connie's face. Either way, Danielle was thankful for the reprieve.

"I think that is your and Major Napier's effect. However, the 5th Battalion D Company had a higher level of personal cohesiveness by the time I had joined the company. Granted that was several years after its formation."

Danielle sipped her cream-dosed hot chocolate which was about the same as licking a stick of butter. "You're saying we're too unfriendly?" That didn't come out right at all. She and Pete had been entirely too friendly all day since their nighttime aerial combat test.

Her phrasing caused Sofia to smirk in a friendly-nudge sort of way that Patty still totally missed. Thank goodness.

"No." If Connie caught it, she ignored it and proceeded with a comforting forthrightness to answer the question at face value.

That was another of the things Danielle had learned about Connie over the last month, the woman was a straight-shooter who proceeded down a path until it was completely handled, and then moved to the next topic.

"I think that your focus on skills has been admirable. These are very unique craft that require a unique talent and last night proved that we have excelled. Beating Lola, Trisha, and Claudia. I agree with John, that was an exceptionally unlikely outcome despite your additional possession of the Chinook."

"*Your?*"

"Another factor to make my point," Connie continued calmly. "I should have said *our* without thinking, yet I didn't. Friendships have been very slow to form within the 5E. Powerful working relation-ships, yes. Friendships far less so in my observations."

"I'm...at a loss. I...don't know how to have friends." To hide her unease at such an unexpected revelation from herself, Danielle bit off a piece of her hot dog, unsure why she'd salted and peppered it. Because she'd thought it was eggs and hash browns? She discovered that she still despised hot dogs even with salt and pepper.

Connie eyed her for a long moment. And in that instant she knew that Connie was much the same. Danielle suddenly felt very close to the quiet mechanic. What had it cost her to leave the 5D? Had she had friends there?

"Well," Danielle gave up and shoved her unpalatable meal aside, keeping only the bacon and orange juice. If she was the senior officer here, aside from their commander, it was time she started acting like it. "Having our first meal together as the five women of the 5E seems like a good place to start, doesn't it?"

"Of course. It is a wonderful place to start," Sofia bubbled.

Connie considered, glanced around the table, and then nodded once in simple agreement. There was a deeper meaning there, one that was terribly important to her.

Danielle could feel it herself. These women would be important to her. They would fly together, fight together, and become friends as only women in a combat zone could be. She had the tiniest glimpse of them possibly being friends for life—which would have been an unimaginable horizon only moments before.

Patty was staring straight at Danielle.

"So, Pete was that good, huh?"

Danielle could feel the heat rushing to her face. He had been; more than good. All she could manage was a nod, but everyone's laughter made her feel as if she might actually belong somewhere. Maybe even right here.

---

"Do I even want to know what they're laughing about?" Pete hacked off another chunk of his steak and looked across at the five women. Damn but they were a sight. And Danielle…shit! The woman glowed among them. He'd wrung out both of their bodies and he could feel himself hardening anyway with his need to do it all over again.

"Nope," Big John rumbled out. "You can trust me on that. You really don't want to know."

"Who's the chick again?" Mickey "The Mighty Dozer" Quinn asked. The man fit his name. He was a big Alaskan native, not as big as Big John, but close. Pete felt small sitting at the table with the two of them.

"That chick is my wife," Big John rumbled out, but after a month of flying together there was no question of Dozer referring to Connie.

"Lieutenant Sofia Gracie is an Avenger pilot. The 5E gets a dedicated stealth drone and she's the one flying it." He recognized the look in Dozer's eyes. "And don't even think about it." Of course his own thoughts were plenty preoccupied.

Dozer flinched and looked at him, "Right. Sorry, sir."

Big John slapped Pete on the back so hard he was glad his elbows were on the table or he'd have face-planted in his steak.

Pete decided that if he didn't want to know what was making the women laugh, and ten times as much he didn't want to know what so amused Big John.

---

DANIELLE FINALLY BROKE DOWN and went back for a proper breakfast. She thought up a topic change on her way back to the table. She *needed* a topic change. The way Pete's eyes tracked her to the chow line and back sent prickles up her skin.

Sofia might say he loved her, but that wasn't on either of their rosters. Though she and Pete certainly needed each other; there had *never* been sex like his anywhere in her experience. The raw force of his personality had battered at her until she could only hang on and go for the ride he'd taken her on…but, oh my God, what a ride! She couldn't wait to climb aboard again.

She carefully didn't look at Pete though he was only two tables away.

"Good girl," Sofia whispered to her as she sat back down. The woman's wink was sly and friendly. Pete was back over Danielle's right shoulder, but thankfully the women were to her left so she could avoid constantly glancing over at him.

"Your Avenger," Danielle went for her topic change, "it needs a name."

"It's a drone, so we could name it *Danielle* for being a force of nature," Patty suggested. "No. Wait. We already have one of those." This time the laughter around the table was friendly and Danielle could feel herself melting. She was no longer standing off to the side observing; instead she was participating. Welcome. Maybe even wanted.

"Or *Dorothy* for killing the Wicked Witch of the West," Connie put in. "Though it was technically her house that did the work, probably suffering severe damage to its foundation. That always bothered me as a child, Dorothy gets the credit, but it is the house that—"

"My baby, she is no *drone*. She is an RPA. Remotely Piloted Aircraft and I am her pilot." Sofia sat bolt upright, fists on her hips and her dauntingly curvaceous chest thrust forward in defiance.

"*Ripley* for Sigourney in *Alien?*" Zoe jumped in with no fear despite being new to the group.

"*Robin* for Mrs. Robinson from *The Graduate.*"

"No! My Avenger is very sexy and very dangerous, but not evil. *Absolutamente não!*" She held up a palm for emphasis.

"*Raider* for *Raiders of the Lost Ark?*"

"Hello, female heroine rule, remember?" Danielle put in. She was rather proud of slipping that rule past Pete without his noticing until after all his birds were named.

"Or *Raven* for Marion Ravenwood in *Raiders?*" Zoe again, with a shy smile that bothered offered and welcomed. Danielle had liked her at first meeting last night, and even more so now. She was a good addition to their team.

"Ooo," Sofia purred, "that one is right. She keeps Indy in his place, doesn't she?"

"*Ms. Raven* it is," Danielle declared.

And she finally allowed herself to glance over her shoulder at Pete. He might be a powerful force, but her new friends had dubbed her a *force de la nature*. She was Spiderwoman. The Number Two of SOAR's newest company. Befriended of four pretty damn impressive women.

And in that moment Danielle knew what she wanted.

*Yes, Pete,* she thought to herself. *I too am powerful. You had best be ready for me.*

She offered him her blandest smile before turning back to her friends. This time Sofia offered no wink and Patty no smirk.

But beneath the edge of the table, Connie briefly squeezed her hand in acknowledgement.

Yes, now she understood Connie and Big John.

Danielle knew what she wanted. And it wasn't just for another amazing tumble among the helicopters.

Patty started some story about a gunnery sergeant who thought he could outshoot her. But Patty was a girl raised hunting duck in late summer and deer, moose, and bear with her grandda each Thanksgiving vacation in the woods of Maine. Apparently the gunny had then tried to out-cuss her, but Patty had also grown up playing on the fishing docks of Gloucester throughout the school year and working the fishing boats in the summers.

After being with Pete Napier, Danielle knew she was done hunting. She didn't want anyone else. Ever.

---

"Major Pete Napier?" a cute blond orderly appeared next to Dozer. The man hooked a thumb toward Pete.

She gave Pete a pert salute, and a radiant smile that his face typically earned him. She handed him a sealed envelope and, when he did no more than salute back, she was gone. It was hard not to admire her loose-hipped walk, but all it made him think of was Danielle's unself-conscious elegance.

Danielle's walk wasn't a tease like the orderly's, nor a declaration of power like Sophie's sensuously confident stride. Danielle's walk spoke simply and clearly, here is a woman eminently sure of herself. No need to entice, she was simply, wholly herself.

It was the same startling way she made love. She gave as freely as she took. Not submissive, but as an equal. He'd never forget that first time when he'd taken her with blinding, unthinking-animal need, and she was the one who had sounded triumphant afterward. Whereas he'd been shattered; a thousand shards scattered at her feet in supplication hoping she would grant him more. And she had.

"You gonna do something with that?"

Pete glared at Dozer and wondered how the hell the man knew about himself and Danielle. Then he noticed that the man was looking at the sealed orders Pete was still holding.

As he started to tear it open, Big John's hard elbow slammed into his ribs. As Pete jerked in surprise, and grunted hard at the force of the blow, he tore the envelope and the orders in half.

He pulled out the two pieces of paper and slid them together so that he could read across the tear.

Big John leaned over his shoulder to read and offered a low whistle.

"What?" Dozer leaned in trying to read them upside down from across the table.

"The 5E is declared active and ready for deployment," Pete managed.

"Hot damn!" Dozer and John high-fived across the table.

Pete scanned the rest, rising to his feet as he did so. He barely heard their questions trailing after him.

He moved up beside Danielle, interrupted something that had them all laughing again: Patty's guffaw, Sofia's laugh, Zoe's giggles, and Connie and Danielle's quiet smiles. He handed her the orders.

"Is there a reason that you have torn these in half?" she teased him as she began reading. She stopped after the first line and turned to face the other women. "We have done it. We are declared ready."

"Wow!" "In four weeks?" "That is so excellent!"

"Thank you," Danielle sounded so sincere to her crew that Pete felt like an idiot. He'd never for a moment thought about thanking John and Dozer, Rafe, Julian, and the others. Even though it was as much their doing as his.

"Keep reading," he prompted her.

She did and then looked up at him wide-eyed. At his nod, she turned back to her companions, "Time to saddle up, ladies. First mission starts now. Hope you like sushi."

And that fast, Danielle had her people moving. She didn't even have to call out to the other tables where the crew were scattered and chatting over their finished meals. The women of the 5E were in motion? Then the whole company followed.

He finally began to understand the advantages of having women in the field for more than the immense competence they had shown him over the last month.

Moving as a true unit for the first time, the men and women of the 5E dumped their trays at the dishwasher's window and formed up loosely to follow him to the hangars.

Of course, even though they were side by side, he wasn't so sure that he and the others weren't actually following Danielle.

# CHAPTER 10

"Six hours it took to break down the helicopters far enough to fit into a C-5 Galaxy transport," John moaned as he finished the last inspection on the reassembled Chinook helicopter now parked in a secure hangar at Kadena Air Base in Okinawa, Japan.

Pete agreed, it was always a long, pain-in-the-ass process to move a big bird like the Chinook across long distances. A couple thousand miles was no real problem, the sixty-five hundred miles from the NTTR to Japan, was a whole different matter. They could do it, in a forty-hour flight with multiple mid-air refuelings over the open ocean...it was easier and safer to take it apart enough to stuff it on an Air Force jet.

The hangar, not as new as the one at Mother Rucker or as dusty and dry as the one at the Nevada Range, was still similar enough that Pete found it to be terribly disorienting.

Their external scenery had been an exchange from an arid desert airbase in the dead of night to a hot, tropical airbase in the dead of night. Their internal scenery could have been a hangar on any US airbase in the world right down to the huge American flag hanging on the back wall.

He'd served a lot of time here in Japan, frequently flying the edges of Korean and Russian airspace. Even crossing it a few times. But inside the hangar he was in some weird bubble of technology, surrounded by four helicopters he still wasn't used to seeing, and the crew he was still getting to know, though he'd learned to totally trust.

"It's because you're on the goddamn Chinook," Patty was teasing John. "My Little Bird was ready in fifteen minutes."

"Pipsqueak little machine," John said bitterly but with no malice in his tone that Pete could detect.

It wasn't really fair. For transport on the massive C-5 Galaxy transport jet, the Little Bird only needed to have the fuel tanks drained and then fold the rotor blades back until they hung over the tail. On the Chinook, it was necessary to remove not only the six massive rotor blades, but also tear down the rotor heads as well.

Pete was impressed as hell that they'd done it in only six hours because the stealth modification added a lot of shapes and layers around the normal, large-to-begin-with rotor heads.

"Then twelve hours in transit aboard a roaring steel can," Rafe whined continuing the chronicle of the last twenty-four hours.

"Run by the U.S. Air Farce," Julian tossed in. The Air Force had command of all of the big transports.

"And Connie took us all for way too much money at poker," Pete decided it was time to shift the mood of the crew.

"That's my gal," John was suddenly beaming. "Of course if she shared her winnings instead of taking my money too I might be happier." The game had raged for hours over the Pacific, and Connie was the winner by a wide margin.

It was clear that John couldn't be prouder. And Pete half suspected that Connie's winnings would find their way back to John at vacation time or perhaps as a surprise savings account at their retirement. Connie didn't seem like a gal into frills, glad as could be to serve in the Army and let the military provide life's necessities.

"Took you seven hours to rebuild the Chinook," Pete decided maybe John didn't deserve to be both happy *and* have a loving wife like Connie.

John groaned once again, "Don't remind me."

Deserve. Did Pete deserve a woman like Danielle? Wow! There was a loaded question. Did he feel like the luckiest shit on the planet for getting to bed her? Oh yeah.

But what had he done to deserve her attentions? That was far less clear. He'd been consistently grouchy about forming the 5E, then driving everyone like mad to excel because of *his* desire to get back in the field.

"Why are you even with me?"

"'Cause you're the boss," Big John thumped him on the shoulder.

Pete definitely needed his head examined, perhaps starting with a swift smack. He looked around for Danielle and instead spotted a team of four men who entered and crossed the hangar floor with the smooth grace of top operators.

One moved like an officer despite his big pack. The other three were also humping packs, even bigger ones. Two of the three had beards and civilian hair. The third was clean-shaven... No, another woman in the service. They were everywhere all of a sudden.

"Hi Pete," Lieutenant Commander Luke Altman came up and shook his hand; a crushing grip that Pete gladly returned.

"Hey Luke," he'd carried Commander Altman and his SEAL team on any number of missions. Altman was one of the very best the Navy had to offer. "What brings a bunch of SEALs to Okinawa?"

"You do."

Pete gave himself a moment to digest that. They'd had the helos together for about seven minutes and, *ding,* on cue, in come the operators. He could feel Cass McDermott back there pulling strings.

Luke dropped his pack to the concrete floor and the other three did the same.

"Didn't know you had women in the SEALs," Pete bought himself another moment to consider things.

If Luke was involved, this op went way higher up the pecking order than just Cass. Joint Special Operations Command was in on this one.

"No offense intended, ma'am," he addressed the woman. After all, it didn't pay to tick off a Navy SEAL.

"I have Nikita," Luke shrugged "Night Stalkers have..." Luke looked him up and down, "you! No offense intended Nikita."

She simply rolled her eyes at her commander's back.

"I felt that," Luke said without bothering to turn to her.

It was the sworn duty of every service member to look down on anyone in another branch. Pete opened his mouth to say something about having learned how to be a wimp by watching SEALs—

"Are you now one of the women of SOAR, Major Napier?" Danielle appeared at his elbow as if magically transported.

It was unnerving how easily she did that to him. She was the only person who could slip past his situational awareness. The woman he should be most sensitive to, and she did it to him constantly.

"You must be very proud to be one of us. Do you wear a dress often?"

"No. Do you?" Pete shot back at her.

"Only when someone takes me dancing."

"Lady," Luke grinned at her with a lascivious smile and Pete resisted a sudden urge to flatten the SEAL commander up against the side of the DAP Hawk parked close behind him, "if I weren't already married, that would be a date. What about you, Pete?"

"Me? Do I look like I dance?"

"I don't know. Grass skirt, a couple white orchid Hawaiian leis. I think you'd make a picture."

"Don't forget the ukulele," Danielle was being of no help at all.

"Would you dance with a man if he played the ukulele?" Luke asked her.

Danielle looked at Pete as if she was trying on the picture for size. A smile teased along the edge of her lips. He knew what that smile felt like when he was kissing her back at the NTTR, but he'd never seen it before.

He'd hadn't seen this smile because for a month he'd kept her at arm's length and ignored the pain he'd caused them both by refusing to even acknowledge their one kiss. And now he'd done a hell of a lot more than kissed her and it was one of the best things to ever happen to him.

Unlike the radiant blast of her "happy smile"—which made her beyond gorgeous—this one made her impossibly cute.

"Hard to imagine, isn't it?" Luke said. "Loving anyone who plays a ukulele."

"Hard enough to imagine even dancing with one," she admitted.

"I. Don't. *Play!* The ukulele."

Danielle ignored him and turned back to Luke. "He also said he doesn't dance, should we trust him on that?"

"Pete's always been more of a tromp on 'em and leave 'em kind of guy."

"Shut up, Luke. Or I'll be telling stories on you that'll burn your team's ears."

"Hell, Pete. You can't threaten a SEAL and expect to be left alive."

"Sir," Nikita spoke up for the first time. "I think you said that we need him for this mission. Won't be much use to us dead. Perhaps we can kill him for you afterward?" Her voice was mission-asset deadpan.

"See why I keep her around?" Luke snapped his fingers and pointed at an open spot of floor next to him.

---

DANIELLE DIDN'T HAVE to wonder what the signal meant for long. In moments the other SEALs had grabbed a fold-up table from where it leaned against the hangar's wall and set it up where Luke had pointed.

He reached into his pack and pulled out a long map tube. Nikita had a worklight plugged in and moved over. All of the Night Stalkers gathered around the table as the SEAL commander rolled out the map. The SEALs dropped into a line standing at ease behind their commander, like a personal body guard.

Danielle tried to look at them without looking. She'd flown with a few Delta operators, they tended to be smaller men. Whatever Delta's selection process was, it favored lean, whip-strong men of average height.

The SEAL commander and the two men topped six feet and Nikita wasn't far behind them. They stood at ease, but looked lethal. You could look at a Delta and wonder what his day job was. You looked at a SEAL and they exuded power and physical conditioning. Even their loose camo pants couldn't hide the powerful swimmer's legs. There was never a question about what a SEAL did for a living.

Standing safe in a friendly hangar, the Night Stalkers still all wore their sidearms. The SEALs had that plus massive knives strapped to their thighs. Another at the ankle. Their rifles were not strapped to their packs; rather they'd carried them in, and only rested them against their packs close to hand. She felt safer simply for having them here.

Then she looked down at the map.

"Uh, that's China. Or at least a part of it."

"Is it?" the Lieutenant Commander stared down at it in shock. "Well, I'll be damned. You're right, little lady. Pete, you should definitely take this lady out dancing. Though she's smart, so maybe not your type. Unlike Brittany or Lucy or—"

"Eat hot shit, Luke!" Pete's growl spoke of a long friendship.

So Pete liked them dumb? Yet he certainly seemed to like her. This would *assurément* be an interesting ride.

Time for a subject change.

"China?"

"Yes," Luke threw some internal switch and became all business. "The Jiangnan Shipyard is China's premier large shipbuilder. They are presently building a pair of the world's largest Coast Guard ships." He tossed down several large glossy photos.

She knew enough about ships to know it was big, but not much more.

"Three times more displacement than our largest Guardie—if you don't count our two broken down ice breakers. Fifty percent bigger than our destroyers and missile cruisers. The only thing we still have that have greater displacement are our helicopter and aircraft carriers."

"So," Patty pointed a finger at the image, "you're saying these things are big?"

Pete rolled his eyes, but Luke nodded matter-of-factly.

"Big and heavily armed," and he listed off an impressive array of armament. "She also carries a pair of Chinese Z-8 helicopters."

That got everyone's attention. Night Stalkers might not be impressed by deck-mounted guns on a ship no matter their number or size. But the Z-8 was a heavy lifter. It could move a lot of troops quickly and even mount missiles; a far more formidable opponent than the Augusta Westlands that served on U.S. Coast Guard ships.

"What are they doing with a Coast Guard ship that big?" Rafe was a good strategy man, which made him ideal as the DAP Hawk pilot.

"The Chinese are dredging sediment and then building man-made islands on top of submerged reefs in Vietnamese and Philippine waters, an area called the Spratly Islands. They're building military bases on them, seven hundred miles from their mainland. You can't protect those without a Coast Guard ship that can cruise for a long time and bring some serious firepower to guard them."

"And we're supposed to do something about them?"

Luke looked at her for a long moment before replying, "We didn't come to Japan for the sushi."

No, they hadn't.

They had twenty-four hours off, between the completion of the mission plan and launch. A day and a night.

Not a chance was Pete going to waste that in a barracks bunk and eating in an American chow hall, not when Japan beckoned.

Nor was he going to do it alone.

He commandeered a car from the motor pool shortly after sunrise —managed not to look like an idiot by remembering just in time that Japan was a right-hand drive country. Nothing fancy, just a blah-green Toyota sedan.

When Danielle came out to the car, he wished he'd found a Miata convertible or a Honda S2000. She wasn't a Ferrari sort of woman, but she definitely evoked the need for a convertible where the wind could play with her hair.

She shouldn't appear so startling, after all they'd rarely been apart in the entire last month of training. But it was the first time he'd seen her in civilian clothes. Sneakers, form-hugging jeans, and a nice, simple blouse should not be such a shock, but they were. The nondescript knapsack over one shoulder and dark wrap-around shades only completed the incredible image.

He scrambled out of his seat to open her door. She walked right up to the driver's door and then did that double-take of soldiers who only drove American military vehicles when overseas.

Barely able to restrain himself from wrapping an arm around her waist, he led her to the left-hand passenger door and held it open for her.

"What?" she stopped with the door between them. "No greeting of hello, yet jumping to open my door, even if I don't know which is which. What's going on, Pete?"

He didn't know. They were standing on a U.S. military base. And while she perhaps wasn't the most physically beautiful woman he'd ever known, she was close. However, Danielle stopped him cold like no other woman ever had. Her looks combined with the way she carried herself were sufficient to make grunts stop and stare when she was walking across base, even if hers wasn't the face-slap beauty of someone like Sofia Gracie. To his eyes, all others dimmed in comparison to the woman standing a single car-door thickness away.

"Climb on in."

"Not until you explain that look on your face."

"I don't have a mirror, how am I supposed to know what I look like?"

"You look beautiful."

Men weren't supposed to look beautiful, but in Danielle's whispery French accent it was very hard to complain.

"Also like a rascal."

Pete rubbed at his jaw in order to stop himself from reaching out and doing something wholly inappropriate while standing on a military base. He'd save inappropriate for as soon as he could get her alone.

She did that eyebrow-arch-question thing.

He placed a hand on top of her head and pushed down until she gave in with a smile and sat in her seat. He closed the door and circled back around the car.

What was it about this woman?

Enjoy and depart...

Good times...

No attachments…

None of the tools he'd used up until now to manage relationships fit Danielle Delacroix.

*This is so stupid,* he told himself as they drove out through the security gate.

*Why's that?*

Pete ignored his own question—resisting the desire to pound his head against the steering wheel—turned north across the Hiji River, and drove through the Toguchi District. In minutes they transitioned from two and three-story concrete buildings crowded hard against the road's edge out into the neat Japanese farmland.

The woman was so goddamn attractive, he didn't even dare look at her for fear of crashing the car. It had been a while since he'd been in a right-hand drive country himself and Japanese roads were painfully narrow with deep concrete drainage ditches close beside them.

---

DANIELLE STARED hard out the passenger left-side window. The Japanese countryside was so orderly that even the trees looked like they belonged in a museum. They lined up in perfect rows of impossibly uniform size, ten meters high and one hand wide; they looked phony, like a child's drawing of a forest made with a ruler.

The farms were out of some textbook. She recognized potatoes growing in rows so perfect that they must be hand tended. Why potatoes here? It seemed so mundane. But she couldn't ask.

The bastard hadn't greeted her. Hadn't told her that he was glad to see her. She hadn't been expecting him to take her against the side of the car in broad daylight, but she'd expected *something.* Instead, he'd shoved her down and into the car as if he wanted to hide her from view.

Then he'd muttered to himself.

*Stupid?* He thought that being with her was stupid? Taking the risk because of their need for each other *was* stupid from a military point of view. But she had been so looking forward to getting away with Pete. She'd said yes before he'd even had a chance to finish asking.

Then he'd called it stupid and refused to explain when she asked why. Was that how he thought of this? Of her? A risk for sex that wasn't really worth it?

Is that all he thought this was? *Sex?*

Sure they'd had sex on the scratchy grass in the NTTR. But they had also made love in the back of the Chinook. There was nothing else to call it. She'd already been gone on him by that point. Now she was pretty sure she was in love with Pete Napier...and he was worried about the trade-off of risk versus sex?

She could feel the ache in her fingers from clenching the door handle. Pete reached the coast road and continued north, still not looking over at her. Why would he? He was ashamed of his need for her and wanted to hide it away. Apparently she was just a fuck buddy, and that wasn't what she'd signed up for. It wasn't what her heart had signed up for.

The view of the Sea of Japan sparkling beneath the morning sun wasn't the only reason her vision had gone watery.

By all the saints, she was a Québécois. A woman of SOAR and she goddamn deserved to be treated like one.

Danielle was gonna kill the man if she sat here a second longer.

"Let's go back."

"Huh, what? Don't be silly." And the bastard kept driving.

"Stop the car."

"Why?"

"Stop the goddamn car, Napier! Or I'll fucking jump!" her shout was so loud inside the car that it hurt her own ears. She didn't look over, but she could feel his shock.

He eased the car onto the narrow shoulder.

She was out the door and moving before the Toyota had fully stopped. She tucked her knapsack over one shoulder, aimed herself back toward base, and started walking. The pavement was rough-surfaced but in good condition.

And she could hear Pete coming up beside her.

Danielle took an abrupt right turn onto the narrow-sand beach, moments before he reached her.

He cursed and called her name.

She kept moving.

He grabbed her arm.

She whirled and gut-punched him hard enough to drop him to the sand.

Danielle turned to keep walking.

An iron-strong hand clamped around her ankle which sent her tumbling down as well. She should have simply rolled with it and come up onto her feet ready to turn and fight.

But her one arm was caught in her knapsack. And Pete didn't let go.

She face-planted.

Sand was hard when you hit it with your face. It was all down the front of her blouse and bra in an instant. She rolled over to kick Pete's grip free and could feel the back of her pants scoop several handfuls of grit down her backside.

She shook her leg and he let go.

"What the hell's your problem, Napier?"

"What's yours, Delacroix?" His expression was bewildered as he rubbed at his gut. She should have hit his solar plexus so that he didn't have the air to speak.

"You really don't get it?" Danielle didn't know whether to be angry or simply give up. Rubbing at her face to get the fine sand clear, she pulled up her legs so that her ankles were out of his reach.

"Wouldn't ask if I did."

" *'This is so stupid'?*" She did a fair mimic of his American farm-boy accent.

"I," he squinted at her then looked around to retrieve his sunglasses that had fallen to the beach when she'd leveled him.

Hers had somehow stayed on her face.

"I thought I was speaking to myself."

"Out loud, Napier."

"Didn't mean to."

"You called what we were going to do 'stupid'."

"Were? Past tense?" Pete's voice was suddenly sad, like a little boy who had just lost his ice cream.

"Could someone please explain men to me?" she asked the world at large. Which consisted of a green Toyota, several hundred meters of beach, and a horizon's worth of ocean shining beneath a blue sky.

"Don't look at me," he held up his hands in surrender.

She rested her forehead on her knees and began cursing.

***

PETE RECOGNIZED most of the French swear words. Though what *tabarnak* (like a church's tabernacle?) had to do with her present mood, he didn't know. Then Danielle went sideways into Italian followed by something that might have been Spanish mixed with…he didn't know what, but she sounded pretty frustrated.

He reached out to brush a comforting hand down her calf, but felt a sharp twinge in his gut. Damn but she had a good punch.

Her cursing eased off but she still didn't raise her head.

Stupid? This was eight kinds of stupid. He knew so much about Danielle and not just the way she flew and the way she served her country, both of which were so incredible that those alone blinded him.

The one taste he'd had of her back after that first flight had built a whole idiotic world of fantasies about the woman—a set of fantasies that she had totally shattered in the hangar at the NTTR by proving how lame his imagination was when compared to reality.

During their last month of flying together to familiarize themselves with the stealth helos, training together, eating together—and *not* sleeping together—he'd also come to learn about the gentle, thoughtful woman who had crawled up out of a hell he couldn't imagine. A father long gone. A woman who couldn't be bothered to put down the bottle for the sake of her kid. Growing up in a desperate poverty he couldn't imagine, to somehow turn into—

He didn't know what.

No woman had ever so occupied his thoughts, not even Lucy—and he'd married her.

Married her, but never said the L-word except for during "...love, honor, and obey." He'd thought that "honor" was the key word of that ceremony. Which he'd done. She hadn't cared a moment about breaking all three. There was his Hell Hound Cerberus. Betrayal, thy name is…

Not Danielle.

Her curses had softened and ultimately lapsed into silence. She sat on the sand with arms wrapped across shins, forehead on pulled-up knees. He reached out to brush a hand over her head; barely a twinge this time.

"Don't!" she said before he completed the gesture, even though she didn't raise her head.

"What the hell, Delacroix?" at a complete loss he finally dug up a fistful of sand and began pouring it back and forth between his palms.

"How about a sentence longer than four words? And see if you can do it without insulting me in the process."

What in the world was he supposed to do with that? The silence stretched long enough for him to become aware of the black-tailed seagulls. He'd never gotten used to their calls, Colorado didn't have a whole lot of gulls. Here they were revered, the messengers from the goddess of the fishery. They circled and called lazily overhead as if he wasn't sitting on the cool sand sinking ever deeper into trouble he didn't understand.

"Try," Danielle prompted him, "explaining why you're with me if you think it's a stupid risk."

A *what?* "It's not a stupid risk."

"Five words. Wow, Napier, really stretching yourself."

"What's nuts, Danielle Delacroix, is how much I want you."

"You're still talking sex."

"No!" Now he was the one shouting. At his soft, "Goddamn it," she finally looked back up at him. He wished she wasn't wearing sunglasses. Her eyes were so expressive and…

"Then what is stupid, Major, if not risking both our careers for sex?"

*Speak. In longer sentences? Fine.*

"If it was just sex, Danielle, I'd never take the risk. Hell, I can get sex anywhere. Japanese woman can be splendidly compliant and willing if they're in the right mood to—" She didn't need to remove her sunglasses for him to see he was screwing up.

*Oh.*

"If that's what you thought I was saying, I can see why you got pissed."

*Try again.*

"See, I've built all of these defenses against women."

"A lot of them?" Was that the hint of a smile?

"Tons. My whole life I've looked for women who could easily come second to my career."

"And what did you find?"

"I found crap!" Which now that he'd said it he knew to be true, perhaps one of the greatest truths he'd ever spoken. "I might as well have spent my time masturbating for all the involvement I felt with most of these women. They were fun, but—" But he needed to leave that subject immediately. "And then you stand there, a drop-dead gorgeous pilot who can quote Greek tragedies, Batman comics, and flies better than any Chinook pilot I've ever served with."

She was still now. When he needed to read her the most, he couldn't get a clue.

"I want you, Danielle Spiderwoman Delacroix. Like I've never wanted a woman before. To make love to, sure; something you're crazy good at. To fly with, absolutely; something you're even better at than making love, if that's even possible. But there's more there. I don't have the words for it, but when you're not beside me, even for a couple hours, it's like my world stops making sense somehow and I..." his words ran out long before he reached the point he didn't even know how to find, never mind express.

Danielle rolled forward onto her knees until she knelt before him.

Leaning in, her face so close that he couldn't look at her sunglass' reflections of both of his own eyes at once, she hesitated one moment.

"I think you said it just fine, Pete." Then she kissed him.

It might be a risk, but he really hadn't liked how it felt when she'd walked away from him, so he wrapped his arms around her and leaned back until she had no choice but to sprawl forward on top of him. He kept her in the kiss as she lay there and hoped to God he would find some way not to screw this up.

Of course, the stupidest part was that he already *knew* that he would.

# CHAPTER 12

*D*anielle contemplated Pete's back while he sprawled face down on the mattress beside her. The mattress was thin and lying on a polished wooden floor, but surprisingly comfortable. Even in his sleep, Pete's muscles were clearly defined across his back. His strength inherent in who he was.

He'd taken them to a little Japanese inn with rooms perched out on the edge of a cliff over the sea. It was all very native and she didn't understand a single word or tradition. She'd flown hundreds of sorties during her deployments in war-torn southwest Asia (mostly Iraq and Afghanistan), but East Asia might as well be Neptune for what she knew about it. Well, not a *whole* other planet, so maybe Pluto now that it was only a dwarf planet.

First off he had led her to an *onsen,* a hot-spring fed common bathing room.

"Don't worry, men and women are separated," Pete had whispered into her ear before disappearing through another door without any further instructions.

Maybe it was some cheap payback for refusing to actually have sex on the roadside beach while her underwear was full of sand, or perhaps he thought jumping into the unknown was fun.

Which it was, usually.

At the moment she was still too busy trying to deal with Pete's wandering attempt to pin down his feelings. He not only wanted her, he missed her when they weren't together. No one had ever really missed Danielle Delacroix before—except mother when she was too drunk to reach her liquor. Not anyone…until Pete.

In the *onsen*, Danielle had tried to watch the other women out of the corner of her eye and still had to be prompted in friendly tones that she didn't understand a word of.

Strip off everything and place it in an open cubby hole.

No lockers, no keys to carry with.

She was embarrassed at how much sand had still remained in her clothes, but it was such a relief to no longer have it sandpapering her skin that she got over that quickly. The motor pool car would not be recovering so easily.

Removing her dog tags brought her to a stop. It was stupid, but standing among a half dozen strangers who were all Japanese, six or more inches shorter than she was, and uncaring of their nakedness, it was the tags that were the hardest article of clothing to remove. The hardest to trust that they'd still be tucked away in the cubby when she came back.

A woman—perhaps five feet tall, before she'd been bent nearly double with age and osteoporosis and old enough to be her great-grand-*mère*—finally commanded her to remove them with an upward flick of her hands. Then she'd placed them atop Danielle's clothes and gave her a sharp shove toward the next door. The old woman was surprisingly strong.

Following her guidance, Danielle dipped a wooden bucket into a large pool of scalding water, and moved to sit on an ankle-high stool facing the matron. A pair of brusque and muscular women dressed in white that might have been nurses' uniforms moved up behind each of them and began slathering them with a soft-bristle soapy brush.

The old woman chatted away with the other women there. Danielle was clearly the subject, but being taken under the woman's wing—the oldest one in the group by far—apparently opened a path for her easy acceptance.

The elder made a face at Danielle, first wide-eyed and open-mouthed, and then suddenly closed up like someone had pinched her face. Danielle was still trying to figure it out when the bath attendant dumped the bucket of scalding water over her head. Mouth open, Danielle was spluttering and coughing out bath water which all of the women seemed to find completely hilarious.

Another bucket followed the first but she managed to not drink any of it this time. Once the suds were all washed down the central floor drain, they moved to the steaming pool. Those already in the water, made room along the underwater bench that circled the perimeter.

The water was so hot that it took her several tries to immerse herself though she noticed the other women slipped easily into the water—not a one of them had a single word of language in common with her. Pete had dragged her far enough away from Kaneda and the other large military installations that such conveniences were gone, so she did the only thing she could do and let herself float in the water.

The stress of her fight…her *misunderstanding* with Pete drained out of her. And of the month's training. And of her doubts of herself as a woman.

It was funny how Pete, by being so alarmingly male, made her feel so female. It wasn't something she cultivated in herself. Out-perform the men was more her personal motto. Be so competent that they can't ignore you and so pure military that you become a brother-in-arms despite the lack of a penis. Pete made her feel both competent and feminine.

At a tap on her shoulder, she opened her eyes.

The old woman was sitting on the edge of the pool with only her feet in the water. She waved Danielle up.

She needed the woman's steadying hand once she managed to make it up onto the edge, her head swimming lightly with the over-heating. The conversations were quieter now, easier. She was no longer aware of her own nakedness as being out of the ordinary. A perfect lassitude lay over her like a warm blanket.

And somehow, that immensely foreign object known as Major Pete Napier had also become familiar. More than familiar. Welcome? Cherished.

Though he would still be required to learn French if he wanted to be her *amour*.

---

PETE LAY there and let his sleepy mind follow the light tracery of Danielle's fingers over his back and shoulders.

After the *onsen* they'd eaten udon noodles with thin slivers of pork at a foot-high table while wearing thin wrap-around robes. Rather than American udon dark with heavy soy sauce, it was light with anise and rice vinegar, elegantly carved vegetables. Sweet and savory. Mellow and spicy. It was Japan.

She had taken to chopsticks quickly, at least quickly enough that she wouldn't starve, and he was able to spend much of the meal admiring how the robe's silk hid then revealed shapes without clinging.

Then she'd laid down beside him and, even as he brushed his hand over her lovely form, fallen asleep to the sound of the sea rushing over the rocks below. He liked this little *ryokan;* the inn was tucked away where only locals found it. Their room was perched on a cliff edge above the Sea of Japan, and the privacy felt as if it went on forever. The smells of the salt sea on the warm breeze wandered through the room.

He'd felt like a voyeur watching her sleep. It was their first time in a proper bed together, even if it was the Japanese version of one; a futon on a polished wood floor. Even asleep, there was a vibrancy to her that drew him in. Made him want to…serve and protect?

To lose his brain, more like. But he'd watched her sleep until he'd joined her in dreams.

Now the day had passed and the room was rich with the amber light of sunset against his closed eyelids as her hand slid once more down his spine.

"Danielle?"

"Hmm?" her hum was as soft as the evening breeze.

"Don't ever stop doing that."

"Roll over and I'll do far more than that."

Well, that was an invitation that he wasn't going to turn down. He soon lay on his back and, as promised, her fingers continued their light investigation of his torso.

"One, two," her hand traced over one of his arms. "Three," along his ribs.

"Four," her hand slid over his thigh and he finally knew what she was counting—bullet holes.

"Any more?"

"Right foot. Thought I told you about when my little brother tried to amputate my foot with a shotgun. No? Thankfully, I'd only loaded it with rock salt until he learned some basic skills. The rest were, uh, in places I probably shouldn't be mentioning."

She leaned in and teased the first bullet wound with a soft scrape of teeth.

"Nope," he refused her.

Danielle continued teasing him, pressing herself against him.

He managed to resist until she slid a hand down past his waist and cupped him ever so gently. He knew it would just stereotype him as male, but there was a feeling of safety and security when she did that. It was perhaps the most erotic thing a woman had ever done to him. It was so complete a sensation that he could form no thought beyond pleasure.

"One," she whispered against the skin of his arm.

"And two," putty in her hands and he didn't care. "Both in Syria. A couple years apart, before and after the start of the Arab Spring." Her security clearance was high enough anyway.

Without releasing her hand from around him, instead starting a gentle massage that made him so hard each pulse of blood almost hurt as it throbbed, she moved her mouth to his ribs.

"Shit! That tickles!"

"The Rapier is ticklish?"

"I'd prefer it if you didn't sound so delighted by the discovery," he tried to squirm aside without breaking her hold on him because damn that felt good.

"Third?" she attacked him again. He tried to find ticklish spots on her, but couldn't seem to land one quickly enough.

"Myanmar," he finally confessed on a gasp. "A week in the hospital and ten more to recover."

"Fourth?" her voice turned into a purr as she nuzzled the inside of his thigh.

"Goddamn dustbowl," nobody got through two years in Iraq clean. The fact that he'd been flying deep into Iran when he was shot and one of his crew chiefs made the return flight in a body bag was just a technicality.

And then it was his turn to inspect her body. Her skin was like liquid gold, a smoothly perfect covering that he'd never had a chance to properly appreciate.

He leaned in to taste the inside of her thigh as she continued to do the same for him.

They shifted closer and closer until they were pleasuring each other and rising together. They crested on the same wave, holding on as the last of the light bled from the windows and the last of the shudders bled from their bodies.

Still they held each other.

It was the most natural of motions when they shifted so that she lay her cheek on his shoulder. And still her gentle fingers held him.

The way the woman made love, there was no questioning where he was meant to be. Now or ever.

Her *Monsieur* Cupid had shot him straight through the heart.

HAVING slept through much of the day, they spent the night making love and talking about their pasts, the parts you didn't discuss with anyone less than a lover.

Danielle knew precisely what made Pete moan like a man dying, but hadn't known about the unavailable woman he had loved in high school. Or the cheerleader who had taken his virginity in the back of his dad's pickup. "Starting raining on us halfway through but there was no way I was stopping that close to gold. Not a whole lot of cuddling afterwards. I made sure our rematch was in a nice, dry hayloft."

His sympathy at her being alone in the world was sincere. And his anger surprising. The story of her abandoning father and alcoholic mother were so ingrained in her psyche that there was little emotion attached anymore. When she laid out the true depths of the situation, Pete had fumed on her behalf as if it was still on-going and within his power to change it.

And he did, in a way. It showed her what support was like, real support. When someone was so far in your corner that they would fight the battle for you if they could.

For that gift, she had loved him tender.

And shortly before dawn, when they wandered into battle stories of his divorce and the destruction of so many youthful dreams, they had loved hard until it was purged from his soul. They welcomed the daybreak laughing together over the joy of being alive even as the orgasms shattered them.

By the time they were headed back to base, Danielle knew a truth.

She didn't love Pete Napier.

Love was far too simple a word for the depth and breadth of so much feeling. She could spend a lifetime getting to know the man and never have enough.

Though as she relaxed in the car seat and watched the sunrise gild the odd forests and diagrammatically perfect farmland of Japan, she was fairly sure her body had all it could stand at the moment.

But even that thought evoked warm feelings that rippled gently over nerves she'd thought spent. She slid a hand over and tucked her fingertips beneath Pete's thigh as he drove, the connection between them not needing any words as they floated along by the sea.

Well, Spiderwoman had found her own personal Superman and she wouldn't be filing any complaints with the casting department.

# CHAPTER 13

$\mathcal{P}$ete was tracking the USS *Germantown*. She was based out of Sasebo, Japan and the six hundred-foot ship was on the move.

Sasebo, Kadena Air Base, and the mouth of the Qiantang River in China made a neat triangle around five hundred miles on a side.

The *Germantown* was an LDS—landing dock ship—capable of deploying multiple helicopters and large hovercraft at a moment's notice. A powerful rapid deployment force. It would appear to any watching Chinese radar that the *Germantown* was on one of her frequent patrols from Japan down to Taiwan.

Tonight her course would bring her atypically close to shore, though she'd still remain outside both the twelve-mile territorial waters and the twenty-four-mile contiguous waters of China. However, she'd be deep inside the exclusive economic zone of two-hundred miles. While this wasn't necessary to make the passage, it was done on occasion to serve as a reminder to China that the U.S. could deploy heavy forces much farther forward than any other nation could hope to match.

The USS *Germantown* had no need to go to Taiwan—a week ago

Taiwan hadn't been on her schedule until the following month. And she certainly had no need to pass so close.

Her entire voyage and its relatively close passage to China's shore actually served only one purpose, to distract the Chinese from paying any attention to the *Germantown's* sister ship.

The *Ashland,* also based out of Sasebo, also would be cruising toward Taiwan a hundred miles farther offshore. Rather than carrying their usual complement of Marine helos, she was traveling empty. The *Ashland* would be the base for the 5E's operation.

Five hundred miles from Kadena, Japan to Qiantang, China and the Coast Guard ship the SEALs were targeting was much too far for ease of operation. The Chinook and DAP Hawk could operate from five hundred miles out, but the Little Birds couldn't. And lingering on site so close to the Chinese mainland brought on a whole other set of issues.

The Black Hawk and Chinook could stay aloft as long as they could get mid-air refueling every four hours and the crew could stay conscious. But the Little Birds *Leeloo* and *Linda* were limited to two hours and three hundred miles per sortie and then they had to land somewhere to refuel. Thankfully, the position of the *Ashland* placed China well within the tiny gunships' range.

By placing the *Ashland* a hundred and twenty miles offshore, they could fly the night's mission from there. A hundred and twenty miles, two-fifty round trip, right in all four helos' sweet spots.

Pete ordered everyone aloft at full dusk. They slipped out of Kadena Air Base with no one the wiser. Two hours later all four helos landed on the deck of the *Ashland.* Pete had always liked these ships.

Unlike the big aircraft carriers, or even the massive helicopter-carrying LHDs, the Navy crew to run the *Ashland* was relatively small. With the standard complement of a couple hundred Marines and all of their craft left ashore, this should be a very quiet operation.

Pete had considered leaving the Little Birds behind; this op really only required the Chinook and the DAP could offer plenty of protection.

"Don't be a *Newfie!*"

Pete decided it was better to not ask for a translation of this one in case Danielle calling him a Newfoundlander was even more disparaging than it sounded. She'd proceeded to talk him out of leaving *Linda* and *Leeloo* behind by listing her reasons.

"One, if anything goes south in this operation, you absolutely want their power close behind us. If the Black Hawk were damaged or lost, my Chinook would be very vulnerable. The *Carrie-Anne* is an assault craft, not an attack craft. Two..."

Pete didn't know why he'd ever tried to argue with Danielle, every single time he'd tried in the last month, he'd lost. No, he hadn't lost— she'd simply proceeded to prove herself right. Every time.

"...leaving half the team behind for our first-ever mission. *C'est vraiment poche pour le morale.*" At his uncertain expression she translated, "it would suck for morale and you really need to learn French, though that's Québécois. Literally it's *truly pocket* and I couldn't tell you why we say it that way."

Granted, though. It would suck to be left behind.

"Three..."

She never stopped simply because she'd already won—which never failed to make him smile.

"We should have the whole team along because of the unexpected."

Pete had to admit, he did like the layers of backup it provided. He'd always preferred to keep a mission as lean as he could. And if they'd done that at bin Laden's compound, they'd have been screwed. When they lost a helo at landing, the tiers of backup they already had in place made it cost them less than two minutes. Aside from the forty million dollars when they had to blow up the crashed helo.

So, the full flight of the 5E landed on the aft deck of the *Ashland,* taking up all of the available space.

The deck service crew was hand-picked and as lean as possible, but still they kept gawking at the birds as they attached temporary tie-downs. The grapes—purple-vested deck crew who ran out refueling lines to all of the craft—kept tripping over themselves in the desire to look the craft over despite the dimmed nighttime-op deck lights.

"Last chance to swim back to shore!" Danielle called out over the radio. That earned a laugh. In minutes everyone was out on deck, stretching, shaking out limbs, doing some light calisthenics even though the flight to the ship hadn't been all that long. The rest of the night would be.

Danielle headed over to Commander Luke Altman, and Pete let himself drift along to the rear ramp of the Chinook in her wake. The SEAL team members weren't doing any workouts, they were going over their gear once more. That's when he figured something out. SEALs were always careful, but these guys were…

"Hey Luke, I thought you were on Team 5. When did you go DEVGRU?" Which most civilians thought was still named SEAL Team Six, not true for about thirty years.

None of the SEALs reacted except Luke who rose very slowly to his feet.

"What makes you say that, Pete?"

Pete had forgotten quite how big a man Altman was.

"You just made his argument for him, Commander Altman," Danielle spoke as if there wasn't a very pissed looking SEAL suddenly looming over them, his face lit red and dangerous by the ship's night-operations deck lights.

"Your guys aren't moving like I'm used to your guys moving," Pete explained keeping his voice as casual as Danielle's in hopes that Luke didn't decide to break them in two over his knee and toss them overboard. "Team 5 dudes would be kicking back, maybe taking a quick nap."

"We *are* invading China tonight."

"Only a little," Danielle argued. "If you really want to invade China—"

She wasn't about to reveal that he'd just been in Tibet, was she? He could get his ass fried for—

"—there's this rare blue flower I need. It's at the base of a Tibetan mountain that leads you to a monastery high on the cliffs. And—"

Pete and Luke laughed together. Luke in chagrin and Pete in relief. Doubting Danielle's discretion was as pointless an exercise as arguing with her. Yet by the same unfathomable logic, her judgment included being with him. Danielle had said this wasn't just sex between them, and he'd agreed. But what had he agreed to? In her superior brand of perception was he…"The One" for her?

He swallowed hard.

Pete trusted her implicitly, but had she suddenly gone blind? He was a bad bet for a woman like her. Bad bet? A dead loss, more like. He had a proven track record—all bad.

"Tell me again," Danielle was thankfully focused on Luke, "why you aren't going in with a diver vehicle?"

"I would have preferred that, but the Chinese coast is wired underwater within an inch of its life. They have more microphones down there than we sunk outside of Russia's harbors back in the fifties and sixties."

"So, they're more vulnerable up on the surface."

Luke nodded, "You'll dump us as deep in the harbor as you can. We take this Zodiac," he hooked a thumb toward the rubber boat they'd loaded in the back of her Chinook, "and sneak in the rest of the way. Same trick in reverse coming back out."

"If everything goes well," Pete put in.

"Chances of which are…?" Danielle had on that smile she'd shown the moment before attacking him back at the *ryokan*.

Luke apparently didn't know how to read that yet, but he'd learn. The DEVGRU commander shrugged.

Danielle laughed and wandered back to follow her crew chiefs' inspection of the bird. No one redid the preflight on a bird after such a simple flight, but Danielle and her crew did. He glanced around and saw that every member of the 5E was doing it to their craft as well. Just like DEVGRU. The woman was never going to stop surprising him.

"Got it bad, Pete," Luke spoke softly beside him.

"Yeah, I do."

So "bad" that he hadn't even caught onto what Luke was saying until after the lieutenant commander turned back and returned to his own team.

"Sofia, talk to me."

Danielle was flying in the lead. Pete had arrayed the three weaponized birds behind her, the two Little Birds in close, and the big hammer of *Beatrix* the DAP Hawk trailing a half-mile behind so that Rafe could provide the unexpected response to any rude surprises.

"*Olá,* my friend Danielle. It is so good to hear from you."

Danielle opened her mouth to remind Sofia that this was a mission, not a friendly chat over a meal. But before she had a chance…

"Our friends are very, how would you say…grouchy tonight. Many Chinese boats have left the harbor of Hangzhou at the mouth of the Qiantang to move out beside the *Germantown* passing so near with its full Marine Corps Expeditionary Unit on board. Kadena Air Force Command, unaware of our operation, has moved four F-18 jets into a loose formation a dozen miles seaward of the *Germantown.* I think this is a good addition to our distraction. All of the noise they are making is now south of your position and continuing down the coast. Security forces in the harbor are down at least thirty percent."

As she'd been speaking, Danielle could see that Sofia was feeding tactical displays to Pete, but she didn't have time to look at it. Her mind had the bandwidth, barely, but her eyes didn't.

Flying just a dozen feet above the East China Sea at close to two hundred miles an hour took a great deal of concentration. At this speed, rogue waves would slap her out of the sky faster than she could sneeze. A small fishing boat could radio in a warning to the Chinese Coast Guard just as fast as a patrol craft, so she had to avoid every single boat.

It was like racing a slalom course. Turn one, shipping lane patrol vessel. Turn two, fishing boat with outriggers and bright lights to draw the fish to the surface. Through the center of a gate defined by an oil supertanker and a coastal ferry.

She could feel herself freezing up, a little too tight on the controls, not as smooth as she should be. Not rising the extra two feet on a turn to make sure she didn't bury a rotor tip in the waves.

What would Spidey do?

He'd loosen up and swing with it. Let the dark night slide by as he slalomed between various craft and the mapped listening buoys.

She found a smoother rhythm, found the groove as she rolled toward shore. It was…Pete. Not the rhythm of their lovemaking, he always made that gloriously unexpected. No, it was the rhythm of his sleeping breath, perfectly matched to the easy step and shift of the powerful *Carrie-Anne*.

Once she smoothed out, the mission clock finally started moving again. It had been creeping the whole first half of the flight from the *Ashland* toward their target. Now that she was in the flow it was moving apace.

At the outer barrier islands she called, "Ready alert," to the SEALs.

She swirled around the outermost islands, small outcroppings of steep rock.

That marked the threshold as they crossed from the open ocean into the thirty-mile wide outer harbor, so she called, "Three minutes." She could take them another ten miles. Maybe a little more.

She made it four minutes and thirteen miles when everything started happening at once and she called twenty seconds. This was her safe limit even in a stealth craft.

The lights of Hangzhou Harbor and Shanghai city came over the horizon. They had been a distant glow, but she'd remained so close to the water that they remained invisible until she was just five miles out from the rocky mainland. The city was set back several more miles from the wide-open harbor.

Less than eight miles to the Jiangnan Shipyards. She could see the tops of the tall construction cranes, though the ships under construction were still below the horizon.

The ramp light went on as Drake the rear gunner began lowering the back gate.

"Surface craft north and south, three miles distant," Sofia reported.

Danielle's altitude was now two feet, which placed her pilot's seat at eight. That would have been high enough to see the other boats, but Danielle had turned sideways and slid the body of the Chinook down between two wave peaks. By continuing sideways at twenty-five miles an hour, she managed to stay between the waves with the bulk of the helo in the trough. The rolling swells ranged around ten feet high, so they hid half of the *Carrie-Anne*. A passing boat would see only the top half of the helo and the big twin rotors…

Except it was ten at night and her helicopter was painted pitch black.

"Slick," was Luke's compliment which she was too busy to process until after he said, "We're gone," and his voice disappeared from the intercom.

"Clear," Drake reported less than five seconds later and the hydraulics kicked in to close the ramp.

Danielle raised the *Carrie-Anne* just enough to get the Chinook's belly clear of the waves and aimed back toward the *Ashland.*

---

PETE KNEW he was a damn good pilot, but he'd never seen anyone do that with a Chinook before.

He wanted to put a hand to his chest and try pumping some air into his oxygen-starved lungs; he'd been holding his breath without realizing it while Danielle had settled them down between the wave crests.

But he didn't want to miss a single nuance on their interconnected controls to understand how smoothly she'd done it. No wonder she made love the way she did. She must integrate her entire nervous system into everything she did. Her control was so perfect he could just as easily imagine the Chinook was moving her as the other way around.

She stayed breathtakingly low all of the way back to the *Ashland* sliding easily around the obstacles that Sofia identified from her

Avenger flying on high. Danielle didn't rise above ten feet until she reached the ship and had to climb to reach the deck.

An hour and a hundred-and-fifty miles each way and she hadn't done a single thing he could correct.

And if she was going to choose him, he would give up his normal state of idiocy and stop arguing with her.

# CHAPTER 14

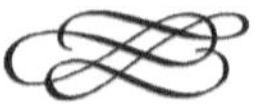

*P*arked back on the deck of the USS *Ashland* a hundred miles offshore China and doing nothing worked for Pete —for under ten minutes.

Sofia had the Avenger aloft to keep an eye on Hangzhou Harbor. The problem was that she and her copilot were flying the RPA in the white control box back at Kadena Air Base. Which made it impossible to just "drop in" and look over her shoulder.

Aboard the *Ashland,* Pete bulled his way into the Plot Room— perhaps the most secure room on any ship—partly by nudging Danielle in front of him every time they met male resistance. At first she wasn't happy with his manipulations, but eventually—if he read her correctly and he hoped he did—she was amused by how well it worked on the swabbies. After all, what chance did they stand against the power of a female Night Stalker.

The Avenger, *Raven* for being an RPA bird—finally one that wasn't one of Danielle's female heroines—could stay aloft for twenty hours on a load of fuel. The side aperture radar offered a surprisingly clear view the distant harbor and the shipyards from sixty thousand feet and a hundred miles offshore.

"Yes," Sofia reported when they were on the right frequency, "I tracked the SEALs successfully to their destination." She rolled back the video feed that she was supplying to the ship as she talked. In moments he was again watching the *Carrie-Anne* sliding along between the boats and the outer harbor islands.

The ship's captain whistled, "Now that's some pretty flying. Nice, Major."

"Thanks, but the Captain was pilot-in-command."

"Which Captain?"

Pete pointed at Danielle standing close beside him. They were all crowded close to look at the big LCD screen showing the *Raven's* feed. He was thankful for the chance to rub shoulders with her in public.

"In that case, that's *real* nice, Captain." The smile he sent her didn't even worry Pete any more. Danielle might have stood a little straighter, but otherwise didn't react. Had Pete sounded so sexist in the past? Probably. Being around women like the ones in the 5E forced a man to reevaluate.

"There," Sofia's voice drew all attention back to the screen. The helicopter twisted, then kept flying sideways with the waves, though there was no way to see on the display why she'd done that.

Moments later, a blip appeared off the stern of the Chinook, and then disappeared.

"If I do not know where they planned to go, I would not be able to follow them." Sofia used a light pen to mark their track on the screen; the blip on the image reappearing only occasionally to mark the track the SEALs were taking.

"Here they made contact with the Chinese Coast Guard super-ship."

Jiangnan Shipyard was a maze of construction. Several vessels ranging from two to eight hundred feet were up in dry docks. As many more floated beside long piers where supplies and machinery were cluttered thickly together. The scattered tracking they had on the SEAL team completely disappeared in the snarl.

"Time of last contact?"

"2215 hours," Sofia announced.

Both Pete and Danielle immediately adjusted the dials on their wrist watches. "That was forty-five minutes ago."

"Nothing since."

Pete glanced at Danielle and she grimaced.

"He said it would take a minimum of four hours."

"Shit! What the hell are we supposed to do for four hours?" Actually he had some ideas on that, but he wasn't dumb enough to suggest it.

---

DANIELLE KNEW the mission plan well enough that she could follow every move, at least every move that the SEAL team wasn't having to make up as they went.

At 2215, Luke and the other three SEALs had arrived at the Jiangnan Shipyard.

Next they'd find their way past the outer breakwater to stow their rubber boat under a dock.

By 2245 the SEALs would scale the ocean side of an eight hundred-foot-long Coast Guard cutter, because the dock side was sure to be guarded. The ship was still under construction so there should be multiple points of entry, they were counting on that.

Inside the ship by 2300 and racing the clock and the Chinese security guards.

She and Pete met up with the rest of the 5E crew at 2400 hours for lunch in the ship's mess.

None of them ate very well.

At 0030, the Night Stalkers attempted to start up a Frisbee game between the helicopters crowded together on the aft deck. There was barely room for the four birds. The stars were lost behind a light overcast and the deck was pitch black except for subtle perimeter lights that warned you of a forty-foot plunge from deck to ocean about five steps before you took it. When they almost lost The Whistler disc over the side, they'd given up on that.

By now the SEALs should have infiltrated the command area of the superstructure. They'd be recording every aspect of the ship from the placement of the heavy deck guns to the best paths for future boarding if they ever had to attack one of these ships. The Activity's intel geeks had gone after the construction plans, with surprisingly little luck. They must be stored on a server that wasn't connected to anything else.

Recording the ship's layout was the *secondary* mission.

Now at 0100, if they were anywhere close to on schedule, they should be entering the Chinese equivalent of the *Ashland's* Plot Room. Modern ships were less about the amount of steel in their hull and more about the computer and control systems being used aboard them. A system had to be able to analyze a target that was still two hundred miles over the horizon as being friendly or hostile. Then they must decide to fire on it before they in turn could actually launch a missile—many of the modern missiles had a hundred-mile range and if the enemy craft was supersonic, safety margins went away far too quickly.

The SEAL team had two *primary* missions—a piece of classic military doublespeak for "don't screw up either one." First find out exactly what electronics were installed on the ship, and second put in an undetectable tap. The goal was to transmit every electronic command to the U.S. intelligence agencies, using China's own equipment and antennas. It would be a variable-frequency, high-density squirt transmission, almost impossible to trace. That's if they even noticed it in the first place.

By 0130 Danielle was eyeing dark corners to drag Pete into for mindless sex. It wasn't that she wanted sex; it was about the farthest thing from her interest at the moment. She simply needed to be doing something. The rocking of the big ship on the relatively quiet ocean wouldn't normally be enough to bother her, but in the near pitch darkness, she always seemed on the verge of catching a boot when she encountered an unexpected angle to the deck.

At 0200 she went looking for him and found Pete in the middle of the aft deck, arms crossed and glaring at the Chinook. Within moments the entire crew was there, as if they'd all homed in together at the same moment.

A buzz of, "This is killing me." "Still no word." "What if—" "How soon—" swarmed to life.

"We go now," Danielle's flat statement silenced the whole group. Because they were sure as hell achieving nothing out here in the emptiness of the East China Sea.

"We don't know when they'll need us."

"It's two in the morning. If they don't need us before six a.m., the sun will be up and we'll have to wait until tomorrow night."

Groans rippled around the group.

***

"WHAT ARE YOU SUGGESTING?" Pete's voice silenced them. He had some ideas of his own.

Knowing Danielle, it was probably the same idea, so he answered his own question. "The *Carrie-Anne* and the *Beatrix* are aloft in five minutes."

Danielle's nod confirmed her thoughts.

"We have four hours of fuel. If they need us, we'll be that much closer."

"*We* don't!" Dozer protested. "My Little Bird only carries two hours. Even if I throw Patty overboard, she doesn't weigh enough to make any real difference."

"Hey!" Patty protested, but was ignored. So she smacked Dozer on the back of the head and he grinned at her.

"The Little Birds will follow either when we get the call from the insertion team or at 0400, two hours to sunrise."

None of the Little Bird pilots looked pleased, but it was the best solution Pete had. If they flew the two main birds a hundred miles closer to the coast and circled, they'd be able to respond to a call in ten minutes instead of forty-five. The increased risk of being spotted the longer they were there was marginal, as long as they were careful.

As they prepared the birds for flight, he and Danielle were alone for just a moment.

"I've got a bad feeling about this, Spiderwoman. Like we're already too late."

She nodded, her eyes wide enough to catch the dim red deck lights.

"Let's get up in the air, then you hustle your pretty ass to the China coast. You hustle it hard."

"Roger that."

# CHAPTER 15

*D*anielle hustled her ass hard.

They were aloft in under five minutes. This time the DAP Hawk was tight on her blind spot; she felt exposed, uncomfortable without the familiar Little Birds also close by. The ADAS camera offered a full three-hundred-and-sixty-degree view, but the back left quadrant was always a weak spot for any rotorcraft pilot. Rafe tucked the *Beatrix* in there nice and tight which made her feel a little better.

Sofia was calling out the locations of marine and air traffic before Danielle was a mile off the deck of the *Ashland*.

For the first half of the flight no one spoke, and Danielle flew on raw nerves. Unable to stand it any longer, she flicked the intercom control to pilots only.

"Talk to me, Pete."

"Sure, you need me to take over?"

"For a minute, sure."

"I have command," his hands were smooth and confident on the controls.

She removed her hands and flexed them, tried shaking out the nerves that rippled along them. Within thirty seconds, she couldn't stand it anymore and took up the thrust control and cyclic once more.

"I have command," she called.

"Well, that was a long break."

"Best I've got."

"Hell, Spidey, worst you've got is better than most folks' best."

"Worst I got? I catch a blade and we all go for a swim unless the Chinese Coast Guard feels like rescuing us."

"I wouldn't worry about it," Pete's voice didn't sound forced in its cheerfulness. Since when had The Rapier become cheerful?

"Why not?"

"Oh, you catch a blade this close to the Never Exceed Speed then we'll all be dead in seconds. After that we'll sink like a stone. In the big picture of possibilities, I wouldn't worry about the Chinese if we crash."

"Since when did you turn so chipper? What have you done with my dark, broody lover?" Danielle swung around an ore carrier inbound from Australia. Sofia, watching from far above, sent her scooting south to avoid the next boat.

"Dark and broody? Me?"

"*Oui!*"

"It was when you said *tu et moi.* A beautiful woman, a hot pilot, and a sexy French accent. Somewhere along the way I decided I was a pretty damned lucky guy. That brightened up my day quite a bit."

"Okay, my handsome hunk of a lover. Guess what?"

"What?"

"We're flying into China. And if we're caught, we'll probably start a war. Definitely tossed in a shitty Chinese jail for spying or treason or something."

"Could be a problem. Unless their cells are co-ed. You, me, a hard bunk. Possibilities."

"Men!" Danielle gave it her best scoff. He might have sex on the brain, but he was making her feel better despite that.

They arrived as close as she dared to the outer harbor barrier islands and turned to circle back out to sea in a holding pattern when the radio crackled to life.

Danielle was glad for Pete's steady hands still riding the controls or she might have actually delivered them into the watery depths outside of Hangzhou Harbor.

---

"PETE. TELL ME YOU WERE SMART," were the first words over the Chinook's radio.

Pete didn't need to recognize Luke's voice, he was the only one who should be on this frequency. Before answering, Pete flipped the intercom back to include the three crew chiefs in the rear of the helo. They didn't need to hear about his relationship with Danielle, but they deserved to know exactly what they were flying into.

"Me or Danielle, can't be sure; we're both pretty damn smart you know. Currently at the outer island of Zhoushan to the south edge of the harbor."

"Good! You're here. That's a relief. We're boxed in. Every goddamn ship that went chasing down the coast after the *Germantown* has come back. There's no way we can move back out to sea."

"Your alternative is for us to fly into a crowded harbor?"

"We've spent the last hour dancing with security forces back and forth across this goddamn cutter. They aren't sure that we're here but they will be pretty damn fast. We got it done, so we need to get out before they get too suspicious."

"Roger, hang on."

Danielle had been circling them slowly off the south entrance to the wide outer harbor. The SEALs were deep in a secure military shipyard along the north shore—nine minutes away—across thirty miles of waters thick with pissed off Chinese Navy and Coast Guard vessels just looking for a fight to assuage their egos after the *Germantown* decoy had blithely ignored them during its passage.

Pete racked his brain for everything he'd read about Hangzhou Harbor and the Qiantang River. Heavy population to the north, very few people to the south where usable land was limited quickly by jagged rocky heights.

North of the SEAL team's current location was even worse. Over the ridge from Hangzhou sprawled the megalopolis of Shanghai.

Coal, ore, and lots of oil shipping would also be clogging both harbors, far more imports than even the U.S. needed. China was sucking mud. Their economy was in screaming growth. They had the labor pool to support it, but not the developed resources. They were switching from being a top global exporter to becoming one of its top importers.

Which didn't help him at all.

It was a city of incredible tourist attractions that he'd always wanted to see.

Two World Heritage Sites; one on a lake and the other inland. West Lake had one of the archetypal gardens that had influenced the rest of China and Japan for over a thousand years. The city had the oldest Catholic church and the oldest mosque in China…which didn't do the trapped SEALs any damn good at all.

The streets of Shanghai were…useless.

The—

"What time is it?"

"0310," Danielle responded.

"What's the date?"

"September—"

"No, the Chinese date."

"How am I supposed to know that?"

"Come on, Spidey. Thought you knew everything." Pete should not be enjoying himself at the moment, but he really was. The adrenaline was buzzing hot through his veins. If he was right, this was going to totally kick ass. And he was going to have the hottest Chinook pilot in the military to give them a chance of pulling this off—they'd need it. And if she screwed up, they'd all be dead so it wouldn't matter anyway.

"Sofia," Pete clicked onto the Avenger's frequency which would relay his call back to her container in Japan. "What's today's date on the Chinese calendar?"

There was a long pause as she accessed the Internet.

"Eighth lunar month. Eighteenth day."

"Perfect! The tide in Hangzhou. What time does it come in?"

Another long pause.

"0350 and—"

He didn't care about the afternoon tide. He flipped back to Luke's frequency.

"Hey, Altman, buddy. I need you to check something out for me."

"What? Make it quick."

"I need you and your team to take your little boat for a scenic cruise northwest, I repeat northwest from your current position."

"Inland? Up the fucking Qiantang River?" There was a very satisfying choking sound in Altman's throat. Unnerving a DEVGRU lieutenant commander was even more fun than he'd thought.

"You must be mid-channel under the Jiubao Highway Bridge in exactly twenty-seven minutes. Believe me when I say there won't be any other boats there."

"Shit! Twenty-seven?" Pete could hear scrambling in the background. "What do I do when I get there?"

"Go surfing."

Altman didn't have time for more than a few choice words before he got moving, but they were very satisfying to Pete's ego.

They'd be even more satisfying if they all survived this.

*D*anielle listened as Pete called the Little Birds to come rushing in, but they were almost an hour out. They'd be no help in the plan's execution, neither would the DAP Hawk. But, he said, they might need all three to cover their escape.

Why didn't that sound good?

Whatever Pete's plan was, it was going to happen in twenty-six minutes.

Next he directed the DAP Hawk to remain outside the harbor and to be ready for all hell to break loose at 0355, right after whatever magical moment Pete had figured out.

She still didn't have a clue.

"Let's fly southwest."

"Southwest?" Danielle looked up at the mountains of Mainland China on the south side of Hangzhou Harbor. What lay in front of them didn't look the least little bit like water. It looked like farmland backed by rugged mountains. "Have you fucking lost it?"

"Trust me, Spiderwoman. I'm spinning a delicate thread here."

"I'll Spiderwoman you right in the snoot! *Merde!* You are so lucky my hands are busy."

"Trust me, Danielle."

And just that simply, she did. She wasn't sure how she felt about his power over her if *Trust me, Danielle* was all it took. And she really did, apparently with her life and her crew's life.

She turned southwest and goosed the *Carrie-Anne*—hard. There wasn't time to think about her heart.

He guided her ashore between Yuyao and Ningbo, which meant nothing to her, but she could see them marked on the tactical display spread on the inside of her visor. They crossed a pair of highways and then she was in topography she recognized. Ridge and valley. Like the back byways of the Appalachian Mountains, the Chinese mountains were coated by lush growth with streams and rivers in the bottom of every valley.

And like Afghanistan, the valleys were brutally steep and unpredictable in their sharp turns. Her predictive software didn't know what to make of the tiny hamlets and ridge-perching villas.

So it was up to real-time and reflexes, which was actually her favorite kind of flying. She still needed the enhanced electronic view, but she had to solve moment to moment the best line of attack on the route.

A narrow twist lead to an abrupt waterfall.

She soared up the face, could practically feel the cool spray that speckled the windshield. Then bursting out among a cluster of riverside homes above the steep falls.

"These people are phoning us in like mad. I can feel it."

"You think they'd expect anyone other than their own military to fly through these valleys? We're probably safer here than out in the harbor. And if they do call us in, radar isn't going to show squat. Definitely not a stealth Chinook sliding through their mountain valleys."

She hadn't thought of it that way.

"0338," Pete called out the time. "C'mon, Sweet Lady. Show me what you can do."

"I'm not sweet!" she managed between gritted teeth.

"Sure you are, Spiderwoman. You're about the sweetest damn woman there ever was. I mean you put up with me, don't you?"

That earned him a snort of laughter from the crew chiefs on the intercom who would be using their miniguns to brace themselves into position and scanning for likely targets.

"Put up with—" it came out as a ragged sputter. She was flying into decidedly hostile territory and he still hadn't told her why or what she'd be doing there.

Pete was deep in communication with Sofia deciding on the best routes, sometimes leaving Danielle on her own, sometimes directing her to cross over into the next valley or start trending north.

If she wasn't putting up with him, then what was she doing?

"0342. Eight minutes to the G15 bridge. We can't be late."

Danielle flipped a control to project the overall tactical display from Sofia's Avenger for a moment. Then she flipped back to the immediate terrain view while her mind analyzed what she'd seen.

0343.

Seven minutes.

"The SEALs are reporting pursuit," Sofia called.

"Let me know when it breaks off," Pete replied calmly.

Man was so goddamn sure of himself. With reason. He was a master tactician who had just led the 5E to the fastest unit certification in history.

Well, if he was going to be so sure of himself, she'd do the same.

The Chinook was too deep in the valleys to talk directly to the SEALs. Radios were either line-of-sight or bounced off satellites, and the Chinook's present flight path sucked for both.

Staying in the deep valleys, she had to keep her speed down if she didn't want to round some corner and fly into a valley's headwall. But if she slowed down at all, she was going to be too late.

"Only Chinese fly in China? Fine."

She tipped the cyclic forward for speed and reefed up on the thrust control with her left hand to climb.

"Come on, *Carrie-Anne,* you leather-clad lady. Fly!"

She cleared the valley wall at 0344 at a hundred and ninety-six miles an hour, the very outer limit of what the Chinook could do.

Once above the ridge line, she stayed high. They'd traveled deep into the mountains south of Hangzhou Harbor to avoid the more populous area. Seventeen miles straight-line flight.

She should be there within thirty seconds of schedule. Danielle kept the nose down.

"Stay on your toes, guys," she called back to the three crew chiefs.

Sofia's data was streaming into Pete's station. He was making adjustments to her course, but there was little he could do now. It was a flat-out race.

"Pursuit is breaking off, Pete," Luke's transmission crackled back to life. "What don't I know?"

"You'll know the signal to move. When you get it, go upriver and go full tilt."

At two minutes out she considered getting Pete on the private intercom for just a moment.

But why should he have all the fun? *Sweetest damn woman* and all that...she left the intercom wide open.

"Petey?" she did her best to make her voice a caress as she crossed over the last ridge south of the Hangzhou and plunged earthward back toward the low farmlands—but now far deeper into China.

"What?" Now Pete's voice was the one that was strained.

"I'm not just putting up with you." She shot over terraced fields, circled wide around the Hangzhou International Airport, and was once again over the water. She was eighty miles farther into China than when she'd left the East China Sea.

"No?" his voice was strained as he called the next order. "Get west of the bridge and be ready to race inland."

"No," she kept her voice smooth and calm as she aimed the *Carrie-Anne* for the middle of the river. It was only a couple hundred yards wide here. The sides were lined with concrete, tiers of concrete. For this channel to fill was going to take one hell of a tide.

Then she saw why they were here at four in the morning and had to swallow hard to keep her voice steady.

"In addition to putting up with you," she slid down low over the water. "I also love you."

There was a *whoop* from one of the crew chiefs.

"But for this," she glanced once more at the nightmare that the cameras were projecting inside her visor. "For this, I'm going to kill you, *Petey!*"

The tide wasn't flowing in, it was *boiling in.* She'd read about the Nova Scotia tidal bore. A wave, often as much as a five feet high, washed up the Bay of Fundy on its way to creating the world's largest tide.

But the Hangzhou tidal bore was a roiling wall of breaking waves two stories high and rising.

"Ramp down!" she called back.

She hopped the Chinook over the Jiubao Bridge just as the tidal bore crashed against its pillars. Spray plumed a dozen stories into the air close behind them.

And then she settled down into the water just ahead of the on-rushing tidal bore.

There was a move called a Delta Queen where a Chinook landed in water, preferably calm water, and allowed itself to sink slightly—just until its cargo bay deck was awash in a foot of water. A racing rubber Zodiac, driven by SEALs with a death wish, could shoot aboard at thirty miles an hour and then the Chinook would take back off. As they climbed, it was always a trick to dump the six or seven tons of water back off the ramp without dumping the boat and the SEALs with it.

Except this water was anything but calm and she didn't dare slow down—this wave was moving with a serious attitude. She couldn't sink partway into the river, she didn't dare. She had to sink partway into the tidal bore wave itself.

She checked the rear-view camera for a moment and saw the unbelievable: on the face of the boiling wave, a tiny rubber boat raced its engine and surfed down the face.

That's why pursuit had broken off, no one was stupid enough to mess with a tidal bore a hundred yards wide, two stories tall, and moving like a freight train. On the plus side, it would be assumed that anyone in a small boat would be dead. The river would be dredged and nothing would be found. So sorry.

Unless she screwed up and they found an entire American Special Operations helicopter at the bottom of the river.

The river twisted and turned here in sharp bends. The tidal bore crashed into one concrete-tiered bank and threw sheets of water thirty, forty, fifty feet into the air. And before it could slosh back down, another wave was reflecting off the other bank.

There was no neat standing wave here, there was only turbulent, muddy chaos.

She managed to plunge the ramp down into the water, but kept the nose of the *Carrie-Anne* held high so that her bird didn't drown.

Danielle was glad she couldn't afford another moment to look back because she'd wager that she wouldn't like what she saw.

"Six inches of water in the bay," Drake called over the intercom.

Danielle did her best to level out at that shallow depth. A foot would be better for the boat, but worse for the leading edge of the wave. Two feet would drown the Chinook and kill them all.

"Ten seconds," Drake called over the headset. She'd have to—

Another bridge loomed in her night vision. The support pilings were too close together and the bridge deck too low. She shot the nose up to dump the water load and climb over the bridge.

In the process, she released a small tidal wave of water out the back of the helo.

"Crap! Tell me I didn't sink them." A Zodiac didn't run well after a couple tons of water were dumped in it.

"No...but they won't need a shower for a long time."

Danielle cleared the bridge deck by inches and dove back down on the other side as the concrete river channel twisted left and narrowed.

"Now!" she shouted over the radio. There was another bridge less than a mile ahead. At this rate of speed, thirty seconds might be too long.

She got her tail in the water again.

"Six inches," Drake called. "A foot."

They needed the extra depth to make sure this worked.

"Five seconds."

It was going to be tight. She slowed down just a little bit.

The roar of the helo's engines was always loud inside the craft no matter how much sound insulation they installed. But now there was a new sound. A crashing of water, a twenty-foot high wall of surf in full breaking roar battering at her extended rear ramp.

The crew chief's curses told her plenty about the view.

"Two. One. Aboard!"

Danielle added lift. She wasn't subtle about it, she hauled up hard.

…and nothing happened.

The roar increased.

There were shouts, but there was no time to make sense of them.

The stern of the Chinook was slapped downward. They were in the wave.

If she couldn't shed water by climbing, maybe she could outrun it instead.

She aimed the nose down into the water to gain forward speed.

Water from the large cargo bay poured forward, washed about her feet, tried to tug them off the pedals. A small wave broke over the radios mounted on the flat console between the pilots' seats.

They shot past a giant golden ball of a building a dozen stories high. The Chinook and the gold ball would make a great photo if anyone was watching at four in the morning to take it. Though even if someone did, it would just look like a bad Photoshop job. A secret U.S. military helicopter—pitch black with no markings—surfing the tidal bore through the heart of a Chinese city at four in the morning. Like a 747 parked on an aircraft carrier, *so* not believable. She hoped.

Danielle kept the nose down despite the cries over her headset. The bridge came closer and closer.

"Now!" Pete screamed beside her. "Pull up now!"

She waited another three seconds, gathering every knot of speed she could, and then tugged back hard, like popping a cork.

The *Carrie-Anne* stuck her nose in the air, going near vertical in her climb, and dumped water out the stern. She knew that the SEALs and all three of her crew would be desperately gripping the interior straps of the cargo bay so that they and their boat weren't washed back overboard with the outgoing flow.

There was a loud scraping sound as the Chinook dragged her belly plates over the bridge rail. Good thing the wheels were folded up or they'd have been ripped off.

Danielle dead-centered a streetlight which smashed Pete's side of the windscreen and then she was aloft. Hopefully the Chinese would discount the damage she caused as the result of tidal bore-tossed debris.

A hard bank to the left and she was once more driving back up into the Chinese hills as the tidal bore continued to spume and thrash its way up the Qiantang River.

# CHAPTER 17

*P*ete had lost at least ten years of his life on that flight.

River water was still running aft, but now it was rivulets instead of a torrent.

"We all accounted for?" he called back over the intercom.

"Except for the shit from crapping my pants, we're all aboard," Drake reported from the rear ramp position.

"Pete," Luke pulled on a headset. "You're a dead man."

"Hey, it was my wave, but I wasn't the one flying."

"Danielle, you're a goddess. Pete, you're a dead man."

"No appreciation for—"

"Hey!" Danielle's complaint cut him off. "Could we get out of China first?"

"Oh, yeah," Pete needed to get his head back in the game. About a third of their electronics were cooked. "What's that smell?"

Luke made a foul spitting sound. "One of the most polluted rivers on the planet and the lady just dumped a thousand gallons of it on our heads."

They still had an intercom. With a little fooling around, he managed to get a radio feed to Sofia off a military satellite. His direct radios linking him to the other helos and the Avenger were all offline.

"Have *Beatrix* wait for us offshore at," he read off the coordinates. "The Little Birds should turn back to the *Ashland*."

"They can't do that," Sofia reported. "Since they left the *Ashland* a Chinese patrol boat has come out to harass her. They don't have enough fuel to reach Japan."

"How about the *Germantown?*" Pete tried to remember how fast it had been headed south and away from the area, but couldn't.

"No. Wait," he heard Sofia rattling some keys on her computer. "If you can order them to turn the ship and have it go north very fast, it should close the distance enough. I think. Maybe."

"Do it."

"They won't listen to me," Sofia complained.

"Drop the Colonel's name. Drop the goddamn President's if you need to, but get them turned. And then order us an aerial tanker, we'll need to refuel both birds if we have to make it back to Japan on our own."

There was a brief pause, then Sofia giggled for a moment and was gone.

"What did that mean?" he asked Danielle.

"With a woman frohm Braazeel," she attempted an imitation of Sofia liquid tones, "You never weel knohh." Came out pretty well actually. "But don't be surprised if the President calls you about issuing orders in his name." Her normal light French accent sounded better.

"Our navs are fried. *Beatrix,* be ready to lead us out," but his mind wasn't really on the last order.

He opened his mouth to speak, to try and express some of what he was feeling for this woman beside him, when the radios and intercom disappeared in a cloud of sparks and circuit breakers began popping out all over the place.

Engines were still running, as was the night vision. They could still fly out of here, but the only way to communicate would be by shouting.

What he had to say would keep well enough until the next time they were alone together. For now, he focused on getting them home alive so that he'd have a chance to say it.

CHAPTER 18

s soon as they were off the C-5 transport jet at Mother Rucker, Alabama, they began reassembling their helos.

The DEVGRU SEALs did their "fade into the night" thing, but Danielle was sure she hadn't seen the last of them.

By midnight the helos were back together. They flew the three miles from Mother Rucker's main Cairns Airfield over to their hangar at Ech Stagefield in tight formation.

A small sign had been added above the entry door's code panel in their absence.

"The 5E," Danielle read aloud as the others gathered around her.

It was all the small brass plate said, but it was enough. It said this was home. She would get some other improvements made here: housing for the crew, convert the old Ech field offices into a training center, and other amenities. But what mattered now was that they had a home base. A place that they belonged.

The 5E tucked away their helos. The Avenger RPA, also reassembled after its journey in the C-5, was in a secure hangar at Cairns Airfield.

Not worried about further damage to the interior of the *Carrie-Anne*, Danielle had taken a fire hose to the interior back in Japan and

166

washed the Hangzhou River out of her Chinook. Hopefully out of her life. She never wanted to try a stunt like that again.

Inside the hangar, a pallet of new electronics awaited them. Connie and Big John moved toward them as if drawn by irresistible magnets.

Danielle rested a hand on Connie's arm, "You just spent six hours reassembling a helicopter after flying all day from Japan. Tomorrow is soon enough."

She could feel the woman's conflict through their contact and then Connie laughed at herself.

"Yes," Sofia joined them. "Tomorrow we work, tonight we celebrate. That is good."

"Any suggestions?" Pete asked from close by her elbow. It didn't take a genius to know what kind of celebration he had in mind. But that was a celebration for just two. Danielle was looking forward to that as well, but this was a time for their whole team.

Everyone was looking to her, waiting for her to speak first. She scanned the faces of the 5E and resisted the alarm that wanted to surge through her. She had moved from being the outsider to becoming the core of the team. Danielle wasn't quite sure how that had happened. It was an honor beyond anything she deserved, so she'd have to figure out how to go about earning it...starting tomorrow.

For now, they still waited for her.

She had no idea of what to do next, and then she spotted the Frisbee in the Dozer's hand.

Danielle turned to Pete The Rapier Napier but raised her voice to make sure everyone could hear.

"Everyone who isn't a complete loser..."

Pete just grinned.

"...grab a set of night-vision goggles. It's time to play."

---

PETE STOOD on the unlit soccer field in the northeast corner of Fort

Rucker. It was a typical Alabama early October night: heading from eighties to sixties beneath a sky so clear that it could be an inverted crystal bowl of stars.

And the NVGs amped that up about ten times, he never got used to the breathtaking splendor of the night sky, even if it was rendered in green and black.

Then he looked at the sign in front of him which showed the layout of the eighteen-hole disc golf course. Hole one was straight along the side of the Fort's soccer field to a steel pole. The upper half was a ring of light steel chains. If a Frisbee hit the chains, it would fall straight down into the waiting basket.

The goggles were heavy on his head, though far lighter than a helmet. Elastic straps over his head held it in place, the battery pack clipped to his belt. The mask covered the upper half of his face and the dual lenses stuck out several inches like alien eyestalks.

They caused the nighttime world to be viewed in a combination of tunnel vision and brilliant apple green. The NVGs registered light and especially heat. Pete saw the crew shining brightly with their body heat, the ground less so, and the steel goals were a cool black in the night air.

He was getting to know the crew well enough to recognize them despite their faces being hidden behind NVGs.

Dozer the Mighty Quinn was distinctive for his size alone; he was also the keeper of the discs and was handing them out.

The DAP Hawks' pilots Julian and Rafe were a Mutt and Jeff duo even now fighting over who would get first toss.

Drake was as long and lean as his Chinook ramp gun.

Patty was by far the shortest one on the team, but could also be easily identified because she was always in the thick of it.

Sofia had amazing curves even in night-vision green and her petite copilot had almost none.

Big John and Connie...they moved like a couple should. Not like his own parents, who got along well enough that he had far more happy memories of childhood than sad ones. Instead they fit together despite their physical disparity.

And then there was Danielle. He'd recognize her in a crowded room in pitch dark without NVGs; she was imprinted that deeply on his nervous system. As integrated to him as any helo had ever been. More so.

"Par three," Dozer said walking up to him. No, Dozer was walking up to Danielle. "But first, I need you to sign The Whistler." He held out the Frisbee with the hole shot through it and a marker pen.

Danielle reached out so tentatively to take it that he almost wondered if she'd refuse. Then she took a deep breath and signed it with a flourish.

She handed it off to Pete and he did the same.

When he went to return it to Dozer, he held up his hands palm out.

"Nope, we're playing teams. And I think you two should play with that disc."

Danielle's hesitation finally made sense.

When Pete had arrived to test the rookies, at least a lifetime ago, Danielle had stood to the side, outside the circle of the crew. Now she was no longer a loner, with no relations in the world except a long-gone father. She now had a place in the world as clearly etched as any family.

Pete shook Dozer's hand in thanks. "You did it just right," he told the man. The big Alaskan actually bounced on the balls of his feet for a moment before looking up and grinning, the only part of his face that showed beneath the goggles.

"You guys go first," Dozer's voice was rough and he backed away quickly.

Pete handed the disc to Danielle, "Honor of the first toss, Spiderwoman."

That radiant smile was a gut punch even in a hundred shades of bright green.

The heat of their hands had left clear imprints on the disc that showed up easily in the NVGs. She cocked her arm and heaved the disc into the night.

Talk about a great way to spike the endgame ball. He missed Nicolai and the guys, but he wouldn't trade this team for the world.

A faint whistle sounded down the soccer field as his and Danielle's handprints spun around together.

---

AT THE THIRTEENTH GREEN, Danielle watched as Pete overshot the goal and the Frisbee flew out into the water hazard of the lake that defined the next three holes, it's little whistle sounding like a laugh right up to the moment of the splash.

Then he tried to make her go in and get it.

Danielle managed a quick twist and a well-planted shove that kept her dry and sent him stumbling waist deep into the water after the stray disc.

Laughter rang out from the other teams who were coming along behind them. Moments later Big John had to wade in after his own bad toss. Big John had immense strength, but Connie had all of the finesse.

Danielle and Pete both cleared the fourteenth without any problems, but it was her turn for the key toss on the fifteenth. It was either four throws to get around the end of the lake or one clean toss across the corner of it; a miss would definitely mean she was going swimming.

"What's it gonna be, Spiderwoman?"

"Stuff it, Napier," but she couldn't keep the joy out of her voice. The game had become a merry mayhem of calls up and down the line. Shouts of laughter. Sofia protesting after each toss that landed in the woods or a bush, saying that if this was a soccer ball she could beat them all to a pulp. Julian shoving Rafe into the lake because the man had stood too close to the shore; leaving both Julian and their shared disc dry.

"Need a better name for you than Spiderwoman," Pete whispered.

She'd been getting used to the name.

"Supergirl isn't enough. Sue Storm. Nope. How about Ripley?"

"From *Aliens?* Get a clue Napier. You're being cliché now."

"Am I?"

Danielle eyed the long toss once again. She could do it. The night was calm, only the slightest breath of air from the west. If she took off the goggles she knew the stars would be a warm carpet across the clear night sky rather than the cool one she saw now.

"Okay, how's this for not cliché," Pete's voice had changed. "Danielle?"

Something in his tone made her turn to look at him. His mouth, the only part of him that showed below the NVGs didn't have even the playful edge of a smile that she'd come to expect.

A slip of nerves echoed up her spine.

"What?"

"I love you."

That was it.

A bald, flat statement.

"You..." she couldn't even breathe.

"I thought a lot about what you said as we dove on the Hangzhou tidal bore. I never thought I could deserve a woman like you. But if you say you love me, I'd be pretty damn dumb to turn you away, wouldn't I?"

She nodded, but her head felt like it belonged to a bobble doll. She tried shaking it, but that felt equally strange.

"You..." she took another deep breath, "...love me? Just like that?"

"No, not just like that. I think it was from the moment you gave me sass about being one of the three Fates after I tried calling you the Hound of Hell. It seems you were right after all. You've snagged my thread, but good."

She searched for something to say, for some way to react. She looked down at her hands which ached with the tightness of her grip. She was holding The Whistler hard. Two patterns of bright green radiated outward from her hands where the plastic had been warmed by her grip. A small dark spot, where the bullet had punched through and left its mark. But whatever the past had done to it, the disc still flew true.

"Okay," Pete continued. "That didn't get quite the reaction I expected."

She looked back up at him still at a loss for what to say, but he turned away from her.

"Hey!" he shouted toward the others. "Members of the 5E. Gather around."

There was chattering and questions as everyone trotted over from their various positions among the closest few holes. When they were all gathered and asking what was up, he turned back to face her. A dozen green aliens with human mouths and mechanical eyes turned to face her.

"Now, let's try this," Pete peeled one of her hands off The Whistler and held it in both of his.

"Danielle Delacroix, our lady who guards the crossroads. I've done many dumb things, but let's see if I can do a really smart one instead. I'm going to risk doing this too soon, because I sure as hell don't want to be doing this too late."

Then he knelt down on one knee and the whispered conversations hushed.

"When you crossed my path, you gave me dreams to pursue. Now marry me and change my life. I swear on bended knee before these good people that I will do everything I can to deserve such a gift."

"And we'll kick his ass if he doesn't," Dozer spoke up and others laughed or murmured agreement.

Danielle considered all of the possible responses and exclamations and doubts.

She didn't need them. She didn't need to think or to hesitate either. How many dreams-come-true knelt before her? So many she couldn't count them any more than the stars overhead.

But she couldn't just let him have her consent so easily, no matter how eager she was to give it.

"Well," she looked up at the rest of the 5E gathered close. At Sofia's clasped hands and shining smile. At how Connie and Big John were holding hands and leaning together with the shared memory of their moment. Now Danielle understood Connie's brief handclasp under the table, and just what was possible if you looked far enough outside the box to finally be able to see into its core.

"I'm going to say yes, but..." she let it trail. Everyone, including Pete, held their breath.

Then she looked down at his upturned face, or at least what she could see of it around the NVGs.

"But, it's my turn and I don't want to hold up the game."

She turned from the man she'd be sharing the rest of her life with and heaved The Whistler out into the dark. It shot over the lake toward the fifteenth pin with a little cry of joy that was the tiniest echo of the one in her heart.

# TARGET LOCK ON LOVE

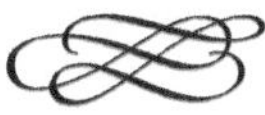

**MISSION:** *If Russia's newest drone flies, then their military may be unstoppable. To block them, the Night Stalkers 5E must deliver SEAL Team 6 to the Kamchatka Peninsula.*

*TEAM:*

***Chief Warrant Patty O'Donoghue***

*— Left her home in Gloucester right where it belongs, in the best-forgotten past, to go fly her beloved Night Stalkers' helicopters.*

***Lieutenant Mick Quinn***

*— Honors his past so deeply that he left his family's Alaskan crabbing boats to join the very best fleet he could find.*

*Fate takes them beyond the last island in the Aleutians and drops them down on a Russian fishing trawler. They must covertly breach the drone factory's security to disable them.*

*The falling in love part? For damn sure that was never in the mission plan.*

# CHAPTER 1

As the Little Bird helicopter bucked its way through the early October storm, Lieutenant Mick "The Mighty Dozer" Quinn wasn't too worried; it wasn't that much of a storm. Especially not by Gulf of Alaska standards. But it did think that slapping their helicopter, the *Linda,* about the sky was good sport and that was making him work for it. It churned enough salt into the air that inside the cabin smelled like being home. The air was unique here: salt, air fresh off the tundra, moisture whipped so hard it tasted alive—he'd missed it to the core of his soul.

Thirty, twenty, and two.

Thirty-knot winds—thirty-five miles-an-hour to landlubbers. Twenty-foot waves—not even enough to slow down his family's commercial crabbing operation. And two miles visibility—if it hadn't been the middle of the night. The storm they were flying into would soon cut that to thirty, twenty, and a hundred yards. As usual, the Aleutian Islands were wrapped in crappy weather and ice-cold water that always found a way down the back of your neck. He didn't miss that, but he still missed working on one of the family's boat.

"This is nuts! Like way worse than even cashews."

The storm was, however, pissing off his copilot. Ready to take on

Mother Nature womano-a-womano, Chief Warrant Officer Patty "Boston" O'Donoghue snarled at her opponent through the windscreen. Patty was always on the attack and she'd be immensely irritating if she wasn't so funny about it. And so damned competent.

"It's—squall line in a hundred yards—doing this just to spite us," she fed him critical information slipstreamed right in with her grousing.

They worked closely together, very closely. Their AH-6M attack helicopter was the smallest manned rotorcraft in the US military's arsenal. It fit just two people, and it was a good thing that Patty wasn't as wide-shouldered as he was or they'd be crammed in the tiny helo's side-by-side seats. Though she wasn't a slip of a thing either; just right, he supposed, for a sassy, kick-butts-now-and-take-names-later Army aviator.

The rear seat could have held two more people. Except the *Linda* was the attack version of the Little Bird—which was why he'd named her for Linda Hamilton in *Terminator II*. The back seat had been replaced by large ammunition cans with feed belts running out to the guns mounted to either side of the fuselage. Just like Sarah Connor, their helicopter was trim and dangerous as all hell.

"It isn't nuts. I used to work on the Alaskan crab boats," Mick nodded down at the roiling sea just fifty feet below them. "My family's probably out there working right now."

"Big whoop, Quinn. I worked the boats on the Grand Banks outta Gloucester." Then she laughed, "No wonder"—it came out *one-de;* her accent always cracked him up—"we went Ah-mee. Still say this hee-ah mission is nuts." The accent that JFK imitators had turned into a national joke was apparently still alive and well in Patty's corner of the country.

The reasons he'd gone Army had nothing to do with the sea. Or maybe everything to do with the sea, but not in the way Patty meant.

"I mean seriously nuts," she waved a hand at the rain-swept darkness ahead then cycled back through checking all the helo's systems. "Five percent falloff in power due to the damp air. Compensating fuel flow."

"*Damp* air?" They had just plunged into the leading edge of the storm with a sharp slap. Rain now pounded against their windscreen as they hustled along at a hundred and fifty miles an hour. The pounding and engine noise vied for which could be louder.

"Barely worth pulling on a sou'wester for, Quinn."

"This mission is no nuttier than you, Boston." Much to his copilot's irritation, their commander's nicknames stuck and stuck hard. When Major Pete Napier tagged you, it stuck, even harder than those of his second-in-command, Captain Danielle Delacroix. Danielle's previous tag for her had been "Irish Patty" but Napier had changed that to "Boston" and all of Patty's protests that she was from Gloucester were dismissed out of hand. Mick saw no reason to ease up on her just because they'd flown together for two years of training and the three months since.

He hadn't minded Danielle tagging him as "The Mighty Quinn" from Bob Dylan's song *Quinn the Eskimo*. He wasn't an Alaska Native, though his family had been up there since the gold rush days. Great-Gran was rumored to have taken an Alutiiq lover at one point—in portraits, his grandma certainly hadn't fit in with her older sisters. Then it had skipped a generation and he liked that he favored Gran; she'd certainly been a tough old bird—still was for that matter even if she didn't ride the crab boats anymore.

Major Napier had taken one look at his broad fisherman's shoulders and tagged him as "Dozer." Danielle had blended the two to Mick "The Mighty Dozer" Quinn.

Didn't matter, he answered to any of them. But Patty couldn't just shrug it off; she really cared about such things.

He stayed focused on flying them through the storm without accidentally flying into the ocean. That's what he cared about, deeply—pun intended. They were now passing over the deep Aleutian Basin. Not that it really mattered. If he made a mistake, it would be the top ten feet of ocean that would kill them, not the ten thousand below that.

Tonight was a typical Night Stalkers' mission, at least for the 5th Battalion E Company. No one could quite agree on what the "E" stood for—other than coming next after the D Company—but "Extreme" was a popular candidate. Tonight's mission was definitely a walk on the wild side: take your four helicopters, fly out into utterly disgusting conditions, mess with the enemy's head, don't get caught.

And so here they were; four in formation, flying west over the Aleutian Island chain in the dead of night.

He flew his Little Bird *Linda* close beside the Black Hawk *Beatrix*. M&M and Kenny flew the 5E's other Little Bird *Leeloo* on *Beatrix's* opposite side. Trailing a mile behind was the workhorse of the outfit, the *Carrie-Anne.* The heavy-lifter Chinook helicopter flown by Napier and Danielle was the key to tonight's operation. The rest of them were just a distraction—three attack helos and one massive transport bird. It had certainly been working for them in the three months since they'd been formed up as a company.

Mick admitted it was a little unusual to be taking on the most paranoid Navy on the planet, the North Koreans. But…

"It doesn't feel atypically extreme," he teased Patty.

He could sense her shrug through their shared flight controls. The collective in his left hand beside the seat didn't lift, but he could feel the vibration of her gesture through the linkage. The cyclic joystick that arced up between their knees didn't even wiggle that much. A pilot learned to isolate gestures from the flight controls.

Mick was damn glad to have Patty riding second on the controls. Flying in tandem like this helped prevent some tiny control mistake that might kill them both. A pilot as good as Patty added another layer of security, particularly in such foul conditions. He always flew at his best with her. Not that he was trying to impress her or anything, she just brought out the best pilot in him.

Along with the rain, the wind picked up another ten knots and the waves another dozen feet. He climbed to stay fifty feet above the crests.

This whole mess had started with the Chinese People's Liberation Army Navy. The PLAN had buddied up with Russia for a massive naval exercise close enough to Japan to give the Japanese a major case of hives. Then, instead of turning for home like good little destroyers and landing craft, they'd driven for US territorial waters. The PLAN didn't push three thousand miles from their home waters just by chance.

"Right of Innocent Passage, my ass," Patty grumbled.

"Kind of my thought as well, but it is the law."

Major Napier's briefing for the flight had reminded them that "innocent passage" was allowed under the UN Convention of the Law of the Sea. As long as they did nothing aggressive, like launching planes or attack watercraft, they could sail right through another nation's territorial waters and say, "Oh, I'm not really here; just in transit."

The fact that the Chinese freaked every time the US came within two-hundred miles of their coast hadn't stopped the Chinese from steaming a loop within a five miles Attu—the farthest west of the Aleutian Islands, uninhabited since 2011. The Pentagon had displayed far more restraint than the Chinese Coast Guard by sensibly doing absolutely nothing.

Then badly misreading the situation—and unaware of the numerous tiny retributions that the Chinese were bound to suffer for a long time to come—the North Korean leader had decided that if the Chinese could cross the American borders, so could he. He'd mobilized every ship that was in good enough repair to risk such a long voyage—all three of them. North Korea's navy was called a "brown water navy" with reason. Most of their vessels weren't even capable of circling from one coast of North Korea, around South Korea, and to the other side—a journey of less than a thousand miles.

Striking for the Aleutians *was* nuts, even if he'd never admit his agreement with Patty just on principal.

The first time, the Pentagon had again turned a blind eye just as they had with the Chinese. The second time the US had sent a pair of jets to do a low-level flyby that hadn't deterred the North Koreans. The third North Korean incursion had passed right between Kanaga and Tanaga Islands in the outer Aleutians—a strait less than five miles wide—to thumb their noses at the Americans.

This time, working their way up the island chain to see just how far they could push it, they had crossed past Dutch Harbor and Unalaska Island within plain sight of the Alaska ferry and innumerable fisherman. Dutch was the largest fishery port in the US and that was too much for the Pentagon. And apparently for Patty O'Donoghue as well.

"The fourth goddamn passage in four weeks is—"

"Is why we're here tonight," he cut off her rant before she could get her Irish up. Because when Patty did, she wasn't a firecracker, she was a battering ram. She made most of the other pilots psychotic after a single hour aloft.

Her sharp humor and passionate emotions worked for him, at least in flight. Whoever she finally latched onto in the personal side of her life would need the patience of Job or to be just as feisty as she was; he'd wager on the latter, with battles royal ensuing into the foreseeable future with both sides enjoying themselves immensely.

At the moment her sights were aimed at Julian, the copilot on the DAP Hawk *Beatrix*—except she hadn't taken any action yet, at least none that he'd spotted. Maybe he'd misread it. At the end of training it had been a mechanic back at Fort Campbell. Before that was a Specialist in the 101st Airborne and then...

Patty O'Donoghue was a looker with her thick, deep red hair and cream skin, and could have her pick. But, man, the woman was a handful.

He wished "whoever" all the luck in the world; they were going to need it.

His idea of an ideal woman was—

"Contact with Korean People's Navy group in thirty miles," Lieutenant Sofia Gracie's voice whispered over the encrypted radio, rich with mellifluous tones of her Brazilian childhood and Los Angeles upbringing. "Correct bearing to three-oh-five."

He could listen to her voice all—

"You gonna fly this thing *o-ah* shall I, dream boy?" Patty interrupted his thoughts.

"Sure, Patty. Like I'd trust you at the controls." Which he did—absolutely—or he wouldn't be flying with her. She was damned good and only flew copilot because he was a little better at the flying and she was a little better at handling the weapons while he flew. He was also Lieutenant to her Chief Warrant 3 for what little respect Patty deemed that to be worth. It earned him the occasional salute, a moderately frequent "sir"—most often ironic in tone—and what he felt was more than his fair share of sass.

No big deal anyway. Mick wasn't more than a second or two late in correcting his flight path to match the other three birds in the flight, all now heading directly toward the tiny KPN fleet. It wasn't like they were flying a tight formation in this weather. His primary worry was not eating a rogue wave on this low-level flight.

"They don't even own a destroyer to send," Patty protested as if the KPN's finest had been sent as a personal insult to one Chief Warrant O'Donoghue. "Their only full frigate has never been seaworthy. They gotta send us *light* frigates, corvettes really. These boys really need to be spanked and sent back home."

"Which is why we're here," though he didn't waste his effort on saying it aloud. Patty was perfectly capable of sustaining the conversation on her own. Gods but the woman cracked him up.

A straight-in approach was safe enough, because the entire 5E flew stealth-modified aircraft. At fifty feet up in a storm, the Koreans' radar wouldn't see a thing of their four helicopters. Of course, if it weren't for the lovely Sofia flying her Avenger drone fifty thousand feet above them, they wouldn't be seeing a thing either.

---

PATTY COULD SEE EXACTLY where Mick's attention had gone; like he stood a chance. He'd been smitten since the first moment Second Lieutenant Sofia Gracie had been added to their team. All of the guys had been gobsmacked because Sofia really was that stunning. Most of them had recovered with time, but Mick wasn't one of them.

Being strictly impartial about it, Mick was a handsome enough bastard in a dark, brooding way. Black hair flowed to his collar, matching his dark eyes. It was that deep, soft voice of his that slayed

Patty, though she wasn't complaining about his fisherman's physique or the way his big hands were so light on the Little Bird's controls either.

The Mighty Quinn was a solid anchor in any situation. He was always so calm and steady, no matter what storm she tossed in his direction to best him.

He was also one of the few that could keep up with her, male or female. No insult to Kenny and M&M in the *Leeloo,* but they just didn't have the feel for the sprightliness of the Little Bird helos the way that Mick did with the *Linda.* Each time she'd flown with them, they'd learned far more from her than she from them. Mick could just as easily be "Magic Man" as "The Mighty Quinn" for what he could make their aircraft do.

Not that she'd ever consider telling him. If his head ever became as swollen as his shoulders, she'd have to copilot from the outside of the helicopter rather than the left-hand seat. The stealth aircraft flew with its doors on, unlike most Little Birds—the door had a lower radar signature than a pilot sitting in their seat. Mick was an easy man to share the cramped space with.

But if he thought all that was enough to win him "Latin Lady's" undying affection, then good luck to him. Patty hadn't seen Sofia pick up even a single hint, not that Mick had dropped one either. Dumb. Guys were so damn dumb.

Sofia was in some whole other class of woman that was way above a guy who was merely dark and handsome. She should be modeling women's underwear or doing Miss Clairol commercials with that swirling dark hair and her Brazilian-brown skin. Or Estée Lauder with those dark, dark eyes.

But she didn't.

She was an awesome Avenger pilot. Of course that meant that she and her copilot flew their remotely-piloted aircraft from a cargo container packed with high-tech gear currently parked at Joint Base Elmendorf-Richardson—typically called a "coffin" for its long, low shape. JBER was eight hundred miles away back in Anchorage, but satellite communications made that irrelevant. Didn't matter that she wasn't physically present, because she did it damn well. She had proved several times that she knew exactly what to do with her drone—sorry Sofia—her jet-powered RPA that flew ten miles up at four-hundred-and-fifty miles-an-hour.

Sofia was also an easy person to like. Maybe there was some way Patty could encourage Mick but sabotage him with Sofia at the same time just for the hell of it. Nah! The few times she'd stuck her foot in someone else's mess, she'd only made it worse...and then gotten caught. Didn't matter; she had faith that the big lummox would find a way to fail all on his own. Too bad; they'd look good together. Of course, any man would with Sofia on their arm.

And now it was time to look good for the North Koreans...who would never see them coming.

Fifty feet up, they should pick up the Korean's top-of-mast radar at ten miles out.

"Five. Four. Three. Two..." She stretched it out but shouldn't have. Right on cue, the KPN's radar sweeps blasted onto the Little Bird's passive detection systems.

"How do you do things like that?"

"*Shit* like that, Quinn. For God's sake, loosen up. And it's because I'm that goddamn good. Not that it matters. Look at the frequency these guys are using," she waved at hand at the console, knowing Mick didn't have time to look down. "They're running tech that the Army retired back while you and I were still pooping up our diapers, or at least you were. I was always a dainty little kid."

"Uh-huh," Mick's grunt might have been long-suffering or it might have been a tease. Man's grunts were hard to read.

"The KPN's radar uses such a broad sweep that we could fly right between their lines of resolution. Even Danielle's big-ass Chinook could do that."

Why was it that the ever so classy Danielle flew the monstrous, twin-rotor *Carrie-Anne?* Of course, flying in a Chinook MH-47G named for the actress who played Trinity in *The Matrix*—the ultimate leather-clad kick-ass heroine—had its points.

Still, Patty could have enjoyed flying her Little Bird with Danielle, not that she wanted to trade Mick even one little bit. Not only was he an enjoyable piece of eye candy, but he also flew like a goddamn genius. And he put up with her, which even not being totally honest with herself, she knew was a serious challenge. Her father had used less kind words.

But Danielle had so much smooth sophistication that Patty knew she totally lacked. If they flew as a girl-girl team, it would have been fun…and maybe a little of the effortless elegance would have rubbed off on her.

"Too bad for the KPN," Mick didn't sound sorry at all, "that we're stealth rigged. All that energy spent looking for something they'll never see."

"Poor bastards," Patty agreed. The storm was beating on them now, thick with rain and hard winds. The KPN's ships were all in the two- to three-hundred-foot range but narrow enough that they rolled hard in the rough waves. Even for people she didn't like, they were *not* having a good day…and the Night Stalkers were about to make it even worse.

"Just makes it more fun," Mick commented.

"You *are* evil and twisted. There's hope for you yet, Quinn," she grinned behind the lowered visor of her helmet which was glowing on the inside with layers of rapidly shifting tactical information.

Mick didn't let his snide out very often, but she always appreciated it when he did.

"Knew there was a reason I liked flying with you." Because whatever else The Mighty Quinn might be, he was a hell of a partner.

She was never as good beside any other pilot; his skill demanded her best performance be even better. *Be all you can be.* Hell with joining the Army, she'd already done that. Earning the right to fly beside Mick Quinn, that took some serious doing.

"Our target will be the westernmost ship," she filled him in. "It's also the biggest, a Nampo class. Twin 30mm machine guns, so don't mess with that. And intel says an RBU-1200—that's a five-missile anti-submarine weapon so we should be fine as long as you don't dump us in the soup."

"Wasn't planning on it," Mick stated it as if he was discussing a change in a battle plan. She really needed to find a way to loosen him up.

"They also have a helo platform, not that they have the skills to launch in this weather. Rumor has it that they're still flying Russian Mi-4 Hounds. You know those things are half a century old. It would be really cool to see one, even parked on a crap frigate. North Korea is the last nation trying to fly them."

"One minute," Major Napier, their company commander, called over the encrypted radio channel from the trailing Chinook *Carrie-Anne*. "Keep them busy."

"Dance!" Danielle called before Napier clicked off.

That was another reason to want to be like Captain Danielle Delacroix.

*Dance.*

It was one of those crazy commands that the captain had cooked up during training—back before they'd been formed into the 5E and Pete "The Rapier" Napier took command.

If Patty could be any other woman, it wouldn't be the curvaceous Sofia Gracie; it would be Captain Delacroix with her soft-spoken Québécois French accent and exceptionally strategic mind. Though if she'd been Danielle, she'd now be married to Major Pete Napier and Patty would have killed his ass in the first month. He'd be damned irritating if he wasn't such a good commander.

So, not Danielle.

Patty would find her boy someday. But he wouldn't be a fisherman, who thought a pretty woman on a working boat was an open invitation. The first real attack on her person had only been averted because she happened to be in the galley and could grab a knife. After that, she'd learned to always have a blade handy and still had to flash it at the occasional overeager asshole to convince them that "No!" meant no. Two of them she'd had to scar but good before they'd backed off.

And it wouldn't be some gung-ho Army pilot too damn sure of himself. If she never heard another airjock say "Come fly me!" then ask if she still had her stewardess uniform, it would be too soon. She'd had enough of those kind of creeps who didn't like the fact that she could outfly every one of their asses. By that time she didn't need a knife, the Army had trained her plenty well in hand-to-hand combat. Switching to Special Operations had only honed those skills.

She glanced over at Mick. And it sure as hell wouldn't be someone who was both fisher and pilot no matter how handsome.

In the meantime she had every intention of enjoying herself. She'd taken up with teasing Julian over on the *Beatrix.* But it was just to mess with his head, there was nothing ever going to happen there. As it was, she'd been having a long dry spell and was just fine with that.

*Dance,* Danielle had said. With that simple command, she'd just instructed each of the pilots to implement evasive tactics based on their favorite music. Better than something *Star Trekish* like "Execute Evasion Plan Delta." The military's top pilots would each dance differently. It made the flight wholly unpredictable and nearly impossible to target. It also meant…

"Oh, man! You are *not* gonna hit me with country," she aimed her complaint at Mick over the on-board intercom. She checked that all weapons' systems were armed and ready in case the North Koreans were dumb enough to actually try and engage American aircraft while sailing in American waters.

"Only the finest," Mick began humming some Tim McGraw song.

"Goddamn it, Quinn. How is it possible that a perfectly respectable girl knows that's a Tim McGraw song? You're ruining me."

"Because a perfectly respectable girl *would* know it was Tim McGraw."

"That's not true!" Patty resisted the urge to stomp a little rock and roll into the rudder pedals as he began making the Little Bird shift and sway.

"It is," Mick continued placidly. "Which begs the question of how you know anything about it."

So much worse than that, she even knew the words well enough to sing along—which she absolutely wasn't about to do. "I'm gonna request a goddamn new pilot; one who knows decent music when he hears it."

He hummed even louder over the intercom until it was resonating inside her helmet.

"Keep it up and you're gonna be so far beyond dead that you'll be way past living like you still had any dying to do."

Patty knew it was a mistake as soon as she said it.

Mick broke into full song with the last line of the refrain, which is what she'd just done her best to mangle. Then he began all over going on all about skydiving and climbing mountains—the helicopter swooping and slipping through the air in perfect time to his music. He wielded a good, deep baritone designed to turn a girl into a liquid puddle.

Well not her.

She fought back with Marianas Trench's *Fallout,* but she couldn't carry a tune for crap so her attempt at punk/emo didn't cut him down even a little.

At that moment, the tall sides of the frigate came into view just a dozen rotor diameters ahead. Which on a Little Bird, with its tiny five-blade, twenty-seven-foot diameter main rotor, wasn't very far.

The ship's high bow was climbing clear of a big wave and then crashing down into the next trough; a very uncomfortable-looking ride. They'd be better off in a fishing boat that could just ride over one wave at a time without all of the bucking and yawing. Military ships were built narrow to move fast, but that meant they totally sucked during a storm.

Mick hit the KPN with the song's line about riding a rodeo bull just to emphasize the point—wasn't right that a country boy could make her laugh so easily—and then he dodged aside as the frigate's forward anti-submarine rocket launcher tried to spear them when the ship took another painful roll.

The ship only had running lights on: red and green to the sides, a white all-around at the top of the mast, a second white below that pointing forward. The deck itself was ink-and-storm dark.

The North Koreans didn't notice that they'd acquired a pitch-black Little Bird helicopter hovering above their foredeck. Of course, the *Linda* was a stealth craft with its running lights out.

Mick slipped up until the Little Bird was hovering directly in front of the command bridge's windows.

"Are you feeling ignored, madam?" Mick asked Patty in an über-polite voice as if they were at some snooty Boston social event rather than a couple of fishers-turned-pilots now hovering over a ship's deck in the middle of the Aleutians.

"Why yes, good sir. I feel as if they aren't paying any frickin' attention to us at all." She raised a pinkie finger from the cyclic control, not that Mick would be able to see it.

Quinn switched to singing the Trace Adkins song about a lonely heart who turned on every light in the house to show his departed lover the way back home.

Oh, what the hell! She could take a hint. So, she joined on the chorus and hit the landing light, aiming it directly into the command bridge windows.

The reaction was galvanic. It was easy to see the several seasick officers leaning against any support—brown water navy indeed. Two seamen, looking far more stoic than their superiors, clung to the wheel.

And every one of them too frozen with surprise to even cover their eyes. Korean deer staring into the headlights.

Perfect.

Because tonight's mission was to make sure that the KPN never looked astern to see what the SEAL team delivered by the Chinook *Carrie-Anne* was doing back there.

# CHAPTER 2

ick watched for the first one to unfreeze; a junior officer twitched like he'd had his butt pinched.

Mick dodged the *Linda* back into the storm with all the agility of her *Terminator II* namesake the moment before the deck lights flashed on.

"Camera." It was their first really close look at a Nampo-class light frigate; though he had no time to look himself.

"Never stopped recording," Patty answered back.

"Good girl," not that he'd expected less.

"Woman!" She sniped back just as he'd planned.

"Where?"

Her growl was music to his ears.

This time he approached from the starboard side, flew directly over the bridge and disappeared to port.

"*Woman*! Like the one who's gonna shove you out on the next fly-by. Then you'll be shipped off to North Korea and no longer chapping my ass."

"So scared. Eek," he delivered it deadpan.

She spared a moment to punch him in the arm, lightly, so that she didn't jostle his control.

Mick focused on keeping the bridge crew distracted. They didn't begin to understand the high technology of his Little Bird. Across the inside of his helmet was displayed the image of any direction he looked. With a thumb control he could look up, down, even straight behind him as if he was sitting alone in the night sky without a helicopter wrapped around him. Outside, multiple mounted cameras routed thermal-enhanced seamless images onto his visor.

A slap of wind tried to slew him into the high bow of the frigate. He lifted enough to clear the railing but kept his landing light aimed directly in their faces as the ship slewed across beneath him. Between the wind and the waves and the crap visibility, this was getting nasty even by Night Stalker standards.

"How are the others doing?" he asked Patty.

"You just focus on keeping us alive and this crew distracted."

"Spoilsport."

"Am not. I'm a woman. I get," and she went for song, "R.E.S.P.E.C.—"

"First ship tampered," Sofia reported over the radio, cutting off Patty's grossly off-key efforts. "The *Leeloo,* she is clear."

Sofia's naturally musical tones only emphasized the degree of murder that O'Donoghue had been perpetrating on Aretha.

"The wet team, it is headed now to *Beatrix's* target."

Mick was damn glad to not be on the wet team. It was a given that SEALs were comfortable in water, but this storm was ugly even from the air. From the small rubber boat that the *Carrie-Anne* had delivered astern of the KPN's ships, it must be pure hell.

*Beatrix's* ship was second. The Direct Action Penetrator Black Hawk was named for Uma Thurman's role in the *Kill Bill* movies; a very appropriate moniker. The DAP Hawk was the most heavily armed helicopter in any military. There were less than two dozen of them—all designed by and built for the Night Stalkers of the 160th Special Operations Aviation Regiment (airborne).

Mick had flown the big helo on a couple of familiarization flights, but he'd always been partial to his Little Bird. Hard not to be impressed by the DAP Hawk's raw power, but he preferred the super-agility of his aircraft. Being less maneuverable, he hoped *Beatrix* was being careful while distracting their target. He shouldn't worry, Rafe and Julian were almost as good a team as he and Patty. He worried anyway.

A hard gust smacked him sideways and he yanked up on the collective to avoid eating the frigate's radio mast.

"Hey look! They do still have an Mi-4 helo tied down on their stern. Ooo! Big wave just buried it in spray. Salt water, fifty-year-old hardware, bad deal guys."

Mick wished he had a moment to look, but that was Patty's job as copilot in situations like this. He actually appreciated the running commentary as she cataloged the ship's features for the recorder that was also capturing the video for later study by whoever cared.

They were playing an elegant trick on the North Koreans. A DEVGRU team—that the public had called by their long-abandoned name of SEAL Team 6 for so long that they'd taken to calling themselves Team 6 anyway—had been launched in a boat by the lurking Chinook helicopter. The team was dodging in behind each of the Korean ships, one by one, and performing a death-defying stunt.

The plan, suggested by the SEALs themselves because they were just that crazy, was to partially disable each ship. Not in a dangerous way, in case they hit a big storm on their way home, but enough to be immensely awkward.

When a particularly tall wave lifted the stern of each ship high enough for the rudder to clear the water, the SEAL team would zip forward in their tiny boat. Undetected due to the helicopters playing distraction games around the command bridges, the SEALs would slap a super-epoxied bar of metal to the hull directly in front of the rudder.

The bar extended out alongside the rudder. The result was that the Koreans would be able to turn to starboard without a problem. But if they tried to turn to port more than a few degrees, the rudder would hit the bar and that was it. Any time they came too far off their course, they'd have to go in a full circle to regain their heading.

For the North Koreans to cut the bar, they'd require calm seas, a skilled diver, and an underwater cutting torch. It was a fair bet that they probably weren't carrying the last item, especially as the bars were titanium—light to handle but with an unusually high melting point.

Even if they were able to cut it, they wouldn't be able to hide the bar itself—it would take a shipyard and new plating to remove it from the hull. Three senior captains were about to be in immense trouble.

"The *Beatrix*, she's complete," Sofia updated him.

The tactical display showed that the heroine of *The Fifth Element*, *Leeloo*, and the *Beatrix* were standing off in case he needed help with distracting his own light frigate, the largest of the three.

---

THE *LINDA* BUCKED HARD, momentarily making Patty float off her seat. She wanted to shriek with delight.

"You a roller coaster boy, Mick?" She leaned forward to brace herself against her flight harness to keep her hand steady on the controls. Still she could barely follow what he was doing. Goddamn, but he could fly.

"Never been on one," his voice remained Mick-steady. He actually flipped the helicopter upside down in a sideways rollover as he shifted from right-side up on one side of the ship to right-side up on the other.

"Hot dog! Wait. *What?*" Patty gasped for breath as the adrenaline pounded. Her efforts to match Mick's imperturbable calm were a total failure. "Did you...Oh Crap!," a searchlight swung their way, but Mick was no longer there, spinning them off over the ocean's darkness, "...grow up deprived?"

"No coasters in Alaska except the little ones at county fairs."

"Well, we gotta fix that."

"You going into the carnival business, O'Donoghue?" When he slewed across the deck again, Patty could see trouble was coming soon.

"I'm not gonna—"

She keyed the mike. "Sofia. Our boat is arming. Only rifles so far, but they're scrambling now."

"Roger," Sofia called back. "SEAL team needs two minutes more."

"—build one," Patty picked up right where she left off. "I'm getting your butt on the next one I can."

"Gee, thanks."

"My luck you'll be a *sicker*. But it's a total rite of passage and you gotta do it. Can you get me right over the deck?"

"Didn't you just say that they're arming?" He moved off their bow.

She flashed the landing light full in their faces down the length of the deck before Mick dodged aside once more.

"Seriously. I've got a special delivery for them."

"Is this something I want to be party to?"

"Absotively! Now do it. Because your only other option is to circle the stern, and you don't want to draw their attention there."

"SEAL Team clear," Sofia announced.

Mick cursed under his breath. It was nice to know he wasn't so perfectly cool all the time.

"The *Carrie-Anne* still has to recover the team and in these seas that could take some doing," she nudged at him.

"Will your *special delivery* buy the SEALs some time?"

"Duh!" Why else did he think she was suggesting it?

Mick played a game of peek-a-boo over the bow: starboard, dead ahead, and port.

Then he yanked up on the collective and slid the cyclic forward. The Little Bird leapt, but she kept a firm grip on the weapon's release she'd pre-rigged back in Anchorage.

He carved a turn back the other way, out of sight below the line of their bow but with her side of the helicopter so close to the waves that she instinctively edged upslope out of her seat. The water was so close that, if not for the g-force and her safety harness, she'd have crawled right into Mick's lap to get away from it.

Exactly amidships, he turned directly for the boat. He climbed sharply to clear the deck and the railings. Armed seamen out on the deck flattened themselves to avoid being hit by his racing helicopter's skids—he was that low.

Damn he was good! She liked that sooo much in a pilot.

Exactly amidships, he went vertical. Directly above the center of the ship's deck, he shot upward rather than crossing the rest of the way to the far side.

It was all she needed.

Patty hit the release.

At her "Whoop! Cargo away!" Mick laid down the hammer again and shot off into the darkness.

# CHAPTER 3

"I can't believe this girl!"

"Woman," Patty snarled at him.

Mick just grinned as all of the other women around the table joined in on her side. He was in too good a mood to care. Someone had to keep Patty O'Donoghue in her place and it might as well be him. She'd been dancing in her seat for practically the whole flight back to Elmendorf-Richardson. Despite her singing the Oompa Loompa song, off-key, for most of that trip, he couldn't begrudge her a moment of it. Though he couldn't believe she knew all the words from *both* Willy Wonka movies, at least the Oompa Loompa parts.

Screw the mess hall. To celebrate, Mick had dragged them all out to the best pizza in Anchorage, or anywhere in his opinion. Moose's Tooth Pub and Pizzeria had been a fixture in his life. They opened when he was eight, and his family had gone on the first night.

It had been to celebrate a big first of his own—his inaugural trip on the family's crabbing boat as cook's helper rather than a passenger. The fifty-mile trip from Seward into Anchorage for some amazing pizza had been his reward. Even though he'd now left the family business, this is where he always came to celebrate. It had also been a fixture of his tenure at the university here.

The owners knew him by name and didn't need to remember his reputation. Showing up with a dozen other Night Stalkers ready for pizza and beer for breakfast at ten in the morning hadn't even phased them. Instead they'd tagged them as rowdies, booted them into a back room, and fed them like you might a starving wolf pack—heavily. Too bad that Commander Altman and his three SEALs had, per usual, slipped away immediately after the mission.

The Moose's Tooth was wood paneled, as welcoming on a cold winter night as on a balmy October morning like this one. A table that could seat twenty-five felt packed with a fifteen of them. Gods, these people were so much larger than life. How in the world had he been lucky enough to work with such amazing folk? He'd done something right; he just wasn't sure quite when.

Napier declared the 5E was off-duty, "dark" for twenty-four hours, so they could actually have beer with their pizza. The Night Stalker rule was twenty-four hours from bottle to throttle. As the 160th SOAR was also on 24-by-7 alert status, it was often tricky getting a drink. Just three days ago he'd been given a week's vacation. Then called back in before he'd even reached a civilian airport. That he was now sitting at his vacation destination but on a mission was a little ironic, even for him; though he was sure that Patty would appreciate it.

In minutes the table was covered with Nashville Nachos and spicy Buffalo chicken wings. Several pitchers of beer arrived. Flight jackets were shed and laughter erupted.

The ship facing the *Leeloo* had tried to dodge the Little Bird with hard maneuvering. It had made the SEALs' job harder, getting clean access to the stern. But the joke of trying to dodge a fifteen-hundred-pound helo with a fifteen-hundred-ton ship wasn't lost on this crew— even if it had been on the North Korean captain. He'd been the first to discover that something had changed and he could only go straight or to starboard.

The *Beatrix* was the only aircraft that had been shot at. Connie Davis had silenced the ship's single rifle round with a brief blast of an

M134 minigun across their deck. The M134 Gatling machine gun sounded like a very, very angry and impossibly loud chainsaw when it unleashed its three thousand supersonic rounds a minute. It would take a heartier crew than the frigate's to retaliate against such a noise. After that demonstration, Rafe and Julian didn't have to do any hard maneuvering at all. They had simply floated above the deck, out of reach of the North Korean's searchlights, with their running lights on. No one had seen that they were a stealth craft, but all attention had been riveted skyward while the SEALs had worked their magic at the stern.

Connie sat very quietly beside her much larger husband. Big John was almost as cheery as Patty, at least under normal circumstances. Not a chance that he'd keep up with her tonight. Besides, he'd been in the back of the big Chinook helping with the delivery and retrieval of Team 6's boat. He and Drake, the *Carrie-Anne's* ramp gunner, had been soaked with Aleutian seawater several times during the operation, which had dampened their spirits a bit. Drake nursed a beer and John simply sat with an arm around his wife's shoulders and grinned at the banter circling about the table.

Sofia teased and taunted with her usual flair. Zoe, her copilot, nursed a beer quietly. The rest of the four helos' crews were joining in, whenever Patty's boisterous laugh permitted.

"So, I just—" Patty kicked back in her chair exactly aligning her head with a giant cartoon drawing of a moose on the wall behind her, giving herself antlers.

"Nope," Mick hid his snort of laughter as well as he could when he cut off Patty. "You don't get to tell your own story."

He stared her down and she quaffed her beer—then made ready to spit the mouthful at him across the loaded table. He almost made a bring-it-on gesture, but knew that if challenged, she would. Relenting only because he didn't want to be eating soggy nachos, he continued before she could launch.

"There we are," he glanced to make sure that the door was closed at the moment and there were only Night Stalkers and no servers in the room. "SEALs in the water. North Koreans hopping mad all over the deck because all they've seen of me is a glaring landing light. Half the time they were *lying* on the deck because of the storm."

"And half the time because they thought they'd be smacked by a whirling dervish. Damn but you can fly, Quinn."

Mick raised a beer in acknowledgement and wondered where the compliment had come from; that didn't sound like Patty. Of course, they'd been laughing together for the entire flight back. It had been a good moment for them both.

"Seriously," she said in an aside to Sofia who'd ended up sitting at her side. "He was incredible."

*What the hell?* Why was Patty buttering him up with Sofia? Sure, the RPA pilot was impossible not to look at—how often did a fashion model end up as a 2nd Lieutenant in any outfit? He'd checked online; she had been. Pretty heavy-duty job for a model to go for, but she'd done it. A real case against female stereotypes, as if his matriarchal family line had given him a choice—didn't matter if she was mostly ashore now, it was still Gran's crabbing operation.

Mick had always felt as if he should have the hots for Sofia, and often caught himself watching her and wondering why he didn't. She fit so many of his ideal-woman fantasies, must be something wrong with him. Wouldn't be a surprise at all if there was. He'd been with some fine women over the years, but wherever the target lock inside him was hiding, it had yet to engage and offer the steady tone of a worthwhile focus.

There were two couples in the group, an incomprehensible event in a military company, but it had happened. Major Napier and Captain Delacroix had tied the knot just a month ago. And the two ace mechanics—Connie Davis and Big John Wallace transferred from the 5D—had arrived on the scene already a couple.

Why not a third? But even if it was allowed, Sofia wasn't ringing his chimes.

He wasn't waiting for some perfect woman, apparently not even when he was confronted with one. He just wanted...

And he was staring again—*Goddamn it!* Even doing something as innocent as sipping her beer, she was like a magnet; if you were a guy you just had to stop and watch her.

No one appeared to notice his lapse, except Patty who was wearing one of those way too pleased with herself smiles.

"I was running out of ideas for distractions," he picked up the story again.

Patty's guffaw burst out and got several people laughing along even if they weren't sure why. When Patty O'Donoghue laughed, it was hard to resist joining in.

He managed, giving her a scowl instead.

She smirked, absolutely thinking the joke was on him. He seriously considered spraying a mouthful of beer in her direction but didn't want to catch the innocent Sofia in the overspray.

"And once I get them all riled up, this one," he pointed an accusing spicy chicken wing at Patty as if he was about to jump across the table and bayonet her with it, "she tells me to fly right over the center of their deck. These guys are fishing out rifles and I'll bet that someone was ranging a surface-to-air missile."

"Here comes the good bit," Patty crowed.

"I get her right over the center of the deck and she unleashes this secret cargo she'd rigged in place of two of the Hellfire missiles without telling me."

"You dropped a pair of dummy missiles on a foreign ship of war?" Major Napier jerked upright in his chair.

That had been his guess too. And he'd reamed Patty but good for it before her laugh had cut him off.

Danielle put a hand lightly on Napier's arm. Most of the women were leaning forward in anticipation, most of the guys were leaping to bad conclusions just as he had. He'd have to remember to ask someone why the gender split. Was it that guys had no creativity in combat and women knew that? Or was it because a woman had thought of it? He didn't like the feel of the latter but suspected both were equally true. Mick decided against asking Patty, she'd get too much smug satisfaction out of it and she was smug enough already.

With masterful timing, Patty waited until all the men had calmed back down. Since he was in on the surprise, he could appreciate her sense of theater. It was just as good as her timing as a copilot.

"Nope!" Patty was so pleased with herself that her big laugh twisted into that rare, high giggle she unleashed only on special occasions. She went from classic cheery-caustic O'Donoghue to impossibly cute Patty faster than a Hellfire could crack the sound barrier.

They had to drop the topic when the door opened and the first round of pizzas arrived. A Greek Gyro sausage pie, a Garlic Lover's with blackened chicken, and a High Protein Land—which had enough meat to satisfy a grizzly bear, and maybe even a Night Stalker.

Once the waiters were gone, and everyone was groaning with pleasure over their first bites, he picked it back up. He'd rather just eat; it had been a long time since his last Moose's Tooth pizza. But Patty deserved her moment in the sun; she'd sure earned it.

"Patty dropped her cargo," Mick said loudly enough to recapture everyone's attention. "It smacked down on the deck and spread everywhere, covering the entire area. As soon as the Koreans recovered from the shock, they were scrabbling about like madmen."

"Caltrops? Those tetrahedral spike things?"

"Marbles?"

"Vegas topless show fliers?"

"A thousand copies of *Playboy?*"

"Better!" Patty crowed as the team tossed out more guesses.

Mick waved his slice of pizza at her for her to take her bow.

"I cleaned out the PX," Patty said it with her voice dropped into mission-debrief neutral. "We delivered a two-hundred-and-three-pound payload of...Snickers, Almond Joy, Twix, Reese's—you name it."

"She gave them a taste of what the West can dish out."

The exclamations and laughter rolled around the table.

Mick tipped his beer in a silent toast to her.

He loved her out-of-the-box brain. She was always surprising him with it.

The smile she sent back was beyond radiant.

Damn! There was absolutely no doubt about the accuracy of his earlier assessment. Chief Warrant 3 Patty O'Donoghue was a *real* looker.

# CHAPTER 4

*P*atty leaned on Mick's arm, not quite sure how she'd gotten there. She drank so rarely that the second beer had blurred reality long before she'd reached the bottom of the glass. She wasn't even sure she *had* reached the bottom of it.

She squinted at the sky. The storm-ravaged night raging over the Aleutians had started as a partly sunny day in Anchorage. Above the Moose's Tooth parking lot, a thin haze now turned the whole sky blindingly bright. Squinting behind her sunglasses wasn't helping. Wait, she wasn't wearing sunglasses. Patty found them tucked up in her hair and pulled them down. It didn't help anyway. No matter how she looked at it, it was two in the afternoon—a Night Stalkers' two in the morning—she was tipsy and hanging onto...Mick. That was the most surprising thing of all.

"Ya know," she could feel her voice softening, but she was feeling too relaxed to reel it back in. "I use-ta be able to drink a whole swordfisheryman's crew under the table. Look what's happened to me. Pitiful! The Army has ruined me for my life's plan of being a lush." She waved a hand extravagantly and almost went down on the parking lot. She held on hard and inspected the surface under her boots. It was just lying there. No ice or snow, not even wet. Nothing to blame it on but herself.

"Just look," Mick said agreeably.

"You don't smile much, Quinn." She squeezed his arm beneath his jeans jacket. "Work out though." Which explained what she was hanging on to.

"I smile plenty."

"Nope! You don't. Looks good on you. Just like the muscles. Sofia would appreciate that. You should smile at her more." She really didn't think it was the beer that was making her this unstable—all she had on was a pleasant buzz. There had to be something else, but she couldn't think what.

"I don't care what Sofia would appreciate on me."

"Sure you do," Patty patted his arm and tried not to giggle at the repetition but couldn't resist Patty-patting his arm again—it was a very nice arm.

"No, I really don't," he placed one of those big strong fisherman's hands of his over hers to secure her grip on his elbow. He used that link to guide her to the Ford sedan they'd signed out of base transportation for the evening. For the day. Whatever this blinding stuff was.

She looked up at those dark eyes. His sunglasses were still tucked in his pocket as if all this brightness was somehow normal. He looked serious, but then he always did. Patty knew that if she was even a little drunk, her judgment went to hell. It was like the Joe Nichols song, *Tequila Makes Her Clothes Fall Off*—which was also goddamned country. Her one bout with tequila and she'd lost her virginity to Timmy Thompson. *Timmy Thompson? Really?* It had been enough to make her swear off boys for the whole rest of high school, and tequila for a lifetime.

"But I'm not that drunk."

"Uh-huh," her hunky pilot nudged her into the car's passenger seat. When he leaned inside and reached across to snap in her seatbelt, she seriously considered nibbling on his ear just to make him crazy. But then he might think she was interested in him and that would never do, because he was interested in Sofia and there was honor among women.

"You don't sound convinced about my soberishness."

"You're a lightweight, O'Donoghue. I don't think that you could ever drink a swordfish steak under the table, never mind a boatload of 'swordfisherymen'."

"I could—"

He cut her off by flipping her door shut and circling around the hood.

She leaned over and locked his door. That would teach him to cut her off.

He raised the key fob outside the window, dangled it in front of her eyes for a moment, and hit the Unlock button. All the stupid doors complied with soft thunks of smug complicity. It was unfair. They all ganged up against her.

"I'm not drunk, I'm just happy," she pointed out once he was in the car.

"Uh-huh." The signature Mighty Quinn grunt.

"It was a good time." It had been. Laughter, pizza, and the relief of another successful mission. The 5E was the first place she'd ever been where her gender hadn't been some awkward barrier. She'd earned her place by kicking ass in a kick-ass team. And tonight they'd really appreciated her for it.

Men like Mick didn't understand how rare and important that was. At least Mick tried, but no guy was ever going to get it. Men were all…

"And you are too interested in Sofia." Was he blockheaded enough not to realize it?

"Nope."

"Of course you are. She smart, skilled, has an accent that could convert the Pope to a life of carnal bliss, and she's drop-dead gorgeous."

"Yep, she's all that." His complacent agreement didn't sit well with her as he drove out onto the Old Seward highway and headed back toward JBER through mid-afternoon traffic.

"Then how come, Quinn?"

"Don't know," his voice went soft. She knew that tone shift. He'd taken her question seriously, so she waited out the long silence before he continued. "By all rights I should be, but she just doesn't do it for me."

"But if that's true,"—and Mick never spoke anything but truth —"why are you always staring at her?" Patty shifted in her seat until she was leaning as much on the door as her seat so that she could look at him. He was watching the road but concentrating on something in the far distance.

"Partly wondering why I'm not interested in her."

"And the other part?" Mick Quinn didn't open up like this very often. She could only recall him drinking one beer, but maybe it had mellowed him just enough.

"Easy woman to look at."

"Eye candy. God, men are such trolls. What do you see when you look at me?" And as soon as she said it, she wished she could take it back. That feeling of euphoria that had followed her since the pizzeria plummeted away faster than a bomb-load's worth of American candy.

Mick glanced over at her as he turned in at the base's security gate. A smile tugged at one corner of his mouth, but he didn't let it out to play.

"I see a royal pain in the ass."

"Great." Exactly what a *girl* wanted a handsome man to think of her.

"Damned pretty one."

Before she could ask what that crack meant, he had the window down. The MP on duty at the gate was looking in at them and asking for their IDs.

Patty guessed she was pretty enough; at least men always said she was. Maybe they just liked her red hair. And that was the problem with men. They liked doing the looking and that was usually all they cared about. For them the next stage after that was getting a girl to go horizontal without any getting-to-know-you first. She'd thought Mick was better than that.

He was. She'd flown with him for over two years and there was no question he was. Any thought of Mick Quinn had the word "decent" automatically attached to it as thoroughly as "sexy" attached to Sofia. "Sexy" slid right off Patty O'Donoghue.

But if a guy like Mick didn't want a woman like Sofia, then what the hell did he want?

Well one thing was damn sure—Patty slouched in her seat as he pulled up in front of the JBER transient quarters—she was nowhere in the running at all. Not that she cared or anything, but she didn't like the feeling.

A woman wanted to feel that she was worthy of any man she took a liking to and finding out that she wasn't up to the standard of one of the best guys she'd ever known sucked! Big time!

MICK DIDN'T NOTICE that Patty was still in the car until he was a half dozen steps toward the three-story white block structure of Matanuska Hall. He circled back and opened her door for her. She was slumped in her seat, her arms crossed tightly in front of her. It always amused him that angry women didn't understand that gesture only emphasized the shape of their breasts—of which Patty's were a particularly fine example—and distracted men even further from whatever was the matter.

In this case Patty was glaring at the dashboard as if it was trying to kill her.

She been so bright when they left the Moose's Tooth, practically shining from within. He'd seen her drunk a few times and she wasn't in any stage of her manically-inebriated modes, but even dead sober her moods could move fast enough to make his head spin.

By any prior O'Donoghue standards, she'd really shone at dinner. Her magnetic laugh had become the keynote sound of the meal. She'd turned a convivial meal into a party, everyone joining in on the merriment until they were helpless to resist; sometimes helpless to breathe from laughing so hard. She'd gotten Major Napier to unwind enough to tell jokes about some rather unlikely corporals and what had happened when they'd tangled with the wrong woman—a brigadier general's exceptionally comely wife. The way he told it, they were all left to wonder if he was one of the hapless enlisteds.

Now, Patty had apparently decided that the world was a horrid place. Maybe she was too hungover to breathe. Even her slightly hyper system couldn't have metabolized such a transition in the seven miles they'd driven. This was also beyond the normal scope of her notoriously mercurial mood swings. Besides, they were typically variations of cheerful and ecstatic. It was one of the things he'd always appreciated about her; even when she was whining, it was from a place of wry humor.

"Hey."

When she didn't react, he leaned in and reached over to unlatch her seatbelt.

She growled something unintelligible about "such trolls" and then she grabbed him.

One moment he was leaning across her; the next she had him by both of his ears. With a sharp twist—that would have hurt like hell if he'd any balance with which to resist the action—she turned his face to hers.

Then she kissed him.

He'd been kissed plenty enough ways to recognize when it was in anger. Patty's kiss wasn't that—it was vengeance. She kissed him hard, in a cobra-strike attack. She drove at him until his lips hurt even when they shifted to a French kiss—accompanied by a deep growl that vibrated between them.

One of his hands found purchase on the steel post of the headrest and he, in turn, drove her back against it. He'd never thought about kissing Patty O'Donoghue, not really, except on really stupid, really lonely nights.

With the choice taken out of his hands, he could absolutely appreciate everything she brought to her attack. The taste of ginger-chocolate cheesecake...the power...the force...the need.

It woke a need in him too. A deep need that rooted so hard in his gut that he finally pulled free despite her tight grip on his ears.

They stared at each other from a breath apart for a long moment.

Then she—thankfully—let go of his ears and slapped her hands over her face to hide her eyes.

"I did *not* just kiss you. Please tell me that I didn't just kiss you. God I wish I was drunk."

"Why?" he answered to buy himself a moment to think. The system-wide shock of kissing Patty O'Donoghue was still roaring through him. Like a helicopter just struck by lightning, it was impossible to tell which of his systems were working at the moment and which weren't.

"Why? You're a blockhead, Quinn. If I was drunk, I could blame that kiss on being drunk."

"But you are, so you can."

"No. Wish I was, but I'm not." Then she did a very unusual thing for her; Patty blushed. Her creamy skin went brilliant red, several shades brighter than her auburn hair.

"Maybe I could buy you a t-shirt that says, *The Devil Made Me Do It.* Would that make you feel better?"

She uncovered one eye and glared at him.

"I could sing you a country song, about the man who done you wrong."

"Aren't you supposed to be angry or something? I'm the one who kissed *you.*"

Mick squatted on the pavement and leaned back against the inside of the open car door but he wasn't ready to move any farther away from Patty just yet. He could use a distraction, but the parking lot of on-base lodging was very quiet at two in the afternoon.

He'd never considered kissing Patty for real. And by how flustered she looked, it was clearly something she'd never thought about either.

"C'mon, Mick. Talk to me," she uncovered the other eye and then dropped her hands into her lap. "What are you thinking?"

"Thoughts I shouldn't be," which was true. She was a fellow officer, but he was a commissioned lieutenant and she was an enlisted chief warrant—which were supposed to stay worlds apart.

"Slow down there, Mick. I'm not looking to get bulldozed by The Mighty Quinn." He liked that she was already recovering and had her feet back under her, at least metaphorically as she was still buckled into the car seat.

"Wasn't quite where my thoughts were going."

And her face closed down hard.

<hr>

RIGHT BACK INTO her same angry cave.

She wasn't good enough.

Patty could still taste Mick on her tongue. Could still feel the pressure on her lips that had far exceeded how hard she was holding him. Now she felt trapped between the seatbelt, the central console that ran between the bucket seats, and Mick studying her through slightly narrowed eyes from just an arm's length away. Far more trapped than when he'd been reaching across for her seatbelt and something had made her kiss him.

Oh God! How were they going to fly together? It was the best part of her life and she'd fucked it up. They'd be even closer together than they were right now every time they were airborne. How could—

"My thoughts were going somewhere else entirely."

Yeah, like how fast could he get her transferred. She was going to lose the 5E—

"I'm thinking that if that's how you kiss when you're pissed at the world, what would it be like to kiss you when you were happy?"

—and she'd lose the friends she'd already made among the women of the...

Mick was just squatting there with that damned half smile tugging at his lips. He was...

"Say what?" Patty blinked but couldn't rewind the statement.

"C'mon," this time he didn't lean in, just reached across her to snap her seatbelt free. Then he rose to his feet and stepped back.

She stared at the offered hand. His face was out of sight, above the line of the car's roof. All she could see was Mick Quinn from mid-chest down, and one of those big fisherman hands held palm up to assist her from the car.

What the hell. Patty took it, figuring she wasn't about to trust her legs at the moment for reasons that had nothing to do with alcohol.

He closed his hand over hers and rubbed his thumb across the backs of her knuckles. It was a question, but one look up at his eyes when she reached her feet made her decide that the question wasn't for her. It was for him.

Without another word, he escorted her to her hotel door…and left her standing there flat-footed.

Mick moved down the hall to his own door, worked the card key, cursed softly, and worked it again. On his third try the door opened and he went in without a single glance back her way; she might as well not exist.

She slotted her own card key, four attempts before she stopped flipping it around and looked at the little arrow mostly hidden by a garish delivery pizza ad. Turning it properly, the door clicked open with much the same smugness that the car door locks had shown.

Okay, maybe Mick was still thinking about her if he couldn't open his own door either.

Because no matter how that kiss had started, the way it had finished meant she was sure as hell thinking about him.

# CHAPTER 5

"I was chatting with Stan McCabe over at the Two-Twelve," Major Napier started talking even as he and Mick set their breakfast trays down on the table the 5E had taken over.

They were the last two to arrive. The rest of the Night Stalkers were already crowded around a long table in the Gold Rush Inn Dining Facility. The evening crowd—which was the Night Stalkers' morning—was mostly Air National Guard grunts, though there were some Army fliers and servicefolk mixed in. The Air Force was based down at the far end of JBER and they used other facilities down at that end of the field.

The floor-to-ceiling curved windows showed a view of streetlights in the last of the fading fall light and a heavy drizzle, chill water that had indeed found its way down the back of his collar as he was crossing from the hotel. Interior lights made it daylight bright inside, enough so that he almost pulled down his sunglasses.

Conversations buzzed through the air and sounded off the high wood ceiling. It made the room feel even more crowded and friendly than it already was. The diners all fit a common motif: military wear and military hair.

The Night Stalkers' table had been easy to spot because many of them grew their hair long. If their main customers—SEALs and Deltas—wore their hair long, Night Stalkers took it as permission to fit right in. In this environment, men with hair over an inch long or women with it past their jaw were clearly marked as Special Operations. As such, they were given an especially wide berth by mere mortals of the National Guard, Army, and Air Force.

The first thing he'd spotted was the red banner of Patty O'Donoghue's cascade of hair down to her shoulders. Patty was sitting between Rafe the DAP Hawk pilot and Danielle, and being her usual chipper self. She looked as if she'd spent a full twelve out cold and then run a 10K before breakfast or something. Health and vitality poured off her, but down at the far end of the table he couldn't seem to soak any of it in. Nobody looked that good after just four hours sleep. Maybe she was doing it on purpose to rub in the fact that he hadn't slept a wink.

He ignored her smug look when he dropped into one of the last two seats next to Sofia.

Mick looked at his watch--seven at night. All he'd had since kissing Patty was four hours of staring at the ceiling. And it hadn't made anything make more sense.

Napier was going on about the Two-Twelve.

"Don't you sleep?" Mick tried to slow him down so that his own brain could catch up.

The Major ignored him, so he turned to Danielle. She was the rational one of the couple and had become their natural leader throughout training because of her incredible strategic vision.

"Doesn't he sleep?"

Napier stopped steamrolling them and glared at Mick. Mick really didn't care, he just needed the major to give him a few moments to catch up. And whatever else Napier did, he never interrupted his wife.

"He sleeps only *un petit peu*," Danielle conceded in her soft Québécois French, but her own happy smile said that she wasn't talking about him being off somewhere talking to the Alaska Air National Guard's famous 212th Rescue Squadron.

Which meant that Rapier had gotten even less sleep because he'd also…

Mick wasn't going to think about what her smile implied. He really wasn't. He'd already spent hours trying to figure out what Patty O'Donoghue's kiss had meant. Actually, he'd spent most of the time trying to ignore the high voltage charge the kiss had pumped into him that a cold shower had done nothing to cure.

The Two-Twelve.

He'd think about them.

Should have stuck with them in the first place.

The 212th Rescue Squadron were the busiest pararescue jumpers in the military. Not only did they jump into active-war hot zones to extract wounded, but the Two-Twelve worked the search-and-rescue detail in the Gulf of Alaska as well as the Alaska Range. In the latter they spent far too much time rescuing the fools who thought climbing the twenty-thousand feet of Denali was something anyone with a rucksack and a pair of crampons could do.

"The Pipeline" to become pararescue took as long as the Night Stalkers' two-years of training. He'd transported these guys on occasion during his time in Afghanistan. Typically, the Air Force flew them in, except when they had to go somewhere truly ugly and then they called in the Night Stalkers. Pararescue jumpers were the ultimate badasses. *Because sometimes even the SEALs need to call 911,* and Air Force PJs were who they called.

Napier was setting them up for an exercise with these guys? Oh man.

"I asked the unit's commander to come join us," Major Napier waved a hand toward an Air National Guard major who dropped into the last open seat next to Mick, holding a mug of black coffee.

"Who's the local here?"

Mick ticked up a finger, "Here, sir."

"Hear you got this lot out for some real Alaska fodder at Moose's Tooth. Good man," he landed a solid slap of approval on Mick's shoulder and then grabbed on and shook him back and forth a bit.

"Pete said you folks were now looking for an Alaska-style training hike. Excellent!"

Mick swallowed down his own reaction and scanned the table. Other than Napier, they were all in shock. They'd been Army for enough years that it was subtle, but it was there on every face. Napier had promised them twenty-four hours dark—welcome to the Army. It wouldn't be a problem for the members of the 5E. After all, a hike meant they wouldn't be flying and the twenty-four-hour bottle-to-throttle rule wouldn't apply.

Last of all he looked at Patty. But she wasn't watching him; she was watching McCabe. And he couldn't read anything into her expression.

---

PATTY WAS WELL aware of Mick's attention and refused to give him the satisfaction of knowing he'd cost her even a minute's sleep. He did look awfully good sitting next to Sofia. Too good. Was that why she'd maneuvered the empty spot to be by Sofia? Because Mick was too good for Patty O'Donoghue?

Damn it! She'd just done it again, except this time she'd done it to herself. Mick was supposed to be her pilot, no more, no less. Well, maybe friend as well, but she wasn't supposed to have kissed him. And she *really* wasn't supposed to be bothered by how amazing a couple he and Sofia made.

At least he looked like hammered shit this morning, as if he'd drunk a pitcher or three rather than a single beer. That made Patty feel a little better. Because she could only think of one reason he'd look that way…he'd slept as little as she had.

ANG Major Stan McCabe gave her the perfect excuse to ignore Mick.

First, he was the poster child, no, the poster *man* of the super-fit warrior. He wasn't the handsomest guy around, not a chance sitting next to Mick, but he was built on an impressive scale. Six-four and all of it muscle; he also had a smile that came out far more easily than Mick's.

Second, Mick had suddenly gone humble when the PJ sat next to him. Mick was always kind and decent, but it wasn't like a member of the 5E to go humble around anyone. But McCabe was a pararescue jumper. Yeah, that made her feel pretty humbled as well.

"We have a team headed up into high country," McCabe's voice was deeper than even Mick's, "for some ice and snow training. We're glad to have you folks along. Don't worry. If you have any problems, we're going up there to practice high-altitude rescue anyway. We're always glad to take on some real-life training opportunities."

For all his easy manners, he'd just thrown down the gauntlet. Patty wondered if Napier was behind that or was it just the normal: one branch of the military baiting another. For herself, the gauntlet hadn't even hit the ground and she'd already grabbed onto it. She knew it was a bad habit, but a challenge was never allowed to slip by Raymond O'Donoghue's little girl. She was going to tackle and take down whatever mess the Two-Twelve sent her way. "Real-life training opportunity" like hell. She'd show them what a Night Stalker was made of, especially a 5E.

"I checked the records," Major Napier began before she could state her acceptance of the challenge. "The last person to do any ice-and-snow work is me, and that was before I joined the 5E. For most of you it was over a year ago."

O'Donoghues were Gloucester fisherfolk, cold didn't scare her a bit. Several of the others were looking unhappy.

"Ready to gear up and go, sir," Patty stated emphatically and glared at Mick, daring him to beg off.

He didn't. Instead, he silently nodded his acceptance which she supposed was better than his trademark enigmatic grunt.

"I don't expect you all to have full ice-and-snow gear with you," Napier surveyed the table, "but Major McCabe has agreed to outfit everyone from the ANG stock. I want you to know that this training is unscheduled and completely optional."

A wave of relief circled around the table. Patty was going to kick Mick's butt big time if he tried to wimp out on her.

"So, I expect to see every one of you in ten hours at the Two-

Twelve's ready room. Oh-five-hundred tomorrow. You'll receive a full kit at that time." Then Napier ended the conversation by standing up with his finished tray and leaving the table. Somehow he'd eaten a full meal while haranguing them.

"So much for optional," McCabe laughed. "He was a total hard ass when we went through West Point together. Nice to see that some things haven't changed. Any questions for me?"

McCabe refused to give out any details about the training mission itself. "Some hiker gets himself in trouble up on Denali at nineteen thousand feet and the Two-Twelve gets a call. We find out information as we go. Our radioman has a script written by our training director. We only know what he tells us, when he tells us."

"Who's your training director?" Mick asked in a voice that told Patty he already knew the answer.

Oh. Of course.

"Caught me! Love local talent!" McCabe slammed another cheery slap against Mick's shoulder, probably hard enough to shatter your average person. He lumbered to his feet, taking his mug with him. Then he looked up and down the table. "We're running this one as real as possible. You'll want to get some rest."

Patty knew she'd been dumb in a couple of ways and she had to talk to Mick before it grew any worse. She'd apologize for kissing him and any other weirdness she'd created by giving in to that impulse, no matter how surprising the results had been.

But when the table had quieted after their initial reactions, she was still at the far end of the table from Mick.

And he was busy talking with Sofia.

Crap!

---

Sofia had Brazil and Los Angeles, both southern climes, for a background. She very quietly confessed her fears about the training mission to Mick in a voice more nervous than he'd credited as possible for Sofia Gracie. Her natural state was one of overt confidence and flamboyance. Vivacious Latina typically poured off her in waves, making the contrast of her present mood all the more startling.

It turned out that her only ice and snow experience had been during a freak storm that had hit Fort Jackson, South Carolina during Basic Training. Her duties were performed in air-conditioned trailers typically thousands of miles from her targets.

Mick felt both deep sympathy and great respect for her. Of all of them, she could have legitimately begged off from the training. An RPA pilot really didn't need to prove Special Operations survival skills. But she'd put that suggestion to rest, fast.

"They will *not* be leaving me behind. My team she goes? Then I go, too," she tapped a finger sharply above her generous chest. It earned her several surprised looks followed by approving nods from those close enough to overhear her. Sofia's voice quieted again until only he could hear it, "But you must tell me how not to look like the fool. That I not like at all."

So, they talked about snow and ice. It was strange, it was like trying to explain Special Operations thinking to a civilian. If they hadn't at least served, there was no common language to explain with.

*You'd die to protect a teammate?*

*Duh!* That was a given before the conversation could even begin. Special Operations soldiers didn't sign up for a tour, they signed up for a career.

Over a second cup of coffee he switched from descriptions of mountain weather and snow conditions on glaciers—which was being very hard to communicate and was probably scaring the crap out of her—to teaching her basic survival skills.

"As long as you can still feel your toes and fingers, you're fine. They may hurt or sting like mad, but that's just a warning; you're still okay. It's when you can't feel them anymore that you're potentially in trouble."

"Layer up: thick socks over thin, thin gloves then thick. Take off only the layer you have to and for as little time as possible."

"When walking, spend as much time as possible thinking about keeping your fingers and your toes in constant motion. It boosts circulation and distracts you from the fact that you're freezing your butt off."

And he tried not to think about Sofia's butt as it was an exceptional one. Besides which, this wasn't the woman who'd cost him a night's sleep. He glanced over at Patty…except she wasn't there.

Nor was anyone else. They were the only two left at the table. Someone else had even cleared their empty trays; it was just the two of them and their two long-dry coffee mugs. The Gold Rush Inn was no longer rushing. A few troops were sitting a halfway across the spacious hall. A cleaning crew was moving through flipping chairs onto tables and sweeping the floor.

Outside the window, evening had long since turned to dark night.

"We should get some sleep," he managed in a mumble. He'd never actually been alone with Sofia in the three months since she'd joined the unit. It was a heady feeling to just sit quietly with such a stunning woman. And to discover the thoroughly pleasant and intelligent person that her beauty made so difficult to see.

He rose and pulled her chair out for her. Easy to admire the way she rose from her seat, too; her simplest gesture reminded him of her surname. Sofia Gracie. Wise Grace, he translated to himself.

Maybe Patty had a point. Maybe he and…

The rain had turned cold, but not bitter, so it wasn't snow. At least not yet. He walked her to her door in the transient lodgings and stood back until he was sure she had it unlocked.

Then Sofia turned to him without moving into the room.

"It is very sad."

"It…what? What is?"

Sofia smiled softly, "It is very sad for me, the way that you are looking at her and the way she is looking at you."

"Who?" But he knew who and felt stupid for even asking. Sofia didn't bother to answer his question.

"We could have a very wonderful time together, I think. But that is all it would be." She leaned forward enough to kiss him lightly on each cheek.

She smelled warm and slightly exotic. And he was just tired enough to lean into the moment.

"I do not want to hurt the woman you fly with, so we will leave that idea alone," she said softly in his ear. "I just will thank you for your help this night. I be much safer tomorrow because of you."

Her words were a warm brush across his tired thoughts.

"Now go," she pushed against his shoulder to get him moving down the hall toward his own room.

He stopped at his own door and looked back.

She was watching him and her sigh carried easily down the silent hall to him.

"Ah, what I could do with such a man."

Her words didn't register until her door had closed behind her and he stood alone in the long, darkened hallway.

# CHAPTER 6

*P*atty hit the Air National Guard's Ready Room at 0430.

She'd heard them last night. Hard not to, she'd been lying awake cursing herself for eight times an idiot and Sofia's door was directly across the hall from hers. Patty had slipped up to the peephole in just her oversized t-shirt and watched them but could only make out some of their words through the door. Sofia's final sigh and what she could do with Mick sliced at Patty.

But even though she watched for fifteen minutes, and then twenty, Sofia's door had not reopened.

Nor had Mick returned to beg entrance.

Patty sorted and stowed her own gear into a large pack. When she returned from the locker room now dressed in long johns, turtleneck, and other multiple layers, Sofia and Mick had arrived as well.

As the ANG's quartermaster issued them gear, Patty could detect no coy looks between them. Mick was always so considerate that it was hard to tell if he was treating Sofia any differently than yesterday, or a month ago.

He didn't treat herself any differently either which was as confusing as hell.

"Hey, Patty."

"Hey, yourself," was her utterly lame response. If he was having issues with her, it didn't show. If he was cozying with Sofia the same night Patty had kissed him, he sure didn't look guilty about it. How was she supposed to know how to act if—

"Vee go now!" Major McCabe roared out in a fake Swedish accent as he rushed into the Ready Room.

"Vee go!" several of the PJs who'd been assisting the Night Stalkers with their unfamiliar gear called back in unison. Some sort of a unit thing.

Patty checked her watch, 0450, ten minutes before they'd been told to even arrive to start preparing. Typical training mission for sure. The 5E had been through enough of those that the full crew was already present and they were all within seconds of being ready despite the premature start.

"We're going high up. Everyone, full snow gear. Put on your Bags."

Patty grabbed hers and started struggling into it. It was a one-piece, dull-green flight suit of fire-resistant Nomex that the quartermaster had issued her along with all of the other gear. Then she began layering snow pants and parka over it.

"We have a climber trapped just below the summit on Mount Hayes at thirteen thousand feet. Exact location unknown. Conditions: three inches fresh snow last night, seven degrees Fahrenheit, zero at the summit, winds light at ten knots. Storm coming. Go! Go! Go!"

A stream of PJs poured into the room and began yanking pre-packed gear off racks. They were moving fast and even with a head start on gearing up, the Night Stalkers were having trouble keeping up.

"Who are my jumpers?" McCabe roared out.

Two of the parajumpers raised their hands and grabbed parachutes from the racks as well.

"Who else? C'mon people, I need two more," Major McCabe's tone made it clear they were going to be Night Stalkers.

Mick looked over at her and raised his eyebrows in a question. Despite what had or hadn't happened yesterday, Mick was asking if she'd jump with him.

The relief that washed through her was strong enough that she didn't even think about the consequences, just shot her hand up.

"You got two," Mick told McCabe.

McCabe gave Mick one of his crippling slaps of approval then pulled down a pair chute-and-reserve rigs.

That's when it sunk in. The winds might be light up on the mountain but at thirteen thousand feet...

It was common knowledge in mountain climbing—a sport that Patty had only participated in as part of her military training—that a thousand feet up was about the same weather change as three hundred miles north. It was October at sea-level in Anchorage. At thirteen thousand feet up...they were effectively going four thousand miles north, somewhere way farther north than the North Pole. Like right over the top and into Siberia. And she'd just agreed to parachute into that?

She looked at Mick.

"And you thought flying into that little rainstorm was nuts," he teased her. But his smile was easy and that he wanted to jump with her—rather than ship her out to another regiment entirely—was enough of a relief that she'd just go with it.

McCabe came over with a detailed map of the mountain.

"Hey, Major," Mick teased him. "You're not trying to kill off the *local talent*, are you?"

Patty appreciated his attempt at humor. It was nice to know that Mick was worried as well despite the calm stance he was presenting.

McCabe smiled easily, "Not today, buddy." Then he called over the other two PJs with parachutes.

"This is Two-ton and Caspar the Ghost," and that was the end of the intros. McCabe jabbed a finger at a high valley on the map and spoke quickly just as if it was a real emergency.

"Yesterday we dropped a radio repeater right in this valley, so that's the signal we all are trying to 'save.' But we can't get a helo in there for fear of causing an avalanche: too much noise and wind."

"Say what?" Patty did not want to be jumping into any avalanches. Or having her jump cause one that would then kill her.

"Which we proved by triggering every avalanche we could yesterday before we did the drop. Anything that was going to let go already has."

"Oh, sorry," Patty clamped her mouth shut. McCabe just grinned at her. If it was Mick she'd get revenge, maybe even against Napier, but McCabe was a major and an Air Force PJ so she decided to leave it alone. For now.

"You'll jump into this snow field. The glacier has been stable here for years and we've never seen any crevasses in this area or I wouldn't be sending you in this way. Using the helos, we'll be landing two teams well below you. The higher team will work their way up to you to assist. The lower team will build an extraction route to help you all get back off the mountain in case the helos can't get back in. We lift in five. Let's go!"

McCabe then simply counted off the remaining eleven Night Stalkers into two teams and assigned a pair of PJs to each of them—for reasons he wasn't explaining, Napier had given Connie and John a pass on the training.

Sofia ended up in the low altitude team. She'd be on their flight, but the farthest from her and Mick after they'd jumped out and her helo had landed. Patty tried not to be pleased by that but wasn't having much luck.

All of the Night Stalkers, including Napier, Danielle, and Sofia—still exuding sexy despite the "Bag" and heavy winter gear—raced out to the two waiting HH-60G Pave Hawks. The Air Force helos had infrared gear, a mid-air refueling probe for lengthy searches over remote areas, and two crew chiefs at the side guns. Other than the common Black Hawk airframe, that was all they shared with the *Beatrix*.

The Air Forces' medevac version of the Black Hawks were dull gray in the pre-dawn light rather than stealth composite-black. Broad skis were attached to the wheels for landing ten tons of aircraft on snow and ice. And the cargo bays were rigged to take stretchers and a lot of personnel, rather than large caches of heavy ammunition.

The rotors were already turning as they ducked low and piled aboard. The blades were high enough for safety but staying low eased the battering rotor wash that was trying to flatten her to the ground out of spite.

Once aboard, Patty checked all of the medical supplies hanging from the insides of the cargo bay and was glad it would be up to a PJ to administer any lifesaving treatments—most of the bags were marked trauma this and blood that. With what they had stocked here, they could perform some major medical operations while still in flight, and she'd bet when they did that the cargo bay wasn't pretty.

Instead, she stared out at the other helo cranking to life in the darkness and rain, doing her best not to think about it. Mick squeezed in tight beside her, because everyone was squeezed that tight. Not because he wanted to be, of course. But her thinking had shifted a fair ways in the last eighteen hours and she wasn't complaining.

"What did you get us into this time, Boston?"

"Me?" Patty twisted to stare at him planting a fairly hard elbow in a PJ's kidneys by accident. "Parachuting out of a perfectly good helo in the middle of the Alaska Range wasn't my doing. You're the one who…"

His smile was easy and friendly.

She jumped when the cargo door slammed shut.

"You don't think that I would have volunteered on my own," he made his protest in all innocence.

"What? You're the asshole who volunteered us," she had to shout the last as the rotors bit air and took them aloft. Like typical helo jocks—including Mick and herself—their pilots cut hard-banking turns, forcing her to lean even harder against Mick. Which felt good in the same way the kiss had.

"Well, I knew you were going to volunteer because that's just the kind of stubborn girl you are."

He hesitated for her to protest *woman* but she refused to take the bait.

"I didn't want you being *nuts* alone, so I figured that I better join in so that I could save your cute ass."

"Right, like I'm the one who'll need saving." Patty wondered about that cute ass remark. It just wasn't the sort of thing Mick Quinn said under normal operating conditions, or even abnormal ones. "How many jumps have you done?"

"Before or after military?"

"Before?" She wished it hadn't come out so tentatively. She had her Master Parachutist Badge but very little ice-and-snow work.

"Okay," Mick shrugged, "you caught me. None before."

She punched his arm, managing not to poke the PJ's kidneys this time, and appreciated his friendly laugh.

"But I got my Master's Badge here in US Army Alaska. I was stationed with the Flying Dragons up in Fairbanks at the time. They like jumping onto snow and ice. As long as you have your laser pick and your bugaboos handy, you'll be fine."

"You're shitting me." What the hell was a bugaboo in snow work?

"Really?" He turned to one of the PJs. "Hey, Caspar. She doesn't have her bugaboos."

"Aw crap," he slapped at his gear and shrugged. "Got no spares, lady. Good luck with that."

There was something about the way Mick was looking at her, just a little too carefully bland. She fisted his ribs, hard. And her hand came away feeling as if she'd just punched him in the bugaboo. Mick "The Mighty Dozer" Quinn was a hard-muscled man.

Whatever it did to her hand, she'd hit him hard enough to knock loose a chuckle as well. Just wait until she got him down on the glacier. He was going to pay.

---

MICK MANAGED A LITTLE SLEEP, but it was only an hour flight to Mount Hayes at the helo's top speed. It was a flight that he wasn't in the pilot's seat for and that was like an itch he couldn't scratch.

Also, Patty O'Donoghue had fallen asleep on his shoulder which was much, much more difficult to ignore. And it wasn't the tickling against his cheek from the bright orange pom-pom on her hat that was so distracting. She slept there like she belonged and it felt just that way.

Sofia smiled at him from the far end of the cargo bay in a kindly fashion. He still wasn't comfortable with what she'd said last night about his feelings for Patty. Patty was…Patty. They weren't lovers. And they weren't supposed to become lovers.

But Sofia had said something about the way they looked at each other. From Patty he'd seen nothing but her typical range of a hundred different emotions racing across her features.

And he'd looked at her how? In some way that Sofia could see and he couldn't.

He hadn't unraveled the puzzle by the time Caspar the Ghost tapped his wrist and held up five fingers.

Mick nudged Patty with a shrug of his shoulder. She blinked at him like a sleepy-eyed cat, once, twice, then wide awake. Rather than surprise or embarrassment, she stroked a hand where her head had been.

"You've a very comfortable shoulder, Mr. Quinn."

"Welcome to it anytime, Boston." And that thought went in all sorts of interesting directions, most of them involving a half dozen fewer layers of clothes and a warm bed.

*He and Patty?* He didn't have time to think anything else as they began their final gear checks. As jump buddies, Patty tugged on various parts of his gear and straps, and checked the positions of the parachute release handle and the cutaway in case the main chute fouled and he had to go for the reserve. The dance of her gloved hands over his harness produced visceral shocks like a stream of static electricity—not painful, just surprising as could be.

When he did the same for her, the sensation didn't go away. The harness strap just above her breasts had his imagination on overload about a shape wholly hidden by all her gear. Her brilliant blue eyes didn't watch his hands, but rather his face.

He almost asked what she was thinking.

But he'd either get back some goofball response, or she'd actually tell him, which he wasn't ready for. And if she asked him in turn, there wasn't a chance that he could come up with a coherent response.

Maybe she didn't have an answer either. The increasing roundness of her eyes staring at him from so close made that seem more and more likely. Mick actually took comfort from that; at least that way they'd *both* be in uncharted territory.

"One minute," Caspar shouted and Two-ton opened the big side door.

The blast of cold slammed into the helo and swirled around the cargo bay.

"Holy shit!" Patty left her heavy knit hat on. It had a gold upper half, orange lower half, red ear flaps darker than her hair, and a red-and-orange pom-pom on top. It made her look like a crazed leprechaun or diminutive Alutiiq goddess...too damned cute either way. She yanked a jump helmet over it. He buckled it under her chin as she pulled down goggles. She did the same for him, but there was no time to appreciate the sensations. Besides, it was freezing.

Caspar and Two-ton knelt side by side with their backs to the cargo door. The two big PJs saluted them and then tumbled backwards out the door. That opened up enough space for he and Patty to move into place.

A peek out showed the PJs popping their chutes. Both had good openings on their mains.

They turned their backs to the door and shot salutes to Major Napier; McCabe had stayed back at base to oversee the operation from the ground—and to play his role of puppet master.

After Mick let go but before he tumbled backward, he spotted Sofia. Her eyes were wide, perhaps in fear. Perhaps in shock at the severity of the cold.

He sent her an encouraging thumbs up.

If she returned the gesture, he didn't have time to see it. Gravity snatched him and he tumbled into the sky.

# CHAPTER 7

$\mathcal{P}$atty didn't have time to wonder at Mick's final signal to Sofia. In seconds she was colder than after an icy Grand Banks wave swept the length of her Gloucester swordfish boat. They were falling from fifteen thousand feet at over a hundred miles an hour.

The wind chill was horrendous.

And the view was incredible.

It was dawn at Mount Hayes, the sun a bright, deep-red orb rising over the spiky rock-and-ice shrouded peaks of the Eastern Alaska Range. The impossibly rugged mountainscape sprawled in every direction except north. In that direction, the steep slopes tumbled down into a broad river valley where the Tanana River flowed west before the far side of the valley climbed anew up another section of the range to the north. Every peak was lit like a brilliant ruddy torch by the low-slanting sunlight. The valleys still huddled in darkness.

It was impossible to get a visual feel of the distance to the drop zone, everything directly below her was stark white. She pulled her cord while still above Mount Hayes and after the briefest moment—when every parachutist was left to wonder if they had a failed chute—she was jerked hard by the harness.

The deafening wind roar, so loud that she only became aware of it by its sudden absence, made the twenty-mile-an-hour descent rate beneath the deployed chute sound like perfect silence.

A glance up, no line twists, the chute had deployed properly. Down, the two PJs were directly below, still circling in to a landing. To the side, Mick floating along a hundred meters over and fifty below her.

"Always gotta be first, don't you?" she shouted over.

"Just keeping you in your place," Mick hollered back, his voice a faint whisper on the wind. Then she heard him on the radio, "Calling Mayday Test victim on Mount Hayes, can you give us a visual?"

There was a pause.

"You're here! Thank God!" By the high tone of the radio operator in Anchorage, apparently the victim was female. "What took you so long? I'm freezing to death and my leg isn't working right. Hurry please!..." And the operator kept transmitting from the mock victim's radio relay in a constant stream, totally blocking the radio frequency for anyone else to use. Radios were one-way-at-a-time devices and when the other party didn't shut up, there was nothing you could do.

Patty offered a few choice words that no one else could hear. It drove home a lesson that she already knew—civilians and radio communication were a mix that should never be allowed.

Unable to do anything else, they flew in to land beside the PJs.

Feet touchdown, roll to calf, thigh, hip, twist onto back and shoulder, and end up rolling to sit and face the collapsing chute. Patty was pretty damn pleased she remembered how to do it right. Of course, the calculated roll had also turned her completely white by tumbling through the foot or so of loose powdered snow.

The stillness in the high mountain basin was as powerful an impact as the massive wind roar of the jump. She could hear every slick nylon ripple of the collapsing chute, even the paracord slipping through her thick gloves was loud enough to stand out in the silence as she gathered it in.

She could hear Mick's breath, caught between heavy gasps in the thin air and a euphoric laugh at the wonder of the experience. Patty noticed that she was doing exactly the same.

The operator playacting the stranded climber had finally shut up which added to the silence.

"Nice attempt, calling the victim on the radio, Mick," Caspar said as he strode up, his chute already packed. "And yeah, that babble stream is a fairly typical response. When they do that, jump up two-tenths in frequency. We do that so that we can still communicate with each other. I got a partial directional on the transmitter as we came down. Somewhere east of us."

"Heads up!" Two-ton called out and pointed westward.

Their four packs of gear came down under a single chute, landing well up a ridge in the opposite direction to the distress call.

"Typical McCabe," Caspar commented without much chagrin. "Rope up and let's go."

And that's how their day began, Caspar, Mick, herself, and Two-ton each spaced a dozen yards apart down a common rope line. All walking away from the casualty toward their gear.

"Shouldn't two of us go to the victim?" Patty called out to the lead PJ.

Caspar shook his head and kept plodding along. "Never split up the rescue team if you can help it. Also, if we don't have that gear by nightfall, we'll be the ones who need rescuing."

"It's hard walking away from even a fake victim."

"Yep," was Caspar's answer, but he didn't slow.

Attempts to reach the radio link returned only brief and unintelligible responses. They finally received a clean response, and then Caspar lied that they were on their way.

She supposed that was what you had to tell a victim—and not that you were walking in the opposite direction—but it still didn't feel right.

It took a breathless hour to reach the base of the ridge where their gear had snagged. Unlike most pilots, Night Stalkers spent little time at higher altitudes. Mission profiles were typically below two hundred feet rather than up at thirteen thousand. High flying aircraft were pressurized down to seven thousand feet anyway, but Night Stalkers didn't even have that adaptation. Despite water and aspirin, a steady high-altitude headache thrummed away in the background of Patty's thoughts leaving her feeling muddy and weak.

But she wasn't the only one taking twenty steps then pausing for a rest. Mick was doing the same. She'd wager the PJs could move along faster, but they made a point about the team moving and acting as one.

Patty stared up at the steep, craggy pitch. Blocks of ice tumbled off jagged rocks. High up, their four packs were strapped together and the parachute had wrapped around a particularly large block.

"Which of you two has more ice and snow experience?"

Mick held up his hand.

"Okay," Caspar said. "You're with me. Patty, go help Two-ton fetch the packs. He's good at this. Man moves like two tons of feathers."

Patty stared at him aghast and then looked back up the cliff. Mick was the one with the experience...which is why Caspar had chosen her. *Training mission. Right.*

Mick was close beside her. For just a moment she let herself lean against him and gather strength.

"I won't need any bugaboos for this, will I?"

His chuckle warmed her as much as their contact.

"Not for this, no," then his face darkened as he stared up at the terrain. "You be damn careful up there, Patty. Do exactly what he says."

"Yeah, roger that."

Coming back dead wasn't on her mission profile today, but she hadn't liked that look on Mick's face.

Two-ton handed her a second ice axe and then unsnapped the safety rope that had connected her to Mick and snapped his own in its place.

"You've got first pitch." It was the first words she'd ever heard him say. Rather than being gruff, he spoke with a simple confidence that of course she could do this.

Patty scanned the steep ridge face again and picked out a route that would keep clear of the worst of the ice. She indicated her planned route with the point of her ice axe.

Two-ton nodded and, resisting the urge to look back at Mick once more, she led off.

---

MICK HAD trouble keeping his eyes off Two-ton in his yellow parka and Patty in her red one as they crawled upward. A two-hundred-foot-high ice-and-rock field wasn't much of an issue. One at twelve thousand feet atop an Alaska mountain in October was a whole different matter.

"Got it bad, brother," Caspar dragged Mick's attention back down from the climbers.

Mick shrugged. It was the only answer he had.

Caspar started leading him across the glacier, climbing the steep ice field on a slant. Mick followed. He was ten minutes out, just looking back to spot Patty's red parka—still in the lead up the ice face—when he heard a soft cry.

He turned in time to see Caspar go shooting by him.

"What the—"

The rope snapped tight on Mick's harness and flipped him off his feet.

# CHAPTER 8

*S*ome piece of training must have remained lodged deep in
Mick's subconscious. Even as he tumbled to land face down
in the snow, he had his ice axe braced high against his shoulder, with
his free hand clamped over the head of the axe.

With a twist he managed to roll face down in the snow which
jammed the point of his ice axe into the flying hillside. He spun from
head first to feet first as the pick dug in. Then he lifted his hips so that
all of his weight was driven down onto his crampon-clad feet and the
point of the axe by his shoulder. But he didn't lift so high that the rope
bearing Caspar's weight could flip him onto his back again.

He scraped to a stop and simply stayed there with adrenaline
surging through him.

*Caspar,* the thought punched through.

Caspar had fallen.

Mick had to—

"You gonna lie there all day, Mick?" Caspar spoke from about a
foot away.

"You're—" then Mick knew. "Training fall. Got it. You secure?" He
asked the question out of protocol, ignoring the fact that Caspar was
standing rock stable beside close him.

"Secure," Caspar reported dutifully. "Long furrow, but not too bad."

Mick eased up and stared at the path his body had plowed through the snow. He had been slow on the arrest. Because he'd...been watching Patty instead of his climbing partner. He knew better. Trust your team, even when they weren't roped to you. Well, he wouldn't make that mistake again.

"Interesting problem, isn't it?" Caspar started coiling the line the ran between them.

"What?" Mick rolled over until he was sitting in the snow.

"Women. Never figured 'em out myself. My ex- had a few words to say about that, I can tell you."

Mick looked up at the red parka. Patty was at a dead stop about three-quarters of the way up. They were far enough away that he couldn't be sure, but she appeared to be looking at him.

Well, that worked, because he sure couldn't stop looking at her.

---

"WHAT'S UP WITH HIM?" Patty asked Two-ton, though she learned that the man rarely responded to her questions unless they were about technique.

She waited as if she expected an answer, because she certainly couldn't move at the moment.

Her attention had stayed on the climb.

Two-ton wouldn't accept less. He'd shown her how to pick a foothold in ice. How to give just the slightest bounce to test each placement of foot, hand, or axe—it stressed the position just a little and if she paid attention, she could feel if it was weak.

Twice he'd led her back down over a tricky passage to show her the challenges of a descent. Twice she'd had to ascend by new routes.

It was astonishing how much information he imparted with every soft-spoken suggestion. They could have reached the packs and returned by the time they were three-quarters of the way there, but it was totally worth it.

Then she'd stopped to rest a moment and look around.

At that instant, Caspar's parka-yellow figure tumbled down the slope. Mick's orange had shot off his feet. They'd fallen fifty yards before Mick did some kind of strange flip and twist that jerked him to halt.

The slam against his harness must have been brutal as he stopped Caspar.

"They're in trouble!" she'd shouted. "We have to go help!"

All Two-ton had done was hold up a finger indicating she should wait.

Caspar-yellow climbed back up the slope to an unmoving Mick-orange.

*He's hurt!* But this time she managed to keep the cry inside her own head.

Then Mick rolled over to sit beside Caspar. After a long minute, they began walking up the slope of the glacier again.

"God damn them!"

Two-ton offered his first smile of the whole day then waved her to continue upward.

She glared up at the packs still fifty feet above them and set off.

No way she was going to look again. For one thing her nerves couldn't take it.

When she reached the packs, it was pure chance that she just happened to see Caspar and Mick glissading down the slope on their butts, using the tips of their ice axes like rudders. Boys! She turned to tie a lowering rope onto the packs.

Hell with her nerves.

Her heart couldn't take it.

---

MICK HAD THOUGHT to keep the pace slow to favor Patty, but he needn't have bothered. The hard work of slogging through the snow at altitude slowed him down plenty as well. He might have gone faster, but the PJs set up a slow but steady pace. Breaks were few, conversation light, but neither were they exhausting themselves.

Back at their landing site, they had to poke around to find where they'd stashed their parachutes. A high, thin cloud cover had moved in and flattened the light, the deep furrow of their out-bound path through the knee-deep snow was almost invisible on their return journey.

He gathered in loops of the rope until he and Patty were walking closely together and could speak slowly between deep breaths.

"Of course, I'm doing okay, Meathead," which told him she really was doing fine. "You're not the only fine Special Ops soldier on this mountain."

"Some of us are finer than others, O'Donoghue." Too late to take the words back, he could only hope she didn't interpret them the way he'd been thinking them. Her form may have been hidden by layers of winter gear and little more than her eyes and nose showing between hat and scarf, but she was indeed very fine. Half a head shorter and half the weight of any of the men, she was still moving lightly despite the hard work and heavy pack.

"Fine, huh?"

Of course she hadn't missed it. As they'd been crossing the snow-field, she'd shifted a long way in his thoughts as well. That final image on the helo, Patty O'Donoghue asleep on his shoulder, was causing him definite problems.

"You gonna elaborate on that, Quinn, or just leave me to speculate?"

With Patty, an elaboration could lead to a hundred more banters and ripostes, which he didn't really have the air for. "Speculate away."

They began ascending a ridge which robbed them of what little breath they had. Before they hit the really steep section, they had a gear break to tighten their crampons.

A two-minute task in the training room became a ten-minute ordeal at altitude. The strap to tighten the spikes to his boots couldn't be easily worked because they were now clogged with snow; he had to strip off his thick outer gloves to clear them. Rest a glove on the snow and it disappeared into the powder, making him dig around blindly until he found it.

When he was done, his ice axe was nowhere to be found, until he remembered the tether that still attached it to his wrist. His thinking was slowing down as well.

When he finished, Caspar was squatting in the snow in front of him. "Last time you ate and drank something?"

Mick looked at his watch. Too long. Saving his breath, he answered by digging out an energy bar and his canteen…and almost lost the other glove. He felt less foolish when he saw Patty doing the same.

"High altitude and dry cold dehydrates you faster than crossing a desert."

Mick nodded, he knew that; had heard it in any number of survival lectures. But now he *knew* it.

"Now repack your canteen with as much snow as you can. Then tuck it inside your jacket near your chest to melt it. Do that every time you drink. You know not to eat the snow?"

Mick nodded. It was just asking for lip and mouth blisters, and crashing his core temperature.

"If you ever fall through ice and have to get dry fast, did you know you can scrub yourself with powdery snow. It's so dry that it will absorb most of the moisture."

He hadn't known that one.

Caspar chatted amiably about different uses and conditions of snow for several minutes as if they had nowhere better to be.

Another five minutes and Caspar saw whatever he'd been waiting for in his and Patty's faces, "Let's move before you chill down."

Caspar led off again.

"Still glad you jumped, Boston?"

"With you, Quinn? Always."

She drifted back along the rope lead to leave *him* to speculate on *her* meaning.

TRACING the small squawks and radio burps of a weakening signal, they finally located the radio repeater in mid-afternoon.

Except there wasn't one victim, there were two, a fact that the "panicked survivor" had failed to mention in her script. Patty stared down at the two life-size mannequins lying in the deep snow. One had a label on its jacket listing symptoms: broken leg, advancing hypothermia, semi-conscious, can't arouse for over fifteen seconds. The second label was far grimmer: DOA. Dead On Arrival.

The steady-paced PJs exploded into action. In seconds they had an IV running into an artificial vein. Caspar tucked the IV bag deep inside his own clothes to keep it warm.

"IV is the best way to raise their core temperature quickly," he explained a piece of information that Patty hoped she never needed to know.

"No hot packs on the extremities. Her heart is barely maintaining core functionality. If we warm the extremities, it will draw critical blood away from the core and flush ice-cold blood back in its place."

Way more than she wanted to know.

"Build up a pair of stretchers."

"A pair?" Patty knew the answer as soon as she asked and turned away to fish the parts out of her pack before they could make an idiot of her by answering. *Leave no soldier behind.* It was instilled in all Special Ops teams ten times more than standard units. They all still said *no man* but they'd catch up soon enough if she had anything to do with it.

Her own reaction to her question was a burning behind her eyes and deep in her heart. It didn't matter that they were mannequins. They were too late for one and possibly for the other. And she'd hesitated. In combat, that could get both her and her pilot killed. Hesitation had been trained out of her long ago—or so she'd thought. Many lessons up on this goddamn mountain today.

Maybe she could blame the environment for her momentary lapse.

During their search, the temperature had dropped below zero. Any hint of sunlight was gone, masked by dark clouds and snow flurries.

"Gets real awfully fast, doesn't it?" Mick knelt next to her in the snow and she felt a little better.

All she could manage was a quick nod.

In unison they both dug into their packs for the rolled-up stretchers. The thick plastic sheet unrolled reluctantly with the cold.

"Load the DOA first," the PJs continued working on the "survivor."

Mick helped her lay the dead mannequin on the first plastic sheet. Pre-attached straps pulled the sides and ends together until the mannequin was cocooned in a toboggan with fore and aft towing harnesses.

When Mick covered its face by cinching down the parka's hood, it was a little too final for her.

Patty pulled both gloves off one hand and rested it on the mannequin's heart. She wasn't the praying sort, so she simply rested her hand there for a long moment and tried to give thanks that this wasn't a real person.

Mick was watching her closely while she pulled her gloves back on.

"What?" It came out harsher than she intended.

"You've got a soft spot in you, O'Donoghue."

"So?" Her defenses were cranked up way too high.

"So, it's both unexpected and sweet." Then Mick kissed her on the exposed tip of her nose before turning to prepare the second stretcher.

She didn't want to wipe it off, but the moisture was cold. The moisture coming out of her eyes was hot and didn't wipe away so easily.

# CHAPTER 9

"We've got to make camp," Caspar declared and Mick couldn't agree more.

The snow was falling hard and visibility was rarely more than a fifty feet. They'd made it down from thirteen- to ten-thousand feet before daylight failed them, but there was no chance of a helo evac.

The two other climbing teams were still too far below them to connect up. The mid-level climbing team had been stopped by a bad icefall and forced to break trail wide around it. The lower team had reached the starting point of the mid-level team but that was all.

Command deemed the "survivor" to be sufficiently stabilized that it wasn't worth the risk of a nighttime descent. Everyone would be spending the night on the mountain and they'd all link up in morning.

There wasn't any such thing as a level spot at ten thousand feet up the side of Mount Hayes, so they dug platforms deep into the snow. The two tents ended up fifty feet apart, too far to shout in the rising storm, but they all had spare batteries for their radios, making communications a non-issue. With the "corpse" parked on the far side of the PJs tent and the "survivor" in the tent with the two men, Mick and Patty might as well be on an entirely different mountain when they slipped into their own tent.

"Cozy," Mick observed after flicking on a headlamp. The tent was big enough for two sleeping bags and their packs, as long as they were very close together. It was tall enough to sit up along the midline...barely.

"Sure," Patty agreed readily. "Way better than a Bahamian beach and a piña colada. I thought we left this storm in the Aleutians." He wasn't going to think about Patty in a bikini with a tropical drink in her hand—an image he was finding way too easy to imagine...especially one of those skimpy ones with a red floral print and...

"Yeah," he forced the image to the background of his thoughts, because it certainly wasn't going away. "You think raining on Anchorage would have tired the storm out." Instead it appeared to have riled it up. Despite the deep snow shelf that protected their tent and being on the lee side of the mountain, the wind still slapped the plastic of the tiny tent with sharp snaps and the rattle of ice crystal clouds blown like gunfire against the nylon.

By the light of his headlamp, they jostled and bumped each other constantly as they lay out insulating pads and sleeping bags. Shedding boots was easy but getting out of the winter gear was far more difficult in the tiny space. They had to help each other and stripping clothes off Patty O'Donoghue was suddenly something Mick didn't want to stop.

With a deep breath and more control than he knew he had, he managed to stop when he reached the "Bag." Even in a shapeless green flight suit that was a couple sizes too big for her, he found a sudden and surprising need to drag her down onto the sleeping bags and try out that kiss again. Topped off by the ridiculously cute red, orange, and gold hat only made the image harder to resist.

Instead, he slid down deep into his own sleeping bag. The tent was warmer than outside, but it was still icy enough to see his own breath. He propped his headlamp in the corner, shining upward. It was disconcerting to watch the thin tent fabric slap so violently above them, but it made for a softer light. He began sorting through their dinner options that had been stuffed in his pack.

"Shredded Beef in Barbeque Sauce, Brisket Entrée, Mexican Style

Chicken Stew, or Pork Rib," he read off while flipping through the Meals-Ready-to-Eat packets.

"Vegetarian Cheese Tortellini, Vegetarian Taco Pasta, Vegetarian Ratatouille, or Lemon Pepper Tuna," Patty sounded thoroughly disgusted. "I'm going to kill the Two-Twelve's quartermaster when I get back to Anchorage. If I get back to Anchorage." She buried her face in her parka that she'd fluffed into place as a pillow. "I can't remember the last time I was this tired."

"Here," he fanned his selection, "take your pick."

If it was a rug, he'd definitely have gotten a burn from how fast she yanked the shredded beef out of his hand. Well, it was the best choice, which would teach him not to make his own selection first. He went for the chicken stew as a close second.

They talked about the day for the ten minutes that the heaters bubbled away warming up their meals.

Silence, other than the roaring wind and snap of the tent, descended as they packed away the calories.

It was comfortable and Mick was slowly relaxing, glad to finally be mostly warm and out of the unrelenting wind.

He was most of the way through his entrée when he noticed that Patty was watching him. Side by side in their bags they were closer together than in their Little Bird helicopter cockpit. It was easy to see that some question was bugging her.

"So ask already."

She shook her head and the ends of her hair where they stuck past the knit cap slipped down to hide her face.

"You've never been a coy one, Patty. Doesn't work for you, so what are you wondering?"

"Not my place."

What wouldn't be her place to ask?

"Christ, Mick. Are all men so thick-headed?"

He shrugged a maybe and munched on a few cheese-filled pretzels to buy himself some time.

"Sofia?"

"What about her?"

Patty put her face back down in her crumpled parka and released a loud scream of frustration.

"I already told you I wasn't interested in her." Though he did recall that moment in the hall when she'd been so close, so warm, and so kind.

"You talked together for three straight hours last night."

"Three hours? Really?" He'd lost complete track of the time.

"You still insist you're not interested in her. What kind of an idiot are you?" Patty threw one of her peanuts at him, which bounced off his forehead. She picked it up from where it fell on his sleeping bag and ate it.

"Based on the tone of your voice, apparently a complete one."

She cleaned up the remnants of her meal and slipped deeper into her sleeping bag until little showed other than her blue eyes and her orange pom-pom.

He let the silence stretch.

"Fine! I'll kill myself with embarrassment later. What did you two talk about for so long?"

"Oh, ice and snow."

"Ice?"

"Uh-huh."

"And snow?"

"Yep."

"You sat with a gorgeous woman for three hours and all you discussed was ice and snow? What's next? Water? Or were you going to jump straight to steam? And why didn't you jump straight to steam?"

"She's never been exposed to either snow or ice before. Sofia didn't know the first thing about survival in winter conditions. No mountain training for RPA pilots."

Patty whistled and her unreadable expression shifted to one of surprise. Then something that might have been respect. "And still she came along on the exercise. Brave woman. Another thing to like about her."

"Uh-huh," he wasn't going to get back into the conversation with

Patty about why he didn't want Sofia.

"I'll be damned." She mumbled it to herself so he decided that silence was the safest policy.

He finished the last of his Wet Pack Fruits side dish and slid deeper into his own bag once the trash was stowed.

"What else did you talk about?"

"The way we apparently look at each other."

"You and Sofia?"

He shook his head and wondered why he'd said it out loud. He tried to speak his answer but wasn't sure he wanted to have such a clear gauge of his own reaction. So he pointed from his face to hers and back.

"You and me?"

He nodded.

"And then?"

"And then she booted me down the hall."

———

PATTY PULLED the sleeping bag over her head. It was hard to think when Mick was watching her with those big, dark eyes from so close beside her.

Maybe this was her moment to die from embarrassment. She'd thought…suspected…conjured so many stupid-ass scenarios of those two that even for her it was pretty spectacularly bad. Maybe—Patty was just an idiot beyond belief.

Mick had talked with the beautiful Sofia about ice and snow?

And how he and Patty herself looked at each other? But there wasn't anything between them. Well, nothing except one rockin' kiss.

"Hello in there," Mick pulled up a corner of her sleeping bag.

She grabbed the edge and pulled it back down.

Patty could feel him toying with the pom-pom that must be sticking out, but she'd have to scoot farther down in the bag to pull it inside with the rest of her. That was actively running away from the problem rather than just hiding from it and she couldn't stomach doing that.

How had she ended up in a tiny tent alone with Mick Quinn on top of an Alaskan mountain? It wasn't like she could go down to the weight room and pump iron for an hour the way she had while trying to burn off the aftereffects of that first kiss.

The way *she* and Mick looked at each other?

If she was going to be honest with herself—and she hated to do that under normal circumstances, which these definitely weren't so she'd give herself a break this one time—she certainly *had* been looking at Mick that way.

He was still playing with the pom-pom.

So what if she had? A girl was allowed to look, wasn't she?

She stuck her head back out of the bag.

"What's wrong with me looking at you? It's not like you're grotesque or anything."

That's when he kissed her.

Unlike her own kiss that had been about heat and anger and men being such total and absolute idiots, Mick's was soft and gentle.

Not testing.

Not demanding.

Just a kiss designed to blow her pulse rate off the charts. A kiss that simply *forced* her to slither one arm out of the sleeping bag so that she could wrap it around his neck.

He didn't break off, didn't check in with her, didn't have a goddamn doubt in the world. How freakin' male was that? Her thoughts were trying to scurry off and scatter in a thousand directions and Mick Quinn had them anchored solidly in place with a kiss that had already forced her to scrap any nav charts she'd ever built about men. This was way better.

When he did finally move, it was to kiss her eyelids closed, a motion so gentle it was like a whisper.

And then a peck on the tip of her nose.

The sigh that slipped out of her was wholly un-Patty-like.

Her thoughts again tried to coalesce, but they only managed to offer up one lucid thought.

"Don't stop now, Quinn. You're on a roll."

When he at long last shifted down to nuzzle her neck they ran into problems with sleeping bags and flight suits. There was definitely too much fabric between them.

"You know," she whispered as she toyed with his longish black hair. "These sleeping bags are designed to zip together. In case one of us has hypothermia or something."

After a few chilly moments, the sleeping bags were zipped together, their flight suits and long johns were down by their feet to keep them warm, and it was the last time she was able to speak coherently. After a while, she didn't even try. Instead she concentrated on keeping the joined sleeping bags up over their heads and Mick as close as she could.

---

MICK HAD MADE love to women in odd places before.

He'd lost his virginity in his bunk aboard the family crabbing boat while it was tied at dock. He and Wilma Cutter, the boat's cook hired on when he'd gotten old enough to work the lines, had multiple trysts there. They'd also used the galley a time or twenty at sea where the storm waves did most of the work for them. And any other place they could find.

Her send-off to college—which had also been her pre-agreed Dear John because though he was staying local at University of Alaska ROTC program, she was off to Berkeley—had been particularly memorable. She'd taken him to her uncle's cabin near the Arctic Circle where they'd made love for as long as the sun was above the horizon…most of twenty-two straight hours.

Since then he'd found willing women in war zones, on Italian beaches, and in the back of a British Challenger main battle tank—a very flexible Company Sergeant Major who had offered an exceptional fringe benefit during a US-UK joint training exercise.

But the upper slopes of Mount Hayes were definitely the most surprising.

It wasn't the location and the circumstances; it was the woman in his arms. As with everything she did, Patty O'Donoghue was enjoying herself completely. Rather than being coy, she threw herself at him.

Every time he touched her it elicited a hum or purr of pleasure. When he did something she particularly liked, she made sure he knew it. Most women left it to the man to guess what they wanted, a mystery to be discovered and learned. And a complaint if he didn't figure it out.

Not Patty.

"Hey, cut that out. Oh God! That! Yes! Do more of that! Never, ever stop doing that!"

Making love to her was neither a quiet nor a languid act; it was an incredible, joyous sport.

When he finally cupped her, she yelped loud enough that he wondered if the distant PJs could hear her despite the storm, then she pressed herself into his palm with a happy burble into their shared kiss.

If only he had—

"You really are a meathead, Quinn." Patty stuffed a foil-wrapped condom into his hand.

"I didn't think that I'd be—" Dear God! Patty was giving back as good as he'd given. Her long-fingered hands explored and caressed while he hesitated.

"My oh my! No wonder you're called The Mighty Quinn."

He kissed her again because he really didn't want a running commentary and he did want to taste her again. He couldn't get enough of how she—

Finally, she pulled away, "Now, Quinn. For crying out loud, now!"

He sheathed himself and slid into her heat, doubly powerful when compared to the cold wind raging so close by. Her body was exceptionally conditioned as only a Special Operations soldier ever achieved. And she knew exactly what to do with it as she gave him more pleasure than he'd ever found with another. He did his best to return the favor and she flew in his arms until they cried out together.

He was wholly spent when the last of the ripples slid along her slender frame down to where they were anchored together, by his need and her legs hooked behind his.

Unable to stop himself, he wholly collapsed down on her, past even propping himself up on his elbows. Missionary was about the only position permitted by the two sleeping bags and he couldn't find the energy to roll them onto their sides.

Patty giggled in his ear as she held him close.

"Damn but you're good at this. If only I'd known how good. Quinn?"

"Uh," was the best he could manage.

"I can't believe how much time we've wasted not doing this."

"Give me a break, Patty. We do that again and I'm a dead man."

"Hmm," she clamped herself more tightly about him as if his death by superior sex would be a small price to pay.

At the moment he wasn't sure he'd argue with that conclusion.

He did finally manage to find his elbows and lift some of his weight off her, far enough away that he could see her by the light that came in through the small gap at the top of the sleeping bags from his still lit headlamp.

Her smile was huge, he expected that it mirrored his own. Her fine features, slightly bruised lips, and just the hint of the long line of her neck were visible. And her sparkling blue eyes. He'd always thought that to be a ridiculous cliché, but he was looking right at her eyes and that's exactly what they were doing. Her beautiful red hair remained mostly covered by her ridiculous knit hat, the only clothing she still wore other than thick woolen socks that presently had their heels pressed into his butt.

He yanked the hat down over her eyes because the joy in them was too dynamic, like an avalanche coming straight at him, and he kissed her.

Her kiss was so sweet, that he knew he was gone. Acerbic, funny, joyous, and beautiful. What wasn't to like about her?

Then he laughed, a single bark. Wasn't it just two nights ago he was thinking whoever Patty became attached to was going to need all the luck in the world to survive?

"What?"

He kissed her again to distract her, because no way was he answering that question. It wasn't a question of who Patty latched onto; it was a matter of who was lucky enough to get her. And somewhere between teasing a North Korean frigate and camping on an ice-cold mountainside, it had turned out to be him.

Mick let himself sink back down on her, because there was no way he could get enough of Patty O'Donoghue.

# CHAPTER 10

$\mathcal{P}$atty shrugged on a parka so that she didn't freeze when she straddled Mick Quinn for "breakfast."

The PJs had called on the radio, "Half an hour to first light. Be ready to go." The call had been the only sound on the mountainside. The storm was gone and the silence was vast.

She'd unzipped the upper half of the sleeping bags to get some maneuvering room and took a moment to admire Mick's chest by the soft light of the headlamp she'd flicked back on. A man was so differently shaped when he'd been born to hard work rather than when he developed it as a gym workout. Mick's chest was spectacular even by fisheryman standards.

Patty leaned down to rub her own chest over his. The powerful sensations of last night hadn't been diluted by a night sleeping in his arms. Well, mostly sleeping. She'd spent part of it awake and watching him in the darkness as the storm quieted. There hadn't been anything to see in the pitch darkness, but she'd listened to his breathing, felt the rise and fall of his chest where her arm lay across it.

That he was an amazing lover wasn't a surprise. Her own intense response to his slightest touch had been a very pleasant surprise. So often she felt that she ultimately didn't satisfy the men she was with, but Mick couldn't have faked the joy he took from her. The joy they took from each other. Maybe the problem hadn't been with her, but with the men she chose. A comforting thought. And if it *was* true, she'd chosen a home run this time.

Was it going to change things between them? She hoped not. Let them both revel in the glorious sex until he tired of her or she of him. Then that would be settled between them and they could return to just flying together. If this flew the course of her normal relationships, it would be over and gone before command could even begin to care. They'd just stay under the radar while it lasted.

But oh! The way he felt in the meantime.

She'd been lulled back to sleep until the radio had awakened her. The call had only shifted Mick from asleep to groggy.

She'd teased him half awake and sheathed him. His eyes had fluttered open slowly, definitely not a morning person. He cupped her cheeks and pulled her into a kiss.

Now his body was awake enough and with a judicious shift of her hips, she slid him into her. There was a deep grunt of pleasure transmitted through their kiss and it tickled right down inside her.

"Not much time," she whispered.

"Okay," and he didn't waste a second of it. He drove up into her with a power that flooded her system with happy nerve signals trying to blow their little circuit breakers. She and Mick were rooted together at hip and mouth. He had one hand clamped on her butt and the other holding her hand where she had it pinned next to his shoulder. Under the warm cloak of the parka they pumped, thrashed, climbed, soared, and with a shared moan that ripped from somewhere deep inside them, the dam broke and the waves of heat pounded through her.

"Never freeze to death. As long as." Her heart was racing so hard and the aftershocks crashing so hard that she couldn't get enough air to complete the sentence in one go. "We can find a way. To do that."

He slapped her butt lightly. "Let's go," long before she was ready to shift off him, but he was right.

She sat up, still straddling his hips, and began dressing.

Mick lay on the sleeping bag a few moments longer like a dead man, except for the rise and fall of his chest as the skin rapidly goose-bumped because she'd taken the sleeping bag with her. And his dark eyes tracked her slightest motion.

Undressing together last night had been an awkward and self-conscious act in a space far too small for the purpose. This morning, dressing was intimate and fun.

She wiggled into her thermal underwear, then yanked up the shirt's hem to flash a breast at him.

He grinned and she slapped away his hand when he reached out to caress. Mick was much more insistent about leaning in to kiss her breast and she was only too happy to give him his way.

"You are so good at this," she finally pushed him away and continued dressing. "Whatever woman trained you, I want to shake her hand."

"I have a good imagination," he grumbled though she could see there was someone back there he was thinking of. "Though my imagination wasn't good enough when it came to you, Patty."

"Was that a flirt? From Mick 'The Mighty' Quinn? Shocked I am. Shocked!"

He brushed a finger along her cheek. Just that slight contact was almost enough to have her collapsing back into his arms, especially as he was still lying there naked and beautiful.

"Shocked," she managed in a soft mumble that sounded dangerously like a girlish giggle of contentment.

When he began dressing, Patty managed to suppress a very womanly sigh of disappointment. It was okay, there would be a later. There had to be. A smart woman didn't use a man like Mick Quinn just once or twice and throw him away. Whatever her other short-comings, Patty knew smart was one of her strengths. Too smart for most guys.

That thought surprised her enough to make her stop while working her way into snow pants over her green flightsuit.

Had that been the problem?

She was Special Operations which meant she was smarter than the average soldier, but also than the average guy. Mick Quinn wasn't average. He was a Night Stalker, too. Even more, he was an officer Night Stalker. That meant he was damned motivated and twice as smart, and that was completely aside from his stellar flying.

Not only did he keep right up with her jokes, but he also encouraged her when she thought out-of-the-box. Like the candy drop on the KPN frigate. She hadn't needed to explain how fractious it would be to have all of the sailors of their largest ship going on to their mates back in North Korea about the wonders of Western candy. He'd trusted her idea without knowing what it was and then lauded it to others afterward, once she'd told him what she'd done.

She'd always gone for guys who looked like Quinn, or close enough, which in retrospect had been pretty damn shallow of her even if it usually proved to be very fun. But not a one of them had thought like Quinn or treated her so well.

"Here, eat this, Boston." He shoved an opened and heated MRE into her hands. Vegetarian Cheese Tortellini for breakfast, could be worse.

While they chewed, they finished dressing and packing everything inside the tent. Finally it was down to just themselves and two packs.

"You ready?"

"Sure, let's get off this little hill."

"Bundle up."

"Why? Storm is gone. It's so quiet that the helos will probably just pluck us off the hillside."

He laughed in surprise and then amusement.

"What?"

"Have you been a little short of breath this morning?"

"I thought that was the sex."

"It was," he kissed her and she'd never get enough of that. The way she went so unexpectedly soft inside every time he did was just... weird. Wonderful, but weird.

Then he yanked down her hat and pulled her parka hood over it. He snapped a rope into her harness and his.

"There is another reason."

MICK UNZIPPED THE TENT CAREFULLY, battering at the snow so that it didn't pile into the tent.

He heard Patty's gasp behind him, but he had to concentrate. He didn't know how deeply they were buried, or what he'd find at the surface. Packing the snow off to either side, he tunneled upward. He was past kneeling and up to a crouch before his hand finally broke through into clear air. Six feet of drift.

A wash of fresh, bitingly cold air blasted down at him mixed with a flurry of snow.

Mick looked up through the six-inch hole he'd punched and saw the blizzard ripping by above them. The wind had little to roar against on a flat surface of powdered snow, so it passed by relatively quietly… and very fast. It would be deafening as soon as they climbed out onto the surface of the snow. It was daylight, but barely.

He ducked back into the tent and saw Patty sitting unmoving in the darkness.

"It'll be okay."

"Duh!" She shook off or buried whatever nerves he'd seen on her face for that brief instant. "We're Special Ops," and in that moment she was.

He squeezed her arm to let her know how much he appreciated her ability to adapt to a changing situation. It was pretty damned impressive even by Night Stalker standards.

"Some things they don't prepare you for so well," she said softly but began cinching up the closures on her hood and prepping to enter the blizzard. So, she didn't have nerves of steel, she just knew how to act as if they were—which had the same result but made her all the more impressive.

Personally, he'd rather stay in their little cocoon than go out in that weather.

"Caspar," he keyed the radio, "this is Mick. Have you punched out yet?"

"Yeah, ugly as ghost slime out there."

"Are we safe to move?"

"Have to," he answered. "And not just because our 'survivor' won't last another night on the mountain. Reports say that this storm gets way worse before it gets better and there's another front behind it. Three days minimum. See you in five minutes."

"Roger that."

" 'Roger that'?" Patty snarked at him. "We're leaving our warm and cozy love nest to crawl into a storm from hell and 'Roger that' is the best you've got?"

Mick keyed the radio, "Patty says that's a 'no go' until after you deliver her hot chocolate, a three-egg omelette with hash browns, and an English muffin with blueberry jam."

She sputtered at him.

"I lost the draw," Caspar replied. "I had to eat the penne with those vegetable sausage crumbles. No sympathy from this tent."

"Sorry, Boston," Mick told her.

"*Strawberry* jam, Doofus," she shot him one of those radiant but smarmy smiles. "Then apricot and after that blueberry. Certain things you need to know about me if you're going to go on bedding me."

As he definitely planned to go on doing that, he committed the information to memory. It was easy to do as her tastes alternated right down the color spectrum: red, skip orange, yellow, skip green, blue, skip indigo, then violet?

"Bet you hated grape juice as a kid."

"But I loved cranberry and apple. You broke my color code, which is better than my parents ever did." Her grin was wicked, then she went serious. "You lead. I'll collapse the tent behind us."

Even though he'd never met them, he could feel pity for parents with such a precocious child. He crawled back out and worked on building tall steps that would get them out to the surface. Mick hoped that it was just a local drift, because if they had to battle six feet of fresh snow the whole way down the mountain, they were in trouble.

Jostling close enough together to evoke memories of last night's hot sweaty moments, they collapsed the tent in the hole it had kept open in the snow, folded it well enough that it wouldn't cause them trouble during the descent and tied it onto his pack.

Ice axes out and crampons on, they roped up with the PJs and the two toboggans. On the descent, the PJs didn't stop for training lessons, which made the key lesson most obvious: do whatever it takes to get out alive.

They took turns battering a channel through the snow. When Patty had volunteered to take a turn, Caspar had gently blocked her.

"You're too narrow, Patty. We need a path wide enough for us to fit through as well."

Mick appreciated how tactfully the man had done it, Patty was out near her limits—not that it stopped her.

She'd passed the same trials he had. They trained Special Operations soldiers for mental stamina far beyond the physical, because it was when the body gave up that the true soldiering began. Patty didn't back down for a moment; "quit" had been knocked out of her vocabulary as long ago as it had been knocked out of his own.

It was a grueling six hours. Finally they reached the second team and the snow was down to three feet of powder. The second team had spent the morning fighting a trail upward and the storm had only partially refilled it.

They should have picked up speed at that point, but all it did was keep them from losing speed. At the line where blinding snow shifted to driving rain from above and chilling slush to freezing mud beneath their feet, the third team relieved them of their burdens. They all headed down the mountain together.

The "survivor" made it down alive, but even the PJs were dragging.

And Mick figured that if he was allowed to sleep for about a week, he'd have made it down alive as well.

Patty was still grimly matching him step for step when they were finally retrieved in the flatlands. An Army bus awaited them for the six-hour drive back to Anchorage. They were whipped hard the whole way as they drove deeper into the storm; rain drummed so hard on the metal roof that it was impossible to talk even if he'd had the energy to try. He was damn glad to be off that mountain.

When Patty collapsed against his shoulder, she was asleep before she got there. It didn't keep him awake for more than a few seconds. But those few were enough to register just how happy he was that she was there.

It was also long enough to wonder at how much his life had changed in the last thirty-six hours. But he was out before he had any time to think about it.

———

"GOT an opening here for you anytime you want," Casper and Two-ton had shaken her hand and Mick's. "That was some damn fine work," they told Major Napier and strode off as if she and Mick had done no more than win a quick game of racquetball.

Patty didn't really remember much else about her triumphant return to Joint Base Elmendorf-Richardson. Partly because it was just the end of another training exercise to the Two-Twelve, so no one made any big deal of it.

She also didn't remember it because she couldn't stop falling asleep. She'd given everything she had and then more as they'd wrestled the toboggans down off the snowy peak. She'd refused to become another victim that would burden her team on the final descent. By the time they were out of the danger zone she knew far too well what it took to wrestle those two heavy "victims" and she wasn't going to become the third.

She'd been led to turn in her gear to the quartermaster, but slept through any chance to rib him about his selection of MREs. One moment she'd been still loaded up in heavy gear and the next she'd been sitting in the Mess Hall and mechanically eating a meal she didn't recall and the next walking along the hallway of the transient lodging hotel.

And now she was in the dark.

The glowing red clock that read 7:30 didn't tell her a thing. First off, what idiot put a clock that ran on civilian time in a military transient lodging? Heavy curtains would have required her to crawl out of a very warm and comfortable bed to see if it was morning or night. Actually either 7:30 would be dark now, a.m. or p.m. Second, she might have slept an hour or a day. But third, since she didn't know when she'd finally been allowed to crash, it was all worse than meaningless. The clock only pretended to have useful information, but it was obviously lying.

Then there was a very small sound that provided an immense amount of information, a soft sigh. She might be in bed, but she wasn't alone.

Next level of awareness: beneath the covers she was wearing a t-shirt that swam on her, she could practically slither out the neck hole and the sleeves reached her elbows. And she was wearing nothing else.

"You'd better be Mick Quinn," she whispered at the form, but received no answer.

She reached out into the dark and found a shoulder. Mick's? Muscled enough to be.

Then its owner, from lying flat on his back, scooped her against him so that she landed with her head on his shoulder and his arm cradled down her back.

Definitely Mick. It was exactly the position they'd slept in up on Mount Hayes and he felt exactly this way. He smelled so gloriously warm and male there beneath the covers.

But he took no further action.

With another sigh, he was back asleep.

Whatever had passed between them—that they certainly hadn't discussed any further during the brutal mountain descent close beside the two PJs—The Mighty Quinn's subconscious obviously approved of it.

The simple move had also awoken every overstrained muscle fiber in her arms and legs. First it was a twitch, then a spasm, then the hand that was lying so comfortably on Mick's broad chest spasmed hard enough that she clipped him in the chin.

After a surprised grunt and a curse, his hands that had been completely lax clamped onto her.

"Easy," he whispered rather than asking *what the hell?* "Easy. It will pass."

In moments her body bucked and writhed with cramps and charley horses. Mick simply held her and let her flail. Eventually the spasms eased and the sharp pains faded back to mere twitches, then thankful calm.

"I salted your food fairly heavily, but you were too tired to eat much of it or drink any Gatorade."

Patty lay still, afraid to speak or even take a deep breath for fear that the shooting pains would start all over again.

"You sweat out a lot of salt and electrolytes at altitude without noticing. We were working hard up on that mountain. And you built up enough lactic acid for a lifetime. I almost punched out Napier when we got down. He should never have pushed us so hard."

"Punching out a superior officer is frowned on in most circles."

"Yeah," he chuckled softly, "especially when that officer is Pete Napier. The only thing that saved me from having my ass kicked and thrown into the brig was Danielle got one good look at you and went after him for me."

"Go, Danielle."

"Yeah. There was something strange though. Napier never does anything by accident. He whispered something to Danielle and she backed right down. Didn't look any less angry, but something else was going on."

Patty felt a sudden chill and snuggled tighter against Mick's warmth as he stroked a hand idly up and down her back.

"Something else..." he tested the words as he spoke them.

"What? Like a new mission?"

"Maybe," she could feel Mick's nod. "Yeah, more than maybe. He wanted us, you and me, to parachute in. Work with the PJs. He specifically wanted us to get that ice-and-snow training."

"No. That wasn't him, we volunteered. You volunteered us." But even as she said it, she knew. "And if someone else had volunteered..."

"Napier would have switched us into their places with a simple,

'Why don't we let Mick and Patty take this one?' Nobody would gainsay him."

"Gainsay. Pretty fancy word for an Alaska fisheryboy."

"Sass. Pretty standard from Patty O'Donoghue."

Since there was no point in arguing that, she concentrated on something else…like how good Mick smelled. Whereas, "I smell like something the polar bear dragged in."

"Better than something the penguin barfed up," he made a point of sniffing her hair. "But not by much."

"Why don't you smell like that?"

"Because I showered. If I tried to shower you last night, I was afraid you would drown, so I just held my nose and stuffed you between the sheets."

Patty sniffed at herself again. "Ick! Real attractive. I gotta shower. Don't go anywhere. I'll make it worth your while."

"Deal."

By the time she was at least sanitary if not fully decontaminated, Mick was fast asleep again. It had been so much fun waking him the first time, she couldn't wait to do it again.

She slipped in between the covers and snuggled up to him. He was out, not even curling his arm around her. She reached down to—

A hard pounding on the door was followed by Napier calling out.

"Up, Quinn. Enough beauty sleep."

"Goddamn it," Patty kept her voice soft because she certainly didn't want the major to know where she'd spent the night. That would not go down well at all. She and Mick in bed together definitely warranted a disciplinary action, if not something far more serious.

"You too, Boston!" Napier beat the door once more before his footsteps tromped off down the hall and he began battering down the next door.

"*Goddamn it!*" She didn't bother to keep her voice down on that one.

Napier might have chuckled as he moved down the hall.

Now what the hell had that meant?

CHAPTER 11

he time was 2000 hours when Major Napier had rousted the team. By 2030 they had breakfasted and assembled in the hangar, all staring at their aircraft in bewilderment. Well, everyone except Napier who looked slightly smug, and the two mechanics, Connie and Big John, who looked harried. They looked as if they'd just been working as hard as the team on the mountain had.

None of the changes were explained which was making Mick feel more than a little frustrated. He hoped that was rooted in lack of sleep and not lack of sex with Patty, because no way could he allow his personal life into his military one.

Napier hadn't pulled him aside; hadn't made a single sign. Mick was a Lieutenant sleeping with a Chief Warrant Officer, even if all they'd done last night was sleep. At least Patty wasn't an enlisted—not since she'd gone Chief Warrant—but it still wasn't right. Yet, Napier hadn't said a word. So still no change there.

It was his helo that was changed.

The *Linda's* two outer weapons' hard points had been replaced by long-range fuel tanks. The weapons that now hung from the inner hard points on his Little Bird were no longer American.

They were Russian.

263

The helos had been repainted, but it wasn't going to fool anyone. The Ugroza missile pod had replaced his Hydra 70s and the Yak-B Gatling gun had supplanted the M134 minigun.

The weapons were absolutely not certified to be on his bird. Their weight and capability were similar enough to what had been removed that it shouldn't be a problem, but he couldn't make sense of the change. Any idiot who looked at those weapons wasn't going to be fooled by the American stealth helicopter attached to them.

Patty shook her head at him sadly from where she knelt inspecting the attachment points, "You always were the slow one on our team, Quinn."

"Me? I didn't say a word."

"Didn't need to. It's all *ov-ah* that pretty face of yours *yawz*," she laid on an extra thick helping of her accent.

He rubbed his eyes. He felt rested; he was never the slow one. But just being around Patty it sounded like he was sometimes…

*It sounded.*

Oh! That was the key.

"The sleeping bear awakens," Patty snorted.

He placed a hand on the top of her head and pressed down. She went from squat to backwards sprawl with a very satisfying thump and a quite descriptive curse.

"My moth-*ah*," he imitated her, "has never once said that she'd wished she'd gotten a dog instead of me for a son."

"Didn't need to," she answered from the concrete floor. "Some things are just that obvious."

He ignored her self-satisfied grin. It was the *sound* that mattered. At night, in the dark, no one would see their Little Bird, not even on most radar equipment. But if they had to fire weapons, they couldn't sound American or fire American rounds.

A quick scan showed similar changes on all of the other aircraft. The *Beatrix,* being a heavier DAP Hawk, now sported a Shipunov 2A42 30mm cannon, which Rafe, Julian, and their gunner Drake, were inspecting with admiration on their faces. The cannon was a nasty-looking piece of hardware even if most of it was tucked inside a composite, radar-absorbent housing.

Stealth American helicopters with Russian armament.

The Chinook was little changed. The crew chiefs' three M134 Gatling guns had been replaced and a massive fuel bladder of four thousand gallons of JP-5 jet fuel now filled the main cargo bay. Add that to the extended-range fuel tanks on *Linda* and *Leeloo*. They were going a long way from any friendly filling station. All the way to—

"Oh man," Patty connected the pieces at the same moment he did and grimaced.

He held out a hand and helped her to her feet.

Napier was down at the far end of the hangar by the Avenger drone with Sofia, her copilot, and a woman with long dark hair who looked vaguely familiar. When they were all done marveling at the changes to their own aircraft, they gathered around them.

Instead of one Avenger drone parked at the far end of the hangar, Sofia's *Raven*—named for Marion Ravenwood in *Indiana Jones*—had grown a twin. As far as Mick knew, only three had ever been built. To have two of them here told him just how hairy this mission might get.

"These," Major Napier rested a hand on one of the drone's blunt noses, "will be forward deployed to Eareckson Air Station on Shemya Island near the end of the Aleutians along with a refueling and maintenance team from the Pac Air Force Regional Support who will *not* be told our mission."

"Not like we've been told squat either!"

Mick laughed at Patty's snide remark. It was the perfect tension breaker. It was definitely frustrating to be heading aloft with no information other than they were flying into Russia. But he wouldn't have dared to drop that in the major's lap. Patty shrugged at him as if to say, *No guts, no glory!*

Napier waited out the laugh before continuing as if nothing had happened. "Sofia and Zoe, you will control the flights from your coffin here. To trade off in rotating shifts, we've also borrowed Captain Kara Moretti from the 5D," Napier introduced the sultry woman with Mediterranean skin and a sparkling wedding ring.

That was it. She'd flown the other drone when the 5E had faced off against the 5E as a graduation exercise. Which meant she was just as exceptional as Sofia and Zoe.

"The *Rita* is her aircraft," Napier completed the introduction.

"Hayworth?" Patty guessed.

Moretti shook her head in a swirl of dark hair. Her smile was sassy and reminded him of Patty even though their coloring had nothing in common.

"Rita Moreno from *West Side Story?*" was Julian's shot at it and others began tossing out ideas.

"MacDowell in *Groundhog Day?*"

"Nah. Though Andie was hot in that."

Mick knew who it was. It hadn't been hard to figure out that all of their aircraft were named for exceptional action heroines, though that trick of Danielle's had avoided her husband's notice until it was too late.

"*Edge of Tomorrow,*" he spoke up and Moretti tapped her finger on the tip of her nose. "Rita was the ultimate warrior. Emily Blunt with Tom Cruise defeating the alien, time-warping scourge across Europe. She, to use Patty's term, totally kicked ass." Since that movie, Ms. Blunt had moved way high on his gotta-meet-that-woman-someday list. Though the other idle fantasies that had gone along with that no longer seemed to matter with Patty looking at him with that goofy grin of hers as if she knew exactly what he was thinking.

Napier scowled at Danielle, who hadn't said a word, for a moment then simply sighed before continuing. "Eareckson is an hour from our destination and the Avenger remotes have a flight duration of eighteen hours. We expect you to keep an eye in the air above us at all times. Stay out of sight but we may need your craft's eyes and ears."

Sofia looked relieved at being left to work from somewhere warmer than the icy slopes of Mount Hayes. Mick had checked in with her on the descent and she'd done better than he expected. She actually understood and integrated their one talk in the Mess Hall straight into the harsh realities in the field. Completely deserved to be in Special Operations.

"Airborne in ten. Let's go!" Napier clapped his gloved hands together and they all hurried to prepare their aircraft.

He and Patty did their preflight in silence, got their engines started, and waited while someone doused the hangar's lights before sliding open the big doors.

By 2100 hours, just an hour after he'd woken up in bed with Patty still beside him, he scooted the *Linda* forward out of the hangar and pulled aloft.

He'd actually expected her to discretely slip off after her shower. Not that he expected her to cover for them, rather that he figured that she would prefer less connection between them.

Mick had taken her into his bed in the first place because he wasn't about to feel her up in the hallway to find where she'd stashed her own room's keycard and because she was so exhausted he'd been half worried that she'd stop breathing. That she'd returned to his bed after her shower had surprised him no end.

It had also pleased him.

Rather than avoiding him after what they'd done in the mountain tent, she had chosen to curl back up against him. If a beautiful woman wanted to be in his bed, his ego wasn't going to complain for a second.

If Patty O'Donoghue wanted to be there, he'd count himself a very lucky man.

And that was the most surprising thought of them all.

---

TEN HOURS and two refueling stops later, Patty groaned dramatically going for the laugh.

She didn't get the response, but that didn't worry her. If Mick was half as tired and stiff as she was from spending so long in the tiny cockpit, then he wouldn't have the energy for a laugh.

Besides, Mick was busy fighting the controls to bring the Little Bird shimmying down out of the dull gray sky. Not a storm front this time, just rotten weather and too damn long in the air.

"The Aleutians. Again," she said with disgust. "Personally I felt that one visit was plenty for this island chain."

"Look at the bright side. We didn't even get to see the islands last time; it was all a night flight."

"You're right, Mick. As usual. Because this," she waved a hand toward the front windscreen, "is so much better."

Desolate didn't begin to describe Attu Island. They were almost a thousand miles past where they'd been harassing the KPN fleet a few days ago. Attu lay several islands and half a hundred miles farther west than even Eareckson Air Station, where the Avenger drones had been staged. And the breaking dawn light wasn't making it any more attractive.

"You know," Patty twisted in her seat once more. "After ten hours cramped up in a Little Bird seat, downtown Paris wouldn't look attractive."

"I bet they have hotels there. Nice ones."

"Probably," she'd never been Paris. Her closest had been to Pau, eight hundred kilometers to the south, to train with their 4th Special Forces Helicopter Regiment.

"We could go."

"I think we have something else we're supposed to be doing right now."

Mick didn't respond.

Had she just turned down a romantic vacation in Paris with Mick Quinn? Uh…maybe. Well, that was stupid by any woman's standards.

Mick had them down close by the shore and Patty guided him toward the southeastern cove on the island. Apparently he wasn't going to be the one to speak next.

"That sounds wonderful, Quinn." Oh man, did it ever.

"It's a date," he said it like he was going to take her out for pizza.

Something had slipped by her but she was so tired that she was having trouble pinning it down. Making a date to be with Mick in Paris felt…normal. Which it wasn't. Or was it? Not thinking clearly, she gave it up for the moment.

She felt battered, even more than she had by the storm on Mount

Hayes. A Little Bird was designed for the quick tactical strike, not for a ten-hour long ferrying flight from Anchorage to the westernmost Aleutian Island that was still part of the United States. In fact, it was so far west that it was east—on the other side of the International Dateline. Only one other island kept it from being the easternmost point of the United States as well as the westernmost of Alaska.

Attu was a lumpy rock fifty miles long and twenty wide. Mostly snow-capped peaks cragging up to three thousand feet. Only one valley was any more than a dent in the mountains and it was barely longer than the old Coast Guard runway that filled it from one end to the other.

Amend that, *abandoned* Coast Guard runway.

Not a single tree showed on the whole island. Just valleys of snarled grasses and a whole lot of steep rock and ice. Patty saw no reason to amend her initial assessment that once was two times too many.

When the four helos got their skids and wheels down, Patty hit the radio transmit switch. She flipped to the low power antenna, so the signal wouldn't travel much outside their immediate group.

"Greetings, campers. We have just increased this island's population by thirteen people and four helicopters. In case you were wondering, that brings the island's population to…wait for it…a grand freaking total of—"

"—thirteen people and four helicopters." Mick echoed her voice. Even his wry tone and accent matched hers.

"Always been a lucky number for me," Mick remarked off air.

"That's because you're a loon."

"I'm not from Minnesota or Ontario."

"Whatever," she was too sore and weary to argue.

"Loons are the state bird of one and the provincial bird of the other."

Patty laughed and Mick smiled along with her but probably for different reasons. Mick was loosening up, making second-level jokes like that. He was so cute.

Patty had gone through very mixed feelings on the long flight from

Anchorage. Initial frustration that their wake-up sex had been interrupted before it began. She'd really wanted to see if what had occurred between them on the mountain had been strictly environmental, or if Quinn was really that spectacular a lover. Having a king-size bed and no opportunity to test the possible results had wound her up and crashed her down.

It was only after they were airborne that Napier's steadfast silence on the topic of Mick and her being in the same bed began to worry her. It was fine. Well, not really, but at least mostly okay that Napier and Danielle were together—they were captain and major after all even if they were in the same damned unit. And Connie Davis and John Wallace were both sergeants. Besides, they'd arrived married. Some prior commander had seen fit to allow it and still let them serve together.

But she was enlisted and Mick was a Lieutenant. Okay, she was a Chief Warrant 3, a commissioned officer like Mick, but not like Mick. They certainly shouldn't be fraternizing, even if they were. Had been. Once.

Maybe the 5th Battalion E Company was *extreme* in more ways than their equipment and their missions. Were they some kind of command-sanctioned coed experiment? She didn't like that thought any more than the rest of them.

Patty had spent the next part of the flight feeling very grumpy about being a lab rat in any incarnation: past, present, or future. And then she'd decided that the answer might be much simpler. The 5E was so clandestine an outfit, that few people outside the unit knew they existed. Well, other than the 5D whose butts they'd whupped (kinda) during the 5E's certification exercise. Maybe it was just a tolerant commander who wouldn't bust her ass as long as she performed absolutely perfectly at every instant.

Having reached that conclusion, her body decided to make another effort to catch up on the physical abuse from the mountain rescue. She'd passed out for the last three hours of the flight, something Patty would have to apologize to Mick for later. She hadn't even known it was physically possible to sleep in a pilot's seat in the Little Bird.

Looking out the windscreen made her wish she was still off in some pleasant dreamland.

On Attu Island, all color had been washed away. There was white snow, dark rock, brown grass with early snow trapped around its roots. A low gray sky and thin mist darkened everything even further.

The only thing that broke the wasteland was the concrete structure and radio tower of the old US Coast Guard LORAN station for guiding ships and planes. Nobody needed LORAN anymore to navigate, not with GPS satellites whirling overhead. In the half dozen years since the Coast Guard had declared good riddance and abandoned ship—or at least abandoned island—the Bering Sea winters had battered the old station.

The U-shaped two-story building showed the wear and tear of Arctic storms thrashing the facade. It too was plain white and added no color to the landscape. The small windows were still intact, but the paint was peeling.

"What a place we've come to."

"Beyond here there be dragons," Mick agreed.

"Did you just make a joke? Mick Quinn. Really?"

"Eat shit, O'Donoghue."

There was another first. She wasn't sure that Mick had ever cursed at her before—she had the foul mouth of this team. Patty decided that she'd take it as a compliment that he'd unwound enough to do so.

Instead, she did what all of the rest of the Night Stalkers were doing, she climbed out of the helo, moving like some billion-year-old biddy.

"I'm like an *Australopithecus* after a hard day foraging in the wilderness that would someday be named Africa."

"You're too tall and nowhere near hairy enough. Which I appreciate."

"You say the sweetest things, Quinn."

"You sure are stooped over like one, though."

If she'd had the energy to circle around the helo, she'd have bludgeoned him with a stone. She didn't.

Instead she helped him secure the bird, covering the more sensitive equipment, slipping tie-down sleeves on the rotor blades so they wouldn't whirl with the wind.

The northerly winds were blockaded from the runway by a ridgeline of tall peaks, but still the bitter fog swirled close about them as she pulled on her cold weather gear.

They pulled visual tarps over the aircraft, so that if someone happened to fly by, extremely unlikely, they wouldn't notice the stealth nature of the helos. The secret that the Night Stalkers were actively fielding stealth rotorcraft wouldn't last forever, but they'd hold off the inevitable as long as possible.

Even as Patty thought that, a Pave Hawk—the Air Force's version of the Sikorsky Black Hawk—came roaring down out of the sullen sky. It landed clean and very close beside them.

She glanced at Mick, but he shook his head. He didn't know what they were doing here either.

As soon as the back ramp was down, a refueling team began running hoses from the Pave Hawk's cargo bay over to the 5E's helos. Their own crew still hadn't touched the large fuel bladder lying in the back of the *Carrie-Anne* Chinook helo. It was clear to see that the refueling crews had been ordered to display no curiosity at all. They barely lifted their heads enough to find where to attach their fuel hoses.

Then two more men came trooping off the Pave Hawk, except one was a woman.

But there was no mistaking what they were or that it meant the 5E was in for a world of hurt.

# CHAPTER 12

$S$EAL Commander Luke Altman had them assemble in the USCG LORAN station's rec room as soon as the Pave Hawk was back aloft.

"Lousy service," Patty whispered in Mick's ear.

He had to agree. The old station was cold and even though the room was oddly intact, it felt truly abandoned. White walls, linoleum floor, four-person Formica tables and rust-pitted-chrome and plastic chairs. Motivational slogans were peeling off one wall, and the bar—with its sign announcing a four-beer limit per person per night—no longer stocked beer, soda, or snacks.

Somewhere a generator groaned to life and the lights over the bar wavered on. Connie and Big John came wandering in.

"The fuel is old and thick," John announced. "But it still fires off. They didn't leave much in the tanks. We'll have lights and some heat in this room and we're pumping heat into the barracks for at least the next few hours. We'll go to bed warm, but probably wake up cold."

Mick and Patty shoved tables together in the still-frozen air, everyone's breath showed in white vaporous clouds, but he could already feel a wash of warm air from the ceiling vents.

"Great service," Mick whispered back to Patty.

"Still no cold beer."

"If there was, it would be frozen and we wouldn't be allowed to have a drink anyway."

"Nitpicker. Besides, that's not the point."

"Then what is the point?" Someday he'd figure out Patty's sense of humor, but he actually sort of hoped not. He liked that she kept surprising him.

"That I can't have a beer even if I wanted to break the rules. Seems awfully stingy. As if the Coast Guard knew we were coming and didn't leave any behind on purpose."

"Do you take *everything* personally?"

"Absolutely!"

They fifteen chairs together around the square arrangement of tables. Patty dragged over an extra, dropped into a corner seat and then stretched out her legs on the extra chair.

How could such a simple gesture send his thoughts churning off into such drastically veering directions? Mick remembered the feel of those legs wrapped around him. He remembered how smooth and perfect they'd looked when he'd slipped her into bed last night, a soldier's legs. A woman's.

He headed for a chair across from her and then caught himself. Was he trying to avoid sitting next to her because it would be inappropriate? Or was he wanting to sit far enough away that he could watch her?

Patty's scowl warned him that he was on the verge of being drastically rude for not sitting next to her. Duh! So he changed course, but it was too late. Connie and then Big John sat to one side of her. Danielle sat to the other.

By the time he got his feet in motion, the only spot remaining was between Danielle and the Team 6 Commander. Luke Altman was bigger than everyone except Big John. The SEAL was six-four of warrior who made even Mick feel a little small and humbled.

His silent fellow SEAL, Chief Petty Officer Nikita Hayward, plugged a tiny projector into a tablet computer and aimed it at a white wall. Nikita was almost as daunting as her commander. Just under six feet tall and strong enough to have survived the Team 6 testing, she stood out completely even in this crowd.

Night Stalkers needed to be both fit and skilled; Nikita was Amazonian. Her dark hair was layer cut and framed an open face. But it was her dark eyes that were that were her knock-out feature. She looked at everyone with a simple frankness that missed absolutely nothing.

Several of the guys squirmed a little beneath her unblinking gaze. Drake, the *Carrie-Anne's* ramp gunner, just stared like he couldn't help himself.

"This," Altman signaled to Nikita for the first slide, "is the Kamchatka Peninsula. The easternmost land of Russia except for a few stray islands even sadder than the one we're sitting our asses on here. Almost entirely separated from the mainland by the Sea of Okhotsk, it's a five-hundred-mile ocean crossing from here. The size of California, it includes: almost two hundred volcanoes with thirty active ones, massive populations of salmon and grizzly bears, and already it's wrapped in snow and ice down to a thousand feet of elevation. The entire area has the same population as Lexington and well over half live in the peninsula's single city, Petropavlovsk-Kamchatsky, also known as PK."

"That makes for a whole lot of nothing," Patty observed and received a nod from the Team 6 commander.

CPO Nikita flicked to the next slide.

The reactions around the table were varied.

To Mick it looked like another drone.

Several people, including Patty flinched.

"Shit!" She scanned the table and then slapped her forehead. "Right, they aren't here. Sofia would freak if she saw this."

"She has seen this photo and your assessment is correct," Nikita offered a rare comment. "I showed this information to Lieutenant Sofia Gracie and Chief Warrant Zoe DeMille, her copilot. Lieutenant Gracie's reaction was 'That! It does not exist!'" It was a better than fair imitation of Sofia's accent when she grew excited. "She then went on at length in Portuguese, which I don't speak, but she seemed quite upset."

One drone looked a lot like the next to Mick. They mostly fell into three categories: cute little ones with tiny propellers, big nasty ones like the Predator and Sofia's Avenger, and the flying wing things. The last looked like the small children you'd get if an F-117 Nighthawk fighter mated with a B-2 Spirit bomber.

And why was he suddenly thinking of everything in sexual metaphors? Worse! Kid metaphors? He caught himself before he could glance at Patty as if she could read the mush that was inside his head. *Definitely* time for a new metaphor.

The drone looked like…someone had mounted a big damn engine onto the middle of a giant black boomerang. Whatever this drone was, it fell into the third category. It was a flying wing thing with a Russian Sukhoi Su-30 fighter jet in formation close alongside. The image looked like an advertising shot—magazine slick.

He scanned the table. Connie was fascinated, others were perplexed, and Patty, the sneak, was shaking her head at him once more.

"Uh," Mick figured he'd take the hit, "can someone explain that thing to me."

"Better make it in small words," Patty teased.

"Sofia was quite right," Commander Altman waved a hand at the screen. "It doesn't exist. According to the best reports we have it shouldn't have its first flight for three more years, or be operational for five."

"Could that be Photoshop?" It was a blue-sky photo. The drone looked as if it had been cut right into the photo with its oddly angled lines.

"I've been assured that this is not a staged photo or Photoshop; it's flying now."

Patty collapsed back in her seat as Altman continued his lecture.

"Lieutenant Gracie's Avenger is an RPA and she controls it, occa-sionally allowing its autopilot to control long ferries or the fussy details of a takeoff or landing. Because it can carry armament, it could be better classed as a UCAV, an Unmanned Combat Aerial Vehicle. But if this Russian UCAV is like our own X-47 tests, it has an extremely low-observable profile and can be programmed to operate autonomously. We've had ours land itself on an aircraft carrier multiple times. In theory, you could tell one of these to fly thousands of miles and drop a nuke at a pre-programmed target and the bomb would have a bigger radar signature while falling than the aircraft that's carrying it."

"Holy shit!" Patty's soft curse was echoed around the table.

It summed up Mick's feelings completely.

"According to everything we've heard from the primary drone labs near Moscow, this is barely off the drawing boards and not expected to be a threat for another five years. This picture is from a previously unknown development base in Kamchatka. We've been asked to fly over and check it out."

No one was able to laugh, not when faced with Commander Altman's deadpan delivery.

And by the silence, Mick guessed that he wasn't the only one stunned past swearing.

---

PATTY DIDN'T CARE what anyone thought or said, she took her sleeping bag, found Mick's room by using her flashlight—the shuttered windows kept out the thin, gray daylight—and joined him in the darkness on his narrow bunk.

They didn't zip their bags together.

He simply shuffled back against the wall. She lay her bag down beside him, crawled inside and buried her face against his chest. He stroked her hair and kissed her atop the head.

"Where does this go, Mick?"

"Definitely Kamchatka," he gave her one of his naive answers.

"No, I…" Then she remembered that no matter what he might show the world to keep them at ease, he was anything but naive.

"Sorry, my 'goofy meter' isn't functioning very well at the moment. It's also not calibrated to you."

"Doesn't matter, Gloucester," he whispered into her hair. He didn't even tease her with his usual "Glaow-chester" mispronunciation; giving her the proper "Glaw-stuh" instead.

"That's better than 'Boston' anyway."

"I was going to come find you, but..." he trailed off.

"It would have besmirched your stoic manliness to be afraid of the dark, especially because it's the middle of the day."

"Something like that."

She liked that she could feel his smile where his lips still pressed atop her head. She snuggled in tighter, felt safe for the first time since the briefing. Well, safer.

"It's easier if you can believe that we're the technologically superior force."

Patty just kept her face buried against his chest and let the words buzz through his breastbone and the bridge of her nose where it tickled a little.

"We cooked up the bomb, even defeated Germany before they could cook up one of their own. Gave us an edge for a while. Once we figured out rockets, we dusted everybody: the moon and all that. We even got the International Space Station. Everyone knows it's mostly ours, we even paid for or built most of the Russian components because they couldn't afford to. Way ahead on night vision and night operations. We have stealth and UAVs cornered...until suddenly we don't."

"It's not fair." She didn't want the world to change faster than she was ready for. "I joined to get away from the danger."

Mick's snort of laughter warmed the top of her head. "You went Special Operations to get *away* from danger? Christ, only Patty O'Donoghue would do something like that."

"No, Doofus. I went National Guard to get away from watching my brother lose his leg to a shark that came up in the seine net. To not watch my brother-in-law get caught in a rogue wave that washed off the boat and widowed my sister when his hold slipped. In the Guard, helo pilots pluck people out of floods and fly training missions. My tours in the dustbowl were brief and…"

"And?" Mick's soft murmur encouraged her.

"And I was bored as shit. I applied for Night Stalkers on a dare."

"That's my Patty."

She wasn't his anything…even if she did like the way it sounded. She'd never actually admitted all this to anyone, but it felt safe, almost important, to tell Mick.

"So why did you stick with it?"

"My reputation," it sounded stupid when she said it that way, but it was true.

"Explain that."

"My reputation caught up with me. You know, all those things you learn on a fishing boat. Safety first, be level-headed in a crisis, hard work is better than the empty net of a waterhaul because it means your family will get to eat that winter. All that crap."

Mick kissed her hair. "Yeah, I know 'all that crap' too."

"Well, my commanders kept recommending me upward. Then the Night Stalkers hooked me with promises that I'd be the best." At the moment she felt like shit. All the underpinnings of her world were crumbling. The Russians were scaling up for another cold war. And they were building *and flying* stealth UCAVs.

She was such a mess. It even bothered her that she was the one who'd been afraid of the "dark" and come running to her lover's arms. Did once even count as "lover"? She wasn't supposed to be curled up in some guy's arms seeking solace, not even if they were Mick's.

"Why did you join?" She could feel the change in him the moment she asked.

While they'd been talking, Mick's hold on her had eased off. Not that he'd moved, he'd just been holding her less hard. Now he pulled her back in tightly enough that she had to turn her head to the side if she didn't want her nose squished against his breastbone.

"It's okay, honey." She wanted to brush a hand down his back, tell him it would be okay and he didn't have to say anything. But her arms were trapped inside her sleeping bag up against her chest.

He took a short, sharp breath. Then a deep, longer one that almost squished her because he didn't ease off on his hold of her at all.

Unable to do anything, all she could do was wait.

He finally blew out the breath in a loud whoosh.

"We lost a boat. Our family lost a boat."

"Oh shit!" Her family had never lost a boat, but Gloucester as a community lost a boat every couple years. And when you lost a boat in the North Atlantic, you usually lost the crew too. It gutted the community. Just because the movie *The Perfect Storm* told the tale of the *Andrea Gail,* didn't mean the losses had stopped.

"The Coast Guard rescue team," Mick continued, "the peacetime version of the PJs we just trained with, flew out and dropped two swimmers. It was sixty and fifty."

Patty pictured a sixty-knot storm and fifty-foot waves. She'd been out working on a boat in that kind of weather a few times and it was sure as hell why she flew in warm and dry helicopters for a living.

"The two of them saved all eighteen of our people. One at a time, in that serious-as-hell weather."

"Wow." There was nothing else to say, it must have been an amazing feat.

"One of the swimmers didn't make it."

"'That others may live.'" Patty blinked hard against the tears. The swimmers and PJs shared that motto.

Most people, especially those inside the military, looked up to the Special Operations soldiers as heroes.

Inside Spec Ops, everyone, absolutely *everyone* looked up to the PJs. Each time one lost his life it was a blow that could be felt all through the community no matter what branch of the military your team technically belonged to. And a Coast Guard rescue swimmer was right up there with a PJ.

"I tried to go into the water for a career. I washed out, wasn't good enough. Air Force Pararescue has a ninety percent failure rate and I was part of it."

Patty tried to imagine Mick failing at anything he set out to do but couldn't quite manage it.

"Our family's lead boat, the one I was on, arrived just in time for us to watch the rescue swimmer get trapped in the wreckage and be dragged under. I couldn't get past that image during testing and it kept me from making the cut. Figured if I couldn't swim, then I'd deliver the swimmers."

"Helicopters," Patty whispered against his chest.

"Helicopters," Mick agreed.

And in that instant Patty knew that she was totally screwed. It had been hard enough stepping up to Mick's standard every day, even if she was a better woman for it.

But living up to the standard that came from that deep, how was she supposed to do that?

Well, she'd better find a way because she'd just learned that she was sure-as-shit in love with this man.

They didn't speak another word. Not when the generator finally ran out of fuel and the heat shut down. Not when the first chill crept back out of the concrete walls forcing them deeper into their bags.

They curled up tightly against each other through their separate sleeping bags and it was a long time before either of them slept.

"Five hundred miles," Major Napier announced as they gathered, each wearing heavy winter gear around the table in the Attu Island USCG rec room.

Mick looked around. They were a tribe of giant snowmen, even the women—but all in non-reflective Night Stalker black. A tribe of pitch-black snowpeople only to be found at the last outpost of the United States.

Pathetic! That was such a Patty-type of bizarre image, and now it was in his head. Mick wondered briefly if she was doing some kind of telepathic thing, showing him quite how strange her view of the world was.

Patty was so layered up it would have been impossible to tell her from Sofia except for the light skin and blue eyes that had tracked his every move. Something was different with her this morning, but Mick couldn't quite put his finger on it.

Maybe she was just cold. Once the generator had run out of the last dregs of fuel, the chill day had worn away at the building's minimal heat reserve. The indoor temperature had fallen to within a few degrees of outdoor ambient—five degrees below freezing. With the onset of evening it was getting colder.

"Five hundred miles and a three-hour flight to the next piece of land…and from here on, neither the land nor the sea will be friendly. Sunset is," Napier checked his watch, "right now." He said it as if it was setting to his command rather than Mother Nature's. With Major Napier, you never knew. Just maybe it had.

He handed around rendezvous coordinates, both primary and secondary in case the primary was occupied by Russians. If it was, the secondary had better be clear because the Little Birds would have to land soon either way.

"This is a hard stretch right out at the fuel limits for the Little Birds, but Commander Altman and I have determined that you are highly necessary assets for the operation's success. If you stumble upon an unfriendly asset and are unable to avoid it, you do not have the spare fuel to engage. Keep flying. The *Beatrix* and the *Carrie-Anne* will be sweeping along behind you and we'll deal with the problem. The ocean is calm tonight, at least by Bering Sea standards. Stay low, move fast, do *not* catch a wave." He aimed the last at Kenny, the Little Bird *Leeloo's* copilot, who was an avid surfer.

"Yes, sir," Kenny "Geek" Rumford, a serious electronics whiz in addition to being a California surfer boy, saluted with all the crispness of a parade ground recruit facing his first three-star general. "Too damn cold anyway, Major Napier, sir."

"Wimp!" His pilot, Malcolm "M&M" Manfred, punched him on the arm. "Life expectancy submerged in this shit is at least four or five minutes, Geek. Where's your board? I'll drop you off on the way."

"Left it stuck up your mama's—"

"Airborne in five," Napier cut them off.

In the chill of the lingering twilight, Mick and Patty preflighted the *Linda* and soon everyone was in the air.

Mick wanted to ask Patty what was the change, because her curious look hadn't dropped behind like Attu Island. And it hadn't changed when the warmth from the cabin heater let them at least unzip their heavy parkas.

But now was not the time.

Flying along at five thousand feet from Anchorage to Attu yesterday had been a casual enough operation.

Departing Attu at fifty feet over dark and formless waves was quite another. Fifty feet up at a hundred and fifty miles an hour placed them under half a second from a watery plunge into the depths.

Patty worked the passive listening devices out to their limits. Infrared, radio, active Russian radar that might be searching for intruders. There would be very few cargo vessels in these waters. Russian, Japanese, and American fisherman were probably the only ships that would be here, though they didn't want to run into any of them either. She'd also be monitoring the helo's well-being and—

"This is *Leeloo*. We appear to have an issue."

Mick felt his entire body flinch at the low-power radio transmission—the first break in an hour of silence. Only by careful training did his hands remain still.

"Go ahead," Napier replied

Mick could see the Chinook using its superior power to quickly close the three-mile gap they'd been maintaining.

"Negative fuel flow from starboard auxiliary tank. We can't fix it in the air. If I find out it was one of those Air Farce refueling dweebs, I'll —" M&M managed to cut himself off.

Mick glanced at Patty and she gave him a thumbs up. She'd already tested their tanks and they were good.

"Point of no return in fifteen minutes," M&M came back on the air but still sounded pissed beneath his professional calm. Without the fuel in that tank, they'd fall from the sky a hundred miles from the Russian coast. And in fifteen minutes they wouldn't have enough fuel to get back to Attu.

The *Beatrix* and the *Carrie-Anne* had mid-air refueling probes that could be extended out to guzzle several hundred gallons of Jet-A from a friendly tanker. The Little Birds weren't big enough to support that much extra equipment; they had to make the crossing on their own tanks plus the auxiliaries that had been mounted on their outer hard points. Except suddenly the *Leeloo* couldn't access one of those tanks.

Now came the tough call and it didn't take Napier more than a second. Damn but the man was impressive.

"*Leeloo.* Turn immediately for return to Attu Island."

The other Little Bird hesitated for a long moment, then slammed a vicious turn. Mick couldn't imagine how frustrated M&M and Geek were at this moment.

"*Beatrix* you will fly escort for the *Leeloo* only until a Pave Hawk from Shemya can take over from you." Because helicopters, especially broken ones, did not fly alone over vast reaches of freezing waters.

Mick could hear Danielle on the radio in the background. Napier and Danielle made such a seamless team that they might have been a single voice.

"A KC-135 tanker," Napier was relaying the information even as Danielle and Sofia were making it happen, "will meet *Beatrix* for a mid-air refuel and then escort the *Beatrix* back to our group while the Air Force Pave Hawk escorts *Leeloo* back to land. Rafe, your DAP Hawk has a strong speed advantage over our *Linda* and the *Carrie-Anne,* use it on the return. We want to arrive at the Russian coast as a unit."

And without the *Beatrix* for escort, the *Leeloo* would have no way to rejoin them. They had just gone from four aircraft to three for this mission; five to four if he counted Sofia's Avenger even now high above them.

Mick watched the tactical display as *Beatrix* fell in close behind the crippled Little Bird. It was said that a helicopter wasn't an aircraft, it was a million parts flying in close formation. Night Stalkers' operational availability exceeded all other outfits. The Air Force barely managed a seventy-five percent Mission Capable Rate across the hundred different models of aircraft they flew—the big bombers ran closer to fifty. The 160th SOAR held a full investigation into every single failure and managed to maintain an MCR percentage in the high nineties outside of scheduled maintenance, the best in the business. But it could never be a hundred and *Leeloo* had just drawn the short straw.

"Better to have poor fuel flow than a rotor falling off," Patty commented over the intercom.

Mick laughed a little, "Leave it to you to find the bright side, Gloucester."

"I'm just a bright-side kinda girl."

"Thought you were a woman."

She made a raspberry sound over the intercom loud enough that it echoed inside his helmet.

Mick kept pushing west. A hundred and fifty miles down, three hundred to go.

"I suddenly feel kinda naked out here," her voice barely a whisper this time.

"I've seen you naked. That's a very good thing." But Mick knew exactly what she meant. He kept glancing down at the tactical display and there was only the one other blip—Danielle's big Chinook, the *Carrie-Anne*, still hanging three miles back. It was a lot of empty ocean. Rolling waves that he couldn't see and shining stars that had slipped out unnoticed some time after they escaped Attu.

"A very good thing right back at you, Quinn."

And it was the first time her voice had sounded normal since they'd woken up this morning.

---

PATTY WAS STILL TRYING to make sense of what had happened. She and Mick had made love once, well, twice but in the same night and morning up on Mount Hayes. And that had been less than forty-eight hours ago.

She'd never gone soft in the head for any man, if she didn't count a multi-year teenage crush on *The Foo Fighters* drummer Taylor Hawkins. A crush she wasn't entirely sure she was over at thirty.

Plenty of men came to her for sex; it's what men thought women were for. Some even stuck around for comfort—as if they were the first to discover that women could be something more. But it wasn't an action Patty ever took in turn. One of Patty's very first memories were being afraid of the thunder and her father's cheery jibe of, "You gotta get your shit together, kid!"

She'd made a career out of having her shit together and not needing to go to someone else.

Being around Mick Quinn made her feel both worse and better. Worse that she'd gone to him seeking solace and better for having found it.

Now she rode her hands on their connected flight controls and could echo the immense skill that simply flowed from Mick. The connection was deep, not just through the controls, but also uncomfortable places that were near the heart she'd never really believed she had. Books and other women described such things, but it wasn't anything she believed in.

"I can take it if you need a break."

"You have control," Mick agreed. And just that easily she was Pilot-in-Command.

"After two years of flying with you, Quinn, you think I'd be used to being trusted." Patty paid careful attention to her flight level. Normally she'd see if she could fly a few feet lower than Mick had been—shave that edge just a little. Not this time. She even let herself float up another five feet so that she could concentrate a bit more on the bigger picture.

"Trust is a big issue for you, Gloucester?"

"At times." And lately, the challenge of entirely trusting herself, which she was *not* going to voice aloud. She had experience with men, but not with what she was feeling about this particular man. This was territory as foreign as the fast-approaching Kamchatka Peninsula.

"**K**amchatka Peninsula," Mick said as they slid along with their skids a dozen feet over the waves in between a pair of rocky headlands. Patty hadn't offered him back the controls and he'd been content to be their electronic lookout. Now it was starting to itch at him.

*Not a damn thing wrong with how she's flying, Mick. So let her do her thing.* The problem was that there wasn't much wrong with her at all that he could see. He had her up on a kind of pedestal at the moment and knew it, but he wasn't finding any easy way to knock her back off it either.

"Looks a hell of a lot like everyplace else we've been in the last few days."

Mick blinked to refocus his vision beyond his visor rather than onto the images and overlaid tactical display projected on the inside. He didn't see a thing…

Right. Middle of the night here versus on Attu or in Anchorage. They all were invisible in the darkness.

The flight had been eerily uneventful. No submarines lurking just awash on the ocean's surface. No coastal patrols. Not even any wandering fisherman working the edge of the continental shelf on the bitter October night.

The report of *Leeloo's* safe return to Eareckson Air Station only to discover a failed valve, and *Beatrix* catching back up with them a half hour from the Russian coast had been the only excitement. The tanker that had accompanied the *Beatrix* had cut and run, they didn't dare climb high enough to top off the *Carrie-Anne's* tanks this close to the Russian coast.

The three helicopters had purposely come ashore in a stretch of deep wilderness well clear of roads or habitation. The coast here was a mix of stark wilderness, abandoned fishing villages, and several defunct military bases. Satellite imagery said they had their choice of the last. Commander Altman had selected a particularly isolated former submarine base. It was defunct and stripped. Even with night vision, it was easy to see the wreckage of the abandonment.

Utilitarian two-story buildings, in depressingly blockish Russian style, were scattered about the narrow valley looking more like a child's spilled toys than a military operation. As they flew deeper into the cove, they had to veer to avoid a submarine's conning tower.

It gave Mick a jolt until he realized that the angle was wrong. It was an abandoned sub, run up on a sandbar, and tilted over at a crazed angle. If it was daylight, he'd bet it was covered in rust and bird poop, but there were some details that nighttime light amplification equipment simply didn't reveal.

Their night-vision gear did reveal the many missing windows in the sides of the buildings. Either a departing slash of vandalism by the workers and soldiers who had spent years confined on these desolate shores, or a raging typhoon. Perhaps both.

The overgrown grounds were scattered with heavy machinery, decaying trucks, and old submarine engines. The detritus of a small military population abruptly vacated stretched far and wide. There was no Congressional oversight committee which defined base closures with phased transition calendars. Here, someone had said "Get out. Now! Last boat leaves in an hour." And they had gotten.

Altman guided them to a small airfield, that and the inlet with its rotting dock were the only two accesses to the old base. No roads crossed the volcanic fields and rugged ridges to this remote location. Along the edge of the airfield there was a line of rusted out hangars that must have been used for protecting any visiting transport aircraft from the ice and snow.

There was no snow on the ground at sea level, yet. But it was the start of October in Kamchatka and he'd wager it would be here soon.

He just hoped that he and Patty were gone before it arrived. He'd had enough of ice and snow for a while.

They made short work of the hangar doors. They were jammed partway open, but a haul line attached to the Chinook and a good sharp yank ripped them off the building. Danielle dragged them off to one side before landing her big twin-rotor aircraft.

Their three helicopters and the very sad remains of an Antonov An-26 twin-prop transport plane filled the hangar. They would now be invisible to any casual flyover. Safely out of sight, their next priority was refueling the helos from the fuel bladder in the back of the *Carrie-Anne.* It took a hundred and twenty-five gallons out of the four thousand available for the *Linda* and made Mick feel much calmer. After they topped up the other two birds—which drank half of the remaining fuel at a gulp—they were ready to depart for a return flight to Attu on three minutes notice if they had to.

For a moment, he stood outside the hangar and looked up.

It was midnight and the stars were burning brightly in a pitch-black sky. With the nearest man-made light at least a hundred miles away, the Milky Way was a sparkling white streak across the sky like Mick had never seen. A fishing boat always had running lights and a helicopter always returned to base at night—if they were overseas in a war zone it was a very brightly lit base for security reasons. Even camping out had a campfire, here they didn't dare to light one.

Patty slid up beside him. He knew it was her just from her footsteps rustling against the dry grass punching up through the pavement.

"Hey, Gloucester." Mick reached out an arm and Patty leaned in against him. "Here. I stole this for you." He pulled the orange-and-gold knit hat with ear flaps and a pom-pom out of his pocket and tugged it down over her head.

"You stole from the PJs?" Patty sounded both terribly pleased and a bit horrified.

"No, just from the quartermaster. And I might have asked rather than stolen it."

"That was really sweet of you, Mick. Are you sure you're the Mick Quinn I've been flying with all this time? Considerate? Thoughtful? Sexy? Doesn't sound like you, does it?"

Mick had always thought sexy is what women were, not men. Like beautiful versus handsome. Before she could continue her rolling dialog he kissed her on a fuzzy temple and whispered, "Look up."

"Whoa!" Patty's voice was soft and he could feel her head tracking skyward until the back of it rested against his shoulder and the pom-pom stuck in his ear.

At least there was something in this universe that could silence Patty O'Donoghue's words.

"Man oh man, if you ever wanted a lesson in how insignificant all our little worries are. Damn!"

Okay, not so much with the robbed-of-speech. In the dark, bundled up like two Michelin tire people, he leaned in to take advantage of her head on his shoulder.

The kiss she offered was sweetly tender, but it didn't stay that way for long. Patty attacked him as if they were lying together naked rather than exposed only from chin to forehead. A hand reached back to grab his butt and squeeze hard.

With the arm around her shoulders, he kept her turned sideways to him so that he could slip his other hand down her front. And even though he couldn't feel her shape through all the layers, he could certainly recall how her breasts felt as he stroked his gloved hand over them.

Her own hand, the one not still clamped on his butt, had been on his chest. Now it was moving downward and in a moment they were going to be having sex while fully clothed in the middle of a defunct Russian military base.

Mick tested the thought and decided that he was okay with that.

Patty must have agreed, because her breast was pressing against his hand as hard as she was pressing into their kiss.

"Ahem…"

They both froze at the sound of a woman clearing her throat from less than ten feet away.

"Perhaps this is not the appropriate moment," Nikita the DEVGRU SEAL. "But I should inform you that we do have devices called night-vision goggles. Perhaps you have heard of them. They allow us to see quite clearly what is happening, even in deep darkness. Especially when bodies are producing significant heat in relation to their back-grounds. I should also mention that everyone else already has theirs."

"I think," Patty said to him drily, "since that's far and away the most words she's ever spoken at any one time, perhaps we should believe her."

"We could always test that theory," Mick whispered into her ear and began moving his hand again, the one that had been frozen in place halfway between breast and waist.

Patty punched him right in the gut to stop him.

"Cut that out, you two." Napier's voice sounded out of the dark-ness. He sounded amused rather than pissed, which meant any courts-martial weren't going to happen tonight.

He and Patty let go of each other.

"Meeting time." Nikita handed each of them a set of night-vision goggles and then led them into the back of the even darker hangar.

---

THE CREW WAS GATHERED around in a loose circle. Two SEALs, four DAP Hawk crew, five from the Chinook, and Mick and herself.

"Lucky thirteen again," she remarked.

"Absotively!" Mick responded cheerily.

"Hey, that's *my* word."

Napier didn't make a sound that she could tell, but Patty's atten-tion was drawn his way somehow. In the green world of night vision, with an NVG rig covering half his face, he managed to look both stern and disgusted at their interruptions.

"Well, it is, Major," Patty refused to be cowed. "Where do I file a complaint? Made up word. One off. Theft with full knowledge, nefarious intent, and malice aforethought. I'll come up with sundry other charges later." In retrospect, thinking of courts-martial for conjugal relations between members of different ranks on the same team, she sort of wished she hadn't said the last bit.

Napier shifted to face Mick. Patty couldn't read the next expression, but Mick nodded in reply. She'd have to remember to ask later… or maybe she didn't want to know. If Napier had been asking Mick if he was sure that he wanted to be with a lunatic like Patty, and then Mick had confirmed his choice, that meant…

His choice? That sounded way more permanent than a tumble in a tent and a grope at an abandoned Russian submarine base. It was way too close to that "loving him" thought she'd had the other night in what must have been a delusional moment. Nope. Decision made. No way in hell was Patty going to ask either man what they were talking about without actually talking.

Instead, she'd ask Danielle.

But if she didn't like that answer either, then she'd be—not to put too fine a point on it—totally fucked. And then—

"Who here knows fishing boats?" Altman's quiet voice sliced off her thoughts.

"Fishing boats?" Patty blinked in surprise and aimed her NVGs at him.

"I do," Mick spoke up.

"No you don't, Quinn." She turned back to Altman. "He knows crabbing boats. Way not the same thing. *I* know fishing boats—sixth generation Gloucesterman."

"I thought you were a woman. Imagine my surpri—" Mick's voice upticked sharply when she landed her elbow in his gut.

"But I thought we were here to look at drones," she refused to react to Mick's happy chuckle. Next time she'd chop him into bait and feed him to the sharks.

"Sport fishing. Dad charters out of Key West," Drake "Mozart" Roman, the Chinook's ramp gunner, spoke up.

Patty scoffed at him, but not too hard. She liked Drake Roman. Besides, Patty herself had tagged him as Mozart. Roman led her to Greek which lead her to frat house and his complete lack of resemblance to Tom Hulce in *Animal House* (the Greek frat house comedy) who had gone on to play Mozart in *Amadeus.* She was pretty proud of that bit of reasoning even if he had refused to take up the piano no matter how often she asked him to. Maybe if she asked him to try the harpsichord…

Of course, she was the only one who called him Mozart, especially after she'd explained her reasoning. Everyone else—after declaring she was *psychotically convolutional*—went from Drake to Duck to Duck-man, with a total lack of imagination. How lame was that?

"Next question is who here speaks Russian?" Altman cut back in.

"Russian fishing boats?" Patty said with as much disgust as possible. She didn't speak a damned word of it.

Nikita and Connie raised their hands. And Mick.

"Since when do you speak Russian?"

"Since Uncle Borya jumped ship in Kodiak and married Aunt Verna when I was a little boy. Verna and I learned Russian faster than he learned English, proper *fisheryman* Russian that would have had Mama soaping out my mouth if she'd understood a word. He still has an accent as deep as his hooks *still* reach. That side of the family long-lines tuna, so I do know fishing as well."

How much didn't she know about Mick? After two-plus years flying together, he shouldn't be able to surprise her…yet he constantly did. Well, it wasn't right that he knew a language that she didn't.

"That does it. From now on sex is only in Russian until I learn it." Then she looked slowly around the circle.

Everyone was looking right at her.

"Please tell me that I didn't say that out loud." And she desperately hoped that her face didn't grow brighter in infrared with all of the heat rushing to her cheeks.

"You're glowing there, Gloucester."

"Eat tuna guts, Quinn. I've changed my mind; no more sex for you. Ever!" He didn't look worried; Quinn was a smart man. She couldn't wait to jump him and receive her first Russian lesson. Time to bite the bullet. She turned to face Major Napier. A deep breath to calm her nerves.

"Wait! No!" Mick held up his hands to protest as if he could read her mind. Probably could. And the fact that he was probably right didn't stop her.

"Care to explain why you haven't court-martialed us yet? While you're at it, could you also explain why if plural is courts-martial, the past tense isn't courted-martial? I'm tired of walking on goddamn pins and needles around my commanding officer, sir."

"Gotta admit, Pete," Commander Altman spoke up. "I been wondering the same thing myself. Your unit. I figure you know what you're doing. But I am finding myself a bit curious. Why is it? You can tell by their goofy smiles they've earned it. Didn't take night vision to pick up on what a blind man could see."

"No."

"No?"

"No," Napier repeated calmly. "I'm not willing to explain my reasons. That's an end to it."

Patty opened her mouth, then closed it again. You didn't argue with a commanding officer, even when he wasn't making sense. *Especially* when he wasn't making sense. Was it some part of West Point training that taught them to play their cards close and confuse the crap out of their people? Based on experience, she'd have to say *yes* to that.

"At first light, you two and Drake will join Altman, Nikita, and Connie on a small fishing expedition. If your boat is stopped, you—" Napier aimed a gloved finger at her chest as if he was going to stab her with it, "—will keep your mouth shut. You will be the idiot girl on the boat who is too mentally deficient to speak."

"Yes, sir," she managed it without sounding too surly.

"First light is in six hours," Napier continued. "I suggest that you spend at least five of it asleep. Dismissed." Then Napier ended the conversation by turning on his heel and walking away.

"Fishing?" Patty turned to Luke Altman because her frustration still needed a target. "You can't fish for drones."

"Oh, but you can." His grin looked positively evil. Of course, being six-foot-four and one of the best warriors in the entire US military made him all the more daunting.

"Humph!" was all she offered him.

"What was that, Chief Warrant?"

"Humph, sir!"

He beamed at her and strode away.

Patty headed over to the *Linda* to fetch her bedroll.

"You feeling okay?" Mick was right at her elbow.

"Sure, why?"

"You didn't keep needling Altman."

"I've got *some* survival instincts, Quinn."

They lay down pads and sleeping bags side by side on the concrete near the *Linda*. They crawled in fast and still mostly clothed. She pulled the bag over her head until some semblance of warmth accumulated inside; the Russian night was bitter. She wanted to talk to Mick...and she didn't. There was definitely something going on here, and she'd wager it was good, if life would just ease off full throttle long enough for her to catch a breath. After two years in Spec Ops, she knew that wasn't going to happen any time soon.

Her hesitancy came from the same place it did before: the question *what if this was real?*

And the only reason she wasn't tackling it was...cowardice. Patty didn't believe in cowardice. People believed in God or government or that cottage cheese wasn't totally disgusting as a diet food. She believed in facing her problems head on.

She stuck her head out of her sleeping bag. The cold slapped her despite the stolen wool hat. *Damn!* More evidence that Mick was decent and thoughtful. More proof that she really was gone on the man. She was totally charmed and Patty O'Donoghue didn't get charmed by people, especially not by men people.

"You gotta cut that out, Mick. You're spoiling me."

He didn't answer.

"Mick?"

His breathing didn't shift. It was exactly like when she'd been listening to it back in Anchorage two nights ago, unable to sleep next to him despite her exhaustion. He'd been zonked out, leaving her wide awake, because he made her feel so damn…happy.

Shit!

# CHAPTER 15

"If this is a typical Russian fishing boat, I feel bad for the Russian fisherymen. Let me tell you, I wouldn't want to go out fisherying in this."

Mick couldn't agree with Patty more. When they'd flown in last night and he'd spotted the craft, he'd assumed it was a wreck left to sink beside the rotten dock when the base was abandoned. Now that he was aboard her, he saw no reason to revise that initial assessment, except that she was actually afloat and showed recent usage. She was sixty feet of sad.

He. Russians called their boats by the male gender.

He was clinker-built, with overlapping boards stuffed with caulk to keep her—him—sealed. Sixty long, fifteen feet wide on the beam, he had a wheelhouse forward and a terribly cluttered main deck. The crane, winches, and net labeled him as a purse seiner. Which Patty was right about; he'd have a hard time running this rig. The condition labeled the boat as old and very, very tired.

"Boat needs a name. Can't go out on a boat without a name. Terrible luck," Patty declared.

Mick edged down the dock, stepping carefully over several missing boards until he could see the stern. A name had once been

298

painted there, but it had long since peeled away leaving only a suggestion of letters and no hints at all of former glory.

"Call it, Gloucester," he shouted over to where she glared down at the boat.

"I hereby dub thee..." Patty looked up at the sky and he followed where she tracked.

The stars were gone and the air was gray with the dawn and then she turned to the volcano towering above the base. Mount Shiveluch rose eleven thousand feet in a cone of ash-covered snow. A cloud of thick smoke, gray with ash, punched up twice the height of the mountain.

"...*Graynose*," Patty declared.

"*Graynose?*" No one else got the reference.

But Mick did, "You are so from Gloucester."

"I keep telling everyone that," Patty complained.

Mick didn't bother pointing out that if she didn't protest about being called "Boston" so much, she'd have long ago won the war on what she wanted to be called.

"The *Bluenose*," Mick explained for everyone else's benefit when it was clear that Patty considered doing so to be beneath her dignity. How the woman thought she could wear dignity and a bright orange hat with a pom-pom he didn't know. "It was the greatest of the Grand Banks fishing sailboats. And I won't offend Patty by pointing out that she was Canadian."

"*Graynose* because this is fucking Russia after all and everything is so goddamn gray," Patty just had to get her two cents in about how clever she was. Which was true, so it worked on her rather than coming across as bragging.

There was fuel aboard and several sets of very authentic smelling clothing. Patty pulled hers on with a vague grimace that might have more to do with memories than the current stink.

Altman and Nikita were as expressionless as ever while they dressed. *Get it done and move on.* Drake rolled his eyes and then dragged on the foul gear with a practiced hand. Mick helped Connie into hers, the short brunette clearly knew nothing at all about boats, not even how to wear the gear that went with them. She was a quiet woman who never complained but was so out of her element here. It was almost like taking poor Sofia up onto Mount Hayes.

"Do you really need to be here?" He turned to Altman. "Does she need to be here?"

"Best mechanic we've got and is fluent in Russian," Altman pointed his finger at her as if Connie was an exhibit on display, not a person. "Cranky old fishing boat—with an engine that I'm promised runs, but who knows how well—that was built and serviced in Russia." He turned back to loading several duffle bags of gear into the boat.

The conversation was done, apparently.

Mick shrugged an apology to Connie. It was hard to tell what her reaction was. No answering shrug of friendly appreciation for his attempt. No flinch at being treated like an asset on a checklist.

Instead, despite being the one least familiar with boats, she moved into the wheelhouse first and through the salt- and grime-smeared windows he could see her inspecting the controls. In moments, the big engine thudded to life and spewed a cloud of black diesel out the smoke stack that stuck up beside the mangy structure. When it didn't settle as it warmed, Connie shut it down and disappeared below. About ten minutes later she returned and restarted the diesel. It had smoothed out and the black cloud shifted to a clear, mostly, plume of heat that merely shimmered the air.

She stepped out of the cramped wheelhouse and onto the deck, glanced at the stack and nodded to herself. Then she faced Altman.

"I left it slightly out of tune. I think that having a truly smooth-running engine on a boat of this age might appear as an anomaly even if there isn't a single thing wrong with Russian heavy engineering. If you want to actually run out the nets and do any fishing to look authentic, I'll need half an hour to rebuild the winch."

"Do it," Altman said and she turned to the task. Altman looked at Mick a little round-eyed. "I'd heard she was good?" He made it a question.

"Scary good," Mick agreed. "If you hang with us more, you'll find out just how good."

"It's an idea." Before Mick could ask what he meant, Altman tipped his head toward Patty. "What about her?"

Mick had been watching Patty move about the boat. She moved without question or hesitation, cleaning things up automatically as she went. Boat hooks slammed into clips. A corner of a net lifted up and practiced eyes scanning its condition before dropping it back to the deck with disgust. All so smoothly that most of it wasn't even conscious. No one could fake that kind of competency.

"This is her space. Let her run with it."

Altman nodded. Mick's word was good enough. Couldn't Altman see how familiar she was with such craft? No, he was a Special Operations SEAL who could drive anything from a diver delivery vehicle—the small subs used by SEALs for underwater infiltration—probably up to a destroyer. But he wasn't a commercial fisherman.

"O'Donoghue," Altman called to her. "Take us out."

"You bet, boss. What would I be called in Russian?"

"*Ya bol' v zadnitse!*"

"*Ya bol' v zadnitse,*" she repeated dutifully, even hitting the accents well. She had a good ear.

Mick tried to stop his laugh, but he couldn't get control of it. Connie and Nikita were smiling but holding their mirth in by studiously inspecting the *Graynose*. Drake didn't speak Russian, so he'd missed the joke.

Which left a very irritated looking Patty glaring right at him.

"What?"

"Never trust a SEAL," Mick pointed at Altman, doing what he could to deflect her attention, but it wasn't working.

"What's so goddamn funny?"

Mick would have to get Altman back for this later; he was enjoying himself far too much.

"Quinn?" Her tone was only the leading edge of an "Irish Patty" threat level.

"Your first lesson in Russian," he tried to dodge one last time.

"Is…?"

No way out. "How to tell someone that you're a pain in the ass."

She huffed out a breath that would have stirred her bangs if she'd had any. "Oh, like that would be a surprise to anyone." Then she turned back to the task of getting underway.

Mick knew he was screwed. Patty wouldn't take it out on a Team 6 SEAL; she'd find her retribution on a much more accessible target. Himself.

---

PATTY SHOWED Mick and Drake how to run a purse seine fishing net. Nikita picked it up quickly as well. Altman was hopeless which made her feel somewhat better. Always nice to find at least one thing a superhero couldn't do. Kryptonite for Superman, purse seining for Mr. SuperSEAL.

Then they ran their first haul and actually pulled up a load of fish. Most swam free due to poor technique—that she of course razzed them about—but they still pulled up a couple hundred pounds of salmon. She showed them how to slip the bottom wire so that the bottom of the "purse" didn't close and the fish could swim free.

Some fish, being too stupid to live, were caught despite the crew's worst efforts and she had them thrown into one of the hold tanks. Altman had wanted to throw them back overboard. Patty pointed out that being seen having a lousy fishing day wouldn't raise an eyebrow; being seen dumping a catch would attract far too much attention.

Connie ignored the whole operation once she saw how it worked and continued moving around the boat servicing various systems.

"Careful, Connie," Patty called out to her on another of her passes through the wheelhouse. "You're going to fix the boat so much that the real owner won't know what to do with it."

"This boat is hurting and, worse, it isn't its fault. I can't *not* fix it."

"Makes sense." Patty had taken the wheel as a form of protection, it kept her from doing the cold and ugly scut work of fishing. And it kept her marginally warmer in the semi-enclosed cabin. But she couldn't move around much and the damp cold was really settling in.

She tried to think of something to talk to Connie Davis about to distract herself from the mundane job of "fishing" their way down the coast toward the coordinates Altman had asked for. But she couldn't. Connie spoke so seldom and—

"You have a problem."

"I have about a hundred," Patty sighed and then startled when she realized that for the first time in their acquaintance Connie had initiated the conversation.

"That's the problem. The way to solve them is to address them one at a time. I can't fix the boat, but I can tune an engine, repair a winch, and tighten a linkage. You see it as a fixed boat; I perceive the individual elements of a mechanical system being consecutively refined."

"Meaning that I should stop trying to fight a hundred battles on a dozen fronts and..." Patty reached for it but could seem to land the thought.

"And fly the route. You are an exceptional Little Bird pilot and an even more exceptional copilot."

"Good enough to make SOAR anyway."

"No!" Connie spoke as vehemently as Patty had ever seen her. "You only see that because you fly with Mick Quinn who is as far above nominal as Trisha and Claudia are in the 5th Battalion D Company. That's three women and one man I've met who are the best Little Bird pilots flying anywhere in the 160th SOAR. Mick Quinn is the one who is able to live up to *our* standards, not the other way around."

Patty felt like the slow child in school who had just been spanked.

"You fly for the 5E," Connie continued in a tone that was passionate by Connie standards. "A SOAR company specifically assembled around our skills—which includes you. A Team 6 SEAL Commander has put you in charge of delivering him where he needs to go. Own it." The last was a command.

"Right. All I have to be is the perfect copilot, gunner, fisher, and mountain climber."

"Don't forget lover."

"Right. And— Hey!" Patty glared at her.

Connie smiled broadly, an unusual event in itself.

"That was tricky."

"I'm a Night Stalker."

With those simple words Connie spoke an absolute truth. Unlike Patty, she hadn't twisted it into a joke with "So sue me" or something similar. From Connie it was a bald statement of fact. And she was right.

Patty had been fighting to be what she already was. What a waste of energy was that!

Then she focused past Connie and watched Mick "The Mighty" Quinn working the nets on a Russian fishing seiner. He'd gotten the others working in an easy rhythm that looked authentic even to her trained eye, except that they weren't catching anything in some of the richest fishing grounds she'd ever seen.

Had she caught something? Mick Quinn had bedded her and collected his manly "prize." But rather than acting as if he'd gotten all he wanted and was now done with her, he was treating her as if he wanted even more.

That worked, because so did she.

"Connie, could you take the helm for a minute?"

"That would be a good idea, especially if we don't want to ram that reef."

Patty twisted around to look back out the front windows. They'd left them grimy and smeared, again because they didn't want the boat to look too clean. Despite that, she'd have been able to see breakers to mark a reef, if there were any to be seen. A look down at the ragged chart that had been left for them showed a broad reef not half a kilometer ahead.

She corrected their course to swing well clear of that. Connie couldn't have seen the chart from where she stood, so how—

"Eidetic memory," Connie explained with a sigh. "I looked at the chart the first time I started the engine."

That explained a lot about the woman's strangeness. Connie could tell you how many times you'd...

And Patty saw the resigned expression on Connie's face. The woman was decidedly odd—SOAR's quiet mechanical genius—and it was clear that she now expected Patty to have any of seven different cataloged reactions that Connie was used to getting. So, Patty would do something different.

"Thanks. Guess I'm not the only one who belongs in the 5E. You have the helm. I have a man to go terrorize. I'll be right back."

Connie blinked once, then a second time in slow surprise. Then that smile cracked open again, "Terrorize a couple for me."

"Deal, sister." They traded high fives and Patty strolled out onto the deck.

# CHAPTER 16

"There," Nikita indicated with a nod.

Her observation sent Altman moving into the wheelhouse and retrieving his high-power scope. Then he hunkered down behind the gunwale to look out.

Mick followed the sight line but didn't see anything out of the ordinary. Kamchatka had started out impossibly foreign. Black sand beaches, backed by grasslands and forests turned autumn shades. Like Alaska, the landscape was harsh enough that there wasn't a wide variety of species, but the ones that survived were dramatic. He recognized the dusty, dark green of spruce, the yellow-gold of larch, and the brilliance of white-barked birch.

Beyond them, rising in a jagged line of sentinels, volcano after volcano defined the horizon. These weren't the broad lava domes of Hawaii or the grand old mountains of the Pacific Northwest. Kamchatka bred its volcanoes like a children's drawing: steep, up past a mile tall, with circular calderas at the top. And now, most of them were coated well down their sides with thick snow. The lower limits of the snow lurked only a few hundred feet above sea level. Another few weeks and it would reach right down to the beaches.

Here and there in the jagged chain, one spewed out a long column of white steam. Of the ones he'd seen so far, only Mount Shiveluch, the volcano perched above the abandoned sub base, was violently active. Even here, thirty miles south, its bold head and massive ash plume marked the sky.

They hadn't passed a single other craft in the first two hours of work. In the third hour, they'd passed three, one close enough to exchange a wave. As far as he could tell, the real fishermen hadn't even wasted the energy of lifting a set of binoculars to inspect their craft.

Even in that short amount of time, he'd grown accustomed to the stark scenery. What had Nikita seen that sent Altman into the cabin to pull out a high-power scope? Finally Mick could pick out the faintest glint of white on the shore. Even then, only out of the corner of his eye when they were riding over a wave crest. SEALs were damned impressive to have spotted the tiny anomaly.

Mick's hands were raw and sore from the freezing cold saltwater, but the feeling was an old and familiar friend. A part of him did miss being out on the ocean, though he'd have preferred a better prepared vessel. The *Graynose* had no luxuries such as life preservers or even an emergency radio. They had their own satellite radios and the Chinook was standing by in case they needed a scramble rescue. But the hull was sound and the weather mild. All in all, a beautiful morning to be out fishing.

Though it hurt him every time he slipped the purse wire and let the catch swim free. His fisheryman blood didn't approve.

Fisheryman. Gods but Patty cracked him up.

As if he'd evoked her by just thinking about her, Patty strode out onto the deck. Hands rammed deep into her pockets, she squinted up at the sky, then back at him. She dodged piles of netting and the occasional fish as she worked her way back to him at the stern rail. She stopped a step from him.

"How can a woman so damn beautiful also be so damn cute?" Mick flicked a finger against her pom-pom.

"Thought I was a girl."

"No. The person who I crawled into a double sleeping bag with was a hundred percent woman."

Her brilliant blue eyes inspected him carefully. No poor Russian fisherman would wear mirrored Ray Ban aviator sunglasses, so they'd all agreed to abandon their standard eyewear, even if it meant squinting most of the time. So, he could see her beautiful blue eyes, but he'd wager the squint had nothing to do with the brightness of the day.

"We've got a problem."

"Damn straight. No time for sex, barely enough to talk."

Again, that narrowed inspection.

"What are you thinking, Gloucester?" Did they really *have* a problem and he was missing something.

"That's not the problem."

"Are you going to tell me? Or do I just have to stand here and admire how amazing you look in that hat with a secret Russian drone base spread out behind you?"

"Really? Where?" She spun away from him to look off to starboard.

Mick tipped his head up to look at the sky. The woman was going to drive him mad.

And high above him, he saw a tiny flash of silver, little more than a sun flash.

Mick did his best to casually walk over to Altman with his scope and drag an oily tarp over him.

"What?" His voice was muffled, but he didn't try to shed the covering.

"Company. About five o'clock, very high." Under cover of the tarp, Altman shifted so that only the tip of his scope was visible as he turned it upward.

"Notify Sofia," the tarp called out to him. "Tell her that she has an Orlan-10 medium drone and she needs to stay clear."

"Get the nets back out," Mick moved back to the crew. "You too," he told Patty.

"What the hell, Mick? I—" then she caught his tone. In that

moment the puzzled woman was gone and the soldier was in her place. That didn't mean he couldn't tease her anyway.

"I need to get your pretty ass fishing. We've got surveillance. No!" He grabbed her earflaps to keep her head in place. "Do not look up. Fish." He turned her around and shoved her toward the job, hopefully as one man might shove another—he doubted that slim redheads were standard fare on a Kamchatka fishing boat. There was no way to tell if they were under observation or not, but it was better to be safe.

He went to the wheelhouse.

"I've already called her," Connie was tucking away a satellite radio. "I only dared risk a single, encrypted squirt transmission. I didn't want them spotting us if they have a radio frequency package aboard. She reported back that she is staying another three miles above it and the Orlan is only designed to look down. She's loaded with four Hellfire missiles just in case there are any issues."

"Good. Thanks," Mick started to turn back for the deck.

"Are you the Captain?"

He looked back at her. "I guess. As much as anyone."

"Okay. Then do you want to know about the Stenka-class patrol boat that's coming our way, or should I keep that to myself?"

Mick hesitated for a moment, hoping it was more of a joke than it sounded. When Connie didn't offer anything else, he struggled to keep his voice as calm and casual as she did. This was apparently her idea of high humor and he didn't want to spoil it for her.

"Stenka?"

"Two hundred-ton category. Thirty-seven meters long, 1960s vintage. They were passed from their Navy to the Russian Coast Guard. A couple torpedo tubes and a trio of machine guns big enough to make short work of the *Graynose*."

"O-kay." Of course Connie Davis would have all of those details on tap. "Anything else?"

"Sonar says that we're coming up on a rich patch of fish."

The depth-and-fish finder was the only electronic device on the boat that worked, but he didn't care about fish at the moment.

"Can you estimate the crew size?"

"It's designed for a complement of thirty-two to thirty-four, but with the staffing problems the Russian Navy is having, especially in the Pacific fleet, I'd say twenty-six. An awful lot of fish here."

He was not going to ask why twenty-six and not one number up or down. He'd learned not to ask Connie questions like that because she would always tell you why.

He ignored the fish comment, and also Nikita's sniper rifle tucked in a corner of the wheelhouse. One spray from a deck gun and the best sniper in the world couldn't save them.

Back on deck he spotted the patrol boat standing out from shore. It was heading straight for them. He tried to remember. Had they seen another fishing vessel in the area? He didn't think so. The other southbound boat they'd passed had been standing out to sea, apparently to circle wide around this heavily patrolled no-entry zone.

He'd need something to allay their suspicions. He needed…

"Thanks, Connie," he called back toward the wheelhouse. He didn't pause to hear if she replied.

"Get that net out," he shouted. "Way out. Gloucester!"

"Yo!" Patty moved fast.

"Show me that you know what the hell you've been talking about. You have ten minutes to fill that net. I want to be knee-deep in fish in fifteen."

Even before he finished speaking, she had the net spilling overboard in a long slide that looked as liquid as the water it was plunging down into.

"Altman, you keep your ass hidden."

"Some weapons would be handy now," the tarp replied. Gods, he was becoming as unhinged as O'Donoghue.

"Nope. Not a shot! If you're wearing one, make sure it stays hidden."

"One?" The tarp scoffed.

Mick ignored him.

"C'mon, comrades. Get me some fish!" He joined Drake at the rail, watching the purseline wire to make sure it didn't snag as the net continued to run out.

It felt forever and a month before Patty shouted a hold on the net. Nikita eased down the brake on the net spool until it finally stopped spilling overboard.

---

Using hand signals, Patty guided Connie in a wide circle back to the leading edge of the net. There she gathered up the lead buoy and with it the other end of the purseline.

Please God, let there be fish here.

# CHAPTER 17

She and Nikita dragged it to the pursewinch and hit the winch hard. Connie had totally rocked fixing it—which Patty had thought was a pointless exercise at the time. They might be a spy boat, but they really needed to look like a Russian fishing trawler. She liked the turnabout was fair play, using a Russian seiner to spy on the Russians.

She didn't know what Mick's urgency was, but there was no mistaking the tone of command he exercised so rarely. It was a new side of him, captain of the vessel and looked damn good on him.

The winch roared to life dragging the two ends of the wire aboard and pulling together the bottom edges of the net so that this time the fish couldn't sound downward and escape. With a groan from the old ship, the rings came aboard and the purse was closed.

Patty leaned over the gunwale to stare down into the net. *You wanted fish, Quinn, boy-oh-boy did I get you fish.* The net teemed with Pacific salmon, in this season all Coho silvers with some smaller Arctic char mixed in.

The *Graynose* had no vacuum for emptying the net. Brailing up fish in a smaller net was a slow process and Mick sounded like he was in a big hurry.

Was it the Russian drone somewhere overhead? She'd been told not to look up, so she hadn't. But why would a high-flying drone suddenly have him so on edge? That's when she spotted it. On the water, a flash of light caught her attention—a boat. A big one was heading their way. It was the size of factory ship, come to collect their catch.

It was gray, just like everything in Russia. Then she spotted the diagonal stripes of color on the sides—the white, blue, and red of the Russian flag. Russian Coast Guard. Instead of cranes to crossload fish, it had…deck guns.

She didn't know the plan yet, but if Mick said he needed the *Graynose's* deck awash in fish, she'd give it to him.

Instead of dipping the fish out of the big purse with a smaller net, she grabbed a boat hook and snagged the net as far out as she could. "Loop a line there," she yanked it up for Drake.

Mick and Nikita were doing the same thing on the other side.

She met Mick at the main winch with the newly attached lines.

"Let's find out just how good Connie is. This trick can fry a winch that's in factory-new condition, never mind an old workhorse like this one." She slapped the lines in place and hit the winch throttle.

The entire boat groaned under the load as the winch tried to haul the first third of the loaded net aboard.

"Yank the fish out onto the deck, as fast as you can," she shouted.

Mick and the others rushed to the rail and began pulling twenty- and thirty-pound fish aboard by their tails. It was a race to unload the leading edge of the net fast enough that the overloaded net didn't burn out the winch. Her muscles were soon burning from the work-out. If they still had fish like this in the Atlantic maybe she'd still be fishing there. The entire boat was shuddering, but the winch continued working.

Connie idled the boat slowly backward, easing the pressure slightly. A dangerous maneuver that could run the prop right into the net and leave them adrift with a snarled prop and a destroyed net.

Patty almost called her off, then she saw just how big the patrol boat was. It was deceptive. She'd thought it was smaller and closer, but it kept coming until it loomed large on the horizon.

"Russian only now, comrades," Mick called out. "Patty, keep your mouth shut. Connie too. Your accent is Muscovite, something I'd rather not have to explain."

*Fine!* Though she kept the thought to herself. She was going to learn Russian so fast, that she'd make Comrade Quinn's head spin.

"And don't use the word *comrade* whatever you do. It really pisses off the new Russians."

So much for that. Though since she didn't even know the Russian word for comrade, it wouldn't make any difference—unless of course it was "comrade". She went on with hauling fish aboard and keeping her mouth shut.

The deck was already a snarl of tangled net and hazardous with a thick slippery layer of fish. They snagged the next section of the net and once again fed it into the winch. It moaned in agony, but it ground the net aboard. They all grabbed and dragged fish out of the net until they had to shake out their arms every now and then just to keep them functioning.

A PA system blared out so loudly in Russian that she almost leapt out of her boots. While she'd been hustling, the patrol boat had pulled up alongside. It was twice the height and three times the length of the *Graynose.*

And it was commanded by an idiot.

Even as she had the thought, a rolling wave slipped under the fishing boat's keel and tipped her steeply over to starboard. Her crane on that side, unused at the moment, scraped a long gash right through the Russian-flag paint colors down to bare metal. Impressively the crane held, but it gave Mick an excuse to start spewing out what Patty could only assume was loads of his Uncle's invective.

She couldn't look away from Mick in that moment, as he stood on a wreck of a fishing boat chewing out the Russian Coast Guard in their own tongue.

It sounded damned sexy and she couldn't wait for her first private lesson.

As she turned back to her work, she wondered what *suka blyad* meant. Mick made it sound very nasty.

---

"IF YOU BREAK MY CRANE, you buy me brand new one, you bitch motherfucker!" *Suka blyad* was a fixture of Uncle Borya's vocabulary that Aunt Verna had never been able to purge. Russians used it as casually as Patty O'Donoghue used *shit.*

"What do you mean where's Uri?" Mick hoped that was the guy who had rented the boat to the US military. "Do you see him here? Uri is sick. We are fishing for him. But his gear keeps breaking." Mick kicked the brailing winch and blessed Patty for not using it even though Connie had fixed it, because he definitely needed something to kick.

"Now go away, we're busy." He did his best to ignore the line of men at the ship's railing, eight of them with rifles pointed down at him and his crew.

"You are fishing in a military restricted zone," the PA roared. "This is a closed town. You are not permitted here."

"I am just an honest Russian trying to make a living. I am not some poacher," which he knew was a huge problem throughout Kamchatka. "Now *otva 'li.*" Of course there wasn't a chance that the guy was going to fuck off, but Mick could always hope.

He made a show of looking around the deck and then shouting, "Where's that drunken son-of-a-bitch Luka?"

Nikita hid a snort of laughter poorly and Drake didn't understand. Patty was busy wrestling with a fish that was as big as she was—an out-of-season Chinook monster that had clearly fallen in with the wrong crowd to be swimming with silvers. Patty and the ninety-pound fish made a very cute image, but he'd have to think about cute later...after they'd gotten out of this alive.

Nikita managed to remain deadpan as she pointed toward the rumpled tarp in the corner of the deck. Giving up her boss pretty easily. He'd have to remember to tease Altman about the loyalty of SEALs; again, hopefully later.

He stalked over to the tarp. Along the way he grabbed two-feet of gorgeous silver salmon that had spent its last gasp. He yanked back the tarp exposing Altman curled up as if asleep. The scope he'd been using was stashed under a coil of rope.

Mick slapped Altman's shoulder hard with the salmon, thoroughly enjoying himself. "You useless drunk. Next time, I'm putting you in the net with the stupid fish. Go help."

Altman made a show of staggering to his feet. He mumbled something very guttural about how Mick would rather screw a fish than Patty, grinned wickedly, and shuffled over to help the others drag aboard the thrashing fish.

"You must leave!"

As Mick had hoped, the captain had gotten off the PA and now stood at the rail looking down at him from among his men.

"Yeah, yeah. Once I have my fish on board."

"Now!" The captain shouted loudly enough to not need the PA.

Mick cursed those of his people who had stopped working in order to pay attention to the shouting officer. It let him buy a moment.

The captain didn't look like an idiot, he would know that they couldn't move the boat at the moment without simply cutting the net.

Mick looked sidelong up at the man. His uniform was a working man's outfit, not some Moscow-appointed popinjay—at least so Mick hoped.

He made a show of looking down at the salmon still in his hand, and then as if just thinking of the idea, Mick laid it across his palms and held it out as a peace offering. Then he tossed it upward, flat, so that it paused in the air just within the captain's reach.

For a brief moment of hesitation, almost too long, the captain considered.

Then he reached out and snagged the silver by the tail. He hefted it a few times, then grinned down at Mick.

"*Milen'kiy ryba.*" Nice *little* fish.

Mick looked at the squirming mass on the deck and spotted Patty's monster. At least ninety pounds of brightly-silvered female Chinook.

"Luka, make yourself useful," Mick jabbed a finger toward the fish.

Luke Altman grumbled, retrieved the wrong fish by about eighty pounds, holding up a tiny runt and giving Mick another chance to berate him. At Mick's curse on his father's family, Altman hefted the monster as if it weighed as little as the runt. Mick reminded himself not to ever tangle with the SEAL commander.

One of the patrol boat's crew quickly lowered a line.

Mick cinched it around the fish's tail and it was gone aboard the Russian craft in a moment.

"Now get out of here, *mu'dak!*" The captain walked away from the rail with two seaman carrying his new fish behind him.

"Asshole to you, too," Mick said under his breath. He'd wager that the crew wouldn't get a single taste of the bounty of salmon roe caviar that the Chinook had been carrying with her. He offered a one-finger salute to the captain's back. By the crew's smiles, he'd read the situation right.

The patrol boat moved off, but didn't return to shore, instead waiting within easy range of their deck guns.

Mick spared one glance at the drone base they'd been scouting, still little more than a cluster of white specs in the far distance. They sure weren't going to get any closer by sea.

"Okay people. Let's finish up and get the hell out of here."

# CHAPTER 18

*O*nce more they were all gathered in the back of the cold hangar as dusk rolled over the abandoned submarine base. As she and Mick walked up to the group, Patty leaned close and whispered.

"Damn, Quinn. You were pretty magnificent out there," Patty tried to make it sound like a tease, but it was absolutely true.

"Careful with those compliments, Gloucester. Might swell up my head." Exactly what she'd figured he say.

"The way you smell, I'm not real worried. But if I ever want a shining knight in stinky, slimy slicks, I've found my man." And she had, which they still hadn't talked about. Now was not the moment, so she chose a different topic.

"Well, that exercise was useful as shit," she addressed Altman as they arrived at the gathered group and sat in the circle of recovered chairs. "And now we all smell like fish. I stink so bad I can't even make jokes about how Stenka-class patrol boats stink." Patty tried not to think about it. It had been most of a decade since she'd wallowed in such a stench.

They'd tossed every fish they could into the hold's tanks. That one catch had taken two hours to load aboard and stow under the Stenka's watchful eye. Whoever Uri was, he'd just gotten a hell of a bonus at no charge.

"And the nearest goddamn shower is in Anchorage."

"I'm sure," Commander Altman spoke up, "there'd be some Russian sailors glad to soap your back if you want to turn yourself in."

"Only person I'm interested in having do that stinks worse than I do." Patty imagined Mick, soap, and a hot shower. That was a hell of a nice thought as she suppressed another shiver brought on by the plummeting temperature.

Mick shrugged. "Ocean is only about a hundred yards that way. Always glad to scrub any part of you, O'Donoghue."

"That ocean is like a billionth of a degree above freezing solid. You're psycho, Quinn."

He didn't deny the charge as he turned to Altman. "So, was all this worth the trip down the coast?"

"Absolutely! We confirmed the location of the drone base and that sea access was unlikely to be successful. Their active response verifies the importance of this location."

"I still smell like a fish," Patty protested.

"Fish are quieter," Napier observed drily.

"So…what? Am I as ugly as a salmon too?"

Napier opened his mouth, then closed it to look at his wife when she rested a hand on his arm.

"This is not an argument you will not win, *n'est-ce pas?*"

It was a pity that Danielle was so nice; Patty could really get into tangling with someone at the moment.

"While we were busy fishing, Sofia was not idle," Nikita shifted the conversation before Patty could decide who to target next. She did notice that after a day on the water with her, Drake was sitting very close to the female SEAL. *Setting your sights on a SEAL warrior? That takes guts. Go Drake.*

If Nikita was aware of Drake's riveted attention, she didn't show it. With her tablet and projector, she was now splashing images against the back of the hangar wall. The scarred and faded concrete made them a little tricky to see.

It took a moment for Patty to get her head wrapped around the image, but once she was oriented to the sea and the white building they'd seen only as a bright spot on the horizon, she could make sense of it.

The Russian drone airbase was a straightforward affair, not all that different from the sub base the Night Stalkers were now illegal squatters in. Again, a deep cove between protecting headlands, but at the airbase the headlands climbed as high ridges making a long, protected valley. Down the center of the valley was a paved runway surrounded by several small hangars, what appeared to be a machine shop building based on all of the materials stacked outside it, and a set of barracks almost as depressing as the ones here.

At the inlet's shore was a long dock and—

"Is that the stinking Stenka-class patrol boat?"

"Feel better now that you got that out of your system, Gloucester?"

"Much," she nudged her shoulder against Mick's in what she hoped looked like a comradely gesture. How was she supposed to keep her hands off him when contact even through two parkas felt so electric?

Altman rolled his eyes at her. Then he had Nikita lead them on a tour of the base's image.

Beside the Stenka was a smaller supply ship, about half unloaded. She zoomed the image in at various points of interest.

At the machine shop she zoomed in so closely that Patty could see the color of some idiot's hair. "Doesn't he know he needs a hat in this kind of weather?"

"This is still mild for Kamchatka," Connie noted in one of her matter-of-fact tones. "The current temperature is thirty-seven degrees Fahrenheit, though it will fall into the low twenties tonight. Mid-winter here will settle solidly in the tens, with the occasional cold snap down to minus forty."

"Altman," Patty turned to the SEAL commander, "you better get us out of here before it hits minus forty or my ass is going to be frozen to this chair." She could see that she'd hit his teasing limit and decided she'd take her own advice and stop attacking the most dangerous man within several thousand miles. "How the hell did you get this image anyway, sir? Full base view with resolution down to that dude's hair color is just crazy."

"The Avengers were just upgraded with Argus."

Patty looked around the table and saw everyone had the same reaction she did. It took her a moment to find a way to give voice to the sensation.

"I *love* the 5E!"

There were cheers of agreement from everyone. Argus was a concept camera that had survived a few test flights, at least that's all she'd ever heard about it. Someone had deemed it as mission ready and the 5E must be the first team anywhere to get one.

The Argus camera was almost two-gigapixels; a hundred times more powerful than the best smartphone camera, backed up by enough electronics that it could shoot streaming video at full resolution. While Nikita's little tablet computer wouldn't be able to keep up with it, it meant that Sofia and Captain Moretti back in the Avenger's control coffin would be able to track any movement they wanted. They could even rewind the video right back to the moment they'd first arrived overhead if they needed to track someone's origin.

Altman completed the tour of the base.

Patty collapsed back into her chair trying to absorb the sheer volume of information.

"What's missing?" Altman asked the group. "Took us a while to figure it out."

Patty studied the image. Nikita had zoomed it back out until it showed the whole base from the Stenka-class patrol boat to…

"Could you zoom back a bit more?"

Altman smiled at her, but it was Mick who spoke up before she could.

"There's no back fence. The runway ends and then there's nothing but wilderness."

"Taiga forest," Altman confirmed. "Miles and miles of open-spaced larch, pine, and birch. It stretches right up into the center of the Kamchatka Peninsula. It is a disorienting, trackless wilderness primarily populated by fox, wolf, and bear."

"Bears," Patty had always thought it would be cool to see a bear some day.

"The Kamchatka brown is only a little bit smaller than the Alaskan grizzly. Making it the third largest bear there is after the polar bear and the grizzly."

Okay, maybe not so much with seeing a bear.

"With the sea so well guarded," Altman continued, "the taiga is also our best route in."

*Please, please see no bears.*

# CHAPTER 19

"You're a lucky bastard, Quinn," Patty commented over the intercom.

"But it makes sense," Mick did his best to offer sympathy as he flew the Little Bird up into the hills behind the submarine base.

"I know it does. But now I know how M&M and Kenny really felt when they had to turn back."

That was true. He'd have hated being in her assigned role on this mission, too. No Night Stalker liked being left behind the action, even in a crucial role.

He stayed low, rarely more than twenty feet above the tips of the trees as he circled all of the way around the massif of the Shiveluch volcano. His night-vision display showed the ash cloud spewing forth from the snow-covered peak as a thick mass. He gave it a wide berth before descending down into the Kamchatka River valley.

They'd stripped the extended-range tanks and the Urgoza missile pod off the *Linda*. The Little Bird now carried only the Yak-B Gatling gun on one side, and a small bench seat on the other. There was no room for them inside the tiny helicopter as the small back seat was filled with the ammo can for the Yak-B. At full dark they had gone aloft with Altman, Nikita, and Connie perched on the seat out in the cold wind. They were facing sideways with their feet dangling down toward the nearby treetops.

At the planning meeting they'd considered fast-roping in from the DAP Hawk or the Chinook, but the roving Russian drone had worried them. Being stealth didn't mean they were invisible.

Stealth tech was properly called LO—Low Observable technology. They were still visible to radar and heat imaging, just much, much less than your average helicopter. And the Little Bird had the smallest signature of any of them.

The *Beatrix* or *Carrie-Anne* would have to remain well back from the Russian's drone base, at least twenty kilometers to be safe. The Little Bird was designed for stealthy in- and ex-filtration; they could deliver the team within just a few miles of the target with no one the wiser.

"But why you?" Patty's voice was as worried as he'd ever heard from her. "You're a fucking helicopter pilot, not a SEAL."

Then it hit him, she wasn't whining about the mission at all. She was afraid for his sake, not her own.

"Oh sweetheart," Mick was glad they were the only two on the intercom. He wished he could just wrap Patty in his arms and hold on to her. He *knew* he was in over his head but… "My Russian is the best and most authentic to the region. I'm the team's best protection if we get stopped."

---

PATTY KNEW HE WAS RIGHT, but that didn't make it any easier to swallow. Of course he had to go. They needed someone to stay with the helicopter anyway, but—

If only she knew Russian, then—

But she didn't and they actually needed her here. As a Night Stalker Little Bird pilot, she was used to waiting, that's what pilots did. They didn't go walking into a foreign military base with a couple of Team 6 SEALs. The risk factors were off the charts, even if the choice made sense.

At least she was out here at the leading edge. The others were stuck back at the sub base—loaded up and ready to race to the rescue if all hell broke loose. But they were over twenty minutes away at top speed.

Even though they'd all agreed it was the best disposition of assets, Patty couldn't stop worrying at it like a sore tooth.

At least she could keep the rest of her fears to herself. Mick was flying them through intense terrain and needed to focus. *Business,* she told herself. *Keep it strictly business.*

"You've got to swing west here," she told him. "The small fishing town of Klyuchi on the Kamchatka River is due south of us."

Like an artist with a brush, Mick swirled them aside until they had passed well upstream of the small town. A small town that also hosted the Klyuchi air base. During the Cold War it had been filled with Russian interceptor jets. Sofia's imaging showed that it was now mainly transport aircraft, but there were a pair of attack helicopters that they really didn't want to disturb. The ground here in the central valley was already white with snow.

Turning south and east, they climbed again into the rough ridge-and-valley country of the coast. Patty fed Mick information, trying to anticipate his needs moment to moment. There was a palpable silence when Mick was using all of his concentration. She'd come to recognize and respect that.

"Vertical descent off the next ridge, watch for downdrafts based on prevailing winds."

"Next fork in the valley, swing south. The opening to the north is a false lead."

It had taken her a while to learn what he needed and with how much lead time, but that had been two years ago. The give and take simply flowed effortlessly between them in some high state of synchronicity that Patty had never found with any other flier. And even though they'd still only had the one shot at sex—which had been truly great—the fact that it had the same feel as this moment didn't elude her. She and Mick simply…worked together.

She guided him through a snow-coated saddle between a pair of dormant volcanoes—"Updrafts on the other side here"—and then Mick descended sharply. He kept so low that the nearby treetops were often higher than they were.

"Coming up in five hundred meters on bearing one-three-five," Patty called out. Then she set a flashing beacon on the terrain map to project on the inside of his visor.

This was the final reason that had tipped the mission in the Little Bird's favor. On the Avenger's Argus-camera images, Patty herself had spotted a tiny clearing, not more than ten feet larger than the *Linda's* rotors. She'd have cursed herself, except that it was perfect. A deep hole in the trees meant they could park the Little Bird close to the base yet it would be invisible to anything except a direct overflight. And even then, the black, stealth aircraft would be very hard to spot.

Mick settled into it like the pro he was, shut down the helo, pulled his helmet off, and rested it on the top of the cyclic control.

Then he popped his harness and grabbed her.

Mick's kiss slammed into her system and all she could do was groan beneath the weight of the pleasure and the pressure of his lips. She hung onto his shoulders, their Russian Bizon submachine guns clanking together where they hung across their chests. She wanted to strip off her survival vest and shred the fabric that separated them. To feel Mick against her, skin to skin, she craved it like nothing before in her life.

His own need fired hers but there was no time.

He finally pulled away with a foul curse in Russian.

"You!" His voice was rough as he spoke to her from inches away in the darkness. "You had better be here, *right here,* when I get back. God damn it, O'Donoghue. God damn it!" And he was gone to join the others.

Patty watched them disappear into the woods, feeling every bit of his frustration right down into her gut.

She'd never wanted to need a man.

But she needed Mick Quinn more than she needed to fly.

Well, if she'd ever wanted proof that the feeling was mutual, Mick "The Mighty" Quinn had just given it to her and how. Her body was still buzzing, her lips stung, and his foul curses—so unlike the Mick she knew—still rung like music in her ears.

Now all she had to do was wait. It was an hour past full darkness. The mission was planned to last three hours. First light wasn't for another nine hours.

"You better be back to me before nine hours, Quinn."

She sat alone in the silent cockpit. Her only company was Mick's helmet which his violent exit had knocked askew. It still perched atop the cyclic control joystick, but now its empty visor appeared to be staring up at her.

"God damn it, Quinn. You better be back right here, too. If I have to fly into that base to save your ass, we're all dead." Not that it would stop her from trying; it was simply a choice of last resort.

Damned Russians couldn't leave well enough alone, could they? Cold War II. It was as if they *wanted* it.

Fine. Well, Mick wasn't the only one who could tell the Russians to *otva 'li.*

She estimated the direction of the Russian base and flipped them the bird.

---

MICK HAD TAKEN the essential survival courses like SERE but felt like a buffoon in clown feet trying to follow Altman. Altman led, Mick was in second position with Connie close behind. Nikita moved silently at the rear.

He felt naked wearing only cold weather gear, the Russian submachine gun, and a GSh-18 handgun. Night Stalkers were supposed to wear SARVSO survival vests and FN-SCAR combat assault rifles. They were supposed to wear Kevlar helmets not woolen caps. And most of all, they were supposed to be wrapped inside the best helicopters that the United States military could manufacture, not tramping through the Russian wilderness on a near Arctic night.

However, on the plus side, he was with a pair of DEVGRU SEALs. In addition to the same weapons he carried, they had yard-and-a-half long SV-98 silenced sniper rifles over their shoulders.

Altman had said the weapons were hopefully for show, not for use. They would be the team's passport into the camp and would also give them the perfect excuse to wear Russian night-vision gear—which was about ten times heavier than US gear—but a sore neck was far better than being blind.

Once explained, the cover was remarkably simple. No one in Russia has access to the class of weapons they carried except Spetsnaz. The four of them were armed as Russian Special Forces. Of course they would carry no identification on a mission. And, of course, they would be the only fuckers crazy enough to be walking through the Kamchatka wilderness without even field packs.

When asked about not having any of those, Altman had shrugged. "I thought we might need the weapons. Can't say that I planned on walking in the back door this way."

That made Mick feel so much better…*not!* Oh gods, he was channeling O'Donoghue. Though being with a Team 6 SEAL who was making it up as he went was still probably the best guy there was to be following.

It felt like hours before they saw the first lights of the Russian base even if Mick's watch insisted only forty minutes had passed since he'd kissed the crap out of Patty O'Donoghue.

That had been a serious amount of fun. He could turn that into a major pastime. Not that he had ever gone for the dumb ones, but Patty was far and away the sharpest woman he'd ever been with. And she could make him laugh even when it was ripping his heart open. He'd managed not to turn back to look at her through his night vision until they were well under the trees.

In the NVGs, Mick saw her flip him the bird, telling him that Patty would do far worse than kill him if he came back dead.

Even now she could make him laugh.

"Okay," Altman called his attention. "Walk like we're the roosters of the world. We've just walked across the breadth of Russia and it was easy. Now we just want a hot shower and a random fuck."

"No thanks," Connie said softly. "I'm married."

Mick wasn't sure if he was supposed to laugh. Altman and Nikita's silence said that they didn't know either.

At least not until he heard Connie's own soft laugh. "You guys. Such squares."

And she led the way into the Russian camp.

# CHAPTER 20

$\mathcal{P}$atty kept trying to think of ways to make the time pass, because as far as she could tell her watch had stopped working. Counting to a hundred took less than a minute. Counting to a thousand…she always peeked somewhere in the two hundreds.

The helo was immaculate. She'd long since memorized the operations manual. She considered pulling out her personal smartphone and reading an e-book she had stored on it. Except that would kill her night vision and she wanted to be ready the second they returned.

Of course that wasn't even physically possible yet.

Her laggard watch insisted that, if they were still on schedule, they'd reached the base only twenty-three-and-a-half minutes ago.

Nothing from Sofia who would be watching from above. Of course she wasn't supposed to transmit even a squeak unless there was a problem. Which meant that everything was going fine except for Patty's mental state.

For a while she leaned forward and looked upward, trying to watch the entire starlit sky that was visible from her clearing in the forest. Maybe, just maybe she'd be able to see the Avenger momentarily eclipse a star.

Yeah, right.

At this distance, spotting the fifty-foot aircraft was like trying to spot a dime twenty yards out—in the dark. While a sniper with a decent scope could hit that dime every time, Patty was more of a fire-a-missile-up-their-ass-from-an-AH-6M-attack-Little-Bird kinda gal.

She was either going to go mad or think about Mick. And if she thought about Mick, she'd go even crazier. Sure, she loved The Mighty Quinn; it wasn't worth arguing that point anymore. The question of what to do about it was far more elusive.

Napier's refusal to answer how married couples were possible in the 5th Battalion E Company only made it all the more unlikely. Traditional military practice said that there were two avenues. One or the other of the couple could resign and go civilian before they were caught. The other option was going dual military. The MACP—Married Army Couples Program—worked fine for general troops, those who spent most of their time cooling their heels and doing training at some base or other. Even if deployed, they were rarely both deployed at once and never to the same action.

The 160th SOAR was not general troops and a couple either served in the same unit...or never saw each other. And serving in the same unit meant being deployed together and no unit did that. Except the 5D and the 5E.

If somehow she and Mick could—

"Whoa!" Her shout of surprise slapped back at her inside the Little Bird. "Hold on there! How in hell did the M word slip past your guard, O'Donoghue?"

Marriage had been no part of her early life's plan. Someday, sure. When she wanted a good man to keep her bed warm in her dotage.

"Patty O'Donoghue's boy toy now open for applications," she wanted to giggle at the old line, but it sounded more like a strangled choke.

Suddenly the M word was square in her sights and she was getting the clean tone of a missile lock.

"No way. Get out of the kill zone!"

But her attempts to wave the mere concept of marriage aside merely emphasized that she was sitting alone in the Russian wilderness talking to herself.

Which led her right back to her original premise, Mick was trying to make her insane.

And it was working.

---

THE ONLY GUARD the team met was at the personnel entrance to the main hangar. He looked lonely and cold, and apologized for raising his rifle the very first moment he got a good look at their equipment.

*Full points to the Team 6 SEAL,* Mick thought. Altman had it figured. They were obviously Spetsnaz and that was scaring the shit out of the poor guard.

Now it was his job, with his Uncle's Kamchatka fishing trawler accent, to close the deal.

"Just doing your duty, *Starik!*" Mick clapped him on the shoulder. It meant *Old Man,* about the closest Russians had to *Buddy. Tovarishch* wasn't even used by old communists anymore. The youth had long since turned *Comrade* into an ironical insult.

Altman fished out a clear bottle, mostly empty. He took a hit off it then handed it over.

"*Spasibo!*" The guard looked infinitely grateful. Being a good man, he took a massive swallow but didn't finish it before passing it around the circle.

Mick didn't need the slight headshake from Altman to not swallow any. He tipped it up, kept his tongue over the mouth, and then pulled it back down and returned it, offering a sharp gasp as if the alcohol burned his throat.

When the guard gestured to offer it to the women, Mick just pushed it back toward the man. "We have other ways of keeping our women warm, *Tovarishch.*" He gave the final word a full, ironical twist. The guard was young enough to have been trained by members of the

Soviet Union who would have taken great pleasure in disciplining anyone of the New Russia.

The guard laughed and smiled, then slipped to the ground. Altman and Nikita caught him on the way down. Altman took back the bottle and stoppered it.

"Falling asleep on duty will get him latrine duty. Doing so while supposedly drunk will get him far worse," Altman explained as he pocketed the bottle.

There was no keypad on the door, just a simple lock. Nikita knelt and pulled out some picks. Ten seconds later they were inside and confirming the lack of alarms.

"Feeling too safe out here in the wilderness, Comrades," Mick whispered quietly.

Thirty seconds later, they had confirmed that they were the only ones in the vast building.

As they'd spotted from the fishing boat, there was an Orlan-10 drone parked close by the main doors. With another positioned close behind it.

The rest of the hangar was taken up by four very nasty looking aircraft in various stages of assembly. A complete one stood on its wheels close by the door.

"Skad UCAVs," Connie confirmed and moved toward the partial aircraft as if in a dream.

"Pictures, Mick. Every angle and a video of each one."

Mick pulled out a low-light camera and went to work.

"Software," Connie said, shaking herself awake. "That is the key to aircraft now. We need the software."

"Here," Nikita moved unerringly toward one particular station. It took Mick a moment to figure out why; it was the only one that was a complete mess. She flipped through the papers rapidly, checked under a keyboard and then a mouse pad, then under the mouse. She left it on its back and began typing as she read what was written on the bottom of the mouse.

The screen flashed to life. Nikita plugged memory sticks into external ports.

Mick went back to taking photographs.

A very quiet and intense four minutes later, he couldn't think of another angle to photograph the Skad and moved on to the Orlan-10. He was just wondering whether or not to try pulling the covers on one when a low whistle brought him hustling back.

"Two clean copies," Nikita announced. And yanked out the memory sticks. She handed one to him and he copied all of the pictures onto it. She took it back and gave him the other copy of the software. By now they'd been inside the building for five minutes and had two copies of everything.

While they'd been making the copies, Connie had slid into the programmer's chair.

"Isn't that interesting," she seemed to be talking to herself.

"You know about software as well as mechanics?" Then Mick cursed himself for asking such an extraneous question during a mission.

Connie ignored him as she scrolled blocks of code faster than an air battle shifted tactical screens.

"In modern day…the physical mechanics…"

It was as if his question was slowly jerking a response from her in little dribs and drabs while her main attention was processing the information on the screen.

"…are just a small factor…in performance. The…software now controls…most of the ultimate…capabilities of the…craft."

Six minutes gone and still she was scrolling screens faster than he could focus on them.

Then her voice shifted abruptly.

"I need fifteen minutes," Connie didn't wait for an answer as her fingers flew across the keyboard.

They'd rehearsed this a dozen times back at the sub base. Maximum mission time was to be ten minutes from first contact.

Mick pulled Altman and Nikita aside. "How long is the guard's knockout good for?"

Altman didn't bother checking his watch. "Twenty minutes to

groggy, thirty to fully awake and praying to God that we were just a hallucination. If he isn't caught sleeping, he'll never report us to anybody. Sofia observed that last night they changed the guard at 2000 and 2400 hours. It's 2230 right now, so that part of it should work out."

"Do we drag her out?" Nikita asked softly.

Mick was about to nod that they'd have to, but Connie didn't give him a chance.

"Don't," Connie spoke once again in her parsed, jerking way. "Right now I'd be leaving a big digital thumbprint across their software. I need fourteen more minutes." And then she leaned in as if she could meld with the screen.

"I bet we could drop a bomb right now and she wouldn't hear us," Mick tucked the camera and the memory stick back in his parka's pocket and made sure it was sealed in.

No reaction.

For a ten loud heartbeats, Altman frowned at a spot somewhere near Mick's shoulder.

Mick wanted to reach up and feel if it was growing warm under SuperSEAL's x-ray vision.

The only sound was the brap of Connie's keyboard, as loud and dangerous sounding in the silent hangar as the chainsaw-burr of an M134 minigun.

"Go!" Altman grabbed Mick's lapel. "You head for the helo. We need to separate these two copies of the data. As soon as she's done we'll either follow or find another route out."

Mick tried to ask what other route, but Altman was already shoving him toward the door.

He was able to stop Altman's strong-arming him right at the threshold to the door only by grabbing the door frame.

"You don't bring Connie back safe, you'll be the one who has to deal with Big John. He's a very protective guy, you know."

Altman slapped him on the arm, "I promise you that if Connie doesn't get out of this alive, neither Nikita nor I will either."

Mick nodded. It was exactly the answer you'd expect from a Team 6 commander.

He ducked through the door, checked that the guard was still passed out, and high-tailed it for the taiga forest.

---

PATTY HAD TAKEN to thumping the back of her helmet against the head-rest of her pilot's seat. It didn't make her feel any better, but if she counted five between the thumps, it gave her something to do that actually let the watch move forward in time. In slow excruciatingly motion, but forward.

Altman's plan stated that they were forty minutes to base. Another thirty to infiltrate and find the right building. He'd allotted them ten minutes inside and another hour to get back.

By her best estimation she had thirty-eight minutes before it was even time to start worrying, never mind panicking.

One. Two. Three. Four. Five. Thump.

Thirty-seven minutes and fifty-four seconds.

One. Two. Three. Four. Five. Thump.

Thirty-seven minutes and forty-eight seconds.

One. Two. Three. Four. Five.

*Thump!*

The entire helicopter shuddered with the impact.

Patty opened her eyes but didn't see anything unusual through the night-vision cameras mounted on the outside of the helicopter.

One. Two. Thr—

*Thump!*

Something heavy crashed against the front of the helo. Still nothing to see. Whatever it could be, it was closer than the area of the external cameras.

She shoved her visor up.

Nothing but pitch darkness. The starlight that she'd been watching earlier was blocked by a dark shape—one that took up half her view out the windshield.

Again the helicopter shook as if being struck by a ginormous hammer.

Deciding to risk a light, she pulled a flashlight out of her thigh pocket and aimed it out through the helicopter's windscreen. The Little Bird offered exceptional visibility. The windscreen was essentially one piece of curved Plexiglas from the rudder pedals to up behind her head. A small console rose between the two pilot's seats to about chest high, but the view from a Little Bird was spectacular. At least normally.

She couldn't make sense of what the flashlight revealed though. Something thick and brown was pressing against the outside of the windscreen blocking her view all the way up to the level of her eyes.

Then it moved.

A gigantic furry face turned to look at her, blinking in confusion.

Patty tried to think of how to respond, of what she could do. The bear's head was bigger than her entire body and they were looking right at each other from less than two feet apart.

The massive brown bear snorted the air several times—great puffs of hot air that briefly fogged the outside of the windscreen hazing her view of his huge brown eyes.

She could see every wrinkle of his nose as it tried to puzzle out the light's origin.

After a long moment's consideration, the bear must have decided that she wasn't food, or something that needed a good tromping. It looked away and returned to scratching its back against the nose of her helicopter.

Then it ambled off into the darkness. She didn't remember to pull down the visor until the last of its fat butt was disappearing into the trees. And the recorder hadn't been running. No picture to prove her story.

But she couldn't wait to tell Mick anyway.

She hadn't even had time to be scared, hadn't thought to be. Just two vastly different creatures, each in their own habitat, staring at each other across the Plexiglas void.

She looked down to put away her flashlight the moment before something else smacked into the helicopter.

"Goddamn bears!"

She yanked the flashlight back out and shone it out the windscreen.

Mick lay against the windshield.

And his face was covered in blood.

## CHAPTER 21

Someone was cursing at him. A long vivid stream of invective in several languages. Or maybe just cursing at the world in general.

He wanted to curse back, but he couldn't. He didn't have the wind. His side hurt so much from running at his flat-out limit that he couldn't even move. He'd already been moving at a fast jog for a while when he'd been attacked.

He'd sprinted from there.

Then he recognized the voice even though she'd wandered off into Viet or maybe Thai.

"Gloucester," he managed to gasp out. Thank God.

She could curse him all she wanted as long as he'd finally found her.

Patty grabbed his arm and he yelped. He couldn't help himself.

"What the hell, Quinn?"

"Wolf. Bit my arm." He tried to lean down to see if she smelled as wonderful as he'd remembered.

But she spun away before he could.

"Where is it?" She shone a flashlight into the woods. She had her handgun out, ready to kill it. His own personal redheaded action heroine.

"Gone." Really gone. Good and gone. Gone for good.

"You're all bloody."

"Wolf's blood," Mick raised his Bizon 9mm. "I messed up its brain a bit." The submachine gun had been short enough for him to ram it right into the ear of the hellhound that had surged out of the darkness to latch onto him. He'd only saved his throat by getting his right arm up in time. How strange. *Methods to Survive a Dog Attack* had always struck him as a wasted bit of training for a helicopter pilot and now it had saved his life. Leave it to the Army to cover all the bases, even the ones that looked totally stupid…until they saved your sorry ass.

"You just never know."

"Never know what?" Patty was looking up at him.

"Pretty Patty with the big blue eyes." Even in the vague sidelight of the flashlight's beam, they were brilliant.

" 'You never know what,' Mick? Where are the others?" Once again she spun away just as he was leaning down to sniff her hair. This time he got a good whiff though.

She smelled like fish.

"The others?" The urgency of her tone cut through his wandering thoughts.

"They're coming. Or maybe not." He knew he wasn't making a whole lot of sense so he struggled to focus. "They're going to follow. In fourteen minutes. Maybe more as I ran a lot. Unless they don't."

"And if they don't?" Patty started guiding him toward his seat in the helicopter.

That was a good idea. He didn't want to risk almost shooting his arm off again if there was another wolf.

"And if they don't, Quinn?"

"Altman promised he and Nikita would make sure Connie got out safely."

"How will we know?" She buckled his harness for him. Which was good. The adrenaline was going away and the shakes would follow.

And his right arm was starting to really hurt.

She climbed in the other side and turned the cockpit light on low.

He looked at his coat sleeve again, just as he had after extracting his arm from the dead wolf's mouth. No tooth holes, just an in and out where the bullet had passed through a fold of cloth near his bicep, right after passing through the wolf's brain. He probed a finger through the hole but found no liquid heat of spilled blood and no pain. A clean miss. The thick parka and a quick shooting had saved his arm, but the forearm where the wolf had clamped down really really hurt.

"How—"

"Sofia will call."

"Okay."

And there was pretty Patty again, now sitting beside him in the *Linda* and staring into his face.

"You sure that's not your own blood?"

"I'm sure. Damn, but you're a looker, Pretty Patty. I love Pretty Patty," he'd said it before and he'd say it again. Actually, maybe he hadn't said it out loud before.

"You're a nut, Quinn," she patted him on his shoulder. That didn't hurt.

"That's true," he admitted. "Because I'm nuts about you. Maybe that makes me certifiable."

"That makes two of us certifiable."

And then the shakes slammed into him as the last of the adrenaline slid away and he finally realized just how close he'd come to death.

---

PATTY WAS STILL HOLDING him when the call came in from Sofia.

She didn't know which of them she'd been holding on for. To comfort him as he was slammed time and again by the shakes? Or herself for how glad she was to have him back beside her.

When the worst of it had passed, she didn't ease her hold and he continued to lean into her.

"So close," he whispered. "So close. I'm sorry Patty. I almost broke my promise to get back here. That was all I could think as that wolf tried to kill me. I promised you I'd come back."

"And you did, Mick. You kept your word," as, of course, Mick Quinn would. All of her doubts of the last few hours washed away. She didn't just love Mick Quinn. If they survived this, she was damn well going to marry him and he didn't get a vote in the matter. Because to lose him would kill her.

"I've been injured before, but never faced death. Not like that. Hot, immediate, and horribly violent," his rough voice tore at her heart.

"It's okay. You made it. It's okay," Patty did her best to reassure them both.

"Who knew death had such stinky breath."

She pulled back enough to look at him again. He'd scared the shit out of her first with the blood and then with the babbling incoherence. That he'd said he loved her somewhere in the middle of that didn't quite count, but it was very promising.

She wanted him to say it again, even in babble. But now, with the adrenaline gone, he'd come back to coherence.

Then the "stinky breath" line.

"Don't I even get a laugh?"

Mick Quinn had just delivered a joke about almost dying and wanted a laugh for his punch line.

And she gave it to him; couldn't help herself. It bordered on the hysterical, but that didn't matter. He was okay. The battered and wolf-bloodied man looking over at her had those same gorgeous eyes she was used to.

She leaned in to find some not-so bloody spot that she could kiss, when the encrypted radio squawked to life.

"Team of three using alternate evacuation route," Sofia announced. "*Linda* cleared for return to base."

Patty didn't key the mike in response, that wasn't protocol. Instead she powered up and Sofia would know they'd received her message when the *Linda* took off.

# CHAPTER 22

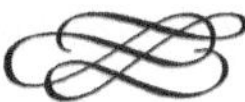

Mick's right arm was horribly tender, every move sent sharp twinges, sometimes down to his fingertips and sometimes up to his shoulder and neck—he'd probably wrenched it but good blocking a hundred pounds of leaping wolf. These twinges were less intense than before. Way better than the moment Patty had grabbed his arm; which was infinitely better than the screaming agony as he'd extracted his arm from the dead wolf's mouth.

He flexed his fingers and wished to God he hadn't. His lame attempt to suppress a sharp hiss of breath was thankfully masked by the high whine of the accelerating turboshaft engine.

So he nestled his right arm in his lap and watched Patty fly.

"You're very smooth."

"Why thank you, Mr. Quinn. Now shut up, I'm busy here."

She'd taken it completely the wrong way. Or maybe not. He remembered the smooth soft heat of her in their joined sleeping bags atop Mount Hayes. Nobody felt that good, not even in late night fantasies. But Patty O'Donoghue did. Someday he'd get a chance to test if that was real or imagined, and it had better be soon.

He let his left hand float on the collective, enjoying the connection from his hand to hers on the linked controls.

Smooth, so very smooth.

And he was utterly exhausted. Too little sleep last night, fishing all day—it was hard work catching nothing all day—and once again it was the middle of the night.

Maybe they'd get to leave Kamchatka tonight. They were barely three hours to Alaska. If they could get even halfway under cover of darkness, they could be back to Anchorage the next day. It all depended on how fast the other team was moving.

Patty swooped the *Linda* through the saddle between the two dormant volcanoes that stood as sentinels over the pass between the drone base and the Kamchatka River valley.

A world of white, lit plenty brightly by the ambient starlight to show up clearly across his visor.

He blinked to shift his focus.

Patty O'Donoghue. She was shorter in her seat than he was, but taller than some pilots. Her flightsuit topped by her survival vest and her gun hid any hint of shape. The blocky helmet covered her flowing hair and the lowered visor hid everything but the tip of her chin.

Yet still he'd know her anywhere. Some part of his brain had cataloged her so completely that he'd instinctively know by the way she handled the controls, by the way she moved, by the way she breathed.

Patty hadn't reacted when he'd said he loved her. He'd also been yammering like a seasick drunk on his first sport fisher.

Mick opened his mouth to tell her, but she'd told him to be quiet so she could concentrate. Busting her concentration during a nap-of-the-Earth flying mission would be a lousy choice, so he kept his peace.

His brain switched on enough that he refocused inside his helmet and began watching the tactical displays.

"Swing wide for Klyuchi," he reminded her.

"Thanks. Welcome back, Quinn." There was enough salt in her tone that he knew he'd spooked her with his wandering responses.

"Glad to be here," he'd leave it at that. So glad to be next to Patty that he could barely stand it.

Past Klyuchi, they climbed out of the Kamchatka River Valley, once again circling wide around Mount Shiveluch. The abandoned sub base lay eleven miles the other side of the volcano. Almost home.

They crested a long ridge that ran vertically down the side of the mountain. Just as they crossed the pinnacle from west to east, a bright flash burned across his display.

The Little Bird's threat warning screamed with the tone for a missile.

But the missile was heading away from them.

Patty carved a turn to go back the way they'd come.

"Where the hell did that missile come from, Quinn?"

"Working on it."

Ignoring the sharp protest from his arm, he reached out and ran back the recording. It looked as if the missile had materialized in thin air with no point of origin.

Unless…

He ran the tape again. There was a tiny blip of heat signature, far dimmer than the missile's, that followed a different course. Then he recalled the empty space at the far end of the hangar they'd just raided. He hadn't given the spot any thought, but now he knew what was normally parked there, a finished Skad UCAV.

Mick decided that he had to risk the radio.

"Sofia. They're test firing a drone in our vicinity. Find it."

"One moment. I was watching the *Beatrix* pick up the rest of the team offshore from a small skiff. They're safe aboard."

"Get away from this thing," he growled at Patty.

"Glad to. Tell me where the hell it is."

The heat trace had been small, but he should be able to see it now that he knew what to look for.

There was only so much heat masking that could be done on a jet engine's exhaust. It was an issue on all stealth aircraft.

But it wasn't there.

"Come on, Sofia."

If he couldn't see its heat signature that either meant that it was gone or…that it was headed straight for them so that its own fuselage hid the hot exhaust flowing to the enemy's stern.

He flipped on the jamming packages, hoping to block any radio transmissions it might be sending back to base, or from base giving it a firing solution. Especially any images of a nasty little American helicopter flying around in its airspace.

"Climb, Patty. Get above this thing. It sees best looking down."

She climbed the side of Shiveluch. They'd been near the peak and would soon be up in the ash cloud above the caldera.

"Yes, up into the ash cloud. Maybe it will be hot enough to mask our heat signature."

"Attention *Linda*," Sofia's voice was urgent. "Connie Davis says to evade only. Do not use electronic blocking. Their software is designed to go aggressively autonomous on loss of signal from base."

"Now she tells us."

A heat plume of another missile shown bright, close in front of them.

Patty flicked them aside from the missile.

Mick hit the decoy flares to distract the missile and he fired the Yak-B Gatling onto the point of origin. He managed only brief bursts totaling just a few seconds. In that time nearly two hundred rounds of half-inch Russian bullets hammered into the drone.

The missile followed the bright hot flares that he'd shot out to the sides, but the attack had come from too close. The missile exploded close aboard and shrapnel pounded against their frame with pings and rattles and a few hard bangs. A few red lights blinked on, but nothing that sent a message into his deep-training that screamed disaster.

For an instant, they hovered, stable above the lip of the caldera. To one side were the barren snow-covered slopes of the volcano. To the other, so close Mick was looking right down into it, the great bowl of the rocky caldera spread below them. At its center, a boiling pool of lava was mostly hidden behind great plumes of hot ash cloud. It lit the cloud in a dark, malevolent red.

"Did we make it?" Patty asked softly.

Mick began flipping through the status readouts when he spotted the Skad drone close below them. So close that it clipped the caldera's rim not fifty meters away.

A massive flash bloomed up from where the drone crashed into the side of the mountain. Maybe the Russians had a new, highly explosive fuel. Or perhaps having lost contact due to his jamming signal, the drone had decided to switch off the safeties on all the weapons it was carrying. Either way, it was a massive fireball, coming right for them.

He heard the boom, even over the roar of the Little Bird's engine. The shockwave spun them out over the caldera, tumbling them through a full flip.

A dozen readings that had been rising toward redline bloomed into full alarms. Now his imminent disaster signals were reporting numerous reasons for instant panic.

In cascading failures, hydraulics, oil pressure, even fuel flashed up red alarms.

"Losing lift," Patty reported with the sudden calm that came with being a trained Night Stalker pilot in a potential crash situation. He felt it come over him as well. He started trying to reset breakers, select alternate systems, even— Nothing was getting any useful response from the crippled bird.

"Hydraulics one and two failure," Mick flipped switches. "Backup at fifty percent and falling."

"Have to land."

Mick began searching for a landing spot.

Not going to happen. They'd been knocked into the caldera by the blast and were now down below its knife edge. The steep sides of the bowl offered no flat spots. The center was glowing with an angry red pool of molten rock.

"Prepare to jump," Patty had reached the same conclusion.

A piece of training that never worked in reality. It was beyond last resort, it was suicide. But it was better than riding the helicopter down. There was now no question where it was going to end up.

"Rudders going soft. I'll hold it as long as I can at ten feet."

"Roger that." Mick popped open his harness, unlatched the door—

ignoring the slice of pain his arm sent to try and stop him—and grabbed the emergency kit from under his seat.

He wished it was him at the controls, not Patty. That she would be the first to try and jump to safety. But you didn't take control of an aircraft away from the pilot-in-command during an emergency.

"Fifty feet," he called out, trying to spot a good place, but there weren't any. "Forty."

Mick reached over and hit the release on Patty's harness for her. He had to close his eyes against the anguish slicing up his right arm as he reached over her to unlatch her door. Give him a car's seatbelt and an angry woman tugging on his ears in order to kiss him any day.

"Thirty. Twenty. See you in a sec, Gloucester."

At ten feet up, Mick kicked his door open and jumped into the void.

# CHAPTER 23

_P_atty blinked to clear the sweat that was pouring down into her face. The moment Mick had opened his door, a wave of hot, sulphurous stench washed into the cabin.

Mick had been right; death had very stinky breath.

She rode the helo another fifty feet downslope to make sure she was clear of Mick's landing zone, skidding on a cushion of blazing hot air.

The _Linda_ was just five feet above the harsh rocks and moving too fast, but Patty was out of options unless she wanted to go swimming in a pool of lava.

She wrenched back on the cyclic and yanked up on the collective for all it was worth. The _Linda_ cried. Every system alarm roared in panic, but she stalled into a hover.

Patty shoved open the door and jumped. She landed hard, banged her helmet harder, then rolled to get down into a crevice between two boulders as the helicopter crashed around her.

Rotor blades battered against the tops of the rocks. Metal groaned and crunched. Something caught and the tail spun by close over her head.

When she dared peek, she saw the *Linda* shredding herself in the flailing death throes that marked all helicopter crashes. Bits and pieces flew in every direction.

*A million pieces no longer flying in formation.*

The fuselage flipped and bounced. The engine's whine still roared loudly enough to hurt right through her helmet.

Then it tumbled downslope and plunged into the lava pool right side up.

Most of the rotor blades were broken off, but the stubs still whirled frantically above the surface—hopelessly struggling to still lift the sinking and melting fuselage clear of its doom. Soon only the stubs of the rotors remained spinning above the surface.

A strong hand yanked her out of her crevice.

"Mick!" She tried to hug him, but he was already dragging her upslope. She banged her shin twice before she managed to get her feet with the program. Unable to see where she was going, she shoved at her visor, but it was badly star-cracked and stuck. She pulled off the helmet and heaved it down toward the molten pool. Mick didn't have his either.

"What's the big rush? We made it."

"Fuel and weapons."

*Shit!* Now she wished she'd kept the helmet. They raced up the steep slope. They'd gone less than a hundred yards with that much more to go when there was a loud *Crump!* from behind them.

Mick shoved her down behind a boulder and huddled over her.

Bits of burning helicopter began pattering down around them.

More than that. Bright bits of lava rained down all around them. A basketball-sized glob landed not more than a yard from her nose. She watched it in fascination. A glowing orb of yellow-orange; she could feel its scorching heat like a hot sunburn on a cold day. It sputtered and spit as it turned dull orange, dark red, and finally began forming threads of blackness as it cooled. It had transformed back into being a rock. Molten rock.

"Quinn. I think we should get out of here. Fast."

More lava rained down, a small piece skidding off her parka sleeve and leaving a cut line where it had melted away the outer material in an instant.

He started to race up the slope.

She cried out even as she saw his misstep. His foot had broken free a rock and sent it tumbling to the side. In moments, he was sliding back down toward her. She dug in her feet and braced for the impact.

He slammed into her, but by leaning forward she was able to stop him. If he'd kept going, he'd have landed close beside the melting *Linda*.

"Follow me," her shout felt small in the vast and lethal caldera. "Step where I step." She grabbed up a four-foot chunk of rotor blade that had been broken off during the crash and used it to poke at unstable looking sections of the slope ahead of her.

She didn't wait for his nod, but moved upslope rapidly, testing each step as Two-ton, the silent PJ, had showed her. As she went, she poked her rotor-probe into the slope ahead just as she had before with the ice axe. That had been ice and rock, this was ash and rock, but the idea carried across well enough.

Patty glanced back and saw that Mick was moving well close behind her. Beyond him lay the last signs of the *Linda*. Even the last stubs of the rotor were gone, just the pattern in the lava of where the five blades had briefly laid on the surface and cooled it slightly.

Then the lava spit again and more globs were lofted skyward.

Patty didn't stick around to watch where they were going to land.

She turned and ran.

---

"WE CAN NO SEND ANY RESCUE," Sofia told him over the radio. "The flares you make and the explosion of the Russian drone lit up the top of the mountain far around. Helicopters they are coming from Klyuchi Air Base. You must hide."

"Roger that."

At least Patty didn't scoff at him for his lame radio response under these conditions. He expected that they were both just too damn glad to be alive.

Mick looked at the snowy mountainscape below them. They were hiding beneath the lip of a boulder fifty feet below the outside of the caldera. He'd scrubbed his face with snow until Patty said he'd gotten most of the blood off.

"Well, it's just like Mount Hayes," Patty remarked. "Snowy peak. Handsome companion. Squatting in the snow."

"Kamchatka Peninsula. Melted helicopter. No cozy tent. Gobs of molten lava raining from the sky. Russian military coming to kick our butts."

"Okay, not so much the same. So, where do we hide?"

"You're great, you know that, right?"

"I am?" Patty made it sound like innocent surprise.

He wanted to kiss her, but that was a road to complete distraction, so he kept it casual. "Sure. Not another person living that I'd rather crash into a Russian volcano with."

"How about if you include dead people?"

"Them too."

"Okay then. So, where do we hide?"

Mick had managed to hang onto the small emergency pack: water, food, basic medical, and a thermal blanket big enough for one.

Patty still wore her survival vest, which could make roughly the same claims. No gloves except for the thin ones they typically wore while flying. No thermal pants, though they still had their parkas. He could already feel the cold nipping at him and his pulse hadn't had time to slow down yet.

"Got to get off the mountain."

"Shouldn't we be tied together?"

"No rope," he'd already searched through the pack. "Closest we've got is some duct tape."

"Well, I'm not going to risk being separated from you. What do we do, tape our hands together?"

The idea of strolling hand in hand with Patty O'Donoghue down the face of Mount Shiveluch had its points. As did the helos that were probably already warming up their engines at Klyuchi Air Base. Or already enroute.

"I feel the need…" he said.

"The need for speed," Patty finished the saying for him. "I feel it too, any bright ideas, Quinn?"

He pulled out his thermal blanket. Using the duct tape, he started fashioning it into a long tube, closed at the narrow end and open down the long side.

Patty groaned when she saw what he was doing, pulled out her own foil rescue blanket and lined it up inside his own.

"I know," he whispered to her. "Just don't think about it too much."

He'd gotten the idea from the snow stretchers they'd used high on the slopes of Mt. Hayes to transport the "injured" and "DOA" mannequins.

"Great!" Patty put on a totally chipper tone. "Injured or dead. Two utterly *awesome* choices."

Mick took off his coat and taped it to the inside as padding in case they hit any rocks. It wasn't much, but it was the best he had.

When Patty started to shed her coat, he stopped her.

"No, your coat will shield both of us. How are you at tobogganing?"

"Lousy. I always crash into trees. And a big hill in Gloucester is like fifty feet high."

"Well, this one doesn't have any trees, so that shouldn't be an issue."

"Mick, it's ten thousand feet high."

"And we're dead if we stay here."

Patty muttered something under her breath.

"What was that?"

"I said: Before, I was only going to make you go on a roller coaster."

"This'll be so much better, I promise." And he actually laughed at his own tease. Then he laid out the foil toboggan and made her sit her butt down in it. He tucked the closed end of the tube over her boots and taped it in place.

Digging around in the pack, he found their one set of night-vision goggles. The visor on the helmets were useless without the information feed from the helicopter, so he'd shed his as dead weight and was glad to see Patty had done the same. He turned on the binoculars and almost yanked them onto Patty's head.

No. She said she was lousy at sledding.

He pulled them on himself and climbed in behind her, pulled himself close so that her back was against his chest.

"Hey!" Patty leaned forward again.

He shifted the Bizon submachine gun from across his chest to over his shoulder, then tried again. God she felt so good leaning back against him. He slid his hands under the harness of her survival vest, but over the parka, and squeezed her breasts just because he wanted to.

"Hey!" Patty didn't sound upset this time.

He pulled his legs in, wrapped them around her waist and hooked them over her thighs. He grabbed Patty's chunk of rotor blade and pushed off. The reflective-blanket toboggan began to slide.

Mick locked his legs tightly around her waist so that they wouldn't be separated no matter what happened. If they found a crevasse, well, they'd die together which was probably better than locked in a Russian prison as spies.

As they started to pick up speed, he did his best to watch ahead and steer them, dragging the tip of the rotor blade like a ship's rudder. His arm complained bitterly and he ignored it; there was no longer time for such things.

Her hair fluttered up on the growing wind of their descent and brushed across his face.

To the odor of fish, she'd now added the stench of sulfur.

Charming.

Patty flew downward through the darkness. The snow spray kicked up into her face. She had to keep shaking her head to clear the snow away because no way was she taking her hands off Mick's thighs.

In moments they were rocketing downward and the wind was a solid roar. Terminal velocity in freefall was a hundred and twenty miles an hour. Terminal velocity tobogganing down a Russian volcano felt pretty close to that.

Tears were being ripped from her squinted eyes. She could feel them freezing along her temples in the wind chill. Unable to see anything anyway, she closed her eyes and hung on.

When Mick leaned to one side, she leaned with him.

When he leaned to the other side, she went that way as well. The snow was deep and powdery. Whenever they slowed too much, she'd raise her feet and the nose of their foil toboggan along with them and once more they'd fly downhill.

It was impossible to talk.

She opened her mouth to shout and so much freezing air and snow pummeled into her lungs that she spent the next thousand feet or so trying to choke it back out.

The ride went on forever. And for all of it she was lying back against Mick. She was rapidly freezing into a popsicle and it was about the closest she'd ever been to heaven.

"Hang on!" Mick shouted. Then he shifted, wrapping one arm tightly around her waist and clamping the injured one protectively over the top of her head.

She opened her eyes just a second before they ran out of snow.

They hit the ash field going at least fifty.

Mick curled up around her, forcing her to go fetal. They tumbled and rolled down the slope for a long time, finally skidding to a stop in a jumble.

She didn't dare move.

Mick wasn't moving either. The silence was deafening; Mount Hayes had been far noisier.

"You still with us, Quinn?" Her whisper sounded like a shriek.

"I think so. Let me check," he buried his face in her hair and breathed in. "Must be. I like to think that if this was heaven you wouldn't still smell like fish. Maybe this is hell, because you definitely smell like sulfur."

He recovered his parka, though he was shivering so hard that she had to zip it up for him.

Miraculously, he still had the NVGs, so she took them and pulled them on herself. They scouted around and found the chunk of rotor blade back up where Mick had tossed it aside at the snow-ash interface. They had too few resources to be throwing any away. Besides, it would be a very American object, even if it was ten thousand feet below the crash site.

Returning to Mick—who had folded up the foil toboggan and stuffed it in his pack—she took Mick's hand on his good side. They both staggered like drunkards down the last of the ash slope.

They had landed on a ridge of ash between two badly broken glaciers. The crevasses and spikes of either ice field surely would have killed them.

"You done good, Quinn, steering us here."

"Blind luck, I assure you."

She kept scanning upward but didn't spot any aircraft overhead. Hopefully the Russians were all heading to the drone's crash site now several miles behind them. There was no American wreckage at the site, outside the caldera.

They'd have no reason to search inside the caldera. Even if they did, all except a few tiny scraps had been melted.

If there was enough left of the drone to see the bullet holes or even recover some of the bullets, they'd find nothing but Russian manufacture. They'd be chasing their own tails for ages trying to figure out who shot down twenty million dollars of experimental aircraft.

Provided they didn't capture a pair of lost and wandering American pilots.

She'd finally shifted Mick to following behind. Blind in the darkness, he had a hand locked on the back of her survival vest and was skilled enough that they'd been making okay time.

Still, the stars were fading by the time Patty found what she was looking for.

She guided him up to the face of the glacier.

"It's warm," she watched his profile as he raised his face to the moist air.

Then she led him inside.

Patty checked in with Sofia who told them to keep out of sight. The slopes of Mount Shiveluch were crawling with Russian military. Hopefully the Russians would give up by nightfall, but during the daylight it would be too dangerous to travel.

She looked around and didn't know if she'd ever want to leave.

The ice cave in the bottom of the glacier had been carved by a thermal hot spring. Somewhere up under the ice, volcanic heat and glacier were combining to make a flow of warm, crystal clear water.

The cave was twenty-feet high, wider than her family's living room, and went back fifty or more paces that they could explore walking upright. The ceiling was a broad arch from one side to the other. The surface rippled like pillows.

The base of the cave was mostly boulders, originally caught up in the ice and then freed by the winding stream's warmth. But there were areas where the finer particles had melted out and been gathered into small beaches.

Its best feature was the dawn light. Shining golds and reds glittered at the cave's entrance. The ceiling above, through the thin ice and snow, was a wash of the most brilliant blue she'd ever seen.

"Color of your eyes, Gloucester," Mick said following her gaze upward.

"Twelve hours before first possible rescue. Ready to catch up on your sleep, Quinn?"

His slow smile told her that there wasn't a chance of that.

She nodded back at him, unable to find the words.

"I'll scrub your back if you'll scrub mine," Mick finally said.

"Okay," that sounded fantastic to her. "But you have to wash off your own wolf's blood."

Shy wasn't anywhere in Patty's personal inventory, but neither was bathing naked with a man she loved. At least not yet.

Mick dipped his face into the stream and scrubbed at it until she nodded her approval. The water, she knew, was hot-springs warm, and the ambient air was comfortable enough once back from the cave opening itself—despite being beneath a massive arc of ice.

Still unable to speak, she sat on the small sand beach and watched him undress.

This was not some man barely seen as he snuggled down in a sleeping bag. This was Mick "The Mighty" Quinn shining in the multi-colored ice cave. Broad chest, six-pack abs, and powerful legs.

She watched as he shed the last bit of cloth and then stepped up to her. He took her hands and coaxed her to her feet.

He was so perfect. Even the purpling bruises of the wolf's bite on his forearm—the thick layers had spared him any punctures—only added to the image. How was it possible she was the one he wanted?

His dark eyes studied her and she had to look away from the strength of his desire that shone there. He slowly undressed her, until she too was standing helplessly naked before him.

Patty swayed on her feet, light-headed and dizzy. For once unsure of herself because no man had ever looked at her the way Mick Quinn did.

When he swept her up in his arms, she turned totally girl and just curled up against his chest. He could do anything he wanted to her and she'd be helpless to stop him because she wanted it so badly. From

Mick Quinn, everything was welcome. Absolute trust in flight had somehow transformed to absolute trust in relationship.

She tried to think if she'd ever before found such a place of perfect contentment. *Nope. Not once.*

Despite his injury, he carried her as if she were a bride crossing a threshold and she remained curled against his chest as if she'd be there until the end of her days.

Then he let her go and she was falling.

With a splash she landed in a wide pool of the stream's warm water.

"Goddamn it, Quinn!" she shouted as soon as she could stop spitting out the water she'd swallowed.

---

IF SHE DIDN'T NEED to cool off, Mick sure as hell did.

The sight of Patty naked and so damned perfect had been seared into him. He knew he would do anything for her. There were also a lot of things, a whole lot of things he wanted to do to her…or perhaps *with* her.

He'd needed a little distance before he collapsed at her feet and begged her for any morsel she might deign to give.

Even lying back in the stream's water with little more than her snarl showing above the surface, he couldn't stop looking at her. The clarity of the water flowing over her body wasn't helping matters. Her shape was exquisite, a fantastic blend of completely feminine and undoubtedly soldier.

He sat down in the water to at least partially hide the throbbing evidence of his own need for her. Mick grabbed her ankle and yanked it hard enough to pull her face back underwater.

Then while she was still spluttering out her shock, he scooped up a handful of the warm sand and began scrubbing the bottom of her foot. As he worked his way up her body, she soon started a running commentary. First, with each scrub he was a "total meathead." But that soon changed to approval of each thing he was doing.

He couldn't even focus on the words. Instead he simply paid attention to when her sentences grew more and more fragmented, finally shattering under the harsh gasps as she struggled for breath.

When he raised her hips from the water to taste her, her cry echoed about the ice cave.

When at long last he laid her out on their spread clothes and took her, it was his own groans that echoed hers.

PATTY WOKE in her favorite position, curled in Mick Quinn's arms with her head resting on his shoulder. Her foil emergency blanket was spread over them, but the cave was warm enough that it was all the cover they needed.

The evening light had turned the cave into a shadowed, mysterious place beneath a ceiling of such dark blue that she caught herself wondering why there were no stars in it.

In twelve hours they had spoken no words. Discussed no futures. Made no promises or protestations.

For most of the last twelve hours they had simply enjoyed themselves and each other. She'd never known a man's body as thoroughly as she now knew Mick's, and he was such a responsive lover that she suspected that she'd barely begun to plumb the depths. Something she could easily spend a lifetime exploring.

She slid on top of him.

This time she was going to get her wake-up sex.

With impressive resiliency, Mick's body allowed itself to be teased to life. She cracked open another condom—they'd each been carrying a fair supply which had made them laugh before they'd jumped each other for the third time.

Mick's body shuddered to life as he let out a murmur of pleasure.

She poised herself over him, clutching the foil blanket about her shoulders—when a deep voice sounded in the cave.

"I thought you two might want some rescuing. Am I wrong?"

Patty twisted to glare over her shoulder, accidently ramming a knee into Mick's ribcage, waking him the rest of the way with a harsh grunt.

"Yes, you're totally wrong. Go away, Altman! I'm busy."

"Busy?" Napier said from close behind the SEAL commander. "Looks like you're getting ready to kill the boy. Will you be biting off his head when you are done with him? Like a praying mantis?"

"*Non!* She will not," Danielle spoke up. "Night Stalkers women do not kill their *véritable amour* except with the love of their hearts."

Patty pulled the foil blanket over her head and buried her face in Mick's chest. "True love" was right up there with the M-word as uniquely embarrassing truths to have been spoken aloud by one of her commanders.

"Your ass is out in the wind, Chief Warrant," Altman addressed her. "Must say, it ranks right up there with my wife's. Lucky man, Quinn."

"I have to agree with you, Commander. Though I'd say that Danielle's is—" was all Napier got out before Danielle cut him off.

"You! You will avert your eyes and say not one word or I will start comparing you to Lieutenant Quinn *en détail.*"

Mick reached his arms around Patty, stroked them down her back, and retucked the foil behind her buns.

"Someday we'll get a break," he whispered into her ear. "I'm willing to keep trying until we do. How about you?"

She nodded against his chest, but was still too embarrassed to face her commanders.

CHAPTER 25

Thirteen hours flying time saw them back to Anchorage. And Mick had spent most of it asleep in the back of the Chinook. The rest of it he'd spent marveling at finding Patty nestled in his arms each time he woke.

With the early departure of one Little Bird, the demise of the second, and a mid-air refueling courtesy of the US Air Force—because Attu Island was buried in a harsh storm—the heavy rubber fuel bladder in the Chinook's cargo bay was only half-emptied. It made a very comfortable mattress for the return flight. A giant, Jet A-fuel filled waterbed.

During the endless hours of debriefing, the investigators—who he was fairly sure were CIA—offered no complaints about he and Patty losing five million dollars of helicopter that would come out of their budget. The intelligence harvest on the Russian drone was huge.

First read was that its capabilities were far less complete than first feared. The airframe existed, but many of the electronics and software packages were little more than frameworks for what would still take the Russians years to develop.

After the round with the CIA, they'd been sent to sit with some engineers as they were the only two pilots who had flown against one or shot it down. Not that there was much to say from an engagement that had lasted under thirty seconds. They seemed quite upset that neither he nor Patty had the foresight to pull the *Linda's* recording log during the crash.

Then…

Mick had needed serious therapy once they escaped the debrief teams.

He knew exactly where to get it.

Fifteen minutes after they had all made good their escape from JBER, they once again were tucked away in the back room of the Moose's Tooth surrounded by pizza and beer.

Mick made damn sure he was sitting next to Patty O'Donoghue this time. Their chairs were so close together that they were drawing wry smiles from everyone around the table—even M&M and Kenny who were still ticked about missing out on the mission—and Mick didn't give a damn.

"To a successful mission," Altman called out and everyone raised their glasses. "And a safe return." He winked at Mick who winked back.

"Crap!" Patty jolted against him, nearly planting an elbow where she'd placed her knee so solidly in his ribs in the ice cave.

"Our Frisbees. Not only didn't we play a game of Ultimate Frisbee on Russian soil while we had the chance, they were in the back compartment of the *Linda.*"

She looked deeply put out by it.

"I'll get you new ones," Mick promised.

"Won't be the same. Those had history," she pouted for display. Then she beamed at him in that way she knew he was defenseless against. "You'll get me tournament quality, glow-in-the-dark ones?"

"Promise," and he sealed it with a kiss. A kiss that Patty heated up until catcalls sounded around the table. Then she sat back abruptly and fluttered her eyelashes at him.

He pulled the orange and red hat, that had somehow survived the mission, down over her eyes.

"To being totally under their thumbs," Napier toasted with a smile. Altman and Big John joined in on that one as the women laughed.

It was hard to imagine a giant like Big John unable to stand up to any whims of Connie Davis…or maybe it wasn't. Mick recalled that no one had tried to argue when Connie had insisted she needed fourteen more minutes.

"What were you doing to their software anyway?"

Connie blushed slightly, not something he'd ever seen before. By the expression on Big John's face that was a new one on him as well.

"They have acceleration sensors aboard their aircraft. They need to track and control the g-forces to make sure they don't overstress the airframe."

"So you switched it off?"

"Seems a little obvious," Patty nudged him. She'd kept her hat down and was pretending she was lost as an excuse to knock a hand repeatedly against his face. He could see a bit of the bright blue of her eyes through the stretched knitting, so he shoved her hat back up on her forehead and she stuck her tongue out at him.

"Far too obvious for my lady," John confirmed. "I'm guessing you set up a failure."

"Not directly," Connie replied. "Too easy to trace. I set it so that when it reached a g-force that was far from critical—one selected each time by a random number generator to make it harder to trace— it would set off a sub-routine in another section of the software. The engine control software would set up a high-frequency and very powerful oscillation that would ultimately shatter the welding compounds that the Russians prefer to use in their airframes."

"Which means the aircraft will test flawlessly on the ground and in simple flight…" Mick was damn impressed.

"But will fall out of the sky under various hard maneuvers," Patty said in wonder. Then she stood up and reached across the table. "High five, girl." Connie reached out and between them (mostly Patty) they managed to knock a pitcher of beer (mostly full) into a Santa's Little Helper meat-red pepper-and-cilantro pizza (thankfully mostly eaten).

"I estimate," Connie concluded, "that will set their program back eighteen to twenty months and add eighty-seven to ninety-two million dollars to their total program cost."

There was a respectful silence around the table.

"I think," Major Napier said softly, "that deserves more than a toast." Then he dug something out of his pocket and grinned wickedly.

He rapped whatever he held twice on the table, hard.

"Coin check!"

People began digging in their pockets.

Mick didn't even bother trying. He hadn't been coin checked in all of his time in the Night Stalkers and had long since stopped carrying the coin from his days at Fort Drum. His commander there had handed out commemorative unit coins so often that they'd become meaningless. To produce one of Goodman's coins was an embarrassment and Mick would rather buy the round of drinks for not having one—for that was the usual price for being unable to produce a unit coin.

At least he wasn't in it alone, only about half of the table managed to produce a coin in the allowed ten seconds after being challenged.

"Let's see 'em," Napier demanded.

Connie and Big John both had coins from the 160th SOAR 5th Battalion D Company. They were beautiful pieces. Inch-and-a-half, die-struck, brass coins. One side had the unofficial Night Stalkers' badge: Pegasus with raised sword and laser-vision eyes. On the obverse face, a Black Hawk helicopter with the regiment motto above —Night Stalkers Don't Quit—and "5D" below.

Altman and Nikita both had coins with the American flag on one side and the SEAL Trident on other side. Six stars had been worked in around "The United States Navy."

"We don't exactly advertise who we are, but the six stars are for Team 6."

Made sense.

Other coins were produced from various units they'd each served in.

Napier had been idly tapping his on the table. If there was ever a man who didn't fidget, it was the 5E's commanding officer.

"Let's see yours, Major," Mick called out.

Napier looked down at his hand as if in surprise. "Oh. Mine? Well, it's far better than any of these other ones. Even yours, Luke. Sorry. This one trumps the table." Then he laid it flat on the wood and slid it out toward the middle.

Everyone stood and leaned in to get a better angle on it.

Having the highest-ranking coin always won any coin challenge.

It had the Night Stalkers badge on the back, along with the motto.

Then the major reached out and flipped it over.

In the center was a simple large "5E."

Danielle craned her neck to read aloud the words which circled around the edge: "The fine men and women who," she reached out and turned the coin to read the other half of the circle, "make it such an honor to command."

Then Napier picked up the coin, the light brush of brass on the wood table, a huge sound in the silent room. He rose to his feet with a scrape of the chair.

He formally saluted Danielle. "Captain Delacroix. My honor." Then he shook her hand and handed her the coin.

Mick could feel the tightness clenching in his throat as Napier's wife rose to her feet and returned the salute. "The honor is mine, Major Napier."

Napier dug in his pocket again and moved to Patty.

"Chief Warrant O'Donoghue. My honor." And they traded salutes. Patty was openly crying as she replied and accepted her coin.

"Lieutenant Quinn. My honor."

As Mick saluted then shook his commander's hand. "The honor is mine, Major Napier," almost stuck in his throat. He took his coin and decided it was better than any medal or promotion he'd ever receive.

They each stood in turn and remained standing as he completed his circuit of the table. He also gave a coin to Nikita and Altman who were both obviously touched.

Once again at his own chair, he saluted the room sharply. With a pounding stomp to full attention, they all returned the salute.

"I never wanted the 5E. I already had the best team there was, or so I thought. I was a foolish man. I could never find any better than you people."

With a soft whisper of, "Nor I better than you," Danielle leaned forward and kissed her husband as tears rolled down her cheeks.

---

Patty held the 5E unit coin clutched against her chest with both hands. She'd never so belonged anywhere. She'd always been the misfit, doing well, but the misfit nonetheless.

People were sitting down around the table and she knew them and they knew her. She'd flown with them and completed a critical mission, while right in the core of it. She'd saved lives and she'd lived up to the Night Stalkers motto.

"You okay, Gloucester?" Mick was looking up at her.

She looked down at him sitting close beside where she stood.

There was another place she belonged. As close to Mick Quinn as she could get. As copilot, as fellow soldier, as lover, and as…

Patty looked over at Napier.

Conversations were restarting elsewhere around the table.

Major Napier, though holding his wife's hand, was looking directly at her. He offered her the slightest nod.

The major understood the depth and power of that bond. That it could coexist with duty.

She offered back the smallest nod and refocused back on Mick Quinn. She allowed herself a long look into his dark eyes, but there was no question, no hesitation any more. Her love for Mick was as clear inside her as a call to survive against all odds.

"Okay, Quinn. Decision time."

"Fine, what's the question?" As if he didn't know.

She held up her coin, "The 5E. We're stuck with each other now."

"Uh-huh."

"So are you getting on one knee? Or am I?"

Mick grinned at her and rested his coin on cocked thumb, ready to toss it aloft.

The smile that she sent back to him started so deep in her heart, she couldn't have stopped it even if she'd wanted to. Her heart had a hard lock and clear tone on Mick "The Mighty" Quinn. A lifelong lock.

"Call it," he said.

"Heads."

Mick tossed and caught the coin, and didn't show the least chagrin when the "5E" head stared back at him. He knelt before her.

Patty figured they were in this together, so she knelt before him, too, touching her knee to his.

Mick dragged her into his arms and confirmed the target of his own heart's destination with a kiss that sent her blood roaring louder than their cheering teammates.

# TARGET OF MINE

**MISSION:** *Honduras ranks as the world's most dangerous country. It's up to the Night Stalkers to join up with SEAL Team 6 and go undercover on a Caribbean cruise liner to take down a deadly conspiracy.*

*TEAM:*

**Crew Chief Drake Roman**

*— Likes his job just fine, working hard and kicking the enemy's butt. He never aspired to more, until sent undercover as the ultimate mercenary. Is it too late to channel his inner alpha?*

**SEAL Team 6 Chief Petty Officer Nikita Hayward**

*— Lost her past to a mercenary outfit gone bad. Assigned undercover as the mission's leading lady? Just don't make her wear a goddamn dress.*

*The Night Stalkers fly the stealthiest helicopters in the US arsenal. But when their unique skills land them on a tourist ship cruising the Caribbean, the mission is only just beginning to go south.*

*Art dealers, a police sniper working the wrong side of the law, a conspiracy, and a very upset cruise line hotelier are the least of their worries when the heat between them starts burning hotter than the Honduran sun.*

*Note: A special thanks to the amazing Cristin Harber for the loan of Team Titan. They belong to her. More at www.cristinharber.com*

# CHAPTER 1

*R*ain sucked.

Philippine September-monsoon rain really sucked.

In a full flightsuit and helmet it was thick, hot, and disgustingly sweaty.

Worse, it was creating mayhem with their midnight attack plan.

Drake Roman hung on to his M134 Minigun with both hands as the Night Stalkers' DAP Hawk helicopter *Beatrix* banked hard to avoid a hundred meters of island that came out of nowhere. The tactical readouts were showing nothing but a wall of water thick enough to block most radar signals, and the infrared night vision was totally useless because everything was the same temperature—wet.

His flight harness cut into his shoulders as he leaned against the turn. Levering himself forward, Drake stuck his head out the window, trying to see ahead through the unlit darkness. The rain was coming straight down, but the Hawk moved at over a hundred and fifty knots, so even in the slipstream of the hull, he couldn't see squat as the rain drumbeat on his helmet.

The crew chiefs' seats faced to either side from close behind the two pilots' seats. His Minigun was on a traveler that reached out the side window and gave him a full range of fire from directly sideways to straight ahead and from level to straight down.

Right now he just wanted someone to aim it at.

On the first pass, the other crew chief had taken a hit, a bad one by the sound of it. With Carl out of action, the pilots had twisted sideways, giving Drake the primary action side, so Carl was someone else's problem. He had an aircraft to defend.

Normally able to strike from a thousand meters away, tonight's weather was forcing encounters to be up close and personal.

"I'm in crew chief starboard seat," a new voice announced on the intercom, "I've got Carl patched and sedated." Anyone else, he wouldn't have registered more than the fact that the position was occupied and Carl was alive—a welcome surprise. But Chief Petty Officer Nikita Hayward of DEVGRU—also known as SEAL Team 6— spoke with a smooth, soft Southern accent that had messed with him since the day he'd first met her on a mission a year before. Never did him any good, but damn he liked that voice.

The wall of water broke—one instant in the midst of a biblical downpour, the next in clear air—to reveal a narrow beach and a high vertical cliff capped by dark jungle. Probably be dramatic as hell in the daytime. At night it was just another obstacle to not smash into. At the base was huddled a line of small boats.

They flew less than a hundred meters above the sea and less than that from the soaring cliffs. With the break in the downpour, the tactical readout inside his helmet's visor finally painted a clear image.

Tourist boat. Tourist boat...and another tourist boat. They were tied up just outside the surf line. Abandoned to the nightly monsoon, they'd be washed clean for tomorrow's tourists who came to mob the dramatic beaches of Palawan Island, Philippines, along the South China Sea.

Except it wasn't only tourist boats huddled here tonight and the Night Stalkers of the 5th Battalion E Company had been waiting for just such a night to take care of a problem.

Someone had made it abundantly clear to the Philippine military to not interfere in this region. The AFP had recently lost three heli-copters, two boats, and twenty personnel before giving up.

Drug-runner, gun-runner, pirate—it didn't matter. Tonight was the night they were going down.

Technically, the US couldn't help, at least not in any obvious way. They couldn't admit to attacking any Philippine nationals without putting their new military base leases at risk. The Philippine govern-ment had given the US military access to five new bases in addition to Subic Bay with the understanding that they'd help defend the country, not attack it.

Regrettably, the local criminal element didn't feel the need to honor any such unspoken agreement. The 5E were here to give them a lesson tonight in the hazards of ignoring that.

Their company had drawn the mission because they specialized in never-having-been-there operations—Black Ops. The very blackest. Though this wasn't one of those.

Tourist boat…tourist bo—

The next boat flared with heat signatures of ten people on a night when no one in their right mind would be afloat. Hard radar returns, as if their boat was loaded with more than tourists or local fish. There was metal on that boat, a lot of it.

He saw the hot flash of gunfire from yet another boat just emerging out of the curtain-like edge of the deluge. Multiple targets.

The bastards had already taken the first shots, hitting Carl more by chance than skill—which satisfied the 5E's rules of engagement for this mission: *do not fire first.* They hadn't.

But paybacks were about to be delivered.

Big time.

**"W**hat the hell did you guys do to my helicopter?" The mechanic was practically screaming. Like he'd never seen a shot-up helo before. It wasn't as if he was new to the 5E.

Nikita stood off to the side of the hangar next to a long folding table, checking through her gear. It was late afternoon and their four helicopters had just unloaded from the C-5A Galaxy transport. After the long flight home, they'd been reassembled and then hopped to the 5E's private corner of Mother Rucker. Fort Rucker, Alabama, had gained that name for the brutal standards of the Army flight instructors stationed here and, even though Nikita wasn't part of the 5E, she'd adopted the name.

"She only has a few holes in her," Drake Roman protested loudly. "*Beatrix* done good!"

"Thirty-two," another mechanic, this one with a clipboard, spoke up. "Thirty-two holes. Who knows how much damage to internal systems we'll find when we peel off the skins. If it wasn't a Black Hawk, you'd be dead."

By Nikita's estimation, that count was low for a standard mission with the 5E, but mechanics enjoyed whining. Besides, they didn't count the holes that had been put in Carl.

"Told you she done good," Drake patted the side of the damaged helicopter.

The helicopter wasn't the only one who'd done good. Nikita had flown a half dozen missions with the 5E over the last year and they were becoming her favorite assignment. They weren't designated as a Special Mission Unit, unlike her own DEVGRU SEAL Team 6, but they should be. Most of the time Delta Force and DEVGRU didn't get anywhere without tapping the Night Stalkers of the 160th SOAR.

The Special Operations Aviation Regiment (airborne) delivered her team wherever they needed to go, and always showed up to get them back out no matter what unholy hell was breaking loose. Of them all, the 5E was both the smallest and the most effective. They only had four helicopters: a monstrous twin-rotor Chinook, the lethal DAP Hawk, and a pair of Little Bird attack helos. And they were all stealth rigged—making them some of the rarest helicopters anywhere. In addition, the company had one of the most advanced drones yet produced for their exclusive use.

To her knowledge, the only other company who rated any stealth rotorcraft was the 5th Battalion D Company and the 5D only had two. Which was how the 5E rated their own private corner at Ech Stagefield on Mother Rucker whenever they were home. These assets were best kept hidden.

"What is wrong with those people?" Drake stood directly across the folding tables she'd set up to sort her gear. He stood only a few inches taller than her own five-ten. He was lean, but soldier fit with dark eyes and darker hair. And he was pissed.

"Why do you feel so defensive about your aircraft?" Nikita went back to sorting her ammo to determine how much she needed for restock. For some reason, which her commander Luke Altman wasn't sharing, he and she had returned with the 5E. Usually they would do what the rest of the SEAL Team had done, just melt away after a mission. Standard protocol was to go back to the DEVGRU base at Naval Air Station Oceana in Virginia and do a full breakdown of the mission to extract lessons learned. Then start into skills training while waiting for the next call-up.

"Because she did great!" Drake apparently just needed to rant, so she let him. He'd get down to what was actually bothering him eventually. He turned back to glare at the mechanics.

That's when she recognized the stain pattern on the back of his flightsuit. The outline of the crew chief's seat back was marked across the fabric—clean where the seat back had been, dark brown where Drake's arms and shoulders had stuck out beyond the edges of the seat.

Carl's blood-spray pattern. There'd been a lot of it.

She'd stabilized him with a tourniquet around the stump of his mostly missing arm. And a pressure patch to the mess that was his other shoulder. Glue to close a few more holes. He was still listed as critical at the Antonio Bautista Air Base hospital in the Philippines. The chances of Drake Roman's fellow crew chief ever leaving there except in a box were slim.

Nikita remembered what Lieutenant Commander Altman had done for her on a similar occasion.

She walked over to the unlocked weapons cabinet where the team had been stashing their mission weapons. She grabbed a pair of MK11 sniper rifles, slipped on suppressors, and selected a couple boxes of ammo.

"Hey, Roman!"

"What?"

When he turned, she threw one of the rifles to him.

He caught it and looked down at it in surprise. "What?"

"You once said that you wish you could shoot like I did."

"Uh huh." He'd been her rear guard during a Peruvian mission a few months ago. Six targets, all out past fifteen hundred meters. She'd taken down all six before they figured out what was happening. It was what SEAL snipers were trained for.

"Well, it's never gonna happen."

That earned her a perplexed smile. "Great. So what's with the rifle?"

"I figure that I can't make you a worse shot than you already are, so anything has to be an improvement."

He laughed. It was bitter, but it was a laugh. He was one of the top helicopter gunners anywhere. But a Minigun fired from a moving platform like a helicopter wasn't a sniper weapon—it was a blunderbuss.

"Besides," she stepped out of the shadows into the sunlight and so-familiar heavy heat of the late Alabama afternoon, "I figure I should get you out of here before the mechanic shoots you, or the other way round."

"Fine."

---

DRAKE TRIED to shake off the tightness in his shoulders but wasn't having much luck with it. They felt as if he was turning into the hunchback of Notre Dame. He had no idea why he was being so twitchy.

Even after a year stationed at Mother Rucker, he wasn't used to the Alabama heat. He peeled his flightsuit and chucked it over on the laundry pile. The shorts and t-shirt he'd worn underneath weren't much better. Alabama was a land where sweat didn't evaporate, it clung.

When Nikita did the same, though, he could feel his mood improving.

She was the first and, as far as he knew, only woman to make DEVGRU through the front door and it showed on her body. She was of a medium build that fit her perfectly. But she wasn't merely strong, she was carved. Not like a bodybuilder with bulging biceps and six-pack abs. She was carved the way an artist would shape her in cool stone or, better yet, warm wood—not an extra ounce of flesh, but what was there was perfect. Soft, smooth...and tough as hell. Her brunette hair was always pulled back in a painfully tight ponytail that made her look panther sleek. And her light brown eyes were always watching.

He followed her out of the hangar and onto the stagefield. Ech was designed for helicopters only. It had five short runways for practicing mass landings and takeoffs, or emergency procedures. The concrete was rough with a thousand scars from auto-rotation practice and helicopters sliding to a grinding halt on steel skids.

But not a single aircraft had landed here other than the 5E since they took over the field last year. Their four rotorcraft were never left out on the apron. Instead they were immediately rolled out of sight into the field's lone hangar. The field purposely looked abandoned and unused, weeds growing up through the cracks in the concrete and the surrounding field in need of a good mowing. At the rate it was growing, maybe they should skip mowing and just bale the area as hay.

The only change to Ech Stagefield in the last year was that the hangar was now highly secure and there was a new two-story housing unit big enough for each of the 5E's fifteen pilots and gunners to have their own tiny apartment in addition to a few guest spaces—those had only ever been used by the SEALs. It included a communal kitchen / dining / briefing room, but most of their meetings were held out at the small cluster of picnic tables between the offices and the hangar.

Ech was surrounded by thick 'Bama forest on all sides: towering longleaf pine and willow oak, hickory and beech, prickly holly and sweet bay. He'd learned the trees when he found out Nikita was from Alabama—not that he'd ever had a chance to show off that bit of knowledge. Even a year here and it still smelled strange, particularly on the quiet evenings when his nose was expecting the Scotch pine, oak, birch, and maple of the New Hampshire hills where his family kept a summer home up on Squam Lake. The only entry to Ech was by air or a narrow dirt road through the forest.

He tromped along behind Nikita as she led him across the tarmac and out into the grassy field.

"Walk softly," Nikita's voice was barely louder than the banging in the hangar behind them as the mechanics got to work.

"What does walking have to do with shooting?"

Nikita stopped and he almost ran into her.

"What?"

"Are you here to learn or to whine like a little pissant, Roman?" Soft Southern with a razor-edged tongue.

"To whine like a little pissant!" At least *that* felt like he was getting something done.

"Okay," Nikita turned back toward the hangar.

"What? No! Wait."

She stopped.

He closed his eyes but all he could see was the blood all over the DAP Hawk's cargo bay. Just wait until the mechanics had to clean that up. Then they'd be sorry. Maybe as sorry as he already was. He'd done what he could, swabbing out the back of the DAP during the long flight home. He'd nearly punched his pilots Rafe and Julian when they offered to help. Carl had been his fellow crew chief, so it had been his job to do and he'd done it alone. Actually, he'd been a rear ramp man on the big twin-rotor Chinook when the 5E formed, but Major Napier liked to cross train his teams by shuffling them around on occasion. Drake had hit the *Beatrix* Black Hawk three months ago and it had fit him just fine.

He managed a deep breath and opened his eyes. Nikita was still standing there, as impassively as ever—more beautiful than a Grecian statue, waiting for him to choose.

"Okay. If it gets my mind off…" he couldn't finish the sentence. "I'll learn anything."

Nikita nodded and continued to lead him out into the field. "To take your shooting to the next level, you gotta leave emotion behind. Emotion changes heartrate and reaction time. And it breaks concentration. Those are the obvious effects."

"What are the unobvious?"

"Emotion blurs perception. To shoot at truly long distances, out past a thousand meters or more, your entire being must be perceiving the shot flying true far downrange or you'll never hit your target."

"Sounds like mysticism, but put those damn gunrunners back in my sights,"—that's what they had to have been by the scale of the explosions when the 5E had finally destroyed their boats—"and I'll show you what I'm perceiving downrange."

"Look behind us."

He turned. Through the thick growth of the late-summer-tall grass, he could only see one heavily trampled clear line, his own. Nikita Hayward had hardly left any impression at all.

*Walk softly,* she'd said.

Drake gazed back at the line of helicopters parked in the hangar beyond.

That's what the 5E did: their stealth aircraft walked softly and carried a damn big stick.

"Okay. Show me how to do that."

# CHAPTER 3

"What the hell are we here for?" A big voice boomed across the twilit airfield, making Drake break off in mid-clip to see what was going on. They were deep in the tall grass, so he actually had to rise up on all fours from his prone position beside her in order to see.

Nikita sighed—the man had the attention span of the goddamn gnats that kept hovering about them. Even for someone who was hurting, he was being chaotic. That he had hit the target at all over the last hour was a testament to his skill.

Ever since she was a child, she'd always found shooting was a great way to relax, giving her a simple focus that cleared her mind of other problems.

Not Drake.

"Come on, Roman. I thought you were serious about learning this shit." Drake was a seriously decent shot for a helicopter crew chief. She felt that there was hope of training him to be actually good. Maybe not SEAL Team 6 sniper good, but definitely operator level.

"I am."

"Well, then you're gonna have to learn to focus. You can either be a sniper or see what shiny objects are glittering nearby to distract you."

With practiced speed, the hangar doors were being raced shut before the intruder could round the corner of the hangar and see the line of stealth helicopters.

"Right. Sorry." He turned back and caught her looking toward the stranger continuing to shout out his impatience.

"Chief Petty Officer Nikita Hayward!" Drake's voice was soap opera dramatic. "I'm shocked. You call that maintaining focus?"

"Screw you, Roman." At least she'd stayed lower, looking between stalk and seeds so that she'd be less visible. Drake's head was popped up like some stupid gopher just asking to be shot in the head.

"Anytime."

"Yeah, I already knew that about you." Sergeant First Class Drake Roman was a damn handsome flyboy and knew it. It had taken him under thirty seconds into their first mission together last year to make it clear that the offer was open whenever she was interested. Absolutely not! Though, oddly, he'd never renewed the invitation and that bothered her at times. It was as if he was up to something, but she couldn't figure out what. Normally she had to beat guys like him back down more times than kudzu vines crawling into the vegetable garden.

Her attention stayed on the newcomer standing in front of the now sealed hangar that housed the 5E's four helicopters. Strangers were not supposed to come to this corner of Mother Rucker. This was exclusively the territory of the Night Stalkers 5th Battalion E company. Outsiders not welcome.

He was a big guy, classic broad-shoulder type. Walked with the arrogance of a US Army Ranger, but there was something else about him. Something that didn't fit—completely—aside from the babe at his side.

The babe would have looked like an over-built sidewalk hussy with her leather clothes, long brown-black hair, and come-fuck-me boots, if it wasn't for where she was. Mother Rucker was one of the most secure military bases in the country, and Ech Stagefield was perhaps the most secure part of the fort—it was a seriously long way from the Miami strip. Besides, what crazy-as-shit person wore leather this far south of the Mason-Dixon line?

Nikita unclipped the Leupold telescopic sight off the rail of her MK11 rifle and turned to inspect the guy.

He was ignoring Pete and Danielle—the 5E's commander and chief pilot—standing right in front of him. Instead, he was looking right at her. He shouldn't even be able to see their position. They hadn't dug in their shooting site, but the sun was down and the light was getting iffy. Besides, she and Drake were fifty meters out into the tall-growing grass.

The smile he sent her way was chilly at best. It made her wish she wasn't merely using the scope, but had swung her entire rifle his way just to chap his ass. Then he turned his attention to Pete and Danielle. The leather-clad babe had followed his line of sight and now *she* was watching them.

Nikita checked the parking lot. Latest model Ford Expedition SUV, black, top-of-the-line, windows all tinted, fancy chrome wheels —all the geegaws. It fit right in with their flashy style.

"Should we go over?" Drake didn't yet have the sniper instincts that would have made it a whisper. Thankfully, the light breeze was blowing from the hangar toward their position, so their voices weren't likely to carry in that direction.

"You that desperate to get near a busty woman in leather, Roman? Besides, we'd just be sent away again if it's anything important. Command talks to you when they're good and ready—not a moment before." She felt foolish for stating the obvious. After snapping the scope back onto the rail, she double-checked the alignment marks.

"We've got incoming. Whoo-doggies, do we ever," this time Drake whispered, but it sounded more like awe than caution.

"You're not from Texas, Roman, so cut that out. Your Southern sucks even worse than your Yankee."

Nikita glanced over and saw the woman was coming their way with a swing of hip like she really did belong working the Miami strip —though definitely the high-rent end. Drake was gonna be useless until she was gone, so Nikita waited her out.

"Hi, honey. Aren't you the cutest thing?" The woman laser-focused on Drake. Her voice had that sexy, breathless quality that always seemed to grab men by the balls. She had long sleek hair that defied the humidity, fair skin, and dark blue eyes.

Drake really was a goner. For a reason that eluded her, Nikita found that irritating. Not that she had any claim, but they had fought together and this woman was—

"You can call me Sugar."

She had to be kidding. Even her honey-smooth words were lipsticked carmine red. The accent was real though. Maryland or maybe Virginia—somewhere up north.

"What are you shooting today?"

Like the overeager puppy dog he was when faced with a large set of breasts, Drake held up his MK11. "It's a sniper rifle."

"I can see that, Sweet Cheeks. May I?"

Before Nikita could protest, Drake had handed over his weapon. No SEAL in their right mind would ever relinquish their weapon short of a court martial. He was only a Night Stalker, but still it was no damn excuse.

"Sugar" gave the rifle a quick inspection that showed more familiarity with weapons than Nikita would have expected.

She shouldered it without asking permission.

Nikita jerked her sidearm, but Sugar was aiming downrange toward the target. If she turned it anywhere else, Nikita would take her out first and ask questions later.

Sugar snicked off the safety and unleashed five rounds, two heartbeats between each shot. Nice and steady. Good weapon control. Absorbed the kick of the 7.62 mm round through her shoulder and down into a back-braced leg. Her stance wasn't military, but it was good.

Nikita ducked her head to her own scope and checked downrange. First shot high, the other four rang steel—near enough to dead center to make it impossible to tell if there was any drift. The target was six inches at six hundred meters, so it wasn't a hard shot, even in this light, but it was far better shooting than most civilians could manage. As good as Drake had done.

Sugar handed the rifle back to Drake. "Your scope is set a half mil too low. Watch out for the catch on the trigger at the last pound of pull. If your shots are drifting to the right, that's why. You should have it fixed. I've seen that in the MK11 Mod 0s before." Her accent almost disappeared when she was talking weapons; in its place was a sharp professional.

Drake was clearly past noticing such nuances, or perhaps even past speech.

Sugar looked at Nikita and probably would have cracked her bubblegum if she'd been chewing any. Instead, she slapped a hand on her own leather-wrapped behind with a loud smack as she turned back toward the field. "Book and its cover, dearie, book and its cover. Y'all c'mon in. There's gonna be a powwow if I know my man." And she strode back the way she'd come, hip swing and all.

Drake didn't look aside for a single second—total brain death.

"She sure got your number, Roman."

---

IN THE PAST, Sugar most certainly would have gotten his number—in a past before Drake had met Nikita Hayward. Built babes in leather shooting high-power rifles were definitely his idea of seriously hot—wasn't a man alive who wouldn't agree. But it was no longer any contest.

Sitting next to him in the tall grass was five-foot-ten of SEAL Team Six in female form. And not just female—she was Lieutenant Commander Luke Altman's right hand. Whatever it took to be that in the male-ruled world of Special Operations, she had it. She embodied it. Nikita was the most amazing woman he'd ever met...not that he'd ever seen her give any man the time of day.

M&M's attempt to get her attention while they were in the Philippines was so dismal it couldn't even be called a decent try. Kenny got nowhere at all.

Himself, he'd searched for tactics, an *in* on the powerful Nikita. He'd even watched the movie *La Femme Nikita*, the *Point of No Return* Bridget Fonda remake, as well as both television show spin-offs about the exquisitely lethal assassin, in hopes of gaining any insight from the fictitious character that he could apply to the real-deal SEAL.

Drake had almost taken a run at her when the SEALs were along on a mission with them into Russia. Every single approach he'd cooked up had sounded stupid in his head and some tiny bit of common sense had left them all unvoiced. But to watch her shoot...it was a thing of true beauty. Lying together in the tall grass—doing nothing other than target shooting—was more of a start than he'd managed in a year.

No matter how much fun she was to watch, the hip-swinging Sugar wasn't even in the same world. Besides, she had "her man."

"Was she for real?" He'd always thought of himself as a great judge of women, but Nikita was slowly teaching him that he was only a great judge of the subset of women willing to slide into bed with him. Nikita wasn't one of those. He found her wholly unreadable and that, as much as anything, had snagged his attention until even looking the other way was impossible when she was around.

"Give me your weapon."

Nikita aimed his rifle downrange and, even though it was dark enough for the first fireflies to begin showing off, she fired a single round with hardly any hesitation. He heard the bright plink as the bullet hit steel. She handed the weapon back.

"What?"

"She's for real. Thought you knew how to zero a scope. We can cover that next time if you want."

"I know how to zero one. But I'm not used to shooting such piddly little guns. I just shifted down a bit instead." At first he'd thought he'd been missing high because the distance to the target wasn't what he thought it was or because Nikita was so distracting or... He'd run out of excuses and simply compensated by aiming lower. The pull to the right? That he'd missed entirely. Exactly what he didn't want to do, look like a complete doofus in front of an ST6 SEAL.

"It's better to zero the scope if you're taking multiple shots like this. Less of a distraction. And if you don't know how to fix that trigger, I can show you." She flicked on a flashlight and began collecting her brass from the deep-shadowed grass. He did the same until they could account for all of their rounds, including the five that Sugar had shot.

He actually didn't know how to repair the trigger, but he'd find someone else to show him how to fix it, then swear them to secrecy.

"A sniper in the field never leaves a trace that they were there," and she didn't. When they were done, there was nothing but two flat spots in the grass that would have disappeared soon enough. She leaned down to fluff up the bent grass. After admiring the view of a bent-over Nikita for a moment, he did the same. All evidence of lying close beside her for an hour, erased.

He hefted the MK11. A dozen pounds of rifle good to eight hundred meters and past a thousand in a pinch. The same basic cartridge as his M134 Minigun, though he typically fired eighty rounds per second instead of one every couple heartbeats. Being shot-perfect was less critical when he was throwing two pounds of lead per second versus half an ounce per shot. Personally, he liked the power of his M134, but there was a cleanness, a purity to what Nikita did, shot by shot, that he could appreciate.

As they walked back to the main hangar, he could see by the lights through the high windows above the closed doors that some of the others were gathering in. Most were still in the hangar working over the helicopters and their gear, preparing for whatever came next.

The 5E's commanders Pete and Danielle, who flew the big Chinook, were front and center. Rafe and Julian, the two pilots from his own Black Hawk crew, also came over. The drone's copilot, Zoe DeMille, rounded out the gathering.

With just four helicopters and one drone, the 5E was the smallest company in the Night Stalkers by far. But they were the only team to be a hundred percent stealth equipped, garnering them the edgiest assignments. Drake wished he knew quite what he'd done right to be here so that he could make sure to keep doing it.

They'd flown against the 5th Battalion D Company in a training exercise, and beat them more by luck than anything. It hadn't hurt that they had "borrowed" two of the 5D's mechanics for their first missions, but the "loaners" had been shifted back to Fort Campbell to take over the future-tech group for all of SOAR. That's when he'd switched to the Black Hawk, to fill in the gap left by Connie Davis. Now with Carl down, there were going to be even more changes.

A massive black SUV with tinted windows was the unknown vehicle in the parking lot.

"Wondered when you'd notice. Now you're going to have serious truck envy too," Nikita sounded thoroughly disgusted.

He just shrugged nonchalantly, but he thought it was seriously cool. Way better than his ten-year-old battered-blue Ford Ranger.

Another vehicle rolled in, a base Hummer.

"When it rains…" Drake recognized the passenger before he climbed out: Colonel Cass McDermott, the commander of the entire Night Stalkers 160th Special Operations Aviation Regiment. Drake hadn't seen him since the night the 5E was formed up right here at these picnic tables a year ago.

"…Oobleck falls from the sky."

Drake looked over at Nikita.

"I'm a Dr. Seuss fan. So sue me."

He laughed at the sudden image of Nikita Hayward as a little girl intently studying a book about a boy trying to save his kingdom from sticky green goo falling out of the sky. The mission to save the kingdom made sense for a future DEVGRU SEAL, but Nikita as a young girl was almost impossible to imagine. Though if she'd worn pigtails as a kid, he definitely wanted to see a picture.

It was difficult reconciling her looks with who she was. By her looks she could have been the nice girl next door. But he'd seen this "girl" swing on a sixty-pound pack as easily as he could sling a rifle, and he'd watched her shoot to kill.

The casual ease of her soft Southern accent would never have flown at Andover Prep—whereas his own moneyed Boston had fit right in. She was like an education in how narrow his world had been before joining the military. But any thought that Southern meant slow or mild was blown away by one look in her brown eyes—she missed nothing of what was going on around her. He could see her mind working every moment behind those eyes.

At the picnic table, Pete and Danielle sat facing the two strangers. The two couples were eyeing each other in silent suspicion. Even Danielle's unflappable Quebecois politeness appeared strained.

"Who are—" Major Pete Napier and the big guy snarled at each other almost in unison. Then they held a glaring contest before both turned their ire toward the Colonel.

Colonel McDermott pulled up a chair and sat at the end of the table as if joining a jovial party.

Lieutenant Commander Luke Altman, Nikita's boss, came to stand on Drake's other side. Not many men could make him feel small, but Altman was even more physically imposing than the stranger. Luke Altman wasn't even the sort of guy you'd eventually call by his first name—he'd never be "my buddy Luke", he'd simply be "Altman" or maybe Lieutenant Commander.

By the time they were all gathered around the table—five of the fifteen Night Stalkers who made up the 5E, two SEALs, the pair of strangers, and the colonel—full dark had descended and, along with it, an Arctic chill that had nothing to do with the balmy September night. The cicadas and frogs seemed to be the only ones happy at the moment.

Drake did his best to pretend that he wasn't trapped between the two ST6 SEALs, but was standing there because he belonged—lined up like they were a Greek chorus to narrate the drama about to unfold. Someone fetched a Coleman lantern and dropped it on the table, lighting everyone in strange shadows. Someone else dropped a case of beer on the table—which meant no flights tomorrow, no battle flights anyway. He wanted to step forward to take one, but neither of the ST6 operators moved, so he stayed put.

"So tell it," Colonel McDermott said to no one in particular as he twisted a cap off a beer.

"Why?" The big guy snarled back. And in that moment, Nikita knew what he was because no one who was still military would talk back to a bird colonel that way. He wasn't a US Army Ranger, he was a *former* US Army Ranger.

"Mercenary," it came out as no more than a whisper, but his gaze shot to her. His smile built—it was *not* friendly.

"I'm a *contractor*. Always on behalf of my country. My Titan team takes on the messes you military types couldn't handle if your lives depended on it. What are you, missy?" He grabbed two beers, opening one for the woman beside him. Then he tipped his own toward Nikita like he was aiming a gun.

Titan. Probably the toughest military contractors in the business. They were the baddest-ass door-kickers out there. Their rep was good. But still goddamn vigilantes—just ones with a big budget and a government sanction.

Nikita wouldn't mind telling him exactly who she was, but DEVGRU operators didn't go around announcing themselves to the general public—except for a couple of the guys on the bin Laden raid with no sense of silence. Luke Altman had never even said a word about it, though she was fairly sure he'd been in on that mission.

This guy needed a different answer.

"I can tell you what I'm not."

"Oh, bring it on," he thumped his beer on the table, then crossed his arms over his big chest and glared at her. In a pissing contest, you didn't look away, so she couldn't see how the others were reacting except for Sugar. She sat close beside the big man and was slowly shaking her head in amusement—as if she knew what was about to land on her companion's head and couldn't wait to watch. Nikita could almost like her for that.

"I'm not from a team that levels an entire South American villa in a bang so big that I could hear it while stretched out all comfortable in my bunk at Fort Bragg," which was not her real base. That was at

Naval Air Station Oceana in Virginia Beach along with the rest of DEVGRU.

That got his attention. He clearly didn't like that she knew that about him. She'd always kept track of the main "contractors." Ever since— No! She wasn't going to think about that.

"No running attacks back and forth across the hills and hollers outside Charlottesville, Virginia. No gun battles shredding up multiple floors of an Abu Dhabi hotel. Y'all Ranger types are great at kicking down them doors. When I go through one, nobody—and I mean *nobody*—knows I've been there, asshole." Name calling was lame, but she couldn't stop herself. And where the Southern hick was coming from she had no idea. But Nikita knew where her emotional heat was coming from, had spent most of her adult life trying to ignore it. Now she had her past chilled down to the point where it took someone like this over-confident bastard to drag it back to the surface. She didn't appreciate it.

"How the hell do you know all—" The guy shut his trap and glared at her, his eyes momentarily shifting from merely black to carbonized steel. Then he glanced around the circle and she could see him start thinking—finally. She didn't look aside, but had the impression that all of the others were remaining impassive, revealing nothing.

Sugar started to giggle. She tried to hide it in a swallow of beer but didn't make it.

He glared at her.

Sugar broke into laughter and began poking at the man's ribs with a red manicured nail. "She got you, J-dawg. She so got you. That's exactly who you are."

"Shit!" *J-dawg* scrubbed a hand over his face. A smile actually cracked his stern features. "Between Sugar and Nicole, you think I'd have learned about women who know how to fight."

"Just wait until Asal grows up. Our girl will teach you a thing or two about warrior women."

He pulled his companion in and kissed her on top of the head with a surprising tenderness. "She already has, damned kid."

He eyed the circle of people once more, keeping his arm around Sugar's shoulders a moment longer.

This time Nikita let herself look around as well. Of the five Night Stalkers present, two were women and neither of them looked any happier with this guy than she felt.

"Not my best meet and greet, I suppose."

"No shit, J-dawg!" For a moment Nikita wished she was her movie namesake rather than a SEAL. *La Femme Nikita* wouldn't hesitate for a second to unsling the rifle over her shoulder and see how a mercenary liked staring down the barrel from two meters out. That's how welcome he was.

"Only Lily gets to call me J-dawg. Name is Jared. And I'm the only one who gets to call her that. She's Sugar to the rest of you."

"Lotta rules there, *J-dawg*." Not a chance in hell of her cutting a mercenary any slack.

He inspected the circle again, then pointed at the line of her, Drake, and Altman. "What are you three? You sure aren't flyboys."

"Hello! Not a boy!"

J-dawg ignored her and looked to Colonel McDermott, who had apparently been enjoying the whole scene.

"Who the hell are they?"

"The two on the outsides are the reason you're here." Then McDermott scowled at Drake, "The guy in the middle? We'll be damned if we know what he is."

She couldn't tell if Drake was unhappier with McDermott's tease or her laugh right in his face.

# CHAPTER 4

The base commissary had delivered a stack of pizzas. Drake figured that if you ever wanted to know the location of every top-secret outfit on a base—and be welcomed into the compound every time—you just had to get a job as an on-base pizza delivery driver.

Drake had managed to stick close beside Nikita as well as snag three slices of fully-loaded pizza to go with his beer, more than sufficient solace for his battered ego. He'd been razzed more times than the sirens had called to Odysseus for the way he spoke—he was an Army sergeant with the speech befitting a West Point officer—so it was no big deal. Though he could have done without Nikita laughing at him.

Everyone was calling the guy J-dawg and he bristled just like a junkyard dog every time. If the guy would just chill, it would go away, but Drake expected that chilling wasn't in the guy's repertoire.

Well, it might eventually go away for everyone except Nikita. Something had crawled way under her skin worse than a whole troupe of ticks on a hound.

Drake always did his best to take his own name's advice: Drake the male duck. He just let it all slide off his back. He'd had to bust his ass to make Night Stalkers, but only because *everyone* had to make it into such an elite outfit and he'd wanted in. The rest of life? He did his best to just swim through, and it came easily—especially the women. The women before Nikita anyway.

He'd never gone for the difficult or tricky women before. Wasn't worth the time. For every one of that type, he could mow down a half dozen or more. But something about the DEVGRU SEAL sitting beside him, and her glowering at J-dawg, made him want to work for it this time. He bet himself a twenty that it would be worth it. He wasn't yet ready to bet money on whether or not he'd succeed. All of his normal lines wouldn't do anything but push her away, so he hadn't even tried them.

"Now, tell it, Jared," the colonel thumped his bottle on the table for attention. He was the only one who hadn't gone all J-dawg on the guy. "Nikita, keep your mouth shut and let the man speak."

"Nikita?" Sugar looked at her with surprise. "Hayward?"

J-dawg looked at his wife, who continued to watch Nikita. "What?"

Sugar just shook her head, "Times I wonder how it is you manage to stay alive, J-dawg."

"Easy. I'm too ornery to die," he spoke around a mouthful of pizza.

"Next time," Sugar informed him, "think before you argue with the first woman to make the cut into DEVGRU."

He stopped mid-chew and narrowed his eyes at Nikita. "No shit? SEAL Team Six?"

Nikita didn't say a word. It was obvious that she didn't like having her name out there.

Sugar must have noticed, "Don't worry, honey. Your secret is safe with me. I only heard because I have low connections in high places. And J-dawg hardly speaks anything to anyone aside from me and Asal except in incomprehensible snarls and grunts."

"I knew you guys recruited women for when you went under-cover. But one actually made the cut? Like through the front door?" J-dawg asked Altman, ignoring his wife's tease.

"You seem kinda slow when you don't like a new fact, J-dawg." If

Nikita's words could kill, Drake figured J-dawg would be a dead man. He must actually be too ornery to die because he was still breathing.

"We have a grand total of one who came directly in as a full-on operator," Luke Altman grunted out. "So watch your goddamn step."

When the pizza first arrived, Altman had ended up across the table from Drake, between Sugar and Zoe. Instead of leaning forward to look at Jared around Sugar, he kept looking across the table at Drake —as if he was the one Altman was threatening.

Drake nearly choked on an over-large piece of pepperoni. First, he wasn't doing anything more than thinking about Nikita. And second, this was a DEVGRU lieutenant commander threatening him. About the only guys in the military tougher than that were Delta Force…and there would be an argument about even that.

"Alright," J-dawg rinsed down the last of his pizza with a slug of beer.

Still, Altman was watching Drake as if nothing else was going on.

*Okay! Okay! I got the message: don't hurt the lady.* It was more likely that if he did, Nikita would be the one to break him into tiny bits like so much kindling. If ever there was a woman who could take care of herself, it was her.

"So my Titan group took over this other outfit—" J-dawg restarted.

"Global Security International," Nikita snapped it out like an accusation.

Drake had never heard any of what she'd said about the guy. Titan and Global were just so much of a mystery, but she knew. He'd also never heard her speak this way. Maybe *why* she knew all that was tied up in her reaction to them.

"Yeah, GSI," J-dawg nodded and the slash of anger that crossed his face said that Nikita wasn't the only dangerous one at the table. "Those assholes deserved the title of mercenary. They were scalping on government contracts, trafficking with foreign powers, all the bad shit."

"Like attracts like," Nikita growled it out.

"Can it," Altman stated mildly, but there was no doubt about the direct order in his tone.

Nikita looked down at her empty plate, but Drake was close enough that he could feel her practically shaking with suppressed rage. One of the best-trained warriors anywhere and a gutful of rage seemed like a lousy combination to him. Using the cover of darkness and the edge of the table, he patted her thigh in what he hoped was a comforting motion. The clenched-tight muscle eased a little. When he left his hand there, she didn't remove it or even make any motion to shake it off.

He picked up his next slice one-handed.

THE CONTACT SHOCK of Drake's hand stilled Nikita's nerves enough that she didn't know how to respond.

Drake had good hands. Not merely big and strong, but he had great control. It was why she'd first noticed him. Most people simply yanked the trigger on an M134 Minigun; Drake coaxed it to life. He managed all of the necessary suppression and destruction with a third less ammo than any other helo crew gunner she'd ever seen. That's why she'd thought there was a chance he could learn to shoot well and been willing to spend an afternoon with him.

That hand on her thigh, the first time they'd ever touched, was a whole different matter. It was exactly the right amount to pull her back from the cliff edge that lay so raw inside her that her past had threatened to overwhelm her present.

She managed a breath, then another. Finally a third as J-dawg continued his story.

"So, we're cleaning up GSI's files. Running down the people they were using. Mostly arms and drugs. GSI was only starting to get into people—human trafficking, mainly for the sex trade—but we shut that down first of all and shut it down hard. I've got a team that's...uh, particularly touchy on that subject and I let them loose." Then his smile went evil. "They're damn good at what they do."

"However," the colonel prompted from where he leaned back into the darkness of the Alabama night.

"However," J-dawg continued, "there's a mess in Central America that needs cleaning up on the quiet."

"Let me guess," Nikita couldn't help herself despite Altman shutting her down. "The State Department didn't want to send in a bunch of out-of-control door-kickers like yourselves."

J-dawg grimaced in disgust, "Almost an exact quote. I've got a team run by my second-best man—"

"Why not your best?"

"Because *I've* been busy," this time the smile was genuine and Nikita could almost like him for that. Special Operations soldiers needed a certain amount of arrogance to survive. "My second team specializes at working in the gray areas, but..." He shrugged.

But no matter how good his team was, they weren't the 5E and they definitely weren't DEVGRU. There was a long silence broken only by the plink of moths battering themselves against the lantern's glass.

"The current party in power in Honduras," Colonel McDermott leaned forward into the light, "is both democratically elected and friendly to the United States, which makes them a popular target. So far, one of our teams—assisted by a group of wildland firefighters— has managed to stop the most serious coup attempt, which was touch-and-go but they did it. We'd like to make that permanent as their president is finally working to clean up the corruption. It means that you need to go in, find whatever it was that GSI was financing, and get rid of it."

"Without anyone the wiser." Nikita was the first to voice it, but she could see the others had reached the same conclusion.

"Not the local government. Not their military. Certainly not the media. No one," Colonel McDermott confirmed. "I don't even want Sugar, with all of her connections, to be able to hear about it except from us."

It's what the 5E and DEVGRU were best at, being completely invisible.

"We have GSI's files," J-dawg signaled Sugar and she extracted a thumb drive from somewhere within her tight leather and handed it to J-dawg.

Nikita wondered what else Sugar could extract if the situation turned ugly. All civilian weapons were supposed to be turned in at the base entrance, but Nikita wouldn't be trusting the results of a contest between a gate guard's diligence and the razzle-dazzle of Sugar's deep cleavage and tight leather.

"It includes my contact info as well as Parker's, if you need him. He's the one who put this together for you. Best data geek there is; he's got every scrap of info GSI knew in here." He set it in the middle of the table, then let out his evil smile once more. "Well, other than what was in a dead man's brain."

Unsanctioned killing on American soil. This guy gave her the creeps, no matter how much the leader of GSI had deserved it. Buck Baer's reputation had always been bad and it was a relief to know he and GSI were gone. Nikita wouldn't be happy until all "contractors" were six feet under like the bastards deserved.

She reached for the drive, then hesitated. She glanced at her boss, then Pete Napier—the major in command of the 5E—and, receiving a nod from both of them, finally took it. She wanted this one. Taking down a GSI operation would appease a small part of the pain inside her.

"You fix it, shooter," the head of Titan glared at her. "Whatever it takes, you goddamn fix it."

"Sure thing…J-dawg."

Sugar's laugh filled the darkness.

# CHAPTER 5

"You look like crap!"

"Thanks, asshole."

Drake wanted a do-over. Too late for that. "Haven't you slept?"

Nikita just shook her head and plinked a finger against the computer screen.

Keeping it casual, he wandered over to the counter and made a cup of coffee. The morning light was shining into the kitchen-dining area, at least enough of it to not turn on the overhead fluorescents. The original stark-white walls were now covered with posters, so many that they were overlapping. There were the hot helicopter shots, of course, but mostly it was travel posters: China, Russia, Laos, the Philippines, a lot of Central and South America. The common theme was that the 5E had been to every one of those places on the quiet.

No need for any pinup posters or hot-girl calendars, not with the stunning women of the 5E in the residence. There were a couple of big group shots of the 5E and one of them with the 5D out on the Nevada Test and Training Range—*that* was his kind of pinup. Funny, it was only now he noticed that Nikita wasn't in a single one of them.

And the one time they'd caught Altman in a photo it was only half his face over someone's shoulder.

The main part of the room was filled with a big U-shaped table set up for meals and meetings. A cluster of chairs and couches faced a big-screen TV that was mainly used with battle-game consoles—some nights the entire company would get online together and duke it out. The other sidewall was a bank of computer workstations, at one of which Nikita sat sagging in her chair.

"You want?" He held up a coffee mug.

She shook her head, so he wandered back to her and looked over her shoulder.

"What's the issue?"

"The issue is that these GSI contractors kept crap for records. What Titan gave us hardly tells us a thing. I've scratched up a couple of names and an amateur-hour contact method that came right out of a bad movie. Nothing about who they might be, how many there are, nor even a location. I tracked a whole lot of money and more than a little not-approved-for-export military hardware, including several helos rigged with serious armament, but I can't tell where it goes." She dropped back in her chair with a groan.

"Gaps in the data, or a second set of books?"

"No other records according to their guy Parker, and this work is good enough that he's probably right."

Drake set his coffee mug on the table and dug his fingers into her tight shoulders. She sat up straighter and leaned forward enough to give him access around the chair back. Nikita groaned as he dug in. She twisted her neck right and left; he could feel her spine crackling through his fingertips as he eased clenched muscles. He drove a knuckle under her shoulder blade as he pulled her shoulder back with his other hand. Her muscles fought the motion, so he dug harder... and it finally released.

"Oh, yeah," she groaned softly.

"So," Rafe, the pilot of Drake's Black Hawk, came in and hit the coffeepot. "It's good for her. How is it for you, Duck-man?"

"You make him stop," Nikita answered before Drake could tell

Rafe to go screw himself, "and I will replace that useless piece of jelly you use for a brain with a month-old cabbage."

Drake took that as an invitation to run his hands down her triceps. Normally his hands could reach right around a woman's upper arms —not even close on Nikita. He dug into the bound-up muscles there, working back toward her shoulders.

"Hey, I'm next," Zoe called out as she wandered into the room. She was a cute little whip of a thing: Scandinavian blond with dark roots, bright blue eyes, and a constantly cheery attitude. She looked like she should be in social media marketing, not flying fifteen million dollars of Avenger stealth drone.

Out of the corner of his eye, Drake could see Altman roll in. Nikita's commander stopped for a long moment and Drake was careful not to look in his direction. Eventually, he crossed behind Drake—without maiming him, which Drake would count as a plus—and hit the kitchen.

By the time half the crew was in, Drake decided he was pushing his luck. With a final squeeze of her shoulders, which she answered with a slight shrug of thanks up against his palms, he let go. His hands tingled with her warmth. He'd have to remember to thank his big sister next time they spoke. Years ago she'd needed a practice subject for her masseuse license and been between boyfriends. Hennie had discussed what she was doing to his muscles aloud, and over the years since, more than a few girlfriends had succumbed with a happy sigh after he applied what he'd learned.

He hadn't given Nikita the massage with any illusions that it was more than a massage, but he still liked how she felt. Again the contrast of the hidden strength and the beautiful woman. He worked out just as much as the next grunt, but he could feel that she lived at a whole other level of fitness. Maybe he'd start hitting the weights harder.

She picked up his coffee mug and took a sip, "Ack! Crap, Roman! How much sugar did you put in this?"

"Two packets." Army coffee, even when he made it instead of one of his teammates who didn't give a damn, was still the bitterest substance on earth. What it was about Army coffeemakers that always scorched the flavor, he'd never figured out.

"Weenie," she razzed him loudly enough for anyone to hear. But she offered him a smile and kept drinking it, so it was hard to feel bad.

Breakfast came together fast. Drake almost asked what he could get for Nikita, but went with keeping his mouth shut instead. Normally a woman would like the solicitousness, but maybe not a SEAL. Also, it would be like singling her out for being a female—which he'd just done with his massage. He tried to picture himself digging into Altman's shoulder if the SEAL commander had been the one who'd spent all night in the chair. Wasn't going to happen.

During his indecision, Nikita grabbed a breakfast burrito out of the freezer, tossed it into the microwave, then took it and his coffee over to the table. He went for dumping boiling water over a bowl of instant oatmeal and called it good with a fistful of raisins and a spoon of brown sugar. And a fresh cup of coffee—with two sugar packets, by god—he followed her to the table. But rather than sitting next to her, he went for his normal spot, four seats away from Nikita.

He did it because he wasn't thinking about her, at least not that way. Not the way he might have after giving her a massage, or lying in the tall grass while she showed surprising patience in teaching him gun handling. It had taken half an hour before she'd even let him fire a round; it was all about positioning his grip and mental attitude.

*You gotta think slower, Roman,* she'd spoken softly and patiently—the gentle trainer inside the tough soldier. *Think slower?* Not about Nikita Hayward, he wasn't.

Nope, he definitely wasn't thinking about how much he wished he'd noticed what she was doing and stayed up with her last night so that he could at least pretend that her lack-of-sleep tousled look had been his doing. Her hair had lost parts of its habitual ponytail and was now a soft, enticing cloud about her face.

None of that. He didn't want to get any teasing from the team. More importantly, he didn't want her to get any.

Rafe kicked Drake's chair, hard enough that it wasn't an accident as he sat down in the next seat over. Julian's elbow as he sat on

Drake's other side was just as "mistakenly" and solidly planted in Drake's ribs. So much for plan A.

"Hey, I've got this tight spot right here," Rafe pointed at his shoulder.

"I can tell you where the Duck-man's tight spot is," Julian squawked at him from the other side, following it with crappy fake-duck sounds.

The two were the pilots of the Black Hawk that he was gunner on and were always carrying on like they were the funniest guys in the entire Night Stalkers regiment.

"Yeah," he answered Julian. "Maybe I shouldn't be sitting between you two, because I know right where your tight spot is."

Rafe punched his arm while Julian groaned and then the three of them laughed together.

<hr>

NIKITA WATCHED the guys messing with Drake. It would have been funny if it hadn't given her some thinking to do.

Drake hadn't been like the others. Most of the male crew had come on to her at one point or another, and one of the women as well. Drake had only tried the one cheap pickup line way back at the China mission and then backed off. She wondered if it had been only a joke to protect his reputation. Since then, he'd been a decent guy.

He was too well bred for her taste. She wanted a challenge and Drake was too smooth and slick in his ways—it was obvious what he was: overeducated Yankee far too used to getting his way with women. He even sounded kind of posh, Boston maybe. Nikita rolled her shoulders—they felt seriously better. She'd have protested when he touched her, but his thumbs had landed right on a hard knot from hunching over the keyboard all night. That and the memory of his hand on her thigh last night. He hadn't asked what was messing her up, he'd just helped her back from that edge. Instead of sliding up her thigh, he'd eventually squeezed once lightly in reassurance and then withdrawn his hand with no one the wiser.

Altman dropped into the seat next to her. "Hayward." He made it a question even though it sounded like a statement.

"Commander?" She made it a statement even though it sounded like a question.

He eyed her over his fried eggs, toast, and sausage. "Got anything to tell me?"

Not about the shit going on in her head. "When the team is all sitting down." *Nothing personal going on here. Just business.*

He eyed her for a long moment before accepting her evasion with a nod. The rest of the crew trickled in. They were on no hard schedule today, but it was just 0600 and the whole crew was up. It actually made sense. They'd been in the Philippine jungle for three weeks, always flying at night and sleeping during the day. Philippines to Mother Rucker, Alabama, was twelve hours time difference. Staying awake all night, she was the only one now out of sync with the clock. Usually they all were out of sync, because the Night Stalkers weren't called that for flying in the sunshine.

As the last of them were settling, she grabbed her laptop and turned on the projection screen.

"Target is Honduras."

"A new poster!" Drake chimed in.

"A new…?" She must be more exhausted than she'd thought if she missed the reference. There was no Honduras travel poster on the walls of the 5E common room.

Others were looking around the room double-checking as if they couldn't remember all of the places they'd fought over the last year. Actually, the 5E's operational tempo was high enough, maybe they couldn't.

She turned back to her report.

"Last year a team of heli-aviation wildland firefighters from Mount Hood Aviation received a contract to fight fires in the Honduran countryside. In the midst of their contract, they were shanghaied by an unknown group of men. One of Mount Hood Aviation's Firehawk helicopters—civilian version of a Black Hawk—

became instrumental in halting a coup staged against the duly elected president."

"Duly elected," Drake cut in, again breaking her rhythm, "is a tenuous term for Honduran politics. They've had presidents who were polling below twenty percent win elections, perhaps because they were vocal supporters of the army and the military police who were the ones manning the polls." He was right and she could see that many didn't know about the mess that Honduras called leadership.

"That was a prior president. This one *was* duly elected, with only minor complaints from UN observers and very few riots during the voting process. It's no longer our concern."

Drake nodded his concession on that point. She didn't know what to think of him. Was he trying to be helpful or playing one of the male power games that would force her to hurt him—bad. She was too tired to think about it now. Focus on the briefing.

"Honduras is also the murder capital of the world. The entire country runs about ten percent worse than Detroit. This is not a happy country, nor has it been for a long time—again outside the scope of our rules of engagement. It is estimated that thirty members of the coup attempt died that night. How the civilian team in an unarmed Firehawk did this is unclear, and command has the *who* and the *how* marked as need-to-know. By their methodology, I expect it was a Delta Force action."

That earned her everyone's full attention. If she had said that back at DEVGRU command on Naval Air Station Oceana, it would have incurred a buttload of comments about the SEALs now having to clean up Delta's mess because they couldn't finish a job or some such crap. Ever since DEVGRU's founder Richard Marcinko had declared that if there was water in his canteen, that was close enough to the ocean for a SEAL, ST6 and Delta had coexisted uncomfortably on the same tactical turf of elite counter-terrorism.

"Maybe they used fire," Rafe waved a piece of pancake at the screen.

"That's another way to bring the heat," Julian made finger-flexing motions like an air massage, "or you could—"

"Shut the hell up and let Nikita speak!" Drake took advantage of his position sitting between the two and smacked both of his teammates on the back of the head.

They turned to retaliate and Nikita sighed at the unavoidable interruption. She was never going to get this briefing done and it was pissing her off.

Major Pete Napier spoke for the first time, "You two don't shut up, I'm giving you latrine duty."

"No way, Pete. Who would fly our helicopter?"

"The goddamn base janitors for all I care! Now close your yaps and listen."

---

THEY SHUT UP.

Drake thought everyone knew not to antagonize Major Pete Napier before he'd finished his morning coffee, or ever, for that matter. Drake had been planning on getting the guys back for what they'd said about Nikita being his tight spot. Even better? Having the company commander shutting them down for him.

He smacked them both on the backs of their heads again, just because it felt good. And they wouldn't dare retaliate after Pete tromped all over them.

He exchanged a look with Nikita. There was a deep chill in her eyes, practically Arctic despite their brown color. Okay, maybe he shouldn't have so enjoyed smacking his two teammates. Or maybe that was simply how much she disliked anything that wasn't squared away military.

She returned to her briefing while Drake resisted the urge to crawl under the table.

"The people killed were identified as primarily military: shooters and a general, along with a key member of the opposition party. However, based on what minimal information GSI kept, it appears there was a much broader operation in process than merely a military coup toppling a president. I found traces of smuggling: gold, drugs, weapons, people, you name it. Money laundering is probably part of it too, but there is something much broader going on. The Honduran government is helpless in this. And believe it or not, that's all we have to go on."

"And the US government gave it to us, that means small and quiet. We need an intel team on the ground," Altman declared. "Scout detail: me, Nikita, Drake…who else speaks Spanish?"

A couple hands went up around the table.

"No pilots," all of the hands went back down. None of the other three gunners.

"I need another woman. Zoe," Altman pointed to the drone's copilot, whose hand had been among those initially raised, "you're in."

Drake raised a hand.

"What is it, Sergeant Roman?"

"I don't speak Spanish. My languages are Japanese and German."

Altman scowled at him, "Then why do you know about Honduran politics?"

Drake shrugged, "Just one of those things. I followed a rabbit down an Internet hole and emerged days later. Their politics are among the wildest of any country; it makes for great reading."

"You still current on what's happening down there?"

"Yeah."

"Then you're in because who knows what knowledge we'll need. Just don't speak when we're in-country. You and Zoe, me and Nikita. We'll look like vacationing couples and see what we can find out."

Drake wished the team pairing was different, but he was glad to be along for the ride. And he supposed it made sense; the massive SEAL commander and the little slip of a drone pilot would definitely make an odd couple.

"Pete," Altman was moving on. "Find a way to get your team quietly into place. Costa Rica, offshore, something. That's why I'm not taking any pilots. Nikita, hand off your research to Mr. Honduras there and get some sleep. Drake, you find us a way in and where to start."

Pete nodded, "Everyone make sure that your gear, weapons, and aircraft are fully serviced and restocked. By nightfall, we're ready on zero notice. Sophia, grab a senior instructor with top clearance to cover for Zoe on your Avenger drone. Everyone clear?" No one would dare to do more than nod in agreement when Pete Napier used that tone.

Breakfast was cleaned up and everyone had left for the hangar in under five minutes.

Nikita simply sat at the table, staring down at her plate and half-empty mug long gone cold.

Drake cleared it for her.

By the time he turned around, they were alone and she was asleep with her arms sprawled on the table and her head cricked sideways between them.

"Come along, you," he coaxed her back to her feet.

"Didn't sleep on the damned flight back either," she mumbled. Which meant she'd been awake for at least three straight days, maybe four. The last couple days in the Philippines hadn't exactly been conducive to rest and relaxation.

When she almost face-planted over her chair, he slipped a hand around her waist. She did the same and suddenly they were as close as a couple of teenagers walking along hip to hip. Now he was the one who wanted to stumble.

Thankfully her room was on the main floor, though at the far end of the hall. No stairs to navigate.

"Is there anything special I need to know about the files?" He needed something to think about other than Nikita draped against him. His palm had landed on the curve of her hip where it dipped upward to the soft valley of her waist. It wasn't decent behavior, but he wanted to pull her in closer. Taking advantage of her current state, he did. For just a moment he could pretend.

Then she slipped her hand into his back jeans pocket, raising his blood pressure about a jillion points.

"You've got a nice ass, Roman."

He managed to guide her through the door between the common room and the residence without breaking their connection. Unlike the poster-plastered décor behind them, the hall was standard, unremitting, military-base beige with gray carpet, best practices posters that no one had ever read, and a couple too few lights. The place would pass well as a cheap motel anywhere in the country. It wouldn't normally be wide enough to walk side by side, except for their current sideways clench.

"Look who's talking about having a nice ass. I assume that's the main qualification to become a DEVGRU SEAL." He'd certainly noticed hers, he just never thought he'd get a chance to be talking about it.

"Helps if you can swim. You know, SEAL and all. Sea, air, and land is what we are, but sea always comes first. Can you swim, Duck-man?"

"Only when I'm trying not to drown."

"You're a sad case, Duck-man."

"How's that?" They reached her door, but she didn't seem to be reaching for her keys. Taking a deep breath, he began checking her pockets because if he didn't get away from her soon he didn't know what was going to happen. A few hand brushes, which he did his best not to enjoy (but failed miserably at), located them in her back-left pocket.

"You shoot like a heli-weenie. You've got the hots for busty babes in leather. And you barely swim." She appeared to be talking to a poster on how to recognize athlete's foot.

He slipped his hand into her back-left pocket and earned no complaints. By the time he had her keys extracted, he knew for a fact that DEVGRU women absolutely *did* have the best asses in the military—even if Nikita was the only one.

"So damn much I gotta teach you if you're going to be a decent man."

"Like what?" he unlocked the door and guided her into her room. Just like his: double bed, small desk, a hand sink, and a dresser. The difference was that she had five rifle cases stacked in a corner and three field packs that he knew from past experience were armor, ammo, and tons of the tech gizmos that SEALs always seemed to have. Her clothes probably wouldn't fill a daypack.

"Like," she grabbed him by the belt, spun him around, and shoved him back against the door—slamming it shut, hard. "Like I'm tired, not drunk. You want to cop a feel, you better do it right." She reached around his hips and double-grabbed his butt, then she leaned in and kissed him hard when his mouth opened in surprise.

He certainly wasn't going to argue and leaned in to the kiss. Her mouth was spicy with her breakfast and sweet with a taste that must be her own.

Drake went to slide his hand down her spine. A dip of back muscle made her belt span the gap and his hand slid inside her pants instead of outside. He was rewarded with a handful of delightful, cotton-clad muscle.

She hummed with pleasure for a moment. Long before he was ready to stop, she tipped her head sideways onto his shoulder.

"You're a good kisser, Duck-man. At least I won't have to teach you that," each word tapered softer and softer.

The last one never got its final consonant.

"Oh," she roused for a moment, "the password on the file is 'Sweet-Cheeks'—one word, two caps. Figured you'd appreciate my using Sugar's nickname for you." Then she was out.

"You're not drunk, but you're not conscious either."

She didn't answer. Her body slowly went limp until she was a deadweight leaning into him and pinning him against the door.

"And here I am with my hand down your pants."

No reaction.

"And talking to myself."

Extracting his hand, he pulled her tightly against his chest to keep her from slipping directly to the floor. Doing his best not to enjoy the moment, Drake slowly walked her backward toward her bed. He had to nudge her legs along with his own. They were in the closest contact possible while still clothed, from toes to her chest pressing against his to her hair brushing against the side of his neck. He wanted to twist around and sit back on the bed, pulling her the rest of the way into his lap.

Controlling himself, he lowered her onto the bed. There was no way in hell he was going to be undressing her. It was September in Alabama; she wasn't going to freeze on top of the covers. He undid her boots, then did his best to arrange her so that she wouldn't wake up a dozen hours from now with an intolerable kink.

Drake studied her for a long moment. He didn't feel like a cad doing so, despite her butt-warmth still very real on his palm. Instead, he looked at her just in case he never had the chance to hold her again—he wanted to remember this moment. He brushed her hair out of her face and resisted running his hand down her lovely neck.

*Get out while you still can, Duck-man.* It was good advice, which meant that normally he wouldn't follow it, but this time he did.

He was back at Nikita's laptop with a fresh cup of coffee a minute later.

When Altman checked in on him shortly after, he was past blushing about the "SweetCheeks" password and deep into the file, enough to have a feel for it.

"Nikita did a lot of good prep here," Drake said without turning. "Give me a couple of hours and I should have a handle on it."

Altman thumped him on the shoulder, a lot harder than would be appropriate for a "well done," but Drake wasn't going to point that out.

He'd sometimes wondered if Luke Altman and Nikita were paired off. They communicated on some other level. It might just be a SEAL thing, but he couldn't be sure.

Then he thought about her kiss and was glad that he was facing away from Altman because he couldn't stop his own smile.

## CHAPTER 6

"I uncovered a travel reservation in GSI's name," Drake looked very pleased with himself. "They were headed to a meeting in Honduras and apparently the owner liked to travel in luxury."

"I think you found this because you didn't want me to sleep." Nikita had managed five hours. Though she could have used fifteen, before Altman was kicking the bottom of her bed.

"We leave for Miami in fifteen minutes," Altman used his command voice. Actually, in her two years with him, she'd come to believe it was the only voice he had. "Shower, dress summer casual but upscale. A light engagement kit."

Light engagement meant she'd only brought two sidearms and one rifle in addition to her clothes, spare ammo, and a diving knife. Upscale was a problem: her nicest clothes couldn't pass and clearly there wasn't time to go hit a wardrobe supply or go shopping. Well, back-of-her-closet shit would have to do.

Once she could stop blinking against the painful midday sun, she saw that it wasn't a Black Hawk waiting for her either. Instead, it was a sleek Bell 429 in a VIP configuration with comfortable armchairs and a minibar from which she grabbed an energy drink. Nikita had gotten ready in ten minutes and still was the last one on board—its rotors were already spinning up. The five leather chairs faced each other: two turned backward and three forward in the wide-windowed rear cabin. Altman and Drake sat in the back-facing seats, Zoe was across from Altman, which left her across from Drake. Rafe and Julian were up front in the pilots' seats.

Drake's smile shifted from pleased about discovering the travel arrangements to tentative in a way she wasn't used to seeing on his features.

It took her a moment to catch up with why. For ten minutes she'd been at a dead sprint getting showered and ready. Now she remembered a tight ass in her hands paired with a jungle-steamy kiss—he could kiss even better than he could shoot his Minigun, which was saying something. She definitely wanted to try that again when she was conscious. But she wasn't going to be admitting that in front of her commander, so she went with a short nod and didn't trust herself with a "good morning."

"Oh my gawd! What is wrong with you people?" Chief Warrant Zoe DeMille rolled her eyes at Nikita as the helo lifted into the air. Zoe wore fashionable bright yellow shorts and tank top. Her white-blond hair was back in matching clips that emphasized the dark roots and she sported big, thick-rimmed round glasses—frames in matching lemon-yellow—that Nikita had never seen before so they must be merely decorative. Zoe even carried a ridiculously poufy jacket in the same yellow despite the warm day. She looked as if she'd popped right out of a designer magazine.

"What?" For lack of any other options, Nikita had worn a tight black t-shirt and her only skirt, a summer weight in floral blue that her mother had picked out for her ages ago and she hadn't worn since. She had one pair of strap-on sandals. Her running shoes and boots were in the pack she'd stuffed into the cargo area. It wasn't as if there was a whole lot more back at her apartment in Virginia.

She could tell that Drake liked the way she looked, and she liked how he looked in tan khakis and a simple, sky-blue, button-down men's shirt. Again, keeping that to herself.

Altman had dressed the same as Drake, except in dark pants.

Zoe was still in a snit. "We so have to fix this before we land. You people are a disaster. They're never going to buy in that we're wealthy passengers. You said wealthy, right?" she asked Drake.

"Passage for four in something called an Oceansaway Suite aboard the *Oceanwide Whisperer.*"

"Oceansaway suite on an Oceanwide cruise? Oh my *gawd!*" Zoe's Valley-girl accent was coming on strong in her obvious excitement. She didn't know that women from Southern California actually spoke like that outside of the movies. "I have a cousin who works booking cruise trips. That is awesome. Oceanwide is one of *the* luxury lines."

"There are luxury lines?" Nikita had never been near a cruise ship except during training exercises for taking down a terrorist attack on one.

Zoe smacked a palm against her forehead. "Where have you been, Nikita? Carnival Cruises are for people who want to party. Disney for families with kids. Princess for people who want to be pampered, treated like, you know, royalty. Holland America draws an older crowd who still want to go out and see the culture and not just whatever party or sports thing is going on. Oceanwide is trying to take on Crystal and Silversea for the luxury niche and doing an awesome job of it."

Nikita blinked as she tried to absorb and categorize all that. But at the speed that Zoe talked, she'd already forgotten two of the cruise lines names. She'd thought a cruise ship was a cruise ship.

Zoe glared about the cabin. "Next you're going to tell me that you are planning on landing at Miami International and all crowding into a taxi to the ship. Please tell me that you guys aren't that dense. Pretty please?"

Nikita could see by the look Altman and Drake exchanged that it was exactly what they were planning.

Zoe grabbed a headset, "Julian, we want to land directly aboard the ship—on the ship, not near it, not on the dock, on it. Get in touch with them and find out how to clear the helideck, these ships all have the capability in case they have to do a medevac at sea. And make it so that we arrive during the very busiest loading time. We want everyone to be looking at us."

"No," it didn't sound right to Nikita. "We're undercover. We want *no one* to be looking at us."

Zoe hung the headset back on its hook without changing her instructions to the pilots. "Look, we are immensely wealthy, arrogant, and probably crooked contractors who have totally bought into our own hype. We're arriving in a very pretty helicopter. We want to make a splash, right? We're undercover, but our characters aren't."

"Right," Altman nodded, ending that part of the discussion. He smiled down at Zoe in approval. She was definitely the pixie in this crowd. At five-four she wouldn't even reach Altman's shoulder and she was one of those vibratingly slender types. She almost seemed to shimmer, blurring her own edges until she might disappear if you glanced aside for a moment. She also didn't seem to understand the incredibly-rare approval that one of Commander Altman's smiles represented.

"They won't see *us*," Zoe fluffed her hair to make her point. "They'll see our arrival. Well, they *will* see us if we can't do something about the way you three look."

Again Nikita scanned their clothes but didn't see the problem.

Zoe rolled her eyes.

Altman scowled down at her. That, at least, was his normal neutral expression. When he was ticked, he went grimly unreadable.

"Okay, good," Zoe pointed a finger at Altman. "That works. Big, tall, handsome, and dangerous-as-hell." She leaned close to pluck the sunglasses from his pocket and slide them on him. She studied him a moment longer, then undid a button on his white dress shirt, then another.

Nikita was surprised that Altman didn't put her down hard for getting inside his personal space, but he just sat there as she ignored his glower and did what she was doing.

"Delicious," Zoe grinned. "Keep that fierce expression. You're the muscle of this outfit. You're the one all of the women will be looking at...and not a one will remember your face, not when they can see enough to imagine your beautiful chest, Luke." She even patted him on it.

Nikita had never heard anyone call Altman by just his first name, not even the captain who commanded DEVGRU. Nikita also hadn't ever looked at Lt. Commander Altman in that way. He was simply her commander. But now that she did, he looked amazing: muscular, handsome, and lethal. And when he noticed her inspecting him, very fierce.

"You two," Zoe turned to face her and Drake. "You two are a problem. At least you have the good sense to buy designer shirts, Drake."

Nikita looked at it, but it just looked like a button-down shirt to her.

The only sound during Zoe's silent study was the beating of the rotor. Nikita had never been in a non-military helicopter before. On military helos you needed a headset or helmet just in order to survive. This aircraft must have used up half of its useful payload on sound insulation; they didn't even have to raise their voices to speak.

Outside the window, she could see that they soared over the Chattahoochee River and into Georgia, then moments later crossed into Florida where the river bent to the west. On their current line, they'd pass close over Disney World. Maybe she could get them to drop her off so that she could climb on a roller coaster and get some sleep there —at least that would make more sense than what was happening around her now.

She didn't like feeling slow, but the speed at which things were happening...Zoe seemed to be the only one keeping up with them. And then there was Drake Roman. Now that Nikita's brain was coming back online, she was starting to second guess her actions last night. She remembered how good he'd felt.

Heat crept toward her face until she ordered it to stop as she considered why what had happened, had happened. It had started... when? When Sugar had strode out into the field and fused the nerve endings in Drake's gonads. Nikita had wanted to...mark her territory like a *junkyard dawg*? No! That was the merc's style, not hers. She was a SEAL operator, first, second, and third. But she'd—

"Take off your shirts."

"Say what?"

Zoe did point-and-swap motions at Nikita and Drake. "Trade shirts."

Drake shrugged and began unbuttoning his shirt. He was lean-framed, but his chest and abs were soldier-fit. She remembered how he had felt when they were pressed together last night—this morning—whenever it was. Nikita had wanted to simply curl up against him. Actually, that's exactly what she'd done and he'd felt glorious. Now she could see why.

---

DRAKE NOTICED NIKITA'S ATTENTION. And Zoe's as well, which was flattering, but it was Nikita he'd been trying to figure out since the start of the flight.

Her good morning nod of acknowledgement had been curt enough that he'd wondered if she indeed didn't remember when she'd pinned him against her bedroom door.

*Tired, not drunk.*

So maybe irritated and wanting to pretend it hadn't happened, which was about what he'd figured on while he dug through the data, then started chasing the leads that Nikita had bookmarked for further research.

But now she also offered a thin smile. No, she wasn't smiling *at* him, but she was definitely smiling.

That in itself was unusual enough for her and he'd found it very encouraging.

As he took off his shirt, she wasn't taking off her own. Instead she was simply watching. When she realized that he'd caught her at it, she reached back over her head and yanked off her t-shirt in a single pull, then held it out.

"A sports bra?" Zoe sounded aghast.

Drake had seen Nikita strip off a shirt that was soaking wet from a hard workout to change into a fresh one before. He'd seen her peel off a shirt, rank with Burmese swamp water, to wring it out. He'd seen her in just a sports bra any number of times.

But never had it been full frontal while sitting toe to toe in a leather-upholstered luxury helicopter. Whatever Zoe thought was wrong, he couldn't find a thing. Nikita Hayward in a sports bra was a vision. Add that to the memory of her kiss and he was a very happy man at the moment.

Nikita took one look at him and heaved her t-shirt into his face.

He handed over his dress shirt with a formal courtesy and couldn't wait to see her in it. He tugged on her t-shirt. Between her strength, his leanness, and their similar height, it wasn't a bad fit. A little tight, but hopefully that made him look more muscular than he actually was. It was warm with her scent. Maybe he'd never give it back, or wash it.

Nikita started to pull on his dress shirt.

"No. Lose the sports bra." At Nikita's fulminating look and Altman's even darker one, Drake wished he'd kept his mouth shut.

"He's right," Zoe agreed. "It will give you the devil-may-care attitude to make up for—" she waved her hand at the rest of Nikita's outfit in disgust.

Nikita and Altman shifted their scowl to Zoe, which was a relief, but it didn't fluster Zoe for a second. She had more spine than he'd expected, facing down a pair of DEVGRU operators.

"Do it!" He'd never have thought that Zoe had a fierce mode, but she did and it was formidable.

Nikita snarled at Zoe, who continued to be unflappable. Then she turned to face him and Altman, "Both of you close your goddamned eyes."

As much as he hated to, he did.

"Cover them!" It was a DEVGRU death-threat tone not to be argued with.

Then there was a movement of fabric just barely loud enough to hear above the rotor's beat and the engines' muted roar.

"Wow, you've got great breasts."

Zoe's exclamation almost had Drake uncovering his eyes to see but he caught himself in time. Then cursed silently, wishing he hadn't restrained himself.

"Seriously, Nikita. What I wouldn't give to have grown a pair like that." Zoe was lean all the way down. It looked very good on her. Why didn't women get that sometimes lean looked awesome?

To distract himself he tried to imagine Zoe with breasts more on the scale of Nikita's, which actually wasn't distracting him at all.

"No, like this," more fabric sounds before Zoe announced it was okay to open their eyes.

Her transformation was so dramatic that Drake almost didn't recognize the woman across from him. She'd let her hair down. It fell neatly to the past collar of his shirt—open far enough down to reveal a very nice cleavage.

Not the serious kind, like Sugar's, pressed together and ready to burst forth at a moment's notice.

Instead, Nikita's cleavage revealed two soft swells of flesh that invited the eyes to linger and—that's exactly what he couldn't do. The shirttails were tied together above her flat stomach, offering more to admire. And she'd rolled up the skirt's waistband until the bottom of the hem barely reached mid-thigh.

Zoe had produced a filmy yellow scarf from somewhere in her outfit and tied it as a decorative sash to hide the roll-up of the skirt. It emphasized Nikita's narrow waist and made it look like she had even more womanly hips than he already knew she did.

Again, he'd admired her legs plenty of times in workout shorts and running shoes. But in the helicopter—with his shoes only inches from her sandals—her legs were astonishing.

"*Roman*," Nikita's voice was a threat that he was spending too long checking her out, but he couldn't help himself.

"You're gorgeous."

"I can also open the door and drop you into the Gulf of Mexico from five thousand feet." The bad-ass version of flattery gets you anywhere.

"Better than a mangrove swamp," he glanced outside to see that they were just skirting the Florida Gulf Coast as they headed south and if she threw him out it could go either way. "I've never been a fan of mangrove swamps. They're snarly and smell awful."

"Dead man," she left the threat clear in the cabin.

He made a point of scanning her body and outfit one last time, "Totally worth the price of admission." Even if he never got to touch her again, the way she looked was a memory worth keeping.

Nikita still wasn't sure what to do about Drake as they slid to a hover above the vast white ship. He gave no indication to Altman that they had kissed, which she was thankful for. He was doing a less-than-thorough job of not staring at her. Every time she turned from whatever merry chatter Zoe was carrying on, his eyes were riveted on her.

Was she so transformed? It was just clothes. Zoe had tried to apply lipstick and other makeup, but Nikita was having none of that no matter how Zoe alternately whined and cajoled.

At first, the direction of his attention had been thoroughly predictable. But as the flight continued, he'd taken to watching her face. He spoke almost as rarely as Altman and she couldn't read what he was thinking.

Or was Drake still thinking about that same splendid kiss that she was?

She welcomed the distraction of their arrival and stared down at the ship. She'd trained on everything from a five-meter rubber boat to an aircraft carrier, but none of that had prepared her for boarding a cruise ship as an elite passenger.

The *Oceanwide Whisperer* cruise ship was halfway between an

Arleigh Burke destroyer and a Nimitz-class aircraft carrier in length, but it rose for eight full decks above its tall freeboard. In a space that would house four thousand navy personnel, there would be six hundred passengers and four hundred crew to take care of their every whim. The minimum stateroom aboard would probably bunk four to six swabbies. By the degree of Zoe's excitement about their suite, it was probably bigger than the admiral's quarters on a carrier group.

"How is this real?"

From above she could see a small swimming pool that had an oversized circular hot tub off each corner. There was lounge seating, shuffleboard, and a miniature golf course all surrounded by a running track. The wood-planked bow of the ship, several stories lower, had been cleared and Rafe and Julian settled the Bell 429 into the relatively tiny space.

A line of people was waiting for them. Four stewards, two male and two female, in natty white uniforms, and a fifth, clearly in the lead, dressed in dark blue.

"Remember," Zoe said just before she opened the door. "It's all in the attitude. Drake, you're in charge, flaunt it. Nikita, you're his gal—you're the most desirable woman around. Luke is the muscle. Sorry, that's just the stereotype looks we have and when they're expecting a cliché, I figure what the hell, let's give it to them."

"And what are you?" Altman grumbled at her, truly living his role.

"Me? I'm just the hanger-on, slave-to-fashion, good-time gal. Maybe if she's lucky, moll to Mr. Senior Hunk Bodyguard Luke," she teased Altman.

Nikita had never in her three years serving with Altman seen a woman tease him. By the surprise on his face, it was something he'd never seen either.

"Four stripes on her epaulettes," Zoe whispered as the ship's officer came over to greet them. "It means she's one of the top people on the ship. We've done good."

A customs official barely glanced at their passports, then left as the officer stepped in to greet them just past the edge of the slowing blades. She was a tall, handsome woman with neatly short blond hair.

"I am Norma, the hotel manager. Please allow me to welcome you aboard the *Oceanwide Whisperer*. I'm so glad that we were able to accommodate your late reservation changes."

By the woman's partially masked grimace, Nikita would guess that the former head of GSI may not have been the most welcome of guests.

"I don't think that you'll have any problems of that nature in the future," Drake had picked up on the cues as well, but he shouldn't be too polite. The team needed him to be the arrogant military contractor.

Out of sight, Nikita slipped a hand down onto his butt and pinched him hard.

He reached back and snagged her hand, "It seems that someone is eager to get to our suite after the long flight. If we may?" He made the statement appropriately lascivious as well as managing to make it a command. He also kept her hand tightly clenched in his so that she couldn't attack him again.

The stewards and luggage were already gone.

Over the side of the boat, Nikita could see the long lines of people just now working their way from dock to ship up a pair of ramps. Some simply walked aboard, others gawked and looked terribly like first timers (a good lesson for her in what not to do), and several strode up the ramp as if they owned the ship. However, she noticed that even they glanced up with curiosity as the helicopter climbed back aloft. Then their gazes slid to her and she stepped back so that the tall railing would block their sightlines.

Drake's tug on her hand led her through a hatchway and into a narrow corridor. It was nicely appointed, the rug a pattern of a Victorian drawing room instead of the more expected nautical theme. The walls were actually wallpapered, not painted. It would have been homey if the hall hadn't stretched apparently on to infinity. She suddenly had the creepy suspicion that she'd just stepped onto the hotel carpeting in *The Shining* and that a pair of identical twin ghost girls would appear at any moment farther along the corridor.

She didn't hear a word that the hotel manager said, but she figured that was appropriate for her role. Zoe was right. Their method of arrival had sold them as worthy of the hotel manager's—Nikita supposed that a floating luxury hotel was an apt description of the ship—personal attention in the middle of a busy boarding process.

Nikita started feeling less like a woman lost in a whirlwind of changes she couldn't keep up with and more like a SEAL. DEVGRU operators were like the Bruce Lee quote: *The superior warrior is a normal person, with a laser-like focus.* This role was no different. They were—

She caught a glimpse of herself in a tinted mirror in the elevator lobby. Nikita did a double-take—what the hell had happened to her?

"I know," Drake leaned in and kissed her lightly, then brushed his fingers through her hair. "I dragged you off your favorite beach on no notice. You can fix yourself up once we're in our suite."

Fix herself up? She'd never been a dress-up kind of girl. Not as co-captain of the volleyball team and captain of the decathlon team in high school, definitely not while working for the bastards at Curtis Contracting, and there'd never been a call for fancy attire as a SEAL.

But the woman in the elevator lobby mirror, with her tousled hair, bare midriff, and long legs, was positively stylish.

In the elevator, as they were whisked upward, her instincts checked for lines of attack or escape. Mirrored access panel directly overhead—hard to spot the seam unless you were looking for it. How open was the elevator shaft on a cruise ship and what places could it be used to access if clandestine motion was needed? Then she focused on what was reflected in the panel—a clear view down her own cleavage practically to her belly button. This shirt didn't hide anyth—

"Here we go," Norma announced as the doors whisked open.

Nikita tried to clamp Drake's loose shirt to her chest, but he still held her hand. She went to clench the shirt closed with her other hand, but Zoe slapped it aside.

Altman held a palm across the gap, holding the elevator doors open to let her go first. He'd never done that for her. He'd always treated her as just another SEAL, except for when an assignment called for an undercover approach; then he treated her like just another *female* SEAL. Now he was standing all formally, waiting for her.

—Until Zoe pinched him!

Altman jolted, glared at her.

Nikita was hard-pressed to hide her laugh. Zoe winked at her.

"Check it out," Drake snapped at Altman.

The lieutenant commander didn't appear to appreciate being reminded of his role as bodyguard—especially not with a hard pinch to his butt. He stepped first out of the elevator and made a show of scanning up and down the hallways before signaling that it was okay to leave the elevator.

---

Drake was having fun with the role of chief mercenary as the hotel manager opened the suite's door. For one thing he got to order around a DEVGRU lieutenant commander like a hired gun. Wasn't a merc in the world who could command that kind of clout. It also gave him an excuse to hang on to Nikita's hand even when she kept trying to extract it. *The arrogant merc is in control.*

"Oh yes, this will do nicely." He'd been on a couple of cruises with his family, but they were definitely on the inside stateroom budget. This suite would do more than nicely, it would do better than any hotel room he'd ever been in.

Coral and crystal motif—the suite wrapped around the front corner of one of the decks high above the bow. It offered a trio of floor-to-ceiling windows with views both forward and to the port side off their private verandah. He was definitely going to be spending time in those loungers. Inside, leather chairs clustered about a dining table. Another seating group included a couch and offered fine views of both the outdoors and the big screen television. A small marble service bar completed the scene.

Through one door was a connecting suite with bed, bath, and a small seating area. Through the other was a master bedroom *en suite* with its own access to the verandah, a writing nook, and a big walk-in. The bathroom was to die for and gave him some very clear thoughts about Nikita, him, and a locked bathroom door.

The air was pleasantly cool despite the hot, muggy Miami afternoon.

"Honey," he pulled Nikita in and kissed her quickly, though not too quickly. It was a fine balance between playing the part and having Nikita or Altman pummel him to the thick mocha carpet. "I know I didn't give you time to pack properly. Why don't you run down to the boutique and get a couple of nice outfits?"

"Excuse me, Mr. Roman," Norma the hotel manager was still with them. "The shops do not open until we are at sea."

Drake blessed his habit of keeping a couple hundred dollars in his wallet emergency fund ever since he got stranded in Poughkeepsie, New York, once when a broken ATM machine had come between him and the last train out for the night. He drew them out hoping that Norma couldn't see that only smaller bills made up the rest of his cash.

"I'm sure you can fix that for a special guest like my Nikita," he passed off the money in what he hoped was a properly discreet handshake.

The manager attempted to demur, but finally accepted that the problem could be solved.

"We simply won't charge your account until we're at sea, Mr. Roman." Norma handed them each their boarding passes. "Use these to charge anything to your room. And you'll need them to register your departure and return through security at any port, if you choose to leave the ship."

Drake was impressed that they bore their names and likenesses though he'd only transferred the reservations five hours ago.

"Fine. Fine. Now go, honey. And get something filmy for...later. You know what I like."

Nikita's warm brown eyes were almost jet black in warning about exactly what line he was on the verge of crossing.

"And take Zoe with you," because she was clearly enjoying the whole scene as much as he was. Drake slapped Nikita's behind lightly, because he felt it was in character. It was only as his hand landed there that he remembered how it had felt to hold her last night, however briefly. His mouth went dry at the memory.

The three women exited the suite.

"Well," he watched the door close. "That went better than I—"

A powerful hand grabbed him by the back of the neck. A moment later he was slammed face-first into the wall. The coral wallpaper didn't look nearly as nice from a half-inch away.

His "bodyguard" spun Drake around and pressed his forearm hard enough against Drake's throat that he couldn't speak. It was probably a few careful ounces from the pressure needed to crush his windpipe. He tried to swallow, but there was no getting his Adam's apple past Altman's forearm.

"What the fuck are you playing at, flyboy?" Altman's face was only inches from his own and he looked beyond pissed.

Drake tried to breathe in but only managed a lame squeak.

Altman eased of a fraction of an inch.

"She kissed me," he sounded like Elmer Fudd, or maybe Bruce Springsteen after a hard night of drinking. Either way it hurt like hell to manage the three words.

Altman blinked at him twice, then backed off enough that Drake slid down the wall until his feet hit the floor. It was such a surprise, his knees almost went out from under him as well. He hadn't even known that Altman had lifted him up as easily as Perseus lifting up the Medusa's head after chopping it off. For once Drake could sympathize with the mythic monster—it must have hurt even worse than this.

"Try explaining that one again," Altman was still only inches away.

Drake wrapped his hand around his throat, impressed to find it wasn't, in truth, severed. He didn't risk the pain of repeating himself.

"When?"

"Last night," maybe he sounded more like a frog. One that had been the subject of a roadkill accident. "This morning. Whatever it was when I helped her to bed after the meeting. She was too exhausted to even walk."

Altman's fists bunched hard and Drake wondered if he was about to die.

"And you—" Altman ground to halt. He looked even more dangerous than Major Pete Napier when he was angry, and that was saying something—the commander of the 5E didn't take shit from anyone. "You kissed her back."

"I'm not an idiot, Altman. A woman like that kisses me, damn straight I'm gonna kiss her back." Now that his own expiration didn't appear to be imminent, he was starting to get pissed. "What? Am I treading on ground you want for yourself and she won't give you?"

Altman's growl said that maybe confrontation wasn't the best tactic to take with a DEVGRU SEAL. But...in for a penny, in for a pound.

"By the way, I don't give a good goddamn what you think. If Nikita lets me, I'll damned well kiss her again. Up to her, *not* you or me."

Altman managed five stiff steps away until he was standing at one of the big windows. Beyond him lay the MacArthur Causeway and the sprawl of Miami Harbor.

"You got an issue with me, Altman, spit it out."

"It's not you. It's— Shit!" Altman turned and dropped into one of the chairs.

Drake crossed to the bar. Crown Royal XR—the former head of GSI had expensive taste in whisky. He poured two fingers each into a pair of tumblers, decided that Altman wasn't the ice or splash-of-water type, and then poured a third finger into each one. He walked over and handed one to Altman before sitting down across from him.

The whisky soothed Drake's aching throat. The warmth slid down into his stomach.

"Okay, Lieutenant Commander. Better if we have it out now before the ladies get back."

The SEAL stared at his glass a long time before knocking back half of it. "I'm just trying to protect her."

"From who? Me?"

Altman shook his head and continued to study the thick brown carpet. "From herself."

# CHAPTER 8

"Oh my gawd, girlfriend. You *really* don't get it, do you?" Zoe's wink asked forgiveness after the fact for the familiarity.

"What don't I get?" Nikita looked helplessly about the small boutique. Not a black t-shirt or pair of camo pants in sight. She did most of her civilian clothes shopping at thrift stores because they were cheap and what the hell did she care. She almost swallowed her tongue when she glanced at the price tag on a simple white blouse.

The shopkeeper hovered in the background, doing a very credible job of not being irritated at being called to work early by the hotel manager.

"You're with Drake Roman...*the* Drake Roman," she said it loudly, with a tone of awe.

Nikita tried to shush her, but Zoe didn't even stop for a breath.

"I heard that when the military took out that al-Shabaab camp in Somalia, that it was actually Drake Roman and his boys. And that coup in—"

This time Nikita did shush her, with a hand over Zoe's mouth. But Nikita could feel Zoe's smile against her palm and finally caught on. "We aren't supposed to talk about those things," she managed to play along.

Zoe looked properly chagrined and they both glanced guiltily toward the shopkeeper, who was listening avidly and doing her best to pretend she wasn't. *And so the rumor mill gets started.* To what end, she wasn't sure, but Zoe seemed to know what she was doing.

"So," Nikita did her best to put her nose in the air. "If I'm with *the* Drake Roman, what should I get?"

"Oh, I'd start here," Zoe's grin was wicked as she reached for a lacy bit of nothing. The La Perla bodysuit didn't even pretend to cover anything. In fact, it was designed to *not* cover *anything*. It also had a four-figure price tag.

"Not a chance!" Then to mask her out-of-character reaction, "I think that Mr. Roman needs to be much nicer to me before he deserves me in that."

"How about for me and the luscious Luke then?"

Nikita couldn't have heard that correctly. "You aren't seriously thinking about…" Or was she?

Zoe put the bit of lingerie back on the rack and shook her head. "No. But it might be fun to shock him with it anyway."

"Can we be serious about this?"

"Oh, Nikki," Zoe shook her head. "Clothes shopping is never serious."

The nickname from her past stopped Nikita's protests by overwhelming her with memories she didn't want.

Zoe began walking among the racks and pulling off item after item. When she had an armful, she guided Nikita back to the small changing room. "Start with these."

"Start?" There were more fancy clothes here than she'd worn in an entire lifetime.

Zoe ignored her as she pushed her into the changing room. Thankfully, she didn't stay after hanging up the items she'd grabbed. Nikita had been sufficiently mortified by the comment about her breasts on the helicopter.

At the threshold, Zoe looked back over her shoulder. "It's obvious you haven't slept together yet." Thank god she kept her voice down this time.

Nikita resisted the urge to ask how she knew that.

"How good a kisser is Mr. Drake Roman?"

Nikita sighed, "Very good." She could still remember the fire that had lashed between them as they'd held each other hard. Judging by that, sex with Drake would be very rough and tumble, and very good.

"Crap! I should have known. Sooo envious!" And she was gone.

Nikita picked up a flowing silk caftan of tropical colors with a plunging neckline; definitely no bra could be worn with this one. At the other end, it would be barely long enough to cover her underwear. How was a woman supposed to sit in such a dress?

It turned out, that wasn't the worst of the options Zoe had chosen. Behind the caftan hung the black La Perla bodysuit.

---

"It's not my story to tell."

"Bullshit!" Then Drake wished he'd spoken more softly. The whisky hadn't numbed his sore throat nearly enough. "You try to kill me, then tell me I don't get to know why. Spill it, Altman."

"You this much of a pain in the ass to your commander, Roman?"

"Are you kidding? You've flown with Pete Napier. Do you think I'd be still walking around if I talked back to him?"

"But *I* get your shit?"

"He never tried to kill me either. So he gets a pass. You don't."

Altman stared down into his glass. He hadn't touched it after that first big swallow.

Drake sat back and took another sip of his. Was this what it felt like to be Altman or Napier? Assured, calm, drinking a quiet whisky in a luxury suite? Well, maybe not the last. And looking at Altman, maybe not the first two either. But an odd contentment had come over him, as if for only the second time in his life he was in the right place at the right time.

The first time had gotten him into the Night Stalkers. He'd been a decent gunner for the 101st Airborne. Then the Night Stalkers had come up short a man when one of their crew chiefs stepped off his bird and onto a landmine in an area that had supposedly been cleared. They'd needed a new gunner for a mission that night and he'd been available. Once he'd had a taste of what it was like to fly with them, he'd fought like a madman to get in. They were the best people he'd ever flown with. It took him two more years before he flew with them again, but he'd made it.

He wondered where that feeling of rightness would lead this time. He'd only had it that once, so banking on it turning out well might be presumptuous, but he'd bet on a good hand until someone forced him to fold.

"Nikita comes from a shit past," Altman finally ground out.

Drake's contentment froze in that moment and the whisky suddenly churned in his guts. Someone touching her who wasn't—

"Not like that," Altman was looking right at him. "Though I like seeing that you're the kind of man that would piss off."

"Damn straight!"

Altman just nodded before continuing. "Got in with a merc outfit. A bad one. One that didn't like spending the extra money on intel, even though she had the lead right in her hand but needed a payoff they wouldn't give her. Got her dad and her fiancé killed in a single mission."

"Oh, crap!" That sure explained her reaction to the GSI guys.

"They were a lean outfit, *so* lean that she was also on the comms when they went down. Talk about a lady who's had a world of hurt…" Altman knocked back another big swallow of his drink.

"That's what gave her the drive to take on ST6 selection." Drake knew it was true even as he said it.

Altman nodded. "Volunteered Navy. SEAL track from day one. Before she made it through boot camp, someone gave me the heads-up to come watch her. I did. You know from making it into the Night Stalkers that it's ninety percent mental."

"And ninety percent brutal." For the Special Operations teams, being motivated or excellent wasn't enough—you had to be both.

"You got that right. She's got it, that indefinable *it.* But I wasn't kidding when I said to watch your goddamn step with her. There's something inside that's hurt and angry, and real goddamn dangerous. She's got a hard control of the former and can use it to direct the latter where I need it. You crack that barrier and screw up one of my best people and you've got me to answer to. We clear?"

Drake considered the idea that Nikita wasn't as tough as she looked. That wasn't right. She was tougher. Her strength ran all the way to the core, or SEAL Team 6 wouldn't have let her in to begin with.

"We're clear. But she's—"

And he heard the door open behind him. He glanced over his shoulder as sandals slapped across the suite's marble foyer. Two women laughing together. At least someone had been having a good time.

They stepped into view and Drake jolted to his feet.

Nikita wore a...he didn't know what to call it except amazing. Two sweeps of pleated white fabric swept around either side from behind her neck. They rode over her breasts and crisscrossed on her abdomen before disappearing around the back. A flirty black skirt barely reached mid-thigh. She was completely covered, but with deep cleavage, a bare midriff, and long legs.

"You were right, Zoe. Look at them."

Drake couldn't turn away to see Altman's reaction.

"Do a spin," Zoe instructed Nikita with an elfin laugh.

Nikita twirled about. The only thing covering her back was her hair, reaching only a few inches onto her shoulders. The two sweeps of fabric actually melded into the dark skirt at the base of her spine.

Drake strode up to her, "Remember how I said you were gorgeous?"

Nikita nodded uncertainly.

He slipped his hands around her waist and onto that beautiful bare back. He whispered for her alone, "I lied. You're way beyond gorgeous."

NIKITA DIDN'T KNOW what to do with him.

Drake had always been a pleasant enough, smooth-mover of a guy who had the added benefit of being an excellent gunner and crew chief. But the man confidently holding her in the cruise ship's luxury suite was someone else entirely.

Without forethought or intent, she leaned into him. She'd never needed anyone to lean on, but somehow, leaning on Drake Roman felt…safe. Not that she'd ever needed safe.

When he kissed her, she eased into it. Unlike last night's hot and heavy, there was a sweet tenderness to it.

"Yes!" Zoe's whispered cheer, which she probably would have accompanied with a fist pump if her arms weren't full, was enough to pull her back from it. But the warmth and peace stayed with her as she eased away.

Altman was watching her carefully. She couldn't read his thoughts but his look made her want to hide her face against Drake's shoulder, so instead she retreated another step.

"There's more," she said to fill the awkward silence and signaled to the shopkeeper, who had been thrilled to help Zoe carry the purchases. They'd probably made the shop's quota for the whole trip in a single go. She'd finally thrown the last of her caution to the wind when Zoe had suggested they could just bill the whole shopping trip back to Titan and J-dawg wouldn't dare argue. She'd liked the sound of that. Even better, he'd probably whine the whole way, and then they could sic Sugar on him to get him back in line. On that premise, they'd made a few purchases for Zoe as well.

"This way," Zoe flashed a big smile, then led the shopkeeper into the master suite.

"I'll take the top one," Nikita snagged the first of several dress bags out of the shopkeeper's hands. "I got this for you, Drake."

She'd bought it as part of the role they were playing, but now it seemed more intimate and personal. Nikita slipped the white Armani jacket from the black plastic and held it out, open and ready for him.

Drake turned and slipped his arms in. She tugged it up onto his shoulders and ran her hand down the lines of the back. They'd guessed at his size and done well—actually Zoe had.

When he turned, he was dazzling. He still wore her tight black t-shirt and tan khakis. Combined with the white jacket, he looked both wealthy and dangerous. With the power of his light kiss still on her lips, she was having trouble meeting his eyes.

"Oh, the fit is perfect, I am so glad," the shopkeeper inspected Drake with a professional eye as she came back into the room. "No need to take it to our tailor." But it wasn't only the jacket she was looking at. Whether it was because of how handsome he looked in the jacket or if she wanted to see the *notorious Drake Roman* was unclear. But he definitely made an impression.

Drake reached for his wallet.

"Oh, there is no need, Mr. Roman. Your lady-friend has been most generous already." She'd signed a big tip on to the room charge just for J-dawg.

As she left the suite, there was a small gasp of surprise, then the shopkeeper spoke softly. "Good afternoon, Arthur." Her tone, which had warmed up the instant Zoe had gathered a third of the shop into the dressing room and had remained cheerful and friendly through-out, went distinctly cool.

"Arthur" rapped his knuckles on the open door. "Good afternoon," he stepped into the suite without so much as an invitation. He was a lean man in a sharp suit that looked inappropriate for the setting—as if he was trying too hard. His overly cheery smile faded as he inspected the four of them carefully, instantly dismissing everyone except Drake.

"Yes?" Drake managed a decent mix of arrogant and curious.

"I'm sorry. I was expecting someone else. I had understood that this was Global Security's suite." But he didn't back out. Global Security International, GSI. Arthur had just said the magic pass phrase.

"*Was* is the *operative* word," Drake replied without even an eyeblink of hesitation. His voice chilled like the haughty person he was supposed to be and Nikita wanted to warn him about doing too much.

She'd spent the night deep in GSI's files, so she knew the source of Drake's reaction. Not only mercs, but by the end they'd added kidnapping of women and children to their list as part of a blackmail attempt.

She slipped her hand around Drake's arm to caution him, but decided that playing the dumb brunette was to her advantage at the moment.

Arthur blinked slowly though she could see his mind working quickly. "A…change in circumstances?"

"Let me just say that after our…*acquisition* of GSI, their people are no longer a factor. I'm now looking out for their business interests." Who was this man she was holding on to? It certainly wasn't Drake Roman the pleasantly thoughtful Night Stalker gunner. This was a dangerous man who could easily command an entourage and stage a lethal takeover of a competitor.

A part of her wanted to shove him away, disgusted with the merc attitude she knew all too well from her days at Curtis Contracting. But another part of her wanted to hold on tight and stay close to his unexpected power.

The ship's horn blared to life somewhere above them, a muted roar through the closed windows.

"Excuse me. Departure is always an exciting time aboard a cruise ship and I should leave you to enjoy it. Especially as you are traveling," he nodded toward Nikita, "with a friend. But perhaps I may interest you in attending an art auction during your cruise," he produced a card. "The gallery is always open for viewing and the first auction will be tomorrow evening."

Drake took the card, glanced at it, then dropped it on the bar counter instead of pocketing it.

"We'll consider it," then his dark and dangerous mood shifted. He kissed her lightly on the cheek. "I am completely at the mercy of whatever whim takes my lovely lady."

"Of course, sir," Arthur agreed smoothly and then withdrew.

Drake led them all out onto the wrap-around verandah. He leaned heavily on the forward railing, which offered a sweeping view of the dock and the many islands that dotted Miami's harbor. Blue sky, shining water, islands packed with luxury homes, it was quite the scene. A glance down revealed dozens upon dozens of other passengers doing the same thing they were, leaning on their own suite's verandah railings to watch the busy harbor.

"Did I do okay?" *There* was the Drake Roman she knew. She'd been right to hang on to him.

She kissed him on the cheek this time and whispered, "You did great!" It was an intimate moment, and one she rather enjoyed.

---

ALTMAN'S SLAP on his back didn't dislodge Nikita's hold on his arm, which was good or it would have knocked him over the railing and into the ocean far below.

"Next time I need an undercover badass, you're my boy," Altman almost smiled.

"Amazing what three years in the Yale drama department can do for you."

"If you went to Yale, why aren't you an officer?" Zoe was standing on Altman's other side.

"Because I never went back for year four. I enjoyed acting. I enjoyed actresses especially," then he felt stupid for saying that aloud. He was going to need to negotiate an unlimited do-overs license with Nikita. "But I wasn't anything special and I spent an entire summer getting cut at first-call auditions in Seattle just to prove it. That's a major theater town and I didn't get a single casting—only got a handful of callbacks."

"Theater to military?" Nikita's voice had changed. It wasn't just like she was continuing the role from the suite; it was warmer. As if she was genuinely interested.

"Granddad on my mom's side flew Hueys in Vietnam. Was flying lumber in Seattle—picking hard-to-reach timber out of the deep forest with an Erickson Aircrane. While I was losing all those auditions, I stayed with him and Grandma. Every night he'd tell me stories over a beer. On the days I couldn't even line up a tryout, he'd take me aloft with him. Liked it better than a whole lot of stage doors slamming in my face."

A trio of dockhands were gathered on the concrete dock in bright yellow vests and hardhats. Nearby was a massive bollard with a six-inch-diameter line run around it and back to the ship. The dockhands were just waiting. Finally one answered a radio call, then the three of them walked up to the heavy line and flipped it off the bollard and into the water. The ship began cranking it aboard.

Then with another horn blast and a low rumble that he could feel through the handrail, the dock began moving away. The cruise ship was so massive that it felt as if the island was gliding aside and not them. But he was. For better or worse, he was trapped in his new role.

"And now I've gone from military to mercenary."

"Military contractor," Nikita corrected him. "They never call themselves mercenaries."

"You mean *we* never call ourselves that."

In answer she continued to face the dock moving away from the ship but squeezed his arm where she clasped it, either in friendly conspiracy or as if seeking strength against something she despised. He was content with it either way.

"What do you make of your new friend Arthur?" Zoe was clearly used to the departure process and didn't spare it a glance.

"He's hitting the Internet on us right now," he and Nikita practically spoke in unison. "That's why he pulled back and retreated," Drake finished.

"Nope," Zoe shook her head. "Not us. He's researching *you*, the great Drake Roman. He doesn't know the rest of us from a hole in the wall."

"Or care," Altman agreed. "You saw how he ignored us, which is good. Let's keep it that way."

"Perfect! Is it too late to get the helo back?" Drake searched the sky though they were probably halfway back to Rucker by now.

"What's wrong?"

"What's wrong? Arthur is going to run a search and it will go *ping!* Sergeant First Class Drake Roman, 160th SOAR, 5th Battalion—"

"Dishonorably discharged eleven months ago," Altman cut off his rant. "Misappropriation of government property, to wit: four million in sanctioned military hardware including air-to-ground Hellfire missiles and Miniguns."

"I did what?" Drake tried to breathe. "A dishonorable what? But I never—"

"Apparently you pulled a lot of high-end strings and called in favors so that you didn't go to Leavenworth along with your fellow conspirators. He can check the back news articles, it actually did happen and there were parties unnamed who were 'arrested and released'."

"But—"

"Instead you formed DR, Inc. According to your hype, Drake Roman can *doctor* anything anywhere as long as it's military. Parker, Titan's data geek, has been planting wild and nefarious exploits for DR, Inc. in all of the wrong places. You also have a website. If Arthur knows where to look, he'll find out that you can be very bad news."

Nikita bumped his shoulder with hers, "It's not our first rodeo, Drake. We know how to set up a cover fast."

"Couldn't you at least have changed my goddamn name?"

Altman shrugged, "Easier to work with your own name. Your civilian passport remains valid. Due to the short notice, there wasn't time to change it anyway."

Drake stared out at that the blinding waves that rippled across Government Cut and the Atlantic Ocean beyond.

*Easier?* If Granddad heard about this, he would stroke out.

# CHAPTER 9

"Are you sure we can't order in?" Nikita was looking at the cocktail-dress clad woman in the mirror.

"Not a chance!" Zoe had been fussing with Nikita's hair, trying to make it look like something. "We are so taking you to the salon tomorrow. Hair, manicure, the whole bit. You look fabulous though. Again, wish I had your body."

"Will you cut that out?" Because Zoe looked fabulous herself in a classic little black dress. Offset by her pale skin, blond-dyed hair, and bright yellow pumps with flirty bows that matched the one clipped into her hair, Zoe looked perfect for the first evening's dinner.

The woman in the mirror, on the other hand, looked like a trussed turkey. Her bright-red dress was a curve-hugging sheath above the waist and a fanciful floral lace over the pleated skirt that ran down just past mid-thigh. The only saving grace had been her refusal to buy heels of any sort, but the red leather strapped sandals weren't much better, even if they were easier to walk in. The dress covered far more of her skin than anything else she'd worn today, but it made her feel far more revealed. This wasn't merely sexy—which would be confusing enough—this dress shouted, "Look at me!"

"I look—"

"Seriously hot. Now remember. Your life's purpose is to make Drake happy."

"Slave girl doesn't suit me well. Can't I just kill him—or myself, either one—and be done with this," she turned the other way and tried smoothing the lace that insisted she had very womanly hips.

"Not slave girl. You're the woman so amazing that no one but the great Drake Roman could deserve you."

"You're fast climbing onto my shit list of people I would maim to get out of this."

Zoe laughed and pushed her out of the master bedroom that Altman had made very clear that the women would be sharing. Their clothes were stowed as couples so that the maids wouldn't notice anything amiss, but their sleeping arrangements would not be.

Nikita decided that was probably just as well.

But she would still rather stay here tonight, in the suite. The bathroom was nearly as big as the bedroom, and definitely larger than her room in the 5E's barracks. A generous tub for two, toilet and bidet, two sinks, and a shower stall that could accommodate a party of six. She could get room service and never leave.

She stepped into the living room at the same moment Drake stepped through the opposite door from the small suite next door. He had looked good in white Armani and black t-shirt. In the Armani with a dress shirt almost as dark as his eyes and a tie the same red as her dress, he was startling.

"You need a shave," was all she could think to say.

He rubbed a hand across his chin, "Altman thought I should leave it."

"Ye-ah!" Zoe placed her vote and Nikita knew it was a lost cause.

Drake looked both sophisticated and, with the shadow of a beard, rugged. It made her remember more about his kiss some forever time ago like this morning. Hot and rugged.

"My question though," Drake leaned toward Altman in a conspiratorial whisper, "is how did we luck out to get to escort the two most beautiful women on the ship?"

Altman's answer was an equally conspiratorial fist in the ribs—except Drake winced like it actually hurt.

---

THE PRE-DINNER MIXER in the Wave lounge included the occupants of the ship's eight high-end luxury suites, the captain, and Norma the hotel manager. It also included a hosted, high-octane bar and a small flock of stewards constantly circulating with tiny *amuse-bouches:* oysters served in those white Chinese soup spoons with a Thai salsa, prosciutto-wrapped shrimp on tiny metal Neptune's tridents, eggrolls the size of his pinky with more flavor than any he'd ever had before.

Drake opted for whisky, in keeping with the Crown Royal XR that had been delivered to his room, and handed Nikita a flute of effervescent champagne that practically made her giggle. Altman had somehow talked a beer out of the bartender, and Zoe had the champagne as well.

He wasn't sure what he was supposed to be saying to anyone. Oddly, it was the deeply reserved Nikita who took the lead in the introductions.

"Drake is in project management, specializing in conflict resolution at the international level."

"Oh, Drake took me to Rio last month. He had work there, not for me to know about, of course. I stayed in the Fasano Rio spa—really, you must go. The Filipino face massage is to die for. After that we went to one of those nature reserves and stayed in a treehouse where the only way in or out was on a zipline."

"Drake is in international transport of specialized equipment. We just returned from Kenya. If you ever need to get away, you simply must rent Kilulu Island. The villa is charming. It has a pool, a full staff, and the whole island is so very private." She actually managed a coy look and a blush as she told that one.

He wasn't the only one with an acting background. Nikita was practically dripping with brainless, fawning jetsetter—until he wondered quite who she was.

By the time he could get her aside, he'd been introduced twelve different ways to stockbrokers, bankers, an airline executive, mistresses, and somebody's boy-toy. He could overhear Zoe doing the same thing in her effervescent tone as she sometimes hovered at Nikita's side and other times at the silent Luke's.

"What happens when they compare notes?" He kept his whisper urgent.

"They already are," Nikita replied with a perfect placidity, slipping back into her normal self, which was a relief. At least the cool and soft-spoken SEAL he knew, even if he didn't understand her any better than the flirty airhead.

"But—" Drake had been saying that a lot lately. "I'm not—" But he was. Every description had, in a way, said the same thing. However, Nikita had said it so many different ways that it was making his head spin. He looked at his glass. Still half full, he'd been careful to pace himself. Maybe drowning his woes in whisky would be a better choice.

"Everyone here now knows that you're an international man of mystery who is wealthy, can afford to send me to the highest-end spas and resorts—which I know about because Mom likes watching the travel channels and we do it together whenever I'm home—while you do dangerous, secret work. We're giving you an instant reputation."

"For what reason? Wait," the pieces began clicking into place. "Because word has a chance of getting back to Arthur, the art auctioneer, and whoever his cronies are."

"Precisely; can you imagine a circle of people more likely to buy his 'art'?"

Drake scanned the room. His mom was a banker and his dad a named partner in one of the major Boston law firms. Dad came from old money, which had opened the doors to Boston society. The joke was that none of the four of them had enjoyed the society events, but Dad's parents were deeply enough rooted in it that his family couldn't avoid attending.

Drake could practically hear his sister Hennie giving them a running commentary on each person.

*I know that black coral is illegal, but I just had to have it. So I had Henry purchase a vintage piece at ten times the market value.*

*My yacht may be twenty feet shorter than yours, but mine has a chef trained by Mario Batali himself.*

*Oh, the tourists on Martha's Vineyard are just hideous this year, so we've rented a villa in Nice.*

Their family was always the slightly odd group giggling among themselves during the various mandatory outings.

Hennie would have a blast with this crowd. Old men with jewel-bedecked twenty-somethings. Widows and widowers on the prowl for someone of the proper class—*money.* One bruiser who just had to be with the Russian mob. There were only two couples who looked happy to be together and were making a real point of ignoring everyone else in the room. Under normal circumstances, they would be the ones that Drake would gravitate toward.

These were not normal conditions.

"Mr. Roman?" Drake tried desperately to remember who the man now shaking his hand was.

Banker—Ranker— "Mr. Rankin." Drake resisted the urge to crush down on the hearty handshake of someone who had never picked up anything heavier than a martini glass.

"I wonder if we might have a moment," he glanced sideways at Nikita. When they'd first been introduced, he'd barely glanced at Nikita despite how incredible she looked. Maybe the man only made love to his money.

Drake tried to think of a way to keep Nikita at his side, but her presentation of being his mistress-of-the-moment had been so thorough that he couldn't come up with one. At a loss, he kissed her briefly, patted her bottom just to mess with her head, and told her to go mingle.

"I have a competitor that I was hoping I might talk to you about."

*And I have an FBI contact that I'm probably going to be reporting you to.*

Nikita was going to have to do something about Drake's fascination with her behind. The gentle pat to send her on her way, the playful slap to send her shopping, and the way he'd grabbed it hard when they were kissing in her room back at Mother Rucker. He was confusing the crap out of her…which was half the reason she'd been playing the brainless airhead. He wanted to treat her like that in public, *fine!* She'd *be* that in public.

It fit her chosen role, so why was it irritating her?

Only partly because it now meant that she couldn't accompany him as he and Rankin moved off to stand at a window and look out at the sunset as they talked.

It also thrust her once more into the social whirl that was like nothing she'd ever been through. Without Drake to hang on to, she felt lost—adrift on a sea that had rules she didn't begin to understand. Her attempts to latch herself on to Zoe were intercepted by many of the men. Several of whom had no compunction about talking to her breasts. What they wanted was only too clear. She barely resisted correcting their habits with a hard body slam to the floor.

Others talked to her breasts but they talked about Roman, seeking more stories. She reached into her research of GSI's files and embellished liberally until she felt like she was spilling tales of fictional supervillains. Nikita made sure that her stories at least half the time conflicted with the first round of stories.

*You're going to treat me like an airhead, Roman, that's what I'll deliver.* On the plus side of that role, it meant that everyone would underestimate or even totally ignore her until it was too late.

She finally forged her way to Zoe.

"Refuge!" she pleaded.

"You bet, Nikki." Zoe slipped her hand around her waist, causing Nikita to put her arm around Zoe's shoulders and feel the comfort of a friend. "What do all of those bad boys want? I mean, I saw how they were looking at you."

"Half want to dial my escort service, even with their wives or mistresses or whatever they are standing right next to them."

"No brainer with the way you look. How about the other half?"

Nikita looked about the room. There were a number of very pretty women in the room. Though much of the beauty seemed overly studied. The only reason she stood out in this crowd was that she wasn't bone thin. "The other half want to know what Roman really is."

"And what is he?" Zoe's voice was teasing. "Other than hunk handsome?"

"He certainly seems to like patting my behind."

"Smart man," Zoe agreed as if that wasn't somehow outrageous. "Your boss won't touch me."

For a moment she thought Zoe meant Drake and decided it was a damn good thing he didn't take any liberties there or she'd bust him a good one. Then she realized that Zoe meant Luke, which was too totally outrageous to even think about.

She had to look around the lounge twice to spot him.

It was a SEAL tactic, finding exactly the right tempo of the room, then match it to become invisible. He stood close by one of the exits looking quietly casual by himself. But Nikita knew the stance: he was on alert for anything out of place. From his position by the exit, he had a clear view of the entire space as well as the two other entry points, both currently blocked by brass standards and a loop of red velvet rope to keep this a private party.

His eyes locked on her for a moment in one of his scans, then he barely nodded before continuing on about the room. Altman was lucky. Of them all, his role alone matched who he was. Whether it was the bodyguard or the SEAL watching the entire room, the feel was the same.

Nikita was feeling much closer to a psychotic break.

Dinner was no better. Normally when she was undercover, she and another SEAL were paired to simply look normal walking down a street together, observing security they were going to have to bypass, defenses to surmount, and targets to infiltrate.

At the dinner table she had to play the merry hostess and would have failed miserably without Zoe's assistance. Drake appeared completely at ease with the situation. Fine, let the two of them take the lead role and she'd go sit beside Altman in his forbiddingly too-dangerous-to-even-approach guise. Except she couldn't.

Dinner led to reserved seats in the large auditorium that could seat half the ship's guests to listen to a horrendous mashup of Cubano salsa and Jamaican steel drums that everyone seemed to inhale as the new sound of the century. Then quiet drinks at the late-night piano bar—seats around the piano instead of back at one of the shadowed tables, of course.

"What are we doing, Drake?" She'd had five hours of sleep in four days, more drinks than she typically had in a year other than a friendly beer or two after a mission, and she was ready to collapse.

"Being visible," he whispered under a predictable but not unpleasant version of *What a Wonderful World.*

"Can we be invisible now?"

"Sure thing, sweetheart."

"You sound like Will Smith in *Men in Black.*"

"I was trying to sound like Humphrey Bogart."

Nikita considered laying her head down on the grand piano they were seated around and weeping.

"Got it. Come along." Drake slid his arm around her waist and helped her to her feet.

Nikita didn't know what was going on. Endless corridors, elevators, more corridors. Normally she could dig deep and gut out anything. With Drake taking control, she didn't need to maintain. As a result, she ended up in a head-wobbling space.

When she looked at the woman in the lobby mirror this time, she was practically lying against the handsome stranger that had replaced her Night Stalkers crew chief. Her head rested on his shoulder and, surprisingly, was content to remain there. His reflection turned enough to kiss her on top of the head before the elevator arrived.

If she hadn't known the sunny and sexy woman of this afternoon, she knew the elegant, clingy woman even less, but couldn't rouse herself to protest.

When the acceleration of the elevator threatened to take out her knees, she let it. The handsome warrior swept her into his arms.

In the mirror in the elevator's ceiling, she appeared helpless yet content to merely nestle.

"We pushed her too far. Damn it but I'm an idiot!" Nikita could as much feel as hear what Drake said. "Five hours sleep in four days. I just wasn't thinking."

"We all should have seen it," another gruff male voice replied.

"Almost there, Nikki," someone whispered encouragement from close by. Nikki. The last person to call her Nikki was…

"I don't want to remember," she turned her face into the shoulder of the warrior who carried her and hung on.

"Then don't."

A door, another. In moments the dress was gone and a nightshirt had taken its place. One last time strong arms lifted her and lay her down on soft sheets.

The last thing she remembered was a kiss on her forehead.

CHAPTER 10

"Where am I?" Nikita was used to waking up in strange places: barracks, barns, blown-out buildings they were hiding in, African huts, and the backs of military transports on sea, air, and land. She couldn't begin to make sense of luxurious sheets, fine wood furniture, and the crystal vase on her night table. She had a night table—filled with tropical flowers. That was perhaps the strangest thing of all.

She flopped over and was greeted with a sweeping view of an island and turquoise-colored waters. Sheer curtains fluttered in a sea-scented breeze. And when they fluttered aside, she could see Zoe stretched out on a lounger in the sun, wearing a bikini that was as scant as she was—yellow, of course.

Nikita grabbed sunglasses, then stumbled out and flopped into a chair on the suite's verandah. It offered her a bird's-eye view of Key West. She'd flown out of the Naval Air Station here on any number of missions and recognized the unique look of the town from above. The cruise ship was far and away the tallest building in town. The palm-lined streets were a breezy and comfortably warm mid-seventies—because that's the temperature the town always was.

"How long was I out?"

451

"What day is this?"

"Ha, ha, ha."

"Well, you've missed Key West. They'll be reboarding in an hour or so. You've been out for fifteen."

Nikita plucked at her long nightshirt, "Who?"

"Drake, but I made him promise not to peek."

"But he did anyway."

"I'm not so sure. He was so busy being pissed at himself for running you into the ground like that, I'm not sure he was noticing anything."

"At least it wasn't Altman. That would have been too mortifying."

"Besides, you don't get to have both men."

Nikita raised her head enough to inspect Zoe, but she was still flat on her back, working on her tan. "You're going to burn." That was a safer topic than whether or not Zoe was actually interested in doing more than joking about Commander Altman.

"Wearing SPF-gazillion, but it feels awesomely awesome. Don't get much sun in a drone coffin."

The cargo containers that housed the ground-station controls for flying drones had always been called coffins, which Nikita tried not to see as morbid.

"Besides, I always was super-fair skinned. That's why I finally gave in and went blonde, at least mostly. I know healthy tans are out, but pasty white is a sad way to be, too."

"Where are the men?"

Zoe flapped a hand toward shore, "Drake didn't want to leave you, but I've seen Key West a couple of times. So, I kicked him out before he woke you to ask if you were sleeping. If they're doing their jobs, they're out there being manly and spreading more rumors. If they pick up any women who aren't us, I'm going to be very upset."

Nikita decided that she would be, too. Very upset. And that was an irrational enough thought to force her back to her feet.

"I need a run."

"They have a track here, up on the top deck. A hundred and fifty meters."

"Twenty seconds a lap? I'd get dizzy."

"It's a jogging track, probably cluttered with couples strolling hand in hand and calling it exercise. They do have weights and treadmills."

"A gym. Excellent!"

"Fitness Center."

"Doesn't matter," Nikita yanked on Zoe's ankle hard enough to almost pull her off the lounger. "You're going, too."

"No! I want to become fat and lazy. That's what cruise ships are about."

"I thought they were about Arthur and the Honduran bad guys."

"Crap!" Zoe clambered to her feet. "Reality sucks."

---

DRAKE DIDN'T KNOW when he'd ever been so happy.

Zoe's three-letter text, "Gym," when he was just back aboard through security, sent him scrambling upstairs to change. Once their suite's butler had told him where to find the fitness center, he'd tracked them down.

After a day like today, doing a workout with Nikita was exactly what the doctor ordered—maybe, if the gods were smiling on him, they'd have a wrestling mat. Then again, she was SEAL-trained in hand-to-hand combat, so maybe not.

Because this mission was extremely compartmentalized, McDermott hadn't wanted to involve the other agencies directly. Instead, he'd sent a very simple request for any information on outstanding GSI operations in Central America. That was enough to make someone in intel look at what had actually been going on—then Internal Affairs had taken over and slammed a lockdown on all information requests. Some oversight committee landed at the center of a witch hunt, which had shuttered all further information that might have flowed to the 5E.

The only message to escape the fray was a single and utterly useless note: *No Global Security International operations authorized outside Southwest Asia region.* All that told him was just how far off the reservation GSI had gone. No record of anything going on in Central America and whoever had been their government contact—probably inside the CIA—wanted no hint of involvement with anything else. Actually, it also told him they were entering the Minotaur's Labyrinth of the wholly unknown monster. Now it was only a question of how soon the beast GSI had created would try to devour them.

Deciding that they'd be better off drawing out the beast, he and Altman had spent the entire day probing the ship's elite passengers under the casual circumstances of Key West. Drake had never spouted so much drivel in his life, not even when playing the mad and ridiculous constable in a summer stock production of Shakespeare's *Much Ado About Nothing*. They'd learned nothing. Not from Rankin the banker, the Russian mobster, or any of the others.

As to the cruise line's officers, his fabricated reputation had proceeded him and they all clammed up tighter than a submarine about to dive deep for cover. Hopefully Altman left ashore on his own would do better, though Drake doubted it.

Drake finally locate the Fitness Center in the stern of the ship a couple of decks down. He had to go through the spa—past beauty salon, massage tables, the "thermal center" with its hard tile couches, treatment rooms where women lay with gray or green facial masks— to find the workout room. Along the way he'd had to dodge several particularly fit men and women in ship's uniforms asking if he wanted this treatment or that. Perhaps a sauna?

In the exercise room, after being briefly dazzled by the sweeping view of Key West, he spotted Zoe spinning a cycle exerciser faster than a hummingbird's wingbeat.

"Where's Luke?" was her idea of a greeting.

"Still ashore, drinking with a group of the ship's officers. Telling stories and spreading lies." Then he turned and got an eyeful. There were a few other people in the gym doing workouts—civilian workouts. Stair-stepping to the beat of some Broadway show tune, or rowing slowly enough that even George Washington's fully laden boats could have beat them across the Potomac.

And then there was Nikita with her back to him.

Five-ten in silken running shorts and a black t-shirt. Her ponytail swinging side to side as she ran in what he recognized as a military ground-eater. Sweat was just starting to make her shine as her long legs ate up the distance that the treadmill was handing out. She wasn't watching the CNN broadcast on one screen or the advertisements for the next port's exciting excursions on the other. Nikita was staring straight ahead at the blue ocean and just now shifting from a warm-up pace to a light run—good, he was only a few minutes behind her. She ran as if she was loping easily through the primeval forests, not working out on a luxury cruise ship.

"You going to watch her or do something about it?"

He gave Zoe the finger without bothering to look away from the magnificent athlete before him.

She merely laughed and kept spinning.

The treadmill beside Nikita opened up and he stepped onto it. Glancing at the program she was running, he hit the same.

She was so focused on her run that she didn't even notice him. Well, when she was ready to, he'd be here. Meanwhile he would run out some tiny portion of his desperate need for the woman he'd cradled in his arms last night.

Women never cost him a night's rest—it just didn't happen. Well, it did, but only when they were sharing a bed and neither of them were interested in using it for sleep.

Last night, after he'd finally finished berating himself for forgetting that even a SEAL had limits, he'd been stuck with the feel of her in his arms. That, far more than how Nikita Hayward looked wearing nothing but underpants, had cost him the night. Women were to be enjoyed, not cherished. But when he'd held her tight to his chest carrying her down the hallway, he'd felt so strong.

When she'd begged him to not let her remember, in a voice so sad that it didn't seem possible it had been uttered by Nikita Hayward, he had felt truly helpless.

And all through the night he wished he was still holding her, to somehow protect her against her own past.

CHAPTER 11

$\mathcal{N}$ikita powered ahead.

She hadn't needed Zoe's laugh to tell her that Drake had shown up. She hadn't even needed the hint of his reflection off the TV screen—she'd felt him when he'd entered the room. There had been a ripple as other women had turned and paused long enough to admire. Men suddenly moved more briskly on their machines as if needing to show themselves to be up to a standard they'd never meet.

Her mind was turning to mush on the subject of Drake Roman and she didn't like it. They ran for three kilometers before she wondered if she might be losing her mind.

"I'm not a woman designed for cruise ships," she snarled at no one in particular and pushed the speed button up another two klicks an hour.

"Nope," Drake agreed happily, and punched his own pace to match.

She told herself she wasn't going to look at him, but she did. He'd already stripped off his t-shirt and flipped it over a handhold. His skin was just a shade darker than hers, to go with his black hair. And his chest—

Nikita looked away. She remembered that chest and what it felt like to curl up against it. Between the exhaustion and the atypical amount to drink, her barriers had crashed down. The anger, the fear, the grief had threatened to overwhelm her. Until a voice like a benediction called down upon her desire to not remember, "Then don't."

And she hadn't. Instead she had buried her face in his chest and allowed herself to be taken care of with none of the hard time she'd given the docs and physical therapists the couple of times she'd been injured in the line of duty.

"I'm waiting," she managed between two breaths.

"For what?"

"For the great...Drake Roman to tell...me exactly what...he thinks...I'm good for...if not cruise ships." Her breath was starting to run short, but she'd just given him a bad straight line. She punched in another kilometer an hour.

"I'll ignore the obvious," Drake managed in a single breath as he again matched her speed.

Nikita leaned into the run and waited him out.

"Instead I'll tell you why I've been...so attracted to you since the first moment I saw you."

At least the bastard had the decency to take a breath in there. She considered pushing up another klick per hour, but wouldn't be able to speak if she did. Besides, now she was curious.

"My mom and my sister are both...seriously strong women. In spirit and mind...if not athletic."

It was nice that he was finally running short of breath as well.

"You are the only woman...I've ever met...who makes them look average."

Nikita stumbled and almost lost her pace as she looked over at him. Nothing about her body or her face or some other thin compliment.

Drake glanced at her for a moment, his dark eyes not looking aside as he held the pace. Sweat was dripping down his forehead and off his chest. He seemed to grow even taller as he ran beside her. Then he looked away and punched for another notch of speed as if he could somehow run away from what he'd just said.

Nikita matched him. "Why…never say…any…thing?" She managed against the blistering pace.

Drake shrugged and cricked his neck to one side as if he didn't know either.

He hit the speed button once more, which precluded all conversation.

She matched him and they simply ran. There was no glancing aside. Not at this speed. There was only the pounding of feet on rubber tread. The hot burning of legs driving ahead, fighting to hold their pace. Sweat stung her eyes and they burned, but she didn't care.

She could do a fifty-kilometer hike with a full field pack. She could jog along for hours with a light kit and her rifle. At this pace, all she could do was lean into it and go.

Five minutes…ten? She couldn't tell. The television screen changed from Key West to Belize to Coxen Hole on Roatán Island, Honduras. Overly perky hosts "reported" on screens filled with reef diving, parasailing, dune buggies, and ziplines.

Somewhere in the distance the ship's horn bellowed a warning —*get aboard or be left behind.* And still they ran.

There was no question of talking now. Their breath rasped in and out. Disharmonious, desperate.

Impossibly, Drake slapped the pace up once more.

With no idea how she could maintain it, she did the same. The setting was now for a four-minute mile—a record no woman had yet achieved.

It was unsustainable, but she'd be damned if some gorgeous flyboy was going to outrun a DEVGRU SEAL. There was honor to maintain.

Her arms were pumping so hard to keep her balance that they, too, ached with lactic acid buildup.

He groaned aloud against the agony of their run.

And still it built.

Thirty seconds.

A minute.

One and a half.

The scream of frustration ripped from her throat as her body fought to deliver what she demanded of it.

One forty-five.

One fifty.

Drake's snarl beside her was furious as he slammed ahead, struggling to sustain the pace.

One fifty-five.

Two minutes!

In final agony they cried out together as they both slammed down fists on the emergency stop buttons.

The treadmills slowed rapidly.

Two steps.

One more.

She let it carry her to the end of the belt. Stepping down onto the floor was almost impossible because her legs were shaking so hard.

Drake grabbed her hand and dragged her along, stumbling behind him, through the crowd that had gathered to watch their contest.

Flashing impressions: a dozen passengers, spa attendants, a trainer, Zoe's smile.

"No one comes in!" Drake snarled at somebody, then pulled her through a door marked "Men's Showers".

He yanked her forward, then tugged her about so that her back slammed against the cedar paneling.

He crashed into her. Kissing her as she groaned with need for breath and for Drake. She hooked an aching leg behind him to pull him in tighter and she dug her hands into his hair.

His hands were on her. There was nothing gentle. None of the surprising tenderness of last night. She didn't want it.

She wanted him. The way she'd never wanted anyone.

His hand dug under her t-shirt, under her bra, and he was the one who groaned with pleasure.

Her own hands dove into his shorts and clenched on his butt just as they had in her room at Mother Rucker.

Nikita hauled him so tightly against her that he thought he might break through the fabric between them.

He hadn't asked permission.

His need had him manhandling her. He couldn't stop himself.

"Now! Goddamn it, Roman! Now!"

So much for asking.

He yanked down her shorts and underwear. He retrieved the protection that an angel of grace had made him stuff in his pocket when he left the suite to come find her.

There wasn't time to be gentle. He wanted to caress, to appreciate, to please.

Not a chance.

He wanted to take and Nikita was offering it with as much desperation as she'd run. Gods, how she'd run. He'd never pushed himself so far past his limits, and still he hadn't been able to match her. She was beyond magnificent.

So he sheathed himself and he took.

No finesse. No grace.

He simply took her.

Everything that had built in him, he poured into her body.

She wrapped both legs around his hips and let him plunder. When she cried out, he swallowed the cry and added his own.

Never had a release so pounded through him as the one he found in Nikita. She clung and shuddered against him until he was shakier than even the run had made him feel.

When the releases stopped slamming through both of their bodies, he still couldn't let her go. His arms wouldn't unwrap from their tight clench about her ribs. Her legs, still ankle-locked behind him, kept pulling his hips even harder against hers—to be answered each time with a soft moan of delight.

He buried his face against her neck and breathed her in.

Heat, sweat, and a smell as rich and elusive as the Alabama forest at sunset.

Maybe he'd never let go.

Drake had simply "taken" women before. A fast, consensual screw and goodbye. Once there hadn't been so much as a kiss. He'd received a very surprising send-off as the Elvis Presley character going to war in the musical *Bye Bye Birdie*. During the final scene break on closing night, the innocent "Kim" had delivered exactly what the lusty "Birdie" had been wanting, and she'd managed to fit it in between the finale and the curtain call. Fast and furious on her bedroom set, which had been rolled deep into the backstage shadows—she'd never even had to lift her skirt when she knelt down over him as she wore nothing beneath. He always thought of her whenever he gave the line about liking actresses.

Now he couldn't let Nikita go. His heartrate finally settled. Her legs slipped from around his waist until she was supporting her own weight, and still he held on.

"That was…something," Nikita whispered it softly.

"Something," he agreed. "Though I'll be damned if I know what."

She wiggled a little. "You're still holding on to me."

He was. "I am." Not breast or butt, not dug into her hair, just wrapped around her and holding on.

Nikita wiggled again, "Aren't you going to—"

He kissed her to keep her quiet. Didn't she know that there were moments when a guy needed time to figure out what the hell had just happened? The blood reaching his brain was still minimal for survival.

"Drake," she pressed her hands to his cheeks. "You can let go of me now."

He could.

Except…he wasn't ready to.

"Nope. I'm not that stupid." He eased back a half step, ready to pull her deeper into the locker room—and collapsed into a wall. His shorts and underwear were still around his ankles.

Nikita was also totally disheveled. He'd gotten her pants down and off one leg by nearly ripping off one of her running shoes. One leg had a sock, the other still had shoe, sock, and her own shorts and underwear. Her t-shirt was shoved up enough to see that he'd freed one breast from her sports bra but not the other. She didn't appear to have noticed that yet.

He righted himself and pulled off the rest of her clothes over her ineffective and not terribly strenuous protests.

A naked Nikita was a breathtaking sight. Curves hinted at by her sportswear, suggested by her first outfit from the cruise ship's boutique, and so promised by last night's dress, were astonishing when unadorned.

"Shower," he explained, which stilled the last of her protests. He definitely had to get this woman into a shower with him.

Then he stepped out to drag her toward the nearest stall—and collapsed into the wall again. His own ankles were still snarled up in his shorts.

# CHAPTER 12

*N*ikita allowed herself to be coaxed beneath the steaming spray, partly because she didn't want to walk through the ship reeking of sweat and sex. But where she'd thought to get herself cleaned up, Drake had other ideas.

Sex with him had been just as rough and satisfying as she'd expected. Sex was meant to be enjoyable and it had been. Though with Drake it had also been much more. To have someone like him totally lose self-control over her as a woman was a revelation.

But a different man awaited her in the shower. He worked shampoo into her hair with a deep scalp massage. With soap and a washcloth, he made sure that not a square inch of her skin was untended, even the bottoms of her feet, which had turned out to be ticklish in a way she'd never been with anyone else. She didn't need any spa treatment when she had Drake Roman to take care of her. She braced her hands against the wall to keep herself upright as he worked over her body. It was so soothing that she was slow to pick up on what else he was doing until it was too late.

She was already halfway to gone before she noticed. He was so gentle that she couldn't find the energy to protest until he delivered another wave of release that stole her breath as it rippled through her body.

He washed himself off before she could recover enough to even think about returning the favor.

"Let's go. We don't want to be late for dinner. Or the art auction."

She leaned against the wall a minute longer before she could dredge up any interest in getting dressed. Men in her experience might give pleasure as long as they were receiving it as well, but for one to make an experience completely about her was unheard of. She was having trouble reconciling the man who had slammed her back against the wall and taken her with such delicious power with the one who had gently coaxed her body to a second release in many ways as overwhelming as the first.

Tender was not something she expected from Drake, nor any man in her experience. Poor Barry always had come to her bed like a soldier—hot and ready for action. He'd been kind and fun, but there was no question about who was having the sex and who was receiving it.

Drake was—

"The clothes fairy has left us a present," Drake announced. He held up a pair of clothes bags.

He was still splendidly naked and already recovering.

"If only we had time, lovely Nikita, but duty calls." His protests did nothing to stop his body's continuing reaction. Taking a deep breath and releasing it as a very complimentary groan of frustration, he pulled a towel off the rack and heaved it at her face. "At least cover up something before you kill me."

Nikita had never been shy. She'd been one of the only women around Curtis Contracting. Nobody messed with her because her dad was Curtis' Number Two, but shy didn't stand a chance. Living with a SEAL team of ultra-fit, ultra-raunchy males? Modesty didn't stand a chance either.

"Aww. Is poor Drake having trouble controlling himself around sexy women?" Not that she'd ever been called that—at least not by anyone who didn't land hard on his ass half a second later. She tossed the towel over her shoulder and let it drape down between her breasts, but not cover them.

Drake's eyes went darker and his expression was very intent.

She eased across the wooden slats of the shower area with the light tread of a sniper stalking its prey until barely a breath separated them.

She could see that Drake was nearly blind with need for her and his body confirmed the assessment.

Was she channeling Sugar somehow? Maybe she understood the woman, so competent in her craft but still sidelined for being female in a male world. So Sugar made a point of packing a physical punch that no man in his right mind could ignore.

And yet Drake had. Oh, he'd watched Sugar surely enough, but he'd watched Nikita far more—even without the tight leather.

Before she'd left, Sugar had said something to her that Nikita hadn't understood at the time. "That boy is just so gone."

When she'd asked gone on what, Sugar had just offered one of her merry laughs and followed J-dawg back to his monster SUV. Well, now Nikita knew. Drake wasn't merely gone on her, he was "so gone." She could feel the incredible rush that she could have Drake forget about everything in this instant if she wanted to. She'd never had such a sense of power over a male, especially not one like the "great" Drake Roman. It was a gloriously heady feeling right up there with sex.

But he'd said that they didn't have time. Pity.

He still held the two clothing bags in one hand. She unzipped the first one, spotted a dress, and plucked it from his fingers.

"Later, Roman."

When she turned to walk away, he grabbed her arm and pulled her back. For half a second she thought he'd take her right there and then. Instead, he dumped his own clothes bag at his feet and held on to her upper arms with both hands. He wasn't looking at her chest or hips. He was studying her eyes from just inches away.

"Say it like you mean it," his voice was so rough that she barely recognized it.

She tried shifting her arms, but his grip didn't ease. She was suddenly a little afraid. There wasn't a chance that he'd try to hurt her, besides, she could take him down a hundred different ways if he tried. But his intensity was so all-consuming. She could feel its shadow all around her. "Drake..."

"I'm serious!" He shook her lightly. "Say that there is a later, because I don't want whatever this is to just be about pounding one another up against some handy door or wall."

Nikita tried to see her own reflection in his dark eyes. He wouldn't allow any flippant answer. But she didn't know what else to give. Only once in her life had she promised there would be more and she'd lied. Instead she'd sent Barry out on a mission with too little information and he'd been captured, then tortured to death in the Congo—and not even for information, just for sport.

Yet for Drake—how was she supposed to make an acceptable answer for Drake Roman?

A part of her wanted to, needed to. A part of her didn't dare.

Fear. That was one thing that had been trained into a Special Operations fighter more than anything else: fear was to be recognized and addressed.

Whatever it was that she feared in this moment couldn't be allowed to stop her. Caution her? Yes. Stop her? Not without a damned good reason.

The gaping wound of her past said she had a good reason. That she should just turn and walk away.

But Drake's look wasn't only demanding, it was also pleading with her.

That she couldn't ignore.

She leaned in just enough to rest her lips on his, but not enough for their bodies to brush together. "There will be a later," she whispered against his soft kiss.

"Okay," he nodded slowly to himself and she could see the tension ease slowly back out of him. "Okay," he repeated it like he hadn't heard himself say it the first time.

He finally let her go and reached down for his clothes bag.

She began drying herself off.

Nikita just hoped that this time her promise didn't kill him.

DINNER PASSED IN A BLUR.

He'd barely a moment to appreciate Nikita in the dark blue sheath dress that draped around her and swept to the floor; though he planned to be thankful for those few seconds the rest of his life—she was stunning.

It must be one of the formal nights aboard. His good charcoal two-piece and freshly polished shoes had appeared from his own bag.

He held the door open to the men's shower as formally as he could for her to step out. Thankfully, only three people were waiting. He handed off the two bags, which now only bore their gym clothes, with a "Make sure these get to my suite after they're cleaned" to the first ship steward he passed.

Zoe wore a huge grin as she eyed Nikita—until the moment she spotted Nikita's hair. They'd done what they could with it and Drake didn't feel guilty for a second about what he'd done to it. With a characteristic "Oh my gawd!", Zoe grabbed Nikita's hand, then rushed her along the corridor to the beauty salon.

Altman stood in a simple black suit with a black turtleneck. His arms were crossed over his chest and he was glaring at Drake.

Drake figured his luck was holding when, before Altman could kill him, a steward arrived to guide him off to drinks before dinner.

Drinks aboard wasn't some grab-a-beer and chill for a few affair. It was a social hour that felt more like twelve.

He thought he had a good handle on the situation. Everything with Nikita was moving too fast and not fast enough, which he hoped meant they were in the middle ground and were progressing at exactly the right speed. He had no idea to where, but that described most missions in his life, so he was okay with that. Knowing he simply wanted more was enough for now.

His professional reputation was sufficiently menacing now that a small bubble of space had formed around him at the bar, even when Altman wasn't adding his looming presence.

The Russian mobster crossed the space to size him up and pass the time of day. An Italian prince—were there still princes in Italy? He didn't think so—well-gone on a brilliantly blue drink, barged through the invisible barrier to offer him a price well into six figures for Nikita. He'd have to remember to tell her that one. He also double-checked his wallet and wristwatch to make sure he still had them when the man departed.

He watched the odd dance, as badly arranged as an unchoreographed stage play, reflected by a mirrored wall placed to make the bar seem larger than it was. Everyone was backlit by the failing day. Without thinking, his theater training had him standing in the center of one of the few spotlights so that he stood out from the crowd all the more. Everyone here was merely a mirage except—

Then he'd forgotten everything.

He spotted Zoe first, very attractive in a green jewel-tone gown that revealed almost nothing on the top, but offered an eye-catching slit that showed a very nice leg and spiked matching sandals. He tried to see if Altman noticed, but it was hard to tell if he focused on her specifically or just as a new addition to the crowd. Maybe he had someone at home, but Nikita had said he once had, but she didn't think so anymore.

Then Drake spotted her. He'd been thinking about other things too intently in the men's shower to do more than glance at long, deep ocean blue gown. Now, as she stepped into the room, chatter dropped by half and he couldn't hear the other half because his ears were ringing.

The gown was a long sheath that gathered asymmetrically above her waist in a bow. The beaded top emphasized her figure and the semi-transparent mesh across her cleavage declared her exceptional form. It was sleeveless, allowing her powerful shoulders to humble all pretenders. And the salon had done a feather cut to her hair, tapering from front to back, exposing her face.

He didn't remember crossing to her until he was holding her hands and staring into her face.

"You know that it will never pull back in a ponytail again?"

"Shit! I didn't think of that when Zoe was pushing." Then she glanced around and almost blushed. "That wasn't exactly in character, was it?"

"No, but it was infinitely reassuring. I like knowing that you're still Nikita Hayward despite how amazing you look."

She studied his eyes for a long moment, then leaned in and kissed him lightly.

That's when the evening blurred on him. Such a simple gesture. His looks had afforded him a kiss whenever he wanted one. But one from Nikita in such a public setting, and he could suddenly see them as a couple.

Somewhere beyond this setting. Despite his family's heritage, they would never be in places like this again. He and Nikita would be out hiking, sailing, shooting, something active. And he could picture it like it was already true.

"Someone offered me a lot of money for you."

"Show me who and I'll kill the bastard." Again, the powerful woman emerging from the beautiful one.

"No. I don't want you so much as tearing a fingernail. You're worth over six figures to me already. And in that gown, I'll bet the price has gone up to seven."

"You mean out of this gown." With the harshness of her tone, he was almost tempted to point out the "Italian prince" to see what happened.

"That," he whispered in her ear, "is for nobody but me."

Again, that long, unreadable SEAL gaze.

He'd meant it as a joke.

Then she nodded her assent.

It was his last coherent thought.

She no longer clung to his arm, but instead held his hand, releasing it only at dinner so that they could eat.

## CHAPTER 13

*A*rthur slid up to them so smoothly as they arrived at the art auction that Nikita almost looked to see if he was on wheels. His smile widened as he inspected her from clasped hands to sheerly masked cleavage.

Drake's hands slowly tightened in hers until his grip was as powerful as the moment he'd dragged her into the men's shower, except this time it was shaking with raw fury. Maybe she could get used to having someone feel protective about her, even if she didn't actually need it.

She considered trying to push her chest out further just to see if Drake would test the strength of his fist against the man's jaw. Now probably wasn't the moment.

"We're so glad you could come. It is early in the cruise," Arthur alternated between talking to Drake's face and her chest, "therefore we will be auctioning only a few choice pieces tonight."

Three dozen paintings had been moved from the tiny shipboard gallery to the piano bar. A pair of easels and a podium had been set up at the far end of the room. Out the window, the Caribbean sunset was ending in rusty skies and black waters.

Nikita scanned the room for potential weapons and spotted very few. Tables were screwed to the floor. The bar was open, but clearly rigged for rough seas. Each liquor bottle was clamped into inverted brackets with press-to-pour spigots. The piano sported a massive chain from the base of the sound box down to a U-connector mounted to the floor. This place was fully prepped for stormy sailing.

Of course she could brain Arthur with the edge of her hand, if she dared strike out while wearing this dress. For fear that her chest would fall out of it and give Arthur a thrill, she didn't even dare to raise her arms in order to check out her strange new haircut that tickled her neck.

No one had ever looked at her the way Drake had at that first moment.

When Barry had "staked his claim" on her, he'd simply made it clear he'd shoot anyone who touched her.

Drake didn't boast or warn. Instead he looked at her as if she were the most captivating woman in history and he was the lucky one in this situation.

Which didn't mean he wouldn't pound the crap out of Arthur if she didn't do something soon.

"I know so little about art," she paused long enough for Arthur to have to look up at her face. "If I were to start collecting, what do you suggest I begin with?"

"Mr. Roman's predecessor was always partial to the work of Myora Folsum," he waved a thin-fingered hand toward a particularly awful nude.

Nikita supposed the work was well enough executed, but it was more a *Hustler* centerfold sort of image than even a *Playboy* one— there wasn't even a pretense of artful. It was just a woman's body. The artist hadn't even included her full face, letting it trail off the edge of the canvas so that she existed only from her lips down as if that was all that mattered.

"My predecessor's taste is not mine, I assure you." Drake's dangerous snarl warmed her heart.

Arthur didn't pitch a different painting, instead he looked suddenly worried. Was it loss of a commission or— She double-squeezed Drake's hand as a warning, as much as she could against his still powerful grip.

He glared over at her. The tiniest shake of his head said that he got the message but didn't give a damn.

She knew there was a reason she liked him.

"I think we will pass, Arthur," Nikita offered, not trusting Drake to speak. "Take me dancing, Drake. Won't you please?"

Drake didn't move, instead staring at the man until Arthur seemed to shrink before him.

"If you or the people you represent wish to proceed, know that I am a man of business—not on given to pandering prurient whims. Approach me directly or not at all. No messages or codes tucked into canvases—I couldn't care. My business succeeds just as well in one locale as another." He waved a hand at a small painting of an African family group in tribal dress that was only spared from being racist by the sympathetic eye of the artist.

Not giving Arthur time to answer, Drake turned aside and would have walked off without her if they hadn't been holding hands.

"When can I get back to my goddamn helicopter?" He snarled as soon as they were beyond earshot.

She let him steamroller along until they reached the very bow of the ship and stepped out onto the foredeck. He led her all the way to the rail. The sunset had left the evening cool, which was refreshing on her face, though she shivered at the unexpected contact with her shoulders. Strapless wasn't exactly her style.

Moments later Drake slipped his jacket over her bare shoulders like a cape. And while she didn't need the warmth, feeling his body heat wrap around her was such a pleasure she might never give it back.

The constellations Capricorn and Aquarius shown in the sky, higher than she was used to. Rather than flying straight overhead, Cygnus the swan was hidden behind the upper stories of the cruise ship as they headed south toward Belize, their next port of call.

"What's our next step?" She didn't trust herself to think more about Drake the man. It was far safer to focus on Drake the warrior.

"How the hell would I know?" He leaned on the railing and stared out over the bow so she couldn't see his face.

The open ocean always surprised her at how much it didn't smell like anything. Dead algae and seaweed gave beaches their fishy smell. Breaking waves churned salt into the air. Yet the four-foot rollers of the Gulf of Mexico added nothing to the air and only the slightest motion to the ship. This was no Navy ship—it ran with stabilizers that could flatten out the least roll for its passenger's comfort.

The last of the day's light had turned the sky blood orange. A land mass lay low to the south and east. It must be Cuba, the only major island for a long way south of Key West. They would pass it in the night on their way to Belize in Central America.

That left them two ports of call to solve the riddle or this whole trip would have been a waste. She leaned back against the railing close by Drake and looked up at the towering ship, outlined against the glowing sky. It rose four more decks above them, the control bridge a single sweep of glass like a dark eyebrow immediately above their own suite.

Looking at their suite's verandah, she could see Altman and Zoe standing side by side, outlined by the light behind them. Both looking down at her and Drake.

What did Altman see? What did he imagine had become of his prize pupil, the first female SEAL, as she lounged next to her lover in a thousand-dollar gown that she'd just as soon throw overboard?

"I don't know how to do this," she told the fading light.

"That makes two of us," Drake's whisper was a caress that she couldn't stand to turn and face.

"Are we talking about the mission?" Nikita kept her voice low as if Arthur or one of his cronies might hear.

"Or are we talking about us?" Drake's voice was hushed as if he was afraid the world would hear.

"I wasn't," she swallowed hard. "But I guess we are now."

"What happens when the mission is done?"

"Shit, Roman. We've never even shared a bed."

"We will tonight," his tone left no doubt. "Then what?"

Nikita spotted a flash of light on the uppermost deck, no brighter than a cigarette lighter.

A highly trained instinct about the color and shape of the flare had her slamming a fist into Drake's arm. She let half the momentum knock him sideways and used the other half to push herself away from him.

She felt a sharp slice of pain in her upper arm—and the distinctive hard *plonk!* of a bullet hitting the rail.

"Incoming!" She hissed at Drake. He'd been facing the wrong way to see it. "Observation Deck," she called out loudly, hoping that Altman was still at the suite's rail and would hear her.

She dove behind a large steel anchor capstan. Drake went down behind a bench, which was lousy protection, then glanced back at her. She pointed up toward where she'd seen the flash of light.

Another round came in. There was a loud *clang!* This time it hit on the back side of the capstan she was crouched behind. No sharp crack of a supersonic round. The small flash she'd spotted indicated a silenced weapon, which would act as a flash suppressor as well.

She was never going to leave her rifle in the suite again, not if she had to wear it under her dress at a fancy dinner.

Drake took advantage of the moment and rolled to a more secure spot close behind a large anchor resting on the deck.

Unless they could get beneath the overhang of the bridge, they were defenseless.

Five breaths, ten, she held her position.

She was considering a bolt for cover, but knew that patience was her friend and the shooter's enemy.

"Wait it out!" Drake hissed at her. "Do you see the shooter?"

"Just the flash."

If only—

A sharp whistle cut the night. It was high and far away, but it was easily heard.

Long-short-long-short. Pause. Repeat.

Altman. The letter C in Morse Code for All Clear.

He'd heard her and reached the Observation Deck in record time.

As a test, she snagged Roman's jacket from where it had fallen as she rolled to safety and held it out.

The letter C sounded again.

She peeked cautiously through a gap in the steel fixture that had saved her from the second shot.

The silhouette of a man stood right where she'd seen the flash of light.

Against the now red sky, he held his arm up in silhouette, fingers shaped like a pistol. Then he circled a hand over his head to rally up, then pointed straight down at the suite two decks below his position and two decks above theirs, indicating that they should meet there.

She raised a hand to pump a Hurry Up in acknowledgement, but only managed a sharp curse.

"Goddamn it!"

"What?" Drake whispered from where he still lay, not having understood or seen Altman's signals.

"I hate being shot."

⁂

"What do you mean she was shot?"

"That does seem to be the question of the evening," Drake said drily. He'd been the first to ask it. Then by the first steward he'd found and demanded to know the way to the infirmary. Then by the doctor and now by Norma the hotel manager as they each joined the growing crowd in the tiny two-bed infirmary on Deck 2, two levels below the normal passenger areas.

Down here the corridors were steel and windowless. A token bit of carpet stretched between the elevator and the infirmary, but the rest was gray-and-white painted steel. Luxury was for passengers, not crew. The doctor was out of his depth with a gunshot wound; he was more geared for seasickness and elderly patients suffering heart attacks.

Thankfully it was only a clean meat shot on the upper arm. The bullet hadn't made much of a hole going in or out, so a dab of glue, a wrap bandage, and an antibiotic were all that was called for and the doc was able to manage that—though he and Nikita had kept a close eye on him.

Altman came in.

"She okay?"

"I'm fine," Nikita growled from where the doctor was making her lie still, or trying to.

"She's just fine," Drake answered for her.

"Hey, I was *shot*," Nikita changed from dismissive to seeking sympathy with all of the agility of a Spec Ops warrior.

Drake ignored her, "What did you find?"

Altman held out a pair of brass casings. "Two rounds, .22LR. You said there was no supersonic crack, so they were fired from a hand-gun, not a rifle. I also followed your lead. I got only fragments from the capstan, but I dug this out of the wooden railing."

"You did what?" Norma the hotelier still wasn't up to speed.

He'd give her more time.

"You'll need to fix it; I had to dig a little," Altman held up a six-inch MK 3 knife.

"Those aren't allowed on board," Norma was still out of the loop, trying to make sense of what had just happened.

Altman's smile said that he was sick of the cruising life and was having fun keeping her off balance.

Drake ignored them both, plucking the round and casings out of Altman's palm and turning to show them to Nikita. Beautiful woman, lovely gown, lying back just as he'd hoped—except on a hospital gurney, not a luxury bed. Somebody was a dead man and he was going to start with Arthur.

They inspected the hardware together.

The bullet was heavily deformed by the impact with the wood, but was definitely a .22 round. No way to get rifling marks, not that it would tell them much without a lab and the weapon. The shooter had gone, or blended back into the crowd by the time Altman showed up.

Short of frisking every passenger in the Observation Lounge, he hadn't had a whole range of options.

"I think that's a bit of blood caught in the furling," Nikita pointed.

"Who the hell besides us has weapons on this boat?" Drake spun back to Norma as the rage shot back to life inside him.

"You have weapons on the boat? Those are forbidden. You can't…" she trailed off and swallowed hard. She was the one who had let them board directly from their helicopter—exactly as she'd probably always let GSI board. The pieces were starting to connect together for her.

"Who else besides us?" Drake repeated, resisting the urge to shake the answer out of her.

But Norma was shaking her head in a dazed fashion. "No one else bypassed security. The Captain's safe should have the only weapons on board."

"Does he have silenced .22s?"

"Silenced? Like with…" she made a helpless gesture in the form that might have been an extended gun barrel.

"Like this," Altman pulled out a six-inch silencer from his shoulder holster, holding the lapel aside just long enough for her to get an eyeful of his Glock 19 with laser sight.

"No," Norma managed in a strangled tone. "No, the captain doesn't."

Altman grunted. For the first time on the voyage he was smiling. "Somebody is being bad besides us. Lousy damn shot, though, to miss you both from no more than fifty meters." He tucked the silencer away.

"Didn't miss completely," Drake returned the bullet and casings to Altman. "And someone is going to go to hell for that one."

Zoe came in. "You okay, Nikki?"

"I'm fine, if the doctor would just stop hovering."

"Doctor," Zoe rested her hand on his arm. "We're done with you now, thank you so much."

"But she—" then he winced.

Drake hadn't seen Zoe tighten her fingers about his arm, but they were right over a nerve cluster that was going to leave his hand numb for hours if she didn't back off quickly.

"And you're not going to say a word to anyone about this without our permission, right?"

His knees buckled slightly for a moment, then she let go and patted his arm in a friendly fashion.

"Uh," he stumbled backward into a cabinet that rattled with equipment but freed him from the clench of the harmless-looking blonde in the green evening gown. "If you need me—" He didn't complete the sentence as he raced out of the tiny infirmary.

"She okay?" This time Zoe was asking about the hotel manager.

"Yes," Drake decided that Norma was either the best actress in the world or was actually in shock that such a thing could happen on her cruise ship.

Altman apparently agreed as he closed the door, with the four of them and Norma still crowded into the small space.

Nikita swung to a sitting position and went to stand, but Zoe pushed her back to stay seated on the bed. Then, to forestall argument, Zoe hopped up to sit beside her, her feet swinging in the air. It was just as well; if they all five were standing they'd have to all be hugging to fit.

"Norma," Drake had to repeat her name before she focused on him. "We're US Special Operations Forces here undercover. No one can know, not even your captain. You certainly shouldn't, but we can't have you throwing us off the ship either."

"But someone shot…" she waved a hand at Nikita. "And you have a gun…" the other hand waved helplessly toward Altman.

Drake would bet that LCDR Luke Altman was armed with a lot more than one. It wouldn't surprise him if Zoe was as well, though he couldn't see where she'd hide it in that clingy gown.

"You're going to have to treat us just the way you did the members of GSI. Courtesy and caution. Can you do that?"

He could see the experienced hotelier in Norma slowly pulling herself together. Her spine straightened. She tugged at the hem of her immaculate jacket. A quick hand checked her short blond hair. Then, with a blink of her blue eyes, she was present.

"But who shot you?"

"It wasn't Arthur," Zoe chimed in. "He's still at his auction. I asked around and he hasn't left the podium since you were there."

"Arthur?" Norma looked close to losing her poise again, but she held on.

"Yes. You'll want to line up a new art handler. We'll leave him in place for now, but if they were desperate enough to move against us, I don't expect that he'll be with your cruise line much longer."

"You can't be right about Arthur," it almost sounded as if she was begging.

"Next time they'll need a better shooter," Altman bounced the bullet and casings against his palm before tucking them away.

"Or maybe they already have one," Nikita was squinting into the distance, looking at something far outside the room. "Steady seas. Deck lights were low but bright enough. Two misses…"

"Two misses?" Drake tried not to explode. Tried not to let loose the terror that his suit was going to end up with another splatter pattern on its back, but not with Carl's blood this time. "You were shot!"

Altman hissed at him to keep his voice down.

"I think…" she tipped her head sideways, then nodded once and looked directly at him. "It was an accident."

"People don't get accidentally shot on cruise ships."

"I think I was," she held up a hand to stop him before he could fume more. "I saw the muzzle flash. I knew I only had a split second and I punched you to drive us apart and out of the way."

Drake ran a hand over his upper arm; it hurt like hell when he pressed on it. "Good punch." He hadn't noticed it until this moment.

"Thanks. But we were standing far enough apart for me to be able to punch you. I think I put my arm in the way of the bullet. What if they were aiming *between* us?"

"The second shot was dead center on the capstan," Altman confirmed. "As if the shooter wanted to be sure they missed."

"Scare tactics," Nikita confirmed.

Drake managed a smile for her sake. "Damn good thing they don't know what kind of a woman they're trying to scare."

Nikita's smile was far more genuine than his, "Damn good thing."

He brushed a finger down her cheek, "Remind me never to get on your wrong side, Nikita Hayward."

"Deal, Drake Roman," she leaned into his caress.

## CHAPTER 14

Nikita could never get tired of Drake's caresses. If only there'd been a chance to last night.

Along with the precautionary antibiotic and the local anesthetic—that the doctor had needed more than she did to dress her wound—he'd apparently given her a shot with enough painkiller to level a horse. She'd been staggering by the time they reached the suite, with Drake's jacket once more draped over her shoulders to hide the bandage.

This time she was still conscious enough to remove her own dress. Though she'd need Zoe's help to put on the t-shirt, because she couldn't feel her own arm.

No powerful arms lifted her into the bed, but that didn't matter. By the time she hit the pillow, she was out.

"C'mon, sleepyhead," someone was tugging on her foot. "You don't want to miss every port of call."

She managed to open her eyes.

Drake was smiling down at her.

"How is it that you always look so good and I feel like shit?" He looked far better than good back in his black t-shirt and tan chinos.

"Good living and I stay off the drugs."

Her head was still muzzy with whatever the doctor had pumped into her last night. She tested the arm. Sore as hell, but not anything worth writing home about.

Drake was busy throwing open curtains. She didn't even know if he or Zoe had slept beside her last night.

"Come to bed and maybe we'll discuss the good living part of that."

He circled close and once more brushed a finger across her cheek. His easy smile disappeared and his expression became deeply intent and serious. "If the next boat ashore wasn't in fifteen minutes, I'd take you up on that."

"Let's miss a boat."

"Zoe found out through Norma that Arthur signed up for permission to go ashore. He'll be on that boat as well and I'd like to have a chat with him." He dropped into a chair to wait for her.

She'd like a few words with him as well. Nikita rolled out of bed and onto her feet. She had to close her eyes for a moment as the world wavered sharply, but then it steadied. Stripping off her shirt, she headed for the walk-in closet. Disgusted that she was still probably "the babe" of the outfit, she went for the light cotton blouse whose price had so shocked her when she first entered the boutique, and capris in a dark lavender. Two minutes flat she was back in the bedroom with her hair and teeth brushed. And—damn Drake for being right—all her efforts at a ponytail were completely foiled.

Drake was sitting in the armchair with his feet propped on the bed.

He was shaking his head, but his eyes didn't move from looking at her.

"Damn, woman. I could really get used to being around you."

*Right.* He'd been in the room when she'd stripped on her way to the closet.

She kicked his leg hard enough to hurt, "Thought you were in a hurry."

"You're enough to make a man think very slow thoughts." But he clambered to his feet. "Metal detectors at the ramp. No weapons bigger than a four-inch knife allowed."

"Shit!" She untucked her shirt and pulled the nice little Glock 36 Subcompact Slimline out of the small of her back and returned to the closet to lock it in her rifle case.

"Extra rounds?"

She pulled the two clips out of her back pocket and tossed them in as well.

"My kinda gal," he took her hand and led her out into the suite.

"That didn't take the two of you nearly long enough," Zoe protested from the chair she'd been slouched in.

"Don't you ever think about anything other than sex?"

"Hunter-killer drones. But other than that? Why bother."

Altman was already by the door.

---

ARTHUR DIDN'T LOOK happy when Drake led his entourage as the last ones on the open taxi boat, but he was too buried in the crowd to make an excuse and rush for the exit.

Belize City harbor was too shallow for the big cruise ships. Even their mid-sized model couldn't make it in. But the city had a jitney service of hundred-passenger open boats that had rushed out to unload the cruise ship and take them the twenty minutes to shore. For twenty minutes, Arthur wasn't going anywhere, so Drake sat in his seat and ignored him.

A very curved lady with skin the color of warm chocolate and hair curling well past her shoulders stood up front. In charming British English she told the passengers about the wonderful opportunities to be found in Belize. There were apparently still open slots in diving, caving, river rafting, and Mayan temple jungle tours. He let her liquid accent lull him into a comfortable semi-trance state as they powered toward shore.

Nikita curled up against him and appeared to be just as content as he was to take in the sunshine, the sea air, and the twenty minutes of peace.

"We are now arriving in the Tourist Village. There are many shops and restaurants to explore here if you are not traveling farther afield on one of our tours. We do wish to caution you to be careful beyond the boundaries of this area. There are clear signs posted. There are parts of Belize City that I regret to say are not very safe and you certainly don't want to be caught there after dark."

After weaving through various anchored boats—mostly luxury yachts in the eighty- to hundred-and-fifty-foot range—the jitney nudged up to a dock and unloaded from the same ramp. They'd been last on, so they were first off.

A glance to Altman, and he and Zoe hung back. Drake led Nikita slowly up the dock and toward town. So slowly that Arthur would have no choice but to catch up with them as the crowd cleared. Zoe and Altman would make sure that he was herded along.

They were three quarters of the way down the nearly empty pier when they all came together. Zoe's idle chatter warned him that the gap between them was now under a dozen meters. He turned aside.

The big industrial piers with their cargo containers were in another section of the city, away to the south. This was a tourist transit pier, colorfully decorated with a scattering of old maritime equipment tucked here and there under the well-spaced palm trees that he supposed would be considered a festive air.

Arthur had to know he was in a pincer, so he followed them until all five of them were in a tall palm's shade.

"It would have been easier if you had bought the painting," Arthur sighed. "I had to go to rather a lot of difficulty to avoid selling it last night."

"So you had us shot at to make up for it?"

"Shot at?" that surprised him enough that he tipped his head down to look at Drake over the top of his sunglasses. "Who shot at you?"

Altman's curse was emphatic.

"*You* are supposed to be the one telling *us*," Drake couldn't believe this was happening. He'd had it all figured out in his head; or part of it anyway. He hadn't behaved the way GSI historically had, so Arthur's people were applying pressure to make them behave. A decidedly weak scenario, but that was all he'd been expecting from these people.

Paintings of nudes and patently obvious art dealers struck him as awfully lame fieldcraft.

"Okay," maybe Nikita had some ideas. "If you didn't shoot me—"

"You were actually shot?" Arthur's astonishment didn't look faked, but Nikita ignored him.

"Who else do you have aboard for this operation?"

"No one," Arthur started looking around as if someone other than Drake was about to shoot him. "There isn't an operation. What kind of an operation? Did you need one for being shot?"

Drake grabbed him by the lapels of his summer jacket and forced him to focus. "Who the fuck tried to kill Nikita?" He agreed with her that it had been an accident that she was shot, but she could have just as easily leaned in to kiss him, or he her, and taken a bullet to the head.

"I swear to god I don't know," the man's voice actually squeaked.

"Shit!" Drake cast him aside hard enough that he'd have crashed to the ground if Altman hadn't jammed a hand against this back.

Either he was just as clueless as he appeared, or he was in deep. Head of an operation could perhaps pull it off, but that was too movie-villain evil to be credible. He'd vote for sniveling weasel in over his head—but watch out for scheming bastard.

If it was the former…

He grabbed Arthur's lapel and yanked him in again until their noses were just an inch apart.

"You want to get out of this in one piece, you find out who else is on that boat. And you don't tell them, you tell me or her," he nodded toward Nikita. "On second thought, don't go near her. She'd be far more likely to throw your sorry ass overboard than I am."

This time when he shoved Arthur away, Altman simply stepped to the side and let him stumble to catch his balance before racing off.

"Any bets?" Drake asked the others.

"Twenty says that he's just as useless as he looks," Nikita pulled out a bill to make her point.

Altman eyed her, "I'm still on the fence about him."

"Personally, I thought he was going to pee himself," Zoe sounded delighted. "This is so much more entertaining than sitting at a drone's ground-control station. You," she poked a finger against Altman's chest, "definitely have to show me more, Luke. Much more."

Altman looked down at her finger as if it was a dangerous weapon to be treated with great caution.

The four of them were the last ones off the pier other than a pair of ship's crew who were standing beneath a small white awning in full uniform just in case someone had a question three hours from now.

At the head of the pier, Drake spotted a familiar face—a pair of them.

"You've got to be shitting me."

---

NIKITA STARTLED. She'd never heard Drake swear, except about her being shot.

There, just outside of security, in front of a row of glitzy tourist shops thick with bad ugly t-shirts and tiny collectors' plates with pictures of a palm tree, stood Jared Westin and Sugar.

Drake blew past the pier's security guards. In a dozen steps he had grabbed J-dawg with a pincer grip around his windpipe and pinned his back against a palm tree even though the guy was a couple inches taller and several times broader than he was.

"Do you have a shooter on the boat?" Drake was practically spitting in his face.

"What are you talking about?"

"Do you have a goddamn team on board our boat?"

J-dawg narrowed his eyes and looked down at Drake, not appearing to even notice the death grip on his throat. "Did you say a shooter?"

"Just answer the goddamn question!" Wherever the mild-mannered Drake Roman had gone, he was awfully far away.

Nikita noted that the rest of the team had circled up, masking the action as much as possible. The waterfront was mostly quiet; the initial blast of cruise passengers had moved farther into the city until the next launch arrived. The only local paying them any mind was a little girl in an *I Heart Belize* t-shirt and eating a chocolate ice cream cone. She was watching with avid interest.

"No," J-dawg sounded like he was talking to an idiot schoolboy. "I do not have a team on your boat. Now answer my goddamn question. Did you say shooter?"

In answer, Drake released his hold on J-dawg's throat. He shot out a hand so fast that it surprised even her instincts. He grabbed her good arm and pulled her to him. Then he slid up the sleeve on the other one and showed him her bandage. There hadn't been time to change it, so there were some spots of blood seepage from last night.

J-dawg's eyes went as dark as Drake's had last night.

"Somebody did that to Sugar, I'd annihilate the bastard." His voice went just as rough and scary, too.

The two men shared their agreement with very mano-a-mano looks.

"What is it with over-protective men?" Nikita had to yank a bit to recover her arm from Drake's grasp.

"Aren't they just the sweetest little things when they do that?" Sugar was smiling up at her husband.

Nikita wasn't sure about sweet. She was getting sick and tired of being "the babe" of this whole operation.

"When I find him," Drake wasn't over it yet, "annihilation is the least of what I'm going to do."

"I'll hold him down for you," J-dawg muttered and pulled Sugar close. "Any guesses?"

Drake just shook his head. "It must be someone who really doesn't want GSI returning to Honduras, but that's all we've been able to come up with. Up half the night sketching out scenarios, didn't find squat that made sense. Shooter is aboard. Silenced .22. That's all we know."

Nikita looked at her three teammates and saw the dark circles of their sleepless night. And she'd been asleep, well drugged, but she didn't like feeling useless.

The kid who'd been watching them all so intently while she ate her ice cream leaned against Sugar's other side and earned a hand around her shoulders. She'd watched Drake attack J-dawg as if such things happened every day.

"Yes, Swimmer Girl, she's mine." Sugar noticed the direction of Nikita's attention. "Asal saved my life on an Afghan hillside and I jes' figured that returning the favor was about the only thing I could do."

"She fought like a demon for the kid," J-dawg said with obvious pride. He turned back to Drake. "You've got a good grip. Glad you didn't use it." There were still five red fingerprints on his neck but he hadn't even flinched. How strong *was* this guy?

It was time she took control of the situation.

"If you don't have a team on the boat, *J-dawg,*" Nikita dragged it out, "what the hell are you doing here?"

Asal answered for him in a high, girl voice and acceptable English, "Checking up on his invesrent."

"His investment?"

The girl nodded and then began practicing the word to herself.

"What investment?"

J-dawg shrugged, "When we took over GSI, we took over all of their bank accounts, too. I get all the bills for everything charged to them, including this trip." Then he looked her up and down, once, assessment with no trace of a leer. "Hope the rest of what you bought looks this good on you. It better, it was a hell of a bill."

"Good!" She still didn't want to like the guy.

"You've got taste. Keep it all."

"*I've* got the taste," Zoe piped up. "She's hopeless. Black t-shirt and camo pants are her idea of a Sunday formal."

"With a McMillan Tac-50 over my shoulder. I always wear a good rifle with my Sunday best."

J-dawg roared with laughter at her joke. "Now that *is* my kinda woman. You pay attention, Asal," he reached over to scrub the kid's hair. "You wanta grow up to be just like Lily or this lady here."

Asal studied her for a long moment, then nodded as if she'd seen something in Nikita.

"Are you deluded enough to think that the clothes would be a bribe, J-dawg?" Zoe asked. "What are you expecting in return?"

Nikita appreciated that Zoe was reminding her of just who they were dealing with.

"A gift, Pint-size. Just a gift."

"So, what are you doing here? A family vacation snorkeling on the reef?" Zoe waved a hand at the waterfront. It had a case of the late-morning sleepies, not even a cat was stirring. The only boat on the move was a water taxi scuttling across the wide mouth of Haulover Creek—the river that cut the city in half.

"Not so much."

Nikita felt slightly nauseous and didn't think it was the last of the drugs seeping out of her system. "You've got assets on the ground in Honduras? A bunch of trigger-happy goons that we're going to stumble on where we least want to?"

J-dawg finally stood up from where he'd been slouching against the palm tree Drake had slammed him into. "Colonel Be-damned McDermott said I'd never get another government contract as long as I lived if I put someone on the ground there."

"So where are they?"

Nikita saw his eyes flicker aside for a second at her question. They all turned to look while J-dawg cursed at being caught out. A couple hundred meters off the harbor wall, among the anchored motor yachts, was a long, dangerous looking one. Black, sleek, and at least a hundred feet long—it looked as dangerous as its owner.

"Real subtle, J-dawg. Real subtle."

J-dawg had led them to a place called Baymen's Tavern. It was actually an outdoor restaurant at the Radisson Hotel with a sweeping view from the north side of the peninsula that formed Belize City. They sat beneath the shade of a massive umbrella. The tall palms around the edge of the patio rustled lightly in the sea breeze. The waitresses were efficient and a pleasure to look at. All very high-end.

"This place is upright, respectable—"

"Family friendly," J-dawg cut him off.

Drake could only laugh.

"Come down here with just the team, I can show you where to get real food, but it's deep in a bad quarter. Food is worth it though."

Drake would bet on more than just the food by his expression, though with the way he acted about Sugar, it was probably for memories past, not futures planned. He didn't like what Titan did, but he understood Jared's need to protect, even if Nikita didn't. It wasn't a conscious, thought out, or innately macho plan. It was simply a fact of life—nobody was getting to her without going through him first. He could see that whatever else was going on, he and Jared were in a hundred percent agreement on that point.

"Family changes a man in surprising ways," J-dawg looked at Sugar and Asal who were discussing the meal. He said it with the contentment of a man well pleased with the way his life was going.

Asal was working her way through an appetizer of chicken tenders like she'd never stop.

"Kid hasn't slowed down eating since we pulled her off that mountain six months ago. Stays thin as a rail, just keeps getting taller. Most of the way to starved when we found her, probably set her metabolism for life."

Asal had ended up between Sugar and Zoe. Drake had made sure Nikita sat between him and Altman. J-dawg was across the table with a lazy arm on the back of Sugar's chair. Without even noticing, Drake had mirrored J-dawg's position with an arm behind Nikita. It was surprising that Nikita hadn't chopped it off and fed it to a piranha or whatever Belize had. Maybe he'd leave it there and see how long before she noticed. The open spot at the end of the table was in glaring sunlight and not even the mad-for-sun Zoe had taken it.

"So, Jared."

"Finally gonna use my damned name. About time someone in your outfit did."

"What *are* you doing here?" Drake had opted for ice tea instead of Belikin Beer, much to Jared's disgust.

"Already told you that."

"I don't buy *checking on your invesrent.* Try again."

"My mess to clean up."

"Not according to Colonel McDermott," even Nikita's tone seemed to be easing around Jared. She only sounded disgusted rather than her usual murderous.

"Still mine. I should have taken them down years ago. Would have saved a lot of people a lot of pain. You want someone who should have been shot by his own men in the field, head of GSI was the poster boy."

"How can you—" Nikita flopped back, clearly angry again, and knocked Drake's arm off the back of the chair without even noticing.

Jared leaned in hard and fast enough that Drake leaned forward ready to block any attack on Nikita. "Because a lot more of my unit would have come back alive it wasn't for him."

Nikita jumped to her feet. Her face wasn't red with anger, instead it was the palest white, as if all the life and blood had been drained out of her.

When Drake tried to rise, she placed a hand on his shoulder, keeping him in his chair. Then she simply turned and walked away.

"J-dawg," Sugar said sharply as she rose. "You did not just say that to her of all people." She sounded pissed as hell, as primal a force as Jared. For the first time Drake could see that, despite how she might look, she was actually a good match for him.

Also, she obviously knew exactly what trigger Jared had just hammered his fist down on.

"Zoe, would you mind staying with Asal?" Sugar didn't wait for an answer.

When the two of them were gone, Jared looked across the table at him.

"What the hell did I say?"

Drake tried to figure out how to say it without punching Jared a good one, but Altman saved them both by speaking up first.

"Did you hear about the mess that took down Curtis Contracting?"

"Sure, cheap bastard strung his own men out to dry. Wouldn't authorize the fee for the intel some chick had a lead on. Chas Hayward and Barry... Wait. Didn't Nikita say her last name was Hayward?"

"Chas was her dad. The other guy was her fiancé. She was the 'chick' stuck holding the bag." Altman's voice was grim.

"And I just said... Aw, shit."

---

"Whoa, Swimmer Girl. Just whoa some."

Nikita didn't want to *whoa*. She wanted to break her fist in some man's face. She wanted to take down Marcus Curtis so hard that he'd never do more than crawl again.

She hadn't even had the satisfaction of taking him down herself. He'd gotten drunk that night and decided to prove how tough he was. Apparently not as tough as the switchblade that slit his throat after he beat a whore halfway to death. That had been the end of Curtis Contracting as well.

Sugar finally rested a hand on her arm, "My legs aren't as long as yours. At least slow down enough that I don't have to run in this heat."

"You're the one who wears leather all the time." But Nikita slowed her stride. Finally grinding to a halt somewhere a lot less nice than the Baymen. But the sign said "Tavern", so she turned in.

It wasn't like a 'Bama bar, all battered pickups and neon beer signs out front. Inside also wasn't all battered tables and country boys nursing long-neck Budweisers.

The only thing lined up out front were poor people. The only thing inside were people with enough money to buy a beer and maybe a bowl of chicken escabeche soup. Shorts, short-sleeve shirts, and flip-flops were the dress code. She and Sugar must look like aliens from another planet.

The walls had once been white and the floor was still concrete. But the beer bottle handed across when she asked was just as beaded with sweat as the one in the peeling poster of a bikini-clad babe holding it between her breasts.

She dropped into a wooden chair at a table that rocked a good ten degrees when she set her bottle on it.

Sugar sat down across from her.

"Why *do* you wear leather?"

"You already know that."

Nikita nodded. She did.

Sugar answered anyway. "Thought I was defining self-worth with the way I could draw those boys. Showing them I was just as tough as they were never seemed to make any difference. They just saw these," she cupped her breasts, "so I gave them that. No one saw more, not until Jared. He taught me there was more to me than I knew."

"But still you wear leather."

"Jared *is* male. He likes it plenty, he just sees the woman behind the leather as well. Asides, it's a part of who I am now. Not gonna be leaving that behind just because I fell in love with the man."

Nikita sipped the cold beer, which soothed her parched throat.

"Just like you being all in love with Sweet Cheeks doesn't change who you are. It makes you better."

"It makes me get shot and doubt my sanity."

Sugar smiled, "Yes on both accounts. Though I got shot when I was still in the ATF, back before Jared."

"You were a field agent for Alcohol, Tobacco, and Firearms?"

"A few of my low connections in high places. At least I was until Jared blew my cover trying to save one of his crew's life. Still not sure if I've forgiven him for that. Now I'm mostly just a guncrafter."

"You're Lily Chase?" There couldn't be that many top gunsmiths named Lily.

"Was. Took Jared's name, mostly because we adopted Asal."

Nikita wondered if you could ever really know anyone. One of the best gunsmiths working was a busty babe in the modern version of designer buckskin.

Sugar handed her another beer while Nikita looked at Miss Belikin Beer Bikini Girl in the poster again. She could have been the twin of the jitney boat tour guide. Maybe she was the same woman. Or maybe she was a banker making extra cash on the side.

Drake was like two different people. Or maybe more. The womanizer gunner. The angry man who wouldn't let anyone help him clean up his fellow crew chief's blood. The glorious male who had pounded into her against the shower wall yet whispered so gently that it was okay to not remember while he carried her in his arms.

"Can you ever really know someone?"

"Where would be the fun in that?"

She didn't know. But she wished she couldn't remember.

---

"YOU SURE you don't know what's going on down there in Honduras? We land tomorrow—next port of call is Roatán. Anything would help." Drake wasn't sure when he'd switched from ice tea to beer. Altman had as well. Zoe and Asal had gone off to the hotel pool, leaving the three of them at the table with their beers.

"Why didn't you just buy the damned picture?"

"It was tasteless, crass…"

"So was the bastard who ran GSI. It was a goddamn lead. Get the painting."

"Why? You like nudes?"

"Yes, as long as her name is Lily Westin. You?"

Drake had to admit there was a nude he was very partial to himself. "But that stupid painting—I don't like playing games."

Jared crashed a fist down on the table. "Dammit! Listen, GI Joe. This whole goddamn thing is a game. You think that half the shit I did while I was on the inside made any sense? You think even that much makes sense on the outside? Do you have any idea how much they pay me for what I do? It sure shouldn't be so much more than you make. What kind of sense is in that?"

It was one of the reasons that the people who served didn't like the mercs, but only one of them. Few were like Jared and Titan. A lot more were like GSI and Curtis.

"How does it make sense that you guys are cleaning up GSI's mess and not me?" Jared growled at his beer bottle as he worked at peeling off the label with a thumbnail.

"Are you still harping on that?"

Jared shrugged but didn't look up.

"When Titan can launch people like SEAL Team 6 and the Night Stalkers 5E, you let me know."

"Okay. Point taken. Can you at least explain to me why I never even heard about the 5E until I drove onto Fort Rucker a couple days ago?"

"Because," Drake could see Altman eyeing him, but Drake wasn't drunk. Well, not drunk enough to reveal state secrets. "Because like Nikita said, when we go through a door, no one knows we've been there."

"WHAT ARE you fighting so hard against, Swimmer Girl?"

"Don't want to repeat the past." Nikita considered another beer even though she hadn't finished her current bottle. She considered getting blind drunk and missing the boat's midnight departure.

"Doesn't work that way," Sugar pushed aside the empty plate of Belize Rice and Beans. That again changed the balance of their wobbly table and Sugar had to grab to rescue her beer.

"Sure it does." For a crappy bar in a bad quarter, they served an amazing version of the traditional dish. It was rich from the coconut milk used instead of water. The heavy spices and the thick gravy from the stewed gibnut meat—whatever kind of local animal that was, Nikita didn't want to know—soaked up some of the beer in her belly, but not too much.

"How is your past going to repeat?"

Almost everything. Maybe she could just stay in the present because the past and future were whacked-out worse than a plugged cesspool. She leaned back to stare up at the fan whispering overhead. It was close to sunset and the few bare bulbs above the bar did little to light the space. In this semi-twilight moment, it almost looked merely disreputable.

As she looked back down to answer Sugar's question, a big man sat at their table and a hand clamped around Sugar's wrist.

And it wasn't J-dawg.

"*Y*ou two will come with me," his English was as thick as a swamp with Spanish.

"Fuck off!" Nikita had been about to say something important, but now couldn't remember what it was. "Private conversation."

With his hand that wasn't pinning Sugar's wrist, he did one of those flashy gang moves to flick out a switchblade instead of just opening it.

Nikita glanced at Sugar, who just grimaced. *Amateur!*

The way Sugar's eyes flickered up behind Nikita told her that she was wrong.

*Amateurs!* More than one.

Sugar jerked her arm toward her chest, dragging the man closer by his grasp on her wrist. Under the table, she planted one of her spike-heeled boots between his legs and hard into his crotch.

His scream hurt Nikita's ears.

She felt hands come to rest on her shoulders from behind. With a hard shove off the floor, using all the leverage her SEAL-strong legs could give her, she flipped her chair over backward.

Her attacker stumbled away, knocked aside by the back of the chair.

When her back hit the floor, Nikita used her momentum to continue into a backward somersault. Halfway through she lashed out with her feet and caught the guy's kneecap. There was a satisfying crunch up through the leather of her sandal as his knee broke and doubled over in the wrong direction.

Her continued roll knocked him onto his back with his leg doubled up under him. She rammed a punch into his sternum. Her aim was off but she was in a hurry. Instead of just knocking the wind out of him, she might have broken a couple of ribs as well.

A third attacker had Sugar by the hair, dragging her head back hard.

Somehow, Nikita still had her beer bottle in her other hand. She heaved it into the guy's face hard enough to startle him into easing his grip on Sugar, maybe breaking his nose as a bonus.

It was all Sugar needed.

With a sweep kick, Sugar knocked his legs out from under him. As he fell forward, Sugar managed to get her hands behind the guy's head.

Nikita kicked the table closer and Sugar rammed him down, chin-first onto it. By the look of the blood coming out of his mouth when Sugar let him fall to the floor, he was going to need a new jaw and some teeth to go with it.

They surveyed the scene.

The first attacker was still on the floor holding his crotch with one hand, but groping for his knife with the other.

Rather than kicking his knife aside, Sugar planted the pointed toe of her boot into his temple with a hard enough kick that he stopped having interest in anything other than bleeding. His cellphone lay close beside him and Sugar put a spiked heel through its heart with a satisfying crunch of glass and metal.

It had happened so fast that the other patrons hadn't had a chance to do anything other than draw back and look aghast.

They looked at each other, then down at the table still standing between them.

Sugar laughed. "Table is stronger than it looks."

Nikita nodded.

"The past isn't," Sugar's suddenly fierce, dark-blue eyes were studying Nikita.

Maybe.

---

"WHY DON'T I like that sound?" Jared had Asal riding on his shoulders.

Drake didn't like it either.

The women had been gone for hours, long enough that it had become an itch, so they'd all gone looking for them—Altman and Zoe starting to the north, Drake and Jared with Asal working from the south. The problem was that the trail had gone cold and there were five hundred cruise passengers reconvening on Belize City from their adventures, all in time for a pre-sailing dinner. Asking shopkeepers if they'd recently seen two pretty women in nice clothes didn't work.

They'd rapidly worked their way out of the Tourist Village and into the rougher section of Belize City.

There were a lot of sounds that were strange in this city, but the whoop of a police siren was a very distinctive one.

Drake spotted it racing by two blocks over, closely followed by a wailing ambulance.

"Really don't like that sound." They broke into a jog, Asal clamping both hands around Jared's forehead like a stoic captain weathering the tossing seas.

Around the corner and two more blocks up were a trio of flashing cop cars and a second ambulance.

Altman and Zoe came out of a side street and joined them as they reached the police perimeter.

"There," Asal pointed from her perch atop Jared's shoulders.

They forged forward as a unit, brushing aside the few policemen foolish enough to get in their way.

In the midst of it all, Sugar and Nikita were standing at ease, as if merely watching a parade go by. It might have worked as a ploy if not for the three cops hovering close beside them with their notepads out. They'd been at the center of whatever was going on.

Drake barged through, knocking a protesting sergeant and his notebook to the side.

"You okay, honey?"

"Honey?" Nikita looked at him in surprise. "When did I give you honey privileges?"

"Your apartment in Alabama? In a men's shower maybe?" Drake was just glad to have found her. He'd missed her through the long slow afternoon—actually missed her. That was a strangeness he hadn't noticed until this moment when he suddenly felt so happy to be standing next to her again.

"Maybe," Nikita sounded as if she was in a much better mood than she'd been in days.

That's when the gurneys started rolling out of the hole-in-the-wall tavern. Three big guys, looking awfully battered.

Drake glanced at Nikita and Sugar. Neither of them looked the least bit hurt, though they were making a point of straightening their clothes and finger-brushing back their hair.

When he met Jared's gaze, the man's smile was electric. *Don't you just love these women?*

He did. Drake slipped a hand around Nikita's waist and she let herself be pulled against him. He truly did.

---

ONCE THE POLICE let them go, they strolled together back toward the ship's pier. Just three couples and a kid talking softly among themselves.

Other couples and groups were wending their way through the warm evening back to the ship, none close enough to hear quite how bizarre the conversation of their group might be.

Nikita had always liked that feeling of being special, being elite. It was her dad's doing. Chas Hayward had taught her young about the high of being better than everyone around her. Better at martial arts, better at shooting, better at noticing details that no one else did. Curtis Contracting had fed that too, at least until it all came apart. Being a Team Six SEAL absolutely did that. But being in this little circle of specialists was something else. Here she wasn't *better than*— she was *part of.* That was something else ST6 had taught her to understand, but this moment was somehow stronger and more powerful.

"I chatted with the bartender before the police arrived," Sugar was explaining. "These guys were complete strangers. And a couple of the patrons said that their Spanish accent was wrong. Any Belizean would have more Creole or British influence."

"Wish we could ID the bastards." J-dawg's growl said that whatever else he might be, he cared deeply about Sugar. Nikita could hear it in his voice.

Even mercenary bastards had feelings. Who knew. And now that she'd count Sugar as a friend, did that mean she had to accept J-dawg as well? That concept she didn't like so much.

"I forgot to ask the damn cops how long it would take to get IDs."

"Oh, we already know that without asking," Nikita said in an offhand way.

Sugar's smile said that Nikita was doing a fair job of channeling Sugar's strong-woman attitude.

"It's going to take them a *long* time. Those three didn't seem like the chatty types."

Their group had reached the head of the pier, where J-dawg and Sugar wouldn't be able to follow past security.

While J-dawg and Drake cursed over the news, she turned aside to where the lights on the pier made a dark, shadowed area behind a wide palm. It was also out of sight of the pier's security watch.

She and Sugar reached down their blouses and pulled out the three men's wallets and passports.

"It may take them a *very* long time without these," Nikita held them up.

The others' laughter made it feel like she was taking a bow at the end of one of Drake's stage performances.

"Careful with those," Nikita stopped Jared from flipping one open. "We took fingerprints of each person on the inside flap."

Jared peeled it open carefully, "What did you use for ink?"

"They each seemed to be leaving a lot of blood around. We also smeared a dollar bill on each of them so that there'd be plenty for a DNA sample."

"IDs look fake as hell. Whatever port authority let these aboard should have his eyes examined." Jared took all three wallets, "I'll get these to Parker right away."

"Hold it," Altman reached out to stop him, but Jared fended him off.

"You people have a boat to catch. And don't worry. Parker can get to any database he needs to."

"*That's* what worries me," but Altman desisted.

"What worries me is this." Nikita reached into the edge of her bra where the damn cards had been poking her.

She held out the men's three cruise ship passes.

"And this," she nodded to Sugar.

Sugar opened her leather vest and lifted her blouse enough to extract the long barrel of a silenced Ruger 22/45 LITE. It was a lean, nasty gun accurate out to seventy meters plus—well past the distance from observation deck to bow. The shooter had put those two shots exactly where he'd intended.

"Scare tactics with the gun. Then a kidnapping attempt. Someone is trying to spook your team," Sugar concluded.

Nikita took it from her. They hadn't had time to inspect it carefully before. She dropped the magazine and held it up to the light.

"Full," Drake said looking over her shoulder.

"So no way to tell if this was the weapon that shot at us, but the model and silencer make it likely."

"Please tell me you hurt the man bad."

"Well, I can tell you one thing, Sweet Cheeks," Nikita leaned in and kissed Drake on the nose. "After what Sugar did to him, he may never have sex again."

# CHAPTER 17

hey waited until the ship was dark and quiet before they
went on the hunt. They were two hours out to sea and the
ship was rolling a bit in the heavy side sea, but not enough to make
them misstep.

This time they were all armed. For the sake of the security
cameras, they made a show of going out as couples, two couples
acting like they were just going for a walk to stretch their legs. Down
one long deck to the grand staircase near the end—all red carpeted
and brass hand-railed.

On Deck 8 they turned away from their quarry and made a point
of window shopping along the corridor past the closed boutiques
where they'd spent so much of Titan's money.

On Deck 7 they explored the selections in the library. Drake took a
Connelly thriller he'd been wanting to read. He couldn't imagine that
Nikita had actually been paying attention when she'd a selected diet
plan title that promised to burn away fat without exercise.

"It looks like the kind of book my empty-headed self might select,"
she explained. Then, as if embarrassed by herself, she dropped it on a
chair as they left. He set the Connelly with it, liking the juxtaposition
—the two sides of Nikita Hayward.

On Deck 6 they meandered most of the way back to the bow.

At side-by-side suites, 612 and 614, they traded nods with Altman and Zoe that would look as if they were wishing each other good night. Both doors had "Do Not Disturb" signs dangling from their door handles.

Zoe slipped the keycard into 614, which had belonged to two of the three henchmen. Nikita did the same on 612.

The electronic locks released at the same moment and flashed green.

In unison they jammed down on the handles, swung open the doors, and pulled their weapons as they moved inside.

Drake was first in.

"Daylin?" A sleepy woman's voice.

A step behind him, Nikita hit the lights.

A lean woman stared at him wide-eyed for the length of two heartbeats, then drove a hand under her pillow.

There was a sharp click and spit close by Drake's ear. The woman yelped as Nikita's round punched into the pillow and there was a loud clank as her bullet hit metal.

The woman flinched and jerked her hand back to her chest. As she did, she knocked aside the pillow, revealing a twin to the gun that Sugar had taken in the bar and delivered to Jared.

The prone woman was smart enough to not go for this gun again.

Altman came in through the connecting door with Zoe close behind and picked up the weapon while Nikita kept her covered. He dropped the magazine and nodded, "Two rounds shy of full."

Drake didn't remember moving until his face was inches from the woman's. "Why did you shoot her?" he pointed back at Nikita.

"I did not! I missed," her accent was thickly Spanish.

"Same accent as our three *hombres,*" Nikita confirmed where she still had the woman centered in her sights. "And you didn't miss. My arm still hurts like hell."

The woman looked aghast. "I was ordered to shoot you. A final test it might be...have been. They never said I would be shooting American woman. I was not ready for such things. So I aim away."

Drake glanced back at Nikita and earned an I-told-you-so look for his troubles.

"Daylin know I am crack shot. Now they no longer trust me. That is why they leave me on ship today."

"Sure," Zoe chimed in. "They trust you so little, they gave you gun Number Two."

"They also give this," she went to raise her other arm.

Drake saw a flash of metal and was all set to dive away when there was a sharp clank and her arm stopped abruptly. She was handcuffed to the bed.

"With just the handcuff, I could scream for help. With a *pistola* on a cruise ship, I would be in very much trouble if I was found." Then her dark eyes went wider as she looked at the four of them grouped around her bed. "Or am I now in more troubles? Did you kill Daylin and the others? Now me, too? Are you kill squad like Daylin say?" Her voice kept rising.

Drake did his best to shush her. He would have to admit it was an odd setting. A cruise ship suite at two in the morning, softly aglow with indirect light. A slender woman with dark skin, black hair that spilled in a soft wave to well-curved breasts that were barely hidden by the thin blue nightgown—handcuffed to the bed while four fully-dressed Special Operations soldiers looked down at her.

"We are not a murder squad," Nikita said with disgust.

"What about when Daylin comes back? He will be very angry. Where is he?"

"I expect he will be in a Belizean jail for quite some time. We're arranging for the three of them to be extradited to the US on the charge of attempted kidnapping of Americans."

Her shoulders sagged in relief. "He cannot kill me from there. Then maybe you could unlock these cuff. Daylin make it too tight and my hand it...*zumbar*...tingle? Yes? All day."

"Do you have a key?"

"Daylin put it in the safe, but he does not give me the combination."

When Drake looked at him, Altman shrugged. "I could pick the handcuff lock. But since we need to see what's in the safe anyway, you should just cozy up to our friendly neighborhood hotel manager."

"Shouldn't we search first?"

"You cozy, we'll search. Not a lot of hiding places in a standard suite." It was a much simpler arrangement than their own. There were only five spaces: bathroom, walk-in closet, bedroom with big-screen TV, small sitting area with big-screen TV, and a verandah barely large enough for two loungers.

Drake picked up the phone, punched for the operator, and began convincing her that he in truth did want to talk to the hotel manager despite the hour. Stating his name turned out to be the key in the lock —he was on some sort of preferred passenger list. If they only knew.

"Hi Norma. Drake Roman here. Sorry to wake you, but could you join us in Suite 614…Yes, 614." He should have called from Room 614's phone. He didn't want to greet her with the handcuffed woman wearing only a skimpy negligee in 612.

"Don't forget to tell her to bring a master key for the room safe," Nikita said as she came out of the closet and headed for the bath.

He passed on the message, making it clear that she should come alone.

Norma made it in record time, every inch of her ship officer's uniform in its proper place.

The safe turned up nothing except more ammunition, the woman's passport, which matched the fake ID they'd found in her purse, and the crucial handcuff key. Zoe pointed out a charger, but there was no cellphone. It must still be in Daylin's pocket.

"Sugar spiked it with a boot heel. Very dead," Nikita explained as she searched under the mattress.

When they showed Norma the gun, she nearly wilted under the burden. "In a decade of cruising, I have never had a gun on a ship before."

Her suspicions began turning on them until Drake suggested that she deliver the weapon—along with the contents of the safe, except the woman's passport—to the Captain to keep under lock and key, preferably until they were again in Miami in four days' time. Nikita also handed over the three men's cruise ship passes.

"What about her?" Norma nodded to the woman. She now had one of the ship's complimentary white terrycloth robes over her shoulders and was massaging her wrist. "We have a lockup, but the crew would see her and there would be many questions."

"For the moment," Drake took the handcuffs and the key, "she will be staying with us."

"My name is Esly Escarra and yes, I know my passport says Joan Smith. I was DNIC sergeant in San Pedro Sula. As *policia* sergeant in crime and drugs division, I tried to be honest."

Not what Nikita was expecting. A gang member, a hired thug, but not a cop.

The five of them were seated in the lounge area of their big suite. She and Drake on one sofa, Altman, Zoe, and Esly in the three armchairs across a low coffee table. Esly was now dressed in simple clothes that made her barely passable by cruising standards—wouldn't have without her good figure and nice, though still tentative, smile.

"Daylin, he was my captain and my lover before he change sides. Now he is…how do you say?"

"On the take?" Nikita decided that just maybe there was someone worse than mercenaries: those pretending to do one job while actually doing another.

"On the take? English idiom is very strange. The *take* was very nice and we live very well. Eventually I must arrest him or join him. The decision is not hard in Honduras, especially not in San Pedro where much of Venezuela's cocaine leave for Mexico and America. Honest police have very short lives there. But I never shoot one. Daylin? Maybe he did. I do not know. I am more Daylin's protection, his…he is with woman so he look like a good man? Yes? The other two were his lieutenants." Then her eyes gazed into the distance for a few moments. "He was always nice to me, but the money changed him very much. If he is truly gone, I will miss him only little amount."

"Why shoot at Nikita?" Drake still sounded pissed as hell about that.

Esly shook her head. "I do not know very much. There is a big project—'more money than drugs' Daylin tells me and very much less dangerous. But we must scare away American contractor. GSI, he told me, were no longer needed for this big project. First we attack their women—he say they always travel with many women. Then, if that does not make them to go away, we attack them. That is all I know."

Nikita shook her head. "Your Daylin was not a smart man. The best way to make a mercenary like the head of GSI angry is to attack his women."

"Works for me, too," Drake's growl was so very male.

Esly sighed, "No, he is not very smart. But he was kind to me and better than many as lover. Are you good lover?" She aimed her sudden tease at Altman. Her self-confidence was amazing for a woman who had faced a "death squad" after being handcuffed throughout the day.

Nikita couldn't resist smiling, but Luke Altman's face didn't shift in the slightest as he declined reacting to her tease.

"So, Esly shoots to miss and loses Daylin's trust. Daylin goes for staging a kidnapping in Belize City."

"Daylin," Nikita confirmed, "ends up bloody when Sugar rams her spiked boot heel into his crotch."

Esly covered a quick burst of laughter with a hand over her mouth. No, she wouldn't be missing Daylin for long at all. If Drake were suddenly removed from her own life? Nikita didn't like that thought at all.

"Somebody in Honduras…" Drake took Nikita's hand and held on to it as if that would protect her from whatever came next.

It was silly, they were safe in their suite, but still she was charmed.

"...took every bit of weaponry and tactical advice that GSI would sell them and now wants to cut them out of the profits. Which would have made GSI even angrier and more dangerous."

"Wait," Esly looked from one face to another, "you are not this GSI?"

"No," Nikita decided to keep it simple. "No, we're not."

An hour later they were none the wiser.

Daylin, and through him Esly, had been hired to scare off GSI. They weren't likely to be scared off, especially not after the amount of capital they'd invested in Honduras. They'd been paid for it, very well, making an outfit as greedy as GSI hungry for more, not less.

"At least we can all agree on one thing," Nikita finally summed it up.

"What's that?" Zoe finally managed to take the bait. Drake and Altman were beyond speech.

"This is certainly the single most screwed-up, frustrating, really-pissing-me-off project I've worked on since—" she almost said *joining ST6*, but Esly was still there with them, "—the last time I was on a screwed-up, frustrating, really-pissing-me-off project."

That earned her grunts of agreement from the two men.

They had sent Esly's fingerprints, taken with the help of Zoe's mascara, to Parker along with the suggestion to look in the Honduran police files. Esly and the three jailed kidnappers came back with positive IDs almost immediately—exactly matching Esly's story right down to each one's rank and matching picture. He also provided home addresses; Esly's and Daylin's were the same.

Daylin had apparently kept the broader scope of the plan to himself, and his destroyed cellphone had probably been swept out with the rest of the trash in the bar.

# CHAPTER 19

They handcuffed Esly to the bed in the back suite—this time less painfully and with her cooperation: "I am the unknown. I understand."

Altman pulled a chair close enough to the bed to prop his feet on the mattress. He'd wake up if Esly so much as rolled over.

Zoe was out cold on the couch close by Luke.

Nikita slouched lower on the couch in the main room and rested her head on Drake's shoulder. She'd never been so comfortable around a man. She could go to sleep leaning on him, and maybe not even wake if he moved. He felt that safe to be around.

Drake rose to his feet and looked down at her. He tugged lightly on her hand.

"What?"

At Drake's eye roll, she let him pull her to her feet, though she was unsure what was happening, at least for the first three steps. He was leading her toward the master bedroom.

"But—"

"I'm tired..."

And Nikita was surprised by the rush of disappointment that he was leading her to the bedroom to sleep. It was so strong that it almost took her breath away.

"…of not having you in my bed."

Drake Roman in a bed was the best idea she'd heard all day, "But this is my bed. Yours has a pretty Latina handcuffed to it."

"Po-ta-to. Po-tah-to. Besides, I want my Southern belle, not some dangerous Latina." Drake closed and locked the door.

"You're saying I'm not dangerous?"

"There's a difference between dangerous and lethal. You slay me, Nikita."

The room was lit by the bright wash of a nearly full moon shining off the ocean and through the wide-open verandah doors. Plenty enough to see by.

She moved away from the door quickly because the urge to take him here and now was nearly overwhelming, but she'd had enough of vertical surfaces. She agreed: bed. Definitely. Nikita peeled off her shirt and bra as she followed him across the carpet.

"Hey, cut that out," Drake was glaring at her as she shucked shoes, pants, and underwear.

"I thought the point was to get naked," she tossed her socks on the pile of clothes.

"I was looking forward to undressing you myself."

"Why?"

While Drake puzzled over how to answer that one, she grabbed the hem of his own t-shirt and yanked it upward. He mumbled a protest as she peeled it over his head and off his arms.

She had his pants undone before he grabbed her wrists.

"Hold on there, little lady! Just slow down for a second." Drake's John Wayne was better than his Southern, marginally. His pants hung enticingly loose on his hips but didn't slide down. She reached, but his strong grip kept her hands inches from his waistband.

"I thought you wanted sex," she tried again and failed. Drake was far stronger than he looked—though she already knew that.

"Did I say that I wanted sex?"

"Well, we're not going to just get naked and then sleep."

"I didn't say that either."

"Then what?"

After another moment, he slowly released her hands.

"Then what?"

In answer, he raised a hand to her face, cupping her cheek in his palm. Then he leaned in to kiss her, so softly and gently that she couldn't tell when it shifted from mere contact to warm kiss. His other hand slid around her waist and pulled her tightly against him.

His dangling belt buckle dug into her hip, so she moved back enough to bat his pants and underwear off his hips, then let herself be pulled against him once more after he kicked the last of his clothes free. Drake's chest was just as much a revelation this time as it had been during their first kiss. She pressed against it more and more, every inch of contact a new discovery. The simple sensation of touch had never been so desirable, so necessary. She felt as if she'd go mad if she didn't get—

Overbalanced, Drake collapsed backward onto the bed, his tight grip taking her with him.

"At least we made it to the bed this time," she rubbed her face against his chest as his hands dug into her hair. He didn't guide her, no pressure to aim her attention at his crotch. Instead he seemed to be merely playing with her hair. When she lay her ear on his chest to listen to his racing heart, his hands went quiet and merely cradled her head against him. She listened to it for a long time—seconds, minutes, ten beats, a hundred...she didn't count, didn't try to keep track.

Drake coaxed her the rest of the way onto the bed and onto her back. While he shed his socks, then backtracked to his pants for protection, she lay back, closed her eyes, and prepared herself for the wild ride to come. Sex with Drake was so good. They'd only had the one opportunity, but it had been wonderful, hot, and steamy.

The hand that brushed down her neck was so unexpectedly gentle that she could only gasp at the contact. She felt a shiver that had nothing to do with temperature.

Nikita lay there and could only let her awareness follow that single point of contact. Down her neck, tracing back and forth across her collarbone, down between her breasts until her stomach muscles clenched tighter than after doing a hundred crunches when he rested his palm there.

She managed to open her eyes and look at Drake. The moonlight was bright enough to reveal his face but not his expression. His attention wasn't following the line of his touch. He wasn't staring at her breasts. He was watching her face.

"What are you doing?" Nikita didn't recognize her own voice it was so breathy with surprise.

"Enjoying myself. What are you doing?"

She hissed at the sensation of his fingertips tracing up the side of her breast, then circling around. "Feeling," she managed. She was feeling the sensations as they rippled over her skin like tiny waves lapping on a tropical beach. For years she'd learned about focused attention down range, on the target. Now her focus was narrowing inward until she was aware of no more than the exact path of Drake's touch, a point of fiery sensation and a trailing wake of pleasant tingles.

Then an underwater explosion's worth of heat lashed through the point where his mouth took her breast. A groan escaped her. The more her body reacted, the slower and gentler Drake became. He delivered no fiery heat, instead he coaxed it out of her until she burned for more.

"Drake," she managed on a broken breath.

"Hmm," he responded a lazy time later after nuzzling her neck.

"If you don't do something more and damn soon, I'm going to have to kill you."

"Hmm," he kissed her on the mouth while his hand slid down her body and returned—traveling somewhere between dead slow and full stop.

Her body was begging for engines full ahead. Her life always begged for that. She'd been born her father's daughter and never looked back—charging into the fray whether it was playground tag or full-force suppression of a terrorist training camp.

"I don't know how to do this." Nikita curled against his hand as he slid it between her legs. She could feel his smile against her temple when his lips brushed there.

"Just be yourself, Nikita."

"Myself," she breathed in deep, pressing herself harder against his hand, "is expecting the men's shower wall."

But he didn't give her that. He coaxed and teased and enticed until she finally gave up, having no idea what was happening next—not from him, not from her.

Instead, for only the second time in her life, she was completely out of control. The first time was when everything went south during the operation in the Congo and the bastards had turned the radio on continuous transmit so that she couldn't leave, couldn't do anything but listen. It never stopped though she begged it to. No one could hear her with the transmit key locked down on the other end.

And now with Drake, she was past reason. Her body and her emotions were in as helpless a whirl, but this time she spent every second begging that he *wouldn't* stop. She rose to meet his every touch, ached for him until it was a full-body sensation.

When he finally entered her, there was a rightness, a completeness that she'd never found before. As if, for just this once, she was somehow whole.

---

DRAKE DIDN'T KNOW what to do with the tears soaking his shoulder. He tried to brush them away, but Nikita clung to him so tightly that he couldn't do anything more than hold her in turn.

She didn't weep or sob, but the salty tang of her tears was a thousand times stronger than the mid-ocean air drifting in through the open doorway to the verandah.

"What's with the tears, honey?" He cradled her gently. Never had a woman so responded to him. He'd meant to make love to her, but had become so involved that it was more as if "making love" was a third thing that would have interfered if it had been in bed with them.

There had only been him and the magnificent woman now clinging to him so tightly.

"What tears?" Nikita's voice was rough with them. "I'm crying? But I never do that. Not since—"

And he held her tighter as she froze. She didn't struggle to get free, but she didn't relax either.

"Not since… It's been a long time," she faded to a whisper.

"Then I'll take it as a compliment that you felt safe enough to cry on me."

"Felt safe? That is not at all what I felt. Well maybe it is. But that's not all it was. It was—I'm rambling."

"Don't stop now," it never did his ego any harm to hear how he'd made a woman feel. And he truly and deeply wanted to know how he'd made this particular one feel.

His answer was a gentle fist in the ribs. "Not feeding your fantasies of male prowess, Duck-man."

"But they're such good fantasies."

This time she pushed away, not hard, just as if she was ready to go. He didn't want her to, but he never argued with what a woman wanted. She didn't turn on a light, or head to the bathroom while scooping up her clothes. Instead she went to the edge of the verandah and leaned on the doorframe, looking east over the ocean, silhouetted in moonlight.

She looked strong and mysterious. Warm despite the cool light.

He slid out of the bed and wrapped his arms around her from behind. She leaned back against him, wrapping her arms over his.

"I heard every word of their deaths. Every cry. My father must have known they were transmitting. The only words he ever said were, 'I love you, Nikki. Tell your mom that you two are the best thing that ever happened to me.' Other than that, he never made a single sound, even when his torturers promised they'd stop if he did."

There were no tears in her voice or sliding down her cheeks now. Somehow he was now holding both his lover and an ST6 SEAL at the same time.

"Barry never said my name once. For all the pleading and begging and crying he did, he never once said my name." Then she turned slowly in his arms and looked up at him from a breath away. "I haven't let anyone past my guard since."

Drake studied her in the moonlight, memorized every feature from the curve of her cheek to the shape of her lips as well as he could.

She waited and he knew what she was asking.

It should be a hard question. It was certainly one that he'd been an expert at avoiding for an entire lifetime. A lifetime that so far had been filled with no one like Chief Petty Officer Nikita Hayward.

He had wanted to make love to her to bring her closer to him. It had worked. The catch was that it had worked both ways and now he couldn't imagine letting her go.

"I would say your name: first, middle, and last." And once he said it, he knew it was true.

And still the SEAL watched him as the woman held him.

He slipped sideways onto one of the wide loungers and tugged her down beside him. There was a shelf with handy blankets and he pulled one over them.

She curled up against him and together they watched the night sky.

He had nothing to say. His life had been so easy compared to hers. All he could offer was to hold her.

There was only one word that would describe how incredible she felt. How important she felt. He kissed the top of her head where it rested on his shoulder and whispered it into the night.

"Nikita."

CHAPTER 20

"Storm's coming."

Nikita raised her head enough to look over Drake's chest and out the master bedroom's doors. She didn't remember exactly when they had moved indoors. Cygnus had flown out of sight over the other side of the ship and Pegasus had proclaimed the zenith when they shifted locations.

Now, the rising sun was masked by deep red clouds. The sky above was still blue, but the old sailor's adage had more truth than not: *Red at night, sailors delight. Red in the morning, sailors take warning.* A storm arriving from the east across the open reaches of the Caribbean Sea.

That wasn't the only storm coming. Last night Drake had awakened something in her.

Not merely an insatiable need, but the firm conviction that her need had only one focus: Drake Roman. Up on one elbow and looking down on him as he sleepily rolled his head to look at her, she was captured as well as any swamp bullfrog staring into a flashlight.

His smile for her was soft and gentle, but she could feel where her leg lay thrown over his hips that *his* need for *her* was awakening fast—even faster than he was.

No complaints from her. This time, when she straddled over him,

518

there was none of the confusing tenderness of last night. No new experiences that she'd never imagined possible. But neither was there the frantic satisfying of their bodies like after their race.

Yes, the sex was fast, hard, and ripped through her body with mind-wiping pleasure. But afterward he pulled her down until she lay full upon his chest and she had her face tucked into his neck so that all she could smell was the rich warmth that was so distinctly Drake's. That too was amazing. More amazing than the sex in many ways.

There was no hurry to get up and get dressed. No impatience. She'd learned that when men were done, they were done. Not Drake. He stroked her body from her knee—still tucked up in kneeling position—down thigh to hip, up and over her back, into her hair or brushing her cheek, even tugging lightly on her ear, before returning via her shoulder, the side of her breast, her ribs, and back to her hips. It was soothing, gentle, loving…

"Wait!" she mumbled into his neck.

"Wait what?"

"What are you doing to me?" She pushed up onto her elbows and looked down at him.

"What do you mean?" But there was a smile tugging at his lips that said he knew exactly what he was doing.

She was never, ever the slow one in the room. SEAL training had only enhanced her natural tendencies to observe and analyze any situation. "You're trying to slip something by me?"

"Me?" Now he was definitely smiling, no attempt at innocence other than his tone. "When would I ever be able to slip something by the incredible Nikita?"

"Wait a minute! There was something…last night…" and then she had it. She'd asked without asking if he cared enough about her that her name would have been somewhere on his lips if he'd been in Barry's position.

*First, middle, and last.*

"I was only asking if you'd think of me if—" somehow everything went that wrong.

"I would," his smile shifted toward leer. "I'd think about your breasts," she had pushed herself up high enough that he managed to get his hands on them. "I'd think about the incredible things you can do with those beautiful hips," he wriggled his own beneath her.

"*Roman.*"

"I'd think of your beautiful, ever so expressive face that shows exactly what you're thinking and feeling no matter how much you think it doesn't."

She put her face back into his shoulder to hide whatever it was saying without her permission. That forced his hands back to her ribs.

"And," his voice shifted to completely serious, "I'd spend my last moments thanking the lucky stars for every instant I got to be with you."

Nikita pushed back up to glare down at him. "I don't need poetry. I need truth."

"Oh. I can do both. I know for a fact that I will never meet another woman like you. Known that since the first moment you stepped onto my aircraft a year ago. And now that I've discovered that making love to you is beyond spectacular," he wriggled his hips again, but his tone remained oddly serious. "I'm completely sold. All in. Sign me up."

"Making love to me? Is that what last night was?" Compared to Drake Roman, even everything with Barry had been merely sex. But she wasn't comfortable with—

"That's what I'd thought to do."

"But instead?"

"Instead," he shifted his hands up to cradle her face, then kissed her ever so lightly. "Instead I made love *with* you. There will never be another woman for me other than Nikita Hayward. You're stuck with me now."

"Sure, until the Duck-man finds another willing babe."

"I've been with three women since I first met you. I didn't even bother sleeping with the last one, which pissed her off quite a bit, and that was nine months ago. None of them were up to your standard."

"But *you* are?" Nikita wasn't sure where the tease came from. And for the first time this morning, Drake frowned.

"No. No I'm not," he looked aside for a long moment before

looking back into her eyes. His had gone almost black and his expression was once more shifting to the powerful warrior she hadn't met before their treadmill race. "But I'm sure as hell going to do my best to live up to your standard from this moment forward."

She wanted to make a joke about all the grunts who aspire to DEVGRU standards but didn't stand a chance. She could have teased Duck-man the gunner about that. But Drake Roman the warrior? No. The tease dried up in her throat as she looked down at him. Him she believed.

This time, when she leaned down to kiss him, it had all of the power of last night's gentleness as well as this morning's heat. How could she not believe in a man like him?

It was even more true than she first understood as his arms slid around her.

She didn't believe in men, had trained herself not to. Oh, she believed in Luke Altman, but as her SEAL commander, not as a man.

But Drake Roman? Him she believed in with all her heart.

"This is our last chance at figuring out what's going on. Our ship is in Roatán Harbor only for today. We sail at midnight."

Not sure what to do with Esly in public just yet, Drake had ordered morning coffee into the suite as the ship docked. The butler had delivered it along with fresh croissants, then been quite put out that he hadn't been allowed to stay and hover. Apparently, high-roller guests would never deign to pour their own second cup of coffee.

"I'm hoping that going out and being very public will attract some-one's attention. That's why I didn't order breakfast; we'll eat ashore as well. As much as I'd like to leave the women behind—"

"Screw that!" Zoe managed to beat Nikita's protest by only milliseconds. Esly may have kept her mouth shut but her look said plenty.

"But as I don't want to be lynched by my own mob," he offered Altman a shrug and received a grimace of commiseration. "You do understand that so far you women have been the main targets?"

"Part of that was my fault. Again, Nikita, I am very truly sorry I shoot at you," Esly apologized sincerely and the other two seemed to forgive her with easy smiles. God help him, he was never going to understand women.

"So here are our rules of engagement today. *No one* leaves the group. Zoe, you're glued to Altman. Nikita, you to me. Even if J-dawg shows up across the street and Asal is choking on a French fry—no one leaves the group."

He glared around the table until he received nods from both of them.

"What about me?" Esly stared straight at him with her impenetrably dark eyes. "I do not want another day handcuffed to a bed."

"How do I trust that I'm talking to police sergeant Escarra and not Daylin's lover?"

Actually her face said a lot about the latter no longer being true. She had said she would miss Daylin only "a very little amount" and she seemed to be over that already.

Esly shrugged. She was smart enough to know that no amount of promises would count.

Drake saw Zoe and Nikita exchange glances and knew the decision was already made. He could fight it or go with the flow.

"You're with us," he said it before the women could say it for him. "Anyone asks, you are extra protection for Drake Roman because you walk like a policeman."

"Policewoman," Zoe and Esly said together.

Drake sighed, then looked at her across the table. "If anything happens to Zoe or Nikita while you're with us, whether by you or because anyone else gets past you, I'm going to take it out of your hide personally. *Comprende?*"

Nikita destroyed the moment by remarking drily, "See! I knew that you spoke some Spanish."

She'd clearly been hanging around with Zoe too much.

---

NIKITA, in all her missions, had never wandered about a tropical island like a tourist before. A well-heeled tourist.

Drake had simply called back the butler, who had been ecstatic to have something to do. By the time they reached the dock, a late model Toyota Hiace van, complete with driver and a bilingual tour guide, was waiting for them. They were an older couple, but it was clear that the wife, Mercedez, had once been a great beauty.

"I am fourth generation in Roatán. I will show you the best of everything." Her energy was cheerful without being overbearing. Before they even traveled the few kilometers to the far side of the island, she had already made it clear that they were all one friendly group for the day.

"Where is the fifth generation, Mercedez?" Zoe asked.

And the brilliance of her light dimmed for a moment. "My daughter was murdered during the riots following the 2009 coup. I have no future generation. I now live through my sister's son. His father is mayor of the island and a good man. They both are good men."

Nikita knew full well that kind of pain. To lose a daughter must be even worse. She offered her sympathy, but couldn't think to do anything more.

"We wish to see the island, Mercedez," Drake replied when she asked. "And as odd as this may seem, we wish to be *particularly* visible while we are doing it."

That earned them all a long, assessing look, which she then covered with a radiant smile. "Of course. To fellow tourists or to… locals?" She was sharp and was making it clear what kind of locals she was talking about.

"I wish I knew, Mercedez. I wish I knew."

She nodded firmly, "Then we must start with breakfast at the Lobster Pot on Sandy Bay."

Crab and lobster omelettes were served under big umbrellas. The sandy beach at the Lobster Pot was fine and white. The score of sailboats anchored close ashore explained the dozen other tables with couples and families enjoying a casual meal—and their table was *particularly* prominent.

For a few lazy hours they seemed to pass every person from the cruise ship several times as they wandered through Carambola Botanical Gardens, lush with a zillion plants Nikita had never seen before. Plants weren't exactly high on her list—other than the edibles she'd learned about during survival training—but the gardens were spectacular. Trails wound through the forty-acre patch of jungle revealing trees with leaves that were bigger than she was, in the form of fronds, twists, and massive banana leaves of green so pure it almost hurt to look at. Impossible flowers grew at every turn from tiny lavender-tinged stars to cascades of white-and-yellow orchids so alien looking that they *could* be creatures from another planet.

Zoe started making up wild science fiction stories about their evil plans to conquer the earth.

Drake joined in on the same theme.

In the poor flowers' defense, Nikita countered with wild tales extracted from Dr. Seuss about a lovely tropical princess and the flowers that tried to be as beautiful as she was when she walked among them each day.

The laughter was easy. She'd never been so thoughtlessly comfortable in a group. In a way, she walked beside herself, separate from the smiling woman with her hand tucked in the handsome gunner's elbow, laughing with trained killers and two tour guides. Who was this woman acting as if she was in love with the man beside her? Nikita knew it was herself, and yet it wasn't. Maybe she and not the flowers was the one wrapped up in a Seussian tale, trying to live up to an impossible standard.

Nikita knew the warrior. That woman she understood completely. This one—with the feathered haircut that fluttered every time she turned to look up at her man, whose stomach was sore with laughing rather than with inverted sit-ups, whose body was still loose with the memory of how he had made love to her—no, *with* her—this one was a stranger to her.

Then Zoe had delivered the ultimate reality check.

"Let's go clothes shopping."

Nikita had decided she would rather die, but the tour guide

whisked them ten kilometers up-island to Junk Boutique in French Harbour.

"This sounds promising," Nikita whispered to Zoe.

"For Esly. Her wardrobe is horrid. It just won't do if she's going to continue being with Drake Roman, Inc. We have standards."

Which was true. "But Junk Boutique?"

"We are a small island," Mercedez overheard her question and replied with her cheerful but unstoppable charm. "We have several very good designers here. This is where they sell. Casual and couture. It is also on the center of the main walking street of our second largest and most pleasant town."

Through the morning it had become clear that Mercedez was practically adopting Esly. By now they appeared thick as thieves, leaning their heads together and laughing. It was almost as if Mercedez had found her missing daughter for a brief moment.

The shop's window, in a stone building that looked as if it just might have been here since the ships of the 17th-century buccaneers had filled the bay, included a cheerful array of trinkets and a very skimpy bikini that she could see was giving Drake ideas. Thankfully the shop was little bigger, though much better stocked, than the one on the ship. Nikita was able to use that as an excuse to sit out on the bench just in front of the store with the two men and the driver, letting Esly and Zoe go in with their guide.

Across the street was a short beach with a good bay.

"The largest fishing fleet in the Western Caribbean," Emmanuel the driver nodded toward the boats anchored throughout the bay and along the piers.

The traffic and pedestrians of French Harbour swirled around them. Not with the hurry of Mobile or the frantic rush of Norfolk, Virginia, near DEVGRU's base. No one was in too much of a hurry to greet Emmanuel, who rarely spoke more than a word or two but was apparently well known and liked. English, Spanish, black, white, brown—the populace was more mixed than a Navy mess hall. Fashions ranged from khakis and t-shirts to flowing caftans. Every person seemed unique, yet they all seemed to belong.

And, once she managed to get over the near miss of a life-threatening shopping trip with Zoe, she was able to appreciate that this too fit with Drake's plans—Mercedez was serving them very well. Every single person who called out a greeting to Emmanuel carefully inspected the people he was escorting. The island patois was hard to follow, but she caught snatches of questions.

Drake had introduced himself to the guides as a businessman seeking new opportunities throughout Central America. A businessman who had an entourage and required Altman and Esly as his putative guards.

Esly had walked off the ship standing tall. The cautious, carefully-spoken woman who had shared their suite since last night had stepped into her role, looking almost as fierce as Altman, especially after she pilfered a set of Altman's dark, wrap-around shades.

Emmanuel was very circumspect about his current customers, and that alone seemed to speak volumes to those who talked with him.

Esly emerged from Junk Boutique looking even tougher than when she'd gone in. The changes seemed minimal: sturdy boots, a light jacket with a military flair to it, and a brilliant yellow blouse with a low enough neck to accent her dark, creamy skin and generous cleavage. But the alteration in appearance was substantial. She looked tough and sexy at the same time. Maybe Nikita should introduce her to Sugar. Mercedez also emerged with a black clothing bag and wearing what Nikita now recognized as a very expensive smile.

Nikita couldn't help laughing and Mercedez only looked a little abashed—she'd taken them to her own store. But Esly looked both sexy and powerful in her new clothes, which said Mercedez was also good at what she did.

"I am hoping that it is okay I buy two dresses. Zoe said I must," Esly was saying.

Drake was nodding his okay, but she was looking at Altman.

"I look very good in these dresses. Perhaps I can wear one when we go to dinner tonight."

Nikita looked over at her commander. He eyed both Esly and the smiling Zoe cautiously, but kept his mouth shut despite the fact that he now had two women teasing him. Altman was a smart man. It was a no-win scenario.

"Now," Mercedez said cheerfully as Emmanuel loaded the dress bag into the back of the van. "Maybe we should all go swimming along with the dolphins. That is very popular with many people."

Nikita hadn't brought a suit. The string bikini in the window mocked her, but she ignored it. Or tried to. It was far too easy to imagine Drake getting her into it.

"Or perhaps we have done enough in public places for you," Mercedez winked at them all. "I know a very private beach of beautiful sand and tall palms trees where the swimming is far more casual."

Nikita opened her mouth hoping to come up with any other suggestion when she spotted Arthur coming toward them along the street.

She called out his name with relief as a welcome distraction.

At Nikita's call, Drake looked up in time to see Arthur's reaction: oddly pleasure, not dismay.

"I am so glad I found you, Mr. Roman," he bumbled through the locals going about their business and finally came to stand close in front of the bench they were gathered around.

"Why is that?" He tried to stamp down on his irritation at the interruption and knew he was doing a lousy job of it. The image of going swimming off a tropical beach with Nikita, with or without bathing suit, had rocketed to the top of his mission list. And now, of all irritating beings on the planet, he had to contend with Arthur. If he ended up being the key to all of this, Drake was going to turn in his Minigun.

"Norma has been pushing me for a way to help you. And I've been thinking on it very hard."

"I'm not buying your damned painting. Wait. *Norma* has been pushing you?"

"She can be a very persuasive woman, Mr. Roman, and she seems to have taken quite a liking for you. I finally thought of something this morning but you had already left the ship. That's why I'm so glad I ran into you."

Drake checked sideways, but Nikita simply shrugged. He suppressed a sigh that now he probably wasn't going to get to see what that shrug would look like rising out of the warm ocean as they skinny-dipped.

"Spill it, Arthur."

The man waffled from one foot to the other. "It isn't very much; I only hope it can help. I was told to make sure that Mr. Baer of GSI was informed that this painting was available for purchase." His stance stabilized as if he was now done.

"Who told you to sell it to Baer?" Drake was getting tired of this.

"I don't know."

Drake cursed and rose to his feet.

Arthur stumbled back and almost crashed into Zoe. Esly reached out a hand and clamped on to Arthur's jacket like she was clamping an unruly kitten by the scruff of the neck. She held him in place. Drake could get to like her.

"How can you not know?"

"That's not how it works," Arthur continued in a hurry. "We aren't actually part of the cruise line. My company contracts to run the gallery, present art education programs for the passengers, and hold auctions. We have stables of artists we buy from frequently as well as freelance artists. We try to make sure that there are paintings for every taste, including a few exceptional pieces."

"You're not saying—" Drake remembered that damn nude far too clearly.

"No. No." Arthur shook his head. "The technique is good though. Borrowing from both the Dutch Masters' depth and Art Deco's clarity of line. I feel that the composition is somewhat lacking, however..."

He trailed off when he caught sight of Drake's expression and cleared his throat carefully.

"Items are accumulated, sorted, and distributed to the ships in containers. I get a provenance sheet on each piece and a cost. I make a commission on every dollar above cost that I can sell a piece for."

"And the provenance sheet said to sell this to GSI."

"Not exactly. Sometimes we have frequent travelers with known tastes and we try to make sure to have a piece or two from their favorite artist or style aboard. This was noted as a definite purchase for Mr. Baer—he buys every one and insists that he always sees them first. He pays rather well for paintings in this particular series."

"There's a series of those goddamn things?" Drake managed a deep breath but it didn't calm him. "Can we see the sheet?"

Arthur reached into his pocket and pulled it out.

"You're not earning points for proactive helpfulness, Arthur."

The man blanched white. Even hard-core method actors weren't so obvious. Maybe he was authentic.

Drake inspected the sheet, didn't see anything unusual except the note: *Definite purchase for GSI.* He handed it to Zoe, who struck him as most likely in their group to have a clue about something like this. She inspected it more carefully than he did, then shrugged.

"Is there anything unusual on that sheet?"

"Nothing," Arthur shrugged.

"Or the case it came in?"

"A simple cloth bag with a rigid protection board. It would be very unlikely that I ever shipped a painting to a client in the same bag it arrived in so I doubt if there would be more information there," then he blinked several times. "But I'll check if there's anything else that came with the painting. I can't imagine there was. I knew Mr. Baer would be aboard because one of that series of Myora's paintings was in this sailing's collection. Who makes sure that they are sent to me? I have no idea. Inquiries into how our buyers work is…not encouraged." He grimaced with the face of prior experience.

Drake nodded to Esly, who let Arthur go. He was so insubstantial that he seemed to waver at the sudden release.

"We need to see the painting," he couldn't believe he was saying the words. "Now."

"So, you *will* be purchasing it?" The overeager art salesman was back as if that's truly all he was.

"Don't push your luck."

"I can promise you an excellent price," Arthur seemed to realize that he wasn't making any headway and pulled out his cellphone, "I can have it delivered to your suite; my assistant is still aboard." He placed the call. "All set. It will be waiting for you."

"How did you find us here?"

"Oh," Arthur pointed at the boutique behind them. "I wanted to get something pretty for Norma."

"For Norma," Drake felt as if his ears were ringing and he couldn't make enough sense of it to answer the call.

"She's just the most wonderful woman, but she doesn't see herself as beautiful as she truly is—too many years of working the cruise ships can do that to you. I've been trying to show her otherwise."

"They have several stunning nightgowns. Very pretty, very tropical," Zoe prompted him.

"Oh my. Exactly the kind of thing I was hoping to find. I must be the luckiest man there is. Good day, Mr. Roman. Good day," he nodded to the rest of them and hurried inside.

"Is he for real?"

Nikita rose from where she'd remained on the bench and kissed him on the cheek. "First Sugar and now Arthur. I suspect they are both for real. You do seem to attract some very odd sorts, Mr. Roman."

"Present company included," he hugged her back and kissed her temple. Over the top of her head he saw the elegant bikini that would have looked so good on Nikita. He cursed to himself over lost opportunity and turned to Mercedez.

"I'm afraid that our day has been cut short by business."

# CHAPTER 23

"I hate that painting even more in daylight," Drake sat on the sofa. He couldn't stop staring at the hideous thing. The nude was so blatant. Too realistic to be ignored. It was almost as if a naked harlot was lying in their midst.

"You only hate it because you have taste," Nikita curled up on the couch beside him with her bare feet tucked under her. He had his arm over her shoulders and if Altman or Zoe had anything to say about it, they were keeping it to themselves.

Esly sat in her armchair, unaware of anything out of the ordinary —like a Night Stalker getting cozy with a Navy SEAL.

Altman inspected it again. "There's no card, no secret inscription carved on the frame, we don't have x-ray vision to see if there is actually a copy of *Dogs Playing Poker* underneath it." They had tried holding it up to the muted sunlight lost behind the heavy clouds, but learned nothing that way either.

Zoe tipped her head back and forth to inspect it. "Maybe her head is on another of his paintings and her missing foot on yet another. If it's a piece in a larger puzzle, we're nowhere."

"I can't believe that there's a series of these goddamn things," Drake managed a deep breath but it didn't calm him.

He went to the window and stared out. They were docked in Mahogany Bay, a narrow, deep-water inlet five kilometers from the town of Coxen Hole. There was room to squeeze in two cruise ships. Beyond the dock a small quaint "village" had been set up—half souvenir shops and half tour providers. Beyond that lay a forest as thick as and even more foreign to him than the Alabama one. Here all he could smell was the sea.

It would have been prettier if not for the high layer of thin, gray clouds that had moved all the way across the blue sky since dawn. It reached to the mainland, sixty kilometers distant across the turquoise water gone dark blue beneath that sullen sky.

"I know this place." Esly was from Honduras, so he wasn't sure why she sounded so surprised. But then Drake turned and saw that she wasn't looking at the view, she was looking at the painting.

"What place?"

"It is *la cascada*, a, uh, waterfall near El Carbón. It is deep in the national park."

He hadn't even looked at the background of the painting as a picture, merely to see if it hid words or a map.

Drake grabbed his satellite phone and punched a speed dial.

"5E Tours," someone answered. "How may we help you today? We have special discounts on heli-diving, heli-jungle tours, and women's lingerie."

"Say what?"

Then the voice registered.

"Rafe!" Drake was so glad to hear his pilot's familiar voice that he forgot to use the lieutenant's title, which was just as well with Esly in the room. "How close are you?"

"Flying, driving, or walking?"

Drake looked at the phone and tried to make sense of the question. Finding no clue as to what game Rafe was playing, he put the phone back to his ear.

"We've been in place for a couple of hours, but we were told you were already off ship. I guess you're back. Been enjoying your luxury transport? It's a very pretty ship, by the way."

Drake stepped out onto the verandah and looked down at the dock. Nikita followed him out. She spotted them first, resting a hand on his shoulder to get his attention, then pointing. Most of ten stories below he spotted two guys sitting on a bench in the shade. Both wore outrageously loud Hawaiian shirts. The two of them appeared to be wrestling over the control of a phone. Rafe was short and very dark-skinned. His copilot was tall and even lighter-skinned than Zoe. The two of them were the butt of endless Mutt-and-Jeff jokes.

"Look up and forward," he instructed them. He and Nikita waved and in moments they were waving back. "Be with you in ten."

<hr>

"Damn, Nikita. You look like a major babe in that outfit," Rafe offered a wolf whistle.

Nikita wasn't sure how she could possibly be a "major babe."

"And Zoe, way hot!" Julian offered her a high five that she smacked hard.

"You two are awfully cozy." She followed Rafe's attention down to her hand with some surprise.

She'd come down the ramp with her hand tucked around Drake arm as if it was a completely natural thing to do. Perhaps because it had been a perfectly natural thing to do. This whole romantic whatever-it-might-be was getting out of control. Except it didn't feel as if it was.

"These two not so much," Julian pointed at Altman standing stiffly beside Zoe.

"And this must be Ms. Escarra. Our friend Parker has told us so little about you." Rafe bent low over her hand and kissed it.

"Hey," Julian protested. "Stop trying to hog the hot women."

Esly looked at Nikita in a bit of a panic.

"Do not worry, Esly. It isn't just you, they're always this irritating. They're our self-appointed comedians—at least they like to think they are."

"I do not mind. Two such handsome men, I very much am not

minding. Also, having no reason to complain. I am mostly happy that I am not dead yet and that I do not kill you, Nikita."

"Nor anyone else…according to *our* records," Rafe was suddenly serious, almost nasty. His flirt of a moment before was now schizophrenically set aside between one breath and the next. Usually he made it easy to forget he was the officer in charge of a forty-million-dollar war machine and that both he and his helicopter were known for their fiery temper.

"The only people I ever shoot was in the line of my duty," Esly raised her chin.

"Before you went to the fucking dark side and—"

"Can it, Rafe," Drake stepped right up in his commander's face. "Old ground. Already covered. Moving on now."

Rafe glowered and Nikita almost wondered if they were about to fight over the woman.

But Julian gave Esly a reassuring wink. Then he looked at Drake, "What the hell happened to you, Duck-man?"

"What do you mean?"

"What do I mean? Standing tall, looking like you're ready to take on my fellow pilot to defend your women," Julian punched his shorter commander in the arm hard enough to receive a snarl. That was Julian's gift, he could always joke Rafe out of one of his dark moods. Nikita had seen it enough times to know it was conscious on both their parts and not just part of serving together. They were a team as assuredly as she and Luke were. Just as assuredly as she and Drake weren't. When the mission was over— She wasn't going to go there.

"Shit!" Rafe scrubbed at his face. "Sorry about that, but you're supposed to pick a goddamn side and stick with it."

"Yes," Esly nodded. "I know that now. But it was better than ending up dead in the streets. I already knew too much. If I refused when they said I must switch… You do not live in Honduras. Do not pretend that you know its problems."

Nikita liked that she said it simply, without anger or pushing back against Rafe's load of attitude. She could see the quiet-spoken police woman despite the pretty clothing they'd purchased for her.

"But something sure happened to the Duck-man," Julian went for the distraction and it served to finish shifting Rafe's attention.

His eyes finally focused on how closely they stood.

"I didn't do this to him," Nikita protested but didn't back away. "Drake did it to himself." It wasn't in her power to transform a man so wholly.

Zoe's sharp laugh was soon joined by Esly's.

"Oh, my friend, Nikita," Esly actually hugged her. "Of course you did. It is the power we women have on men."

"I'd rather shoot them," Nikita grumbled out. That was so much easier. Get assigned a target, complete with a long-and-bad history, then infiltrate, acquire, take down, and exfiltrate. This whole trying to understand the man beside her was much harder.

"We have the VIP helo at the local airport because we knew you were coming in today," Julian was explaining to Drake. "The rest of—" he glanced at Esly, "—our people are offshore."

Nikita didn't know of an aircraft carrier group in the area. So either a helicopter dock ship or a littoral combat ship was parked outside of territorial waters. Or in Belize's waters, which were less than a hundred kilometers away.

"We'd like to go on a sightseeing tour today," Esly finally spoke up.

She hadn't struck Nikita as being stupid in any way. But she…was teasing Rafe just moments after facing him down.

*Go, Esly.*

"I would so love to see the pretty islands of Roatán and Utila from the skies. I have never seen Honduras from a helicopter."

"Lady," Rafe protested, "you know that we're busy here. Besides, there's a tropical storm coming. It's supposed to stay out to sea, but it's still going to make for some very lumpy air."

Julian caught on immediately of course, but Esly was able to string Rafe along for several more pedantic declarations before he noticed his copilot's big smile and figured it out.

# CHAPTER 24

*D*rake could think of far worse ways to travel than a luxury helicopter flown by two of the best heli-pilots in the military.

Whereas the whole maid-and-butler treatment in a cruise ship's luxury suite was actually creeping him out. It was like everyone was always watching him, the entire ship's complement was—and not just the crew who were paid to look after their rich passengers. Nikita and Zoe's rumor campaign had definitely taken hold and he couldn't go anywhere without being nudged for exciting tales to fill the other passengers' boring lives. Thankfully, there'd only been one other like the banker who had actually tried to hire his clandestine services to deal with a competitor.

Word of the treadmill race, and many hints of the steamy aftermath, had also gotten out. That story didn't appear to need any help from Zoe to spread far and wide. He was propositioned in the dining halls, in the bars, and on the gangway by women ranging from a very sultry Frenchwoman who happened to mention she had just started *lycée* this year (how did the French look so mature when they were just starting high school), to an Italian grand dame offering him the keys to her Amalfi villa at any time—bringing along "the girl" was optional, but only if she liked the *right* kind of games.

Sanctuary had not been achieved by clinging ever more tightly to Nikita. For her part, she merely appeared amused, or perhaps bemused.

He'd taken on a mythic persona and the only ones who could see through it were all on this helicopter. And he wasn't even sure about that much. He often caught Nikita looking at him, just watching, as if she didn't know him at all.

Once again he and Altman were in the back-facing seats.

"Okay, Altman. You've got to admit that we are two damned lucky guys," Drake nodded across the narrow cabin toward the three women.

Altman grunted something that might have been agreement, it might not. What did they do to people when they turned them into SEALs?

Across from them were three very attractive women who couldn't be more different if they tried.

In the middle sat the dark, sultry Esly. She wore the tough-as-nails outfit on a killer body.

Zoe was across from Altman, still just as cute as hell in the outfit she'd been wearing all morning—an airy silk caftan in wild tropical colors that was constantly falling off one of her fine shoulders. The plunging neckline could only be worn by a woman as lean as she was. And it just brushed her knees.

On Nikita it would be...he pictured it...then tried to picture anything else, but couldn't. On Nikita's taller, more powerful build, she'd reveal deep cleavage rather than an expanse of smooth skin. And it would land ever so high on her thigh. That he definitely had to see. He looked at her dressed in a long flowing skirt of woodsy colors, and the simple white blouse that said it wasn't about the clothes at all, it was all about the woman inside them.

And it was true.

They left Roatán and flew sixty kilometers across the storm-dulled Caribbean Sea. After they made landfall they flew the same distance again up into the rugged hills of eastern Honduras. Drake spent much of the flight chatting softly with Altman about just what it had taken for the first woman to become a SEAL. Slowly at first, but warming to the tale of his prize protégé, he revealed just how impossibly high Drake was shooting if he was going after Nikita.

Standard Navy SEAL indoc and testing sounded brutal not even counting the infamous Hell Week that weeded out two-thirds of the candidates to make it even that far. And compared to the DEVGRU SEAL intake pipeline…

*Time to* really *gear up, Duck-man.* Because going for her was Number One on his personal mission list.

---

"It is all so different from the air," Esly sounded deeply perplexed.

Nikita had finally switched seats with Esly so that she could look more easily out the window. Julian had fished out a small pair of binoculars and handed them back for her to use.

The rolling eastern mountains of Sierra Rio Tinto National Park were covered in trees completely foreign to Nikita. Southern Alabama was mostly river flood plains and bottomlands of the Tombigbee and Alabama Rivers. Even Cheaha Mountain, the highest point in the state, topped out at twenty-four hundred feet and had a resort lodge and RV park atop it.

The mountains of eastern Honduras climbed little higher, but they did it in steep slopes covered in dense jungle. Trails were few and roads fewer as they flew further inland.

Nikita had carried out missions in these kinds of jungles and they were hard work. It always seemed she spent half her time trying not to be bitten or even eaten. It was her first trip to Honduras, but she'd been plenty close. She'd had to shoot a variety of fauna: a cougar in Nicaragua, several charging wild boars in Guatemala, and there'd been a time in Panama where it had been touch-and-go as to who got who first—her shooting a Mexican drug lord brokering a major deal or the jaguar that had been stalking her hideout through the long, motionless afternoon.

She didn't like these jungles.

They were following the Sico River up into the hills as well as they could, but it meandered as it flowed, occasionally disappearing entirely in dense growth. The flat light of the overcast sky wasn't helping: hiding instead of revealing terrain and water.

She alternated between looking out over Esly's shoulder and Zoe's.

"You have changed him, you know," Zoe whispered without turning as Julian announced they were crossing from Sierra Rio Tinto to Sierra El Carbón National Park—again. It didn't look any different to her.

"We have gone too far," Esly spoke up. "Make the pilot turn us back. We are very close. I have not been here since my first lover when I was sixteen, but I remember it well. I will know when I see it."

Drake passed Esly's instructions to the pilots and they circled.

"How have I changed him?" Nikita kept her voice low.

"The Drake Roman I know was always a follower. Good at what he does, damn good. Like he's born to it. But it still felt like he was just loafing."

"You have to be better than good to 'loaf' along in this crowd."

Zoe nodded her agreement, "He is. And if you doubt that, look at who one of the 5E's most eligible bachelors is attracted to."

"What…"

Zoe turned, her bright blue eyes only inches away. "You, you goof. Drake Roman is completely and totally gone on you. How many other female SEALs do you see in the military who qualified the hard way? None. Duh! Delta has what, two or three now? That puts you in a very elite category. I don't think he understands yet what it means that he's attracted to such an amazing woman. You really, really make me wish I could be more like you."

Nikita sat back and stared straight ahead. Between Drake's and Altman's seats she had a small view out the forward windshield. So far the flight had revealed more jungle-covered peaks undulating ever higher into the distance. They'd overflown a line of high-power transmission towers leading to a big construction site lower on the river. Now they were headed back that way.

She'd actually been envying Zoe her apparent ease with the world around her and with her own body. Again Nikita faced that strange dichotomy of the SEAL who knew exactly what to do with her body and the woman who didn't have a clue.

Esly and Drake were both leaning forward and looking down at something, probably still trying to trace the elusive river toward the unknown waterfall.

Drake Roman.

Zoe was right. Nikita had always liked him well enough, as much as she ever liked anyone. But now Drake stood out from the crowd. And not just in the ship's dining room, but in the crowd that included two top pilots, and maybe even Luke Altman. There was a focus, a drive that Drake had never revealed before.

Nikita had wondered at Zoe's original selection of each of their roles, placing Drake in the character of Head Mercenary. It was not a selection she ever would have made. Now she couldn't imagine it being anyone else. And if he was leading a contracting firm instead of flying for the 5E, maybe, just maybe she'd be willing to work for him.

Oh god, she was losing her mind!

There was no way she was leaving DEVGRU, not until she was too old to maintain the training level. And certainly not for a merc outfit, not if God herself was in charge.

But Drake was an amazing man to serve with. He hadn't been mad when she'd been injured, he'd been furious. When Rafe had threatened Esly—a team member in only the most tenuous sense—he'd tromped down on it. He commanded loyalty as easily as—

Esly's shout of excitement said that she'd finally spotted what they were looking for.

At the same moment, dead ahead, Nikita saw a telltale spark in the jungle.

# CHAPTER 25

"Incoming!"

Her shout had Rafe slamming the controls in a hard evasion to the north. "Where?"

"Downriver. Range two thousand meters, minus."

As he twisted the helo around and plunged toward the trees, the side view opened to the east. They'd overflown somebody who now was very unhappy about their return.

"I'm guessing that we finally found what we're looking for," Zoe spoke up.

"I'm so thrilled," Altman tone was impossibly drier than usual as he actually teased her back. There was no time to be surprised.

Nikita could see whatever was coming at them still burning fuel against the dark clouds. And it turned!

Not an RPG—rocket propelled grenades didn't have guidance systems. This was a guided munition of some sort, but not a SAM. Surface-to-air missiles were generally supersonic and would have fried their asses already; an American Stinger or Russian Igla hustled along at Mach 2, ten times the speed of a helicopter. From just two thousand meters, they'd have been dead already.

The Bell 429 wasn't a DAP Hawk. There weren't countermeasures. Nothing aboard to return fire.

"It's following," she shouted.

Drake and Esly were now staring at it as well.

As the helicopter twisted down and away, she turned in her seat to follow it but lost it. No more heat trail.

"Too small to show on this radar," Julian called. A civilian Bell's radar was all about not hitting another helicopter or a massive squall line. Actually, their helo was new enough, it should be able to see one of those stupid hobby drones as well.

Which meant whatever was following them was very small.

Rafe began twisting and turning the bird in hopes of losing its track.

"Bank hard right and climb!" Nikita shouted out.

Zoe was forced against her as they carved the turn. Maybe, if her guess was right—

She was looking too high to see the explosion, but she saw the flash coming from close below them.

The helicopter pinged and rattled as shrapnel peppered the helicopter.

There was a sickening twist—the kind that reminded her of other helicopter crashes.

"Someone find me a landing zone," Rafe called out as warning alarms began bleating from the cockpit.

Everywhere Nikita looked—which was a wide range as the helicopter began spinning awkwardly—was jungle. Tall trees and helicopters were a lousy mix. She'd gone down once very memorably in an Alaskan cold-weather training mission and never wanted to do it again. The only reason they hadn't all died had been because they were on the verge of a scheduled night parachute jump and been fully geared up.

Her team made it out, though one lost a foot to a bad tumble and a slice of the rotor blade. The two pilots had died high in the trees.

"Waterfall," Esly called out. "There was a large pool below a waterfall. Would that work?"

"If I can reach it," Rafe banked them carefully back toward where they'd been shot as he bled altitude. They were already below the ridgeline, soon they'd be below the treetops. At least they would be out of the line of fire that way.

"Whoever shot us is going to come looking for us," Drake was looking right at her.

She nodded, exactly her thought. "Julian, do we have a flare gun aboard?"

A moment later, he tossed a plastic case backward between the pilots' seats.

It hit Drake in the head as the helicopter slewed one way, bounced off Altman's lap as it carved the other direction, and Zoe managed to grab it. She popped the latches and turned it to Nikita.

As she was reaching for the flare gun, they almost lost it to a gut-wrenching yaw that meant the helicopter had almost no time left aloft.

"Shrapnel must have caught both the rear rotor and a main blade," Drake shouted to her.

"Perfect!" She managed to grab the bright orange pistol and the three flare cartridges. She shoved one in the gun and the other two deep into her pocket. She then clutched the weapon to her chest with both hands to make sure that she didn't drop it when they impacted. It was the same training that had let her hang on to the beer bottle in the bar fight—never let go of your weapon.

She'd enjoyed that fight.

The trees were now flashing close by either side of the helicopter. If a rotor blade clipped one, they'd be going down hard. *Trust the team. Not in your hands.*

Instead she thought about having a beer and a girl talk in a rowdy bar with Sugar. She actually hoped that she'd have a chance to do that again. She'd bring along Zoe, maybe Esly too and—

A blade caught and the helo twisted hard. Flew backward for a moment, then continued around in a corkscrewing flight.

Trees...

The river running away from them...

More trees…

A massive waterfall towering over a hundred meters above them…

Trees…

Another view downstrea—

They plowed into the water, tail first. A horrendous shearing sound of ripping metal sounded close behind her as the rear rotor disintegrated.

The twist continued, tumbling the helicopter on its side.

The rotors beat water and shattered just as surely as if they'd hit concrete. Out at their tips they were spinning at nearly the speed of sound.

The helo flailed and jolted for a long moment, but the water buffered the motion.

With a last ratcheting grind, the transfer gears sheared. Then the racing turboshaft engines ingested a load of river water and died.

In slow motion, the helo tipped the rest of the way onto its side.

Zoe lay on her and she lay on Esly, their seatbelts only keeping their waists in place.

One heartbeat. Two. Three. The engines gurgled to a shattered halt.

All stable. As a bonus they apparently weren't going to blow up right away. She'd have to send Bell Helicopter a thank you letter.

"Go! Go! Go!" Altman shouted. He opened the high-side door, the downward facing one offered a clear view of rounded river rocks beneath the water.

In moments, they were out. No obvious blood or breaks.

She pointed at the First Aid kit floating in the water and Drake grabbed it as he followed her out.

"Nice landing, Dude," Julian's voice was thick with sarcasm as he climbed out the pilot's door.

Nikita could barely hear him over the roar of the waterfall. Instead of a clear fall, it spilled down over a massive, water-carved rock face thirty meters wide and twenty stories tall. A fine mist of spray filled the air over the broad pool at the base of the fall. Jungle crowded close to all sides. Even taking root up the rocky face to either side of the cascade. It would be a breathtaking view if she had time to admire it.

"Hey," Rafe replied as he crawled out of the cockpit favoring one wrist. "Any landing you can walk away from is a good one."

"You call that good? This helicopter ain't walking away from anything. So who is gonna tell the Army they have to buy a new one? It isn't me, I can tell you that much. The base commander is gonna be so pissed."

"Why?" Drake asked him as he crawled out last after helping Zoe.

"Because we only borrowed it to go to Miami. I sort of didn't bother to tell him we were taking it to Honduras with us. It's his personal bird."

"Okay," Rafe tried to use his bad hand, which wasn't working. He did a tumble and flop into the water, then stood in the waist-deep current. "Then it's definitely you that gets to tell him."

The two of them kept at it as they were splashing toward the shore, though Julian had a solid grip on Rafe's upper arm to guide him along and keep him steady. The river was warm and not moving too quickly here.

She still had the flare gun in her hand.

"Herd them to shore," she shouted at Drake. "And get them behind something solid. Bind Rafe's wrist."

"Yeah, he broke it, just hasn't noticed it yet." He dragged her against him for a quick kiss. "Don't go blowing yourself up. I'll be pissed as hell if you do." Then he headed to shore.

No insistence that he should do this next dangerous part because he was the guy.

Nikita located the cap to the fuel tank. She cracked it loose, and fuel began to spill because of the mostly inverted angle of the helo.

Drake didn't even treat her like an equal.

She checked to make sure everyone was ashore and mostly out of sight. The timing on this was going to be tricky.

He treated her as if she was the DEVGRU warrior and he was the Night Stalker. Even a lot of her teammates didn't do what he'd just done. Drake actually treated her as if she knew what she was doing.

She sure as hell hoped she did.

She popped the fuel cap all the way off and Jet A spilled out, adding a sharp slap of kerosene to the thick moldering jungle and brightness of the fresh water mist. Most of the fuel ran down the hull and into the open passenger bay door. A trickle of it spilled into the river as well.

The shore was too far away to trust that this would work from there. She had to sink the first shot.

She swam halfway toward shore.

No one in sight except for Drake, peeking around the side of a tree.

Nikita stood up, hoped this wasn't the last time she ever saw him, turned, and fired.

## CHAPTER 26

*D*rake barely had time to cry out before Altman grabbed him from behind and dragged him back behind the tree.

Nikita had fired the flare gun nearly point blank into the helicopter's gas-filled rear bay.

Then she'd dropped as if cut down where she stood—and the helicopter exploded.

Bits and pieces of it slashed through the leaves overhead. To either side of the massive tree they were hiding behind, shrapnel zinged by like…like…shrapnel!

Large chunks of helicopter slammed into tree bark and stuck there, quivering with the force of impact. Half of a pilot's seat landed in the brush not half a meter from where Julian was splinting and binding Rafe's wrist.

Then the bits and pieces that had been blown upward began to rain down in a bright patter, landing all around their refuge.

Still Altman wouldn't let him go.

"Goddamn it! She's—"

Altman released him barely in time to save himself a hard elbow to the ribs. A last piece of helicopter, an unidentifiable shred of metal, slid off a higher branch where it had hung for a moment, and disappeared into a bush covered with impossibly blue flowers the size of his head.

Drake struggled back to his feet. The helicopter was shredded; only a few jagged edges of the wreckage stuck out above the water. A large section of the hull, still fiercely on fire, starting bobbing down the river. For a hundred meters downstream, spilled jet fuel burned on the surface, making the center of the river a streamer of flame.

Then, right in front of the conflagration, Nikita rose from the river's depths like one of those James Bond fantasy scenes. The cotton blouse was now sheer over her breasts, her hair slicked back in a wet look that reminded him of the shower they'd shared, and the skirt that clung to her legs was like an artist's afterthought.

She surveyed the burning remains of the helicopter, nodded her head, clearly pleased with herself, and began wading toward shore.

"Shit, woman! Are you okay?" She walked right by him when he tried to lend her a helping hand over the slippery rocks along the shore.

"Sure. I was afraid that if I missed and left a flare burning in the jungle due to a bad shot, they'd see it. These things aren't all that accurate," she held up the stubby orange flare gun. Nikita stepped from the river like a Navy SEAL despite the fact that she looked like a river goddess.

Before he could argue with her sense of urgency, he heard the heavy beat of a helicopter's rotor blades echoing up the valley—maybe two birds. With the roar of the waterfall, it meant the enemy was close.

"Cover our tracks."

Thankfully, between the bare rocks and the soft mat of undergrowth, it was only the work of seconds. Drake dropped dead branches to cover their wet footprints over the rocks and Nikita spread leaves across a muddy patch. They withdrew into the woods only a moment before a pair of helos swung into view far downstream.

"Bury yourselves in case they have infrared."

Drake almost pointed out that the temperature here was at least body heat, maybe hotter by the way he was already sweating, so they wouldn't stand out, but thought better of arguing with a river goddess SEAL.

As he helped scoop branches and dead leaves over other team members, he wondered at his presumption for wanting to be with such a woman. She could have the pick of anyone anywhere. By what earthly reason could he even hope to be with a woman like her?

They slid side by side under their own cover; he made especially sure that her white blouse was well hidden.

Of course he wasn't a goddamn idiot. He was going to stick as long as she'd let him despite his inability to figure out why she let him.

The helos made one high pass, then one of them descended to barely ten meters above the burning wreckage. Bell TwinRangers, painted black with a gold racing stripe and no other insignia.

He could see Nikita reloading the flare gun.

"Don't even think about it!"

"Tempting though, isn't it?" Her smile looked particularly evil.

The TwinRanger hovered not thirty meters away, broadside to them. The cargo bay doors had been removed, making for a large opening that would be an exceptional target. An M240 machine gun was mounted on a swivel and by pure chance was aimed almost directly at them. Yes, it was very tempting. But it would be an easy shot in both directions.

Four-man squad: pilot, copilot, and a pair of gunners. They were mercenary stereotypes right down to black t-shirts and camo pants, black baseball caps, shades, and M16s.

Then he glanced at the second bird still hovering a hundred meters up, near the level of the top of the waterfall.

He nodded upward and Nikita looked aloft.

The second bird had a side-mounted M230—five and a half feet of bad-ass chain gun—and a 7-tube rocket launcher on the other.

"Let's not piss them off, what do you say?"

"Spoilsport!"

He nudged his hip against hers under the foliage, she nudged him back, and he couldn't help smiling. Together they turned back to watch the low-hovering helicopter's inspection of their crash. It would have helped if there'd been a body or two, but he'd rather his team stayed alive.

Apparently the lack of any bodies on fire didn't bother the bad guys for long, as the helicopter pulled up and away after less than twenty seconds.

No one moved until they were well clear.

"Well, that was fun," Drake sat up shedding leaves and branches. He brushed the worst of it out of Nikita's hair as others emerged.

"What the hell was that?" Rafe's arm was now bound against his chest in a sling.

"Raytheon Pike by how it behaved." It was the only weapon Nikita could think of that fit the performance parameters.

"Shit!" Altman was pissed. "That's leading edge. We only got those ourselves at the beginning of the year. If this GSI guy wasn't already dead, I'd fry his ass for selling those to unfriendly powers."

Drake hadn't even heard of a Pike.

Nikita took pity on him. "It's a sweet little laser-guided missile about the length of your arm that can be fired out of a handheld grenade launcher. Good to about two thousand meters. Proximity fuze. I'd hoped that last bank and climb would fool it."

"Might have," Julian agreed, "if we had a Black Hawk. Seven people is the TwinRanger's payload limit, plus it's hot so the air is thin, and our rate-of-climb sucked. Nice call, Nikita, even if it didn't work."

"Working enough. We're still alive."

"What now?" Rafe's voice said that the pain was beginning to register. Nothing stronger than aspirin in the First Aid kit.

"Did anyone bring lunch?"

Everyone turned to look at Drake like he was insane.

"Either we can hike out through fifty kilometers of jungle filled with bad guys without a map or," he pulled out his waterproof satellite phone, "we can wait until dark and call in the rest of the crew to come fetch us."

"Then's there's the third option," Nikita spoke softly.

$\mathcal{N}$ikita would have preferred to go alone, but Drake had insisted on going with her when she'd come up with her third option.

Altman hadn't shut him down. Instead he'd done his zero-expression face, leaving the decision up to her. Drake had proved his skills, but she was worried about his stealth—that took a lot of practice. Still, a second set of eyes would be useful.

To avoid any possible booby traps set in the jungle, they slipped a couple of logs into the river and then floated down the current with them.

"I imagined going swimming with you," Drake floated along beside her. "There was this bikini in the shop window that—"

"Wasn't going to happen," Nikita peeked over her log to check for any approaching rapids.

"But you're a SEAL."

"In a wet suit armed to the teeth. Not in a Drake-fantasy string bikini."

"Well, you in a soaking wet cotton blouse was pretty damned fantastic."

Nikita hadn't thought about that. She should have put on a bra this morning, but again, the unbuttoned look had seemed to fit her role better.

They drifted half a kilometer before Drake spoke again.

"Any crocodiles around here?"

"They're lousy at climbing waterfalls and we flew over several others on our way here."

"Exactly my point," Drake looked side to side fearfully. "That means that any that made it this far up river would be like the Special Operations Forces of the crocodilian empire."

Nikita palmed a faceful of water at Drake, who laughed.

Their laughter didn't carry them very far downstream. They came around a corner and quickly swam to the northern shore by mutual consent.

On the southern shore was a massive fence topped with multiple coils of razor wire. They dug in and watched.

Beyond the fence, the jungle had been sheared off—clear-cut for the construction site they'd flown over on the way out. The clearing stretched for hundreds of acres smack in the middle of a national park.

There was a well-worn pair of ruts along the inside of the fence line. They didn't have to wait long to see who was using it. More heavily-armed, black-t-shirt-and-camo guys cruised by in a black Toyota Tundra. They wore dark sunglasses and serious expressions.

"Pros," Drake whispered. He glanced at his watch so that he could measure the time between patrols. Good idea. "All look like Americans with beards. These are far bigger guys than the natives we saw in Roatán."

"Fucking mercs," Nikita whispered back. "When we circled back to find the waterfall, they must have decided that we were showing too much interest in their compound and it was best to take us out."

"Tourist helicopter lost without a trace. And in other news at eleven..." Drake intoned.

"Yeah. Exactly the sort of contract you'd expect a merc to take."

"Can you really picture J-dawg or Sugar taking this deal though?"

Nikita glared at the compound for a long moment, hating it. If someone gave her a B-2 stealth bomber, she would carpet bomb the place. But...she...liked the Titan people; it was hard not to like J-dawg when he was toting around a young Afghan girl on his shoulders.

"Hey, Nikita! Shake it off. No emotion, remember."

"I'm not shooting right now. I don't even have my damned rifle because of ship security. I *want* my rifle." And that's when she heard it in her own voice. "Shit! How can you stand to be around me, Drake? I'm a screwed-up mess."

"Yeah! But you're my *favorite* screwed-up mess."

Nikita had to think about it a bit. It wasn't like she had a long list of people she was close to, but that didn't make it any less true, "And you're *my* favorite mess, Duck-man."

"There!" Drake pointed. A rising wind out of the east had swung the trees aside for a moment. A three-story, steel-framework guard tower came into view for a moment. Once they'd spotted it, it was easy enough to see. Nikita tried to gauge how far they'd floated downstream from the waterfall. Close enough to two kilometers to answer the question.

"It fits. That's probably where they fired from. But what didn't they want us to see?"

Nikita pulled out the binoculars that Esly had held on to through the crash. She scanned the compound carefully, softly listing off what she saw.

"Five big excavators. Half dozen dump trucks. None moving. One of the earth movers is a burned carcass. I don't see anybody working. I don't even see any buildings. Nothing but a wasteland of churned soil." Which was a metaphor for her emotions that there wasn't a chance she'd be considering.

"Look at the hills."

She turned her binoculars but all she saw was jungle.

"No, just the general topography."

Nikita lowered the binocs, but still didn't get what Drake was on about.

"The current Honduran government approved a lot of new dam building, a whole lot of it. They did it without environmental impact statements and ignored a lot of agreements with towns and local tribes. There have been pitched battles back and forth ever since. They've got murder squads hunting down environmentalists—one article said that was now the job in the country with the shortest life expectancy. Huh!"

"What?"

"I didn't pay attention to where all the bad blood was. This must be the spot."

"Our unfriendly boys in black." Sometimes talking with Drake was almost like talking to herself. They simply thought the same.

"Probably."

"What about the hills?" But he saw different things than she did. Patterns. And she was learning that he was good at it.

"See how the rise on either side of the river sweeps back into ridgelines? It would be an ideal spot for a dam. This whole valley would be filled, right back to the waterfall and probably over it."

"Okay. Dam going in. Unhappy environmentalists. Mercenary kill squad…" she couldn't quite put it together.

"Not only set up by GSI, but probably bankrolled by them. Now someone wants to cut them out of the loop. Esly's buddy Daylin and his boys were brought in to clear away the upper-level contractors as thoroughly as the environmentalists."

They watched as a helicopter came in from the south.

"More gun boys?"

"No," they were right at the limit of what she could see even with the binocs, "white shirts and black slacks. Suits."

"We need to know what's going on."

"No we don't. Just clear out the mercs."

The truck went by again. They were so stereotypical mercs that he couldn't tell if it was the same truck or not. He checked his watch: twenty minutes on the dot.

Nikita watched them go by and groused again about not having her rifle.

"They can always grow more mercs. We need to cut off the head of the snake, not just some of its scales. I need an in."

As if in answer to his prayer, Drake's phone rang. It was loud enough to make both him and Nikita jump, but far quieter than the river splashing over the nearby rocks between them and the compound.

"Mr. Roman?" It took him a moment to recognize the voice of the ship's hotel manager because it was so unexpected.

"Norma?"

"Yes, I'm glad I reached you. I have a very insistent party on the line trying to reach the occupants of Suites 612. I thought that might be of interest to you."

"Please patch them through," he considered warning her that she'd be safer if she didn't listen in, but that would be pointless and outside his control. Instead, "Be aware that I may lie a little."

She laughed nervously, then there was a loud click, "Here's your party."

There was no secondary click of her leaving the circuit.

"Daylin?" a male voice asked.

"No longer a factor," Drake lowered his tone more than normal, trying to sound nastier. It sounded good to him. Like Arnold Schwarzenegger's, "I'll be back."

Nikita leaned in so that their shoulders were touching. He tipped the phone so they could both hear, but he didn't quite dare to put it on speakerphone.

"Buck Baer?" The voice was disdainful. "I thought we made it clear that we were done with your services."

"He also is no longer a factor."

"Then who am I speaking with?"

They exchanged names and there was a short pause...perhaps the length of a quick Internet search.

"Mr. Roman. What is your intent here?" Apparently the disinformation plan was solidly in place as now Franshesco Gutierrez's tone was very cautious.

"I, shall we say, *acquired* all assets of Global Securities International. I am interested in continuing any mutually beneficial business relationships, but under my purview, *not* the former management's." All of his practice over the last days aboard ship at meals and in bars was paying off—he managed to say it with a straight face, or at least with a straight tone over the phone.

He made a face at Nikita, who gave him a thumbs up.

"Perhaps we could meet somewhere quiet this afternoon to…"

"I'm presently out on a private excursion."

"Ah, yes. Daylin did mention that you were traveling with your mistress before we, uh, lost touch with him."

Drake let all of the cold chill that washed over him spill into his voice. "Yours is not DR, Inc.'s only investment in the area. I can—" Nikita put a hand on his arm to warn him off.

*I can disassemble you far faster than GSI put you together.*

"I can meet you for drinks at eight this evening?" Drake wished that he had a cellphone tracker so that he could see if the person he was speaking with was presently at the construction site just across the river.

"That is…possible."

"Good. I will be at the front gate of the El Carbón dam site at that time."

"That won't—"

"As you know, I'm on a ship that leaves port later tonight. That is the only time I can spare, and I always do my own site risk assessments myself. I will meet you there. End of conversation."

There was a long pause. "I shall look forward to that. Ask for me; I will be there." And he was gone.

"Norma?"

"Ye-es?" the hotel manager's stutter of embarrassment at being caught was sweet.

"Could you please have my white Armani and a nice summer dress for Nikita delivered with a rental car, preferably an up-armored SUV, to the town of El Carbón by nightfall?"

"Hey," Nikita frowned and Drake ignored her.

"I can take care of that for you, Mr. Roman." Much more in her comfort zone.

Nikita nudged her shoulder sharply against his in protest.

"Also a set of casual dark clothes from Nikita's wardrobe and…" he drew it out just to make Nikita crazy, which was clearly working. "Her black rifle case."

Nikita's smile finally made him able to picture the young girl reading her Dr. Seuss, suddenly happy to have her toys. She must have been a serious handful as a kid.

*Couldn't just fall for some timid, stay-at-home babe, could you, Duck-man?*

There was no response over the phone.

"Norma?"

"I will…take care of it personally, Mr. Roman."

"Thank you, Norma. It would probably be best if you made the car reservation in the name of GSI's former chief, Buck Baer."

"Mr. Roman?" her tone shifted enough that he knew what was coming next and didn't force her to ask the question.

"Yes, Arthur was actually very helpful today and appears to be clear of any intentional wrongdoing."

"Oh, thank goodness," the relief in her voice spoke volumes.

"I have to ask," and Nikita's look said he shouldn't, but it was too late to stop now. "You and Arthur?"

"He isn't the most…impressive of men," her voice grew softer than he'd yet heard, or ever expected to hear. "But he is a good man despite that and he's being very good to me. I'm glad he didn't do anything to get himself in trouble."

"He didn't," Drake couldn't think of what else to say. His parents had an A-plus marriage, as did a few military couples he worked with, but he didn't know many others who did. "Please keep who we are under wraps until after we're gone."

"Of course, Mr. Roman," and the hotelier was back. "I'll now see to everything."

He hung up and looked at his watch.

"Six hours until sunset. Oh, what shall we do with the time?"

"Hike back upstream without getting ourselves killed, bitten, or poisoned," Nikita eased back into the jungle away from the camp.

"Spoilsport."

---

*No,* Nikita told herself, *not a spoilsport. Sensible.*

Sensible because she'd wanted to have groaning sex right there beneath the eyes of the watchtower. Because she wanted to lose herself in his arms and not just for an hour or a day.

They clambered over tall roots that splayed in all directions. They backtracked around patches of foliage too dense to penetrate and jumped narrow, steep canyons carved by rushing streams heading down to the river.

What had been a twenty-minute float was a two-hour battle of hard labor to return through the fading sunlight that slipped past the high, leafy canopy and dappled the jungle floor. By the end of the journey, the sun was lost behind the heavy gray overcast.

Once they rejoined the rest of the team, the planning began.

As with almost everything else on this trip, Nikita decided that her role in the plan they put together completely sucked.

# CHAPTER 28

The major sent out the two Little Bird helicopters to extract them from the twilit jungle.

Or to at least move around the pieces on the board.

Drake could only smile as Nikita kept griping about not going with Commander Altman, but it was clear that her place had to be at Drake's side. Besides, if ever there was a one-man army for a special assignment, Drake knew that Luke Altman was it.

Then their Little Bird, nearly as silent as the night birds whose calls filled the forest, set him and Nikita down on the road a half kilometer outside El Carbón. He enjoyed the stroll through the descending darkness with Nikita. It was easy to imagine walking like this with her, making it a regular part of what they did together, talking about not much of anything.

He told her about his big sister, who stood five inches shorter than he did and just how much that continued to make her crazy.

She told him about the life with her mother before the Curtis Contracting debacle had shattered her family. Even back then it had been mostly just the two of them as her father was always away on "assignment." Yet she'd still turned out to be Daddy's girl, mostly interested in the shooting and hiking.

The wind, which had buffeted the Little Bird, was now building through the high trees, rattling the leaves together almost as loudly as the various birdcalls. Whatever they were, they weren't chickadees or cardinals. There was a moving cacophony of clicks, buzzes, throaty rattles, and other birdlike noises, warning of their progress along the darkened road—they certainly didn't sound like any birds from New England or even Alabama.

The small packs they'd been handed during the brief flight had lightened rapidly as they each drank several bottles of water and ate two meals' worth of rations.

By the time they reached the village, lit only by a few stray indoor lights, he wished he'd thought to grab a flashlight. The "main high-way" through the region had turned into an agility test of stumbling among unseen potholes.

Their rental was waiting—and it had gathered a large circle of gawkers in the small town. No wonder. It was a town with only three buildings that were two stories high; the others were better than shacks, but not by much. Donkey carts, not cars, were the standard.

And there, in the center of town—as defined by the tiny cluster of buildings huddled together along the road—sat a shining black Toyota Land Cruiser. He and Nikita picked up their own following as well, mostly children eager to see the two white people who had walked into town along a road that stretched empty for over twenty kilometers before the next community, farther up into the interior.

Behind the Land Cruiser, a small white pickup was parked with two men sitting on the tailgate.

"Senor Baer?" The rounder of the two men struggled to his feet and asked.

"*Si*," Drake nodded, hitting another third of his Spanish. He only remembered at the last moment that he'd decided to keep posing as GSI so that his own name didn't appear on any paper trail in Honduras.

The man replied with a long fluid cadence of which Drake didn't catch a single word.

Much to the man's consternation, Nikita was the one who

answered with something that might have been questions or might have been music. He was going to have to learn the language just so that he could listen to her speak it so beautifully.

The man handed her the keys and a card and looked relieved to be rid of it.

"*Bueno,*" Nikita finally finished and turned to Drake. "He says that this is an armored version to B6+ standards. That covers us through all the 5.56 mm ammo and most of the 7.62, up to armor-piercing. Our clothes and gear are inside. We simply call this number and tell him where the vehicle is when we're done with it and they will fetch it back."

"Wonder what the insurance waiver is on this thing. Norma done good. Remind me to tip her well."

"Let's just be glad that J-dawg is paying for it, both the rental and the massive tip."

"Roger that. *Gracias,*" he used up the last third of his vocabulary on the two men. They drove away as fast as if there was going to be a gun battle right here in the middle of El Carbón. Unlikely, as they had gathered quite a crowd of locals by that point.

"I'd be more comfortable if we got out of town first." She went straight to the driver's door.

He thought it was amusing, until he saw the puzzled look on the crowd's faces. In this culture, the man would always be the one to drive. He stepped up and plucked the keys from her hand.

"But—"

"You're messing with my macho, woman." Her glare as she circled to the other side warmed his heart.

---

NIKITA HAD WANTED to go straight to her tactical clothing. Norma had even packed her boots and she was going to kiss the hotelier the next time she saw her.

"No," Drake had insisted as they changed by the soft wash of the dome light spilling out the back of the SUV on an empty stretch of dark, dirt one-lane. "We have an image to maintain. And you're the surprise."

That's why she hated her role in this. There was only so far she was willing to compromise.

Before putting on the dress, she strapped a Glock 19 on one thigh, her knife with three spare magazines on the other, and slipped the Glock 36 subcompact and its spares into a purse that Zoe had made her buy because there were no pant legs to hide an ankle piece. Now she felt halfway to human. If only she could think of a way to slip five feet of sniper rifle under her clothes...

Roman had pulled on a fresh t-shirt and slacks, strapped on an ankle piece (which she envied), and shoulder-holstered a pair of Glocks under his jacket. Then he leaned back against the open door and watched her. Steady, calm, and armed to the teeth—he looked so damn good. His smile said he knew it, too.

No.

His smile said she was standing naked except for her underwear and her weapons in the middle of a dark road in a hazardous country.

"Damn but you're a picture, woman."

"I'm not a fantasy poster-babe."

"You sure as hell are. What I wouldn't give for a camera at the moment."

"That would be good. It would give me something to break over your head, Duck-man." How was she supposed to keep herself from being dazzled by him? Nobody ever saw her the way Drake did. She almost wished that Norma had packed that ridiculous bit of La Perla frippery just so that she could pull it on at this moment and then tell him he wasn't allowed to touch her.

"If only we had the time," his voice was soft as he reached out and brushed a thumb down her cheek. Not her exposed breasts, not her bare waist, but her cheek.

She struggled with the unexpected tenderness as she wrestled the dress on over her head and her weapons. It made her feel...what? Desirable? Drake's every glance and gesture made her feel that.

Exposed? Absolutely, as if he could see parts of inside her that even she couldn't.

But there was something else.

She turned her back to him, "Zip me." What stupid men had designed dresses so that a woman needed a man to get her in and out of them? Bastards.

Roman zipped her in, then slipped his hands around her waist and held her tightly—so tightly it was even harder to breathe than the dress' tight waistband made it.

Wanted? There was no question that Drake wanted her. Nor that she wanted him. She could finally accept that a man had gotten so far past her shields that she wanted him deeply.

"When we get out of this, Nikita, we're going somewhere and you're mine. Completely mine. You hear?" His voice was intense and his arms squeezed even tighter about her abdomen as he buried his face in her hair.

That's when she knew what Drake made her feel.

Loved. Sugar and Zoe had both said Drake was "gone" on her. She hadn't understood. Maybe they hadn't even understood, not fully.

He wasn't *gone* on her, he was in love. That was something she truly wasn't ready for. But the words that came out weren't careful or a rebuff. They were soft and...feminine.

"Yes, Drake. Completely."

Now she had a new question: why was that answer *not* scaring the crap out of her?

# CHAPTER 29

"You touch her and you're a dead man," Drake kept his voice low and calm.

The gate into the construction site was reminiscent of an army base guard station. Multiple stops, alternating concrete barriers forcing a slow, weaving drive to enter, massive floodlights fighting back the jungle darkness. And at the far end of the gauntlet, they'd been asked to climb out of their car.

When the guards went to inspect the inside, he'd hit the remote door lock on the key fob. The SUV had sealed itself with a smug click from all four doors and the rear hatch. There were items in there, like Nikita's rifle, that were best kept out of sight.

That hadn't exactly set the tone for a friendly welcome.

Then one of the guards had slung his rifle over his shoulder and moved in to frisk Nikita.

"I won't repeat myself. Do *not* touch her."

The guard glared at him, then made a point of looking at his three companions, all armed with M16A4s before sneering at him. The guard took the last step and raised both hands chest high to make it clear exactly where he was going to start patting her down.

"I tried to warn you."

When the man glanced his way, Nikita shifted into action.

In a blur Drake could barely follow, she pulled the man's KA-BAR knife out of his own sheath. With it, she slashed the carry strap on his M16. Snagged it by the grip with one hand as it dropped and aimed it at the guard who had been standing well back so that he could provide cover protection for the three closer guards.

She heaved his long knife, point first, into the ground, drawing everyone's attention down.

Then, on the upswing of her arm, she yanked the guard's SIG Sauer P226 out of his holster. She continued the upward motion and rammed the big pistol up under his chin hard enough to make him squeak.

While everyone was watching her in surprise, Drake pulled his pair of Glocks and rested the barrels on the temples of the two guards closest to him.

All four gate guards froze as if cast in concrete, their eyes went wide.

"Nikita, can you please tell me why people just don't listen to a simple warning?"

"Lack of education, Mr. Roman."

"You," Drake nudged one of them hard enough with his pistol to draw blood that began to drip down his temple. "Give us one good reason not to continue the lesson." He'd finally found a problem with the Glock: because it had no safety, there was nothing to make a threatening click when he flicked it off.

"Because the tower guard will drop you where you stand," he'd gotten over his surprise and shifted to anger. The tower they'd observed from across the river, looming above the front gate, had actually blocked their view of the gate itself. He wished it was still afternoon and he was once again lying close beside Nikita under the trees. Now the rising wind blocked any sound of the nearby river.

"Really, that's your answer? Whichever one of us the tower guard targets first, the other one will still have time to kill at least two of you, but probably all four. You've got to do better than that."

A Mercedes sedan rolled toward them from inside the compound.

It didn't come from a distance—one moment it wasn't there, the next it was already in motion with its lights on. Whoever it was, they'd been waiting outside the floodlit perimeter to see how the first meeting played out.

The sedan stopped twenty meters back and a man in a suit stepped out of the driver's side.

"What did I tell you boys about these people being guests?" He called out as he got close.

"They wouldn't allow us to inspect their car," the guard facing Nikita's M16 from too close a distance didn't sound happy about it.

"Or check them for weapons," the man with the dribble of blood easing down his temple was still pissed.

Drake ignored them and focused on the man. "Mr. Gutierrez, I presume?"

"Franshesco, please, Mr. Roman."

"Then I'm Drake."

Franshesco. One of the most prominent members of the Gutierrez family, with dirty fingers in far more than large construction contracts. They also controlled shipping, a small airline that specialized in moving very questionable cargo from Colombia to Mexico, and much more. He was into everything ugly in the country.

"What do I do with these?" Drake nudged his pistol once more against the man's bleeding temple, earning him a hiss of anger.

"I couldn't care. They're replaceable."

"Hear that, boys?" he asked the guards. "Next time you're looking for work, contact Drake Roman, Inc. On second thought, don't. We're looking for people with skills." Then he made a show of reholstering his weapons slowly as if he had no worries in the world about the two angry and armed men standing less than a meter from him. It was a calculated risk but he figured that it made him look more like an arrogant mercenary. That, and Nikita was still armed to the teeth.

As a kid he'd always wanted to be a Wild West cowboy. Not cowboys and Indians or Pony Express, but a gunslinger on the streets of Tombstone, Arizona, had sounded good—sometimes on the side of the law, sometimes not, but always *The Blazing Guns of Justice.* It had sounded good to a kid anyway. That's how he'd gotten into acting, now that he thought of it. Funny that this was the first time he'd ever played the role of gunslinger. There was a certain satisfaction to closing that circle.

Now he just had to survive that closure.

He let Franshesco Gutierrez come to him. His handshake was good and his smile appeared genuine on his dark face, but unlike Arthur, Drake would bet that the guy was a good enough actor to make any impression he chose.

His suit had the perfect fit of custom-made and the watch was a very distinctive U-Boat, recognizable at ten paces away and worth over seven grand. He had the broad shoulders of a military man, but his walk said businessman with a passion for fitness. He was the sort of man who would pack a .44 Magnum long-barrel revolver because that's what Clint Eastwood had carried as *Dirty Harry,* the renegade cop.

The man was as smooth as an upper-crust Boston banker and probably just as trustworthy.

"This is my assistant, Nikita."

She offered him a tight nod, more of a twist of her neck, but hadn't yet eased off on her stance.

He recalled the sexy look of the outspoken Sugar, dressed in leather and firing a sniper rifle in an Alabama field. It was a good memory. But nothing compared to the quiet woman who had just disarmed a pair of heavily-loaded mercenaries while wearing a white Marc Jacobs summer dress with a flowing skirt spangled with blue flowers. She was spectacular...and still not moving.

"We'll consider this lesson taught," he said softly.

———

NIKITA COULDN'T LET GO.

These were exactly the sort of men Curtis had always hired.

Had her father been one of these? Was that *all* he'd been? Big, tall, Chas "Lumberman" Hayward—so called because he was built on the scale of Paul Bunyan—had always been her idol. But what if?

What if his refusal to speak at the end hadn't been to protect her, but instead had been the same raw, stubborn pride these idiots were portraying? Even the guard, up on his toes to ease the pressure of where she was jamming the barrel under his chin, was still glaring at her in fury at being outmaneuvered.

Had her father been so shallow? A part of her knew that for truth. He had only done two tours in Afghanistan, never climbing out of regular Army. Then a merc outfit. Not one of the good ones, which she finally had to admit existed as she knew which select few of them were good.

She finally looked across at Drake. A gunner for the Night Stalkers 5E. The 160th required five years in the service before you could even apply. He'd flown with the 10th Mountain Division for six, then fought his way up to the most elite helicopter company of them all.

Would her father have stood in front of Esly to protect her from Rafe's suspicions?

Would her dead fiancé?

Those questions earned her a *slim maybe* and a *not a chance.*

Drake *was* the man who a young Nikita had thought her father and Barry were. That she had struggled all her life to be worthy of. She'd fought merely to win the admiration of a dead father. Yet by doing so, she'd won the love of a true warrior.

These two guards in her sights—over-armed, over-arrogant—didn't deserve to walk the same dirt as...

"Nikita?" Drake's soft call was like a slap of reality.

She thumbed the magazine releases, dropping them out of both weapons, cleared the chambers, and let both the rifle and the handgun drop in the dirt. Turning her back on the men, she stepped over to stand close beside Drake. She didn't take his hand, because it would slow down their reaction time.

He didn't reach for her either, though under any other circumstances he always reached out for her when she was close. At first it had been strange; now she missed the simple intimacy.

But there was no question that this was where she belonged, standing side by side with him. In that moment she knew that she'd never find a better place to be.

"Perhaps, Franshesco," Drake continued smoothly as if she wasn't assimilating a new reality for her life, "you can offer us a tour of the situation before we discuss whether we can benefit one another."

"Why certainly," and he began leading them toward his Mercedes.

"Let's take our vehicle," Drake turned for the armored Toyota Land Cruiser. The safety of the steel box was a good tactical advantage and also a good reminder to get her head back in the game.

The first thing Nikita did after being put in the back seat behind Franshesco was to pull her purse weapon and aim it through the seat at his heart. She'd wager that when they'd armored the vehicle, they hadn't loaded up the seat backs. There was something slippery about him that she didn't trust at all.

***

DRAKE WASN'T sure quite what had come over Nikita. Whatever the reason for the change, it had been amazing to watch. The guard who she'd disarmed had been so angry that Drake had been sure it was going to end in blood. The guard's blood.

Then, when she cleared and dumped his weapons in the dirt and turned away from him, he'd deflated like a popped balloon. Drake actually had to pull the Toyota around him as he continued to stand there with two firearms, two magazines, and a knife scattered about his feet. If they came back this way, Drake was glad that they'd be doing it in a vehicle rated safe to higher than an M16's ammunition.

As he glanced that way, he noted Nikita's position, with a gun to the back of Franshesco Gutierrez's seat. Whatever had changed in her, she hadn't lost her focus. She was as much telling him as threatening Gutierrez: *I don't trust this man.*

He heard her loud and clear; neither did he.

"There isn't much to see here, Mr. Roman." He pointed for Drake to follow the perimeter road, the headlights slashing narrow paths through the darkness. "We are having problems with the locals, but nothing we can't handle."

"What are you doing about the European banks pulling twenty-four million euros in funding off the project? I don't think that Sino-hydro will continue building your dam without being paid. Also, I don't see that you have enough long-term collateral to offer them for the Chinese banks to step in. Your political environment is too unstable—they are notoriously conservative investors." That accounted for most of the article he'd read about the murders of two leading environmentalists only a week apart. He'd never thought he'd use those boring Boston-society parties that his father's parents had dragged him to, but without them he wouldn't have understood the financial implications and maneuvering. Apparently everything had a reason if he could only find it.

"We will find other funding," but Gutierrez didn't sound happy about it, perhaps his first honest emotion.

"In the meantime, your investments sit idle. I see that you have cleared the construction area, but have done minimal work since then."

"We are simply assuring the safety of our investments to date so that they will be ready as soon as additional financing is obtained."

Meanwhile, Drake was observing what he could. The perimeter

fence, a work of military beauty near the main gate, rapidly tapered to little more than coils of razor wire as it ran along the deeper jungle. That explained the frequent perimeter patrols. Out here, eyes watched him from the forest. The headlights revealed a deer and a few specimens that looked like furry pigs. A flock of white bats flitted across the beam of his lights but were abruptly batted aside by a blast of wind. Didn't they know a storm was coming?

He reminded himself that the guard tower had been well enough armed to take out their helicopter from two kilometers away. Four or five guard towers could cover the whole area of the construction site...but he didn't see another tower as they drove. Security was a stupid place to cut expenses.

That told him a lot about Franshesco Gutierrez. Not only wasn't he military, but he probably didn't listen much to his security advisors. Not to Buck Baer while he'd been alive nor whoever was on site now. Gutierrez was removed enough from the day-to-day operation to be worried only about the money.

Drake knew in that moment that Gutierrez was going to find out what Drake knew and then do his best to get rid of them permanently. Drake Roman, Inc. wasn't being considered for anything. Instead they were being assessed for what scale of threat he represented.

No joke about the storm coming. Stray branches and leaves blew past his windscreen. When he could see the jungle, the trees were swaying heavily in the gusts.

So Drake kept the conversation light and matter-of-fact as they cruised the perimeter fence.

He had most of what he needed to know. Security was mostly concentrated at the point of entry and at least one alpha target was on site, sitting right now in his vehicle. Drake checked the odometer, had to remember it was in kilometers, and decided that the patrol's timing was correct for a single Toyota constantly driving the perimeter. There was bound to be at least one more vehicle somewhere, but not out on patrol.

No, taking out the mercenaries wasn't the challenge. The problem was Gutierrez and the other suits who had arrived on the helicopter this afternoon. How to remove them without just dropping a bomb on their heads.

He knew that the third helo was still here because the first call he'd made once they'd retreated into the jungle this afternoon was to Zoe's boss, Sophie Garcia, back at the 5E base on Fort Rucker. She had the Avenger drone aloft and on station above the construction site in under three hours. The clouds from the approaching storm had blocked the view, but they didn't slow down her radar in the slightest.

She'd reported two armed helos and one unarmed, all on the ground in the center of the site, well clear of the perimeter. But everywhere Sophia had looked, there were still no buildings.

He had to solve that first.

---

Nikita listened to the conversation, but couldn't make any sense of it. It was as if Drake really was looking to turn this into a serious business discussion. He acted as if the clock wasn't ticking and he had all the time in the world.

"You want to add three more towers, though I'd recommend five. I can source the steel for you. Your best price elsewhere minus ten percent."

"I notice your boys are still using the M16A4s. You should set them up with something decent. You know that the US military has almost completely phased them out."

"Your outer layer security is fixable, but it's only single tier. I'd suggest at least two more layers if you're having the kind of issues you've mentioned."

He offered a new earthmover at cost when their headlights lit up the burned-out one. "Engine fire," Gutierrez had explained, not that she believed him—it was scorched from one end to the other.

It was as if Drake was commenting on every single piece of their security. Then she realized that's *exactly* what he was doing. They had each taken an encrypted radio from the Little Bird. She'd tucked hers in the rifle case because there was nowhere to hide it on a dress. But

Drake must have locked a frequency onto transmit and had just given a running narration to the rest of the team still aloft.

It gave her the creeps because it was shades of the militia that had tortured her father and Barry to death on an open frequency. But it also made her want to kiss Drake, the Duck-man was as sneaky as a DEVGRU SEAL.

Finally they dropped Gutierrez off near a small hut. Close by was a pair of Toyota pickups, another Mercedes, and the three helicopters. There was no way the people needed to man them would all fit in that shack.

That they weren't invited in was a very bad sign.

"Are you sure I can't run you out to your Mercedes at the gate, Franshesco? We are headed that way, after all."

"No, Drake," all Mr. Bonhomie. "I'll have one of the boys fetch it for me. I have some business I need to take care of here. We will definitely be in touch. Thank you so much for coming to Honduras and introducing yourself."

They appeared to shake hands sincerely. Nikita climbed into the front seat, keeping her sidearm ready, out of sight behind the still-open passenger door.

The instant the doors closed, Nikita practically shouted, "What the hell, Roman?"

He just stared out the window at the shack as Gutierrez went inside.

"Drake?"

"They're set up underground. These guys are ready for a siege. They're dug in."

"Then we have to dig them out."

"Or entice them. Too bad they're going to try and kill us first."

That was news to her. "Any time soon?"

"Not sure," Drake dropped the Land Cruiser into gear and turned for the main gate. "But I'd say yes. They don't want Drake Roman, Inc. any more than they wanted GSI. They think that hired guns equal security."

Nikita pulled the side lever and laid her seat down so that she could crawl into the back.

"Where are you going?"

"No chance in hell am I gonna die while wearing a goddamn dress."

Drake's chuckle made her smile…until she tried to figure out how to pull down the zipper on the back of her dress by herself.

CHAPTER 31

rake stared at the gate from a few hundred meters out.

"They're going to kill us sooner than I thought."

Nikita slid back into the front seat. He hadn't seen her looking like this since the Philippines. Camo pants and jacket, boots, and enough magazines of ammo on her vest to stop a small army—perhaps even a mid-sized one as she also had her long Tac-50 sniper rifle out of its case and propped in the foot well.

"There's the lady I fell for. Wondered where you'd gone."

"I got tangled up in some idiot he-man's idea of a wardrobe. Won't happen again so I hope you enjoyed it." He could easily hear her smile in the dark.

She shoved something in his lap.

"Here's your jacket, unless you want to be an Armani-white target."

A blast of dirt whipped against the side of the SUV, rattling it loudly, though the armored Toyota was too heavy to sway in the gust of wind. The storm was almost here.

He changed into the darker clothing as he continued to watch out the windshield.

Drake had doused the lights on the Land Cruiser the moment the glow of the main gate's floodlights came into view. Now they were parked atop a small clear-cut rise, looking down at their welcoming committee. The security was outlined in a circle of light that had been punched into the jungle's darkness.

The four guards all had their M16s off their shoulder straps and in their hands. He only saw one other up in the guard tower. They weren't watching the gate. Instead, they were all facing into the compound, waiting for his arrival, not knowing he was already here—in range of their weapons but hidden by the darkness. A distant crack of lightning said that ploy wasn't going to work much longer.

He turned on the windshield wipers as the first of the rain started to fall.

When someone knocked on the window, he nearly leapt out of his clothes. He risked turning on the dash lights. There was just enough glow to light Luke Altman's smiling face.

Drake rolled down his window, the only one that still operated after armoring. The fresh smell of rain washed in. He could feel the red dust of the Honduran soil being knocked down. Soon it would be slick and muddy, but after most of a day and an evening in the jungle, it was a relief.

"Hey, Altman."

"Hey yourself. Nikita, nice to see you in proper clothes again."

"Asshole," Nikita replied cheerfully.

"So, looks like they're waiting for you."

"Looks like," Drake agreed.

"I might have an idea on that."

Less than a minute later they were ready.

"Do it," Altman slapped him on the shoulder.

But Drake hesitated. He wasn't sure exactly why at first, but then he focused on what his instincts had seen before his thoughts did.

The every-twenty-minute patrol. He glanced at the dashboard clock.

If they were on schedule…

He waited. No one commented on it. They simply waited in the rain along with him, trusting whatever was making him hesitate.

A minute later a black Toyota pickup was coming along the fence line, its lights refracting high off the raindrops before it fully came into view. The two guys in back were hunkered down in ponchos, not even pretending to look around them.

Drake estimated the timing for both his SUV and their truck to arrive at the gate at the simultaneously.

"Now!" He dropped the Land Cruiser into gear, checked one more time that the steering wheel was well tied off, then flicked on the headlights as he stepped clear. At just engine idle, it began rolling toward the gate.

He walked over to Luke and Nikita.

"Why are you lying down in the mud?"

"If you want to catch a stray round, that's fine with me," Altman said flat-voiced.

"Not with me," Nikita complained. "Get your ass down, Roman. So much to teach you, it's just sad." She was watching the unfolding events through the scope on her rifle.

He got down fast. His instincts were too used to being wrapped in a helo's armor.

"They've seen it. Raising their M16s."

The Land Cruiser continued to idle forward, slowly gaining speed. It wasn't much of a slope, but it would be enough to make sure that it didn't get stuck.

When it was half the distance down to them, the guards opened fire. Their muzzle flashes were brilliant yellow despite the big floodlights shining above. The rounds sparked off the armor and bullet-proof glass. A few ricochets whistled by overhead and Drake was glad he was lying in the mud.

"Changing clips."

They resumed burning rounds. The headlights finally went, but the SUV just kept rolling. The pickup pulled to a stop and the occupants piled out to add their firepower.

"Watch the tower," Nikita announced.

A heavy machine gun began chugging away, its roar loud even at this distance.

"It's just a Mark 48. Still marginal against this armor. Looks like he figured that out."

"About time," Altman grumbled.

A streak of white arced down from the tower and onto the SUV. The Pike missile hit the driver's window and blew a massive hole in the side of the vehicle. As if that wasn't enough, the tower gunner fired a second round through the hole.

Unable to contain the internal blast compression, the entire roof and window section of the SUV flailed upward. The heavy door armor on the other side was all that saved the two sets of guards on the ground, keeping the Pike's shrapnel within the vehicle. But the force of the explosion was enough to bowl them all off their feet and send them tumbling.

The Land Cruiser veered off course slightly.

"Damn it!" The SUV was supposed to cripple the tower.

Instead of hitting the base of the tower as planned, it lodged in the storm fence between the empty Toyota pickup and the tower.

"That's why I came early," Altman pulled a small box from his hip pocket. He had taken supplies from the Little Bird this afternoon and floated downriver himself.

He dialed in a frequency and pressed a trigger. Two of the four legs on the tower blew out. In slow motion, the tower collapsed over the burning remains of the SUV, blocked the front gate, and the guard shack at the tower's top shattered the parked black pickup. The tower gunner dove clear at the last moment, but just lay stunned in the mud.

"Let's go!"

Together the three of them raced downslope through the battering rain. They arrived before any of the guards had shaken off the effects of the double explosion so close by. In moments they had them cuffed with zip ties hand and foot. There were only two Hondurans among them, the rest were US ex-military or worse.

A bright crack of lightning illuminated one of the Little Birds landing just in time to help finish the job. He, Nikita, and Altman all grabbed night-vision goggles, then Drake pointed upward without looking.

"Nikita, floodlights."

In moments she'd shot them out.

He flicked on the power switch and his world went to the familiar thousand shades of green produced by NVGs.

He continued securing the downed and now blind guards.

Then the Tac-50 sounded again, a round hitting metal very close by with a sharp clang.

He turned in time to see Nikita's second Tac-50 round hit the Mercedes sedan. Head on in the engine block. A hiss of steam rose from under the hood.

---

"I HAVE AN IDEA."

"Hit me," Drake replied.

So Nikita did. His surprised yelp was only partial payback for making her wear a dress to a gunfight.

Esly had been on the Little Bird and was now kneeling on the least happy of the guards, who was face down in the mud. It was the bastard Nikita had disarmed earlier—she should have shot him while she still had the chance.

Nikita walked up to him and at her nod, Esly turned his head to face her. She flicked on a flashlight for his benefit, not hers.

"Were you the shooter of the environmentalists?"

His eyes went wide at her transformation.

She placed the business end of her Tac-50 an inch from his right eye. The sniper rifle could throw a half-inch round well over a mile. At an inch, the bore would look like a cannon.

"I suggest you answer her question," Esly prompted him with a hard knee to the kidney. "She isn't as patient as I am."

Nikita clicked the safety off and braced as if she was about to fire.

"No! It was Hank. Not here! Not me!" His panicked accent placed him from New Jersey. "He's back at the underground base. Hank pulled the trigger on both of them; he insisted it was his right as leader. We were just patrol. All we did was track and secure."

Nikita kept the gun aimed at him.

"I swear. It wasn't me."

*His right.* Killing an innocent was—

Oddly, she didn't feel a desire to pull the trigger on the downed guard. Tonight she wouldn't have; he wasn't a sick animal to be put down. But in the past she'd have thought he was. Now he wasn't even worth her time.

She huddled back up with Altman and Drake as Esly finished tying everyone up. Ankles as well as wrists.

"We need to get this guy Hank out of his hole in the ground and have him come here."

"Easy," Altman shrugged. "But what do we do with him once we get him? And in order to flush him, we're going to spook off the people we really want. I don't have a plan for them."

Nikita gave a sharp whistle to Esly, who came trotting over. She wore a holstered sidearm, an ammo vest with a half dozen clips, and carried a loaded M16.

"Well, you didn't shoot us in the back," Drake told her. "Guess that means you're okay."

Altman's grunt made it clear that he'd been comfortable enough around her to not object to her arming herself.

Nikita ignored both the men. "Esly, how connected is Mercedez?"

"Are you joking with me? She is a woman who knows everybody and everything."

"Do you have her phone number?"

Esly tapped her forehead and smiled.

Nikita pulled out Drake's phone and handed it to her.

"What am I asking her about?"

She glanced at Drake and Altman, but they hadn't put it together yet.

"Ask her how to reach the most corrupt military commander at the nearest military base. Call it a hunch."

Drake smiled slowly as he caught on. "Gutierrez would definitely need the local protection of these guards, but he'd also have an ear inside the military. Let's see if we can't cut the whole head off this snake. And now that you mention it, I'd like to ask her a question myself after you're done with her."

Drake's look could have covered anything from calling in a bomber to pulling her into the darkness for a quick tumble.

It was the moments when he was being most creative that she couldn't read him.

# CHAPTER 32

Once they had the information from Mercedez, Drake had placed another call, stepping away from the others to place it privately. He'd need an authentic reaction of surprise for this part of his plan to work. He also didn't want the others to reject it as being too stupid for words. Drake could see it in his head; he just hoped that the reality matched when it caught up with them.

For the third call, because Altman spoke Spanish and Drake didn't, Altman then played the role of Gutierrez. He placed a panicked call to the military commander that Mercedez thought was most likely to be involved with siphoning money off a big construction project in his area.

Altman started nearly hysterical, then escalated from there.

Drake could only assume he was on script, since he supposedly was shouting something like: "Not just the local crazies. They have helos and are in-bound. Get up here now. Low profile. Only your most trusted. We can't risk exposure of your role in—" Altman hung up the phone mid-sentence.

Drake was going to start Spanish lessons the minute he got back to base. Maybe Nikita would give him private lessons; he liked the sound of that. Though he'd suggest somewhere drier. It wasn't a cold rain, but he was soaked right through. At least it wasn't Philippine monsoon—if he never hit that again, he'd be a happy camper.

As soon as Luke was done, Drake got on the radio up to Zoe. She had taken over running the Avenger drone from a small screen and set of controls rigged in the back of the other Little Bird.

"Black out their cellphones. I don't want the military able to call Gutierrez."

Zoe acknowledged and began working her drone magic.

Drake checked his phone. It took less than ten seconds before his two wavering bars of signal plummeted to *No signal.*

"How long do we have?" he asked Altman.

"I could hear the general shouting orders in the background and he sounded seriously upset. La Ceiba military base to here in a Huey, which is about the most advanced helicopter they have in their fleet… Half an hour at the earliest, forty-five at the outside."

"The timing is going to be tight. Let's go with Stage Two now. Time to take out the rest of their security."

Drake walked over to the pile of gear that Esly had gathered as she stripped off the guards' gear. He picked out one of the guards' radios and keyed the mic.

"Main Gate to Base! Main Gate to Base! We've got a problem here." He copied the New Jersey accent of the trussed-up guard.

Altman pulled out his sidearm and fired six frantic shots into the jungle.

Esly unleashed her M16 at the fallen tower's shack for half a clip on full auto. She must have hit some stored munitions, perhaps the stockpile of Pike missiles, because the shack suddenly shredded itself and a fiery plume roared several stories up into the night sky.

Drake turned off the radio and tossed it back on the pile. "I think that should do it."

"Oops," Esly didn't look the least bit sorry, but she did put a fresh clip in the rifle.

Drake clicked back onto the encrypted radio to the Night Stalkers team circling above them. "Zoe, you can jam their radio frequencies now as well."

"On it," he heard a quick rattle of keys on the keyboard. "There. Our encrypted radios are in a different frequency band, so we should be fine, but they're blacked out."

"Roger that. Okay, Esly. This part is up to you and Altman. Nikita and I have to run."

Esly gave him a hand sign that might have been a "Hurry Up" military signal or might have been a fist pump prior to starting a happy dance.

He grabbed an M16 and a stack of magazines for himself, and a couple of the guard's jackets. After a quick stop to make sure Altman was clear on what was happening, he chased after Nikita, who was already halfway to the horizon.

Drake wished she hadn't shot the Mercedes sedan; he could certainly use it at the moment. The rain, slashed at him by the hard-gusting winds, pounded so hard on his head that it almost hurt. He couldn't wipe his eyes fast enough to clear the water streaming out of his hair. Maybe Philippine rain wasn't so bad.

---

NIKITA WAITED, crouching by the burned-out earth mover. She considered giving Drake a moment to catch his breath when he reached her, but where was the fun in that?

She started to rise but then saw the two Toyota pickups racing by along the perimeter road and settled back down. There was no way for them to see her, as she and Drake had been moving directly across the construction site because it was the shortest distance rather than following the road. And between the rain and their own camouflage clothes, they probably wouldn't have been seen at three paces, never mind three hundred.

"They're moving awfully fast," Nikita knew that would be a logistical problem for Luke and Esly, dangerously narrowing their engagement time.

"Should I have stayed and waved a Caution sign at them or something? I don't see a way to slow them down."

Nikita dropped into a prone position and swung out the bipod legs on the Tac-50. She'd done so much training in so many weather conditions that the increasing rain only crossed her attention as a blurring of her sight lines. Rain didn't affect something as big as the rounds the Tac-50 fired.

"You're kidding me, right?"

She ignored him and focused on the first pickup in the line, then the front half of it, then the front right tire, then the leading edge of that tire. Using the markings in the scope, she used the typical length of a quad-cab full-sized pickup to estimate the distance. At nine hundred meters and a target the size of a truck tire, she didn't need to factor in much for temperature, humidity, or Coriolis effect. The wind was the major factor, kicking in the high twenties out of the southeast.

Nikita tracked the leading edge of the tire long enough to get a feel for the truck's speed as it jounced along the rough road. At its current speed, it would travel twenty-two meters in the full second it would take her bullet to fly the distance between them—almost exactly three times the truck's length.

She swung her rifle ahead more by instinct than thought, fired, and worked the bolt. But she wouldn't have to fire again. It had been clean. Keeping her line of fire centered in the scope's field, she saw the tire enter her field of vision just in time to have a hole punched in its sidewall.

The truck stumbled badly. The driver was good enough that he didn't flip and roll despite the rough ground. But it slowed them abruptly from sixty kilometers an hour to fifteen. The truck following close behind them nearly rammed into the back, skidding wildly in the mud to avoid a collision.

As they straightened themselves out, the two Little Birds descended out of the night sky and turned on blinding searchlights, one fore and one aft.

In moments, Altman and Esly appeared to disarm the mercenaries.

Nikita watched long enough to see Esly boot one in the balls particularly hard after she tied him up. Apparently she'd found Hank.

Drake tapped Nikita's shoulder and they were up and running again.

"Shit, woman! How did you make that shot?"

"I could teach you."

"But then you'd have to kill me?"

"No, then you'd be a SEAL."

Drake would have laughed if he'd had the breath. He'd been able to match Nikita on a treadmill, barely. Over open terrain he was flat out when she was still in graceful-gazelle mode, carrying the rifle that was almost as long as she was and weighed twenty-five pounds to his M16's nine with the ease of a relay racer's baton.

"What direction will they be coming from?"

Not able to spare the breath, he pointed the M16 due west. That was the direction of La Ceiba military base.

Nikita veered in that direction and he followed her.

They'd been racing toward the helicopters parked near the shack that covered the entrance to the underground offices. Now they were running west. Fifty meters, a hundred, two hundred.

"This should do it," she spoke as if she was finishing a morning stroll, not a hard 3K run.

She lay on the ground facing west.

He lay beside her, but facing the other direction, back toward the parked helicopters.

Drake stared at them for a long moment before he saw the problem...nothing was moving. "They're staying in their bolt hole."

"Now what, genius man?"

"Genius man?"

"Would you prefer Mr. Mercenary Man, sir?"

"Sir?" Drake nudged an elbow against her ribs. "I like the sound of sir."

"Maybe try a panic call from Hank?" She ignored him.

"I can fake a random guard's voice, but I don't think we can play that card twice. Besides, I didn't bring one of their radios because I have Zoe blocking their frequencies."

"Well, we have about five minutes to flush them out."

How to flush a rabbit out of its hole? Going in the front door would just drive them in deeper. Or out the back door. The problem was, he didn't know where the back door might be.

Had they built underground because it was a convenient and safe place for their construction headquarters, needing only a simple couple of rooms? Or was it a complex arrangement for other purposes? How could he know when—

Then he had it.

He patted the nearest part of Nikita, which turned out to be her splendid behind, earning him a sigh of exasperation.

Then he tucked in the earpiece for the encrypted radio.

"Zoe?"

"Here, Duck-man."

"Do you have anything on your Avenger drone that you could rig to act as a ground-penetrating radar?"

"Would an *actual* ground-penetrating radar do, or do you want something else?"

"You brought—"

"You didn't say what we'd need, so I had Sophie load up everything I could think of."

"I could just kiss you, Zoe."

"If you do, Nikita would pound the shit out of you. So keep it to yourself, Duck-man."

"Roger that."

Nikita made no response from close beside him though she had to be listening in.

"We're right on top of a rabbit warren here. I need to know where it goes."

"Give me a couple minutes. My baby is up at forty thousand feet."

"You have thirty seconds."

"Stingy," Zoe complained. But it was well under thirty seconds later that he heard the loud *whoosh* of the Avenger slicing by close above them. She must have descended under full thrust. It was amazing she hadn't ripped off the wings with that maneuver, but that's why she was an Avenger pilot and he was merely a DAP Hawk crew chief.

For a full minute, it swept back and forth making multiple passes. For a full minute, he lay there trying not to be driven deeper into the mud by the blasts of wind-driven rain. If it was this bad here, Roatán and the ship—over a hundred and fifty kilometers deeper into the storm—must be getting hammered.

"These are rough, but it looks as if there's a small complex and it runs south, away from you and toward the jungle, but doesn't reach it. On the last pass I did a thermal scan and I don't see that anyone has come out."

"Okay. Drop a pair of JDAMs on their backdoor."

"How about a few SDMs instead? The radar and the jamming packages took up too much space and payload for me to carry any of the bigger weapons."

"A pair of small diameter bombs should serve my purpose just fine." At two hundred and fifty pounds each, they'd shake the place hard without doing much damage.

"SDMs. Wow!" Nikita spoke loud enough to be heard over the ripping wind while they waited for the next pass of the Avenger. "They *have* put you in a bad mood."

"They tried to kill, then kidnap, you. Then that guard was going after your breasts and I'm sorry, I have prior claim to that territory."

"*That territory?*"

"Your breast territory. I have rights of sole passage until you revoke them. No two-bit mercenary hired hand gets to trample all over *my* territory."

Nikita's reply was smothered by the pair of bombs that struck a few hundred meters to the west. Great fountains of dirt fountained upward, lit in the darkness by the central explosion like a blooming night flower. What kind of flowers did Nikita like? He didn't know.

Considering that she was a DEVGRU SEAL, probably exploding ones just like these.

Dirt spattered down all around them along with the rain, but nothing big was thrown this far.

He waited for nine heartbeats, then on the tenth saw a stream of people scrambling out of the hut and racing to the parked helicopters.

"Bingo!"

"Good timing," Zoe announced over the radio. "I have three birds incoming from the west that must be Gutierrez's military connection. Ten kilometers and closing."

The trio of Gutierrez's own Bell TwinRangers began cranking to life. The underground caverns must have shaken hard because there were no stragglers. The timing of the meeting between the two helicopter groups was going to be too close. Nikita's Tac-50 had an effective flash suppressor. His own borrowed M16 didn't—and they'd be able to see where his shots were coming from.

That would ruin the whole play.

He draped the guard's jackets that he'd taken into a jumbled pile in front of him, weighting them in place with a couple of stones so that they did blow away. Then he nudged the muzzle into the folds of the jacket and flipped the firing mode to semi-auto. He'd just have to hope that the jackets hid his muzzle flash.

"In sight," Nikita whispered.

"Hold...hold...hold," the first two TwinRangers crawled aloft. These were the two armed patrol ships that had flown out to check on their downed 5E helicopter at the waterfall. The VIP craft was still waiting for the last people to board.

"Tell them to hurry," Nikita whispered. Both helicopter groups had to be aloft and nearby at the same time for this to work.

"Remember not to actually shoot them down."

"This is crazy."

"You want to face five heavily armed helos with a rifle?"

"I'm not that crazy."

"Just crazy in love with me?" Wow. Time for another one of his do-overs. His timing sucked.

"*Definitely* not that crazy," but she didn't sound upset. "Damn it, Roman. Don't make me laugh when I'm about to shoot at multiple gunships loaded with corrupt military."

Laughter wasn't exactly the response he'd been hoping for.

The third of Gutierrez's helicopters—the transport with the suits aboard—made it aloft. The two gunships were hovering fifty meters up waiting to take up guard positions.

"Go!"

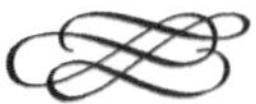

Nikita began firing at the three helicopters incoming from the military base. Firing a half-inch round out of a high-precision sniper rifle, it was actually hard *not* to shoot them down. It should be two shots right through the windshield. Dead pilot and copilot. Crash. Done.

But that wasn't Drake's master plan.

So, instead, she shot at one of the skids and missed. The wind had continued to pick up and was playing havoc with the bullet's and the helicopter's flight paths.

She worked the bolt and aimed for something bigger. She dropped a round on the FLIR turret hung under the helo's nose. It would knock out their night-vision camera, but it shouldn't go through the frame and kill anyone.

Nikita could hear Drake firing down by her feet. *Snap!...Snap! Snap!*

She chose another helo and shot it high in the windshield. Her round would either skip off the windshield or punch through into all of the electronics directly over the pilots' heads.

It took surprisingly few shots before Drake called hold.

In moments the military Hueys and Gutierrez's TwinRangers were in a full-fledged battle directly over where he and Nikita lay in the mud.

It had been so simple. The two groups of helicopters had approached each other with their radios out of commission due to Zoe's jamming. Add in a nighttime rainstorm and a panicked evacuation.

A few shots head-on at each group of helicopters with no detectable origin, and they'd each assumed the worst and attacked each other.

"There goes one," Nikita called out as one of the military's Hueys appeared to stumble in the air. It didn't autorotate down, it plummeted.

Drake tapped her shoulder and led her racing back the way they'd come.

As they circled behind the parked earthmoving equipment, a helicopter flew close above them. The blast of wind said that it was far bigger than any of the helos currently fighting it out in the storm, but the sound was odd, far more like a washing machine flying away from them than a five-ton DAP Hawk flying toward them. Stealth-rigged. It settled on the mud for the briefest of moments and she and Drake piled aboard.

She was glad to be sitting once more on a hard steel deck instead of the red mud of Honduras that had penetrated her every pore. She was sopping wet.

Someone at the crew chief position handed her a headset.

She recognized one of the gunners from the 5E's big Chinook helicopter but couldn't remember his name at the moment.

"How goes the battle?" she asked over the intercom.

"The locals," Julian called from the front seat, "are tough contenders this year. They're not to be put down lightly, sports fans. Each side is down one bird, and I mean down as in hard. Nobody walking away from those."

Nikita looked out the open cargo bay door, but the battle must be on the other side of the aircraft. The DAP Hawk was circling back out of the way. She dangled her feet out the door and over the abyss.

Someone—Drake—snapped a harness around her waist. She felt him tug it to make sure that she was securely attached to the frame. Then he slid his feet out beside her. For a moment they both just sat with their rifles across their laps, staring out at the wind-torn darkness.

She leaned her shoulder into his and just listened to Julian's play-by-play as the DAP Hawk jounced through the turbulent winds.

The Honduran Navy was down to one as the second bird autorotated into deep jungle, snared high in the trees, and exploded long before it hit the ground.

Julian's slow circle brought the construction site back into view.

Drake pointed an arm.

Three helicopters spinning and twisting across the sky. Actually two doing the dance and one hightailing it out of there.

---

"Gutierrez," Drake knew he was right. "Julian, we can't let that third bird escape."

"According to some asshole crew chief with delusions of grandeur —and no, I'm not telling how we're gonna whup that back out of you —I'm not supposed to shoot them down. Any other suggestions, Mr. Genius?" But he climbed, circling wide around the continuing battle, and laid down the hammer to chase the departing aircraft.

Drake looked down at the M16 in his hands. That wasn't the answer.

If the military won, they would declare themselves heroes. If they lost, well, they'd probably be declared heroes anyway.

But if Gutierrez was shot down, there would be far too many questions. He was too important. Everything could come to light. But if he escaped, he would just start all over again somewhere else. Still, there couldn't be any cause to look beyond a conflict with the military.

Drake watched the last two helicopter pilots battling it out. Neither was Night Stalker caliber, but they knew their machines.

Their battle was lit in strobe flashes of lightning and distorted by sheets of rain. The drops stung his legs where they dangled out in the DAP Hawk's slipstream, but neither he nor Nikita pulled their legs in.

Instead they watched.

Watched until the military Huey made the first mistake. Apparently noticing that Gutierrez's aircraft was slipping away, it turned to shoot him down.

The remaining armed TwinRanger raced directly at it with a fusillade of fire streaming off its side-mounted M230 chain gun.

Realizing his mistake, the military pilot carved a hard turn to bring his own weapons to bear, but they were too close.

The two helicopters tangled their rotor blades as they passed. They twisted and slammed their tail sections together as they sped by one another. A moment later, they were both gone from sight, plunging into the river at unsurvivable speeds.

So much for the military solving the problem. Now Gutierrez was free—unless Drake could stop him.

Stop him but make it look like an accident before they lost him in the storm.

The storm!

"Julian."

"Yes, Mr. Roman of the dangerous reputation?"

"Screw you."

"You wish. Only the finest of the ladies get to play with this body."

"Julian," Drake started over. "Is he following the power lines?" Drake could picture the tall transmission lines climbing the hill toward the interior, away from the storm.

"He's right over them, following their break in the jungle to keep out of sight."

"Does he know we're here behind him?"

"No, he's now flying at a standard cruise speed."

"What happens if we fly over him?"

"Not much."

"I mean *right* over him. Like a couple meters."

## CHAPTER 35

*Family mourns loss of Franshesco Gutierrez in storm-related accident.*

Nikita read the headline on the suite's bedroom television screen again and tried to feel sorry about it, but she couldn't. The bodies of Gutierrez, two bankers suspected of drug running, and a dirty chief of police known for his generous payoffs were found in the crashed helicopter. Of course none of those details were listed, but command had confirmed who they'd been.

"Why was the entire head of the snake onsite for a meeting?" she asked Drake where he lay beside her.

"Because," he poked a finger in her shoulder, "they were worried about the great Drake Roman coming their way. Your rumor campaign was big enough that it got back to them somehow and must have scared them spitless."

Nikita remembered the moment that their DAP Hawk had over-flown the Bell TwinRanger. A flash of lightning had strobe-lit the moment. The down-blast of the DAP Hawk's massive rotors disrupted the air flow over the much smaller Bell helicopter, and its blades had lost all lift.

Another flash, this time of man-made lightning as the helo

snagged one transmission line with one skid, twisted, and laid the tail across the other. It had lain there for a long moment, arcing and flashing with light, before the rotor sliced one of the massive wires and then the aircraft plummeted down into the clearing. There had been no explosion, but they had landed on a boulder field from fifty meters up. There was no question of survivors.

The newscast flipped to the next news item and Drake chuckled beside her.

"Show off," she accused him and he didn't argue, instead pulling her more tightly against his side. Nikita snuggled as she joined his laugh.

*Police sergeant goes undercover to unmask environmentalists' killer.*

Nikita couldn't help smiling back at the image of a grinning Esly, soaked by the rain, standing with her M16 over a dozen well-bound mercenaries. Drake's move of calling in the press had been a brilliant way to make sure the entire site's security detail was taken out of operation. Apparently the guards had tried to tell stories of the 5E team, but Esly had simply said, "Others who wish to remain anonymous for their safety offered some assistance." It made it sound like a locals' movement seeking retribution for the killed environmentalists, which would only make the whole event more popular.

"It's nice to see her really smiling again." They'd left her to ride back at the head of the police column that carted them all away.

*President declares Esly Escarra a national hero.*

"He didn't have a lot of choice, did he," Drake asked the screen rhetorically.

*Tropical storm Kyra gives coast glancing blow.*

They both sat up as the images flashed across the screen.

The ride back to the ship had been a wild one as the storm buffeted the Roatán coast. It had been a dozen times more violent on the island than it had been up at the El Carbón dam site. At midnight, in the heart of the storm, they had fast-roped down from their helos onto the top deck of the cruise ship as it wallowed and bucked against the pier despite its protected harbor. She and Drake from the DAP Hawk, Altman from one Little Bird, and Zoe from the other. With no one the wiser, they'd reached their suite. Drenched, filthy, but back in their suite. A quick call to Norma and they were all logged as being back aboard—much earlier in the evening.

Drake had declared it would be best if they were found here. Less chance of an official connecting their leaving the ship with what had happened up in the hills. He had proven himself as a strategist so many times that no one questioned his judgment anymore.

But no one had slept until it was reported back that the three helos had flown through the storm wall and safely landed on their ship in the relative calm of the eye.

The newsfeed shifted from showing the mainland to footage of the islands:

French Harbour had been hammered.

Fishing and tour boats were cast up on the beach, others were sunk at their piers.

Houses had been damaged.

Then Nikita saw the palm tree rammed through the front window of the Junk Boutique.

She was up and half-dressed before she knew it and Drake was right there beside her.

Out in the main suite's living room, Altman and Zoe were also dressed for hard work.

At the ramp, the ship's attendant tried to convince them to stay aboard. "The seas are too rough for us to leave today, but we *strongly* suggest that all passengers remain aboard."

They brushed past him, though it took a while to find a truck making its way toward French Harbour that they could hitch a ride on.

Where Drake led, Nikita and the others followed. He was a sergeant and Luke Altman a lieutenant commander. Drake was actually the lowest ranked of the four of them, but there was no question who this team's leader was.

They arrived at the Junk Boutique ready to go to work. Mercedez was inside with a mop. She was in a good mood despite the damage, "I am better off than others. It is only broken glass."

As a team they managed to pull the tree back into the street. Emmanuel found a roll of thick plastic in the back room and they soon had it tacked over the window. Then Mercedez shooed them on their way with a sincere hug for thanks.

The sky was still overcast, but the rain was no more than an occasional spatter and even that tapered off as they worked along the street.

When they reached the harbor itself, Nikita saw that it had been the worst hit. It wasn't long before Altman found the local tour divers and began going down with them to help refloat sunken boats. Nearby, Zoe used her magnetic charm to turn the people working at random along the beach into a team that dug half-buried boats out of the beach sand and hauled them back into the water.

Nikita stuck with Drake. They lifted, moved, dug, and consoled people until both her muscles and her heart burned, but still they didn't stop.

When they managed to get a restaurant put back together enough to make food, they were served the first lunch. Zoe and Altman soon joined them and they sat out at the end of a pier with their feet dangling over the turquoise water. The harbor waters were active without being rough. The fishing boats that survived and those they'd been able to refloat or relaunch bobbed at their moorings once again. A group of children were making a game of swimming out to floating plastic furniture and hauling it onto the beach.

"What next?" Nikita would be content to sit here all day, her shoulder brushing Drake's each time one of them lifted a conch fritter for another bite. It was hard to imagine being anywhere other than at his side.

"I don't know," Drake said softly.

She'd meant what was next after they'd eaten, but Drake wasn't scanning the beach for the next task, he was looking at her.

"You tell me."

The conch seemed to stick in her throat as she looked up at his dark eyes. The subject of the future hung between them. She turned away before the sadness overwhelmed her.

In perfect irony, the midday sunlight finally broke through the parting clouds and the turquoise water seemed to turn golden.

If this was like any other mission, they would return to US soil and she'd catch the next flight to Virginia Beach. As much as she enjoyed working with the 5E, they had accounted for less than ten of her missions over the last year. Without them she'd fought piracy in the Persian Gulf, tracked kidnappers across Africa, taken down terrorists in Indonesia, and any number of other missions.

"I could," it hurt to say, but she forced it out, "switch—"

"Hey," Zoe's shout interrupted their whispered conversation. "I know that boat."

Nikita looked up as a massive black motor yacht idled into the harbor.

Zoe jumped to her feet and finally managed to flag them down. The boat turned and headed for the pier.

They all rose to their feet to catch lines and greet them.

Nikita couldn't bring herself to finish the sentence. She loved being a DEVGRU SEAL. But life without Drake Roman—she didn't know if she could face that.

***

DRAKE PULLED Nikita tightly against him as Jared's boat finished nosing alongside the pier. Drake buried his face in her hair and kissed her on the temple.

If a man ever needed proof that a woman loved him, it just didn't come any higher than what she'd been about to say.

He whispered for her alone, "If you *ever* even hint at leaving DEVGRU for me again, you're really going to piss me off. Just so you know."

She turned her face into his shoulder as if hiding there. "Then what do we do?"

Drake smiled, "I think I have an idea on that one." But he wasn't ready to give it a voice yet.

Nikita looked up at him and, after a long look, gave him a kiss that promised a lifetime if he could just figure out how to make it happen.

A massive hand crashed down on his shoulder, "Damn, military!"

Jared had a hold on both his and Nikita's shoulders and was shaking them like clothes on a line during a storm.

"Hey, mercenary," Nikita gave it right back to him, but her smile said she was no longer reacting to her past. Drake was so proud of her. How in the world was he supposed to tell an ST6 SEAL that he was so proud of her it made his chest hurt?

Jared shook them some more. "You weren't kidding about the whole 'being invisible' shit. Been watching the news feed and there isn't even a goddamn hint you were there. That was damn sweet work. Damn sweet."

"I think," Sugar eased up beside him, "that may be the highest praise I ever heard from J-dawg."

Asal nodded her agreement from close beside them.

Drake handed her his plate, which had one more conch fritter on it. She nibbled a corner, paused, and then began eating it happily.

"I got the names and faces of those mercs," Jared was practically effusive. "They were all GSI hires, which means they were bad news anyway. Can't believe you caught Hank Jaffer; I've been after that bastard for years. I spread the word that if any of those assholes ever get out of Honduran jail, Titan will be taking down any outfit that hires them—all the way down. They're blacklisted for life."

Drake slapped a hand down on Jared's shoulder, partly to stop the dual-shaking thing he was doing. A group of men and women lined the rails of the boat and looked down at the proceedings. The men were like miniature Jareds, a wide variety of types and all military tough, though none of them were as big as their boss. The women didn't look any less dangerous.

Nikita went up on her toes and actually kissed Jared, which shocked him into silence and thankfully made him finally let go of their shoulders.

Sugar gave Nikita a sideways hug, "Knew there was hope for you, Swimmer Girl."

"Hey," a voice called from up the pier.

Drake turned to see Esly striding along it.

"Do you have proper entry stamp for that boat?"

Nikita and Zoe threw their arms around her and the three women hugged.

All he got was a punch on the arm.

"What's it to you?" Jared growled.

"Careful, Mr. American. You are now talking to the Roatán Island Chief Minister of Security."

Drake laughed. "Mercedez *is* well connected."

Esly joined his laugh. "Yes, she had the mayor create this job for the new 'National Hero.' My duties are to ensure that the Bay Islands, including Roatán, remain safe for tourism no matter what disaster is the mainland. So," she turned to Jared and scowled at him. "Tell me if I should trust these people or no. They look like bad element to me."

Jared simply glowered, not able to hear the tease.

"I wouldn't trust them," Nikita was the first to speak.

"Not for a second," Drake crossed his arms over his chest.

"You wouldn't believe the kinds of things these guys do," Zoe chimed in cheerfully.

Altman simply stood beside Zoe with his arms crossed as well.

"Unless..." Drake trailed it out.

Jared glared down at him.

"Unless they were willing to help pitch in on the post-Storm Kyra cleanup."

Jared looked out over their heads and inspected the waterfront.

Drake saw him register the damage the storm had done and the people struggling to put their town back together. Without appearing to notice what he was doing, he reached an arm around Sugar's waist and pulled her tight against him.

"And if I was?" But despite his grumble, there was no question he'd be joining in. His true emotions were always clear on Sugar's face and Drake could see how proud she was of her man.

Drake knew exactly how she felt as he hung on to Nikita.

"Got room aboard for four temporary Team Titan members?"

Drake nodded at the others. "A couple of days' hard work together and we would go a long way to getting these people back on their feet."

Drake didn't need Sugar's glowing smile to tell him he'd done it right.

It was Nikita's laugh that really mattered. The merry sound proved that over these last days they had finally broken the past's hold on her life and now she'd be glad to work side by side with a military contractor, at least a good one like Titan.

They'd fixed her past, but his future—their future—was still a huge question.

# CHAPTER 36

Nikita leaned on the bow rail of Jared's massive boat as it eased out of French Harbour.

The town was still damaged, but it was no longer broken and she could feel the ache of each day of the hard work, deep and good in her muscles.

Drake's arm was warm around her waist. It was just the two of them, leaning against the rail watching the harbor slide away.

Norma had left all of their clothes and gear at baggage claim at the Roatán airport before the cruise ship was finally cleared to continue its voyage. She'd done a fair job of covering how glad she was to have them off her boat.

Jared was now delivering them to the seaside airport for the flight home.

"I'll miss this place." The setting sun illuminated the tropical colors of the buildings—pink, pale blue, apricot—they all glowed in the warm evening. Most of the boats were back at their moorings and piers. There were even tourists venturing into town from whatever latest cruise ship had arrived that morning.

"We'll be back," Drake said softly.

Nikita was torn with a ton of questions. *We?* That was the biggest one, but she didn't know how to face it. She'd thought of little else as they worked side by side over these last days. It had been at the forefront of her mind when she'd collapsed into the luxurious bed aboard —because Jared definitely traveled in style—shaking with exhaustion. It was her first thought when she woke in Drake's arms.

But she'd been afraid to give it a voice. Drake had been right: she couldn't leave the SEALs. *What* she'd done to get there—the why no longer mattered—was as essential a part of her as breathing. The problem was, Drake Roman was an equally essential part.

Unable to voice that question, she faced a simpler one. "When? How do you know we'll be back?"

"Because Esly said she'd track me down and kick my ass if we didn't honeymoon here."

Nikita started to laugh at the first part of his statement, then nearly strangled on the second part when it registered. When she looked over at Drake, he was no longer watching the shore but was looking at her instead.

He was right, there was no question. Not about marrying him and not about where to honeymoon. And now she finally knew what to do with that crazy La Perla lingerie body suit. As her sole concession to girldom, she'd wear it under her dress white uniform on her wedding day so that he could discover it when he undressed her on their wedding night.

"When?" Nikita barely managed to repeat the question now that it meant so much more.

"I'll take that as a yes."

All she could do was nod.

"Then I think the day I qualify would be a good one. A double celebration."

"Qualify for what?"

Drake looked out at the golden water for a long time before answering.

"Remember what you said about what would happen if you taught me how to make that shot? The one you used to take out that racing pickup's tire in the midst of that night's tropical storm?"

"Sure. I said that…then…" she could feel her words slowing down, but she couldn't figure out why.

"That then…" her second attempt didn't get any further than her first. If he meant…

"You said then I'd be a DEVGRU SEAL."

"Uh-huh." She felt a brief flash, little brighter than a round firing out of her Tac-50's flash suppressor. It was deep down inside her.

"Well," Drake finally turned to look at her and he was smiling. "I've been thinking about that."

That tiny spark lit a fuse and began to build. It was an emotion she might not have recognized before this last week. In that long ago past, she might not have felt it at all. But Drake had changed all that.

"I spoke to Altman and to my commander."

But not recognizing what emotion this growing feeling was? That would have been before she'd spent the week as Drake's fellow warrior and as his lover. Before she'd learned to see herself through his eyes rather than the ones of the past.

"There's a DEVGRU training course starting in a couple weeks. They both approved my transfer and application, but I told them it needed one more sign-off."

"No…" It wasn't possible. Since when did anything good come to her other than being a SEAL? Never.

"Why not? It makes perfect sense. You can't leave DEVGRU because it's such a part of who you are. I went from being a failed actor to Army flight crew to Night Stalker. After spending a week with you, even that's no longer enough. It's the logical next step for me. And how we can be together. I thought you wanted that?"

*Wanted?*

"No. I don't *want* that."

She *needed* it.

"Like I need air to breathe." The explosion of feeling was turning incandescent inside her.

"What? You're not making much sense, Nikita." Drake leaned with one elbow on the rail being impossibly handsome as the sun settled behind the distant mainland. It cast red across the coming night sky. *Red at night, sailor's delight.*

It burned away the fear, the anger, all the horrors of the past and lit them so brilliantly with the light of the future.

No longer able to speak at all, she did the only thing she was capable of—she threw her arms around his neck and hung onto Drake as hard as she could.

"I'll take that as a yes, too." Drake eased his arms around her until he held her just as tightly.

Nikita didn't even bother to try to nod. It was impossible to hold that big an emotion inside and it began to spill out of her.

This time she knew exactly where the tears were coming from. From the one feeling too big to keep inside.

They were pure joy.

# TARGET OF ONE'S OWN

**MISSION:** *Special Operations Forces barely miss capturing Pakistan's #1 arms dealer. They know only one thing: he's a champion driver in the most challenging car race in the world, The Dakar Rally. The Night Stalkers and SEAL Team 6 must join up again to face the race of their lives.*

**TEAM:**

**Drone pilot Zoe DeMille**

*— Her career never prepared her for going into the field rather than sending her drone. Driving dune buggies at Pismo Beach throughout her teen years, oddly did.*

**SEAL Team 6 Lieutenant Commander Luke Altman**

*— Trusts no one but his team. Ever!*

*Zoe convinces Luke that they must go undercover to target their prey in the wildest 5E mission yet. They enter the two-week, 10,000 kilometer race across the dunes, deserts, and mountains of South America to track him down.*

*But when Zoe's viral fashion blog—The Soldier of Style—sparks a media frenzy, it threatens the very nature of this Black Op. She can't outrace the madness. And she hasn't a clue how to navigate Luke.*

# CHAPTER 1

The view was awesome from up here. To the far north, the mountains of the Hindu Kush were jagged ice points etched across the limits of the horizon. To the south, the arid wastelands of Pakistan.

At the New Year, all of the peaks were sheathed in layers of snow; only the valleys were barren. Scattered villages, even nomadic groups, showed up as bright spots in her infrared vision, but with little of note in between. It looked like a half-finished artist's painting—ever evolving, never complete. Midnight silence reigned, so near perfect that it echoed. She could almost smell the dry desert air—so clean and clear that it was like cool water on a hot day.

For now, she floated above it all like some disembodied alien: seeing but unseen. Her favorite state. As if she was finally forever disconnected from—

"Zoe?"

Lieutenant Sofia Gracie's voice slammed Zoe back into her chair. One moment she'd been soaring through the night at sixty-thousand feet, so completely in tune with her twenty-million-dollar Avenger stealth drone that she might as well have been up there. The next, she was back in the "coffin"—as drone control stations were called—

staring at the command console for her bird. The air so sterile that it had no scent at all. The vast silence replace by the soft whir of ventilation fans.

Her soul had been in the sky over southwest Asia, but her butt was undeniably planted in Fort Rucker, Alabama.

Some remote pilots got all wound up, "It's not a drone. It's a remotely piloted aircraft—an RPA." Whatever. As long as they let her fly, she was cool with anything folks wanted to call it. She didn't even mind when they said she wasn't really a pilot. All they were doing was proving that they were ignorant dweebs—stroking their massive egos to compensate for tiny, Air Force pricks—and were so not worth speaking to ever again.

She'd left the Air Force behind and good riddance. Zoe had answered the call to become an RPA pilot for the US Army's 160th Special Operations Aviation Regiment and not regretted it even once. She flew with the Night Stalkers, the very best helicopter pilots anywhere. No one could debate that. Not even the Air Force jocks with their big jets…and tiny pricks.

And while she didn't fly rotorcraft, there was no question that she flew with them, over them. She was their all-seeing eye. Her view was a multi-screen array that had once made her head hurt, but now felt second nature. LIDAR (high-resolution 3D laser-scanning radar) on one monitor with image resolution down below a meter even from this altitude, infrared night vision on another, visible light on a third (which wasn't much on this moonless night deep in Pakistan), and finally the RPA's operations and weapons status. Each screen itself multi-tasking with superimposed readouts of relevant data: terrain, targeting, friendly assets, and the like. Keyboard and a pair of joysticks—flight (not the running-away kind) and fight—completed her world.

Zoe glanced over at Sofia, sitting in an identical seat beside hers.

Just once she'd like to look at her commander and not feel inadequate.

Sofia was a tall, voluptuous beauty that her Army coveralls did nothing to hide. Her smooth Brazilian accent made her sound even more beautiful than she was—which was saying something.

Zoe stood five-four on a good day and had all the curves of a computer screen. Of course, they were making curved ones now, which... She sighed and reported. Sofia had been busy on a command frequency while Zoe was doing the flying.

"Air space is clear," Zoe told her. "I'm seeing no ground forces on the move. Couldn't even see our people if they weren't linked up." The Night Stalkers 5th Battalion E Company was on the prowl tonight and really didn't want to be seen as they were deep inside a "friendly" country without permission. Of course, being invisible was their specialty. The only completely stealth helicopter company in the US military, they truly ruled the night.

It felt odd to be flying here. The fact that she was sitting in Fort Rucker, Alabama, half a world away from her team, was nothing new. But she hadn't flown over Pakistan since joining the elite Night Stalkers.

Back when she'd been flying Predators for the US Air Force's 27th Special Operations Group—out of a coffin at Cannon Air Force Base near Clovis, New Mexico—she'd flown over Pakistan and Afghanistan all the time. The hours had been brutally long and the missions emotionally gutting. Authorization to fire in the face of collateral damage—dead civilians—permitted in order to take out a Tier One target. Women and children traveling with the target were deemed by command to be guilty by association and therefore expendable.

"Keep it smooth." Sofia's reminder to stay focused. Maybe she'd learned that from when she walked fashion runways in exotic climes. If she had. Sofia never talked about her past, but it was easy to picture her there.

Zoe didn't talk about her own past either, but that was because she couldn't imagine anything more boring—other than the one part she refused to remember.

Her mother was a stereotypical legal secretary and her father a Pismo Beach, California, car mechanic—a business he'd started with his high school best friend and next-door neighbor. It was a family she'd *never* belonged to. Their conversations weren't exactly what Zoe would call intellectually stimulating. Thankfully, they also hadn't been strife-laden, just...dull. Which so wasn't right for descendants of the great filmmaker Cecil B. DeMille—not even if they were distant ones. As their only child, it had been up to Zoe to amuse herself. For the last nine years it had amused her to fly drones for the US military.

"Two minutes to perimeter."

This was a smaller mission than normal. The 5E only had four birds aside from her Avenger: a massive twin-rotor Chinook helicopter (the cargo van of Special Operations Forces), a heavily-modified DAP Black Hawk (the most lethal rotorcraft weapons platforms anywhere), and a pair of Little Birds. The last two didn't have the range to strike this far from any support so were parked in the hangar alongside her coffin in Alabama.

In the heart of Balochistan Province in "friendly" Pakistan, a ground team had identified a major arms dealer—perhaps *the* major arms dealer. Not only was Hathyaron ("Weapons" in Urdu) supplying the Taliban in Afghanistan, but he'd been doing it since the Americans had first arrived. Hundreds of millions of dollars for weapons and ammunition had flowed through his hands every year.

The bastard had slipped the net more times than bin Laden. He'd left behind booby traps that had decimated teams. He'd mailed informants' heads to the US embassy in Islamabad—with the tongues cut out before they'd had their limbs removed at the neck. This just had to be the night they took him down.

Zoe scanned again.

Still a whole lot of nothing.

More nothing than there should be. No shepherd boy. No traders camped with their mules by scattered campfires. It was as if the land had been undressed.

"It's quiet." Now that she thought about it, almost nothing had happened at the target compound in the four hours she'd been in position.

"One minute to deployment," Sofia announced as she scanned her screens carefully, then they shared a look.

Zoe keyed her mic. She could broadcast without pinpointing the 5E's aircraft for any enemy. They could hear her transmission, which would cover a wide area—encrypted burst signal, of course—but the mission team wouldn't respond, to avoid their response giving away their position.

"*Carrie-Anne*, this is *Raven*."

The big Chinook helicopter of the Night Stalkers 5E was named for Carrie-Anne Moss, who had played Trinity in *The Matrix*. Their own RPA, *Raven*, had been named for Marion Ravenwood in *Raiders of the Lost Ark*. Their whole company was named for dangerous women —just one more reason to love flying with the 5E.

"It's *too* quiet."

Lieutenant Commander Luke Altman echoed the call to the rest of his team.

The two leads on his team, Nikita and Drake, grunted out acknowledgements and shouted the message down the line. Six DEVGRU SEALs—SEAL Team 6's actual name, the Development Group—and six SilentHawk prototype hybrid-electric motorcycles in the cargo bay of a pounding Chinook helicopter. Just because it was stealth on the outside didn't mean that it was quiet on the inside. The US military wasn't big on wasting weight on sound insulation that could be better spent on ammunition or fuel.

The bay was eight feet wide, thirty long, and red as the devil's armpit with the night operations lighting. The helo flew fast and furious, mere meters above the Pakistan countryside to avoid detection, slewing them side to side with every tree or tall boulder.

Not his issue.

His issue was the takedown mission.

He considered dismissing the warning. What did coffin-heads really know, locked safely in their stateside boxes?

But he'd recognized Chief Warrant Zoe DeMille's voice. Not hard to do, since the only other person who could be on the circuit was

Sofia Gracie, with her lush Latinate tones that so evoked her tall, lush body. That was his type of woman: long, leggy, and built. She wasn't big on talk and that was fine with him. But they'd tried it once. Not even enough spark to get them past drinks. Strange. In the past he'd always been able to ignore such shortcomings, but that had shifted recently. He'd be damned if he knew why, but for some idiot reason an awesome body wasn't enough anymore.

Zoe DeMille was the polar opposite of her commander: five-four, flat, and sassy, with hair somewhere between yellow, gold, and white except for black roots down the center. Kind of cute, in a punch-you-in-the-face style.

She'd even gone into the field with them once when an undercover mission called for it. Without her instincts, that mission might have gone down hard. She was no fighter, definitely not built for it (he could bench press her one-handed if she was a free weight), but just maybe she was a warrior despite that.

If only she didn't make it so damn hard to take her seriously. He was always having to discount her flighty civilian lifestyle for which he had no respect at all.

However, her job *was* to be their eye in the sky—especially as the helos were racing along, nap-of-the-earth at better than a hundred and fifty knots—in territory they were *not* supposed to be in. From their low flight altitude, they couldn't see anything past a few hundred meters—a view only two seconds into the future. And to fly even a drone with the 5E meant she was one of the best in the military at what she did, no matter what the woman herself was like.

"Thirty seconds," Nikita pointed out. It was the way his Number Two asked questions, by not wasting time actually asking them. Thirty seconds to their planned insertion point five miles from the target. He'd studied the files and was only too aware of what might lay in wait for them at Hathyaron's compound.

Thirty seconds meant a mile and a half out from that; they'd be audible any second if someone was waiting for them at the outer perimeter.

"Too quiet" because the information was bad and the target would be a dry hole? Happened often enough. Some leak could have spooked the target and they'd be gone. But the intel had come from The Activity—the Special Operations Command's own intelligence service—and those guys just didn't miss.

The other answer was that Hathyaron's instincts—which had kept him alive for so long—had him either bugging out or digging in a ground team so deep that they were invisible.

Which meant they were flying into a trap.

He flashed a signal to Nikita and Drake to prep the team for landing as he turned and called up to the pilot, "On the ground, now!"

"Wel-l," the Chinook's pilot, Major Pete Napier, drawled out laconically like only a true Coloradan ranch boy could, completely belying his radical actions to slow down and land. "Don't that beat all. You SEAL boys never do know what you're wanting, do ya?"

"Just don't put your wheels down, Napier. Might suck if Hathyaron put landmines out this far."

"Might at that," Napier agreed pleasantly as he hovered a hundred feet of helicopter to a stop less than a meter over the dirt. Danielle had sure mellowed his ass by marrying him. Pete "The Rapier" Napier was a changed man since he'd hooked his copilot—no less skilled, just less of a pain in the ass.

The rear gunner lowered the big rear ramp to reveal the night.

Napier had found what looked like a goat trail to hover over.

Luke gave no outward sign. He stood at the edge of the lowered ramp and tried to read the night. He flipped down his night-vision goggles. The NVGs revealed low brush and scrub, nothing of interest—probably not even a goat.

The night was cool—just below freezing. His breathe was as cloudy as a cold winter's day in Maine. Aside from all of the dust being churned by the rotors, it smelled clean. He liked the crispness on the air; it wouldn't be hiding anything. In Beijing or New Delhi the air hurt to breathe no matter what temperature it was, and it had a stench all its own that masked all other scents. He'd have to get well clear of the helo to listen to the night, but he could get to like this place if it wasn't filled with assholes who wanted him and his country dead. Even from here he should be able to see the heat signature if a man had walked through here in the last twenty-four hours. Or if some asshole had come out to bury IEDs along the path.

Nothing.

There was a dead feeling to the air despite the rotor's downwash; a feeling he knew.

"Dry hole," he bet himself, but he didn't tell his team because he wanted the vigilance to be at full-mission high.

"Saddle up," he called aloud, wondering if Napier's Coloradan was rubbing off on him. Better not be—Maine lobsterman and Colorado rancher just didn't mix. Same as Maine farmer and Texas rancher.

Old Maine joke.

*A Texas rancher is surveying a Maine farm and says, "Well, shoot, son. I got a ranch so big takes me all day to drive 'round it in my car."*

*Mainer looks at him for a long moment before replying.*

*"Had a car like that once." Knocks his pipe out against his fencepost and refills it. "Got rid of her."*

Saddle up? *Yeesh!*

# CHAPTER 2

In fifteen seconds, six members of DEVGRU had slipped down the ramp on their silent hybrid-electric all-wheel-drive motorcycles, jumped down the meter of distance aloft that Napier was holding twenty tons of helo, and sped into the night. The big rotors' downwash drove at their backs as they accelerated down the trail, leaning hard into the throttles.

The helo would pull back to some safe location and was no longer his concern. They were Night Stalkers, so he knew they'd be there when it was time for their extraction. "Anytime, anywhere." It wasn't just a motto for them—it was a permanent mission plan.

Luke punched down the trail. He particularly enjoyed missions where he could integrate a motorcycle into the scenario, and these were particularly sweet machines. It took him back to his days racing dirt bikes along the Maine logging roads during long summers. Even though his team was all SEAL trained, no one could keep up with him as he jumped gullies and goosed it hard to climb narrow upward twists. Having all-wheel-drive made the SilentHawk bike exceptionally tenacious. The infrared headlamp lit the terrain brilliantly in his NVGs.

And still the ground remained evenly cold—no stray heat signatures bigger than a rabbit.

The SilentHawk could run over level ground at eighty with no noise except the tires in the dirt, and the chain. You could converse at normal volume while running at full tilt, except for the wind noise. On the goat trail, he rarely dropped below forty until he reached the edge of the original landing zone.

He grinned to himself at beating the others by a full thirty seconds. Not something he'd ever show, but it felt good. Long way from aging out.

Weird to think of that. He remembered older SEALs talking about it, but had never thought about it himself before. He had a decade in. By the end of the second decade, most SEALs' bodies had been so hammered to shit by constant training and hard missions that they just couldn't sustain it anymore. The thought marked some halfway point that he sure wouldn't care crap about for long while.

Parking his bike, he moved fifty meters down the trail and surveyed the night. He knew these smells. Less iron in the dusty soil and a little more moisture than Afghanistan—which meant it didn't catch in the back of his throat or hurt his nose as much. Growing up in the Maine woods, almost everywhere else he'd ever fought was drier—except for his time in Central America with Zoe DeMille. But the bit of moisture in the Pakistani air meant that it carried scents farther than a truly arid desert. No mules. No spent cordite. No hidden enforcer drinking too little water meaning that his piss would be sharper on the air.

The night animals were behaving normally. The heavy wingbeat of a lone owl passed by to the south and a mouse or gerbil skittered along twenty meters off to the northwest.

Nobody had disturbed them and few but a SEAL team operator could be here without doing so.

No lurking guards.

Dry hole.

The others were waiting back by where he'd parked his bike.

"Moving?" Nikita asked about what he'd found. It had always been

Drake who had been the talker of the couple, but their year together since he'd made the jump from flying with the Night Stalkers to fighting with the SEALs had made him quieter rather than drawing her out.

"Ahead slow. On our toes." *Ain't gonna find shit, but no dying in case we do.*

He pointed at Nikita and Drake and waved them down the trail.

Nikita had been the first woman to make it into ST6 through the front door because she was just that goddamn tough. And Drake had proven himself in Honduras, getting Nikita to fall in love with him while he was at it. How did that shit happen?

He'd been there and seen it go down.

He'd given away the bride, for crying out loud, since her dad had gone down ugly years before.

Luke still had no idea how that kind of shit happened.

And their skills? They'd become his absolute go-to pair in the entire squad because they coordinated like no one else. It had taken going through hell and high water—and a fair amount of very fine Scotch one night—to convince his commander to sign off on them both remaining on his team. The results had spoken for themselves.

Signaling "No Relation" Coogan to follow him left, he knew the last two would ride to the right as they came in on the target. Coogan had protested one too many times that he was no relation to somebody and the tag had stuck. Not to the actor who'd played Uncle Fester in *The Addams Family*. Not to Coogan's Irish pub in New York or Coogan's tavern in Boston. "No Relation" was also the newest member of the team and Altman liked keeping him close for that reason. Better trained than dead, though he'd transferred over from another ST6 team so he was no slouch.

Nikita and Drake would know to move slower up the middle to give the two pincers time to sweep wide. That would also allow them more time to check out what was happening ahead.

Apparently the answer was nothing.

No landmines, no tripwires, no claymores, bazookas, machine guns...not even a damned potato gun. They rolled into Hathyaron's compound, scaring up a grand total of squat. Only a caretaker they startled awake...who insisted he was alone. Carrying no weapon except for a Makarov handgun so old Luke wouldn't dare fire it for fear it would shatter in his hand. And no radio. Guy was too frightened to be faking it, swearing up, down, and sideways that he knew nothing. He'd just been told to come watch the place starting this evening.

*Fuck all!* That's what was here. Luke knew it happened, but it didn't make it suck any less.

No need to tell his team to check it out, they were already on it. And he'd bet good money that they weren't going to find a single personal item: no clothing, photos, none of that. He knew that because they wouldn't if it were him.

He climbed off his bike in the center of the main courtyard and studied the soil. This had never been an arms depot—Hathyaron didn't work like that. He was a broker, never actually touching the goods himself. You needed a hundred thousand rounds for an AK-47 or a dozen Strela-2 man-portable missiles? Maybe a Russian Tupolev Tu-22M jet-bomber? He quoted a price and had someone else get his hands dirty with the delivery. It was part of what had made him so hard to find.

Luke studied the heat signatures while the rest of his team moved in. Footprints, some six hours old that must belong to the caretaker, and a few real faders were probably closer to eighteen—about dawn on New Year's Eve. No obvious booby traps. Meant Hathyaron hadn't been spooked; he'd planned to leave. The question now was for where, because the place felt as if he wasn't planning to come back.

The soil hadn't been stirred up by helos. Rather, a lot of tire tracks. Mostly size 245 tires with all-terrain tread appropriate for a Toyota Hilux or a Range Rover. Some narrow P205s for the ubiquitous Toyota Corollas that seemed to be taking over the world. Crap! That's what his dad had always driven. Gutless little rattletraps that just wouldn't die no matter what you did to them. At least not until Luke had pulled the plugs and dumped iron filings into the cylinders, which had destroyed the rings on the day he left for good. Did the same to the bastard's lobster boat on his way out of town.

But there was one heavier pair of tracks.

It wasn't like Hathyaron to have a truck big enough to run 275 duallies with similar tires on the trailer it towed. By the depth of the impression in the loose soil, he'd estimate that whatever he was towing was below the maximum gross weight, but it wasn't exactly light either—there was only a slight bulge of side tread from the flexed tires imprinted on the soil.

The tracks led out the compound's front gate and turned toward Peshawar. He followed them to their source around the back of the main building and up to a sprawling workshop building.

Everything about the compound was traditional Pakistani—wealthy but traditional. It wasn't some heartless concrete fort like bin Laden's place. The man had lived here. But he'd hear, if he didn't already know, that this place had been found and raided. No way was he coming back here any more than Luke was ever going back to Maine.

He peeked through the workshop's window with his NVGs, but what he saw made absolutely no sense.

---

ZOE HAD SLID the *Raven* down to thirty thousand feet for better resolution. At six miles up, she could read the tags on a car's license plate. If there'd been a postcard in decent light, she could have read the address. She set one of her cameras to a wide area view so that there'd be no surprises if someone else approached. She set another to auto-track the first bike off the helo *Carrie-Anne*. That would be six-four of Lieutenant Commander Luke Altman, a full foot taller than she was. He *always* led from the front—except for the one time she'd forced him to follow in Drake Roman's wake.

She'd done it half because the mission called for it, but half to see if she could convince the bull-alpha SEAL to take a secondary role. She still wished she'd had some way to make a photographic series of

Luke's various frustrated expressions on that mission—*The Many Grimaces of Lieutenant Commander Luke Altman.* A bestseller for sure—or at least some great fodder for her social media channel.

Her vlog had begun as a way to show her parents that there was more to life than an under-stimulated, *so-boring* existence. Of course, her actual career was almost entirely classified as top secret, so she couldn't use that at all. She'd started developing her feeds on herself—creating a persona that had been comfortably distant from herself—long before she joined the military. She'd spent a year trying different hair colors and cuts—frequently surveying the results with her various followers. Eyeglasses (all decorative, of course), clothes, shoes…she'd done the research and created an entire flighty persona that had nothing to do with her real personality. Yet it had taken off in a *huge* way. Her loyal following of budget-conscious hopefuls were near fanatic.

Over time, she'd become more comfortable in the role than in the person. Did that mean that's who she was becoming? That…persona on the screen? That didn't sit very comfortably in her, but she didn't know what else to do with it.

*The Cutey-Edge* had changed its name when she'd joined the military.

*The Soldier of Style: Living in the Cutey-Edgy Budget Battlespace.*

She never mentioned joining, it was simply a better name. Fan numbers had skyrocketed. Her fan group, *The Soldier of Style Brigade,* was far larger than a mere brigade. It wasn't the 1.3 million of the US military, but it was fast approaching the half million active personnel in the US Army.

Outside the military, she doubted if one in a thousand believed she actually was a soldier. On the inside, she'd sometimes run into someone in the PX or a chow hall who would startle to find her actually on a military base. Rather than telling them she was a Chief Warrant Two with a top secret unit, she always told them she was just a clerk in Army intel—they'd know not to question her about anything. Or they should. Those who did were quietly reported, even if it cost her a fan every now and then.

Her online reputation had garnered her more than a few dates, and a serious pile of inappropriate propositions from: married men (some of them officers—whose wives she tipped off), overeager teenage boys (especially during her "experiments with leather" series), and the like. *Nothing* interesting, never mind long term.

She wanted a man...*not* boring. At least she knew that much. A writer, maybe an artist. Someone she could understand and who understood her. Someone so not like *The Many Grimaces of Lieutenant Commander Luke Altman.*

Altman had never mentioned her alternate, social self—he barely appeared to recognize her soldier-self from one mission to the next. At first it was understandable, the 5th Battalion E Company was new and the Team 6 SEALs only occasionally flew with them. But over time, the bonds had tightened and it was rare for the 5E to fly for anyone other than ST6. Still, Luke remained a puzzle; no tease elicited more than an infinitesimal frown. Definitely not an artistic, self-aware sort of person. Too bad for Altman that she couldn't stop herself from needling him because he was her polar opposite.

Way back on his first mission with the 5E he'd said he was married. To her mind, that also made him a safe target to tease. Actually, it had almost become mandatory. She'd imagined his home life.

"Welcome back from your latest life-threatening mission, dear."

*Manly grunt.*

"Did you have a good time?"

Another grunt. Then a beer and ball game before hitting the weight set. Better yet, a man cave with the weight set, the big screen TV, *and* the beer fridge. There he'd gather with his SEAL buddies and be...guys.

Such a charming image Zoe wanted to barf.

Yet hadn't he gone on a date with Sofia once? What kind of married asshole did that? He didn't wear a ring, but that didn't mean anything in Special Operations. Spec Ops guys didn't like things that could catch or conduct an electrical charge to an explosive trigger...or reveal the least thing about having evolved to Cro-Magnon rather than Neanderthal—never mind modern humans.

But there was no questioning that Luke Altman was one of the best warriors in the military and it would pay to keep an eye on him. Not hard at all. He might not be the artistic type, but he definitely wasn't a burden to watch.

So, while ninety-five percent of her did her job, looking for some clue as to where Hathyaron had gone, the other five percent followed Luke's progress. Racing ahead of the others to the outer perimeter, then walking away from the heat signature of his parked bike.

Again with the other five SEALs, entering the compound.

His unmoving stance in the center of the deserted site as the rest of his team moved ahead with rapid precision. His very stillness an anomaly that echoed along her camera feeds.

She and Sofia had had the *Raven* RPA circling high overhead since late afternoon and there'd been no movement. The Activity had reported Hathyaron's position two nights ago. Thirty-six hours, and they'd lost the biggest arms dealer in Pakistan somewhere in that window. Satellite overpasses were less consistent than drone coverage, and he must have left during one of the gaps in coverage—he'd know when those were, of course. He'd survived far too long not to. The Activity's call had sent them rushing from Italy where they'd been running missions into Libya, taking out ISIL infections one at a time.

Luke's heat signature was on the move again. Afoot by his speed. Yes, the tiny radar image of his stealth bike remained in place. She followed him around the main house—a two-story structure of typically four-square stucco design. He continued to an outbuilding almost as big as the house.

*"Raven?"* It was the first transmission of the night from the mission team.

"Yes?" Zoe answered, knowing full well what he was asking. Making the man actually speak was half the fun—he was pure gruff-warrior-hero to the core. He'd always looked it too. Clean-shaven with dark hair just long enough to look charmingly scruffy, fitting his roles when he had to go undercover, but not so long that he'd feel non-military. He wasn't like some Delta soldiers who took hairy and bearded permission to untidy limits and beyond. Never attractive to her. She liked Luke's neatness. No wasted actions. No wasted words. And certainly no wasted looks at her—even if she hadn't been watching for them.

"*Raven.*" He said it like *Du-uh!*

"Yes?"

"Zoe! Are there any damn stray heat signatures you can see on this building before I walk into it?" He snapped it out like a single-word curse.

"Nope!" Could she sound anymore facile and airheaded? Probably not. Her normal games never worked with Luke. Maybe it was because he had the sense of humor of a rock.

His helmet's camera feed came online and she split-screened his feed with her drone's eye view of his position. Sofia took over the piloting and flight status consoles. It was fun how seamlessly two women could fly together.

She kept wanting to ask men if they ever did that, but the pilots who had sufficient security clearance that she could actually discuss her job with, counted very close to zero. She should ask Danielle or Pete Napier next time they were back in Alabama—except the Captain and Major were a little daunting in their perfect synchronization. Besides, maybe it was because they were married. Rafe and Julian in the lead DAP Hawk would just assume she was flirting. So not with those two self-proclaimed comedians!

For now, she was the eye in the sky protecting Luke's back.

The insides of the outbuilding were so bizarre that she had to blink as if that would clear the monitor's view. It was an auto shop. No, it was far more than. It was one that would put *any* American service garage to shame. The equipment was all top-of-the-line gear and it gleamed. In a land where dust penetrated everything every-where, this shop looked surgically sterile.

She recognized the gear from her father's shop catalogs—he'd certainly never been able to afford even half of this. It was as if someone had driven up a big, red, Snap-on tools van and stocked one of absolutely everything. Rachet sets, welding gear, computerized emission testers, wheel alignment lasers...everything—right down to the girly calendar, even though Snap-on had stopped those when Zoe was a little girl (Hathyaron had the *Sports Illustrated* swimsuit one instead). She could practically smell the fine sheen of oil wiped over the sparkling tools to protect them, the latent hint of heavy weight motor oils, and the sharp tang of lubes and greases.

"Wow! Stop moving so fast." Luke was just scanning the room, turning his camera as fast as he was shifting his gaze. She couldn't see all the cool toys when he didn't focus on them for long enough.

"It's car shit, DeMille. What do you care?"

*I had such a boring childhood that I used to read Dad's catalogs for fun.* Nope! Not going to find her saying a word about thinking this was cool.

Luke turned to leave.

"Wait. Go back!" She'd seen something. But what?

Luke turned back more slowly.

"Stop there!"

"Didn't know you were into cars, DeMille." She wasn't looking at the tools anymore, though she could tell by the angle of view that he was.

"This place isn't mere cars, you goof. Look at the poster."

"So?" The view shifted and centered on it. The poster hung in the place of pride, centered above the workbench. It was black, with a few silver lines that suggested an Arab wrap around a man's head and shoulders. Below it simply said, "Dakar" and the date.

"It's the Dakar Rally, the toughest car race in the world. The Tour de France-scale ultimate endurance race of motor sports."

Luke took a step closer to it. She could feel him squinting at it in confusion from ten thousand miles away.

It was the announcement poster for the most amazing race ever. And the next run started in just a week.

"Well?" Luke was back to his one-word sentences again.

"Wait a sec," Zoe did a quick search of her social media fan base to confirm something, then looked back at the image of the poster Luke faced.

"DeMille." *Wasting my time here, DeMille.*

She composed a quick message to Christian Vehrs. He was one of her superfans—and a racer in The Dakar Rally.

"It means…" Zoe dragged it out to buy herself a moment.

Christian pinged back immediately, announcing that he was always at her service.

"…that we're going to Dakar."

"Fine print says the race starts in Argentina."

"Uh-huh. Which is why you and I are meeting in Dakar, Senegal, in twenty hours. If you want Hathyaron, get your cute ass moving."

Luke just offered one of his questioning grunts.

Sofia looked at her in some surprise.

Zoe offered her a conspiratorial grin—woman to woman, even if she wasn't half the woman her commander was. "Gotta keep him on his toes," she whispered even though she hadn't keyed the microphone.

Sofia's smile didn't quite buy it.

Zoe wasn't sure why she'd thrown in that last bit. She wasn't a woman who watched men's asses—that was more of a cliché from *Sleepless in Seattle* than reality as far as she was concerned. Though, being a SEAL, his *would* be exceptional. Didn't mean she was actually interested.

Also, drone pilots simply didn't go into the field. But she'd done it once for the Honduras mission and was suddenly itching for an excuse to do it again.

"Really?" Sofia's arched eyebrow—lovely, of course, and only one raised, something that Zoe couldn't do no matter how much she'd practiced in the mirror as a kid—looked very skeptical of her motives.

Zoe nodded, *Yes, it is necessary.* She long ago learned not to look at her motives too closely because she never liked the answers. Not since she was eleven and—

*So* not going there!

Sofia shrugged her acceptance—she'd make sure it was square with the company commander.

Zoe keyed the mic to Luke. "It's on the westernmost tip of the

African bulge. The farthest point into the Atlantic, if you're wondering."

"Know my countries."

"Learned them in fifth grade like a good little boy?"

"Learned them by reading the models' profiles in *Playboy*."

Zoe couldn't help glancing down at her own chest, well hidden by the pilot's uniform she always wore when she was flying. Well, if that didn't just put her in her place. Not a photographer anywhere would waste a single shot on her. Not even for an issue on the hot women of the most secret helicopter regiment anywhere.

Poop!

CHAPTER 3

"What the hell?" Luke flapped his carboard sign at DeMille as she breezed off the plane in the Blaise Diagne International Airport in Dakar, Senegal. No mistaking her, there couldn't be two people like her on the plane—or anywhere, for that matter. Petite, blonde, outrageously flamboyant in bright yellow clothes, and a smile bigger than should be physically possible.

"It means precisely what it says. And hello to you too, Luke."

He flipped the sign to look at it again, as if it would make more sense this time. It didn't. It had been included along with his plane ticket and false ID that had already been waiting at Bagram Airfield by the time he got out of Pakistan and back into Afghanistan.

*Zoe DeMille, Personal Assistant.* In large black letters.

"Not your goddamn ass—"

"Keep your voice down, Luke."

"It is down," he struggled to rein it in. "I'm not your goddamn assistant, personal or otherwise."

"We *are* low profile here," she ignored his protest.

DeMille was anything but low profile. She wore oversized sunglasses—despite it being past midnight—with thick, plastic, yellow

633

rims and pale yellow lenses. Her sundress—again past midnight, but he was pretty sure that's what women called them—was sunrise yellow with blue butterflies sewn on to flutter about the skirt's hem. The combination made her blue eyes stand out, despite the ridiculous tinted glasses. The dress stopped just above her knees, revealing surprising legs. He'd remembered being surprised the first time he'd seen those legs too. DeMille wasn't the size of woman that a man expected to have good legs, but she did.

He very slowly crumpled the sign in one fist, then folded his arms over his chest.

"Oh, you're so cute when you get like this that you just slay me. I swear on my favorite cat's grave."

"Isn't that supposed to be your mother's grave?"

"Not dead yet. Duh."

Teach him to open his damned mouth. Figured she was a cat person. As if there was something wrong with a decent dog. Day he retired from the military he was going to the pound and getting himself a prime, Grade A mutt. Nothing wrong with a dog.

Though there was definitely something wrong with this airport. The country had a perfectly serviceable airport right in the heart of the city, a city that now accounted for over twenty percent of the country's population and more every day. So what did they do? They built a brand new airport sixty kilometers into the desert that was close to absolutely nothing. Open more than a year and the nearest hotel was still over thirty kilometers away—all one of them.

The airport terminal was a shining multi-story edifice with four jetways, three of which stood empty. His plane had parked far out on the tarmac, then everyone had been crowded into buses for the drive to a small door at the bottom of the steel-and-glass terminal.

He'd watched three planes debark over the last six hours as late morning became late afternoon, which accounted for all four flights that were scheduled for today. Not one had used the jetways, except DeMille's of course. She'd strolled off the plane at the head of the line —which meant her pint-sized frame had traveled first class while he'd been crunched in coach.

"You rich or something?"

Behind her came a line of majestically dressed men and women in what he assumed was traditional attire. It was clearly one of those countries where people still thought plane travel was special and dressed up for the occasion. A heavy matron, in full head-wrap matching a floor-length dress of strongly patterned gold on red, stepped from the plane slowly but with immense dignity. A pair of tall, very handsome daughters tended her either side as soon as they were clear of the jetway.

He'd been watching people unload all evening, for lack of anything better to do. The Senegalese weren't as generally dark as the Nigerians, but they were close. They were a damned handsome race. Tall, shining white teeth, clear skin. And the Senegalese definitely knew how to build curves on their women. He wondered what the cultural rules were like about picking women up in bars here.

"Not rich," DeMille dragged his attention back down to her level. "The girl at the ticket counter is a fan and gave me a free upgrade to First Class."

"A fan." He used a tone that had quashed the hopes of new recruits for the rest of their useless little lives.

She just offered him a cheery, "Uh-huh."

Keep that up and he was going to start calling her Tweety Bird: small, yellow, terminally cheery, and far too cute for her own good.

Well, he knew a fan of what, but he sure as hell didn't get it. He didn't work with anyone without investigating their background. Her service record was so stellar that it was hard to believe it wasn't faked —except she was one of only two RPA pilots selected to fly for the Night Stalkers 5E, which said she'd earned every bit of it. But it was Nikita who had shown him Zoe's social media profile.

*The Soldier of Style: Living in the Cutey-Edgy Budget Battlespace.*

It was catchy. Funny even. Didn't mean he understood any of it though.

When he asked if her number of followers was considered a lot of fans, Nikita had taken him to the US Army site. Okay, so the Army was still outpacing Zoe DeMille, *The Soldier of Style,* in popularity. But not by as much as he'd expected—or liked. He'd investigated the site, but couldn't make any sense of it. Too foreign to his way of thinking. He'd finally asked Nikita to break it down for him.

"She plays it clean. Not a single word about her day job. It's as if she's two people, one RPA pilot and one constantly reinventing herself. This site and her fans are all about the latter." He'd tried to watch one of the videos, but gave up halfway through because he didn't recognize the woman at all or understand what the hell she was talking about. The only thing she had in common with Chief Warrant Zoe DeMille was blonde hair and a thoroughly cheerful attitude. But the overexcited-by-fashion bit he didn't get at all.

Old Maine joke.

*Three blondes out walking in the Maine woods.*

*First blonde, "Oh look, deer tracks."*

*Second blonde, "Those aren't deer tracks, they're moose tracks."*

*Third blonde is still looking down, puzzled by the tracks, when the train hits them.*

Zoe DeMille's online persona in the "Fashion Battlespace" was absolutely the third blonde. Why would he want ditzy?

Not that she made a whole lot more sense in real-space either. She was one of those women who looked permanently twenty, except for her service record and those eyes—when they weren't behind yellow-colored lenses.

He remembered those eyes from Honduras. They'd seen things so clearly, and in ways that they never taught in SEAL training. He'd been trained in threat assessment, but DeMille had been deeply attuned to emotional nuance so subtle that even after she pointed it out he often couldn't see it—yet she'd been proven right every time. But this wasn't some phony battlespace. Nor was it a real one. Senegal was one of the very few peaceful countries on the entire continent—not a single war since it gained independence from France in 1960.

"Why the hell are we—"

"Zoe!" The loud cry had Luke slapping for a weapon that he wasn't wearing.

"Christian!" Zoe cried back, pronouncing it to rhyme with Shawn, before tossing her gigantic electric-blue purse—it matched her dress' butterflies for crying out loud—to Luke and letting herself be enveloped in a big hug by the interloper. He was mid-height, slender, elegant in Armani or some such shit—you could smell the money on him from his leather loafers to his professionally trimmed beard —*coming in with a little gray there, dude.*

"To meet you in person! It is such an honor." Well, at least the suave bastard wasn't sleeping with her. Not that he cared. Or had any reason to. *Le Dude* was so French that he should be in a Parisian café… in a movie…anywhere far away from here. Right. Senegal was a former French colony. The French colonialists had differed from the British: the Brits ruled, the French married in. An attitude that still hadn't changed even in the post-colonial era.

"What are you doing on this side of security?" Zoe was standing so close that they looked to be the oldest of friends on the verge of *becoming* lovers. Had they had online sex or whatever that was called?

"Oh, I couldn't wait. So I buy a ticket, *oui?*" He was one of those Frenchmen who was too handsome and knew it. They always made Luke want to squish them like a bug.

Zoe acted like such things happened to her all the time. She looped an arm through this *Christawn's* and walked off chatting away happily.

Squashing him like a bug could be a kindness.

---

Zoe could barely understand a word Christian was saying. It wasn't his accent; her high school French had left her ear well enough adapted to easily understand his heavily-accented English.

It was that watching Lieutenant Commander Luke Altman of SEAL Team 6, without watching him, was *so* distracting. A reflection in the darkened glass of the broken water-bottle vending machine. Another against a window facing the night.

She ached to pull out her phone and snap a picture, even just for herself.

Tall, rugged, pissed as hell about being in Senegal without her telling him why—there just hadn't been time to tell him about Christian's connection to The Dakar Rally where Hathyaron must have gone —and toting along a foul attitude and a bluebird Michael Kors purse. It was actually a knockoff, all her budget could afford, but she'd always liked it. Watching Luke carry it through the Dakar airport now made it her absolute favorite. Maybe that would be her next hair color, though she'd become attached to the daffodil-blonde—which her fans still favored too. It was time to stir them up, but not blue. Maybe she'd go to a true white next.

*Focus, Zoe!* Never something she did well when she wasn't flying.

At the baggage claim, she handed Luke her ticket. "You know which one, Luke," as if he was indeed her personal assistant.

He offered her a narrow-eyed glare. She barely managed not to giggle as Christian led her aside. It would be obvious once Luke saw it on the baggage carousel, but he wouldn't know that.

"So, who is this Luke?" Christian asked in a barely lowered voice as he led her away. "Should I be terribly jealous?"

"He *works* for me, Christian. He doesn't sleep with me." Despite her teases on just that point during their last mission together, he hadn't done a *single* inappropriate thing. Ever. Of course not, why would he? Why would a man like him, who could choose any woman he wanted, be at all interested in someone like her? Even if he wasn't married.

He'd said he was, but she'd seen him head off on a date with Sofia. Her commander hadn't said a word afterward and they'd given no other signs of being together. Just a *Wham! Bam! Thank you, Ma'am?* That didn't sound like Sofia. That totally sounded like a SEAL and she wanted none of it.

"Ah. That is good. Your fans would be very disappointed if the lovely Zoe settled for such an angry man. You need a French lover."

"Like you?" Would she be interested? He was far closer to what she was looking for than the SEAL commander. His charm was as thick as his accent, both undeniably inviting.

"Ah, my wife Leola is Senegalese. She does not have the French view of such things. You will meet her. Meek like a lamb in public. But her name, it means lioness. Curiously, her name is Italian even though she is a pureblood native." He shrugged it off. "She is fierce in the home."

"And in the bed?" She felt decidedly voyeuristic for asking, but as he was French, he took it in stride.

"One look at her and you will know how she is in my bed." His tone spoke volumes.

Zoe only had to look around to know that the Senegalese women were all shaped far more like Sofia than like her. Would Luke treat her differently if she had a real figure?

Now there was an odd question because she couldn't think of why she'd possibly care.

She glanced back to see him carrying her massive zebra-striped suitcase. He ignored the wheels and simply carried it as if it weighed less than her handbag. She'd been unsure of what the future held, so she'd packed her civilian clothes—with enough changes to satisfy her fans for at least a week—and a full military kit except no weapons.

Luke didn't notice her glance. He wasn't looking at her or Christian. His anger apparently forgotten, Luke Altman appeared to be ever-so-casually looking at nothing—which Zoe knew was when he was looking at absolutely everything. A man strolled by him—*close* by him. Moving well into his personal space, which was almost shocking. No one got close to Lieutenant Commander Altman unless he was playing a role. She'd certainly been deep inside his personal space for much of the Honduras mission—atypically so, even for her. It had felt natural at the time…still did in memory and—

If she hadn't been watching, she'd have missed the handoff.

Luke had been wearing a small, efficient backpack before she'd burdened him with her handbag and suitcase. Now, after the man had brushed by him, Luke also carried a small satchel—the handoff so smooth that it had nearly been invisible. They were outside airport security, so she'd wager there was at least a handgun and a good knife in the newly-acquired satchel.

A warm shiver slid over her skin. Knowing that an armed Team 6

SEAL was watching her back felt surprisingly good. Whoever said that having a highly-protective male in your life was going out of style needed to have their head fixed—if she'd had one in her past, her present might have been so very different.

Zoe filed the idea away for her next media post.

# CHAPTER 4

"What the hell have you got in here, DeMille? You know this country never gets below 70, right?" Luke heaved the suitcase, as heavy as a field pack, into the back of the Frenchman's waiting car.

"A Vega II?" DeMille sounded passionately breathless, and was utterly ignoring him. No, purposely ignoring him. It wasn't an accident that she hadn't told him why the hell they were in Senegal, Africa, together. He hadn't missed how often he was a target of her quick tongue.

Altman looked around—Vega was a star in Lyra he'd used to navigate a few times on hikes—but it wasn't even sunset. DeMille was staring at the bright red car.

"Oh, Christian," she whispered, like saying thank you after amazing sex.

*What the hell?*

"I bring it out special for you, dearest Zoe. I knew you would appreciate her."

"The 1962 Facel Vega II. Oh, with the manual four-speed," still in that tone that was supposed to be reserved for the bedroom.

It was a long car that might have been sleek half a century ago—so retro it was almost modern. Two doors meant that emergency egress from the back seat was poor. It looked like some primitive had been trying to design the future but reality had passed him by.

DeMille was busy emoting over original leather. She rapped her knuckles on the wooden panel, which sounded metallic—which she apparently knew beforehand.

When Christian opened the hood, she scurried to look. "The Chrysler 383 cubic inch Typhoon V8." She held both hands to her heart.

"She will go *very* fast," Christian might be talking about the car or about DeMille.

It didn't sound as if she was faking it for the Frenchman's benefit. It sounded as if she actually knew something besides blue handbags and zebra suitcases filled with ten tons of girl-shit.

Why was it so hard to remember that she was an Avenger RPA pilot? She had skills, even if he only understood the one of them.

Not that he understood a thing about piloting either—except for the data feed it provided. *That* he understood perfectly because it was a new key to survival and victory in modern warfare. And no one provided it like the 5E's RPA team. The fliers of the 5E were amazing and he loved what their stealth-equipped aircraft could deliver, but at least half the reason he'd shifted most of his mission load to them was because of their RPA team.

Sofia and DeMille. Two seriously skilled women, who were so different that it was hard to believe they were the same species, never mind the same gender. Sofia was everything a woman should be and DeMille was…

She was talking gear ratios. The damned Frenchman was practically drooling. Well, whatever turned your crank. Christian's hand rested casually at the small of her back as if she was the pinnacle of desirability and not…

*Shit!*

DeMille was like a woman designed just to confuse the crap out of men. Thankfully, she wasn't his problem. Except she was. She'd dragged him to bloody Senegal. While he didn't know what was going on, he'd bet she was way out of her depth.

One of the airport "freelancers" came over with some hustle in mind. He knew the type. Hanging about and always vying to make an extra buck wherever they could. Rather than pull a gun on the guy, he gave him a friendly-seeming grab on his forearm. Pinching the ulnar nerve point, he turned him about and sent him on his way, letting him wonder how long it would be until his arm started functioning again. Take about thirty seconds, but Luke saw no reason to tell him that as long as he didn't come back.

The late-afternoon light blazed down out of the dusty blue sky. The parking lot could hold only a few hundred cars—smaller than the average American grocery store—but it was mostly empty. No sign of long-term parking lots, apparently not needed. Palm trees and irrigated grass made it appear First Worldly.

Turning away from the airport toward the near horizon dispelled that impression completely. Palm trees gave way to twisted scrub and cactus growing from the achingly dry red-brown sand. He twisted a foot and felt the slickness of blown sand over the tarred pavement. Just enough to make him compensate if he was turning a corner at a dead sprint or on a speeding motorcycle. He filed that away against future need.

Done showing off his car, Christian waved Luke toward the back seat. It wasn't small-car cramped, but neither was it the back of his Silverado pickup's Crew Cab. DeMille was half the size, but he was the one crawling into the back—stupid two-doors. How did she keep making him do shit like this?

She settled in the front passenger seat and at least had the decency to slide it forward...then she tipped the seat well back. He reached out to grab the lever and pop her upright, but the back of the seat hit the center of his chest before he could reach the control.

Which left him staring at the top of her dark part and the cascade of blonde hair falling to either side. It looked thick and soft, perfect for a man to run his hands through and—

He was *not* thinking such shit about Chief Warrant Zoe DeMille. Just plain and simple wasn't happening.

She tipped her head back to smile up at him upside down as if she could read his thoughts. Worse, he wouldn't put it past her. It would explain some of why he always felt off balance around her.

Her position also provided a very pleasant view down the front of her sundress that revealed enough to show that, while she didn't wear a bra, she was very definitely female.

*Whatever.*

*Shit!* Now he was sounding like her. Given the choice, he'd rather sound like Napier, despite his new-found Colorado-pilot-Joe Friendly mannerisms while flying his Chinook.

DeMille had placed him here. In Senegal. No idea why. And no way to ask without revealing DeMille's game. Or maybe she and Christian were in on it together.

If she was wasting his time, he'd see that she was busted but good and—

Except that wasn't like her.

So, she did have some clear purpose but enjoyed trying to get a rise out of him by not giving him even a clue. *Fine.* Let her try. He pulled on his shades against the lowering sun and stared out the window to watch the desert give way to concrete buildings. Lots of them. Most of 'em empty.

Damned weird country.

---

ZOE STARED OUT THE WINDOW. She'd fallen into a strange science fiction novel. *The Half-built Apocalypse* or something like that. Her first ever trip to Africa, first out of the US other than some training trips to Canada and Ramstein in Germany. And that lone mission to Honduras. She'd flown all over the world from the safety and comfort of her coffin—most of the time ten miles up, but to see Africa in person from ground-level was overwhelming. She'd thought it would be so easy, like slipping down to Honduras on a luxury cruise boat had been.

Not so much.

At the airport, she'd focused on Christian's Vega II partly because it was amazing, but partly because everything else was wholly disconcerting.

She wasn't so parochial that being one of the only three white people in the entire airport was affecting her, but *everything* was different.

The clothing styles had started it. Men wore button-down white shirts, dark trousers, and leather shoes. That was fine.

The women were swathed from neck to ankle in form-fitting dresses that came in a wild array of colors and patterns. It had taken her a long time to notice among the wild oranges, reds, purples, golds, and every other color both in and out of nature that no two were alike. The colored patterns of the material—which would appear wild in the extreme elsewhere—somehow belonged in Dakar. They were remarkably modest in that they covered the women from throat to ankle, but they also displayed them elegantly.

During the flight she'd been particularly captivated by a teen across the aisle who would be wearing jeans, a slogan t-shirt, and Converse in any Western culture. Instead, she wore leather sandals and a stop-sign-red dress with a gigantic bloom of multicolor painted flowers flowing upward from her hip to curl around her breast and also spilling down over the skirt. It made Zoe's own efforts to push "The Cutey-Edgy" appear timid and reserved. And it made the girl breathtakingly beautiful.

Once away from the airport, the women's lush fabrics were the only color to be seen.

She'd never seen anything like what was passing outside the window, not even the desert towns near Clovis AFB.

Christian was racing the big car along the road like a cross between a luxury liner and a cigarette racing boat. The divided highway—three lanes to either side—boasted perfect pavement, concrete dividers, Western-style exit ramps, and clusters of little orange and yellow taxis that were mere flashes in Christian's wake.

To either side of the pristine highway was an entire city under construction. Mile after mile of three-story apartment blocks, malls, a Yankee-stadium-sized sports arena, and more. And no sign of a single person or car on the side roads except for construction vehicles. Only the highway had traffic and no one using the big, sign-posted exits and on-ramps. This couldn't be normal, could it? She had no way to judge.

Anything.

It had seemed like such a good idea at the time. Hathyaron goes to race The Dakar. Superfan Christian Vehrs lets Zoe and Luke go undercover at The Dakar Rally as his "assistants." They find and take out Hathyaron. Done. Simple.

Except Christian was still in Dakar, Senegal, rather than preparing for the start of The Dakar Rally in Argentina. And now it was all going to hell and Luke was going to just flat out kill her for screwing it all up so badly.

How much of her "instant plan" had been an ego trip of "Zoe knows best" and how much had been real? Was it too late to declare a mission abort? Could she ask Luke? What would he think of her if she did? This empty city was scaring her like an echo of a bitter emptiness that had devastated her so long ago. A city with no life. No purpose. No—

"Yes, dearest Zoe," Christian must have noticed her distraction. "It surprises all people the first time. The president, he decides that the city must grow, so he is building the city before the people come. A vast city far from any services."

At least he didn't appear to have noticed her rising terror before she could throttle it back down—something she had too much practice doing.

"Scam?" Luke asked from the back seat. He'd made no response to her laying the seat back to tease him and now it seemed even more foolish to return it to upright, which left her craning her neck to see over the dashboard. Which felt even sillier.

Christian shrugged. "It is Africa. There is always someone else's hand—how do you say—on the pot? It is so normal, we don't even bother to look anymore."

Luke offered one of his grunts, apparently exhausting his verbal capacity by unearthing an actual word.

She tipped her seat upright and continued watching ahead. Still no detectable reaction from Luke Altman and there was no passenger side mirror on the old car so that she might catch a glimpse of him without turning. The man was a brick—almost literally. Solid, dependable, and just as exciting. No tease penetrated his formidable facade. Had she ever seen him smile?

So the question was, why did she keep trying? He wasn't like her father, content with his small garage and his quiet life. Her father was an open book, a gentle man with gentle thoughts who loved his family and his cars. Yet she couldn't leave the inscrutable SEAL alone. Maybe because she needed a distraction.

Luke thumped the back of her seat, as if he was punching her shoulder. Not about raising her seat, she'd already done that. So why? To remind her of something? Nothing that she could think of.

After the team had cleared out of Hathyaron's compound, there hadn't been time for any planning. There'd barely been time to shower and pack—there was always a sense of flying in a coffin that she had to wash off immediately after any shift. Cold, chill efficiency. As if she had indeed flown the *Raven* directly rather than remotely. She could feel the kerosene of the jet fuel drying and tightening her skin even if she couldn't actually smell it.

It wouldn't bode well if Luke knew that her plan had just imploded.

They finally moved out of the Half-built Apocalypse area and rolled into outer Dakar, the scenery changed only a little. One-story buildings of gray concrete topped with tin roofs were scattered among baobab trees—the fat gray tree trunks sported thin branches with few leaves, looking like forlorn rocket stages dropped end-on into the sand. She only recognized them from having read *The Little Prince* in high school French class.

In the city itself, there were few cars, almost all old, and not all that many scooters. Sheets up on roofs drying in the hot wind indicated that there were finally a few inhabitants. The flat terrain revealed a city with a few taller buildings yet they never seemed to come closer despite their considerable speed.

Focus. There *was* a reason she was here and, short of bailing out of a car going over ninety, she was stuck in a bucket seat of her own making. She didn't want Luke giving her some other unsubtle reminder.

"Christian. You have raced The Dakar seven times, right?" Maybe he knew Hathyaron personally.

"Nine," Christian suddenly lit up, as if he hadn't already been glowing before. Some part of her had been keeping up with his inane chatter about how Zoe was his wife's style guru and how her energy and vitality had captured his imagination as well.

"Ever won?" The conversation killer asked from the back seat with two whole words.

"One does not win The Dakar so easily," Christian replied in a huff. "One survives it. The big sponsors, they command resources that we amateurs can never bring. There are over three hundred entries, and four winners each year. This is not some simple party; it is the Dakar Rally."

"Which isn't in Dakar?" Luke had all the tact of a turnip.

"Alas, no." And Christian looked so sad that Zoe reached out to pat his arm.

---

AND NOW DEMILLE was getting all cozy with the guy? Holding onto his arm while he was driving at twice the speed of any other traffic?

Hadn't Mr. Suave said it was such a pleasure to meet her in person?

Luke sent a secure text to Nikita: *Investigate relations: Zoe DeMille, Christian Vehrs, Dakar, Senegal. Check whatever that site was you showed me.*

They waded into Dakar—the city, not the race. The capital of Senegal, it might seem a Third World city, but only on the surface. Buildings weren't falling apart, they were being built and painted. It was being worked on in a thousand different ways.

After a while, he managed to sort out the new construction from the old. Only after a building was finished did it get a coat of paint. He'd been in enough concrete block towns to appreciate how rare such attention was. They were done up in pastels, mostly pale yellows and equally dull blues, but they were painted. No wild Indian paint jobs here.

The city proper had crazed traffic. The rotaries—probably used instead of traffic lights because the electricity was too unreliable— were so narrow and tight that it was hard to see how a truck or bus negotiated them even without the clutter of bicycles, scooters, and taxis ignoring any rational sense of navigation. All of the vehicles came in the same color—dust-coated red—no matter what their actual paint job might be, but they were there. It meant that they had moved beyond strictly foot-and-moped culture that so much of the Third World never made it past.

However, they still changed lanes as if they were fresh out of the moped era—with psychotic abruptness most SEALs wouldn't attempt. Any opening over half a car-length long was an excuse for hard acceleration, even if a pothole the size of Kansas awaited them.

In his experience, few cities anywhere had pedestrian dress codes. Paris required a certain amount of chic—most of it black. Seattle had a dress code of never looking dressed up. Dakar did as well. Men all wore the ubiquitous slacks and button-down shirt. Some women were in the evocative dresses and others dressed similarly to the men, but all decently attired. There might not be much money here, but there was a pride in who they were. In how they carried themselves.

He also didn't see any beggars on the street. Little kids selling neatly folded packets of peanuts they'd toasted on a small propane burner using a steel wok, but not begging. Fruit stands could be merely a single pile of bananas. One woman sold mangoes into which she'd jabbed a wooden stick and was peeling with a small machete.

He'd make a point of keeping an eye out for where these vendors were, in case he needed to grab a machete on short notice.

The stark poverty was missing. Which was interesting. As if that low, painful layer had been scrubbed clean from the city—or perhaps never been there.

They plunged into the city. Suddenly the massive length of Christian's car commanded attention. But it didn't do him any good as the congestion pressed them down to a slow jog. It let Christian babble even more in his tour-guide role.

*No obvious connections outside social media,* Nikita pinged back. *He responds to almost every post by Zoe, but so do hundreds of others. He's one of the most consistent, though always in his wife's name as he claims she is the true fan.*

He started to type back: *Is hundreds good?* But figured Nikita wouldn't have mentioned it if it wasn't. Zoe. First name basis. Of course Zoe had been Nikita's maid-of-honor, so it made a certain sense.

Luke stared at his phone, waiting for further information, but there wasn't any coming in. He could feel Nikita doing that almost-smile of hers that she'd picked up since marrying Drake. Just daring Luke to ask the next question.

To hell with that. He stuffed the phone back in his pocket.

"The *Deux Mamelles,* the Two Breasts," Christian suddenly had Luke's complete attention. He slipped his hand onto the hilt of his hidden knife—five inches of hardened steel. While not quite his Winkler blade, if that man tried to grab DeMille's breast, he'd find that hand pinned to his own thigh—hard.

Christian instead waved his hand to take in the surroundings rather than making a pass at DeMille, which drastically increased his projected lifespan. But he wasn't indicating some well-endowed woman on the street either—and there were a lot of those to see now that they were barely crawling.

"They stand above Dakar like guardian angels."

Luke decided he had to be talking about the two hills. They weren't much to look at, maybe a hundred meters tall. However, with the severe flatness of Dakar and the flatter Atlantic Ocean beyond to compare them to, they were indeed prominent—and kind of breast-shaped. The far one sported a tall lighthouse in traditional white like an oversized nipple. The near one had some crazy monument that was half as tall again as the hill it stood on. A powerful man, holding aloft a child pointing out to sea, and forty meters of bronze babe on his arm with her hair and skirt billowing out from high on her long thigh.

But what Luke really noticed was that DeMille's hand still rested on Christian's arm. He remembered the feel of that from the Honduras mission where they had posed as a couple. She'd often kept her hand in the crook of his elbow when they were in public, as if it was the most natural thing in the world to her. Natural to *her* maybe. So foreign to him, even undercover, that he could almost feel her fingers there even now. The only people who ever touched him were the occasional bar babe, for the brief encounters that entailed, and soldiers who needed a few lessons in hand-to-hand combat.

Except it was this Christian guy she was touching.

Fine. Not as if he had any claim on her himself. Or interest in her.

The Frenchman just damn well better not touch her in return.

Zoe struggled to make some sense of her surroundings. Everything had gotten so disorienting that even that slightest contact with Christian was the only thing that kept her from flying apart. She'd stopped as soon as she caught herself, but she missed that tiny bit of human contact badly.

They were seated on the verandah of what she supposed was an upscale Italian restaurant. The food was good—though not up to Pismo Beach standards, or even Fort Rucker DFAC standards—but the Fort Rucker Dining Facility had some seriously good cooks working the line so maybe the comparison wasn't fair. Ahead of her lay the Atlantic: nothing but the Cape Verde Islands five hundred kilometers over the horizon until the ocean slammed up against The Bahamas. The sun was easing down toward that watery line in a sky that should be painfully blue but was tinted gold with a hazy red dust.

The ocean didn't smell of ocean. Nothing here smelled right. There was the faintest hint of sea salt, but none of the rich sea-ness of Pismo or the murky thickness of the Florida panhandle just south of Fort Rucker. Instead of the smell of garbage, which she'd expected, there was the smell of livestock.

"But we're in the heart of the city," she'd protested when they'd been stopped along a major road while five cows had moseyed through the intersection.

"That is Farouk's herd," Christian had shrugged negligently. "They make most of their living in this area. Everyone knows them. Phillipe's goats wander less, but you can sometimes see them down that street."

As if on cue, she'd looked and there they were, sorting through the garbage to see what was edible. Apparently almost everything was, as every member of the small herd was chewing away happily except for a pair of baby goats chasing each other in circles.

When they'd arrived at the restaurant, it was almost as disorienting. It was thoroughly Western in design, furnishing, and menu. The verandah perched over a craggy beach with the Atlantic rolling away from them forever.

Between their table and the ocean were tiny patches of sand that had been leveled within rock-walled terraces and were graced with picnic-table sized, open-side thatch roof. There was nothing inside them except more sand, but it might get them clear of the sun during the daytime.

Laughter floated up from a group on the second one past the end of the verandah. Most were astonishingly tall and handsome black men. A group of four white women sat close together—chatting happily away like close friends. She could hear snatches of English and French and some language she'd never heard before, but couldn't make out any of their words from this distance. Their easy way with each other calmed her nerves better than a good belt of scotch—which truthfully just tended to make her sleepy.

Zoe wondered what it would be like to just stand up, descend the stairs, and join them. They were her age, dressed in jeans, flip-flops, and long-sleeved shirts open over t-shirts. They had no particular style, no overt fashion among them. They were...so much themselves.

She would be embarrassed to wear her clothes among them, though they didn't look like the sort to care. She didn't like the feeling but couldn't seem to look away. She made sense in her own world. But her "sense" seemed uncomfortably senseless in theirs.

As she, Christian, and Luke were served with their main courses—hers was seafood carbonara—the group below was also served by someone who had been cooking out of sight under the thatched roof. Great round platters like giant pizza tins were set out. Rice, dark brown with sauce, had been spread in an even layer with a small fish and some vegetables in the center. Everyone gathered around the platters with a spoon and set in to eating, some kneeling on the sand, others sitting cross-legged.

"Watch them," Christian said softly—the first time he'd spoken in less than a merry bellow all afternoon. "They will only eat what of the *ceebu jen*—it means fish and rice and is the national dish—is in the triangular area in front of them, like a slice of pizza."

"But the fish lies in the exact middle." Even as she spoke, someone dug into the fish with his spoon and pried loose some meat. He nudged some into the triangles adjoining his before pulling some in front of himself.

"Everything in this culture is shared. It is called *teranga*. A rough translation is: 'the more you share, the more plentiful your bowl will be.'"

Zoe looked back at their own table. They each had their own section of table, their own napkin, silverware, glass of wine, and white plate of food.

The silent meal continued below them. "They don't have much to say to each other."

"The Senegalese believe that you should do one thing at a time to improve your enjoyment of it. Eat, talk, play music, make love. These are all separate."

Rather than looking at Christian, she caught herself watching Luke, who was already well started on his spaghetti and meatballs.

"Your assistant never talks, so for him it is not a problem," Christian announced smugly before cutting into his eggplant parmigiana.

A wave of sadness washed over her. An old familiar cloak that she had spent a lifetime fighting against with bright colors and outrageous looks.

Why was that simple action of the group below affecting her so?

She had friends. No, *they* had friends. She had…fans.

Zoe had Sofia—who was her commander.

Nikita was a friend. As much as the lone female SEAL had female friends. She spoke almost as rarely as Luke, which probably explained part of why she fit into the team so well. Though they rarely saw each other outside the start or end of a mission, she supposed that Nikita was her best friend. She'd certainly told Nikita things she'd never told anyone else and knew that Nikita had done the same. But perhaps Nikita was also her *only* friend, and that was a very sad thought.

There were the other women of the 5E—who Zoe liked and respected—but she was "other." Peggy, her best friend in high school, had explained "otherness" to Zoe. She had a nurse mom and a cop dad. Zoe's own parents, with their "normal" occupations of secretary and car mechanic, didn't stand out. But Peggy talked about how people always treated her parents as if they never belonged. People lowered their beers at a party when her dad showed up—as if drinking was bad even with friends when you weren't driving. Others set down their greasy burgers and over-dressed potato salad when her mom sat with them, even if her plate held the same.

Zoe was "other." She flew with the 5E, except they flew helicopters into foreign countries and she flew an RPA jet sixty thousand feet above them from a box in Alabama. They constantly risked their lives beyond the front lines and she risked getting a sore butt from too many hours in the coffin's command chair. They didn't treat her differently, but she was and knew it. They told tales of wild countries and wilder missions. She watched them from her eye in the sky.

Or maybe Zoe had no one she could just let her hair down with because she was broken inside. She knew that, but it was completely out her control to fix. That internal breakage they each possessed had created the bond between her and Nikita.

She was so sick of being "other." Of being broken. Of being…

So sick of herself.

*Teranga?* She'd show them goddamn *teranga*.

She jabbed her fork into one of Luke's meatballs and hacked off a whole chunk.

He stopped his own fork with a large twirl of spaghetti halfway to his mouth and watched her, hawk-eyed.

She made a deliberate show of stuffing the whole piece into her mouth and chewing.

Luke made no other action except to watch her as his spaghetti slowly unraveled back into his bowl—his expression as unreadable as the moment she'd thrown him her purse and he'd caught it.

*Fine! Whatev!* She sipped some wine to clear her mouth and spun some of her own pasta onto her fork.

Still Luke didn't move or look away. What did those trained eyes see? What thoughts did that bland expression mask? Not even the hints that most men gave as they told her all about themselves. Luke revealed nothing. He was seriously smart—they didn't forge Team 6 SEALs from dumb jocks—but there was no way to read what was going on in that head of his. Not that she wanted to know.

Zoe sighed and turned her focus back to Christian, pasting on her best smile.

# CHAPTER 6

*L*uke decided to grind out another five klicks. The sun was just cracking over the sprawling city and the dawn temperatures were running about seventy Fahrenheit—fifty above the chilly midnight mission in Hathyaron's Pakistani compound. A welcome respite. It wouldn't become too hot and humid for running here until May or June.

But it felt like he was part of some damned cross country team. Nothing organized, but there were a lot of guys and a few women out for a run in twos and threes. He'd never been in a country so filled with runners—no one jogged here, they ran.

Then between one heartbeat and the next he was running alone.

The muezzins' call echoing from the minarets of the mosques cleared the streets. On the next arm swing, he tapped his fingertips against his SIG Sauer P239 compact 9mm handgun just to make sure it was still in his waistband.

It was hard to believe the low religious violence stats for Dakar. Ninety-five percent Muslim, but if they decided to marry a Christian, it wasn't much of an issue. Highly tolerant. At least some damn place on this planet was—he'd fought in enough of the others. He'd grown up in a deeply bigoted household, which was crazy in Maine because the state was far more Christian white than Dakar was Muslim black. So who had Dad and his buddies been fighting against?

People from away?

Maine was so insular that someone was called a Person From Away if they'd been born "over the line" in a New Hampshire hospital, even if they'd lived the next ninety years without ever leaving Penobscot Bay.

His old man was cracked in the head. Too bad he'd survived whatever it was that had done that to him.

Luke kept pounding along the road, which was giving it the benefit of the name. There were only four or five paved roads in the Ouakam neighborhood where Christian Vehrs lived. Christian was really starting to piss him off, even more than DeMille—which was saying something.

He sure couldn't wipe out the memory of that brilliant laugh in her blue eyes as she'd stabbed up a piece of his meatball. She'd done it as if challenging him. The last fool to challenge him had been a recruit six years ago and Luke'd made the guy eat dirt for being an asshole.

DeMille had taken some of his food without his permission and he hadn't known how to respond. Still didn't. Take some of hers? Stab her hand with his fork? What?

And the smile on that woman. Half the time it made her look like a sixteen-year-old imp up to no good. The other half it made him want to do things so that he'd see it again, because when the cute rubbed off, there was a woman in there somewhere. A woman that a part of him recognized, and he wasn't thinking about his dick. Okay, he wasn't only thinking about that.

She did something to him. He could pal around with his team just fine. Knew how to flirt with women. Except DeMille.

Shit! He was starting to babble like an ensign after his first actual combat mission, which was beyond sad. Like DeMille had planted a hex on him.

*Focus on the run.*

There were a few sidewalks, but it was safer to run on the verge of the road. The sand was often several inches deep with low drifts of plastic garbage and concrete rubble at the crossroads, but the sidewalks were inconsistent with gaps and shifting surfaces. As the morning traffic built, his route was more and more pushed onto the backroads. They were all deep, gritty sand and tougher running. He didn't mind the sand—just made for a better workout—but the twists and turns, with streets ending abruptly or running into a blank wall without warning, made it harder to sustain momentum.

Everywhere there was evidence of the good and bad. New building projects marked every street, backed by another road-ending open sewage ditch or a load of deep red sand someone had dumped in the middle of the road by a construction site. It was so fine that it left a taste of iron rust thick on the air for a dozen meters around. The bootstraps that the city was hauling itself up by were plain to see.

Most of the residences were walled, making it hard to tell what was really going on inside—but there was definitely more than met the eye.

Christian Vehrs' place last night had been a shocker. He lived behind a random steel door in a white concrete block wall that looked no different from any other on the quiet back one-lane. The door had required a sharp kick to open after it had been unlocked, the hinges squealing with grinding sand.

Despite the low theft statistics, a second house door with another lock stood just inside. It opened onto a large room with cool marble floors and Western furnishings. A sectional couch wrapped around a monster big-screen TV that was set to a moderate blare of a soccer game. An inner courtyard thick with trees and bushes was open to the sky. Between a banana and several mango trees, a twenty-foot swimming pool had been sunk into the ground. On three sides, Christian's two-story home wrapped around the courtyard.

Were their private oases and family areas hidden away behind all of Dakar's sterile concrete walls?

The fourth side of Christian's home was a large blank wall with no windows and only a small door.

"Ah," Christian had said. "That is for tomorrow. Tonight is for relaxing and drinking."

Nothing he or DeMille had said swayed that determination. And Zoe still hadn't offered a single clue as to why they were here. No, she had. She'd gotten Christian talking about the Dakar Rally...briefly. But he'd ever-so-smoothly changed the subject before it went far. She'd said they had to come here after she saw the poster for The Dakar. And Christian had raced The Dakar—nine times.

And Zoe had put that together how fast? Under twenty seconds. Perhaps under ten.

Did he trust her? As much as any woman. Which wasn't saying much except for Nikita. And yet Nikita trusted her. Friend of a friend was one thing. Trust? That belonged only to his own action team. He didn't even like integrating with other ST6 squads on a mission and he understood them a whole hell of a lot better than he understood Zoe DeMille.

Luke turned the corner at a European-style bakery that offered a glass display case filled with French pastries and a sign offering pizzas that he'd have to remember how to find later. A cinnamon roll sounded good, but he opted for another lap up and over the Two Breasts.

Christian's wife, Leola, definitely had a pair of those—custom-designed to satisfy a T&A man. Pretty and half her husband's age. Her frank looks had made it clear that he was welcome to come find her if Christian was out.

He didn't know if it was for his own protection or DeMille's that he chose to stretch out on the cool marble outside Zoe's door last night. He'd slept in far less comfortable places, so that was fine.

In the middle of the night, he'd heard the soft pad of feet slapping on the cool marble. He prepared to roll away from the door so that DeMille didn't trip over him. But the footsteps weren't coming from the crack under DeMille's door, rather from the direction of Christian Vehrs' room.

Luke had pretended he was still asleep.

Christian had almost stepped on him before stumbling to a halt. His curse in French didn't sound polite, even if Luke didn't understand it. He'd stood over Luke for long enough that he was mere seconds from earning a hard upward fist in the nuts before he finally turned around and returned to his wife.

How naive and trusting was DeMille that she'd landed them here? Luke was far bigger than Christian, but the man could overwhelm a woman of DeMille's size easily.

Luke was again blocked off the sidewalk and onto the street by a roadside nursery of hundreds, maybe thousands of small tropical plants and a few man-tall trees. It was just a fifty-meter stretch along the road and a few meters wide, but the pots were all touching so there were a huge number of plants. No gardens on the outside of homes, so his guess must be right about there being a lot more courtyards like Christian's inside the city's unrevealing white walls.

A taxi carwash was a hose at the side of the road. For a brief instant, each small Toyota or Ford was its proper color again—two men with whisk brooms cleaned sand out of the inside. By the time one rolled past him a hundred meters later, its color was already hazing with the sticky dust.

He entered the roadway up to the Mamelles lighthouse. It wound a full time around the hill in a steady climb, just like tracing a finger so slowly around a woman's breast, starting at the ribs and spiraling up to...

Too long in the field. Way too long in the field when he realized he was picturing that glimpse of DeMille's breast. First, they were kinda minimal issue. Second, she was...something. Irritating? Yeah, that was it. Just like watching too many Tweety and Sylvester cartoons in a row.

His Maine sense of humor kicked in and made him feel better.

*A tourist asks: How can you tell if a boy moose is attracted to a girl moose?*

*Cain't say, but wouldn't want to be gettin' in his way.*

Imagining tiny Zoe DeMille with a moose-sized rack of horns at full charge could almost make him laugh. Thinking about being the man doing the charging at DeMille...

He kicked harder on the climb. The circle of the two-lane paved road was just tight enough that he could actually lean into the curve.

At the top of the hill, he slapped a hand on the old lighthouse that towered a half dozen stories above him. On his way back down, he forgot to account for the thin coating of sand over pavement and almost flew off the trail into a nasty looking tangle of thorny acacia bushes all snarled with wind-blown plastic.

That would teach him to think about DeMille's breasts. Or DeMille.

Twelve hours in Dakar and he'd had enough of this shit. It was time to get something moving if he had to pin Christian to a wall and beat on him to get it. He blew off the end of his run and turned to cross straight over the second breast beneath the African Renaissance Monument to return to Christian's home.

Time to make sure DeMille hadn't gotten herself into trouble in the hour he'd been gone. If she was even awake yet.

Then to find out what trouble she'd gotten him into.

---

IF one more Dakari man tried to stop her and convince her that she should marry him, Zoe was going to murder him. It was as if they couldn't help themselves.

*Oh look. Pretty white girl. She must be rich. I must flirt.*

At least she hoped it was just flirting, but she'd grown sick of it in the first hundred meters of her run and that had been five kilometers ago.

She'd pulled on a wedding ring for her morning run...which seemed to make no difference at all. At least they weren't aggressive—confrontational but not threatening. But they kept getting in her way.

Asking Leola if there was a gym nearby had earned her a disinterested, "Not at this hour." Zoe wondered if Leola's expression was unreadable because of cultural differences or if Leola just didn't care. It didn't seem like anger. Or curiosity. It certainly wasn't the fandom that Christian had claimed on her behalf.

Zoe needed Christian, but she wasn't dumb enough to trust him. He could just be a superfan who didn't want to admit it. Or was he something worse—something she'd had far too much experience with? It was the first time her professional career had needed her public image and she didn't like the feeling in the least. Lines that should never have been blurred were actively converging—the story of her life.

Last night she'd slipped the carbon fiber knife out of her suitcase and kept it beneath her pillow—it wouldn't pass an x-ray machine, but metal detectors didn't see it. Self-defense rule: don't brandish it unless you're going to use it. Twice pulled, twice bloodied. Not wanting a third episode, she'd also rigged a primitive alarm system using two chairs on either side of her bedroom door. She'd linked them together with three of her belts so anyone opening the inward-swinging door would snag the belts and drag the chairs noisily across the marble floor.

The only sound had been someone moving very close by her door just at dawn. She didn't hear the person arrive, but she heard them depart without knocking or trying the door. By the time she'd ventured from her room, she could feel the absolute stillness of the house. Which had sent her back for a quick change and a run.

She'd have invited Luke along, but she didn't know which room was his. There was an idea in the back of her mind but she couldn't seem to tease it out. If *felt* as if there was some way to recover the situation, but she couldn't make it conscious. Maybe with Luke's help... Except he was still asleep.

Usually a good workout helped her think, but her run had instead earned her nothing except jillions of marriage proposals.

Now she was trying to pump up the energy to do some serious stairs work. Trotting around Dakar, and dodging tall handsome natives with hopes of a rich foreign wife, hadn't really lent itself to the kind of workout her elliptical delivered.

But then she'd spotted the stairs up the front of the African Renaissance Monument. One quick trot up and down had revealed two hundred and four steps, level and in good repair. Eleven flights unevenly broken up between landings, mostly in groups of seventeen. or eighteen. Good. More of a challenge.

Back at the bottom, she closed her eyes for a moment and breathed deeply to make sure she was as well oxygenated as possible.

Then she spun for the stairs and slammed into someone.

"I'm. Not. *Interested.*" It took all her control to not shout it in the man's face. "I don't want to marry…" The "you" dribbled off as she looked up into Luke Altman's face. He hadn't even had the decency to waver when she'd slammed into him. He was just that substantial.

He crossed his arms and looked down at her, then raised his eyebrows at her in a question.

"I don't want to marry you either," she snarled at him.

"Good to know." They were so close she could feel the soft morning breeze speeding up slightly to slip between them. Two bodies creating a Venturi Effect just like an RPA wing's flat and curved surfaces creating lift. And with Luke's impressive biceps and chest, it was sadly apparent which one of them was the flat one.

"Go away. I'm working out here."

He waved a hand for her to proceed.

Screw him. She breathed deeply once more, then turned and began double-timing it up the stairs. Her legs were long enough—barely— that she could have done them two-by-two but that wasn't the point of the workout. Hitting every step clean, she was soon racing upward.

Only when she turned at the top did she realize that Altman was right there with her.

"Enjoying watching my butt?"

"Did enough of that last night."

At the airport was the only time he'd been behind her—for about twenty meters. Great. Like one look at her was all a man needed before he got bored.

She turned and ran back down.

"Go away," she said at the bottom turn before heading back up the stairs to start her third lap.

Luke came up beside her and matched her step for step. He didn't run up the stairs or climb them. He flowed. He had built-in laminar flow as if he was only touching the steps for guidance to steer his flight up the steps. He did the same on the descent. Ten stories twice, she was definitely beginning to feel the burn, but she wasn't going to give in yet. Definitely not with SEAL Commander Altman beside her.

At least he kept away the *Marry me* jokers. They were there, also working the steps hard with their long legs and lean muscles. But now she was "with a man" so they treated her differently. She didn't *need* a man's protection. She didn't *want* a man's protection. They'd certainly done crap at protecting her when she could have really used it.

She turned to face him on the red-brick plaza at the base of the stairs.

"Okay. How do you do that?" She asked partly because she wanted to know, but also to buy a moment to catch her breath without letting Altman see how badly she needed to.

"Do what?" But his smile said he totally knew.

"Asshole." She started up a fourth time.

As she hit the second landing and started on the next flight of twenty steps, she almost fell and ate the brick. Luke had placed a large hand at the small of her back.

"Try not to shift against my hand. Keep your body stable and let your legs do the work."

She'd have asked why, but she was running way short on breath—far more than the climb should account for. Maybe the interval timing of landings and descents was chewing her up a lot faster than the predictable continuity of an elliptical exercise machine.

At first it felt as if he was rubbing his hand up and down her back. Not an unpleasurable sensation—even if he was married. Even if he'd grown bored of looking at her ass in the first thirty seconds. Her efforts to stop the motion only made it worse.

"Stay on your toes."

"This isn't. Ballet. Class," she managed to huff out.

"Not ballet. A stable core from which to shoot accurately."

And she watched Luke sideways as they hit the next flight. His motion was so smooth, even with her jostling against his hand, that he would indeed have a very stable motion from which to shoot accurately while on the run.

With the gentle pressure of his big hand, she had a reference of what her upper body was doing. It was going up with each step, but it was doing it in noncontinuous, bumpy fashion, shoving upward as she reached for the next stair, then easing down as her foot settled firmly on the step. It made her feel like she was a bobble-head doll version of herself.

By the sixth flight, she was getting a feel for it and by the top one, she felt a little as if she was floating upward on a strong thermal rather than driving upward under full thrust. Her legs burned even more, but the feeling of smooth flight was more than energizing enough to compensate for it.

Another lap down and back without a word.

Halfway up, he slid his hand away. And again she almost went down, losing every bit of the smooth rhythm she'd found. She held it together until the top step, then more collapsed than sat.

Her lungs were heaving. Five laps? Six? Ten stories each. After a 5K run. That definitely counted.

"You'll get it." Luke looked as if he was barely breathing.

If she had a cooler of ice water, she'd dump it over his head right about now. Or bury her face in it.

"You work out. It shows." *Wow!* He was using whole sentences. Only two or three words, but grammatically intact.

"Hullo. In the Army."

He shrugged. Because of course a Team 6 SEAL had no need to respect anything in the Army. Especially not an RPA pilot.

"I repeat: asshole. Bet you've been called that a few times."

Again the maddening shrug as if to say, "Maybe." Or perhaps as if he didn't care.

"Bet your wife calls you that." Except it didn't come out funny the way she'd meant it.

Luke's fulminating look might be the first true emotion she'd ever seen on his face.

"Sorry. That was—" unforgivable. "Sorry."

But she was talking to herself. He was already halfway down the steps in that floating motion of his—at triple the speed she'd been moving. So smooth that he disappeared from view long before he was out of sight. He just blended in and she could no longer find him in the gathering crowd below.

"Smooth, Zoe. Real effing smooth."

She stared out at the Mamelles Lighthouse and the broad sweep of the Atlantic. Beneath the morning sun, it was a dark blue with a hint of green. So different from the dark Pacific and the turquoise waters off the Florida beaches she went to on leave—because she sure as hell didn't go home.

No question she was out of her depth here.

A tall Senegalese man, in green tennies and gym shorts that left little to the imagination, reached the top of the steps and sat down beside her. His smile revealed brilliant white teeth.

"You look so very sad," he said in a deep, pleasantly French tone. "Maybe you should leave him and marry me. I make you very happy."

It wouldn't be the dumbest thing she'd done in the last thirty-six hours.

Or even the last thirty-six seconds.

Crap!

---

THERE WERE some things Luke didn't need to explain to anyone—least of all to someone like Zoe DeMille.

He stood in the cool shower and tried to soak the heat out of his body.

It wasn't working.

Marva Hernandez had been everything he wanted. Exotically dark, fantastically built, and hungry for a SEAL. They'd met at McP's Irish Pub and Grill in Coronado. They'd started at one of the outside tables, a cluster of tall tables under the cool trees perched on Orange Avenue. Their group had been thick with SEALs and bar babes.

Even in that crowd Marva had stood out. Maybe that's why Sofia, DeMille's commander, had been no turn on—too much like Marva. He hadn't thought of that but it made sense. Except he hadn't gone after many others lately either. The game had gotten old and maybe even gone stale.

But Marva had everything a twenty-eight-year-old, newly tagged SEAL lieutenant commander deserved: sun-kissed Central American skin, topped with just a hint of her country's lush accent. Marva had done her best to make her speech pure Californian after coming to the US as a teen.

Long dark hair had rippled down to the middle of her back. Her short shorts and that clinging tube top had promised so much—and they'd delivered in McP's bathroom stall when he took her up against the wall later that first night.

Luke turned the shower water colder, but it was already as low as it could go.

The heat wasn't in his groin. He could feel it steaming off his head.

Two years married, his first mission with the Night Stalkers 5E had finished fast and efficiently—something he'd since learned wasn't chance but rather a trademark of the 5E.

He'd meant to surprise Marva by coming home early.

He had.

The first thing he'd seen when he walked into their home was her magnificent breasts, clutched in another man's hands as she rode him hard. A damned petty officer second class from Blue Squadron.

The petty officer went wide-eyed with shock. Screwing an officer's wife wasn't a court-martial offense, but it could easily be a death sentence.

If Marva noticed Luke's arrival, she ignored it and finished what she was doing—crying out in that near-panicked release that she'd said only he could give her because he was just that big and good.

When she came down, that lovely toss of hair and arch of back so burned into his memory that he could still see it now, she'd finally turned to him and waited for his response.

"Back early," were the only words he could think to say.

She'd rolled her eyes at him. "Asshole." Moments later she'd tried to cover it with the typical, oh-honey-this-was-just-a-mistake bullshit, but he wasn't buying it for a second. That one word had burned between them and he could still feel the searing brand of it.

SEAL officers didn't beat the shit out of enlisted men—not if they wanted to stay in the military. No one would say shit if he flattened Marva, but Luke had seen too many beatings of women in his youth to ever do it himself.

Instead, he'd tossed them both out the door without clothes or car keys and called for the MPs to come haul their asses away when they made a fuss—it was base housing after all. Three hours later, he'd dumped every single thing that was hers or the asshole's into his pickup, including their wallets. He'd towed her car—that he'd paid for —to the nearest used lot that offered him cash on the spot, transferred all except one dollar out of their joint account, and swung through the dump on his way out of town to empty the bed of his pickup.

Luke had wanted a photo of Marva's glittering smile each time she greeted him home. It would keep him company on missions and he'd had his phone out. Instead, he'd instinctively snapped a photo that went in with the divorce papers that left her nothing. He'd forwarded a copy to the asshole's wife, which had cost him everything too. And the asshole's commander, which had made no difference at all. There were *many* reasons Luke only trusted his own team.

He lay his head on the ornate brown-and-gold tile wall of Christian's shower. It still hadn't chilled him down.

*Asshole. Bet your wife calls you that.*

"Go to hell, DeMille." She couldn't do it soon enough for him.

# CHAPTER 7

Zoe stood in Christian's garage and tried not to keep checking every dark corner. Her nerves were only slightly mollified when Christian rolled up the big outside door to let in the morning sun. There were still too many dark corners. Too many places where she could be dragged out of sight and—

Gathering every fiber of strength she possessed barely overpowered that horror of memories. She had made a whole woman out of that broken girl. It was so unfair that she wouldn't stay lost in the past where she belonged. Everything about this mission was unearthing that young, naive, trusting version of herself from her restless grave and Zoe hated it. No shower, no amount of scrubbing, no amount of wishing to make that girl go away had sufficed.

*Garage!* She shouted it to herself in panic the moment Christian led her and Luke in here.

*Don't focus on the garage!* There'd been a time she'd loved her father's garage. As a little girl, she had known what tool her father wanted before he did. Could do the fussy work of rebuilding a carburetor by the age of ten better than Dad could.

*Focus on that!*

This wasn't the garage where Dad's best friend from childhood, "Uncle Bob," was co-owner. Where—

She was half a world away from Pismo Beach.

Senegal. They were in Senegal.

Surely she was safe here.

In Christian's garage the dark corners weren't dangerous shadows, but rather pools of cool concrete-enclosed space inviolate to the soaring temperatures outside. The structure was as big as a whole wing of his house—which made sense as it was the fourth wall of his courtyard.

She also took comfort in Luke standing close beside her, even if he was still not saying a word. Her attempt to apologize once more didn't even earn her the narrow-eyed inspection of when she'd hijacked a piece of his meatball last night. Someday he'd learn to use his words. And someday frogs could be princes. SEALs? Not so much. That thought almost made her smile.

The garage wasn't quite the fantastic setup that Hathyaron had hidden away in Pakistan, but it was pretty amazing anyway. Over a dozen cars were parked here, and the Facel Vega II was not the only rare prize. A Plymouth Hemi Superbird and an even rarer 1981 Talbot Sunbeam rally racer also graced his collection. She wanted to go visit each one, but the vehicles in the service bay were why they were here, so she forced herself to focus on those. Which wasn't hard; they looked amazing.

The working part of the garage had room for three cars, a lift, and an impressive array of tools. The parts rack alone was a thing of beauty—ultra heavy-duty shocks and other suspension parts, spare body panels, an extra engine... It screamed off-road rally racing even without the cars.

She wrapped her arms more tightly around herself, still feeling chilled by the space. But the cars helped pull her out of the darkness. All three in this area were Dakar Rally racers.

"They're awfully pretty."

One car was in pieces. A somber black man who was introduced as Ahmed the best mechanic in Dakar was rebuilding it.

But the Renault and Citroën looked ready to roll. They were only recognizable as such because of the prominent logos on their hoods. These bore no other relation to the manufacturers' production cars— custom-built for world rally championship races. Like most WRC vehicles, they were designed to tackle cross-country racing where roads were just a distant memory.

There was a certain romance to them. Wide tires with deep tread to run on sand or rock. High body metal for ground clearance revealed massively oversized suspensions. The roll cage was clearly visible inside the body to protect the driver and navigator in the event of a roll or flip.

"You've upgraded them both to Brenthel Baja kit suspensions." Even without the factory stickers, she'd have recognized the configurations from the dune buggies her father had built for racing the Pismo Beach dunes.

Most of what raced there were just ATVs or the hopped-up buggies that were little more than an engine and a roll cage. But every now and then a serious racer would come into the shop and want their car or truck jacked especially for the sand. If they had the cash, they went for the Brenthel kit. Independent front suspension, solid axle rear—both rugged enough to take the pounding.

"Oh, Zoe. You make my heart go wild. That is how I first find you, is that picture of you at Huckfest."

Huckfest was the annual truck-jumping competition that had run for years on the Pismo Beach dunes. Huckfesters had showed up by the hundreds, with fans in the thousands, to win bragging rights for the longest and highest jumps. The five years it had run had overlapped with her wild teenage years. She'd taken her revenge—mostly on herself, she'd finally understood—by sleeping her way through the camps.

She already knew the gear from her dad's shop, so she could speak the lingo. The men had found the combination of that and the string bikini on her sylph-like body irresistible. She'd flown with more than a few of them. The summer after her senior year she'd gone for a record of her own—"I'll sleep with you if I can jump with you." She shuddered to remember how many jumps she'd made during the two-day event.

A few of the photos, thankfully not any of the bad ones—at least not the *really* bad ones, had been unearthed by her fans and posted to her feeds. There were some skills she wished she'd never learned.

Christian waved a hand at the Huckfest photo's place of honor just above his own swimsuit girl calendar. It was her, the only woman and dressed in that trademark lemon-yellow bikini, at the center of a long line of male Huckfesters with their arms around each other's shoulders, grinning like idiots for the camera. At least she'd finally developed some breasts by then.

She was a head shorter than any of the guys. Well, she wouldn't be revealing the truth behind that photo, she'd screwed every one of them—some before the photo and some after. As if filling in the gaps had made that part of her more rather than less complete. Even did the twin brothers together to squeeze everyone in.

Definitely time for a change of subject.

"Why are your cars here, Christian, and not on a ship bound for South America?" She knew The Dakar started in less than a week and they should already be underway.

Luke twisted to look at her. She could see the light bulb flash on over his head. Hathyaron. The Dakar. Undercover. Each piece fitting except for Christian being in Dakar, Senegal, rather Mar del Plata, Argentina.

Christian sighed dramatically as he ran a loving hand over the smooth hood of the dark red Renault. The Citroën was appropriately lemon—*citron* in French—yellow.

"My doctor, he says my spine will not survive The Dakar so soon after last year's crash." He blushed as if he was less of a man for having impacted his disks. No, it wasn't a blush, it was anger. "I tell the doctor he is a criminal, but he insists that he will report me to the race association if I try to drive. They would take away my FIA license. So here my beautiful cars sit when they should be racing. It would have been my tenth Dakar, I would become Legend."

Legend was the label—and fee discount—that they gave to drivers who had started ten or more races. It was obvious that Christian didn't need to worry about the ten percent discount off the thirty-thousand-euro entry fee. Not when the shock absorbers on each car cost over ten thousand apiece. It was his ego that radiated fury.

Zoe had researched both the Dakar Rally and Christian on the flight over—the free First Class upgrade had thankfully included free Internet.

She'd already known about the former being the most demanding car race in the world. Five thousands kilometers—in vehicles that made Huckfest jumpers look like kids driving Tonka trucks—over terrain that made the Pismo dunes seem little more than sand ripples on the beach.

She'd also found a video of Christian utterly destroying what now must be the pile of parts that Ahmed was working on. Christian had jumped a dune, catching serious air—too much air. He'd flown off the top of the steep-backed dune with his nose almost straight up toward the sky. What had appeared to be a smallish dune from the front had turned out to be a catastrophically far fall on the back.

The car had landed tail first, shattering the rear end. Then the front end had slammed down so brutally that it had folded everything except the driver's roll cage in half. The car had tumbled down the dune like a shattered donut—spewing parts in every direction.

His navigator had only broken his ankle, but Christian had to be airlifted out.

"Maybe you should listen to the doctor."

His fury glared from his eyes for a moment, then she could see him visibly struggle for a long moment before he smiled and looked at her.

"If that is what my Zoe thinks, then I will accept it."

But she'd seen the look in his eyes as his rage had turned briefly on her. It was a look that said he was capable of anything. She casually laid her hand against the handle of her knife where it lay flat against her opposite forearm under her blouse.

While he struggled to regain control of himself—soothing his male ego by showing Luke all of the features of his cars—Zoe was left with a problem of her own.

Two cars in Dakar instead of at The Dakar.

An injured driver.

Her entire plan for hunting Hathyaron the arms dealer while embedded undercover in Christian's support team had just gone up in smoke. What had seemed like such a brilliant idea when she'd thought it up had turned into a boondoggle—something she'd wager Luke Altman wasn't a fan of. And something that even if he didn't report to her commanders, she'd have to.

She didn't have a Plan B. Needing one fast wasn't helping her think clearly.

Luke Altman was tolerating Christian's ego, but that wasn't going to last much longer.

Unable to remain in place among all the shadows, she stepped out the garage door and onto the street. Christian's garage door opened onto a typical Dakar street. It was reddish sand and under twenty feet wide. Two cars could pass, if one edged onto someone's front stoop— narrow mosaics of colored stone swept clean several times a day. Occasional trees dotted the roadside, but the only one she recognized was a bougainvillea vine because of its lovely dark purple blossoms showering the street with its only color.

The sand itself was gritty with bits of broken-off concrete from construction work. A small group of men were working a few build- ings down. One was mixing concrete in a plastic bucket. He dumped it into a battered steel mold. Another man thumped it a few times with a board to settle the slurry, then flipped it upside down in the sand. When he lifted it clear, a concrete block, complete with its two large central holes, joined the rows of the ones they'd already made.

That explained the grit already wheedling its way into her sandals. And the grit she felt inside seemed to make her blood flow sluggish and painful as well.

Across the street, two men sat with ropes in their hands. The ropes led up to pulleys attached to the building's third story, then back down to street level. Finished—and she hoped dried—concrete blocks were loaded into slings, then tugged up to the roof by the men with the ropes. Occasionally a fresh bucket of mortar was sent aloft to the men laboring on the third story. A half dozen others were sitting around, appearing to have no purpose other than visiting with the workers—perhaps their friends lucky enough to actually have a job. In a country where a living wage was $150US a month and unemployment hovered around twenty percent, there were plenty of friends to hang out.

The work slowed at the site as more and more of them began watching her. She wore long pants and a knee-length caftan of spangled sunrise colors that Emilio Sosa had made for her when she'd interviewed him for a post after he placed second in *Project Runway.* She was decently covered—far more than usual—but she'd felt the need for it after this morning. Even that didn't hide her from their attention. The question was obvious on their faces, *Is she single? Would she marry me?*

She wanted to smack the lot of them. And smack herself for believing this was all going to be so easy.

In the other direction, the back lane led toward the main road, a street busy with buses, taxis, and the constant interweave of pedestrians. Across the street she could see a lone tree. Its bole was painted red and blue. Beneath the overarching branches a group of people sat. Friends. Laughter. One making tea with long dramatic pours from one cup to the other. And musicians. Even from here she could hear the music: a guitar player hunched over his six-string as if he was nurturing it, a drummer with his instrument clamped between his knees, and a flute player who swayed with the music.

In moments she forgot about the construction workers and let herself get lost in the music. The flute arced above the noise and hurry of the street; it seemed to float, echo, and beckon. Her heart leaned toward it until she almost stumbled forward.

"He's a *griot*," Christian said softly, coming up beside her, wiping his hands with an oily rag. "Music is very important in Senegalese culture, and some are born to the music as their destiny. The skill is inherited. His father was a *griot* and his father before him."

"He had no choice?"

"Music is not to be denied. Like a bard of Druid Europe, he holds great power. Traditionally, when he died he would not be buried, but rather placed inside the hollow center of a baobab tree that his music may live on. Though I don't think they do that anymore."

A breeze stirred up the cloying scent of oil and grease from Christian's hands. Splotches of oil darkened his knuckles. They reminded her of a past so dark that—

If only she could just answer the flutist's call. She would run down the street and never stop. She could taste the bitter adrenaline in the back of her throat, so sharp she wanted to cough it out, but feared she'd vomit out her breakfast of over-strong coffee, omelet, and Nutella on baguette instead.

The shadows of the garage behind her and the promise of sunlight ahead of her. She'd race away until—

Zoe turned and looked back into the garage. She could see, by how studiously Luke wasn't looking her way, that he was intently keeping track of exactly where she was. If she tried to run, he'd be on her in a flash.

Did that make her feel better or worse?

Trapped?

Protected?

Borderline hysterical?

But it wasn't him or his fine backside that was attracting her attention. Not even the impression of his palm on the small of her back that she could still feel resting there.

It was the cars.

The cars. The empty street. And her desperate need to escape.

# CHAPTER 8

"*C*hristian?"

Luke could feel Zoe's voice through the street noise as much as he heard it. It resonated in some way that confirmed her identity through instinct long before he could have actually recognized it. It was down at the level of a SEAL training gestalt—simply known. When had that happened?

Maybe because, while putting up with Christian's ego, he'd pieced together DeMille's plan...and how it had just broken. The key had been the change in her when she'd entered the garage.

Tweety Bird DeMille—again dressed in yellow—had flown away and suddenly a very serious woman stood in her place despite the flowing clothes that made her look almost ethereally pretty. When she'd asked why the cars were still here in Dakar, he could hear the deep importance of the question. Then her vast disappointment at hearing of Christian's injury was far more than mere sympathy warranted.

And that had been the key to her plan. She'd intended to use her crazy fandom thing to get inside the Dakar Rally undercover to chase Hathyaron.

Chief Warrant Zoe DeMille had never been stupid. He didn't understand her most of the time, but she was as sharp as any Spec Ops soldier. He remembered how fast she'd put it all together while he'd been standing in Hathyaron's compound in Pakistan. No more than a long pause over the radio and she'd thought up and implemented the whole plan.

She wasn't being some gushing fan of Christian Vehrs; she was trying to use the fact that *he* was a fan of *hers.* A plan that had been shot to hell because the guy had busted up his back.

Yet she did her best to appear like a flighty airhead, running on no more than two moosepower. Moose were one of the dumbest animals on the planet—two moosepower was still dumber than a turnip green.

He remembered a young bull that had walked into town and accidentally stepped on a low sports car—except it was an old ragtop. Its huge hoof had punched through the cloth roof and the flooring on the driver's side. Each time it tried to lift its leg, the tendon at the back of its knee caught on the inside of the roof, making it impossible for him to withdraw his leg. So, he had stood there, looking perplexed, while Officer James had tried to figure out how to help half a ton of stupid wild animal that slashed his massive rack of horns at anyone who got close.

He already knew DeMille was smart enough to be flying for the 5E, damn it.

From now on, he was going to proceed on the assumption that she did nothing by accident.

Had she leaned her car seat back into his chest to heat him up by looking down the front of her dress? No. That didn't fit. But she certainly enjoyed teasing him. Though he still wasn't sure why, she must have some reason. Didn't she?

"Christian?" DeMille's voice was sweeter than fresh-boiled maple syrup. Okay, here came Plan B. *Go for it, DeMille.*

"Yes? What can I do for you, my Zoe?" That possessive was going to get Christian in trouble yet. Luke just might leave him with far more than his back screwed up.

"I've never driven a WRC car. Is there somewhere I can try? I'd love to video that for my fans."

And Christian lit up like he was Sylvester who had finally caught his Tweety Bird.

*What the hell? What kind of a Plan B was that?*

Luke glanced at the cars. Two seats: driver and navigator. No rear seat, not in a race car.

Whatever naive ideas DeMille might have about being in control of Christian Vehrs, she was dead wrong. The man was dangerous. Luke hoped that she didn't end up wishing she was dead because of—

"Maybe we could drive somewhere together," she made it a statement, not a question.

Hadn't he just seconds ago thought she was smart. She was being an idio—

"No, wait, your back. How about if Luke and I each drive one. You could ride with Luke and film me for the post."

Okay, not as stupid as he thought...maybe. He still didn't see where she was going with this.

"What do you think?" And suddenly she was up close to Christian with a hand placed on the bemused man's chest, pleading upward into his face as he was most of a foot taller.

It should be ridiculous, but somehow DeMille made it coy and cute.

Yes, cute as hell in the yellow drape thingy over loose slacks and blouse. She was also more concerned about clothes than common sense. These were high-performance race cars—what the hell would she know about those?

"Oh, it would be so fun to drive even a little way." "Oh, it's such a beautiful car that you've built." "Would you really let me drive one even though I've never done a rally drive?" "I have to go change! I can't drive in these clothes." And she was gone, running back into the house.

Christian never got in a word edgewise. She'd accepted his agreement without him ever agreeing. She'd simply kept hammering on every one of Christian's weak spots to keep his head spinning.

DeMille better not try that shit on him, but it sure worked on Christian. The man was in a daze as he prepared the cars. Luke settled in to wait for Zoe, but didn't have to wait long.

He'd leaned back against the hood of the Renault, partly because it was comfortable, but mostly because it pissed off Christian.

But he jolted to his feet when DeMille reappeared in three minutes flat.

She now wore a form-hugging zip-front sleeveless shirt sealed up to her neck—with such a big-toothed zipper that it was easy to imagine pulling it down. The material—like her running shirt this morning—revealed there wasn't a single thing wrong with her figure despite her slenderness. Her chest matched her, complementing her slim waist and good shoulders. Black jeans hugged her hips down to sensible shoes. A yellow leather jacket was slung over one shoulder with a casualness that said she absolutely knew she was on display. Not just on display, but loving it.

She posed by the cars and did one of those coy smile things as Christian snapped pictures of her. They conferred quickly over the display on his camera and Christian plugged it into his phone to post two of the photos immediately.

DeMille had leaned her shoulder against his as she dictated the captions for him to type in.

For all that he'd known Zoe for three years' worth of missions, he'd never really seen her as a woman until she was lying back on the Renault's red hood, perfectly outlining her bright yellow clothes. Did she also have a red outfit in case she'd wanted to pose on the Citroën? What if his car had been blue or green? At least that would explain why her suitcase had been so damn heavy.

Five-four of pipsqueak shouldn't be able to look even half that good, yet she did. Dark, wraparound shades—with electric yellow frames of course—and she actually looked like one of those fashion magazine nymphs. She was sure doing a job of selling it to Christian.

He made one final token protest that DeMille's Tweety Bird mode instantly quashed. When the Frenchman caved to the inevitable and conceded that maybe a short drive was possible, DeMille pulled him down to her and kissed him on both cheeks.

Not on the lips, Luke was pleased to see.

Then DeMille winked at Luke.

For the life of him he still didn't know why.

# CHAPTER 9

Completely aside from her new plan, Zoe itched to find out just what the car could do.

The engine's throaty rumble begged to be allowed out to play. It ran smoothly, in perfect tune, but it had so much power she could feel it vibrating the car right through the seat and the steering wheel. It was a vehicle that begged to move super-fast.

And they were crawling behind a horse cart. The two-wheel cart had been piled high with someone's household belongings: a dresser, bed, some bags of clothes. And the woman sat atop a pile of pillows, clutching a small houseplant to her chest and chatting with the drover as he shushed the horse along. Moving day.

The delay was actually a good thing, even if it was making her crazy. It gave her time to familiarize herself with the cockpit. It was unlike anything she'd ever driven. She'd been in stripped-down vehicles before with no pretty trim and an exposed roll cage—that wasn't the problem. But this dash and the controls weren't stripped down at all.

In front of the passenger seat were two screens the size of tablet computers, though thankfully their screens were dark at the moment —she didn't need more distractions. There were several other instruments including a large compass. Rally racing was as much about navigation as anything. No GPS, no satellite images or ultra-hi-res maps, or even a cell phone was allowed. Old-school navigation. She knew The Dakar used a GPS monitor for the race officials, but it was very specifically crippled so that it couldn't be used for long-range navigation.

The center of the dash was filled with rows of switches. Each time she was trapped in traffic, waiting for pedestrians or a truck to get out of the way—they thought nothing of stopping in the middle of a one-lane road to make a delivery—she studied the panel. Lights, instrument power, yada, yada. There was a jacks switch, which must mean there were hydraulic jacks underneath in case a quick tire change was needed. CTIS she'd read about, but never used. It allowed the inflation/deflation of the tires while driving: softer for sand, harder for rocks or road. She tinkered with the settings until she could do it without looking.

Most of the dash's center was taken up with a very simple display that showed compass heading and speed. Speed was critical. Going even one kph over the limit on any Road Sections of the course could have disastrous penalties of time and money.

In front of the driver's seat, she was facing a wholly daunting change from the typical car or dune buggy. The driver's console had a large digital display for speed, but it also had dials for engine revs, gearing, oil pressure, temperature, transmission fluid pressure and temperature, vacuum pressure, voltage, even altitude and fuel/air mixture ratio. It took her most of the way through the city to get them locked in her head, including the ranges that meant okay versus "oh crap!"

Christian had, of course, showed her how to start the car and shift —asking three separate times if she knew how to work a clutch. Looking studiously fascinated by his droll insults had been a challenge, but she'd managed.

A rally car's display was so much easier to interpret than flying her RPA. Each gauge was only single-layered—a dial or a number— without additional tactical overlays. The center of the steering wheel was covered in fingertip controls from wipers to engine responsiveness. Where she'd expected a stick shift, there was a towering lever that was a handbrake. The shifters were small paddles on the back of the steering wheel.

They'd eased out of the garage onto the sun-scorched street, away from the staring construction workers, away from the dark garage with its shadowed corners. At the blue-and-red tree with its musicians, they turned right and started winding their way out of the city as the flute music shifted and changed to echo the rumbling of their two big engines. And then a long, slow mile behind the horse cart and the woman clutching her house plant. Hard to get a feel for an off-road vehicle on city streets.

The suspension was abominably stiff; she could practically feel every tiny pebble they rolled over, every discarded flip-flop. Every grain of sand.

The clutch was high and tight, just the way she liked. The paddle shifters on the back of the steering wheel let her shift gears without taking her hands off the wheel. It only felt clunky for the first few shifts. Even though she hadn't gotten into third but once or twice as they'd crossed Dakar, she wondered what it would cost to retrofit them to her Mini Cooper at home.

Then she pictured Luke climbing into her Mini. Now that would be a sight. Maybe next time they were both on base she'd try to talk him into trying it just for fun. His shoulders were so broad that they'd probably rub against hers. It would take nothing for him to reach out and rest his hand on her thigh as she drove along.

She wanted someone who couldn't stop touching her. Not for the sex, but just for the contact. If that made her a hopeless romantic, let it. Actually, she preferred the line from *Romancing the Stone:* "A hope*ful* romantic."

Of course not with Lieutenant Commander Luke Altman. But with another man it could be nice. As she'd cleaned up the disaster that was her personal life—mostly by joining the Army and burying the past—she'd started dreaming of what a good man might be like.

She had definite ideas, but wasn't having much luck locating a man who could fulfil them.

She trailed the Citroën quietly in the wake of Luke driving Christian's Renault until they passed beyond the north edge of the city. They rolled off the end of the last sandy road as it devolved into beach sand. To the south lay the grand sweep of Dakar's peninsula. The few tall buildings of beachside resorts and the tiny financial district stood like a dust-fogged child's game. The beach, which had been thick with fisherman skiffs, had emptied as they'd eased north around them, finally reaching an abrupt end to the city.

Christian had Luke stop and she rolled up beside him. She'd wanted the sexy red Renault, but her persona had to take the lemon-yellow Citroën. It matched her clothes, her hair, her social media banners, even her Mini Cooper. Truth be told she was getting a little tired of that color in her life, but not enough to disappoint her fans.

Something in her appearance had to change soon to keep her fans entertained. Usually she could plan before she was ready to change it, but this time it was apparently going to be a total surprise when it arrived.

She could see through his rolled-down window that Christian was contemplating some way to switch over to her Citroën, but she cut him off.

"You have the camera ready, Christian?"

He held up his brand new Nikon Z7, now sporting a big zoom lens. It would shoot 4K video—about a hundred times what she needed for a couple of quick posts. His toy and all of its lenses cost more than her monthly salary. Almost more than her Army pay combined with the revenue from the few select ads she allowed on her site.

Fine.

She waited until they'd all donned helmets, though Christian had been hard pressed to find one small enough for her head...or big enough for Luke's. Luke had let her tease him about that, so maybe he'd finally accepted her earlier apology.

If not, tough!

"How far can we go?" She laid on her sexy, let's-go-jump-a-truck tone.

Christian's eyes went wide, and beyond him at the wheel, Luke's narrowed. Ticked off by who knew what? Studying her? What? They really needed to talk about him using more words.

Christian managed to choke out around a woman-eating smile, "Two hundred kilometers to Saint Louis. There are a few streams, but no rivers or roads. Only one or two tiny villages. We can go as far as you'd like, my darling Zoe." Even his smooth French accent wasn't going to get him where he was thinking this was going.

Wearing his normal silence like a cloak, Luke continued leaning forward with his hands clutched around the wheel so that he could see her around Christian.

*Watching me a little too intently to pretend you don't care.* But that was the only clue she had for interpreting his thoughts. She could *always* tell what men were thinking—pretty simple equation actually: male thoughts about a woman equaled sex. The math was a lot easier than fuel loads and weapon ballistics for her Avenger drone.

Luke was intriguingly enigmatic.

To hell with him.

She wasn't Sofia, dating a married man no matter how pretty he was.

"I've got one more question."

Christian and Luke both watched her in anticipation, awaiting sex for the former and something impossible to interpret for the latter.

"Yes, my darling Zoe?"

*As if.*

She hammered down on the gas and popped the clutch.

The Citroën leapt like a rabbit, spewing a rooster tail of sand all over the still-parked Renault. This was *definitely* no Huckfest truck. The Citroën was five hundred horsepower of a girl's best friend.

She hit third gear and the first beach berm at the same time, catching air on all four tires. Rather than bracing for the hard jar of the landing—a real beginner's mistake—she let her body go loose with the floating sensation.

Airy float...

Airy float...

Splat!

The heavy suspension ate it up, smoothed out the ride.

A street vehicle would have bottomed out or perhaps busted the suspension. In a Huckfest truck, that would have been a hard slap. But it didn't even limit out the springs on the Citroën's seat, never mind the suspension.

Up into fourth, she flew over a washboard area as if she was only touching the very tops of the bumps and skipping the potholes entirely.

Around a curve in the dunes, she slammed into a stream—axle deep and two car-lengths across. Water arced in a massive plume like she was parting the Red Sea. It felt as if she was. Escaping the darkness. If she could only race fast enough, maybe it would never catch her. Maybe she could fly beyond it as she did when linked to her RPA.

Back into third to recover her speed, then fourth and fifth as she headed down for harder sand along the tide line.

A flash of red in her mirror was the only warning she had before Luke took her on the high side with Christian cheering from the passenger seat—not that she could hear him over both engines' roar.

That would definitely never do.

She dropped back to fourth for more power, but every time she tried to get by him, Luke slid the Renault over, closing the gap with the waves. Up the beach was speed-robbing deep sand. The advantage lay down on the hard sand, but she couldn't risk more than a couple inches of water or it would rob her as badly as the sand. A slap by a big wave could completely dislodge her—a dangerous proposition going a hundred kilometers an hour.

Tired of the game, she poked twice at going past him on the low side.

Both times he blocked her.

Then she saw the beach swinging out toward the ocean, followed by a curve inland to make a new cove. It wasn't much, but hopefully it was all she needed.

LUKE BLOCKED HER AGAIN.

DeMille might have spit sand all over him once, but she wasn't going to get away with that twice. She was good, but she wasn't a SEAL. Girl had no idea what she was dealing with.

This time she fell way back, then came racing toward him with an alarming suddenness. He could see her once again lift up a rooster tail of sand several times higher than her car.

Rooster tail? Chicken tail. She was one of those fancy birds with bright feathers in constant need of tending and preening. Damned cute...and flighty—unpredictable from one second to the next.

He didn't understand how he'd missed the cute before. *Because you like your women with breasts built to make a grown man weep.* True, but then why couldn't he erase the image of DeMille as she'd zipped herself into the yellow leather jacket and climbed into a racecar?

Suddenly, the feel of how his palm had fit the curve of her lower back while running the steps at the African Renaissance Monument took on new meaning. It burned where it rested on the steering wheel. He'd felt every muscle, felt the softness and warmth of her skin through the thin moisture-wicking material, far more than he felt the heartbeat of the Renault's engine.

She was—

Catching up fast.

He squeezed over.

"Make her eat surf," Christian called from passenger seat. Whatever his other shortcomings, Christian was mad about racing. He kept giving Luke little tips. Some Luke knew from racing bikes, but others were new, unique to getting the most out of a world rally car.

If Christian was fine with Luke putting his other car into the surf, then DeMille was in for a hell of a ride.

Just as she pulled close behind his bumper, he veered down the sand toward the ocean.

He checked the rearview to watch the splashdown.

DeMille wasn't there.

"Where the—"

Christian was shouting out in surprise, and looking the other way.

DeMille hadn't merely come around his other side. She shot high and hot across the beach and up into the soft sand. Even over his own engine, he could hear her take another gear.

Then she lifted off. Where one cove had ended to bend into the next, the sand had built up high.

Using it like a stunt ramp, she was airborne.

Her massive catch-up speed hadn't been about overtaking him at all. She'd been gathering speed specifically for this jump.

He could only watch in awe.

For a long second, she flew down the beach as if she was her damned drone brought to life. He half expected wings to slash out sideways. Hang time like he'd never seen.

The car twisted slowly, leaning more and more to the right.

If she hit like that, she was going to roll. Bad!

"*Merde!*" Christian managed in a voice that made the same assessment.

Moments before she hit, she turned the front wheels to a new alignment. Then revved the engine hard enough for it to cry out. But it also applied a twisting force that killed the sideways roll just before she touched down.

The tires caught and bit at the perfect angle, jerking her brutally to the left before a brief fishtail that left her aimed straight down the next beach and well out in front. He couldn't have done it better. And maybe not as well.

"Holy mother—" this time Christian wasn't staring at Zoe racing away to the right, but instead straight ahead.

Luke looked, then jolted.

He jammed down a gear for more power and cut the wheel hard. They were up on two wheels, riding the hairy edge of a roll themselves.

One cove's beach had swept outward—and the curve of the next had swept in.

While Zoe was jumping the divide between them, he'd distractedly continued driving out the curve of the disappearing cove. He was now aimed straight for the ocean while the beach swung away in a new direction.

They were slammed hard when they hit the water, but he managed to continue the turn as the deepening sea slowed them. Still he might have gone over if a wave hadn't caught him halfway up his door and slammed him down onto all four wheels again. He sliced for the harder sand of the beach before the wave could drag him out to sea in the undertow.

Four-wheel drive, a powerful engine, and perhaps more luck than he deserved—after watching Zoe when he should have been driving—were all that kept him from unexpectedly setting sail in a Renault racing car.

Once clear of the water, he jammed to a halt on the beach.

He and Christian looked at each other, then in unison turned to stare down the beach.

Zoe's car was a tiny spark of yellow sunshine far down the stretch of beige sand.

"Tell me you got that on video," Luke could only hold onto the wheel and squint against the brilliant sunlight.

Christian's voice sounded as if he'd just had amazing sex and hadn't recovered yet.

"I got it."

*L*uke had tried, but though he'd caught up to her—eventually— no way had she let him pass. A few times she'd had to abandon the beach and race between the imposing baobab trees like slalom poles. Or perhaps like a pinball dodging between the massive gray pillars of the wide trunks with a major tilt penalty if she clipped one.

Once or twice, while racing through the brush, Zoe found a dirt track, but those were usually so rutted that it was less hazardous going overland among the scattered thorn scrub. At least being in front, she only ate a little dust...the Renault in her rearview was coated rust-brown rather than lipstick-red. In the lead, she got to breathe ocean salt and fresh palm breezes when they jogged inland. On the occasions when she managed to reach sixth gear—often topping two hundred kph, over one-twenty miles an hour—even the morning's heat couldn't catch up with her.

Christian obviously knew the route well and several times directed Luke to turn aside. Perhaps in hopes of passing her by in the process. But she'd flown hundreds of drone missions where her job was to go in first, often providing guidance to the manned aircraft behind her. She'd developed a sixth sense that had managed to anticipate each time Luke gave the slightest twitch out of her rearview mirrors.

"Not getting by me that easily, Luke."

He too had answered her every move with a countermove—he couldn't pass her, but neither could she lose him. He drove the same way he ran, with an unexpected smoothness of flow. As if his hand was forever placed at the small of her back, she could feel herself driving more cleanly with each moment they vied for the lead.

Twice he got close enough beside her that she could see him watching her as much as where he was driving. It wasn't a greedy look like Christian's, wanting all that any man ever wanted from her. No, Luke's assessing gaze wasn't quite a smile but it spoke of the joy of the challenge. He was a warrior for SEAL Team 6, of course he was competitive.

Well, she hadn't become a Night Stalker by slouching along.

Half the time she could have jumped a truck better than the Huckfesters she flew with. She and her father often took the trucks and dune buggies he'd built out onto the sand for testing. Her favorite times had been when he had a pair of them ready at the same time.

Side-by-side family races had ranged up and down the dunes.

Lines of attack.

Jostling for the best angle to take the big dune slopes.

Backsliding in the sand from a misjudged climb.

Punching through the flow of Oso Flaco Creek where it drained deeply across the beach.

Bobbing and weaving to shake out the armature and run in the gearbox so that everything ran tight and smooth. By twelve, she could match most other racers on the dunes. By sixteen, no one could touch her—not even her dad.

Those had been her favorite times growing up. She'd always been much more her father's daughter than her mother's even before—

*Nope! Not going there!*

Zoe jammed down a gear and almost ran Luke into the waves. She hadn't even realized he was there, but he backed off fast to save himself. Too bad there was no one to save her.

It was the last time Luke came close to seriously challenging her lead.

She was ten car-lengths in the lead on a long sandy stretch of the beach when the first sign of Saint-Louis appeared. It was a magnificent ten-meter fishing boat pulled up onto the sand—right across her path. It was such a surprise that she almost slammed into it broadside. Thankfully a receding wave left her a low-side gap that she was able to slip through, ducking below the proudly jutting prow. Luke missed the timing as the next wave rolled in and had to take the longer route around the stern through the deeper sand—stretching her lead to fifteen lengths.

The boat was like a canoe with pointed ends that someone had put on a torture rack until it was shockingly slender—almost elegant in how it stretched out to twice the length that seemed proper. A whole line of the long boats were perched upon the beach with their prows aimed out to sea. Dark bottomed, they had white upper sides. Each boat's name—or maybe it was each family's—had been painted down the length of the sides. The entire prow was elaborately decorated with orange, red, and blue images that might be blessings offered to the gods of fishing, or perhaps were simply each fisherman's expression of art.

In the midday heat, the fishermen were sitting in the shade of their boats, mending nets or chatting. Maybe they'd been out for the morning fishing and were now waiting for an evening cast.

She was so busy admiring the boats that she missed when Luke was no longer visible in the gaps between them.

Zoe spun the wheel, sliced up the beach in the narrow alleyway between two boats—barely missed snarling her tires in a piled-up fishnet—and prepared to gun off in hot pursuit before she spotted the red Renault. It was parked high on the beach in front of a single-story beige concrete block building. She eased up through the thick sand and parked alongside it as Christian and Luke climbed out.

Luke smiled at her over the roof of his car. He actually smiled. It was like a gut punch. No, bad analogy. It was like a gut punch by a comfy pillow. It said, *You done good.*

Coming from a Team 6 SEAL officer, it didn't need to say a single word more than that. She couldn't tell if it did say more because it made her look away. Luke Altman smiling was just...wrong. And smiling at her was downright confusing. It hadn't taken a genius to read what he thought of her at the airport.

*The Many Grimaces of Lieutenant Commander Luke Altman.* They had all too frequently been aimed at her in the past. Even on the Honduras mission where she'd thought she was doing important work, she could now see that he'd barely tolerated her presence.

Fine. After this mission she'd swear to never have a good idea again.

Except he was smiling at her.

Why did the man have to be so damn confusing? If he would only remain a mere macho jerk, she'd know what to do with him.

Speaking of which...Christian opened her door as she killed the engine and shed her helmet. At least he was a smooth and well-mannered macho jerk. That she *absolutely* knew how to deal with. He was close enough that she could see the look in his eyes. Except rather than avaricious desire, it was...pain.

"Are you okay, Christian?"

"I am fine. Fine!" He brushed it off but she didn't quite believe him. "The way you drive, my darling Zoe. *Incroyable!*"

"Christian?"

"It was a fantastic drive. You have the gift. Your assistant is surprisingly good as well..."

Luke had come up beside Christian and was actually grinning again. Or still. Or something.

"...and with a little practice, he could be almost as good as me."

Luke's smile grew. He remained half a step behind Christian and she knew that Luke's ego was really enjoying this.

"But you Zoe. The way you flew," he slapped one hand off the other and arced it to the sky, but winced hard and didn't complete the gesture, drawing his arm back slowly.

Luke had noticed it too, his smile turning off like a light switch. He caught Christian's arm as he stumbled and helped him to stand upright once more. Then he probed Christian's back with his other hand. It earned him a spectrum of winces and one deep grunt.

"Doc was right. You screwed your back, my friend," Luke rumbled out.

"It was during your recovery after Zoe's first jump. Not your fault; I don't know how you saved it."

"Almost didn't," Luke continued in a surprisingly friendly tone as he massaged Christian's lower back.

Zoe had been certain that Luke utterly despised Christian. Guy bonding must have happened in the car—like a cloud of shared testosterone or something. If they were bonding over her, she was going to take them both down. She didn't care if they both towered over her.

"Might not have saved us from a swim except for some of that advice you gave me when we first started out," Luke was turning downright loquacious. Maybe he was the one who needed to go see a doctor.

Nikita would never believe it. Zoe wished she'd taped the moment so that she could prove it had happened.

"Let us sit and eat and drink. Then my back will be better."

Zoe looked around and didn't see where they would go.

Christian pointed. "Mama Odette makes the best *ceebu jen* in Senegal."

An old woman sat out on a patio overlooking the beach. She was wizened in a country where fifty was old and sixty was ancient. In her hand was a heavy, meter-long stick and she was beating it into a large wooden bowl placed between her feet with the energy of a twenty-year-old. It took a moment for Zoe to figure out that it was a giant mortar and pestle.

"See? She is already grinding the spices for our meal." It was more the right size for grinding an entire pumpkin than the scant quarter-cup of spices she scooped out of the bowl as they settled in the cool shade of the tin-roofed awning. As a young servant girl served them tiny glasses of mango juice, Zoe could only look out at the strangeness of it all.

Close by her chair, Mama Odette was cooking on a small propane tank—smaller than for most BBQ grills at home—with a single burner fitted directly on top of it. The large steel wok there appeared to be her only cooking vessel.

In front of them was a line of traditional fishing boats baked in the midday sun, looking as if they'd been little changed in centuries.

And off to the side were parked two vehicles at the peak of exotic motor sports—world rally cars.

It was a land of such sharp contrasts.

LUKE WONDERED what had happened to him.

Actually, he knew the answer: Zoe DeMille had happened to him. But that didn't make the feeling any more familiar.

This morning the flighty girl in her lemon-yellow jogging clothes had proved that she had stamina and skills. Six times up ten stories of stairs, he'd been able to see that she improved rather than flagged the more she ran. He had to respect that—even if it was so unexpected that he wondered if he was remembering it wrong. No, her athleticism couldn't be denied. Just because a SEAL's mission field pack could weigh more than DeMille herself didn't change how fit she was.

Next he tried to discount how the small of her back had fit against his palm, but it had preoccupied too much of his thoughts since then to question that either.

In the garage she'd been playing Miss Sexy Airhead, which had been news on its own—the sexy part. The blonde airhead part he'd already known about—or had always assumed before. Christian certainly believed it.

He kept an eye on Zoe and Christian sitting at either end of a small, battered sofa, talking about racing. It was a technical conversation of car handling that he could barely follow, yet he knew that Christian still only saw his Tweety Bird target.

But the way she'd driven.

Luke had initially wondered if she could even navigate the streets of Dakar. The Renault that he'd been driving was an eager car, severely hot to trot. It wanted to dig in and go like a woman in her prime. He'd kept waiting for DeMille to be overpowered by the car and crash it into some banana stand or cream a faded-orange taxi.

But Zoe hadn't just tamed the Citroën, she'd dusted his ass with it!

That jump hadn't been the final trigger for him. Not that it wasn't about the sexiest thing he'd ever seen a woman do—it was. But as she'd outsmarted him for kilometer after kilometer, he'd learned to respect her as well.

He could count the number of people who'd done that to him on a single hand—with most of his fingers folded.

Zoe DeMille had outmaneuvered him at the juncture of the two coves—then kept doing it for two hundred kilometers. Even Nikita couldn't do that. She was an awesome SEAL, but to be so endlessly creative—that wasn't skill, it was a gift.

Some of it was driving skill; Zoe had clearly driven these kinds of vehicles before. But it didn't matter how much of a feel he got for the car—or how many underhanded plans Christian cooked up for him because Christian knew the terrain—Luke couldn't get past Zoe's guard.

The woman who climbed out of the car on the beach of Saint-Louis wasn't the same one who'd settled behind the wheel in the dim Dakar garage. Her hair was matted with sweat from the helmet she'd worn. She'd unzipped that leather jacket, again revealing the tightly clinging shirt beneath, sweaty and dusty now. The immaculate Zoe DeMille looked slightly disheveled for the first time since he'd met her. Even when they'd crash-landed a helicopter into that jungle river in Honduras, she'd surfaced more like a cartoon mermaid than anything else.

Sitting beneath the tin-metal awning, her eyes hidden by her yellow-framed dark wraparounds, she looked stunning. Her easy confidence as those slender hands arced like a bird in flight when she was describing her approach to a jump. The heat-heavy midday breeze managing to tease her hair into soft ripples as she leaned forward and slammed back to imitate a hard-landing, punctuated by a happy laugh.

She might be entertaining Christian, but now she stood tall in his mind. The woman had skills—real world skills that he understood. Escape and evasion tactics that had never been taught by any SEAL course, she'd displayed at the wheel of her car. No wonder she was a top RPA pilot. If she could fly like that when bound by the restrictions of terrain and gravity, what she could do aloft must be seriously next-level shit.

It was only looking at her, shining in the sun as she fluffed her hair with her fingers, that he finally figured out what she was doing.

She actually *had* a new plan. A Plan B.

Plan A she'd cooked up while he was standing in Hathyaron's Pakistani compound. And its death notice was the question she'd asked in the garage: *Why aren't your cars on the way to the Dakar Rally in South America?*

He'd caught that she'd hoped to attach herself to Christian's team. It would have been a great chance to hide in plain sight while they hunted for Hathyaron.

But when that got shot down because of Christian's screwed-up back, he'd thought she wanted to go for a drive just for her social media thing.

Then, when he saw her drive, he'd decided it was a joy ride. He'd rarely had as much fun in a car—front or back seat—as chasing after DeMille. Maybe it was chasing the pretty woman—

Whoa! Had his head really gone there?

It had.

Except that wasn't what she'd been up to at all.

It wasn't the jump that gave away her Plan B—something she might have mentioned that she had, rather than leaving it to him to figure out.

He watched her bend and twist to work out the kinks from two hard hours of driving. Fantastic flexibility that was a joy to watch.

But after racing her for two hundred kilometers over incredibly challenging terrain, her Plan B was so goddamn obvious she could have posted a billboard along Maine Route 1.

It was also brilliant. With all of the cues she'd given, he didn't need to ask what it was—now that he'd gotten his head out of his ass.

If they could convince Christian to take a car to the Dakar Rally and let Luke drive it, he could still chase after Hathyaron. She'd gone out of her way to force Christian into the car with him so that Luke had the opportunity to demonstrate that he had the skills.

Her ploy also forced him to look at DeMille in a new way. She wasn't some overbuilt bitch like Marva. Her apology this morning had sounded sincere and heartfelt—even if she hadn't really done anything wrong except slash open a scar so old that he'd forgotten it was there.

And she had Christian eating out of her palm—he was positively lapping up the crap DeMille dished out. Maybe in addition to being smart, she was also reliable. Novel idea.

She'd slid so smoothly from Plan A to Plan B back at the garage that he could still barely see the transition in memory—not a chance that Christian Vehrs had caught on.

*Not going to The Dakar? Can we please take the cars out anyway?* Then that whole frenetic pitch where she hadn't given Christian time to refuse.

She made Luke feel slow.

*No one* did that! But DeMille had.

They *needed* Christian's willing cooperation. And she'd seen how to get it from the very first second.

How could he help but smile at her. A great driver, funny, cute as hell, and smart to boot. Climbing out of that car and fluffing her hair in the sunlight, what wasn't there to smile about.

She'd befriended Christian. No problem for DeMille—apparently every person with a Y chromosome was her instant friend. No, that wasn't it. Nikita also liked her, as had DeMille's commander. He and Sofia had spent much of their abortive date talking about DeMille. And her flock of rabid fans were mostly women—plus at least one very essential guy named Christian Vehrs.

Luke had better do the same. Being nice to a man who deserved a sharp slap upside the head for how he thought about Zoe wasn't easy, but Luke had found a way there when Christian's back had acted up. He had done plenty of missions with guys who'd screwed up their backs on the infiltration and completed the mission anyway.

Doing a second undercover assignment with DeMille was shaping up to be very interesting.

After dinner, Christian's back was so bad that he could barely get up from the battered sofa. With Mama Odette's guidance, Zoe had raced to a local pharmacy and then dosed Christian with prescription strength codeine, which apparently didn't require a prescription in Senegal.

"Sure! Anything you need: Schedule II narcotics, Cipro antibiotic, cough drops. No problem. All at the pharmacy. Doctors in Senegal are only for when you break something. You go to the hospital if your only other option is dying, otherwise we don't waste the time. And most times, if it is time to die, people just do that rather than fighting it. Let's go! I'll race you back, dearest Zoe. This time I will drive."

"Christian. Your back?"

"Pfft!" he waved his hand airily as if dismissing the concern. Then he tripped on a crack in the sidewalk and would have gone down if Luke hadn't caught his arm. Christian yelped as the motion pulled at his back hard enough to punch through the painkiller.

"A taxi, my friend," Luke kept an arm around Christian's shoulders, looking supportive, but also effectively trapping the man.

As far as she could tell, Luke was being sincere with his kindness. She still needed to find out what that was about. If he was being sincere about that, had he been sincere with his smile as well? As they'd eaten their triangular areas of the *ceebu jen* platter, she kept catching him watching her. A few times he was looking at her body—in such a thoughtful way that she could feel the heat rippling through her, and not as a blush to her cheeks.

But mostly he was looking at *her* as if he'd never seen her before. Sure he had—he'd simply looked through her, not at her. Luke's new state of observation was decidedly unnerving.

"It will be a much smoother ride in a taxi," she assured Christian. It would, but some part of her wanted Christian out of the way, and not just because of his habit of only looking at her body rather than at her.

She decided to trust the instinct, even if she didn't know the cause.

"We'll take the rally cars back to Dakar for you."

Christian's protests didn't alter Luke's actions in the slightest. Christian was soon tucked into the back of an orangish cab and was most of the way to asleep in the back seat by the time Luke had given the driver the address. The four-hour drive would cost him under a hundred bucks and he'd be thankful for it later. At least Zoe hoped so.

The cab had pulled away after Mama Odette gave the driver a lengthy lecture about this being a good friend of hers and she'd know if he wasn't treated well or if he was ripped off or... That's where Zoe's high school French gave up the ghost.

Then Mama Odette had waved and headed inside her house without another word, leaving Luke looming over her until Zoe found herself shuffling her feet on the hot sand.

She tried looking up into Luke's eyes, but the sun was close behind his head, blinding in the bright sky. Looking toward the house felt as if she was trying to stare at their hostess who had apparently had enough of them...or perhaps had enough sense to snooze through the midday heat. Looking at the sea felt like she was avoiding looking at Luke. And shifting so that she could look at him clear of the sun still left her blinded by the sight of him. He'd always been handsome in a rugged, rough-and-ready way, but now he was...

Zoe was losing her mind. This was Lieutenant Commander Luke Altman and she was—

"What's the prize?" He folded his arms over his beautiful chest and looked down at her with those equally lovely blue eyes.

"The prize?"

"If I beat you on the drive back?"

Zoe laughed, "You couldn't even catch me getting here."

"I'm light one passenger now."

"Still won't help you catch me."

"What will?"

"Not being married, for one." Zoe had no idea why she'd said that. That so couldn't be what he was asking.

"Not married." And by the thousand-and-first grimace of Lieutenant Commander Luke Altman she now knew exactly what button she'd hit this morning at the top of the African Renaissance Monument steps.

"But you were… And…" Zoe started piecing it together. "And she called you an asshole. And I said—" Suddenly the fish and rice that had tasted so good before twisted in her stomach like it had come back to life. "I'm so sorry, Luke. I'd never— I didn't— I—"

"Not your fault, DeMille. I don't talk about it much. Try not to remember it much."

"You don't talk much at all."

He scoffed—maybe that was his version of a laugh, but he didn't say anything else, and Zoe again found that she was shuffling her feet.

"Is it something you want to talk about?"

His face didn't change, but she could see his arms tightening.

"I'll take that as a big fat no."

"Smart," he nodded his approval and she felt fantastically tall…at least five-five.

And if he wasn't married? And he'd smiled at her? Then he was thinking… "Whoa!"

He gave her another dose of silence. Maybe he'd meant the double entendre, *What* will *let him catch me?* Nope. Not answering that one. She'd stick with racing cars. Those she understood.

Cars.

"I'll prove you can't catch me."

Instead of a grimace, he raised his eyebrows.

"You take the Citroën." She'd still beat him even if she drove the Renault. She crossed to the Citroën to fetch her helmet and jacket.

"You got a red outfit to wear with the Renault? Not sure it's legal for you to drive it if you don't." There was something sly in his voice. Teasing her about her suitcase? Teasing her at all? That would be an absolute first for him.

In answer, she grabbed her shirt's zipper at her throat and tugged it down far enough to expose the front strap of her bright red bra. She'd long since learned that even being lightly built, a girl needed support when off-road racing.

"Is that red enough?"

Luke's eyes went dark. He didn't move an inch as she made a show of putting on her jacket and zipping it all of the way up without zipping up her shirt first. He hadn't moved when she'd donned her sunglasses and helmet.

It was the first time she'd ever gotten a "male" reaction out of him and it felt like someone had just kicked on her body's turbocharger. Chance had led her hand to grabbing the red bra when she was changing. Which had left her wondering just how desperate she was to get Christian to lend them his cars.

Enough to…?

No! She'd decided that before she'd even returned to the garage. Even pretending just wasn't going to happen. But to have it work so well on Luke Altman—the *unmarried* SEAL Lieutenant Commander Luke Altman—that was a different matter entirely.

She stepped around him, climbed into the Renault, and fired off the engine. Plucking Luke's helmet off the seat, she held it out to him. He took it autonomically but made no move to put it on.

"You got to catch me to get the prize." By which time she hoped that she knew if she wanted him to.

"I—"

She never heard "I—" *what* because she gunned the engine and popped the clutch.

In the rearview she could see him trying to bat the sand she'd sprayed off his face and out of his hair.

———

LUKE SPIT out more sand as he yanked on his helmet and jumped into the Citroën. By the time he'd strapped in, she was a kilometer down the beach—well clear of the fishing boats and accelerating hard.

The shore lay south-southwest, almost straight into the sun. And there was a tiny shining star redder than Mercury far down the beach. He'd be damned if he didn't catch it.

To hell with behaving. Most of the fishing fleet had pushed back out to sea while they ate…much of the beach emptying. He opened up the Citroën.

"Come on, baby. Show me what you can do!"

And the car leapt. They were twenty klicks down the beach before he caught up with her. The Citroën was awesomely powerful. Though catching up to DeMille had seemed a little too easy as if she'd been waiting for—

DeMille slashed up the beach. The tide had come in, so the beach was narrower and all the sand they had to run on was soft. What was she up to this time?

She started carving S-turns in front of him, up and down the beach. Soon, he was enveloped in a cloud of dust and had to slow to make sure he didn't end up in the ocean or wrapped around a baobab. When he finally broke through into clear air, DeMille was again well down the beach.

"Gonna play hard to get, DeMille? Well, two can play at that game."

This time he waited for a long straight stretch that he could see was clear before he attacked. He jounced and rocketed over the lumpy sand, carved by wind and water into knee-high humped dunes. The car was jumping every other one.

Launch…slam! Launch…slam!

He hoped he wasn't about to shatter the car. That would piss Christian off but good.

Luke was almost upon her. Close enough to imagine that he could feel the heat of her. Smell her over the Senegal sea and iron dust. Could almost touch—

And she jolted ahead.

She'd been holding a gear in reserve. Now she was taking the dunes in groups of three. He tried, but he couldn't get the Citroën to fly the way she was lofting the Renault.

No, she wasn't lofting it. She was racing low and fast, as if she'd found the flow of running up the steps and now he was the one who was clumsy like some midshipman jouncing up a ship's ladder.

How?

He tried changing gears and engine power.

No better.

Then he remembered something Christian had said about the suspension. He angled across the dune tops ever so slightly. Not a big obvious zig-zag as she'd done earlier to raise the dust cloud, but an angular attack, up and down the beach. The ride smoothed out and he began keeping pace with her.

Now that he thought of it, he saw that Zoe was doing the same.

Damn but she was incredible, hurling three tons of racing machine over rough ground at two hundred kilometers an hour.

He managed to pull even, but he couldn't get by her. He knew that she was toying with him, but he wasn't going to let her get away with it this time.

For twenty kilometers neither of them could get more than a few meters of advantage. Waves breaking in a white blur to the right. Palm trees close on the left, but the bright sun far enough into afternoon to pound relentlessly against the car. No sound but the engine's roar. No feeling except the twitching of the wheel in his hand and the impact of tires on sand transmitted to his butt.

Ahead by a nose, the length of the front end...

Then catching a bad patch of sand, and suddenly he was staring at her rear bumper, again clawing to keep up.

He was just about to—

Zoe cut over hard in front of his nose. She didn't clip him, but it was a close thing.

His rear end broke free—she'd forced him to brake at a bad moment on a swell of sand, and probably knew that. It took everything he had not to roll or flip. Dumping speed. Handbrake on, then back off. Down two gears and gun it while counter-steering.

The dust and sand was a cloud around him as he finally spun end for end. Running backward down the beach for a moment, then snapping around to aim forward once more.

Finally back under control, he prepared to gun after her. Paybacks were gonna be hell.

Except she wasn't down the beach.

Instead, she'd parked the Renault sideways across the sand like a road block.

DeMille simply sat at the wheel, looking at him out the side window.

He rolled up until his front bumper stopped a single meter from her door.

Never in his life had he needed a woman the way he needed Zoe DeMille. Not Marva. Not the head cheerleader who'd taken his cherry at sixteen—Susan? Cindy? He didn't know. It didn't matter.

He needed DeMille.

But still neither of them moved.

They finally shut off their engines at the same moment.

Shed helmets.

Stepped out onto the hot sand.

Closed car doors.

Zoe didn't move away from the Renault, outlined in yellow against the red.

He couldn't stop moving.

# CHAPTER 12

Zoe couldn't move. Pinned in place by…what?

Not like the shocked disbelief that such a thing couldn't be happening, like so long ago.

Simply unable to set her body into motion. It waited for something. Waited somewhere outside her control. All she managed was to remain standing.

Luke didn't hesitate. By some superhuman strength, he approached her. Not puzzled by her inaction. Not even hesitant.

He stepped to her and lifted her as if she weighed nothing. Lifted her and placed her back against the driver's door. His hand scooped her butt as her legs wound about his hips of their own accord.

She groaned as she tightened her legs to pull them closer together.

This was what she needed. She needed a man. It had been a long time and she needed him so badly that it actually hurt. Zoe needed someone to want her. One who saw her. Who…

His kiss seared thoughts out of her brain faster than the heat of the afternoon sun. His heat reflected her own as she clung and held and bit and beat her fists against his shoulders.

There was no undressing. No time for that.

No pause allowed in this race. Too much need.

He pushed against her, pressing hard between her legs exactly where she needed him. Their first time was going to be fully clothed.

Luke drove against her. Slammed her back harder against the car as he raked his teeth down the side of her throat.

Against the car.

The...*car!*

All she could remember was the car against her back, her own helplessness, and—

Zoe screamed!

It ripped out of her.

Her body's uncontrolled flailing found a target.

She doubled her fists together and slammed them at her attacker. She heard a grunt of pain.

Again, fists joined and raised.

Slam down!

Something caught her fists before they found their target. She fought. She squirmed.

Her body was still pinned to the car.

The *car!*

She couldn't escape. She couldn't free her arms. Couldn't free her body.

Her knife. If only she could reach her knife, she could—

But her hands were trapped. She couldn't break free. Couldn't—

"DeMille! Stop!"

She screamed again, but there was no help. No one to save her.

No one on the lonely stretch of empty beach.

No one to—

Beach?

She was on a beach?

The next cry caught in her throat.

Not in a dark garage that reeked of motor oil and grease?

Pinned against a car by...

"Luke?"

"Welcome back," his voice was no more than a low growl.

"Let me go," Zoe couldn't catch her breath. Each attempt stuck in her throat. A throat that hurt as if she'd screamed until… *Please* let me go," the helpless pleading tone hurt almost as much as the scream had.

Luke eased back, lowering her to stand on the sand. The last thing he released was her hands—he'd caught her joined fists easily in one mighty hand.

When he finally released her, her knees let go and she slid the rest of way to the sand. Pulling up her knees, she buried her face against them.

After a long moment, she heard Luke slide down to sit with his back against the car too, but she couldn't look at him.

"What happened?" Why did she even ask? She remembered, but wished she didn't. Maybe Luke would be kind and not answer the question. She felt unaccountably chilled in the shadow of the car despite the hot afternoon and the scorching sand.

"I was hoping you could tell me."

She could, but it would kill her to open the door on that piece of her past. All she could do was shake her head. She barely knew Luke, and there were places she wasn't ready to go with anyone, especially not some SEAL Team 6 superhero.

Luke remained silent for a long time. Long enough that she was afraid she was going to have to speak first. Even if she couldn't look up at him. Even if she couldn't face…

"I'm guessing there's someone I need to kill. Very slowly and very painfully."

That forced her to look up at him.

He was staring at the Citroën's front end, parked just out of reach, not at her. His jaw was set in a grim line. There was already a bruise forming on his chin and cheek.

Had she— Yes, she'd done that.

"Who?" Luke's voice was still rough with anger when he asked.

"He's already dead."

"Do I tell you *Well done?*"

She shook her head. "Dead, though not my doing."

"You do this thing every time?"

Again she could only shake her head. "First time ever."

"Well, ain't I the lucky guy."

She buried her face back on her knees. For one glorious moment, she'd had exactly what she wanted. Exactly what her body craved. And then— He was never going to touch her again; not unless he was a total idiot. Lieutenant commander wasn't a rank awarded to idiots. At least not very often and never in SEAL Team 6.

"I'm not pissed at you, Zoe."

"No. Don't call me that," she held her knees tighter. "You've never called me by my first name before."

"Considering what I was about to do to you, using your first name seems about right."

"Screw my brains out?"

"Yeah," Luke sounded pretty grumpy about not getting to do that. Or maybe embarrassed at having seen more than she'd ever shown anyone.

"I was looking forward to that, too."

"Then...why?" There were a lot of long pauses when talking with Luke. She supposed that she'd rarely left him big enough gaps to speak. Not that he used all that many words even around the long pauses.

"The car. Being pressed up against—" she shuddered.

Luke grunted.

"It felt...amazing." Now she was doing the pause thing.

"For about six seconds."

"You were counting?"

"Not likely." His soft chuckle actually made her feel a tiny bit better about the whole disastrous mess.

"Do you still want to...?" She couldn't finish the sentence. She couldn't believe that he was even here beside her still. That he hadn't simply driven away in disgust.

"What? An apology fuck for trying to crack my jaw?" It was purpling more brightly with each passing moment.

"No. I mean..." No, it was too humiliating to ask. "Never mind. Maybe we should just drive back to Dakar and pretend none of this ever happened."

"Zoe… DeMille… Shit! Whoever you are, you dizzy broad. Yes I want to. I'm not the sort who is going to hold a rape against a woman. I only hold it against the bastard who deserved to die."

"That's not what I mean."

Luke dug his hands through the sand for a bit before answering. "Better explain yourself then. I'm just a local boy from the Maine woods, not some New Age, sensitive hipster-type." That almost earned him a smile, but she couldn't quite find it yet.

"How can you want me after I…" she nodded behind her toward the car. The car where he'd almost done exactly what she'd wanted before she'd totally lost it.

Luke rose to his feet and held out a hand. He helped her to her feet, but didn't let go of her hand.

"DeMille—no, to hell with that. Zoe, when you're ready, I'm your man. Yeah, the heat right then was pretty hot. But you're my favorite fantasy of the moment." He shrugged. "Kind of sounds like shit coming out that way, but it's true."

"*I'm* your fantasy? Despite being a screwed up mess?"

He shrugged a yes.

A superhero, Special Operations Forces SEAL wanted…*her?* More than the heat of the moment? That was certainly unexpected.

The slutty part of herself, the one she'd tried to leave behind with the Huckfest truck jumpers, wanted to jump Luke right here and now. Ten years ago she'd buried that desperate girl, even holding a ceremony out in the dunes and burning that damned photo that just happened to include every single guy she'd fucked during that year's event.

The sensible military girl knew that guys like Luke Altman weren't for women like her. He should be with…

"What happened with you and Sofia?" She regretted the question the moment she asked it.

Luke offered her a half smile. As if he could see everything behind her question. The nerves about her own slender and short physique. Wanting to have sex with the man who'd already slept with her commander. Being so much less of a woman that—

"Nothing," Luke interrupted the crazed stream of her thoughts.

"What?" Is that how he treated women? Insipient rage was blasting the last of the fear out of her system. "You can call doing it with her *nothing?*"

"No, I mean literally nothing. It was weird. Drinks. A little talk. I even liked her by that point. Not just her body."

"Which looks awesome," And so unlike her own.

"Which *looks* awesome," Luke agreed without the least hint of embarrassment.

She couldn't believe she was discussing her commander's body with a man who had just said he wanted to make love to her. Was she trying to talk him out of it? No, even she wasn't that stupid about men.

"Wasn't enough. Should have been." He looked out to sea for a long moment, then shook his head. "It wasn't. We even tried a kiss, but..." Luke shrugged as if he talked about women with other women all the time. "It wasn't like kissing my sister or anything weird, it was just...nothing."

"Did I mention that you're an asshole?"

His smile slowly reappeared as he looked down at her once more. "You might have."

"Asshole." She went up on her toes and kissed his unbattered cheek.

Not once since he'd helped her to her feet had he let go of her hand. Maybe having sex with Luke wouldn't be slutty, because she didn't want a man between her legs—she wanted *this* man between her legs.

———

LUKE SCANNED the beach for potential threats as he constantly had during the drive to Saint-Louis. On the drive back he'd had other things on his mind.

Miles of empty in both directions. Christian had said that that the nearest road here was four or five klicks back into the bush. The only living things that came here would be the seagulls and the occasional rally car. There weren't even any of the former at the moment.

Just the two of them, the sea, and a whole lot of sunshine. He hadn't wanted Sofia Gracie, but something about Zoe was electrifying his body. And he didn't think it was just the idyllic setting.

He turned back to face her at the unzipping sound.

Zoe shrugged out of the jacket. Then, without looking away from him, did the same with the blouse and finally the red bra.

He knew he should move. Knew this was his cue. But all he could do was look at her. She was strangely perfect. Her small size had nothing to do with the size of the person inside the body. Moments ago she'd had a panic attack. And now she was... Or was she?

"Said I didn't want an apology fuck."

She nodded. Her hair slid across her bare shoulders in a soft cascade as she leaned down to untie her shoes. Once again he was staring down at the dark part in her hair.

"How about sex?" Her head remained down as she shucked her pants. "Consensual sex, Lieutenant Commander Altman. How about that?"

"Why?" What the hell was suddenly wrong with him? A cute-as-hell chick was offering her body. His own body was rapidly making its vote loud and clear.

She stood up and looked at him. Not a scrap of clothing and utterly beautiful. She belonged back in her coffin wearing a flight suit. She didn't belong...he looked around...out here. Palm and baobab trees offered shade along the beach. The Atlantic Ocean rolled practically to their feet. A pair of fantastic race cars parked beside them— ones she'd proven that she could drive more competently than he could fully comprehend.

And this slender beauty stood waiting for him. Not fifteen minutes ago she'd been screaming in terror. Had she stuffed that away? Where? When would it lash out again? If she hit him on the same side of the face, it might fall off. Her blow had been fantastic for someone her size—for a person any size.

She knelt over one of those very nice legs and unstrapped an ankle sheath. Boker Plus Anti-Grav knife with carbon fiber handle and ceramic blade. He supposed he was lucky her legs had been locked around his waist and she hadn't been able to reach it during her panic.

Zoe tossed it atop the rest of her clothes and rose back to stand before him, naked and glorious.

"Where?" He didn't have a blanket and had learned the hard way that sand wasn't great for the guy and totally sucked for the woman when you were having sex.

In answer she leaned back against the driver's door of the Renault.

"You sure?"

She nodded.

No hesitation.

No sign of fear.

Those blue eyes showed nothing but absolute certainty. Was it that she wanted him to purge her past? Or had her panic attack already done that? Or was Zoe DeMille simply that damn fearless? Maybe she'd hypnotized him and this was all an illusion.

Luke brushed his fingertips over her breastbone, tracing the line between those small, perfect breasts. He could feel her heart beating. It wasn't racing wildly.

How was she so strong?

* * *

WHEN LUKE KNELT before her and kissed her between the breasts, Zoe didn't know whether she wanted to laugh, cry, or scream again. Except this time the scream would be from contact shock.

Her father had taught her to love cars. Driving the beach and dunes today—the first time she'd been on sand since the final long-ago Huckfest—had brought all of it back. The bad, the horror, but also the good.

Luke was definitely from the last of those. She'd hurt him and he'd done nothing in return. He'd listened. He'd understood.

Who was the last man to understand her? Had there ever been one?

Christian Vehrs thought she was just some object of lust for him to conquer. Luke moved his hands up her legs, started by rubbing a thumb back and forth where her ankle sheath had been strapped, acknowledging the soldier. Knowing an ankle sheath always left a little irritation, like a wristwatch worn too tightly, he massaged it for a moment. His rough, powerful hands, gracing over her skin like warm water sluicing away the remnants of fear. Of a past she'd make sure never took control of her again.

She fisted her hands in his hair as he tasted her. Breast, belly, hip— each place purged.

And behind her was the rock, the bastion of her young life—a fine car. The metal and glass so warm against her skin it was like coming home. The strength engineered into the car and held there, waiting for a driver who understood how to unleash all of that power. How to see beyond the machine and become bonded with it. To let it drive her as much as she drove it.

She'd loved to drive.

Somewhere she'd lost that, flown instead. If not for the horrors she'd been confronted with in her father's garage, might she have entered The Dakar years ago? Or gone Formula 1?

Luke drove her body the way she drove a car. One moment coaxing her to open to him, to give over control, and the next moment bypassing the obvious to trace the line where butt met thigh.

When she would have begged him to plow straight ahead, he drew a gentle spiral that circled her breast five times or perhaps a hundred from the outer edges to the aching center. And he almost killed her with pleasure when the final contact was not with his fingers, but with lips, tongue, and teeth. His touch convinced her that she was shaped just as she should be. Not like her commander. Not like the curvaceous women who had always plagued her thoughts, but rather exactly as she should be.

This time, when he rose to his feet and lifted her, there was no protest in her. She was so ready to fly.

She hadn't noticed when he undressed. Didn't care that he'd been carrying a condom somewhere—didn't care if it was presumptuous or just practical.

It didn't matter. She gave him complete control and let him steer the course. Let him control her body just as she'd controlled the Citroën. When he took her and pressed into her and drove her hard against the Renault's driver-side door this time, she no longer had the power to protest or accept.

She was past functioning as anything more than a body for Luke to take and use. She wrapped her arms around his neck, buried her face against his throat, and breathed him in. The tears that mixed with his own salty sweat as his body bucked and rolled against hers were not joy, but neither were they sadness.

They were just tears of release. A release that rolled through her time and again until nothing else remained.

Afterward, when she could, she planted a kiss on his collarbone to let him know she was okay—she could do no more. In answer, his arms slid more tightly around her and they remained a long time together leaning against the car as close as two bodies could be.

# CHAPTER 13

"You bastard," Christian sounded more impressed than angry. "How is it that you get Zoe and I do not?"

Luke had no idea. It was like a DeMille-sized bomb had been dropped on his position and he still hadn't recovered. Taking her against the car parked a hundred kilometers from anywhere was a tropical-beach fantasy that still didn't seem real. Going down on her last night in her bed had simply been downright awesome.

Christian, who they should have easily beaten back to Dakar, had returned and been put to bed by his wife hours before he and Zoe returned.

He hadn't remembered holding her for so long in his lap after they'd made love, but when he'd sat down in the sand and she'd curled up there, it was hard to complain. She made no attempt at explaining or apologizing for her crying. Maybe he should have asked, but she'd stopped soon enough and simply remained in his arms. There were also no words about the sex they'd just had. He liked sex, knew he was good at it—which didn't begin to describe what had just happened between them. The warm day and the soft woman had made the passage of time meaningless.

It had gone dark as they'd wound through the streets of Dakar. Leola had greeted their return in a transparently sheer nightgown of purest white that offset her dark skin and hid absolutely none of her exceptional assets. Despite the stunning display, Luke had barely looked at her, which hadn't pleased their hostess in the slightest.

Instead he was watching every single motion Zoe made, all the while wondering what it would be like to touch her ass as she climbed the stairs ahead of him—turned out it was exceptional. Or to once more have his hand at the small of her back as she arched against him —even better. Some day he *had* to see how she would look in a nightgown as sheer as Leola's, but black to offset her light complexion.

She teased, but it was always a cheery banter, not games.

Or maybe it was games with others, but not between them. He didn't think that games of that kind would be possible between them after her past had unraveled on her in his arms. There had been no grand confessions afterward. He'd no more mentioned Marva's betrayal than she'd explained her past. But there were no games. No woman had ever given herself to him so completely.

Zoe in the morning had turned out to be much as he'd guessed— not an ounce of coy in her trim body.

She'd woken like a soldier, one moment asleep and the next wide awake. From curled up against his shoulder, where she'd spent the night, to lying full on his chest and humming happily in a single move as fast as most women might flutter their eyelashes.

Thank God he always kept a couple condoms in his med kit, because it wasn't long before she was arched over him and had finished waking them with awesome morning sex.

If she'd been any bigger, they'd never have fit in the shower together, but they had. While his body didn't recover *that* fast, hers did and he'd made the most of it. Devouring her cries with a kiss as her body jolted against his palm. Even the delicious Marva had never responded the way Zoe DeMille did in his arms. Vibrantly alive and completely frank in her approach to sex. For her, sex wasn't something that was to be withheld, twisted, manipulated until he went mad. No, with her it was simply about using each other's bodies in glorious ways.

Zoe placed a phone call he couldn't quite hear over the buzzing in his ears as he dressed. Then when she had bent over at the waist until she was head down to run a dryer over her hanging hair, he decided he'd better get out of there. If he looked at that fine ass pointed aloft much longer, he was going to be getting undressed again double-time.

Christian was there when he made it out of the bedroom and down to the outdoor courtyard breakfast table.

"You bastard," Christian repeated. "How do *you* be the one to get her? You must explain this."

Not a chance, even if he had a damned clue.

Christian looks so comfortable in his personal kingdom. The large home wrapped around him, the collection of very expensive racing toys in the garage, and the elegant garden. Christian sat at the head of the table that could easily seat twenty guests in the garden; Luke sat to his right. Rather than the heat of the morning sun, they were in the dappled shade of thick palm and fruit trees. Blooms the size of his head covered one tree and as many dusky red mangos hung from another.

Hawks circled high above. A pied crow, darkest black with his proud white necklace and breastplate landed at the far end of the table with a harsh ar-ar-ar-ar. Christian tossed it a chunk that he tore from a baguette and the big bird flitted away with it. A trio of mourning doves were bathing in the small puddles on the concrete around the swimming pool. A flock of small yellow birds flitted onto a blooming hibiscus. Bright yellow. Zoe's color.

Luke could still taste the strong red *bissap* juice that Mama Odette had served with the *ceebu jen*. And the milder but richer taste of Zoe that lingered on his tongue from their last lingering kiss in the shower.

He was definitely losing it if a flock of birds had him thinking about Zoe in ways to give him a serious arousal. Time for a subject change.

"Great pair of cars you've built," Luke offered as a maid brought hot coffee.

"Ah," Christian nodded his head. "Yes, you drive very well. So, *you* win her with *my* car. I think this is very unfair, but *c'est la guerre.*"

"*Guerre?* What does that mean?" French had never been one of Luke's languages. He knew *C'est la vie*, "such is life," but not—

"*Guerre* is 'war' in French," Zoe explained as she breezed out the French doors and up to the table with her blonde hair floating gloriously off her shoulders. Six-foot-tall runway models didn't look so poised as she did when she sat down at the table across from him. "Are we at war?"

"A war it seems I have lost," Christian admitted defeat with a smile and shrug.

The way that Zoe glanced up at him, Luke definitely felt as if he'd won. It wasn't as if they were in any kind of relationship. Like all his forays with women, they'd fade away when he was called up on another mission. Except this time he was already *on* a mission. He'd done it with women soldiers before, but always between assignments, never during one. It was his "way out" of any female trap, "Duty calls. Been great, babe. I'll call ya." Without a single chance that he would.

But Zoe…

"You know, Christian…" Zoe had that tone again. Luke suspected that Christian was about to have the hammer dropped on his head and that he wouldn't see it coming.

"If you were to start The Dakar, even just the first hour of the initial stage, you could capture your 'Legend' status for entering your tenth Dakar Rally."

"But who would drive for me then? Even I must accept I cannot run the whole of The Dakar this year. I already let my navigator go and join another team because I could not race."

Luke felt the blood drain from his head and go straight to his groin. Zoe DeMille was far more than a fantastic driver with a seriously sex-kitten body. He wanted to drag her off into the thick foliage of Christian's garden to show her just what he thought of her. It wasn't just a brilliant plan; it was genius. And she'd found a way to sell it that he knew Christian could never resist.

Zoe rested her chin on her palm and her elbow on the table as she leaned toward Christian. She was wearing a loose top like the one she'd worn on her arrival at the airport. This one was Renault red and from his angle he could see the strap of her bra—lemon-yellow.

Luke wasn't sure whether she was trying to slay him or Christian. He definitely no longer begrudged her the weight of her suitcase. He looked forward to taking that scrap of yellow off her at the first opportunity. Or better yet, leave it on—it and nothing else. Then he'd—

"You, my dear Zoe? You would drive my car for me?" Christian's voice was caught up in the wonder of it. Luke had to admit it was a hell of an image.

But... *What!* It was supposed to be him doing the driving, not—

"And after you *have* to drop out to save your back..."

"Ah, your assistant would be your co-driver. Yes, he is very good, even if not as good as you or me."

Luke would show Christian just how goddamn good he was. And Zoe too... Except, as hard as it was to swallow, Zoe was a better driver than he was. Someday he'd get her out on a pair of motorcycles and see how she did. Zoe DeMille in full body leathers? Oh, he definitely had to see that in real life.

"But how to get my support truck and my car to The Dakar in time? The ship from Europe left weeks ago and is already there."

"I hoped you'd be willing. I already called a friend. He has a transport plane that must pick up a delivery in Buenos Aires. We'll just take your vehicles to the airport with us and I'll have my friend fly them to Mar del Plata for the start—it's barely out of his way. You just buy us the plane tickets on the very next flight out."

Luke now understood the phone call that Zoe had made. He imagined that a C-130 Hercules cargo jet was already en route and would be gathering up Christian's vehicles shortly after they themselves were safely gone.

"Which—"

"Oh, we must take the Citroën, Christian. She and I match as if it was destiny."

The guy never stood a chance.

While Christian pulled out his phone, Zoe looked over at him. Luke couldn't help but smile.

She blushed and looked away. Beyond cute.

---

"I wasn't sure if you'd be angry," Zoe whispered to him when Christian had gone forward to use the 787's bathroom and stayed to flirt with the waitress under the guise of having to stretch his legs.

"About what?" Luke had taken advantage of an overlap of their lap blankets to slide his hand across under the blankets. He ticked his nails lightly along the inner seam of her jeans. It sent a shiver of anticipation along her skin.

"About me arranging for the C-130 without consulting with you. It just made sense and I was sure Christian would agree." She did what she could to keep her voice level, but Luke's lightest touch, even his smile, was doing strange things to her.

He ran his fingers up along her inner thigh until the heel of his hand rubbed against her. She clamped her legs together, trapping his touch there. She'd done it instinctively to block him, but now that she'd pinned his hand there, she didn't want him to move it away. Her wanton past was her past. Since reaching the rational age of eighteen, she'd chosen lovers with care and typically enjoyed her time with them. They invariably made love to *The Soldier of Style* rather than to Zoe DeMille, but she'd learned to live with that.

She didn't know how Luke saw her, never mind *what* he saw in her, but it certainly wasn't her online self. It made every touch of his have more meaning, be more important than it should be.

She never, ever cried having sex. And she'd wept on his shoulder, unable to stop for an embarrassingly long time. And still he hadn't walked away from her in disgust. Instead he'd sat down on the sand

and shifted her so that she could stay in his lap, curl up against his SEAL-broad chest, and simply weep.

Afterward, he'd made a point of dressing her himself, which was good because her body was still warring between numb and tingling with the aftershocks of him wanting her at all and the incredible releases he'd delivered. When the first piece of clothing he'd put on her had been her knife's ankle sheath, her heart had made a strange flip. She had no idea what it meant, but it was undeniably there. He wanted to protect her. Being a man, it was a gift he would never understand the magnitude of to a woman—ten-fold to one who'd been violated before.

Once fully clothed, he'd actually lifted her into the Renault before planting a deep kiss and copping a feel that had left her breathless. This time they'd lined up side by side for the start. They'd run the last hundred kilometers in perfect sync, neither pulling ahead for more than a moment even though they were pushing the cars' limits the whole way.

Last night he offered equally synchronized sex.

Zoe had barely made it through the door of her room without laughing in Leola's face. She'd briefly imagined that being naked beneath a two-thousand-dollar Kiki de Montparnasse negligee robe was how all sexy Senegalese women greeted their guests. All the closed doors of Senegalese homes, each with a nearly naked Leola behind it was so unlikely that it was funny.

Leola and Christian were a perfect match—both in it for whatever they could get. Instead Zoe remembered the people at the beach or out by the tree having tea, simply glad to be together. Real friends. Normal people, belonging. She could see herself with them and that made her like the city.

Realizing that Leola's greeting was intended just for Luke had almost killed her sense of amusement.

Until, unimaginably, it was Zoe's ass he'd grabbed as soon as they'd turned the landing. Her desire to ask if Luke was out of his mind, wanting her over the gorgeous Leola, was short-circuited when Luke brushed her hair behind her ear and then traced his fingertips along her jaw the moment they'd safely escaped to her bedroom.

She'd answered his silent question with just as many words by simply stepping into his arms. This time he'd undressed her and she him. She'd been right about the Sig Sauer compact sidearm he'd acquired in the handoff at the airport; wrong about him having a knife. He wore two.

Always a light sleeper, she'd collapsed onto his shoulder afterward and not had a single thought until she woke in the morning. And that first thought, just as it was now on the plane, had been very simple: *More!*

Luke's hand didn't press harder against her beneath the airline blanket. Instead, he started a slow, circular massage with the heel of his hand, sending successive shock waves of turbulence rushing through her system.

Did he enjoy sending her flying like some RPA pilot? Did he get off on having such complete control over her body that she was utterly helpless? Remote piloting was her job, but his lightest touch stole her breath and mind. She felt she should complain, but her body won that argument before it even started.

"You arranging the C-130?" Luke whispered from somewhere close by.

Zoe had closed her eyes to revel in the sensations that were shifting from full throttle to wide-open turbocharger as well. She managed an "uh-huh" sound, but she wasn't sure what she was acknowledging other than asking him not to stop. Oh, her apology for ordering the plane without involving him first. Maybe that was her form of remote piloting him. Did that make what he was doing to her body more or less manipulat—

He nibbled on her ear and elicited another "uh-huh" that prayed he wouldn't stop.

"Almost as sexy as the way you drive." His whisper, barely louder than the plane engine's roar, sounded so close to her ear that it would have tickled if it didn't feel so good.

So he thought she was sexy because of how she drove? Why wasn't that a surprise? Even as her body continued responding to his touch, Zoe knew it couldn't be about *her*. That would have been too much to ask.

Was this being about her driving better than it being about her online persona? She supposed it was. Driving a race car *was* closer to her true self.

Did that make it okay even if it *still* wasn't about her?

Luke leaned close enough to brush a kiss across her lips. She'd expected a SEAL to be a masterful lover—they were good at so many things—but she'd never expected him to be a gentle one. It was an electrifying contrast. She let her body's acceleration drive her deeper into the seat cushions. At least if it wasn't *about* her, it *felt* as if it was.

Thirty-six hours in Dakar and they were flying to South America. Not just as some "pretend" support team, but in the race where they'd have a far better chance at finding Hathyaron. She still didn't doubt for a second after seeing that garage in his Pakistan compound that he would be racing at The Dakar.

In the last thirty-six hours she'd also gained a lover against whom she had no resistance. And she didn't want any.

She opened her legs beneath the blanket and let him take her the rest of the way aloft.

If this was flying, maybe she'd never come down.

# CHAPTER 14

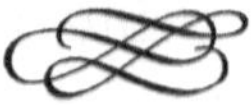

Luke rubbed his thumb across the FIA driver license bearing his picture.

*International Competition Authorization.*
*Authorization is given to this license holder*
*to enter and/or drive in any event*
*inscribed on the FIA Calendar National Race.*

What favors had Zoe called in with the Fédération Internationale de l'Automobile to get these? Or maybe he didn't want to know.

*Think, Luke.* She hadn't sold herself. She'd called SOCOM and told them what she needed. Then Special Operations Command had taken care of all of the details while their plane was en route. She and Luke would now both be fully registered with FIA including any fees and required qualifications—faked but on record. Exactly as he would have called for, if it had been his op.

His op. Up until this moment, some part of him had thought it was. Assumed it was.

Not so much.

This op had been completely in the control of Zoe.

He was…her personal assistant. As stupid as that sign she'd made for him to hold at the airport might seem, it was exactly what he'd become. Not a position he was comfortable with.

Looking around didn't make him feel any better.

He, Zoe, and Christian were queued up in a hangar-sized shed in the Argentine seaside town of Mar del Plata. Of which he'd seen nothing after the thirty-hour flight had landed at midnight. The cars had been waiting as promised, with the keys left at the Avis rental counter—after four hours passed out in a hotel and then straight into the "scrutineering" shed by dawn with nothing but coffee and a chocolate croissant to ease the pain.

His eyes hadn't even focused until they were inside so he'd missed his first look at Argentina. Other than the Spanish and the Latinate complexion of at least some of the locals, they could have been in a steel barn in Brussels. Along this side of the building were dozens of desks manned by clerks who were checking over everyone's documents to make sure they were in valid.

"Scrutineering" was the in-depth inspection of both the drivers and their vehicles to make sure everything was in order. Christian's vehicles (the Citroën and the support truck)—which had made their direct flight in half the time of their own route through Dulles, Panama, and Buenos Aires—were being inspected for compliance with The Dakar Rally's safety and outfitting regulations. He hated flying civilian for that reason, but it wouldn't have done to let Christian see the military C-130 that had delivered his vehicles. That would raise far too many questions.

In the shed they were checking everything from tire size to engine horsepower to making sure that no unsanctioned navigation equipment had been installed. There were a dozen vehicles ahead of them in the long queue and a dozen more waiting to get in. Male drivers were standing near the desks, laughing and joking over past races and hot women, while they awaited their own inspection.

Any of them could be Hathyaron. Hoping to spot someone of Punjabi, Pathan, or Sindhi descent—which constituted seventy-five percent of Pakistan's population—was probably fruitless, but he kept an eye out.

There were a few women competitors in the queue besides Zoe, a very few. A pair were over in motorcycles—tall, powerful-looking women who looked ready to wrestle the heavy machines through two weeks of sand.

A tiny Japanese woman was clambering up into the cab of one of the massive Hino racing trucks along with two barely taller men. The ten-ton trucks took a crew of three: driver, navigator, and engineer. The three of them looked almost comical in the immaculate matching racing suits in front of their gigantic machine. Most folks in the scrutineering shed wore t-shirts and shorts because of the heat.

Then he turned around and nearly rapped noses with a tall flaxen-blonde.

"Hi," she offered in one of those smooth Texas accents that always seemed to add extra syllables to the simplest words. She held out a hand, which he shook while he was busy looking. Tall, with a men's plaid work shirt unbuttoned low enough to allow her breasts to make a fine statement above, with the tails tied off to reveal flat abs and shapely jean-clad hips below. She was a treat all the way from her alligator skin boots to her straw cowboy hat.

"Hi," he managed in his Maine-flat mono-syllabic tone.

"I'm Tammy Hall. And this must be your first Dakar Rally."

Luke nodded and managed to retrieve his hand. He recognized her type. Liked the type; had enjoyed its benefits any number of times. But he could feel the look Zoe was burning into his back.

"Well, if you need any tips, you just feel free to come find me, honey." Then one of the clerks called her name and she moved off with a feline smile (the sort worn by hungry lions) and a toss of her hair that floated half down her back.

"Gonna be an interesting race," he muttered.

"What's that?" Zoe hadn't been glaring at him, instead she'd been cozying up to Christian.

Luke thought about Tammy as he ran his thumb over the license again, so new he imagined that he could feel the heat of the plastic fresh out of the machine. Did the woman actually know she was trying to sell it so hard? He supposed she did, because he knew in retrospect that it had worked on him any number of times. He looked down at Zoe, again speaking intently with Christian and some other guy who stood the way a macho version of Tammy might.

Had Zoe fallen prey to such games? He'd certainly never seen her play them. She teased and flirted, but she never did the flinging-her-body thing. She had to know how cute she was and how easy that would be to do.

When the clerk called for his packet, not sure what else to do, he handed the entire stack over: license, passport, insurance, and whatever other cards SOCOM had determined he'd need to enter.

There must be some way to get back control of the situation, but he didn't see that happening anytime soon. He looked over the barricade at the Citroën. Now they were checking what was stowed in the narrow cargo space behind the driver's and navigator's seats: water, seat belt cutter, thermal survival blankets, flares, a horn, reflective triangle, spare tires, and the like.

For the moment, Luke was merely "support crew." He and Christian's mechanic, the towering, soft-spoken Ahmed, were to drive the support truck. The clerk asked him several questions that he had no idea how to answer, but Christian stepped in and soon they were through the line. He noted that Zoe was asked far less.

Not gender bias. She simply exuded that she belonged. He knew how to do that, but Zoe had unbalanced his world somehow. Being constantly a step behind had to end soon. Zoe'd had her days of fun, but she worked in a coffin and he worked in the real world. Enough already.

They exited the far end of the queue to await the car's clearance. A phalanx of reporters with cameras and microphones were lined up. Behind them, the parking lot was filled with ranks of inspected motorcycles, cars, and racing trucks. All were covered with bright stickers of team and race sponsors. He figured out that these were the ones successfully through scrutineering because large black-and-white racing numbers had been plastered on them. The magnetic decals were on both doors (both sides on the motorcycles), front bumpers, and the rear of every vehicle. It was a far cry from him and a couple buddies running dirt bikes in the Maine woods, or even a SEAL team doing offensive and defensive training in a line of Hummers.

A woman jumped forward and snapped Zoe's picture.

"*The Soldier of Style,*" she gasped excitedly. "You're racing The Dakar?"

Luke was going to shoot himself. This couldn't be happening.

Zoe offered one of those light-up-the-world smiles that she'd used so lethally on Christian.

"I am," she matched the reporter's own breathless speech. Tweety Bird DeMille was back in full force. "I've raced before, of course, but never anything as grand as The Dakar. My good friend Christian Vehrs needed a co-driver on short notice and offered me the slot." She pulled a beaming Christian into the shot. One of these days, after they didn't need him so much, he'd earn himself a bloody stump for the way he wrapped his arm so possessively around Zoe's shoulders and pulled her hard against him. Or maybe Luke wouldn't wait that long. It was one way to get Christian out of the car—make him bleed.

Luke already knew he wasn't the starting co-driver, but now he was completely sidelined, not even in the image. Not that he'd have let himself be photographed. And it wasn't like he cared. Not a chance. Actually, it could be an advantage, now that he thought about it. Lurking in Zoe's shadow might not be such a bad idea. Besides, she threw one easily as large as the far more obvious Tammy Hall without even trying. Letting Zoe *think* she was the one in control wouldn't hurt his ego any. In the meantime, he could get it done.

They all bubbled at each other about the amazing opportunity and the exciting route. The reporter was drawing obvious conclusions that Luke didn't like at all. Zoe wasn't *his.* He'd never even really cared if he had exclusive use of a woman while it lasted—after his ex-wife it never seemed to matter. Yet he wanted to slowly and painfully snap off each one of Christian's fingers where they'd shifted to around Zoe's waist.

The reporter was worth watching. Hot German with cutely short, mid-blonde hair offset by a dark suntan, blue eyes, and nice curves—not quite the eye-poppers of Tammy Hall's. And not a single distracting thought crossed his mind when he looked at her. Whereas looking at Zoe…

Unable to stand watching Christian try to assert his claim on Zoe, Luke looked around again. Theirs was far from the only interview going on. There were lone reporters like this woman "Liesl Franks—freelance," but most were TV cameraman and interviewer-with-a-mike pairs. Interviews were happening in half a dozen languages: Italian, French, and Spanish were most common. But he again spotted the Japanese team that was being interviewed by a crew with a kanji logo on their camera.

Fifteen or twenty interviews were going on simultaneously and he could see the other drivers eating it up just like Christian.

Behind them, rope lines held back a mass of fans stacked at least five deep down the whole line. Before or after interviews, drivers were going over to the line to sign programs, photos, jackets, even across the top of a woman's breasts with a magic marker—one woman had already collected enough signatures there that she was running out of room for others to sign despite her hefty build.

The major drivers stood out because they had a hired entourage of pretty local girls behind them, most wearing sexy tops and straw cowboy hats. There were more cowboy hats in Argentina than at a Texas rodeo. The girls were handing the drivers eight-by-ten color glossies and signing pens, snapping photos for the fans' cameras, and whatever else it was that sexy entourage girls were paid to do.

It was definitely wild.

There was a flow to it though, that their party was disrupting. More drivers came out of the administrative queue, but Zoe was hanging tough with the Liesl woman, forcing other drivers to move around them. Zoe must be eating up her own hype. Sad.

Three hundred and fifty-four vehicles were entered this year with an average of two drivers. Motorcycles only had one driver, but the massive trucks had driver, navigator, and engineer, so the count averaged out. Double that for two support personnel and another transport for each entry. That meant approximately fourteen hundred individuals and six hundred vehicles were involved in the race, not counting the race officials, media, entourage gals, and other hangers-on.

And Hathyaron the arms dealer was one of them. Somewhere.

Let Christian and Zoe bubble along; he hadn't forgotten their target.

It would help if they knew what he looked like. The Activity hadn't been able to even confirm his nationality.

"He's probably a Legend," Zoe spoke from close by his elbow. "Those are the ones who've done at least ten Dakars. It just seems likely after seeing that garage—it represents someone who has invested a great deal of time and learning to prepare for this. Christian will know all of them. Liesl has also covered the last six Dakars and is writing a book about the Legends."

Relieved and without thinking, he wrapped an arm around her shoulders and kissed her on top of the head, causing her to make a happy hum. Zoe hadn't lost track of the target for a single second. She hadn't bought into Liesl's hype, Zoe had convinced the reporter to buy into hers. Any of his teammates, even Nikita, he'd have chucked on the shoulder or given them his "well done" nod. So why did he grab and kiss Zoe?

Liesl hadn't gone away—she prepared to snap his picture.

And he prepared to reach out to grab her camera and smash it.

Zoe simply held up a hand to stop her, then shook her head.

"But—" Liesl protested as she lowered her camera.

Luke absolutely didn't want to be noticed. There was enough of that shit going on in the SEAL community and he certainly didn't want anything else to do with it. The number of "Tell All" books was disgusting.

There were also far too many news articles about ST6 operations. Actually, there'd been a spate of articles on missions that he knew for a fact hadn't been run by ST6, but had been very vocally credited to them—probably by those assholes over in Delta Force. Maybe turnabout was fair play. He liked that idea. Not this mission, but after some future one; he'd definitely be dropping Delta's name. For this one, an embedded-civilian style scenario, he wanted to remain as anonymous as possible.

"He doesn't like to have his picture taken," Zoe tried offering.

"But *The Soldier of Style* has two men vying for her attention. The story. *Es ist wunderbar.*" Liesl tried to raise the camera again.

"Please, no," Zoe already had control of the reporter without her even realizing it.

Luke *did* still have his arm around Zoe's shoulders. He gave a small squeeze of thanks and let her go to remove the temptation for the reporter.

"No pictures at all, *ja?*" The reporter asked unhappily.

"*Nein,*" Luke confirmed—finally they'd hit German, which *was* one of his languages. And somehow that was a mistake.

Liesl eyed him speculatively before a slow smile crossed her face. "Does Christian know?"

"Know what?" Luke offered his best scare-the-crap-out-of-recruits look. Somehow she'd figured out that he was military and that belief —no matter how accurate—couldn't be allowed to persist.

Liesl's smile didn't falter for a moment. It worked on his men without fail. What was it with these women that it didn't even leave a graze on them?

"Nope! He hasn't a clue," Zoe offered cheerfully, totally spoiling his play—not that it had worked any better on her. "Another thing we'd like to keep that way."

"*We?*" Liesl's eyes widened for only an instant before that smile returned two-fold. "*The Soldier of Style.* You really *do* serve!" Liesl had a merry laugh. Whereas Zoe's...

*Huh!* He hadn't heard her laugh much. Wasn't sure if he ever had.

Luke just hoped the reporter knew how to keep her damned mouth shut. A reporter? Good luck with that.

# CHAPTER 15

*S*omehow Zoe had survived the two days leading up to The Dakar.

Now she lay face down, alone on her hotel room bed, and didn't know if she could make it to the starting line.

Sitting at home on her social media feed had kept everything at arm's-length. She put on a show and the fans gave her their love. She never held real-life fan events of any sort. Her need to keep the two worlds of her life completely separate in real life and internally was absolute. Now the blurring of those lines was letting the darkness she kept locked in her past slide to the fore at unexpected moments. Fighting to keep that back was even more exhausting than the constant pressure of the pre-race social obligations.

Between Christian's post from Senegal and now Liesl Franks' stories, her life was rapidly spinning out of control. Liesl knew she had a hot story and had worked out a three-way deal that made Zoe's head hurt worse than her early training days as an RPA pilot.

First, Luke would be left in the background as much as possible— though she'd almost tossed him to the wolves that first day for how he'd been checking out that Texas blonde's cleavage. With him hiding in plain view to search for Hathyaron, it threw herself and Christian together into the foreground. Thankfully Christian was kept distracted by the other Legends, but she had to be constantly at his side to meet and greet.

Not a single one of whom was Pakistani or Afghani this year. There wasn't even a listing of any vehicle from a country between the Arabian Peninsula and Australia except for a lone motorcyclist from India. If she didn't know the nationality of who they were looking for, how was she ever supposed to find them?

Second, there was no exclusivity allowed when giving interviews at The Dakar—publicity was part of the deal. Section 47P of the regulations—the penalties section—stated there was a five hundred euro fine for not stopping in an interview zone. Even worse for being otherwise uncivil—the fine *plus* possible disqualification. Liesl had tacitly understood that she might never be told the real reason the military had inserted a team into the race. Instead, she'd negotiated that she'd have an exclusive on *The Soldier of Style's* inside story.

Anyone else got only the public story: she'd met Legend Christian Vehrs through her fan group and they discovered their mutual love of rally racing. And it stopped there—though most services had blithely ignored that last bit of information. Christian had certainly worked to give them, and himself, the impression they were also a couple.

Liesl got as much of the inside story as *The Soldier of Style* was willing to tell.

The third part of Liesl's deal—that Zoe absolutely hadn't counted on—was that Liesl set out to make her famous. She'd upsold the story to Reuters news service, who had flown in a videographer, and they were both now following her every move. Another thing that thrilled Christian.

Luke occasionally deigned to scoff at her. Or maybe he was trying to make fun of the lunatic situation, but she didn't feel much like laughing. For the most part she hadn't seen him in the last forty-eight hours even though they were sharing a bed.

That definitely wasn't thrilling her so much. The first knock on the door both mornings had been Liesl, even before room service could be begged for coffee. And by the time she'd chased out Liesl,

Christian, and whatever other Legends happened to be hanging out in the suite drinking beer or wine (always French) each night, she was too tired to do more than collapse beside Luke.

That was becoming a major problem. At least she'd assumed that was the problem. Yesterday morning Luke had already been gone when she woke up, and she hadn't heard him come in. For a relationship that was only four days old, not seeing him for the entire fourth day wasn't good.

And now she was waking alone again.

It was a bad sign that left her even less interested in getting out of bed. Having had his fun with her, he was done and moving on.

The Dakar Rally was a spectacle and the city of Mar del Plata was doing its damnedest to make it one of grand proportion. The elegant Teatro Auditorium had run highlights of prior Dakar rallies on its large screen—accompanied by lots of teasing of racers with spectacular crashes, flips, rollovers, or simply getting lost. The Casino Central had thrown a huge bash. And the lobby of the side-by-side Hotel NH Gran Hotel and the Hotel NH Gran Provincial had hosted massive parties.

The lobbies had also been thick with hundreds of vendors from Toyo Tires to Oakley sunglasses, each one doing their best to attract the attention of every driver or crew member. It was a good time for hot Argentine women—hired to dazzle the ninety-nine percent of racers with a dick for a brain as they hawked their rep's wares.

The Dakar was far bigger than just the race or even the vendors— it was an excuse for an epic celebration, South American style. Outdoors had included band concerts, dance troupes, and open-air bars along the seawall and the prime beach of the city. Plenty of "good time" girls working those venues.

Had Luke shifted his attention to one of them?

Or that sexy, built blonde?

Or one of the women on motorcycles? He mentioned motorcycles in almost every other sentence. Of course he spoke so little, that still wasn't very often.

Wherever Luke had gone, Zoe sure hadn't seen him in their bed.

Once again she'd been absolutely right about her attractions as a woman. She'd been born for an era of five-seven Tom Cruise and five-four Michael J. Fox as heroes. The problem was she'd grown up into a world built for the likes of six-foot Chris Pine and six-two Ryan Reynolds.

And six-four Luke Altman.

Nobody ever stuck—not that she cared.

Except this time she did, not that it helped her at all. Maybe Luke was off with Liesl? If so, that definitely wasn't part of any deal Zoe had meant to make, even if Liesl was much more his type. A tall, willowy blonde with a nice, if not dramatic, figure. Zoe had seen them side by side enough to know they made a lovely couple, instead of a goofy one that had people tilting their heads strangely when they deigned to notice her beside him.

If it was over, then—

"Still in bed?"

She managed to flop her head the other way on the pillow and open one eye. That, at least, *was* worth the effort. She felt too tired to take advantage of it, but a naked and still-damp-from-the-shower Luke Altman was formidable motivation to change the direction of her thoughts. If she hadn't been worn out, she might have noticed the shower running and taken some hope there. Was it enough to get her moving? Would it matter if she did? He was already gone, wasn't he?

He smiled at her.

So what if he was done with her. Maybe they could have one last tussle between the sheets anyway. She'd certainly never had a lover of Luke's skill before and wouldn't mind a final encore before he completely drifted out of her life.

Maybe it *was* worth waking up today.

If she did, would he—

There was a sharp rap on the door.

"Go away, Liesl. I'm about to be busy." Hopefully.

"Race day. We must now be moving." Christian called through the door.

Crap!

"Yes, Zoe. *Ein sehr* important day." Liesl, too.

Double crap!

Luke shrugged.

Giving in to the evil plan of the twisty, sadistic Fates (*so not my sisters in spirit),* she clambered out of bed. On her way to the bathroom, she kissed Luke quickly because he was so very pretty standing naked in the middle of their bedroom. She did her best not to groan at what she was losing because even a brief kiss with Luke was a complete toe-curler.

She came away with her t-shirt only a little wet. Her attempts to sleep in one of Luke's hadn't worked. It never stayed on both shoulders, the sleeves reached her elbows, and it fit her like an old lady's house dress practically down to her knees. Real attractive. All it did was remind her of all the reasons Luke shouldn't want her. And since she wasn't getting any sex at the moment, it was a place in her brain she really didn't want to go.

Grabbing the towel out of his hands, she headed for a quick shower. Passing the front door, she popped the handle and called out, "So come in already."

Then she ducked into the bathroom door, leaving a naked Luke on the other side to scramble for cover as Christian and the camera crew walked in.

---

RATHER THAN STANDING NAKED in a hotel suite, Luke felt as if he was melting beneath the midsummer sun in a full-body fire-resistant Nomex racing suit. For lack of better cover, he reached for a throw pillow from the small couch, but was far too slow to really hide anything. Besides, the pillow he'd grabbed was about the size of a dinner plate.

Zoe certainly generated heat in him.

Curled up in their bed with the covers pulled up to her nose so that she was little more than a floof of blonde hair on a pillow, she was about the cutest damn thing he'd ever seen. In one of her tight t-shirts and very brief panties, she was a total turn-on. He should be pissed about her leaving him standing naked as everyone barged into the room; instead he wanted to laugh aloud at the joke.

She teased everyone a little bit, but he now understood that she'd always particularly targeted him. Standing outside Hathyaron's garage building and forcing him to ask for what he wanted when she damn well knew what he meant. The way they'd raced together. Every time she…

Now that he thought of it, he could see it was a pattern that held right back to the start of the Honduras mission. She had teased Nikita and Drake on that mission…somewhat. But she'd never given him a moment of peace.

He stood there naked in the middle of their hotel room, except for the tiny pillow that didn't hide squat.

Then a mental lightbulb went off, one that froze him in place.

*Did she understand how much she liked him?*

*Did he?*

It wasn't just having her in his bed. Since when had he been content to just lie down beside a sleeping woman without waking her to screw her brains out? Never. But he had done just that last night beside Zoe—moving especially carefully so as not to wake her. He'd drifted off happily just listening to her quiet breathing as she snuggled up against him in her sleep. Not that her contact had let him fall asleep very quickly.

It had left him plenty of time to think about her unexpected skills. He particularly appreciated the way her mind worked: seeing a solution and jumping right in with both feet because she knew it was right and to hell with the consequences. Differently built, she'd have made a good SEAL.

"Hi, boss," Nikita and Drake had followed Christian, Liesl, and her cameraman into the room. She smiled when she looked at him, such a rare thing that it momentarily dazzled him. He was impressed they'd made it down here so fast since he'd called them only last night.

"Nice outfit, Mr. Emperor," Drake smirked.

He offered them a nod of greeting. Problem was, his clothes were on the far side of the room and the one pillow wasn't going to get him there across the crowded room.

"Who are you?" Christian stepped up and got in Nikita's and Drake's faces.

Luke used the distraction to ease along the wall to his pack. He rummaged through it and began dressing.

Nikita moved up beside him while Drake was busy not answering Christian. "You treating her well?"

He started to answer, but there was something in her tone that made him finish pulling on his t-shirt to look her in the face. In this moment, she wasn't Nikita Hayward. Instead she was a SEAL so lethal that he'd promoted her to his Number Two on the team.

"Because if you hurt Zoe, I'll goddamn kill you, sir. And yes, it will be *completely* personal." Then she offered one of her most pleasant smiles—one that didn't reach her eyes at all this time—before moving back to her husband's side. She was supremely competent, one of the reasons he'd called for her to come join them. She'd also married a former Night Stalkers crew chief, which meant he was an amazing mechanic—the other reason he'd called the pair.

But dangerous, to *him?* That was new.

Luke finished dressing, including the racing suit and boots—Zoe had ordered them in electric yellow, of course. He rejoined the group but kept his own counsel.

Christian was still ranting (probably didn't like finding Luke naked in Zoe's bedroom either). Luke promised himself to never sleep apart from her for the duration of the mission, just for the Christian Vehrs-irritation aspect of it. He supposed that knowing Luke was here with Zoe and seeing proof were two different things. Or maybe it was that he knew he'd only get to drive Stage One. Perhaps he could feel control slipping out of his fingers. Luke felt empathy for Christian, but it didn't mean he was going like the man anytime soon.

Nikita and Drake were doing a fine job of being SEAL silent.

Liesl smiled like she knew too damn much.

Then Zoe came out of the bathroom.

It was the first time he'd seen her in her racing suit. Because he'd seen her drive, he knew it wasn't just his imagination that made it fit her so well. In her own way, she was as powerful as—

"Nikita!" Zoe screamed, raced across the room, and slammed into the woman's embrace, fitting neatly under Nikita's chin. They held onto each other like long-lost sisters. "Oh. My. Gawd! Luke didn't tell me he'd been able to reach you."

He'd never seen Nikita quite like that. Not even when she'd been falling for Drake had she looked so...soft. There was some bond between the two women that he'd never noticed and, seeing it, didn't understand—but it looked plenty real. It was the way he was learning that Zoe approached everything: with her entire heart.

Nikita understood that. That would explain why she'd become so protective.

And that Zoe was sharing a piece of that with him was a gift he was only starting to understand.

She shot Luke a grin that held only a little bit of surprise. She'd been calling the shots enough on this mission and he'd felt it was time to call some of his own—he'd started by mobilizing Nikita and Drake to come join them.

Luke opened his mouth to explain, but never had a chance as Zoe turned to Christian and plunged right in.

"Christian!" with that impossible level of excitement of hers. Except it wasn't impossible from Zoe DeMille, merely irresistible. Joy seemed to pour out of her every single moment of every day.

Something else he hadn't had a lot of experience with.

"I know, because of the short notice, that you were having trouble getting another good mechanic. Nikita and Drake aren't racing mechanics, but they're absolutely amazing and can help Ahmed, your lead man, with anything we need."

Luke should have known that Zoe would understand the plan without being told.

For the two days between the scrutineering check-in and the race itself, Zoe and Christian had been off in the social whirl of drivers and race organizers. He'd stuck for a little while, then realized that he was a third wheel in more ways than one.

Sure, once he dragged himself away from the stewardesses, Christian had spent much of the long flight from Africa drilling him and Zoe on how to read the Dakar Road Book. The Road Book was the turn-by-turn guide to the race and the only navigation tool allowed in the car.

"One mistake can send you many kilometers off course before you realize it. You will have no choice except to retrace to your last known good point and try again. All the GPS will do is turn on when you get within several hundred meters of a check-in point to guide you in the last bit of the way. Everywhere else, you are on your own with only the Road Book and a compass."

Christian had truly feared that Luke couldn't navigate well enough, but that was only because he didn't know who he was dealing with. The Road Book was far better information than he usually had while swimming or hiking to a mission target. There were only a hundred symbols in the entire map coding system—most of which were pretty damn obvious. One exclamation point meant caution, two meant danger, three meant "Holy crap! Slow down and be careful."

Much of rally racing was about orienteering and land navigation, bread and butter to a Team 6 SEAL—or someone from Maine. From one peninsula along the Maine coast to the next might be a hundred meters across the water, but it could be a thirty-kilometer drive to get back to where they connected by land. And the logging roads he used to run on his motorcycle weren't exactly signposted.

But he stuck out in this crowd because he didn't have a lot of rally stories to share—as in none. And hanging with Christian, it was expected that he did. The guy was a Dakar Legend after all.

The only attention he was getting was pissing off Zoe. Between the various "cute girl" squads and Tammy Hall's occasional strafing runs, he was getting a lot of the kind of attention he always got and he could see Zoe taking it hard.

So instead, he'd gone on the prowl and stumbled on the Malles Motos class, or MM guys—everyone was ignoring the new "The Original by Motul" label except when the sponsor was around. In French, *Malles Motos* meant "Trunks Motorcycles." These guys raced with no support trucks and teams, no camper vans, not even a mechanic. The MM competitors showed up with a motorcycle, a box of spare parts, and a tent. The race only allowed thirty competitors in the class. The trunk box was the size of a SEAL team field pack and was transported from bivouac to bivouac by a semi-truck along with all of the other MMs' gear.

He sat and talked with them for hours.

They told Luke about single-track conditions, climbing the slip face of dunes, high altitude techniques (there were places in the Andes where they lost twenty percent of their power due to thin air), water holes, *fesh fesh* sand so loose and fine that it could mire a bike wheel-deep without warning. If they fell off their bikes in *fesh fesh,* which was almost a given, it was possible for your bike to disappear from view even though it was only a few feet deep. The dry stuff almost flowed like water.

At first he'd thought they were the misfits of the race, taking on The Dakar with no support and no team. But the more time he spent with them, the more he respected them. There was a purity of adventure with them that seemed to be lacking elsewhere. Just rider, machine, and terrain. It also sounded absolutely brutal, which fit right in with his training and career. In a way, they were the hardcores—the Spec Ops guys of The Dakar.

And at this moment, he'd take a ride with the MMs if it got him out of this hotel room.

Nikita threatening him. Drake probably glad to back her up. Zoe collecting staunch defenders right and left as she was fast becoming world famous. Next thing he knew she'd be dropping out of the military and be gone into whatever the hell her civilian world was. Probably end up with some asshole like Christian Vehrs with his smooth French accent and enough capital to front a Dakar Rally car of his very own.

Nope, Luke wouldn't like that image one bit.

"Can we get a move on?" His growl sliced through all the dynamics ricocheting around the hotel suite.

There was an awkward silence as he killed a half dozen conversations, which was a good trick as there were only about that many people in the room.

"C'mon!" Zoe still had an arm around Nikita's waist. "I'll introduce you to Ahmed. He's Christian's lead mechanic from Senegal and he'll put you to work. Actually, he'll totally flip over you. You look so amazing, Nikita."

Nikita was dressed in her usual civilian—jeans and a black t-shirt. Her brunette hair back in its typical ponytail. She maintained the peak level of fitness that was necessary to be a DEVGRU SEAL. He supposed that she did look amazing.

Marriage also agreed with her. When she'd joined ST6, there'd been a sadness that he figured nothing could ever erase. In fact, he'd assumed that it was a key element of her success because that sadness fed a deep-rooted anger that had seen her through the entire DEVGRU selection process—the first woman to pull that off.

When Drake Roman had showed up and started messing with that sadness and anger, Luke had threatened to kill him if he screwed up one of his best operators.

But he hadn't.

Nikita had become even more driven, more impressive, but the sadness and anger no longer drove her. He blinked as he watched her go out with Zoe and Christian. Nikita of old had worn a force field around her that repulsed all boarders. Yet she'd greeted Zoe with a welcoming hug in which he could detect no hesitancy.

Was that another of Zoe's gifts? She'd certainly slid past *his* guard.

"You heard about Pakistan?" Drake was the only one who'd hung back when all of the others had left.

"No, what?"

"Hathyaron's compound doesn't exist anymore."

"What do you mean?"

"About twelve hours after you left, it was bombed by a pair of Chengdu F-7s owned by the Pakistan government. Obliterated the place."

Luke shrugged. "Pakistanis have followed us in enough times."

"Word on the ground is that it was a personal favor requested by

Hathyaron—made *after* we were there. Also, an airport security team at Bacha Khan in Peshawar broke into a hangar. They found several vehicles, including the truck-trailer that left his compound—tire prints match what you sent in."

"Any other clues on the vehicles?"

"You mean before the Pakistan Special Services Group seized them?"

Luke grunted. The SSG was Pakistan's form of Spec Ops and the guys weren't half bad. If they too were doing personal favors for Hathyaron by erasing evidence, that wasn't good news.

"Yeah. Four vehicle drivers, still in their seats. But nobody's talking…in fact, last I heard they still hadn't found the poor bastard's heads or hands. No way to identify them."

"Erasing his trail," Luke nodded.

"The on-duty air traffic controller—the only one who might have identified the plane that had been near that hangar—was found at home, in bed. His head was still there, but a machete had chopped him and his wife into six separate pieces. No rape. No robbery."

It made sense. Brutal, but not stupid.

Would Hathyaron's ego still bring him to The Dakar? Yes, it would. It didn't even have to be ego. If there were any last minute dropouts—there weren't—it would have made him too easy to find and he'd know that. Luke thumped a job-well-done fist down on Drake's shoulder.

Drake shifted from reporting sailor to his normal casual himself. "Funny when it happens to you, isn't it?"

"When what happens?"

Drake was generally mild-mannered. He was the easy-going one, always glad to do what he was told—though fully capable of taking the initiative when necessary. A lot of SEALs wanted to lead; Drake just wanted to be on the team and had proved he had the skills to be.

He started to get angry, which Luke knew how to deal with. But before he needed to react, Drake stopped, then shook his head.

"You don't see it?"

"See what?"

"Shit, Altman, you were never stupid."

"Still not."

Drake made a point of looking over at the bed that was still all rumpled. Luke could see the impression of Zoe's head on *his* pillow, hers still exactly as the hotel had plumped it. She'd already been on the edge of his pillow when he finally dragged himself back to the suite last night. And she'd stayed there.

"Shit, Roman. You talking about what's between me and some woman?"

"No, asshole." The heat suddenly flashed back to life, sharply enough to have Luke stepping back in surprise. "I'm talking about what's between you and Zoe DeMille, who happens to be my wife's best friend. A woman who also saved our asses any number of times back when I still flew with the Night Stalkers." Drake had backed him up against a wall without his even noticing. Drake didn't have Luke's broad build and was an inch or so shorter, but that didn't seem to matter.

"I'm not talking about this." Luke went to push Drake aside, but Drake shoved him back against the wall.

"This isn't from chief petty officer to lieutenant commander, Luke. This is me and you. Just like aboard ship in Honduras. What the *hell* are you up to?"

Luke hit Drake with a palm strike against his sternum hard enough to knock him backward. The bed caught the back of his knees and he collapsed onto the mattress.

"I'm not talking about this with you or with anybody."

Drake sat up partway, rubbing his palm against his breastbone. "You goddamn better talk about it with Zoe. I can see it in her, even if you can't. Like you once told me about Nikita, she's dealing with some next-level shit and if you don't respect that, it's going to blow up in your goddamn face." Then he pushed to his feet and strode out the still-open hotel door without looking back.

Luke looked at the mirror. "Has everybody lost their goddamn mind?"

He was almost out the door when he realized that this *was* the first race day. Tonight they'd be sleeping seven hundred kilometers away. He packed his duffle in about thirty seconds. It took him another ten minutes to locate and pack all of Zoe's stuff.

"Personal, goddamn assistant, my ass."

Hair dryer and brush, makeup, toothbrush, other girl products. From the dresser came underwear, shirts, slacks, and all the rest of it. He found sunglasses, lemon-yellow hair clips, lemon-yellow shoes, and...shit! Too damn many reminders that Zoe was someone he didn't begin to understand.

On his final sweep he found the t-shirt she'd slept in. It was black and worn almost wordless. He twisted it in the light to read: DeMille Dune Buggy and Auto Service.

After what had been done to her there—for he had no doubt about exactly what had gone down—how could she wear that?

It smelled of her. He didn't know what it was, but it was absolutely her. How could something so damn small encompass such a woman? Rumpled together, it barely filled his palm. He rolled it up and tucked it into his own pack.

Luke Altman, personal assistant, hefted his duffle and her suitcase out of the room. For two nights they'd slept here together, just slept. Was it already ending?

The mission would really be kicking into gear now. Was it the relationship-ending signal he was so familiar with?

For the first time ever, he truly hoped not.

Yeah! That and "Don't let the door hit you on the way out" would win him a kewpie doll at the county fair.

Last out the door and all on his own.

Zoe'd been sitting beside Christian in the Citroën for almost an hour. Breakfast of *medialuna* crescent rolls had been eaten while watching Ahmed lead Nikita and Drake over the car. She had a thousand things she wanted to ask Drake, about how a guy's mind worked around women. She wanted to cry on Nikita's shoulder that it was already over before it began. And she didn't want to talk to anybody for fear she couldn't hold it together.

But there hadn't been a chance for any of that before it was time for them to line up for the start. The motos and quads had started leaving shortly after sunrise. The cars were up next and they'd been in line by midmorning.

They sat along the resort waterfront between the two sprawling, four-story brick buildings of the Hotel NH and Hotel NH Gran Provincial. Ahead of them lay the boardwalk and the sea, behind them stood dozens of ten-story apartment and office buildings like a forest wall. She'd had no opportunity to explore, or even stop long enough to breathe the air.

The Dakar was "the event" and touching "the natives" just didn't happen. Were her vlogs—video logs—and feeds like that? Zoe DeMille *is the event. Don't associate with the fans directly. Keep everything* remote, then it will never affect you? What an utterly depressing thought, she really had to cut that out.

One by one, vehicles rolled up onto the podium at the Stage One start. It had a big ramp up, a car-long flat spot over a story in the air, then a slope down the other side. A great arch spanned over the top to support a giant big-screen projection television.

On the screen were close-ups of what was happening on the podium. It let the huge crowd assembled along the waterfront see and hear everything.

Each racer drove up onto the flat and parked. Motorcyclists dismounted, drivers climbed out of their cars, trucks pulled up beside the ramp and their drivers clambered up to the flat spot. While cameras zoomed in, the emcee announced their names and vital racing stats. The crowd, which numbered in the thousands, cheered and applauded just as strongly for the latest car as they had for the first motorcycle hours earlier. The drivers waved to the fans, blew kisses, and shot a thumb's up before getting back in their vehicles.

Once they were helmeted and ready, the timekeeper stepped forward and counted down the seconds to their official start window. At the crucial moment—*Three fingers...Two...One!*—the engine roared to life and they rolled down the front ramp and onto the seaside plaza. A sharp left around the front of the hotel, then out the other side onto Maritime Boulevard to head north. Every two minutes, another team started the race.

The real race wouldn't start until they had wound through the city and reached the end of the roads. There was a fifty kilometer "Road Section" along normal roads where speed limits and other rules of the road had to be maintained. Road Sections weren't race timed, though there was a precise time limit to complete them—no stopping for burgers along the way—and arriving early incurred the same time penalties as arriving late. Road Sections were about exactness of navigation, not speed.

"Selective Sections" were almost entirely about speed. That was where every second counted as the racers left roads and headed off into the wild on beaches, tracks, dunes, or wilderness as the Road Book commanded.

The emcee announced the next driver's name. Even if he hadn't been parked directly in front of them for the last hour, she'd have known all his vital stats. She recited them along with the announcer: Sergey Kanski, Poland, five Dakar starts, three finishes (best two years earlier in twenty-third place), driving for Toyota (one of the biggest teams). His co-driver…

Zoe had memorized every single thing Christian had told her about every single driver. (For example, Sergey was very good to his wife—both the one in Warsaw and the one where he trained half the year in Morocco.) She'd chatted up each driver she came in contact with. Not one had mentioned anything about Pakistan. Nor had one been kind enough to offer a simple, "Hello, I am the Taliban arms dealer you are hunting for. Please may I give you the names and addresses of my Al-Qaeda contacts as well so that you can target them with missiles from your stealth RPA."

Each hour of this mission was more exhausting than the one before. Each night she'd been tortured by the idea that she'd read something wrong. The beautiful service garage at Hathyaron's compound. The poster of the Dakar Rally in the place of honor on the wall. They *had* to lead here…didn't they?

She didn't dare admit her fears to Luke. What would he think of her for having led him here, especially if here was nowhere near his target? He'd think that she had seduced him because she wanted to race. Not because she…

Because she…

Her brain felt as if it was stuttering.

She hadn't seduced Luke. *No, you just stripped naked in front of him on a deserted tropical beach in the middle of an impromptu car race.*

If her four-point harness didn't have her so effectively pinned to the Citroën's passenger seat, she'd be pounding her head on the dashboard. Except that wouldn't really count as she was wearing her helmet.

Kanski got his start signal and rolled off the podium. In moments he was gone down the street—probably well cheered on by both his wives.

They started the introduction for Christian up on the big screen.

"Finally reaching Legend status, Christian Vehrs is starting his tenth Dakar," the emcee shouted out to the crowd who broke into a big round of cheers.

"Christian?" He wasn't moving forward. He'd started the Citroën's engine, but he didn't drive up on the podium.

"Watch this, my darling Zoe. You will see what makes a great driver of The Dakar."

Her own face flashed up on the screen. "His navigator, Zoe DeMille, *The Soldier of Style,* is starting her very first Dakar. We must wonder what is going on there."

The crowd roared its approval of the question though they were craning their necks searching for her in the shadows behind the podium. More than a few lemon-yellow flags were waved over people's heads. Would her commanders think she'd done this because Christian was her lover? A foreign national of uncertain allegiances? Or for her own self-aggrandizement? The numbers on her social media connections had jumped twenty-four percent in the last three days and the race hadn't even begun yet.

Still Christian waited.

"And now…" The timer stepped forward and flashed out ten seconds.

There were penalties for late starts. Christian must know that.

At five seconds, Christian punched in the clutch and shifted into first gear.

"Christian. What are you doing?"

At two seconds, the emcee and the timekeeper both backed up to the very edge of the podium. They'd been warned that something was going to happen. Christian popped the clutch and gunned the Citroën.

Like the good Dakar Rally car that it was, it didn't jolt forward, it leapt.

In just the few dozen meters from their hold position to the ramp's base, it was moving fast and clean.

Christian hit the rear ramp of the podium. The sudden angle slammed her into her seat and elicited a deep grunt from Christian. By the top of the ramp they had enough speed to jump completely over the flat section of the podium, arcing through the air, then slamming down onto the forward exit ramp.

The crowd went wild—the roar so loud that it was a palpable wave.

And Christian screamed!

The end of the front exit ramp dumped them onto twenty meters of paved plaza. A path had been cleared to the north. If they missed turning onto that route, they'd plunge across the plaza, through the packed-solid beach crowd, and then into the sea.

Christian was still screaming in agony, both hands clamped on the wheel.

But he wasn't turning. She had no doubt that his back hurt so much that he couldn't think or react, because his scream still pierced her ears despite her helmet.

Zoe reached out her left hand, managed to grab one of the spokes of the steering wheel and yanked it as hard as she could. It forced Christian to let go and she made another half turn, aiming them down the route.

"Brake! Christian! The brake!"

When he didn't react, she remember the tall handbrake and slapped it back. The hydraulic cylinders slammed the rear brake pads full on. Because they were in still in first gear and the clutch was still in, the engine stalled hard and slammed her sharply against the harness. Her breasts might be small, but they were going to really hurt as soon as the adrenaline let go.

Too bad. She'd been looking forward to Luke fondling her breasts. Or would have been if they were still… Not anymore.

Stopped in the middle of the plaza, she couldn't seem to let go of the wheel.

Christian was grunting. Hurting so bad that every time he even raised his hands to take the wheel, she saw him flinch at the pull on his lower back.

Luke and a pair of medics sprinted up to them at the same time.

They extracted Christian and got him on a backboard.

Somewhere in the background she could hear the emcee talking about Christian's accident last year. A glance showed that some technician was astute enough to have a clip of the disaster on hand and the spectacular end-over-end crash splashed across the big screen above the starting podium. The crowd groaned in sympathy.

"You've got to move this car," a race official was right in her face. "You're blocking the starting lane."

"Drive, Zoe. Drive!" Christian called out as they rolled his stretcher toward the waiting ambulance.

Luke looked at her from outside the car, across the empty driver's seat. She hadn't even released her seatbelt and she still clutched the steering wheel in some haze of desperation that this wasn't happening. Luke didn't climb in through the open driver's door that his hands rested on.

"Move your ass over, DeMille. You're a better driver than I am." Then he slammed the door and was racing around the car to the passenger side as he pulled on his own helmet.

"Get this car out of here. Now!" The official shouted.

"We're both on his team, both entered and licensed. Can we legally take over?"

"Honey, thirty meters from the Stage One podium? It's all yours, just go!"

She threw off her four-point harness and crawled over the console between the seats, then pretzeled herself around until she was in the driver's seat.

Luke slid into the passenger seat almost as fast as she was out of it. "Damn but that's a cute ass you've got there, DeMille."

"Shut up!" If he was done with her, she sure didn't need to be hearing that kind of crap. But if he *wasn't* done with her—he had been naked in their hotel room just an hour ago—which must mean something. Too bad she didn't have time to think about what.

But *cute?* She was so goddamn sick of being *cute* she could spit kittens—which would be even cuter!

Rather than making herself more crazy—if that was possible—she moved the seat all the way forward, snapped on her harness, and started the engine. She was careful not to look at Luke—she didn't want him to see how much she was smiling.

"THE TURNS, Luke! The turns. I only memorized the first six."

Luke was still trying to get his harness clipped. It was set so small, he could barely get his hands around to the adjustment straps. "Follow the previous guy."

"Hello, two minutes, now more like three ahead of us. Got nobody to follow."

He glanced down at the Road Book, then up at the trip odometer. "Sweep left in seventy meters. Then you have a straight run of three hundred meters."

"Great, Luke. At eighty kph, that's my next eight seconds." Her first turn slammed him painfully into the passenger door.

"I didn't learn Stage One—Christian was supposed to do all of it."

"Well, he didn't!"

"Left then a tight right." He risked releasing one hand from his safety harness to advance the Road Book readout. A glance out the windshield showed a line of policemen directing traffic. "Zoe!"

"What?"

"Take a goddamn breath, then follow the line of policemen. In the city, they'll be our best signposts." He finally got the harness set properly, the seat moved back enough that his knees weren't in his chest, and began calling the turns *before* she reached them.

"His scream, Luke. I've never heard anything like it," her breathing was still far closer to hyperventilation than normal.

"Yeah, I could hear it over the crowd. It happens."

"Not to me. Okay, Mr. Super Soldier? I work in a very quiet world. Radio calls from command and helicopters. I listen to ground teams only occasionally. So, I'm not used to people screaming in agony right next to me."

"Zoe…" He knew what to do with a soldier in the field. Dose him down and patch him up until the medic showed up or you needed a body bag. That took care of the injured.

But how long since he'd dealt with someone who hadn't already lived through that harsh dose of a mission turned ugly? Years. What did he do with a woman racing along a city street and beginning to freak?

"Whatever made me think I could do this?"

"You can outdrive a Team 6 SEAL—and trust me, we get serious driver's training. And based on Christian's curses as we raced along the Senegalese beach, I'm guessing you could outdrive him as well."

"I know how to drive, Luke," her voice climbed higher and tighter rather than easing. "That's not the damned issue."

She slammed through the next five turns as he called them out—barely in time. The next one he called too early and she almost blew into an alley through a sidewalk crowd. They should have driven together over some terrain. Their timing was off.

He had studied the Road Book until he could read the directions without hesitation, but she'd been the one to ride with Christian, to practice with him. There was no synchronicity in what they were doing. And when they got away from the city center and the traffic police, he hadn't called out a red light and she'd almost raced into crossing traffic—leaving black rubber on the pavement that they could ill afford to lose. Christian had said they'd go through several sets of tires over the two-week race and the number of spares were limited by the rules.

The time he'd spent with the Malles Motos guys had taught him how to ride the course if he was alone on a motorcycle. It hadn't taught him anything about how to help another driver.

They both needed to breathe.

He slowly got a handle on the call timing. Then he started feeding her information on speed limits, traffic, and other obstacles. Once they had that down, he checked their overall timing on the route—

surprisingly, they were right in the slot. Night Stalkers missions, both drop-off and extraction, were planned to plus or minus thirty seconds. So that part of the challenge was nothing new to either of them. Another bonus.

"You feeling any better?" he asked on a long straightaway that carried them out through Mar del Plata's suburbs that looked no different from any Mexican town he'd ever been through. One story buildings, mostly white with brightly colored doors and the occasional man-tall graffiti littered the roadside. No hovels of the desperately poor, at least not along this route. Just typical—

"Go to hell, Altman." Zoe didn't even glance in his direction. Her hands were clenched so tightly about the wheel, he didn't know how she could steer.

"Sure, if that's what you want, DeMille." He tried to make it funny, but she didn't seem to take it that way. The guys on his team would have at least given him a pity chuckle. Not Zoe.

Fifteen minutes away from the podium, another seventy to the start of the Selective Section.

"You really *are* an asshole." She didn't make it sound like a joke this time.

He considered lashing out at her, pointing out that she was really a bitch when she was driving, no matter how cute her ass was. It sounded funny in his head that way, but he didn't think it would play well.

"So, what's the damned problem, sailor?"

"I'm a soldier, not a sailor. An Army aviator. Okay? That's all I know. For three days I've swallowed Christian's shit and been the chirpy little Girl Friday and 'Oh, isn't he so sweet to let me drive with him?' until I'm ready to gag on it. I've spent hour upon hour at his parties getting my breasts stared at and my butt patted. And—"

"You've *what?*" Imagining someone touching Zoe without permission was—

"Give me a break, Altman. What hole do you live in that you don't know that's how women get treated. Don't believe me? Ask Nikita."

Luke tried to imagine someone doing that to Nikita, a Team 6 SEAL, and not winding up bloody and mangled.

"*And* I still don't know anything!" Zoe hunched over the steering wheel as if it had just been stabbed into her chest. "Is Hathyaron even here? That's the worst of it, Luke, I don't know. I've totally screwed up. All I want to do is crawl back into my coffin, do my job, and never come back out."

ZOE COULD FEEL the hot tears running down her cheeks and soaking into the helmet padding to either side of her face.

And that wasn't even the worst of it.

*Move your cute ass!*

And that's how Luke saw her as well. He was already done with her and still calling her cute. She'd show him goddamn cute! When they hit the Selective Section, she'd pound the car to pieces until he was screaming just like Christian.

She'd never heard a sound like that in her life. Except inside her own head as her virginity, as her girlhood, as her unforgivable innocence was ripped away in a single instant of never-ending torture. And not just once. Repeatedly over years. At first she'd avoided her father's garage for all the good it did her. Toward the end, she'd sought it out just to prove—

"Zoe. Zoe! *DeMille!*"

"*What?*" She shouted back at him.

"*Stop!*"

Her eyes focused and she was almost the one to scream. Slamming hard on the brakes, the Citroën squealed all four tires. When they stopped, the nose of the car rested only a breath from slamming into the undercarriage of a parked truck. It would have shredded their car if she'd hit it.

"Are you okay?"

"Do I *seem* like I'm okay?" Her heart was pounding so hard she couldn't breathe.

"Uh, no."

Zoe hung her head between her arms.

"Want me to drive?"

No. She wanted him to go to hell along with all the other memories. If he was now in her past, fine let him. She was *so* done with it.

Luke gave her silence. He didn't push. He didn't insist. And at the moment, silence was a true gift.

"Where's my next turn?" It practically tore her throat apart to grind out the question.

"Eighty meters back."

She nodded, but couldn't raise her head yet. Breathe. Just breathe. That's how she got through these moments when they slammed her unexpectedly. An RPA was far more forgiving though. If she flew in the wrong direction for three seconds, no one knew or cared. She cracked open the small triangular window at the leading edge of the window—the only part of the car's glass that opened—to get even a little more air and stared at the parked delivery truck. Its driver came around the far side and startled in surprise when he found a Dakar WRC car blocking his door.

"Zoe DeMille?" It wasn't Luke, but the truck driver. Then he rushed to her window holding out his clipboard and a pen. "Please sign this for me. Oh, lovely style, senorita. I will cherish it forever." He continued on in racing Spanish.

She managed to ask his name, then reached a hand out through the small opening to write his name and sign it with a flourish that she'd stupidly practiced for hours, right down to the heart-shaped o in Zoe. She wasn't even going to think about how sad her life was.

A glance at Luke. Still doing his SEAL waiting thing. She was really going to miss him.

Shifting into reverse, she rolled backward until Luke indicated the turn she'd missed. In her rearview mirror she could see the next driver: Pierre Manot, Switzerland, three Dakars, just celebrated his fifth anniversary of marriage to his high school sweetheart, driving for...

She took the turn. Except for turns and warnings, Luke didn't say a word for the next forty kilometers. For forty kilometers she slowly pulled back her dignity piece by piece. No one had ever seen her have an episode that bad. No one. And now he'd seen two of them.

"Who is she?" The first non-racing words between them in half an hour.

"Who is who?"

"The woman you're with." Though why she decided she needed to torture herself with that, she didn't know.

LUKE THOUGHT ABOUT that as he called the next several turns.

Rally racing used to mean getting away with whatever you could in between checkpoints. The checkpoints were never known, so you had to simply make sure that you matched the ideal course timing as closely as possible. And if that meant going double the speed limit to catch back up to the plan after a delay, that's what you did.

Now, with the GPS tracking their every move, speeding was prohibited and it all came down to precision—thankfully something Zoe specialized in. Her flying, her driving, her brain were incredibly precise. Even her *The Soldier of Style* persona—which he'd initially assessed as flighty and inane—he now understood was meticulously planned and maintained. Though he'd still tag it as inane. The only time he'd seen her let go was in his arms.

Who was the woman he was with?

He stole a moment to look over at her, but couldn't think of how to describe her. Words weren't exactly his best play, he was far better at doing and showing. However, taking her out into the low bushes they were presently driving past outside of town wasn't really an option. The scattered one- and two-story homes were no longer crowded wall against wall. Patches of green stood between the house of tan stone or brick.

What was she asking? Was she asking for help in understanding herself? How was he supposed to—

"Fine. Never mind," her growl was worthy of a ticked-off Rear Admiral.

He concentrated on the Road Book for a moment as they were turned south with five extra turns that the course designers must have put in just to be irritating.

"She's..." How was he supposed to describe Zoe? "Surprisingly sexy and—"

"I take it back, I don't want to know." Zoe picked up three more seconds on their laggard time by slaloming neatly around an over-loaded bus before an oncoming hay truck threatened their existence.

Starting with sexy probably hadn't been the best choice.

"She makes me laugh."

"Hard to picture you laughing," Zoe's tone was still acerbic. Okay, maybe he didn't, but she made him feel as if he wanted to. He hadn't had a whole lot of laughter in his life. A mom who bugged out when he was two. A drunken father, with a lobsterman's powerful fists, who thought that beating on his son would help mold his character. They'd both been black-and-blue the day he left for the Navy.

What had he just been thinking about her moments before? Oh, right. "The way she thinks is stunning. And I'd say that your assess-ment about Hathyaron being at The Dakar is plenty sharp enough to continue the mission. Even before Drake heard—"

"The way she *thinks*? You've got some strange criteria, Altman."

He wasn't quite sure why Zoe kept talking about herself in the third person, but maybe after whatever that episode had been, it was more comfortable for her.

Perhaps she was asking him to help her define who she was.

That happened all the time during the sixteen months of SEAL selection and training. That was how he'd figured out who he was. That level of endurance couldn't be done without coming to terms with who you were. Was this Zoe's "Hell Week"? Maybe it was. Seven days ago, he'd been standing in Hathyaron's compound in the middle of winter in Pakistan. Now it was the morning of the seventh day—midsummer in South America.

"She's someone who does her best to make others *not* notice her,"

Tweety Bird DeMille all dressed in yellow was a highly engineered distraction from the real Zoe DeMille, who he was only starting to understand. "And utterly fails because of who she really is." Nikita, he knew, was notoriously hard to impress, yet Zoe certainly had.

"Great," Zoe's tone could dry out burnt toast. "When do I get to meet this perfect bitch?"

"Got a mirror handy?"

Zoe was passing a line of cars and almost clipped the nose of the last one when she jerked back into the lane—not quite squealing the tires.

"Wait." She set herself solidly in the lane. They were now on a nominally two-lane paved road—paved as in the potholes had sharply defined edges where the pavement had cracked off and broken.

Luke held on, but she managed to veer around a particularly deep hole at the last second.

"Who are you talking about?" He could practically hear her teeth grinding.

"What do you mean?" The road was getting rougher, jouncing them harder with each passing mile. He guessed they were reaching the end of the city…and the roads.

"Who are you *sleeping* with, Luke?"

"*You.* Or hadn't you noticed?" Again she made him want to laugh. She had the strangest sense of humor and it just tickled him.

"Not so much these last few days. Who were you with?"

"The Malles Motos."

"The Motorcycle's Trunks? Is that a strip club?"

This time the laugh actually came out before he could stop it.

"In a way. They've certainly stripped away all their support."

"Everything just hanging out there," Zoe's tone still had an odd bitterness he couldn't pin down.

"Yep. Those guys—"

"Guys?"

"—are very attractive."

"Guys?" Did she think he was being like sexually attracted to guys?

No, she was just teasing him again. He wanted to hoot aloud, but decided to play it up instead.

"Awesome dudes. They're running bare bones."

"You mean bare-assed, don't you?"

"Ouch! That'd be an uncomfortable way to run the Dakar."

The GPS flashed on, indicating they were within three kilometers of the timing zone at the end of the Road Section. The arrow indicated that it was well off to their right. He scrolled the Road Book and saw that there was a deceptive turn farther ahead that would send them that way. An earlier turn would probably get them lost deep in some farmer's field. Tricky bastards. They were still on course no matter what the GPS said.

He fooled with the trip computer for a moment, double-checking their odometer reading against their scheduled arrival time. They should hit the check-in station to the minute. A hard jounce rocked the car. If the potholes got much deeper, they'd need alpinist's climbing gear to get out of the next one.

"What are you talking about, Luke?"

"I'm talking about the Malles Motos. Supposed to call it The Original by Motul."

"The French engine oil provider?"

"Yeah. Those guys run with no support except for a small trunk of parts. Do their own service, their own camping, their own route planning, and they ride without a support team. Really impressive." He called out the final turn and he could see the white tents of the check-in point not far ahead.

"That's where you've been these last two nights is hanging out with motorcycle racers?"

"Sure. What did you think I was doing?"

"Being off with someone like one of those Argentine dancers or Liesl or the blonde with the major front-end armature or something?"

"Couldn't get to Liesl even if I wanted to, not with the way she's bolted to your side. Besides, are you crazy enough to think I'd be with anyone else when I've got you?"

"Apparently, yes, I'm that crazy."

Zoe rolled up to the time check-in and pulled the time card out of the special dash holder that Christian had tucked it in.

Had she thought that he'd lost interest in her? Was that why she'd almost crashed them early in the course? Not overwhelmed by the driving, but by their...relationship?

He'd admit they'd left fling somewhere back on the road and he hadn't even noticed. Since Marva had cheated on him and blown up their marriage, he'd only ever had flings. A few of those had lasted as long as a month or two, but weren't involved enough to call them anything more.

For fuck's sake, how had he ended up in a *relationship* after seven days?

Luke decided that it was a good thing he wasn't the one driving.

CHAPTER 17

Zoe waited through the five-minute hold at the timing station. All she knew about the next stage from the Road Book was that there was no mention of dunes. In fact, most of today's Selective Section was technically on roads because the course markers didn't have the dashed line of off-road. But neither was their route going to be even marginally paved. It was technically marked "track," which probably meant just as little as it sounded.

Luke was still with her? What did that mean? (*Means you're still together, you goofball.*)

Actually, it didn't. But if he thought so, maybe they still were.

And if they were, the things he'd said about who he was with… were about her?

He liked the way she *thought?*

The way she made him laugh (even if she'd only ever heard it as a smile)? Except he actually had laughed at her just a moment ago. *At* her, not *with* her, but maybe it was a start.

And…sexy? That was the first thing he'd said—as if such a delusion was possible.

With a roar, Kanski's Toyota leapt out of the holding station beside her.

She checked over the car. She left the tire pressure set to high. On dunes she'd deflate the tires for better traction, but "track" probably meant dirt roads. She dialed the shock absorbers to a stronger response—there'd be no way to dodge the potholes on a track as it was probably more pothole than road. Fuel status was still good—they had to be able to go the entire route on a single tank—no en route refueling allowed. She changed the engine setting from "1," which meant no turbo and very fuel conservative, used for road driving, to the max responsiveness of "4"—all out power. Oil temperature and pressure were—

Their timer handed them a new time card. She double-checked that it was their car number and it was stamped with the next minute before tucking it carefully in the dash holder—losing a timecard incurred a major penalty.

At thirty seconds, she shoved in the clutch and shifted into first gear.

At fifteen, she slid her little side window closed but no longer felt stifled for air. No longer felt the choking oppression of all her doubts. They were still there, but their chokehold had eased from imminent death to mild strangulation. No prob! She was used to that.

The timekeeper started the ten-second countdown.

"Luke?"

"Yeah?"

Five seconds.

She didn't know what she wanted to say, but once the racing started, there wouldn't be a chance for stray thoughts.

Four.

"This woman you're with?" Unbelievably herself.

Three.

"Uh-huh."

Two.

"Um… Please don't give up on her too quickly."

One.

"If you say so." Zoe swore that she could hear the laugh in his voice and that encouraged her more than anything.

She punched the gas and popped out the clutch. The Citroën roared to life. Five hundred horsepower launched them from zero to a hundred kph in less than two seconds. First, second, third, fourth—a four-wheel drift through the first corner—and she launched down the track.

What she could have done at Huckfest with a car like this almost hurt her heart. Well, she'd had enough of that.

Luke wanted her.

*That* was the present and she'd be damned if the past was going to come between them again. It was so hard for her to trust, but if she wasn't going to trust a Team 6 SEAL lieutenant commander, she'd better get her head fixed.

Third gear, second through a tight corner that Luke had warned her about. Out of the turn: third, fourth, fifth…then the world opened up in front of them.

Zoe hadn't been ready for it.

At Huckfest there was a starting dune. Jumpers started from its wide flat top to take advantage of the sharp downslope to build speed. Opposite, there was a high dune to climb, then a single jump over the backside. A momentary sensation of flying, with a view over successive dunes and the Pacific Ocean, then the hard slam like one burst of a sexual release as you came back to earth.

On the race from Dakar, Senegal, to Saint-Louis, they'd been entirely on the beach. The Atlantic had rarely been more than a few car lengths away and their highest altitude might have been the moment she'd made that jump to pass Luke and Christian.

Here, the track led to the Argentine oceanside south of Mar del Plata. It was a strip of dirt atop a cliff. To her right was arid brush—far denser than Senegal's, though that wasn't saying much. To her left was a five-story cliff down to the Atlantic. Senegal was in her past, all the way there across the ocean. She'd do her best to leave her doubts over there.

And if she didn't pay attention, she might well end up there—as a floating wreck.

The track wove back and forth atop the cliff, sometimes mere feet from the drop-off to the beach. Each hummock that she jumped had to include a dose of faith that while she was in the air, the road and cliff wouldn't veer out from under her.

"Two exclamations in half a klick," Luke called out.

Fourth, third, second. She slowed perhaps more than she needed to, but she didn't have a feel for how cautious the course designers were. Three exclamations might be all the way to first gear.

Two exclamations was the sharp turn she'd feared, but it wasn't that sharp.

Zoe accelerated as she swept through the corner—

Then slammed on the brakes and the car jerked to a halt and died as she'd forgotten to drive in the clutch.

She looked out her side window at the face of a boulder larger than the delivery truck she'd almost hit earlier. Its rough face was so close that she could make out individual grains in the towering chunk of sandstone. In the sudden silence, a seagull began laughing off her feathered ass at them.

"Okay, now we know what a two is," Luke said calmly.

"Yeah," Zoe swallowed against a dry throat. She pulled back on the tall handbrake that stuck up from the middle of the console—the size of a baseball bat, there was no way to miss grabbing it in an emergency. She hit the Engine Start button on her steering wheel while holding the brake.

Giving it gas, she released the brake and was once more racing up the track, but no faster than her heart, which was still trying to throttle her. Ten minutes into her first Selective Section and she'd almost knocked them out of the race. What else was she going to run into over the next fourteen days that would try to kill her?

Other than a Pakistani arms dealer?

---

Luke hung on. The car danced and jerked like a living thing.

Its awesome suspension smoothed out all except the very worst of the road's surface, but Zoe's control was shaking them hard.

She changed gears every few seconds: sometimes more frequently, but rarely longer. He now understood the characteristic sound of the videos he'd watched of previous Dakars.

*Roar, roar, roar, ROAR!* with the increasing pitch of increasing gears. *Bwaa, bwaa, bwaa* of downshifts. Then roaring up again.

She downshifted into turns and accelerated hard on the straight-aways, even when they were only a hundred meters long.

Each tiny change of the steering wheel twisted the highly reactive car. Cleaner landings off jumps, smoother slides around dirt corners, counter-steering against acceleration torque—Zoe's hands were in constant motion.

It was a challenge to watch the Road Book and not her.

He remembered that he'd once thought of her as blurred because of the way energy seemed to constantly vibrate off her. Here, in Christian's world rally car, she finally made sense. No Tweety Bird energy spent to distract or tease. Zoe was one hundred percent about milking the most out of the car over specific terrain.

She displayed a fearlessness. She took blind corners on faith. No exclamation marks warning of danger? She accelerated into corners—sliding through them in dramatic four-wheel drifts. Blind jump in the middle of a straightaway—she might slow for the angle of the jump, but not because she couldn't see what lay on the other side.

Then they descended a narrow notch through the cliff and down to the beach.

That was where Zoe shone. Fourth, fifth, sixth gear—wide open at over two hundred kph, a hundred and twenty miles per hour, she flew along. If there was one thing she understood, it was sand.

He didn't recognize what was happening at first. The motorcycles had all started before the cars and were long gone. Their single tracks had been obliterated by the thirty cars ahead of them, leaving their own sliding twin tracks.

But the air, which had been so clear, began misting up. The midday sun blurred by dust, then by sand thrown in the air. Sand thrown by what?

By...

Zoe was overtaking Kanski. A seasoned Dakar Rally driver, who had left the timing area two minutes ahead of them, and she was overtaking him. There wasn't a chance that their car was more capable than Kanski's, which meant that it was Zoe's driving.

As she came even with Kanski and began the battle to pass, Luke could feel his body heating up again.

The memory of just the two of them racing along the Senegalese beach. Of the way she'd felt as he took her against the side of the Renault. The second time she'd been true to her word, giving herself to him as much in joy as the first time had been in fear. She'd bared more than just her body—he'd never felt so connected to a woman than right after she'd first beat on him and then, when all was done, wept on him.

She hadn't done either one again, but it had given him insight into the woman. That there was a woman in there, not just a body for him to enjoy. Had he always been that shallow? Women were for… But Zoe wasn't like that. It wasn't like she had some pre-ordained purpose. She hurt and ached and felt joy and had a dark past that she confronted with towering strength. Were all woman like that? More complex than he'd ever bothered to think about?

Maybe he could ask Nikita.

He checked the odometer again, glanced at the Road Book, then began to smile.

"Zoe," he called to her over their helmet intercom.

"Uh-huh," she tried again to get by Kanski, but he wasn't having any of it on the narrow beach. It was high tide, and there just wasn't that much room to play with between the cliff face and waves.

"Really put the pressure on him. Distract him until he's only paying attention to you."

"Why?" But she was already accelerating hard on his passenger side.

"But don't try to actually pass him."

"Say *what?*"

Kanski came up close to the cliff edge to block her and she slid down toward the waves.

"In about six more seconds, there's a right turn that will take us back up the cliff. Distract him so much that he misses the turn."

In answer, Zoe dropped down a gear and thumped on the gas. A rooster tail of sand shot out the back of the Citroën as she weaved side to side behind Kanski like a maniac, mere inches off his bumper. In the lower gear, there was no doubt that Kanski would hear the Citroën engine's roar like the wrath of the gods on his tail.

He could feel Kanski and his co-driver glancing at each other and thinking, *No way!* Or perhaps, *What the hell?*

Three.

Two.

Zoe had gotten so close to the water that she had two wheels in the backwash of the waves and Kanski was right down there with her, to block. The Citroën's windshield was blasted nearly blind with sand and water despite the wipers being on high.

But Luke sat on the dry side of the car and kept watching ahead for the turn.

There.

"Now! Hard right!"

Zoe sliced from left to right, so close to Kanski's bumper she could have flattened a taco between them. She shot blind across the beach on his word.

Then the wiper managed to clear the windshield and she corrected a few degrees as she punched for more power.

Luke glanced back.

Kanski was in an arcing four-wheel slide as he tried to recover.

"Too little, too late, dude," Luke called out with a whoop.

They sliced into the narrow cleft in the cliffs three car-lengths ahead of Kanski.

"And that's how we do it in Maine!" Luke shouted rearward before he faced forward and scrolled the Road Book for the next set of instructions.

"Ma-ine?" Zoe managed on a bounce as they jumped clear of the arroyo and landed once more on a clifftop track.

"Ay-uh," Luke confirmed happily.

*"Too little, too late, dude* is what they say in Maine?"

"Sure…" Except it wasn't.

"It sounds like you're from *Bill and Ted's Excellent Adventure.*"

"What's wrong with that? I like that movie."

Zoe actually spared him a glance during her latest drifting turn.

"What?"

"I'm just trying not to admit that I like it to. Most people think it makes me weird."

"Idiots. It *was…*"

And they both shouted, "Excellent!" together which left them both laughing.

"Well, I'm not going to start calling you dude. You're a girl-type person."

"So, what *are* you going to call me?"

They passed a lone tree. Luke twisted around and began counting seconds. Kanski was five or six seconds back now. *Most* excellent.

"A lovely, smart, sexy woman who drives like a god and enjoys goofy movies? Damn, I don't know, Zoe. Dudette doesn't seem to cover it."

"That's goddess to you. I drive like a god*dess!*"

The track slashed down toward a stream a dozen meters across. There was nothing to indicate how deep it might be.

Zoe drove through it at speed, blasting water aside, and actually shifted up another gear as she climbed out the far side.

*Goddess Zoe?* She wasn't going to get any argument from him.

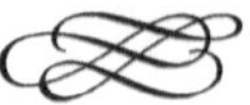

"*E*ight hundred and twenty-three kilometers," Luke announced as they rolled into the bivouac.

And Zoe could feel every single one of them tramping through her body like a centipede army bent on her destruction. Only a hundred and fifty klicks had been on a Selective Section, because Stage One was the easy one—six hundred something had been timing challenges on roads. *This* was the easy one? Someone shoot her now, please.

She and Luke hadn't talked much through the rest of the drive beyond what was needed for the racing itself. But it wasn't an uncomfortable silence, she hoped. They'd simply focused on the task at hand like the good soldiers they were.

On a couple of the longer straightaways, they talked over the import of Drake's news about what had happened in Pakistan. While it was chilling, it didn't shed any more light on what was happening at The Dakar. That conclusion had also cast its own pall over further conversation.

After the emotional drain of the start and the first Road Section followed by the pounding exhilaration of the Selective Section, the long Road Section to the end of Stage One became a timing challenge that ultimately consumed all of their lagging energy, despite drinking water and eating a couple of energy gels. Maybe the gels had energy, but she certainly didn't.

The bivouac had been set up by the assistance vehicles that had hurried ahead—doing their own timed rally race, but only on Road Sections. There existed no Selective Section for the assistance crews.

Santa Rosa de la Pampa might be a city of a hundred thousand, but they weren't in it. Instead, the bivouac was on a tabletop-flat farmer's field far enough out of town to make the tall city buildings no more than a heat shimmer in the distance.

The area was a fenced-off rectangle covering many acres—a one-night-only pop-up city of nearly two thousand people: five hundred competitors, an equal number (at least) of assistance personnel, the same again in media, officials, vendors, caterers and... It was a wild scene, not counting the fans who'd come out from the city.

Then she eased around a corner looking for her lane—tall banners with car numbers flew to indicate where to go—and almost plowed into a dance troupe. A great number of women were moving in two circling lines, one facing each way. Attire ranged from jeans with loose white blouses (the kind that looked silly on flat-chested women but fantastic on the Argentines) to elegant rawhide skirts and vests topped with (what she assumed were traditional) flat-topped, flat-brimmed Old West hats. They all looked like they were having such fun.

And they made her want to hide. For nine hours, her world had become the inside of the Citroën. Her heavy helmet buffered, but by no means blocked, the roar of barely mufflered racing engines. Her seat vibrating to that basso rumbled, when it wasn't being slammed and jarred by rough surfaces and hard turns—which was continuously. The only breaks had been the two timing breaks at either end of the Selective Section and the fastest rest stop ever made by a woman in a full racing suit.

These dancing women were a shock to her world. Over the low growl of her idling engine, she could hear their festive band, the rumble of other cars, the harsh *burrrr-ap!* of a pneumatic impact wrench as someone had their tires changed—or perhaps more dire repairs.

The scent of hot metal and dust had been replaced by hot dust and cooling metal.

She really needed to get out of this car and her gear. Easing around the dance troupe, which was now doing something between a man-eating shimmy and a groin-wrenching hula, Zoe decided it would be a good thing to get Luke well away from them quickly no matter what claims he made.

With only a little direction, she wound her way through the sprawling camp to where Ahmed, Nikita, and Drake had set up. It was only late afternoon, but they had big floodlights rigged in a shop area made of a large pop-up canopy. The rest of their base was a big camper van and a well-stocked service truck.

She rolled up and parked the car where Ahmed directed her beneath the blinding lights.

Liesl greeted her two steps from the car with a videographer and an ice cold Coca-Cola. Because of the latter, it was hard to be angry about the former.

"We're with Zoe DeMille, *The Soldier of Style.* How was your first-ever Dakar Rally stage?"

"Long," Zoe had to reach deep for the bright laugh, but she found it. She was intensely aware of Luke as he swung wide around the camera's field of view and came up behind Liesl and the videographer to watch her. Yellow racing suit unzipped far enough to reveal his black t-shirt like a deep cleavage on his SEAL-awesome chest. His eyes hidden behind mirrored shades. He crossed his arms over his chest and looked absolutely gorgeous. So male and powerful. Unlike the wilting mess she knew she was presenting to the camera.

"What part did you like the best?" Liesl didn't even give her a chance to catch her breath.

The best part? *Finding out that Luke still wanted to be with me.* "I've always enjoyed racing on sand. There were only twenty kilometers on the beach today, but it made me hungry to tackle the dunes." Sand was also the only kind of racing she'd ever done, so that easily counted as the best part of the driving.

"Twenty kilometers that did not go well for Sergey Kanski of Team Toyota," Liesl informed the camera. "He finished seven minutes off the best time."

"He's a fine racer, even if I did manage to get by him on the beach. I used a trick I doubt he'll ever fall for again." Only seven minutes off the lead? She hadn't seen him pass her again. Maybe on the Road Section…though she didn't see how.

She herself had passed several drivers out on the track. Two in racing, one mired in a mudhole, and another car that had gone nose down into a deep ditch and had turtled onto its back on the far side. The two drivers had been standing to one side watching anxiously as a racing truck used a long strap to flip the car upright. She wondered if it was still drivable after it was righted or if they were out of the race in Stage One.

"Zoe? You do not know?" Liesl looked at her in surprise.

"Know what? I only just arrived."

Liesl looked like she'd just swallowed the sweetest chocolate in the world. Zoe wondered where she could get some. Or anything else that wasn't an energy gel.

"What would you say if I told you that out of ninety-three entries in the car category, you are currently standing third, only forty-two seconds off the lead?"

"What do you get if you multiply six by nine?" Zoe replied with the exact quote from *The Hitchhiker's Guide to the Galaxy*. After all, forty-two was the answer to "life, the universe, and everything," according to Douglas Adams. Even if it no longer felt that way.

Luke's bark of laughter and Liesl's puzzled expression was Zoe's excuse to escape. Only Luke understood that nothing was truly important other than finding Hathyaron and the answer to everything else, including the race, might just as well be forty-two. *Hathyaron* was the real question and they were no closer than they'd been nine hours ago.

Then she stumbled to a halt as she spotted Christian sitting in the shade of the canopy.

"How did you get here?"

"I hitched a ride on one of the helicopters."

Zoe hadn't paid much attention to them—which was a major mind warp as her entire job was all about tracking the helicopters of the 5E. It was like a part of her had gone missing. The Dakar's helos—eight Airbus helos so she only knew them by their specs—floated overhead doing camera work, rescuing crashed drivers, and transporting race officials. Also, apparently, severely injured Legends.

"What about your back?"

He shrugged, then winced. After a sigh, he explained. "I have a back brace on under this shirt and enough painkillers in me to not care. But I cannot drive. They say I'm lucky I didn't make myself paralyzed." He sighed again, expressing exactly what he thought of his doctors. "You did very well today, Zoe, so you must keep driving. But this was the easiest stage with the shortest Selective Section, so you must step up your playing. Come. I have videos. I can show you some things you can do better. Then we must prepare your Road Book."

Apparently reaching the end of the race had nothing to do with the end of racing. God but she was tired. Even the Coke, which was now empty without her noticing, hadn't done a thing. Normally, that much caffeine and sugar would hyper her straight into space: don't pass the stratosphere, don't collect two hundred dollars.

She looked for Luke but he was nowhere to be seen. At least she knew he wasn't off with Liesl—because she and her videographer were still hovering just as if they too had been manufactured by Airbus rotorcraft. She was asking questions about her thoughts during the transition moment after Christian had blown his back jumping the podium.

How was she supposed to remember something that long ago?

Almost eight hours.

"Just let me shower first," she headed to the camper. She was slow to get there.

First, Ahmed wanted to discuss all of the details of how the car was performing. Was it pulling left or right, or was it running true? Any adjustments for the suspension that might improve cornering? Was the acceleration strong enough or did the turbocharger need tuning?

"It's already strong enough to give me whiplash every time I need it," appeared to satisfy him. It certainly earned her a brilliantly white smile. Moments later, he was pulling out air filters, checking oil, and all the rest of the things that the geeky part of her wanted to watch and the rest of her couldn't care about at all until it got a shower.

Then Nikita pulled her aside and congratulated her on the stage.

"We need to find Hathyaron," Zoe went for one of the questions that was plaguing her after Nikita had led her away from the others.

"Drake is out circulating with the crews right now. He's listening for Pashto- or Urdu-speaking teams, even their accents. No luck so far."

"Good idea," Zoe wavered on her feet, then realized she was slowly being cooked alive. Nikita had led her out of the busy tent and back into the sunshine. Finally tracing the problem, Zoe unzipped the flame-retardant racing suit right down to her shorts. The hot afternoon air was a cool balm in comparison.

"You need a shower," Nikita took a step back and pretended to hold her nose.

"Duh!"

"The shower in the camper isn't very big, but you can try."

"Try what?"

"To shower with Luke, of course. Though I still can't picture him with a woman."

"I'd have thought you could picture him with too many women." Neither Zoe nor her imagination needed help imagining Luke Altman with a long line of shapely women.

"They don't count," Nikita shook her head. "My commander used to have lifelong bachelor stamped on his dog tags. Now not so much."

"Whoa, Nikita. We're sleeping together. That's all. Using each other for sex," then she sighed, "and not much of that lately."

"Lately? You've been together six days and you're already sleeping together without sex?"

"That doesn't mean anything." But it did. None of her relationships had ever lasted to the point where sex wasn't a nearly nightly (*and morningly*) mandatory event. The problem had been that when the sex calmed down from dating heat to relationship pleasure, her relationships had invariably faded with them. If she understood what was going on, she and Luke had already made the transition due to circumstances beyond their control. And they'd done it without everything falling apart.

"What are you two ladies talking about?" Luke stepped up to them.

"You, of course," Zoe riposted, then wished she hadn't.

Luke's eyebrows raised above his mirrored shades.

"Don't worry, boss, none of it was good," Nikita patted his arm, then walked away. Luke didn't even turn to watch her go.

"Here," he held out a paper plate.

Zoe's body kicked in all at once like her engine dial had just been set to Four—full power. On the plate were two long kebab skewers of grilled steak chunks, with scallions and cherry tomatoes interspersed between chunks. Beside it was a large bread roll and a chimichurri dipping sauce. The feast for her eyes was assessed by her nose as exactly what she needed—together they transmitted their doubly reinforced data stream directly to her stomach, which growled loudly enough to make Luke chuckle.

"Speaking of gods…" She grabbed a skewer, dipped it into the sauce, and slid off the first chunk between her teeth. The outer char and inner marinade combined to make a small piece of heaven. The peppery meat accented by the cool cilantro and sharp vinegar of the sauce made her want to eat slowly to appreciate every bite—and to scarf the whole thing down in a flurry of greed.

Luke rustled up a pair of camp chairs and set them in the shade as far from the bustle as possible.

Definitely speaking of gods, Luke looked as delicious as their meal as he slouched down and sighed happily.

"Any thoughts?"

His leer answered that well enough. She needed a temporary subject change if there was a chance she was going to finish her dinner rather than dragging Luke into the trailer and ripping his clothes off.

"Other than that?" She told him what Drake was listening for out among the other teams.

He nodded that it was a good idea, but grimaced on its chances of success.

"Yeah, my thoughts too. I'm starting to think he isn't Pakistani at all. If he's a foreigner, he could be anyone."

Luke grunted agreement.

"So how do we find him?" She voiced the question for both of them. Their shared silence lasted long enough for her to start on the second skewer.

"Shit!" Luke's final assessment on the situation matched her own.

---

It seemed to take the fun out of the evening.

Zoe had looked so small out of the car. The contrast from Zoe the driver to Zoe standing so much shorter than everyone else was almost surreal. So powerful when wrapped in steel, and so petite when standing beside it. Even the car was taller than she was.

Yet she was the one they all mobbed. Liesl, Christian, Nikita, Ahmed: they all wanted a piece of her. Well, so did he. The long silence of racing fit him well. He'd enjoyed the task of a single focus instead of the normal twenty that a mission required. Turns, speed, timing were all he could control while in the car. No phones or radios were allowed for the Dakar teams except for an emergency satellite phone—with brutal penalties for calling anyone other than the race officials to report a breakdown or accident.

Being cut off had let him shed the mission from his high-priority task list.

He'd stuck with that upon their arrival: listening to Zoe spar happily with Liesl. The woman never ran out of energy. And he didn't want to be running out of energy when they got off alone somewhere—so he'd followed his nose to the catering area just two rows over. He even ran into the Malles Motos crowd, but declined their invitation to join in, apologizing by holding up the two plates of food he was already carrying.

A long day of racing, arriving in camp to good people and good food—life wasn't bad at all.

Except this wasn't his life, as Zoe had just reminded him.

Hathyaron the arms dealer simply had to be here. Zoe had been absolutely right in connecting the dots he'd missed of the heavy tire tracks in the Pakistani soil, the high-tech garage, and The Dakar Rally poster.

To date they'd been moving on the idea that he was Pakistani and that would make him stand out. Except it hadn't. No team from there. No flight that could be traced back.

"Definitely a foreigner." Luke nodded over Zoe's shoulder. She turned in time to see Drake talking to Nikita and shaking his head sadly. No luck on catching an Urdu-speaking mechanic.

She slumped lower in the chair, like all of her supports had just been pulled out.

"Something you need to know about SEALs, Zoe."

"Why doesn't this sound good?"

Luke wasn't sure what she meant, so he kept on anyway. "We train constantly. But there is a great deal of waiting as well. A sniper may lie in wait for days before they get their target in their sights. Patience is hard, but we have thirteen more stages. On this stage we learned he wasn't Pakistani. That's progress."

"That may be the longest speech I've ever heard you give, Luke."

"Huh." Maybe. But he liked talking to Zoe.

"You're right though. When I fly, there is always something I can be doing. We have our 'Road Sections,' flying from the airport of origin to the mission area, but during the 'Selective Section' of the mission itself, there is never any true pause. We're constantly reviewing details, shifting for different angles and better visuals, tracking our team and what situations they're headed into, relaying communications, and the like. Once we enter the battlespace, there's no moment for true rest."

Somehow, Zoe had reached deep and shifted back to her optimism. He could see it in her, sitting upright once more and resuming her dinner. Damn but he was a lucky bastard to have her on the team. Which wasn't the only place he was lucky to have her.

"No true rest here either," Luke leered at her.

The smile she returned as she suggestively slid the last piece of meat off the skewer with her teeth flash-heated his body. He was halfway to his feet to drag her into the camper when Christian hobbled up and handed him a small roll of paper—four inches wide and far too long. Tomorrow's Road Book.

Luke was at least pleased that Zoe's groan matched his own.

It meant that the next couple of hours would be spent sitting around a table together with Christian, reviewing the course and marking up the scroll. Christian liked lots of colors on his markups and had made Luke do that on today's: red for upcoming hazards, bright blue for particularly tricky navigation areas, green for places to make up time, fuchsia for timing waypoints (only a few of which were included; the rest were stealthy ones, hidden along the route at unexpected intervals, but couldn't be missed without penalties), and on and on. Luke had thought about making a color guide to go along with interpreting Christian's version of the Road Book route guide. He was going to go to one color: the bright blue had stood out best in the bright sunlight.

He looked at Zoe for a long moment, still holding the little roll.

She looked back at him, once again slumped in the chair.

"Showers first," he declared. "We'll start this in an hour."

Christian smirked. It took all of Luke's self-control to not put the man down and give him more than his bad back to think about.

He must have read Luke's mood, because the look disappeared quickly enough. Then he held out his hand, "At least I can start on marking the Road Book."

Luke tucked it into his pocket, earning him a slightly more

cautious frown. Christian was starting to wise up. Luke wanted his own markings on the roll…and only his.

The shower did nothing to ease the heat of the day. It was too small to share, but the tiny stall had clear glass sides. Zoe had shoved him in first, then leaned against the door offering ribald suggestions as he took a combat shower: thirty seconds pre-soak, water off for shampoo and soap lather, one minute rinse.

While he was toweling off, Zoe slipped in. After some of the comments she'd made, he almost took her then and there without letting her shower first. She seemed to have tapped directly into his blood flow control, allowing none of it to go to his brain.

He leaned against the doorframe to watch her shower as he dried himself off. But he couldn't think of a word to say. He remembered the look of her naked body on the Senegalese beach, but that view had been very brief before they came together. He'd never simply looked at her naked form. Her hair darkening with the water changed her appearance dramatically. Instead of a cheery blonde fluff to her shoulders, it was a dark curtain down to her biceps that made her blue eyes shine forth each time she glanced his way.

When she stepped out of the shower, he couldn't wait another moment and grabbed her.

"I'm still all wet."

He tackled her with his towel. Squeezing all the water he could out of her hair, he began working down her body. He'd backed up into the tiny hallway and she clung to the bathroom's doorframe for support as he worked her over. Her eyes slid shut and her breathing went short and sharp as he applied the soft towel to her lovely form.

Luke wanted to tease. To draw it out for her, but he couldn't. His slightest touch lit her up like a thermite reaction. Unable to help himself, he gave her what her body was clearly craving. Placing one hand to hold her sweet behind, he massaged her through the towel from the front.

When she came apart, he was almost envious. It was so fast and so powerful. She clung to the doorframe in desperation while the release slammed through her so hard he was half afraid that he'd hurt her.

"Now!" Zoe's whisper was fierce through clenched teeth with closed eyes.

*Now, what?*

"Hurry, Luke. I need you inside me now."

He pulled her from the doorframe. Her grip shifted from the panels to clench around his neck. Three steps later, he had her on the bed in the back of the camper.

"Hurry," she begged again as he struggled to sheath himself when she wouldn't let go.

He slid into her like he'd never been anywhere else. No one had ever fit around him the way Zoe did. It wasn't that he was entering a woman, it was that he was sliding into the best place he'd ever been.

She buried her face in the crook of his neck and together they went up again. As he drove her aloft, as he climbed right along with her, he knew this wasn't about the sex. Nor was it about fears or tears.

This was about him and Zoe. No one else could ever feel this way. This was connection at a level he'd never known existed. Being married to Marva—perhaps standing at the altar had been the very best part of the whole disaster—he'd admired her body and what she did with it.

Zoe didn't treat sex like an art form as the exceptionally skilled Marva had, but she also had no artifice. She simply gave so completely there was no questioning that she wanted to be with him in this moment more than anything and that made it all the more amazing.

He did what he could to delay crossing over the tipping point. It felt as if he perched on the precipice of some decision. He needed to pause, to hold off, even for a just a moment, in order to understand what was happening to him.

But such thoughts were useless.

With Zoe in his arms, they were racing toward a finish line that allowed no turns or delays.

The release gutted him. It left her humming happily against his neck as he wondered what the hell had just happened. His body had no calibration for such a powerful release. It wasn't sex. It was filled with meaning. But his brain had been scrambled even more than his hormones and he had no idea what that meaning might be.

———

ZOE'S BODY HUMMED.

She didn't mind Christian's sly comments as the three of them worked through the Road Book. Didn't care that the nine p.m. route briefing said they were in for even a rougher day than the Road Book implied. The Road Section would be short and the Selective Section horrendously long—the opposite of today. That was fine too.

This had to be just a hormone-fueled temporary euphoria. A mental aberration that she'd eventually recover from, but she hoped not.

It wasn't just her. Nikita, never one to be expressive, had offered no words. Instead, she'd merely hugged Zoe and held her for longer than even when the nerves had hit the bride as she'd been maid of honor at Nikita and Drake's wedding.

When she'd crawled into bed, exhaustion had threatened to take her. It certainly knocked Luke out of circulation.

Instead, she lay with her head on his shoulder and her leg thrown over his hips. The past she'd survived could never have been worth it, but the present certainly put it in perspective. With Luke she was simply Zoe and—she pressed herself against his hip, enjoying the deep heat that stirred to life—that was all he asked of her.

She worked hard to suppress the laugh that would surely wake Luke, because once it started coming out, she might not be able to stop it.

Luke only asked her to be Zoe.

But who in the name of all that was twisted and warped was that?

Chief Warrant 2 Zoe DeMille of the US Army's 160th Special Operations Aviation Regiment (airborne) ready for duty. *Yes sir, you betcha.*

*The Soldier of Style: Living in the Cutey-Edgy Budget Battlespace.* At least to a kajillion fans and most of her previous lovers, that's all she'd ever been.

The Rookie currently holding third place in the Dakar Rally. The officials had ruled that since Christian hadn't made it even fifty meters from the starting podium, she and Luke were eligible in the Rookie category—which they were leading by a huge margin.

Her Pismo Beach-based parents' daughter. A source of so much anger that in a sick way it was almost funny—in how it had twisted and twined its way through her life.

But most of all, she was a top pilot for Special Operations Command and her lover was a high-ranking SEAL Team 6 officer. And life simply didn't get any better than that.

# CHAPTER 19

Any tiny hint of order that had occurred in the Stage One went right out the window in Stage Two.

He and Zoe had regrettably been woken by the alarm clock rather than their bodies, so there was no time for a rematch. But he certainly enjoyed waking up with Zoe curled up against him.

It was also not his standard mode of operations. He was typically gone from a woman's bed by two a.m. If she was in his bed, he'd become an expert at sliding out without waking her and going for a run—typically until she was long gone. Marva had slept well apart from him, sometimes in the other bedroom, claiming that her constant need for him made her too restless.

Zoe was snuggled so tightly against him that they might have made love in their sleep and not known it.

But they hadn't even grabbed a quickie because the alarm clock had electrified Zoe.

"C'mon, Luke. Stop dragging. Race day today."

Being a SEAL had whupped being a morning person or a night owl out of his system—whenever he needed to be sharp, he was sharp. But when he wasn't out in the field on a dangerous mission, he liked to take a *few* moments to wake up. Zoe simply threw her internal On Switch, going from Sleeping Beauty to ballistic missile in two seconds flat. There wasn't even time to really admire her form as she dressed.

A standard Argentine breakfast had filled another thirty seconds of their morning: cream-filled *medialunas*—crescent rolls—with black coffee and a glass of orange juice. Their rank in the standings had placed them early in the starting lineup and had them hurrying to the timing start position just outside the bivouac gates.

The Road Section had proved uneventful.

One minute into the Second Stage, disaster had already struck. Two of the drivers of a Jeep were standing in the low swale between the third and fourth dune along the Selective Section. Brothers Andy and Jim Kyle, United States, seven Dakars each—two of the nine Americans in the race, including themselves. They were looking morosely at their vehicle from a distance. It was intensely on fire, the entire vehicle engulfed.

Zoe had slowed beside them, close enough for Luke to ask, "You guys okay?"

"Blown hydraulics line, we think. Maybe. Shit, I don't know," Jim managed while Andy simply stood there looking numb. And then there were seven Americans in the race.

"Need me to call—"

The guy held up a satellite phone to indicate he'd already placed a call.

"Sorry, man."

The poor guy didn't even manage a wave before turning back to stare at the burning remains of several hundred thousand dollars of race car. Once a carbon fiber body ignited, there wasn't much other than time that could put it out—certainly not the small handheld extinguisher they had aboard with their other supplies.

Zoe let go of the handbrake and opened up the engine with a roar to get up the next dune. Over that dune, a car was badly sand-bogged. Luke had only the briefest glimpse of two guys out in the heat with small shovels trying to dig in a couple of flat traction ramps just like the ones they had stowed in their own cargo area.

"Getting real," Zoe commented drily as she slid down a dune slip face, crabbing sideways around a particularly steep section.

"Seriously," Luke agreed. The GPS flashed on. "Way Point," he called out. Which meant they were within eight hundred meters of the point. They'd have to get within ninety meters before the GPS would mark them as validly reaching the electronic check-in represented by the Way Point.

"Which way?"

"Dead ahead or I would have told you."

"Some help you are," Zoe in race mode sounded pissed at him. No, ultra-intense driver *and* pissed.

Then he looked up and saw why. An insurmountable dune practically blanked out the world ahead of them. There was a low pass far to the left—far enough to add over a kilometer out and another back once through. He could see tracks that showed most racers had gone that way. Close to the right was a far higher pass. It looked as if only a single motorcycle had gone that way.

"Left?" he asked.

But Zoe was already slicing the other way, scooting diagonally up the dune's slip face. He considered asking why, but even the intercom might not overcome the roar she was coaxing out of the engine. Besides, it might be better not to distract her as the car kept threatening to lose traction and roll over onto his side first. Each time, she did something that kept her crabbing upward rather than rolling down.

"Hang on," was the only warning he had as she reached the top. The steep approach had forced her down to second gear, the engine pumping at seven thousand RPM to keep them moving. Great rooster tails shot off the rear tires.

He grabbed the handle on the inside of the door and the other on the center console.

Just as the car reached the crest—and threatened to high-center atop the pass—she cut the wheel hard, slamming them through a nearly end-for-end turn. At one moment they were slicing right over the dune crest, at the next they were racing left along it. Now their left front tire was hooked on the edge of the ridge with the other three wheels having crossed over. She made it back up to third gear and powered up the ridgeline.

Now he was looking down a far steeper dune face than they'd just climbed. Had they crested directly over the ridge, they'd almost assuredly have done an end-over-end down the other side.

"How did you know?"

"Wind carves dunes in strange ways. I remembered one in Pismo when I was still fifteen that did that. I was out in a dune buggy and high-centered on a pass just like that one. Getting stuck was probably the only thing that kept me from really bunging up Dad's newest buggy. Even with the roll cage, I bet it would have really hurt."

By the end of her explanation, she'd reached the very pinnacle of the dune that had blocked their way. Here, at the center of the dune, the back slope was much less steep—merely vicious rather than terrifying.

With a hard snap of the steering wheel, she managed to point them directly down the slope. Fourth gear, fifth, and they flashed through the Way Point several minutes ahead of the route through the lower pass.

"Next heading is 120 by the compass," he slashed a hand sharply to the right, "for five kilometers." He looked at the dunes across their path and knew it would probably take traveling ten kilometers in a zigzag pattern to cover those five.

Though with Zoe driving, maybe not.

***

GETTING REAL? Talk about the goddamn understatement of her life.

She hadn't remembered the dune that had almost battered her as a teenager until they were mere meters from the crest. This one wouldn't have battered them, it could have killed them. Ridge-running with one tire hooked over the top was a new one on her—it had been an act of desperation that had worked by pure chance. She'd meant to get two wheels on either side of that crest and high-center them to a safe stop. It was the only option left to her when she understood the steepness of the face they could never descend except in a tumble. But in only catching the one wheel, she'd learned a new technique. More importantly, it had been enough to save them from a very ugly descent.

It didn't help that one of The Dakar's official helicopters had been hovering only a few hundred meters away for her entire maneuver. She hadn't seen it behind them as she climbed the dune, but as she'd slewed around on the ridge crest, she'd spotted it flying lower than she was now driving. A cameraman leaning out the door had tracked her all the way up the crest. Luke wouldn't know, he had no way to see down where they'd come from because he'd been sitting in the passenger's seat tilted down the other side of the ridge.

She was used to looking down on helicopters—from sixty thousand feet. In the dead of night. Via remote feed from her RPA. But from two hundred feet away in broad daylight? Not so much. In the rearview mirror, she could see that it climbed aloft high enough to film her race down the dune face before peeling off to other tasks.

Near death experience. Wild-ass ridge running. ESPN at eleven.

Definitely *getting real.*

Zoe eyed the first dune of the next set and decided to go straight over it. With a long flat run, she was able to gather enough speed to take it while still in fourth gear. She eased off the gas as her front wheels left the crest, reaching out to pop the handbrake for just a moment. It made the rear wheels drag just enough at the crest that the car tipped from nose high to a level-flight jump. They fell almost three stories before they hit.

The car's suspension and the deep sand ate up the shock, and she was up in fifth gear as they hit to keep pulling them ahead rather than slower-spinning tires acting like an unintended brake that might flip them. The Citroën had taken it with less complaint than her Mini Cooper did when eating a pothole on the highway to Mobile.

"Go, DeMille!" Luke shouted loud enough to hurt her ears.

She slalomed for a low spot around the next dune. Her lover was cheering her on. Since when did that happen? Lovers were always looking for a way to make themselves feel superior. Every relationship she'd ever been in had a built-in power dynamic of making the male feel even more male: the strong one, the teacher.

She was the one driving the race car.

—And Luke was cheering her on!

It wasn't her ears that were hurting, it was her heart. Her brain kept waiting for the subtle (or not so subtle) manipulation. For the wake-up call that said no matter what she did, she didn't really belong. Her heart had no idea what to do with what was happening between them.

Around the next dune wasn't another dune, instead there was a river—that she almost plowed straight into, not always the worst tactic. Except she spotted a head popping up out of the water, and another. Not trusting to brakes alone, she did a four-wheel drift to make sure she stopped before she drove into the river.

Then she realized that the heads were helmeted and on either side of a car that was flooded and floating downriver—driver and co-driver crawling out the windows of their sunken vehicle. She followed them for over a hundred meters, but neither one seemed hurt. She was about to turn around and figure out where to find the ford—and hopefully cross it with better luck than they had—when their car crunched up on a hidden shallow and its roof resurfaced before it stopped.

One of the big six-wheeled racing trucks pulled up to the river's edge and drove across easily—wetting about halfway up their monstrous wheels. As soon as it was completely across, it stopped and one of the crew climbed down.

Zoe had memorized most of the truck numbers as well, though she'd only learned the drivers' names rather than the full crew.

This was Pierre Rousseau, France, seven Dakars, driving ten tons of Kamaz racing truck with a thousand horsepower.

He tossed a six-inch-wide strap out to the guys standing chest-deep in the river. One ducked underwater for a moment to hook it to his bumper, then gave a thumbs-up to the trucker. Rousseau's crewman hooked the other end of the strip to his rear hitch and in moments they had the car towed out of the water. As soon as they dropped the strap, the truck raced away, leaving the car's team to see if they could repair and restart their soggy vehicle.

Zoe looked at Luke. Halfway up the Kamaz's big tires would be near the top of theirs. Deep enough that the current might drag them away if it floated them before they crossed.

"You got this, Zoe. Do it!"

She could only look at him in amazement.

Zoe had lain awake for a long time this morning before the alarm went off, listening to Luke's heart and slow breathing. She'd slept in his arms with no thoughts to her own safety. No knife clandestinely slipped under the pillow—which had freaked out more than one lover who'd accidentally discovered it there. Not even on the nightstand. For all she knew, it was still in the bathroom where she'd stripped down while watching Luke shower yesterday. It might still be there now because she'd never thought to strap it back on. She'd worn a knife every day for over half her life, and suddenly she wasn't.

At his side, she'd gone to the driver's meeting without a thought of carrying her own weapon. When was the last time she'd felt for her missing sidearm—locked in her gun safe back at Fort Rucker? Hours? Maybe even days?

She lined up with the Kamaz's tracks, kicked the engine hard, then popped the clutch and plowed into the river. Her passage blew an arc of spray over Cid and Jabir, working frantically on their car—their second Dakar Rally, Ford car, United Arab Emirates, last year finished forty-seventh.

She stopped to apologize.

"Shit. Don't stress, Zoe. Like we weren't wet already. Just go," Cid turned back to his car. As far as she knew, she'd never actually met them, but they certainly knew who she was. They moved down several notches on her suspect list.

Dropping into first, she eased away to make sure she didn't blast a load of sand on them after the bath. Once away, she punched back up to racing speed.

Zoe looked at Luke, at perhaps the first lover she'd ever had who made her feel completely safe.

Without thought or comment. Without realizing quite how incredible he was, Luke was studying the Road Book to find their next destination.

*Yeah, Zoe.*

Getting *really* real.

———

"How could you do this to me?"

"What?"

"*What?*" Liesl raged at both of them the moment they climbed out of the car at the San Rafael bivouac. "Have you seen the footage? You are the new sensation of The Dakar… *Und es ist nicht mein Film!*"

Christian spun a laptop so that Luke and Zoe could see what he'd been watching.

Luke's stomach lurched as he saw the bright yellow Citroën clawing up an impossible dune face. Knowing what was going to happen didn't alter the sensation. Seeing it in perspective from the helo's vantage point almost made him nauseous. Down on the sand, it was simply what was happening. In the wider world? It looked terrifying.

They'd done *that?*

As the helo climbed and the wider view came into the frame, Zoe slipped an arm around his waist and held on. He pulled her tight against him and held on himself. It was an amazing sequence. Then, in a tapering telephoto, it followed her racing jump over the next dune and the flight down the far side.

"I take back what I said yesterday, Zoe," Christian turned from the replay as another scene unfolded. This time the camera was on the ground and had caught Cid's car failing to cross the upstream ford across the river and then slowly sinking as it washed downstream away from the camera (then a clip showing them back in motion—*Go guys!*). "Maybe I have nothing to teach you. Not many drivers would have dared to take the righthand course. So, until the next disaster or amazing feat, you are the media's darling."

Luke felt Zoe's shudder beneath his arm.

He looked down at her in surprise, but she was very carefully not looking up to meet his gaze. The air whooshed out of him as surely as if he'd been sucker punched in the solar plexus.

That amazing maneuver was pure luck? He wanted to ask, but decided that he definitely didn't want to know the answer. No, it was pure skill, but it certainly hadn't been with any planning.

How far out on the edge was she running this? That one he knew the answer to—about SEAL-on-a-mission far. Damn, the woman was amazing. He'd never met anyone like her.

The fact that he might not ever again was a startling thought that he didn't like at all.

CHAPTER 20

"Go! Be famous for an hour or two." Christian had waved them away after they'd prepared the Road Book. Either his back was paining him too much—or he wanted some alone time with the hot Argentine brunette whom they passed as she sauntered down the lane toward Christian's camp site.

Zoe couldn't help but giggle.

"What is it with men and their little one-track minds?"

In answer Luke yanked her into the shadow of an Iveco truck. Marik Ebbers, Netherlands, Legend with seventeen Dakars, top finish was...

It was something she couldn't remember as Luke quickly proved where his "little one-track mind" was focused without question. For the length of perhaps thirty seconds, he locked his lips on hers and thoroughly manhandled her—one hand on her breast, the other down the back of her pants to haul them together. She managed to slip a hand over those six-pack abs and down the outside of his pants making him groan into their kiss until her head was spinning.

Then he released her all at once, forcing a gasp of need from her, and grinned down at her. "Having a woman like you around? Makes me very one-track."

If Luke really meant what he'd just said…

It wasn't that she doubted him. But until she was eighteen, she'd been just like Luke. And Christian. *Got a pulse? Let's do it.* She'd shed that idiocy at eighteen when she'd burned that awful Huckfest photo of her and the line of guys she'd fucked. Men never seemed to get past that. Christian certainly hadn't.

But if Luke really meant what he'd said, she remembered that transition herself. It had changed the course of her life in so many ways. She'd left men behind—at least random ones—and started working on fixing herself. She'd focused her energy on *The Soldier of Style* and joined the Air Force as an RPA flier.

Resting both hands on his chest and looking up into Luke's shadowed blue eyes, Zoe wondered—perhaps for the first time—*What if?*

Christian would never change. He was too much the privileged boy.

But Luke was a Spec Ops warrior of the highest caliber. What if he was changing? Was she ready for that? How—

"Okay, enough of that, you two."

LUKE HAD SEEN Nikita and Drake coming up behind Zoe. The interesting thing was that Zoe didn't startle away. Instead she turned and leaned back against him as if it was the most natural thing on the planet. His hands had landed on her trim waist. In her turn, she'd laced her fingers into one of them and pulled it onto her so-soft belly as she turned so that she ended up inside his embrace.

It made him feel…like…an ST6 SEAL. When a mission wasn't totally in the shitter, being in SEAL Team 6 was the ultimate power drug. The best weapons, the toughest training, and the most dangerous missions.

Holding Zoe made him feel that kind of powerful, except it was a new kind as well. Strong and protective—that's what it was. As if holding her, he could do anything.

Felt like the old joke about two guys in Maine who get blown way off course in a hot-air balloon. As they were landing near a farmer working his field, they asked him, "Where are we?" The Mainer answered, in typical fashion, "You be in a balloon, you darn fools."

Zoe had certainly blown him way off course. *Where are you, Luke? And the answer? In a relationship with Zoe DeMille, you darn fool.* And he didn't want to be much of anywhere else either.

He looked at Drake and Nikita, chatting with Zoe as she continued to lie back in his arms. They were standing hip-to-hip, so close that they must…have their inside hands tucked in each other's back pockets. So close. So comfortable. It wasn't just that he saw that now. It was as if they'd always been that way and he could finally see it for the first time.

He glanced down at Zoe's black-and-blonde hair. What the *hell* had she done to him?

---

"AHMED SAID he could handle everything the car needed, then shooed us away, too." Nikita's smile told Zoe so much that she needed to know.

*Yes! This was how it felt when it was right.*

Sure, she'd helped Nikita and Drake get together during the Honduran mission. But that heat, that rightness had been there for them from the very start. All she'd done was help Nikita get out of her own way. With the slightest shift, she was able to lay her head back against Luke's chest.

What if Zoe got out of *her* own way? Maybe she'd end up…exactly where she was. Being all wrapped up in Luke's arms was about the best place she'd ever been. It was no longer a question of how long would it last. It was now hoping that it didn't end. Ever.

And that was far too big a thought for the second night of The Dakar.

"Let's go dancing." She tipped her head back enough to look at Luke. "Can you dance?"

She could see where his eyes traveled down the front of her

blouse. She hated when guys did that. But Luke? He'd earned a license to do it as often as he liked. It tickled her no end that he wanted to. The first time, when she'd caught him doing it as Christian drove them from the airport into the city of Dakar, had merely been surprising—and she remembered thinking, *How typically male.* Now she knew that nothing *typical* remained between the two of them. They'd left behind simply sex right along with mere lust and pure heat. She *wanted* to be with Luke. And she wanted him to *want* to be with her.

Apparently too mesmerized by her minimalist breasts to speak, Zoe looked back to Nikita, "Does he dance?"

"Not in my lifetime." Nikita almost laughed. Drake shook his head in agreement.

"Time to learn." She kept one of Luke's hands in hers, grabbed Nikita's with the other, and together the four of them plunged into the social area of the camp.

They followed the sounds of pounding drums and blaring trumpets to the big open area out in front of the mess tent. There was definitely a party going on.

The San Rafael Guerra de Baile, the War of Dance troupe, had taken over the broad field. Men were dressed in clinging black slacks heavily embroidered in gold, and knee-high leather boots covered in bells that tinkled brightly with each leaping step. Their seafoam green, asymmetrical shirts and long black gloves were also beautifully embroidered. Their dance partners were just as colorful: gold heels, kicky little green skirts that poofed out with layers of equally tiny petticoats, which didn't even reach down to mid-thigh, their poofy-sleeved matching tops, and little straw hats trailing bright ribbons as long as their dark, flowing hair.

They were all working the crowd, and with each moment, more race drivers were enticed to join in. Zoe could already feel the beat in her toes and flowing up her body. It wasn't the rhythm of sex…quite. It was the rhythm of how good it felt in anticipation. And how good it felt afterward. The moment where a crow of pure joy wanted to sound out.

Luke gave her one of his, *Are you insane?* looks.

She took both his hands and pulled him down until she could shout in his ear over the driving beat of the band. "Do you think Hathyaron would dance or would refuse?"

His eyes flicked over her shoulder, assessing the crowd, then snapped back to hers in a moment. It had taken him under three seconds to see the pattern once she'd brought it up—he was just that astute. But had she just out-observed a SEAL? No, she'd dragged him into an environment that couldn't be more foreign to him if it was on Mars. She almost laughed at the comparison; he was the God of War after all, just like Mars—or at least close enough that she didn't care about the difference.

"My bet is he would," she shouted again. "He'd let loose because he'd think that The Dakar was the one place he was safe. That means that anyone who refuses is less likely to be a suspect." Then she started to dance backward toward the throng without releasing his hands.

A look of alarm shot across his face.

"You're not Hathyaron, are you?" Her tease got him moving, but it was a close thing. He might have balked if Drake and Nikita hadn't happened by in that moment, arm-in-arm with a male dancer between them trying to show them the steps.

She did her best to catalog who watched but wouldn't join. Some of them surprised her. The stern Russian motorcyclist, Roza Vilenko (two top-three finishes in nine Dakars), danced beautifully. She looked like the female badass from the next *Terminator* movie and moved as well as some of the professional dancers—of course she was doing the men's dance, not the women's. The women's seemed to be mostly about shaking their hips and making their tiny skirts flit up to reveal even more bare thigh.

Tammy Hall was in the middle of them, of course, with her blonde hair flying and her cowboy hat not looking out of place for once. Zoe was pleased when Tammy's attempt to peel Luke off Zoe's arm was rebuffed with utter disdain.

He did one of his who-the-hell-do-you-think-you-are looks and Tammy went away.

Being five-four, she'd never been able to wield that kind of look with any success. On Luke, it was terrifying—which was awesome.

Liesl and her camera showed up at some point. She gained another point in Zoe's estimation by mostly shooting her and Luke when Luke's back was to the camera—leaving him out of the picture as requested. She hoped that Liesl captured at least one with both of their faces so that she could have a copy.

The dance troupe was good. Once they had a driver in their crowd, they were very reluctant to let them out. It gave her enough time to memorize the thirty-six who wouldn't join in. As to the ones who did, out of six hundred drivers, at least a hundred of them were dancing. That left over four hundred who weren't here to change their suspect-likelihood. It was a long shot, but she knew that hunting a target was the accumulation of hundreds of tiny bits of data that just had to be correlated the right way to find an answer.

And while she was doing that, she was dancing with Luke.

It was an evening she was never going to forget.

# CHAPTER 21

$S$tage Three was predominately on *piste*—on track. Dunes were definitely off *piste*—"HP" in the Road Book for the French *hors piste.*

Of course "track" was a strong word to describe the day's route. There was a dirt path that a road grader might have cut through the wilderness fifty years before. Or maybe a couple of ox-drawn carts had once come this way—when the world was even younger than she was.

Zoe could have measured the smooth spots in the road in meters— on a good stretch. The suspension was doing a dance that had nothing to do with a Michael Jackson moonwalk and a lot to do with a Metallica heavy metal show. The Senegalese beach had been so much smoother by comparison that the car had seemed to float while the suspension took the abuse. Not so much here.

Every turn was a slide, because at a hundred and fifty kph, the tires were only catching the tops of each road divot—too little traction to actually call it a turn. Places to accelerate strongly, like a run up to a dune, were replaced with a gear shift every second or so. Down, down, down, headed into a corner, then up, up, up before the next down, down on the twisting track.

The road grader—which hadn't been near this road since the Stone Age—had left low berms of dirt off to either side. As she was still in the top four—she'd dropped down a place but was still within a minute of the lead because Hermann Golschen (eight Dakars, Belgian, Peugeot) had moved up so strongly—she'd had an early start. By end of day, this track would be twice as pitted and even harder to run at speed. Despite how few cars had started ahead of her, every now and then a pair of tracks blew out over the berm. A pair of fresh tracks would shoot out of the middle of a turn. A new path would be plowed through the sparse bushes, then a new notch in the berm where the racer rejoined the road.

This was high desert and completely unpopulated. Definitely the land of Whatever Worked.

"Luke."

"Uh-huh."

"Any off-*piste* forbidden symbols in the Road Book?" In some of the environmentally fragile areas, or farmland, they were severely penalized for leaving the track.

"No."

She didn't need to say anything else. Luke began scrolling ahead in the Road Book. He made a pleased grunt.

"Okay, so, not this turn, but the next one. Straight off the middle."

In the second turn, she punched head-on through the berm and almost flipped. The berm was both softer and wider than it looked. *Have to remember that.* But she managed to keep the nose out of the dirt with a burst of power. Back in Pismo she'd gotten over the first instinct, which was to hit the brakes. Sudden deceleration would have nosed the car down and they'd have burrowed in.

"Ditch!" Luke had been looking ahead.

She gunned the engine and aimed for the highest ground she could see. It made a small lip of a jump—enough that she could fly nearly thirty feet. Looking down at the ditch as they flew over it said that maybe off-*piste* hadn't been the best idea—it was a rough, rocky defile that they never could have crossed on the ground. Landing on the far side in the middle of a massive acacia hedge sounded like a thousand fingernails being dragged across a chalkboard. All the thorns and woody stems certainly weren't doing anything good for Christian's paint job.

"Berm and a hard left."

Zoe jumped back onto the road and slid into a long drift to get lined up once more along the track. They did two more like that, surviving as much by chance as planning.

"Maybe going off-*piste* isn't the best idea."

Instead of answering, Luke shouted, "Dust!"

She raced the engine harder because her first thought was *fesh fesh* —dust so fine that it might as well be quicksand. This absolutely was the kind of country to expect it in.

Except this dust wasn't vast clouds of talcum powder fineness. Instead, it was a hazing of the air, especially on the outside of the turns where a sliding turn would particularly kick it up. Though the leaders had started two minutes apart, she had caught up to someone enough that his dust hadn't settled yet.

"No more turns for a while," Luke was looking straight ahead.

Zoe rarely looked beyond the next hundred meters of track, but she followed his gaze. The flat plains of the Dry Pampas had climbed into the Andean foothills without her noticing. The track did indeed stretch out long and straight ahead of them. Even as she pushed up through fifth and into sixth gear—something she got to use far too rarely—she couldn't help but admire the view.

They were arrowing directly for a vast blue lake. Around them was low scrub in blackish dirt. Beyond the lake rose a towering volcanic peak—pitch black with iced glaciers trapped in its higher folds like a giant sentinel set to guard against their passage. It blocked out a whole section of the achingly blue sky.

"It's midsummer!"

"Not up there. Cerro Galán is one of the biggest calderas in South America. Besides, we're at 4,500 meters."

"We're *what?*"

She'd been preparing a mental list of problems for Ahmed. Something was eating the Citroën's power. The acceleration had worsened all morning until she felt as if she was gasping as badly as the car. And the power bleed-off response had worsened ten-fold through the day's racing. If they were three miles above sea level—higher than any road, paved or not, in the US—it was no wonder the car was struggling.

Come to think of it, so was she. She'd been so focused on the racing that she hadn't noticed, but now that they were on a straight-away she could feel the oxygen deprivation. Her head throbbed, her butt hurt, and her nose and throat were achingly dry. Drinking water didn't help. Having Luke palm a couple of aspirin for her didn't either.

"Say something," she begged him, needing a distraction.

"Well, according to Liesl, don't drive us into that lake. You might float, because it's way saltier than any ocean, but it also has something like 200,000 times the safe dose of arsenic if we sink instead."

"There *is* a safe dose of arsenic?"

Luke chuckled. She really liked the deep, welcoming sound. It was like his enveloping hugs that she could almost disappear into. "Not in that lake. So no swimming, you hear?"

"Yes, sir, Lieutenant Commander, sir."

"Just trying to keep you safe, Chief Warrant."

And the warmth of that truth sustained her through the rest of the harrowing nine-hundred-and-twenty-seven-kilometer drive. They never did catch the person raising dust ahead of them, but they came close. By the time everyone had rolled into the San Juan bivouac, they were back in third.

## CHAPTER 22

"What if he isn't here?"

"He is," Luke tried to reassure her. It was past midnight and her restless flailing had kept them both awake. Seven stages down, they really needed the rest day tomorrow, especially if they didn't get some sleep tonight.

He could hear Zoe was out at her limits. It was a time that every top sailor, and top soldier he supposed, reached. It was a tricky moment. How many strong fighters had he seen hit this wall and tumble back? It was why Hell Week thinned two-thirds of any SEAL class—it's why Hell Week existed. People who couldn't push through those limits might be dedicated fighters, but they'd never be true warriors.

Because of her skills as a pilot, she'd passed into the Night Stalkers, perhaps without ever having tested her limits. Well, driving The Dakar would do that to anybody.

"Maybe he dropped out. Almost a third of the field are already gone. Both of the US motorcyclists have gone out in this last stage."

Luke pondered the grim reports.

One had broken a chain—badly. It had wrapped around the rear

807

sprocket, locking up the wheel at the worst possible moment. How the rider had survived the high-speed flip into a cliff wall had been more miracle than luck. That he'd survived it with only a couple broken ribs and a shattered arm made it God's own miracle.

The other had blown an engine, literally. It was like a bomb had gone off inside it, shattering an entire casing so that the cooling fins had shot like shrapnel into the guy's leg. Dude would be lucky if he kept the leg. Luke had never seen anything like it and he'd seen a lot of bad shit on bikes over the years.

He'd spent an hour checking in with the Malles Motos guys last night. Partly to see how they were doing, but mostly wanting to cheer them up. Neither of the guys who went down had been Malles Motos —they'd both had full support teams—but accidents that bad struck too close to home. Now that he'd seen just what it took to run in the Dakar Rally, he was really impressed that they were doing it solo. If he had to do everything he'd been doing, and on top of it had to service his own ride without any help... Well, he liked the sound of that— what Spec Ops soldier wouldn't—but that didn't make it any less impressive.

But he'd also learned from them that, with only a few exceptions, the first third of The Dakar dropouts were mostly in two categories: amateurs and mechanical failures. Hathyaron's garage said that he was anything but an amateur. And that his ride would be maintained in top form.

"No. Whoever Hathyaron is, he's still running."

She buried her face against his shoulder. "There's got to be some way to find him. He didn't just dematerialize into thin air."

Luke blinked into the darkness, then started laughing.

"What?" Zoe propped herself up on his chest to look down at him despite the darkness.

"You know that you have sharp elbows?"

"Luke!" She was so cute when she tried to growl like a six-foot SEAL warrior.

In answer he picked up his phone and speed-dialed Nikita, then whispered while it was ringing. "Not dematerialize into thin air. But where did he materialize from?"

"Uh," Nikita grunted after the third ring.

"There's a car carrier ship that delivered the cars from France to Argentina prior to the race. When did it leave France?"

"End of November," Nikita mumbled at him.

He could feel Zoe freeze, then she started pounding her forehead against his chest as if she was pounding it against a brick wall. Yeah, it was a real *duh!* moment for him too. But she was doing it hard enough to actually hurt. He wrapped his free arm around her in a headlock before she cracked one of his ribs with her pounding.

She struggled for only a moment before trying to tickle his ribs. Thankfully, he wasn't ticklish there.

"Find out everyone whose car wasn't on that ship. You can cross out Japan and the Americas, too."

"Unless they transshipped through one of those countries to confuse their trail," Zoe mumbled from somewhere around his armpit. He might not be ticklish where her hand was headed, but he was certainly sensitive.

He amended the request to Nikita quickly and managed to hang up just before Zoe latched her hand around him. He grunted hard as she wasn't gentle.

Shuffling her around, he shifted the headlock into a hard kiss. She squirmed against him—closer rather than trying to get away. It was a long wrestling match that left them both with bruises, but much more content.

When she finally slept he wondered how neither of them had seen it. The car carrier ship had left France in November and they'd missed the goddamn arms dealer by only hours in Pakistan on New Year's Eve. He'd had his car *flown* across the Atlantic just as they had—and probably just as clandestinely. Again, his path would be nearly impossible to trace, but at least they'd know that anyone who'd used the ship wasn't their target.

He pulled Zoe more tightly against him and rested his cheek atop her head. It no longer hurt, but he could feel where she'd clobbered him that first time on the beach. None of tonight's bruises would hurt for more than an hour or so—these had been earned in joy, not pain. He wished he could reach down inside her and rip out the pain she carried. Even if he knew it was impossible.

But it didn't stop him from wishing.

# CHAPTER 23

Nikita had the list for him in the morning. Her dark scowl said exactly what she thought about him going back to sleep while she'd done the research and rousted the intel people to get her the ship's manifest. Except he and Zoe hadn't gone right back to sleep for a long, awesome time.

He offered Nikita his best happy smile before returning to his coffee and studying the list. Their layover day bivouac was in Copiapó, Chile, at the southern end of the Atacama Desert. Unlike the heart of the desert—that they'd be passing through tomorrow, which typically received a millimeter of rain per year—Copiapó typically received fifteen to twenty. A whole three-quarters inch of rain per year. Made it a damned weird place to build a city of a hundred and fifty thousand people. Though he supposed the copper and gold mining was enough reason.

He was looking forward to doing the tourism thing with Zoe. Copiapó had jumped onto the world's consciousness with the 2010 Chilean Mining Disaster. It had trapped thirty-three miners seven hundred meters underground for ten weeks—but they all made it out. That was a definite must see.

Did Zoe like flowers and such? There were some nature walks.

There were supposedly some great beaches around the high mineral lakes. He wondered if Zoe had that yellow string bikini tucked away in that suitcase of hers. That he *definitely* wanted to see.

Nikita had gone to get some coffee and was already grumbling her way back. One problem with thinking about Zoe, it was an incredibly distracting hobby. He focused on Nikita's list.

Eighty cars and trucks, nearly two hundred campers and assistance vehicles, many of which had a load of motorcycles aboard. That was in addition to sixty media and thirty officials' vehicles. Over three hundred entrants and barely half of the racers had been on that ship. It helped, but it wasn't enough.

He crossed out the dropouts. The overlaps helped, but there were still a hundred possible candidates for the role of Mr. Weapons, the non-Pakistani invisible arms dealer.

Well, they'd have a quiet day to think of something else without having to worry about a stage race. Ahmed and Drake had the Citroën well in hand under Christian's watchful eye. They had whole sections of the car torn open: wheels off and brakes opened for inspection, a full fluids change, Nikita had been set to clean out the carburetor. A local boy was going through with a brush and already removing his second bucket of sand from every nook and crevice of the inside of the car.

Zoe was still sacked out, exactly where he wanted her to be. She had a scheduled couple hours with the media, but that wasn't until after lunch. Then maybe they'd get out of here for a while. Just the two of them.

"Excuse me." A guy who looked like a hippie well past his prime was poking around. "Is this Zoe DeMille's team?"

Luke saw the guy's eyes register the yellow Citroën, so he already knew the answer to that question.

Her fans were being a major pain in the ass. She was still holding top three. Even the slightest mistake by any of the leaders could change that instantly—missing a waypoint, having an on-course breakdown, even getting lost for just a few minutes could change the whole shape of the race. The leaders were just that close.

The media had made sure she premiered in every "Rookie" segment. Actually, she was overshadowing the race leaders; everyone knew they had a hot story. Per their deal, Liesl was the only one who got the personal interviews, but even those, he knew, Zoe carefully censored.

*The Soldier of Style Brigade* had gone insane. People were flying in to watch the Dakar, easily identified by their lemon-yellow clothing. The racer guys were going wild too, because so many of Zoe's fans were women—both dyed and real blondes. The party atmosphere ramped way up—what happened in Chile remained in Chile—and the male drivers and the rabid female fans were making the most of it together.

And any time Zoe left the bivouac—something she'd stopped doing several stages back in central Argentina, but not soon enough— she was mobbed by fans.

Fans had been getting past security constantly and hunting down Zoe. Christian had even hired some local bodyguards to rebuff anyone who made it this far. And still a few, like this guy, slipped through. Maybe it was because he wore nothing that was lemon-yellow. His hair was as dark as Zoe's part and his eyes as blue. He was a lightly-built man, barely halfway between Zoe's and his own height.

Luke felt a nasty itch between his shoulder blades.

"Who's asking?" Luke rose to his feet and stepped well into the guy's personal space. He shied away with as much spine as you'd expect from a civilian.

"I'm her father, Brian DeMille." He tried holding out his hand, which Luke ignored. "I've always wanted to come to The Dakar Rally, but I never dreamed it would be to see my daughter driving." He was craning around and looking in every direction.

"She said you were dead."

"She…*what?* Why would she say that?"

"You gotta ask?"

The guy squinted at him as if he really did.

"If I were her, I would have said the same thing, rather than admitting to your existence. You're dead to her and it's going to stay that way. Now turn the fuck around and never come back."

"Why would she say that?" Guy was a goddamn broken record.

Nikita was hurrying toward him, holding her palm out vertically in the military hand sign for stop.

"You rape your teenage daughter and you gotta ask why she tells everyone you're dead?"

Nikita skidded to a halt still several steps away with a look of horror on her face.

To hell with her too. It was high time someone confronted the bastard.

"Zoe?" the guy's voice was soft with shock. But he wasn't looking up at him. Instead he was looking off to Luke's left.

He'd been too late to protect her. Luke could feel her there close behind him. He closed his eyes for a moment. The one thing he could do for her was keep her "dead" father away—and he'd failed.

*Shit!*

"You fucking asshole!" Zoe was screaming.

He opened his eyes, but she wasn't facing her father, she was facing him.

"I trusted you. I trusted you and this is how you repay me? To think I thought that I—" She choked off whatever she was about to say.

The depth of her fury made her clobbering his jaw last week seem mild by comparison.

"Asshole!" She spit it out like an epithet. No tease this time—she was in dead earnest. It hurt worse than Marva's dispassionate slur by a hundredfold.

"Oh, Daddy," Zoe turned to her father. She clung to his arm and began walking him away.

It wasn't right. He'd done that to her and she still clung to him? What was wrong with her?

Nikita stepped up to take Zoe's place in front of him before he could follow. She didn't look furious, instead she looked desperately sad.

"*What?*" He knew better than to try and shove Nikita aside—she was a Team 6 SEAL and looked seriously planted.

"You really stepped in it, sir."

He watched over Nikita's shoulder. Zoe and her father had stopped twenty meters out into the lane between the two sections of the camp. To either side were vehicles being gone over by their teams. There was laughter, camaraderie, and hard work.

Not with them. The two of them were hunched together like they were having a deadly serious conversation.

When her father stumbled back, Zoe gathered him into her arms and held him. The two of them stood there in the shining sun holding onto each other like lost souls in a shipwreck.

"Anything you want to be telling me?" Luke couldn't tear his eyes away to look at Nikita.

"Not my story to tell. As far as I know, there are only two people aside from Zoe who know what really happened, and I'm one of them. At least until you did that. Now there are three."

If her father hadn't known and the guy who did it to her really was dead, then... Clearly he himself didn't know shit. Three would be Nikita, now Zoe's father, and...

"Who's the other?"

Nikita stood silent for so long that he finally looked at her.

"Not your story to tell."

She shook her head sadly. Then she did the strangest thing. Nikita, the warrior woman, rested a hand on his cheek.

"You gotta find a way to fix this, Luke. I've seen you two together. You gotta find a way."

Then as she walked away, he heard her say as if to herself, "I just wish it was possible."

She'd never used his first name before.

# CHAPTER 24

Zoe didn't return to the camp at all that day.

Luke had waited. After a couple of hours he'd gone looking for her, but the trail was cold. He didn't have Zoe's number because he'd never had occasion to call her. They'd been attached at the hip since the start of the mission, never beyond shouting distance apart.

He tried enrolling Nikita's help, but she flatly refused. "You're my commander, but she's my friend."

Even his offer to help Drake work on the car was turned down.

"Nothing personal, Luke," Drake had assured him. "But Nikita warned me off—though I'll tell you on the sly that I don't know shit. They're close, those two. Anyway, Nikita said it was better if you stewed in your own juices than distracted yourself with work. Guess she wants you to think about things."

Luke tried to think about what he was supposed to think about, but he didn't know what the hell was going on. Except that Zoe had gone off somewhere with her father—who he'd just accused of being a rapist. No, worse. Who'd he'd just told the secret of his daughter being raped when he didn't know.

He couldn't talk it out with Nikita, who knew something but wouldn't say.

He couldn't talk with Drake without betraying Zoe's trust—which wouldn't be acceptable—because apparently he knew even less than Luke did.

No way on Earth was he talking to Christian about anything to do with Zoe.

Luke pulled out his phone again and stared at it. His contact list held the numbers for his team, his commanders, the intelligence agency, and the supply personnel he sometimes needed. Scrolling through the list looking for friends was a fruitless endeavor, but he did it anyway. It had been ten years since he'd needed anyone outside his team. He'd always figured that was all any man needed and he'd been damned lucky to have the one he did. Ten years since Marva had fucked him over by fucking someone else. Her number was still in his phone for some reason. He must be a real mess if he thought for even a single second she might be able to help.

Definitely a mess, he considered it for five seconds before deleting her entry.

The only person he knew well enough to really talk to didn't want to talk to him.

Even if he had her number.

Finally, he figured he'd find her at the nine p.m. briefing if she was still going to be racing. He picked up the next day's Road Book, but there was no sign of the petite blonde who'd punched a hole in his life.

## CHAPTER 25

"Are you alone?" Zoe whispered when Nikita answered her phone.

"With Drake, but not Luke. Are you okay?"

"Definitely not." Zoe hadn't been this not okay in a long time. She'd just destroyed every fond memory her father had held about his best friend. Mom had been right about one thing at least: Brian DeMille might be a good man, but he was not a strong one.

He was a man with simple needs. He'd loved three things in his life: his wife, his daughter, and his auto business with his best friend. It had been all he'd ever needed. He'd survived Bob's death only because he still had the two of them and the business he loved.

And Luke's accusation had forced her to utterly destroyed all of those happy memories.

Zoe had never been so strong as the moment she managed not to destroy the third. It had taken everything in her to spare him from the last piece of the truth—about his wife, her mother.

The fact that she'd become a target for rape, by his best friend, in his auto shop, had almost killed him. Shattered by that truth, he lay in the medical tent and looked like he'd aged a century. She only *felt* as if she had.

"How's your dad?"

"He's asleep now. The doctors knocked him out. They swear that there's nothing physically wrong with him, but he collapsed like he'd had a heart attack—standing beside me one moment and down in the dust the next."

"Where are you? I'll come and—"

"No, Nikita. I'm okay here with him. But I can't leave him here like this and I can't face Luke. You have to drive with him. Together you can find Hathyaron."

There was a long silence. "I can't."

"Why?"

"I don't have a FIA license. None of us do except for Christian and Luke. You know Christian's back wouldn't survive it. No point in getting a fake one, no one else knows enough to race even if the officials would let us add a team member. Without you, they'll withdraw from the race."

"I," Zoe searched inside and knew the answer. "I just can't."

"You know that Luke feels—"

"Don't tell me!" She didn't want to know. Couldn't know. The blustering bastard had wounded her father past any recovery. In a twisted way, he'd raped her father's past just as surely as "Uncle Bob" had raped hers. She'd thought Luke could protect her; instead he'd permanently wounded the one man she'd ever loved—the only pure thing in her entire life.

"Okay," Nikita's voice was soft. When Zoe didn't answer, "You sure there isn't anything I can do for you?"

"I'm sure."

A long silence later Nikita whispered, "Love you, Zoe."

"Love you." Zoe listened to the soft beep and dead air after Nikita terminated the call. She had one friend in the world. That much she could be thankful for.

# CHAPTER 26

*L*uke didn't eat. He didn't go in the camper. Not a chance he'd
sleep.

Instead he sat out by the car.

He spent two hours meticulously reviewing and marking the Stage
Eight Road Book, knowing it was pointless. Zoe wasn't coming back.

Somewhere way past midnight, Nikita came out to sit with him.
She didn't say a word, simply dropped her phone beside his on the
table and sat with him in silence.

She knew…something. But a bond tighter than superior officer
and tighter than team membership (which was a hell of a bond in ST6)
made her keep her silence. She was the closest thing he had to a
friend, but she still didn't speak.

This went beyond friendship. Far enough beyond that she hadn't
even told Drake—the man she'd married. *Loved* enough to marry.

His need to protect Zoe was an ache that ran through his entire
body. Was that reason enough to marry?

*Idiot!* The one person Zoe needed protection from was *him.*
Goddess Zoe, running Number Three in her rookie Dakar, needed his
protection like she needed a hole in the head.

Nikita said only two people had known who had raped Zoe until he'd opened his yap. He still didn't know. Nikita was one. Which meant the rapist was the other.

But, if her father hadn't known about it... And her attacker was really dead...? Then who was the other person? How many times he'd trodden that loop of reasoning through the long night he no longer knew.

An hour later, he was still nowhere and Nikita still hadn't spoken a word. She'd simply sat like you would with a dead comrade on the long flight back to Dover Air Force Base before they came to bury him in Arlington National Cemetery.

There was a tradition among SEALs. When the coffin lid was closed for the last time but before it was laid in the ground, every SEAL in attendance removed his SEAL trident pin and pounded it into the lid with the side of his fist. When Chris "The Legend" Kyle, the American Sniper, was laid to rest, a hundred SEAL tridents were pounded into his coffin's lid.

He half expected Nikita to pound one into him. At least *that* would make sense. Without Zoe he was a dead man.

Instead, she finally rose to her feet. Reaching down, she tapped the unlock code on her phone and walked away. He could see that it was on the recent calls list. At the very top was Zoe's name.

He watched it for the thirty seconds it stayed lit.

He watched it for the five seconds it dimmed before it locked.

And he watched it lock and go dark.

Luke wanted to talk to Zoe more than anything in the world, but he had no idea what to say.

Just before dawn, Liesl showed up. Apparently a glance was enough for her to assess the whole situation. He couldn't imagine that she was the other person who knew the truth of Zoe's past, so her deep sigh must be for the loss of her insider's scoop. Confirming his guess, she plummeted into the chair. She plinked her fingernail against Nikita's phone beside his. Whether she recognized it or surmised the reason it sat on the table didn't matter.

"Welcome to the human race."

It took him a moment to understand that someone was actually talking to him. He looked over at her in surprise.

"I don't need to be a genius to know that you aren't used to screwing up even if its written all over your goddamn face. I know what you are. Unlike Christian Vehrs, I've covered war zones."

Luke had never been comfortable with Liesl's knowing looks; at least now he knew why.

"You're clearly Spec Ops. SEAL, Delta, maybe Green Beret, but I don't think so. The feel is wrong. You see everything as a threat. Rangers do that too, but they tend to be overeager. I've learned that no one except a Spec Ops warrior sees the world as clearly as a journalist—clearer. Every detail. You probably knew it was me coming just by the sound of my footsteps long before I entered the far end of the lane."

He would have under normal circumstances. The bivouac was dead silent, not even the cooks were awake yet. Instead he'd barely noticed her before she sat down next to him.

"Zoe is a puzzle I haven't quite unraveled yet. Spec Ops in everything but size. Did you know that her standard response to a military fan is that she's a clerk in intelligence? It's brilliant in its way, forestalling all questions. Except clerks can't drive world rally cars in their first-ever race like the very best Dakar Rally racers. She's…ah! She's a pilot, isn't she?"

Luke kept his face neutral.

"But she doesn't see the world the way you do. She walks like a well-trained soldier but also like a civilian. Yet you and she are here together with absolutely no prior history of racing. Yes, I found old rosters that showed neither of you had been in any of the races your vague histories imply you were. What kind of Spec Ops pilot has no field experience? Even the Air Force rescue guys get out of their helicopters once in a while." Then Liesl whistled softly in surprise. "Drone?"

"They prefer RPA—remotely piloted aircraft." Luke couldn't believe that he'd just confirmed every one of Liesl's conjectures.

But she showed none of the triumph he expected. Instead she

simply nodded, fitting the pieces together in her neat, journalist's mind.

"You can't—"

"*Nicht dumm!* National security and all that. I'm a German citizen, but I'm not stupid enough to think that would protect my freedom for a second if I were to betray a black ops mission—which is what this has to be. Besides, I don't believe in doing that. I want my sources to tell me their story because they want to, not because they want a moment of fame for revealing state secrets—even if it's anonymous fame."

Luke slumped back in his chair. Could anything else go wrong?

"What will you do if Zoe *kommt nicht zurück?*"

If Zoe didn't come back, there was no chance to complete the mission. They couldn't stay in the competition. Couldn't be out in the field looking for Hathyaron.

Without Zoe, he—

He couldn't think about that.

"This mission of yours? It's bad?"

The biggest arms dealer in Southwest Asia about to slip through his fingers? The one who'd supplied the opposition in at least the two wars in Iraq and Afghanistan and who knew how many ISIL insurgents and… Yeah, it was bad.

"Does she know that?"

"Better than anyone."

Liesl nodded. "*Gut!* Now you must decide what to do when she comes back."

"But—"

Liesl laughed softly. "How little you know her if you think she could walk away from this. Now you must find a way to make sure that she doesn't walk away from you afterward."

She rose to her feet as if to go.

"Any brilliant ideas?"

Liesl brushed at his hair like he was a sweet little boy. "You'll figure it out."

Then she walked away into the breaking predawn light.

# CHAPTER 27

Zoe stood at the end of the row, watching the team area.

Ahmed was polishing the Citroën—as if it wasn't about to spend nine hundred kilometers traversing the roughest conditions on the planet. Drake and Nikita were breaking down the camp, getting ready to move it to the next bivouac. Christian was hovering.

Luke sat in a lone chair beside the car, as if he had been carved from stone on that very spot. He looked even worse than she felt.

*Good!*

She checked her watch. Ten minutes until their assigned start time.

Zoe waited until there were only six left, then stepped out into the service lane.

Luke jolted to his feet before she made it three steps. He watched her all the way in. No smile—which was good, because it saved her trying to punch his lights out. No frown. Just watching.

She walked right past him and stepped into the trailer, making sure to lock the door behind her. She allowed herself three minutes to try and wash the sleepless night off her face and get dressed.

At two and a half minutes to the start, she stepped back out of the trailer. She had her knife strapped on the inside of her forearm, in the perfect position to drop into her palm if she needed to stab somebody.

Luke—her prime candidate at the moment—glanced down to it, then back to watch her face.

She barely paused in front of him, "If you say one word not pertaining to the race or the mission, I'll walk away and you'll never see me again."

Zoe didn't even wait for his acknowledgement. She managed to climb into the driver's seat without breaking down, without screaming, without her heart shattering any worse than it already was. But that was all locked away on the inside, and she'd never again share what was inside of her with anyone on the outside. *Never.*

She had the engine started and was already backing up while Luke still had a foot on the ground. He dove in and strapped into his harness while she drove up to the Start Line outside the bivouac's entry.

Waving and smiling to the wild mob of her personal *Brigade* who waited just outside the gates was a strictly mechanical act. Many of them reached out to touch the car as it went by. They were rabidly excited by someone who didn't exist outside of her social media persona. *The Soldier of Style* knew no more about herself than Zoe DeMille did.

However this mission turned out, she was done. She'd serve out this tour and get out of the Army. Maybe she'd go work in her father's auto shop. Having lost herself there, maybe she'd find herself by going back.

The timer handed her their card, then began counting down from ten.

She was done with the Army.

Five.

And she was done with Luke. That was a hard thought—no matter how she hardened herself to take it, the idea was a knife in her already dead heart.

"Zoe?"

"I warned you to shut up!" Her yell at Luke wasn't quite a scream, but it was close.

She couldn't do this.

But as she reached out to kill the engine, Luke pointed silently toward the timer.

He was glaring at her when she turned to face him. "Already ten seconds late. Are you refusing the Start? You know that incurs a fifteen minute penalty."

Zoe did know that. She couldn't imagine why she cared, but she knew that.

She shifted into first and drove away.

When Luke called out the first turn, she let the racing take over. *Just race. Then you don't have to think. Don't have to think about the pain on your father's face when you told him his best friend had raped you repeatedly. And don't think about the half lie you told him when you said you'd kept your silence because you didn't want to hurt him.*

Stage Eight was a blur of snapshots.

Much of the track wasn't dirt, but rock. A whole different technique of driving that she had to learn on the fly.

Cerro Mulas Muertas—the Dead Mules Volcano. Towering up to almost twenty thousand feet, only a little shorter than Denali in Alaska, it dominated the high, arid, *dead* plain.

The names of the local geography leapt at her like personal attacks: Lake of the Dead, Crags of the Dead, Ravine of the Dead Mules, the Dead Mountain... *Muertas. Muertas. Muertas.* It fit her mental state perfectly as she plunged over ash ridges, wove around sharply porous boulders of lava that would as soon shred her tires as look at her, and wondered if she was driving on the Moon...or was simply so disconnected that it felt that way.

She remembered nothing else. Didn't hear that she'd moved up to second. Didn't recall a word she'd said during the mandatory stop in the media interview zone. Didn't care when Christian told her she was the prime feature on today's broadcast.

Didn't even care who carried her to bed in the camper, glad to simply be held for a brief moment in the misery of the last two days.

# CHAPTER 28

*L*iesl was looking aloft when Zoe crawled out of bed the next morning. Coffee and *medialuna* did nothing to convince her that consciousness was a worthwhile endeavor.

"How long do I have?"

"Depends if you get your act together today better than yesterday?"

"My act?"

"That is the correct idiom, *ja?*"

"*Ja.*"

"What do you remember about yesterday's drive?" Liesl turned from her inspection of the sky.

Zoe didn't answer, because she didn't have a good one. She remembered little more than the pounding, aching silence in the car as she drove.

Liesl returned to her inspection of the sky. "Is the bottom painted blue to hide it? It is very hard to see as it circles up there so high."

Zoe looked up for a long moment before she spotted the tiny dot, the only thing moving across the blue sky other than a few early-morning hawks. It was about the size of a dime held three car lengths away. Someone had decided that the mission was important enough for Sofia to fly *Raven* down to South America to help.

The mission.

She hadn't given it a single thought yesterday.

By the time she looked back down at Liesl, she felt as if she was standing there naked with no secrets left in her life. She should have asked what Liesl was looking at, rather than simply accepting her question. Liesl had clearly figured out not only that this was a military operation, but also what Zoe did for a living and that someone would be covering for her.

"No," she replied carefully. "They're a dulled aluminum."

"*Interessant,*" was all Liesl said. "It is time for you to act your act."

"The idiom didn't work there, but I get the point."

"Good. You should also know that another of your compatriots is out of the race."

"Compatriots?"

"United States. He was a car driver with a Brazilian navigator."

Zoe closed her eyes. "What happened?" Still the ground seemed to lurch beneath her feet.

"Frame failure." Not unheard of.

"Grind to halt?"

"In mid-jump. The car came down in pieces. The driver and co-driver are both in the fourteenth hour of surgery."

What the hell was Zoe doing here? She was a pilot, not a racecar driver. She wasn't even that: she'd decided to quit. She'd be a car mechanic. And she'd never get behind the wheel again.

"I am going to warn you now," Liesl was once again staring aloft. "After today's race I *will* be interviewing you about the terribly handsome man who carried you to bed last night and threatened to maim anyone who disturbed you."

Zoe looked around for who that might be, even though she knew.

Luke. Again her protector. And her destroyer.

If only she could find some way to forgive him, but that didn't seem likely.

Zoe was far more functional in Stage Nine than she'd been in Stage Eight. She wasn't driving quite as aggressively, which Luke appreciated. He'd never had a death wish, but Zoe had given him a taste of what it must be like to have one.

After he'd put her to bed last night, he'd made a point of going up to Ahmed and Christian and telling them what a magnificent car they'd built. Luke had no question that it had saved his life any number of times during the rough stage.

This morning, Zoe kept leaning forward to the limits of her harness and looking upward—once almost eating a boulder that was in their way as they drove around a scrubby tree.

"What are you looking for?" He risked the question because maybe something was wrong with the car. A crack in the top of the windshield he couldn't see, or maybe the mounting seal coming apart—which wouldn't surprise him after the beating the Citroën had taken yesterday.

"Sofia," Zoe's voice croaked with disuse. It was the first word she'd said to him since her initial threat.

Luke leaned forward to look upward and finally spotted a flash of sunlight reflected off a high-flying craft. He wished it was legal to have a screen in the car with the data feed from the drone, but getting caught with one was grounds for immediate disqualification—which they couldn't afford.

"Hey!" Zoe squawked and slammed on the brakes. She slid to a stop at a Y in the track. There were tire tracks leading up either side, making it unclear which way to go.

Luke checked the Road Book. "Uh, sorry. Left. I guess the trucks must have gone right." The Road Book only told them where to go, with nothing about where other vehicle classifications went.

Cars, quads, and motorcycles almost always followed the same routes, but there were some things ten tons of truck simply couldn't do. So they were occasionally routed off onto another route for part of a stage.

"Maybe best if we both ignore Sofia." Odd, he couldn't even imagine what he'd seen in her before, not with Zoe for comparison.

"I will if you can." It was almost a tease and it made him feel much better.

Then a car overtook them from behind and shot into the left leg of the Y.

"Not for long, buddy!" Zoe had the Citroën spitting dirt in seconds and flew into the lane.

---

"I TRACKED Legends whose vehicles did not come on the ship from France and who are still in the race." Sofia's liquid tones sounded from the small computer sitting on the camper's cramped dining table.

Nikita sat close beside Zoe, which she found very comforting. Drake sat across from them, craning his neck to see the display. Luke stood with his back against the door to make sure they weren't interrupted.

"I have discounted motorcycles based on Luke's analysis of the tracks departing Hathyaron's Pakistani compound. Even a job box and a pair of motorcycles on a trailer would have been unlikely to make such an impression in the hard soil."

Zoe glanced at Luke to check in with him, but she couldn't read him through his mirrored sunglasses. There'd been a time, a brief time, when she could read every thought on his face, but that was gone. Gone along with her lover. Her choice, so she'd have to live with it.

She turned back to Sofia.

The display was an aerial view of the day's Selective Section. Only eleven lines traced their way back and forth across the screen.

"You lost one here to a broken axle," Sofia placed a yellow circle around a line that ended abruptly in the middle of the course. "And you effectively lost another here," she indicated a line that had zigged wide of the course. Obviously lost, it crossed back and forth several times, losing time and distance. "When they'd finally spotted the track and returned to it, they'd missed two waypoints, which incurred an hour of penalties. They dropped from eleventh to thirty-fourth place."

Zoe knew that could happen to anyone. A single moment of inattention—like her entire day yesterday—could be a race-ending event. Someone had been watching out for her that day and she rather suspected that it was a Team 6 SEAL rather than some unknowable deity. She didn't turn to look at him, but she could feel him there. Watching her. Waiting.

Well, he was welcome to wait until hell froze over.

She turned her attention back to the display. "So we're assuming that Hathyaron is a Legend who is still in the race and still running well."

Nobody answered. It had been her original suggestion.

"I know it's probably fanciful, but it still *feels* right," Zoe answered her own question and no one argued. "So tell us about the remaining nine."

"You can cross out this one," Sofia marked which one she was talking about with a red X.

"Why that one?"

"Unless you and Luke are doing something we don't know about, you aren't suspects."

"Okay, I guess we can make that leap. At least on my behalf. Any dark past you want to admit to, Luke?" She'd turned to face him automatically, until his name caught in her throat. It was the first time she'd addressed him by name since... There was a tightness that clenched her body as if she'd been frozen into a block of immovable ice.

He studied her for a long moment through his mirrored sunglasses before replying, "None that I'm real interested in talking about."

Zoe watched him for the length of a breath. So he wasn't interested in talking. Should they talk? It would be even harder than telling her father about his best friend's dark past. Or was he saying that she didn't need to talk about the past if she didn't want to? Or...

She was going to make herself insane if she followed that back-loop much longer. If they *did* need to talk, it was something she wasn't strong enough to face. Not now. But she hated that it had to be soon.

By brute force alone, she managed to turn back to the display, though it was nothing but a bright blur once she had.

"Three cars and five trucks make up our remaining lines," Sofia continued. As she listed off the names, Zoe tallied them in her head. She knew them all by name and two of the car drivers quite well. She almost told Sofia to cross off their names, but feared that she'd already narrowed the field too much and kept her thoughts to herself.

Sergey Kanski of Poland was currently the race leader in the car group—an incredibly able driver—he'd recovered all of the time he'd lost in Stage Two. Perhaps he also had access to Russian military suppliers. He'd have made a splendid Cossack horseman under the Czar—dark and brooding.

Cid and Jabir had recovered splendidly from their float in the river and were currently in sixth. She'd actually have to watch out for them as they were driving like they had something to prove and could well catch up to her before the end. Were they a front for Saudi or Iranian interests? Should she discount them simply because they'd showed a sense of humor at the ford and been glad to chat with her since, despite her success?

Henni was the only other female car driver still in the race. Was her shyness and soft English accent a mask for an evil career? Or was Hathyaron her secretly supportive lover—the team sponsor without being the team driver?

"We need to learn more about the five trucks." She didn't know them well at all.

"Nothing obvious in their bios," Sofia replied. "I'll send all of their names over to The Activity. They found Hathyaron once, maybe they can find him again from some clue we don't see."

"Thanks. Anything else, anyone?" Zoe had to smile to herself at that one. Sofia was her commander, Drake and Nikita were ST6 enlisted, and Luke was a Navy officer. So how had this become her mission?

When no one said anything, they signed off and stowed the laptop.

She looked around again, forcing herself to look at Luke as well—he was part of the team after all.

Still no one spoke.

"I guess this means we're on to Stage Ten."

Nods and shrugs.

She checked her watch. "Almost time for the course briefing. I'll go," she continued even as Luke turned for the door. And barely managed, "with you."

He stopped with his hand wrapped around the door handle as if steadying himself. A moment later he had the door open and was holding it wide for her and the others to exit the camper as if nothing had happened to make him hesitate.

She hadn't imagined it, but what could make an ST6 lieutenant commander show such weakness?

*L*uke waited by the trailer for Zoe to come out. He'd woken just before dawn, feeling suffocated by the light. The night wrapped about him more comfortably than the day.

Nighttime was the heart of a Spec Ops warrior's soul. It was the environment in which technology truly was winning the war. Night-vision and teams like the Night Stalkers had altered the battlespace for the past thirty years. Their enemies were making giant strides, but even the Russians and Chinese weren't crazy enough to offer their technology to notoriously unpredictable terrorist groups no matter how they were aligned.

Also in the night, Zoe slept and he could lay his pad outside the only door into the camper and sleep—or at least pretend to. By day—when she came to life—it felt as if a piece of himself was torn from his body every time she walked away.

Each morning though, he made sure he was away from the door and sitting by the car long before anyone else woke.

"May I?"

Luke jolted. Again he hadn't heard the person approach. Worse, it was a civilian with no training in stealth. And worst of all, it was Brian DeMille, Zoe's father.

"Of course, sir." What else could he say? *No, go away. Haven't I already hurt you and your daughter enough?* Instead, he sat still and wondered if that simple act might be the bravest thing he'd ever done.

"I still can't get used to her as a blonde."

*No, please!* He was *not* about to have a discussion about Zoe with her father.

"Only way I've ever seen her, sir." Apparently he was.

"I'm sorry I put on such a show," Brian said as he dropped into the chair as if dropping onto a living room sofa. By the moonlight, Luke could see that he'd passed more than his black hair and blue eyes on to his daughter. Her features were a refined version of her father's: cleaner lines, a narrower face, but just as shapely.

"I'm sorry for my part in it, sir."

"I'm not a sir. I never served like you do. You are in the service, aren't you? With Zoe?"

"Yes, sir." Brian's quick smile acknowledged the "sir" just as Zoe's would have.

"What are you two doing racing The Dakar?"

"I, uh, I can't tell you that, sir."

"Which means you're on assignment? I've never known what Zoe does for the Army."

"I'm afraid that I can't tell you that either, sir." And Luke could see her father slump in the chair. "But I can tell you that she is perhaps the smartest and most skilled woman I've ever met—and when you meet my second-in-command, you'll know just how high a compliment that is." Luke almost assured him that his daughter worked from a place of complete safety—an RPA control coffin—except she'd been right in the fray in Honduras and now was driving in a race that had killed seventy people over the years and injured a hell of a lot more.

"I've always thought she was amazing myself, but then I'm just her father. That makes me totally biased in her favor. So, like, what do I know?" Brian nodded to himself.

They sat in silence long enough for the stars to begin fading with the dawn.

"He was my best friend. How could I not know?" The first light caught the tracks of tears running down Brian's cheeks.

His best friend? Zoe had mentioned that her father was in business with his best friend from childhood. The fucking bastard. Luke fought against the fury that shook him. She'd probably grown up with him as practically a second father. And then he'd betrayed that trust by…

Then other pieces started connecting. Her fear when they'd first started to make love against the side of the Renault on that remote Senegalese beach. The bastard hadn't merely taken her, he must have done it in the family auto shop—staining yet another portion of Zoe's past.

By what unholy strength had she managed to turn her fear around and make love to him there. No wonder she'd wept in his arms afterward. Awash in her past, she'd chosen to purge the memory and create a different future. He didn't know of many SEALs who could face themselves that clearly and make choices that hard. Certainly not him. The less he remembered of his old man and his battering fists, the happier Luke was. Zoe had faced it head on.

"Is he actually dead or did Zoe make that up?"

"He's dead, thank God," Brian's voice caught. "I don't know what I would have done if he wasn't. I know I could never face him again."

*Never face him again?* Luke was tempted to find the bastard's grave just so he could dig him up and pound on him more than death already had. Hopefully he'd suffered even a tenth of the pain he'd caused Zoe before he finally went down.

"You can take comfort in the fact that she's become an amazing woman, sir."

Brian merely nodded, but the tracks of his tears still caught the light.

*More* than an amazing woman.

Luke finally knew what was wrong with him, why sleep was more elusive than while on watch far behind enemy lines.

She was *the* amazing woman. If he had a choice of any single woman to spend the rest of his life with, it was Zoe DeMille.

Too bad she wasn't speaking to him anymore.

*You gotta find a way to fix this,* Nikita had told him. *I just wish it was possible.*

Yeah, him too. But Nikita, who knew Zoe better than any of them, wasn't feeling very hopeful.

This mission had just become the highest stakes of his entire life.

———

HOVERING JUST inside the camper's door, Zoe watched the two men sitting by the car. Okay, there were worse-case scenarios for how this would play out—she just couldn't imagine what they might be. She'd left her father in a nurse's care thousands of kilometers behind, and now he was here, sitting next to Luke as if it was a perfectly natural thing.

They appeared to be talking as little as men ever seemed to and she prayed that the few words they were exchanging chronicled the weather. *Lost that bet without even gambling, girl.* Talking about the next stage? *Nope.*

Could she crawl out a back window of the trailer and run away? It would be totally chicken, but she *was* wearing a yellow racing suit.

Taking a deep breath, she stepped out and did her best to be cheery.

"Daddy!" It wasn't hard to be cheery with him.

He lurched to his feet and wrapped her in a hug. He held her hard for a long time. She let herself close her eyes and lay her head on his shoulder just as she always used to. Somehow they'd come through this okay.

"I'm sorry you didn't tell me," he whispered just for her. "I guess I'm glad that I didn't know, for my sake, but I wish I'd known for your sake. I was hurt for a while, but I guess I understand why you didn't say anything."

No, he knew nothing about why she hadn't, and maybe, just maybe, she'd come to terms with the real reason. Or would someday. Preferably sooner rather than later, though she suspected that it would be quite the opposite.

She opened her eyes without raising her head from her father's shoulder.

Luke too had risen to his feet, but he kept his hands jammed into his pockets and his expression blank.

"Morning, Luke."

"Hey, Zoe," she could see him swallow hard. "You doing okay?"

Was she? No longer having to hide everything from her father was a huge relief, even if there was still one thing he could never know. She raised her head enough to nod, she was okay—in the most basic sense of the word.

She could see the next question as clearly on his face as if he'd shouted it: were *they* still okay? Having no answer to that one, she closed her eyes again and clung to her father for dear life.

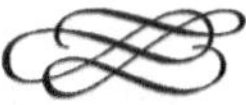

Stages Ten, Eleven, and the start of Twelve through the Andes from Chile into Peru were no more than a blur.

Luke kept functioning, but the lack of sleep was really catching up with him. A trademark of a Spec Ops soldier was that they could sleep anywhere, anytime. Helo flight into a life-threatening mission? Perfect excuse for a twenty-minute catnap. Roaring along at thirty thousand feet in a C-130 Hercules, fully dressed for a highly dangerous HALO parachute jump? Better than a sleeping pill.

Being apart from Zoe during those three long nights of the rally had nearly killed him. He'd gotten them lost twice, once for twenty minutes in the trackless dunes of Stage Eleven. The only comfort was that all the teams were so tired that the screw-ups weren't limited to him.

Sergey ran into a boulder and lost time replacing a tire and doing a field repair on the suspension.

Cid and Jabir didn't high-center themselves on a dune ridge, instead they hung themselves out to dry. They'd tried to jump a depression in the sand but hadn't cleared it. Their front end had hit the far side and then the rear had caught on the near side. The car ended up dangling its wheels a meter in the air while its front and rear ends were buried in the sand. It had taken them a long time to dig down enough to free their car.

Henni had busted her top two gears and finished well behind on the Stage Twelve Selective Section. Her crew would be frantically rebuilding her transmission through the night.

Their own Citroën wouldn't still be in the game if Zoe's dad hadn't joined the team. He wasn't merely an ace mechanic, he was an ace racing car mechanic. He and Ahmed functioned together on some level that neither Nikita nor Drake could match.

The Dakar was taking its notorious toll. There hadn't been any deaths this year, but there were sixteen racers and five spectators still in the hospital with injuries worse than Christian Vehrs' back: shattered pelvises, major concussions, crushed ribs with a collapsed lung —the list was long and gruesome. A kid who'd chased a ball across the road at the wrong moment was going to be playing soccer with an artificial leg the rest of his life. It was by far the worst toll in decades.

The motorcycles were down by a third; though most of his Malles Motos buddies were still in it even if they looked as if they hadn't slept in two weeks. The cars and trucks were down by more than half. A hundred and fifty competitors had been swept off the course by the brutal challenge of The Dakar. Fellow Americans were particularly hard hit and were now few and far between.

They'd started Stage Twelve with a huge sendoff from Arequipa. Peru's second-largest city sat at seven thousand feet, dramatically close to the foot of the nearly twenty-thousand-foot active volcano El Misti. The historic eruptions of El Misti and the two other nearby monster volcanoes had also made it the most fertile region of Peru. If it ever had more than four inches of rain per year, it would be lush instead of merely green. But even that was a relief to the eyes after crossing the Andes and the high Atacama desert plains.

Here the men in Arequipa traditional dress was brown Spanish bullfight attire with black sombreros. The women's dresses landed mid-calf, but more than balanced out the view with far more vivid colors that the Argentine dancers wore—powerful reds and rainbow stripes.

And the food could kill a man with happiness. The bivouac mess had served truly impressive platters of *lomo saltado*. The grilled sirloin beef was stir-fried with onion, pepper, soy, and yellow Peruvian chilis. The spicy chicken stew, *aji de gallina*, was so good that he just might have to learn how to cook so that he could eat it in the states.

Through it all, Zoe had been pleasant but a mile away. She stayed close to her father and it was a space that Luke didn't dare invade. No matter how tiring the stage, they often worked on the car together with Ahmed. She wholly entrusted him to work up the Road Book— which made it a lonely task.

Stage Twelve had left behind the greenery of Arequipa very quickly. The Selective Section was their most varied stage yet. Up ash hills, down off-*piste* wilderness that threatened to shatter the car and their bodies just from the shaking. A small but particularly vicious set of dunes added variety before they climbed once more into the foothills.

They were racing along a narrow cleft that some ancient river had carved through the stone—a tortuously twisted path.

"Zoe?"

"Not now!" She snapped out.

"If not now, when?" It just burst out of him as he called the next turn. He was either about to fight her or blow this all to hell, but he didn't know how much more he could take of her silence.

"How about when I'm trying to not kill us?" She dodged a boulder, rode two wheels up and over a rubble pile where part of the sheer wall had collapsed onto the course, then gunned it down a narrow gut with no turns for a few hundred meters.

"Right. Sorry." And she was right. He announced the next turn, even though they could both see it coming.

SHE HAD to let there be a time. Now wasn't it, but she had to get over herself and just do it.

At the end of the straightaway, she downshifted hard and was preparing to gun into the corner when Luke called out.

"Smoke!"

Black smoke billowed skyward from just around the corner. She pulled back a gear, then another. She crawled around the curve and still was barely slow enough to not run over the man lying in the middle of the track.

He lay sprawled on his stomach. The marks in the sand showed that he'd crawled from his car. The blood on his face made him unrecognizable.

The gas tank must have breached moments earlier and the car was fully engulfed in flame. Zoe knew from her dad that gas tanks didn't just explode like in the movies, but they could make lethal fires.

Killing the engine, she and Luke rushed forward to drag the man farther away from the blazing car. There was no sign of his co-driver.

A brief flutter in the flames, and she spotted the car number. Another US driver, Bernie Cole.

The car that had burned the first day, Andy and Jim Kyle's car burning in Stage Two, the unusual failures of the two motorcycles, the car frame failure, and now Bernie. All registered as entries from the US.

It *wasn't* chance.

"Bernie! Bernie! Can you hear me? Did you see who did this to you?"

Luke was trying to staunch the flow of blood and went shock still for just an instant, then continued his efforts with a sharp curse.

"Bernie? Did you see?" It was a cruel question, his eyes were gone, burned from their sockets. What she'd initially taken for blood all over his face was the black of burns and char.

"Bernie!" She shouted it to avoid being sick. How far had she gone around the bend that she was begging a dying man to help her?

He croaked out a noise.

"Again, Bernie," she leaned her ear close to his mouth. She took his hand, at least it was only bloody and not burnt.

"Man," he croaked softly.

"A man," which was no help at The Dakar where it was ninety-nine percent male. "What did he look like? Help me, Bernie."

"Silver," he gave a struggling gasp. "Man," was the last word he was ever going to say.

She held his hand as one of the race helos came screaming in overhead. It seemed only moments before Bernie was whisked away on a stretcher and the helo was aloft again. Another came in and disgorged men in firefighting gear with tall extinguishers.

They were sent back to their car, "Get moving. Get back in the race. You arrived after the accident, so we can wait until after today's stage to take your statements."

Zoe put it in gear, eased around the fire dying under the blast of the big extinguishers. She slowly worked her way back up to speed, but she felt as numb as she had on that stage after Luke had dumped her past on her father.

"The compound," she finally managed as they rolled into the end of the Selective Section and handed over their timecard. Thank God there was no Road Section today, the Selective Section ended close by the night's bivouac.

Luke nodded. "Hathyaron knows it was US forces that went into his compound."

"So he's killing all of the entries from the United States, but why?"

"In case they— In case we followed him this far."

"So he's just knocking every US entry out of the race—cars, quads, trucks, and motorcycles? But he's never killed before. Maybe that was an accident and he didn't mean to kill Bernie."

Luke's silence was the only reply that was necessary. Then he leaned forward as if looking up at the sky.

"He saw our drone—he'd know to look for it and it's not invisible. He *knows* we're after him."

"And he can't just quit and run because he knows that we'd be on him in a flash."

Zoe eased into the lane and idled her way toward their camp. She parked and turned off the engine but made no move to get out.

Luke waited her out.

She rubbed a thumb at the dried bloodstains on her hands. Bernie Cole's blood. "Why hasn't he come after us?"

"Maybe because you don't look like a Spec Ops soldier?" Luke shrugged. "Or maybe we're next."

# CHAPTER 32

"At least there are only two stages to go," Luke consoled himself as he tried to find the energy to eat. The price was so high.

It had been just a standard—well, perhaps not so standard—mission. But Hathyaron had just made it personal. Yes, his operation had to be taken out, torn up by the roots and shredded. But Hathyaron himself was going to go down and go down hard.

Too bad Cole's dying words about the "silver man" hadn't helped. There were no silver-painted vehicles still in the race. No one was named silver or wore a silver racing suit. There were some older racers, not many, but none had hair that would be called silver. Salt-and-pepper, gray, white, bald. No help.

"Actually, there's really only one more stage," Christian spoke up. "Stage Fourteen, the final stage, has only a very short Selective Section. It is still a race, but very few changes in the standings happen there. It is more of a parade. No, it is tomorrow's long Stage Thirteen through the Peruvian Andes and down to the beach that will almost assuredly decide the race."

Which meant that tomorrow was their last real shot at finding Hathyaron. Something they were no closer to achieving than three days ago. The Activity had come up blank. Hathyaron had erased his tracks so thoroughly that they might as well be starting with the world's population of seven billion to track him down.

Luke considered burying his face in his plate of rice and shrimp. The tiny town of Nazca couldn't put on a show that could touch a big city like Arequipa, but their food was still damned good. He could tell that, even though he could have eaten cardboard tonight and not noticed.

"Luke?" It was a soft voice, in a tone he hadn't heard in almost a week. A voice that stole his breath.

He turned to look at Zoe, something he'd trained himself not to do anymore because it hurt too much.

"I've got to talk to you," she tipped her head out toward the far side of the bivouac.

He nodded carefully. As he rose to follow her, he glanced at Nikita to see if she had any guidance. She only offered an infinitesimal shrug —perplexity rather than resignation, but still no real help.

Once they were well clear of the group, Zoe came to a stop. Luke estimated they were almost exactly the same distance from their camp as when she'd delivered the news that had shattered her father's life.

"I—" he had to try. "I'm so sorry, Zoe. I swear I'd take it back if I could."

She nodded sadly without looking up.

He couldn't find any more words, so he simply stood and ached that it was no longer his place to console her.

"I have an idea. It could get me thrown out of the military, but I still think it's a good idea."

"No! You can't do that!" He had no idea what her idea was, but that was so wrong. "You belong there as much as Nikita. As much as I do!" Picturing Zoe going civilian was the worst thing he could imagine. "You aren't that fluff ball, Tweety Bird *Soldier of Style* you show everybody. You're so much more than that. You're—" Then she gave him a look that told him to shut the hell up. He could only bite his tongue hard at the restraint she'd just placed on him, but he was going to have his say before this was done.

"But I think it's worth the risk because it might help us find Hathyaron. Also there are still two other US teams out there. We can't risk another innocent," she kept rubbing at her hands even though Cole's blood had long since been washed off.

How did she remain so steady? She was a warrior. Well, so was he, damn it. He took one deep breath and refocused on the mission, then nodded for her to go ahead. She could talk all she wanted, but she *wasn't* risking her career. No way was he letting her just hop out of his life like—

"I'm going to tell Liesl who I really am."

Luke shrugged, "She already knows. She just isn't using it."

"I guess I knew that. I mean that I'm going to have Liesl *report on* who I really am. I'm going to give her the interview she's been begging for by being nice enough to not beg. I won't divulge any secrets or break my officer's oath, but anything short of that is up for grabs."

"Why? Wait…" If Zoe told the media who she was, it wouldn't blow her career—it would fucking nuke it out of existence. Probably get her a dishonorable discharge. Spec Ops served at a whole different level than normal soldiers.

However, if she *did* publicize who she was, Hathyaron would hear about it. He wouldn't be able to help it—Zoe was the talk of race. Luke had descended to pushing Christian to the fore at every opportunity until most people would just assume he was Zoe's co-driver rather than Luke. But Zoe stood front and center.

If Hathyaron heard that Zoe was a Spec Ops soldier, would it spook him? Damn straight. But it would also give him a target—Zoe DeMille.

"You're leaving him only two choices," Luke rolled the idea around, but only found two possible outcomes.

"He drops out of the race at this late date…"

"Telling us exactly who he is," Luke finished her sentence. "Or…"

"He'll come after me," she finished his.

"You're willing to set yourself up as bait? There's an old saying in Maine about how it never seems to work out well for the bait."

"No," she brushed a hand over his crossed arms. Just the lightest of touches, there and gone, but it steadied him more than anything else in a week. "No, I'm setting *us* up to be bait. And I'm banking on you protecting me."

"With my life!" And he absolutely meant it.

CHAPTER 33

"This is Liesl Franks with Reuters, reporting from the heart of the Dakar Rally, the greatest car race of them all, with an exclusive report."

They were all crowded around the laptop. Zoe still wasn't used to watching herself on the screen. She'd never gone back and looked at her own online media vlogs once she was sure they were posed the way she'd wanted. If someone had The Dakar Rally news running and one of her interviews came up, she'd made a point of moving on quickly.

This time she watched intently over Christian's shoulder. Her father stood to one side, with his arm hugging her around the shoulders. Nikita and Drake stood between her and Luke. Liesl was there as well, studying the broadcast as it came out.

"We all know about the most unusual performance in recent Dakar Rally history, the astonishing race being run by Zoe DeMille. In her rookie season—in any rally racing—she is not only the top-ranked Rookie, she's top three in the cars classification."

"Hey, you didn't mention me or my car," Christian piped up.

Everyone shushed him.

"It's my goddamn car," Christian grumbled, but everyone ignored him. Zoe had insisted that he not be mentioned, not in this interview. She wanted to protect Christian as much as possible from what was coming next. No one knew what that was except Luke and Liesl.

"Today I confirmed another startling fact about Ms. DeMille's past, or should I say, her present. And I'm hoping to confirm it with Ms. DeMille herself in this exclusive interview."

Several people in their group glanced her way. Zoe ignored them.

The camera pulled back to reveal a very serious Zoe standing beside her. Her hair, rather than falling in its normal ripples down to her shoulders, was pulled back in such a severe ponytail that she almost didn't have hair at all. No thick-rimmed sunglasses, she'd borrowed Luke's mirrored Ray Ban aviators, which were too big for her face. You could see the camera reflected in them as if she was part cyborg. She'd opted to retain the yellow racing suit, zipped up to choke-her high. She looked dangerous, which was a good trick when she was only five-four, but Liesl had a good man working the camera.

"Thank you for your time, Ms. DeMille. Are you enjoying the race?"

"Oh yes. There are such fantastic competitors, they've just been great. And the challenges that the race committee set out have been beyond demanding. I just love this kind of driving."

"And you're very good at it."

"Thanks!" Merry, happy, everyone's friend Zoe DeMille was about to go away.

"Ms. DeMille, I recently found out that you have a very interesting day job."

"What have you heard?" Zoe had shut it down hard. Listening now, she sounded too severe. For a lack of any better idea, she had tried her best to sound like Luke. Her voice wasn't much lower, but the words were sharper, clipped until they were no more than honed, rapid-fire projectiles.

"Is it true that when you aren't driving at The Dakar, you work for the United States Army?"

Zoe had paused a long moment before snapping out an uncharacteristic monosyllable, "Yes!" At least uncharacteristic for her persona.

It was such a contrast to her earlier interviews—the bright and ever-cheery-no-matter-how-she-actually-felt *The Soldier of Style*—that it should really catch everyone's attention. That had been one of Liesl's suggestions on how to make the interview more memorable.

"And not just your average position either, but rather an officer in military intelligence?" She *was* a chief warrant officer, and she hoped that Command—who were sure to see this—would forgive her Luke's suggested white lie. She wasn't technically in an intelligence branch of the service, but her drone certainly was a tool for tactical intelligence even more than it was a lethal weapon.

"I'm unable to confirm or deny that information," her voice now carefully deadpan.

"I understand that you work for an unnamed agency who is deeply involved in supporting Special Operations Forces."

Nikita and Drake gasped in surprise at the on-air revelation.

Her father and Christian spun to look at her.

She stared at the screen as she'd stared at the camera during an intentionally over-protracted silence—could feel that her lips and her expression were just as tight now as they were on her on-screen persona.

"We're done here!" she'd finally snapped out, then stalked off-camera as if immensely irritated. And she had been irritated. She might as well have admitted to being a foreign spy who was operating in a friendly country without permission. Then, and now watching herself, Zoe could feel viscerally just how much she was risking. Thrown out of the military, her working relationship with Luke and Nikita and all of the others would be cut off. She'd known it would be a risk, but if she caught Hathyaron with the trap, maybe it would be worth it.

By airing the interview just before the start of the stage, it wouldn't give the wheels of injustice enough time to chew her up, but now she felt a cold chill radiating from the Pentagon already. The possibility of losing her career felt painfully real.

"Yes," Liesl continued on screen. "Never a dull moment here at the magnificent Dakar Rally. This has been Liesl Franks reporting for

Reuters from Nazca, Peru. Next up, our coverage of the start of Stage Thirteen, the penultimate stage of this brutal two-week challenge."

Everyone starting asking questions at once.

She glanced over at Luke.

He offered her a single nod—it just might have been respect.

If Hathyaron was out there listening, she'd certainly lit the fuse. Now to see where the explosion hit.

*L*uke was having a very hard time not smiling. It was as if someone had jammed a cattle prod up the entire event's backside. Or maybe an armed explosive that had no visible timer.

The crew in the next pit over, who'd been as friendly as any seasoned racer ever was with a high-performing rookie, had lowered a curtain of silence as certainly as if it was made of steel.

*The Brigade* had all saluted her in unison as she'd rolled by them. Most of them were sloppy civilian attempts, but he saw several that appeared authentic. The other media cameras were positioned to eat it up. Liesl was among them, but she was filming the crowd's responses whereas most of the others were filming Zoe. Luke made sure to keep his head tilted down so that no one got a decent angle on his face past the brim of his helmet.

When even the route timer treated them differently, Luke couldn't stop the laugh.

"Fine for you," Zoe snarled as she accelerated off the start. "You're not the one with the bullseye painted on your racing suit."

"We actually *are* Spec Ops, Zoe, not just some intel group. If Hathyaron comes at us, he's in for a very rude surprise. Besides, I got us a little extra help." He glanced aloft, but it wasn't time yet.

"And what's to stop him from using a sniper rifle or a missile on us?"

"He hasn't survived this long by being stupid. He knows that if he does that, we'll have him as point of origin. Sofia has *Raven* down to thirty thousand feet. Hathyaron probably already knows it's there, but he absolutely can't miss it now. Not with his training."

Zoe grumbled, but seemed to relax into the drive. Which was a good thing, the course designers had created a particularly challenging penultimate stage.

The narrow track behaved as if it had stomach cramps. One moment twisted up, the next it unraveled completely only to snarl up in a new direction. It plunged into a dry arroyo and slalomed along a channel barely wider than the car. Worse, it crossed and re-crossed other classification's tracks. One moment they were racing among cars and motorcycles, then the next they'd merged with the truck course. Then, in the blindest, dustiest areas—where it would be natural to follow one of the big racing trucks through an intersection —their courses would suddenly diverge again, enticing the drivers to choose the wrong route.

The navigation was a nightmare. Motorcycles—who had to read their own Road Book on a small scrolling display at the center of their handlebars—frequently strayed off-course and had to double back to pick up the track. Soon the motos, quads, and cars were hopelessly intermixed.

Then, when the track had been closed in on both sides by thick masses of brush like an English hedgerow, the Road Book had the symbol HP with a slash through it—off-*piste* forbidden. They had to stay on the track now or suffer severe time penalties.

"No HP," he called out.

"Guessing this won't be good," Zoe slammed through the gears. The course was so challenging that she was shifting at twice the rate she'd done on any other stage. There wasn't a moment where being in a particular gear was at all useful in the next moment.

They were in a twisting green tunnel several meters taller than the Citroën and never more than twice as wide.

"S-curve ahead," he called out.

A tight right-hander was immediately followed by a sharper left-hander.

Then the car nosed down hard and a brown cloud billowed out forward of the car.

"*Fesh fesh!*" They cried out in unison. Luke slammed the internal vent closed, but already there was a whirl of brown in the cockpit despite the filters.

*Fesh fesh* was a dirt so fine that it acted like water, splashing out in every direction. It also acted like dust, hanging in the air and creating blinding brownouts. Finally, it acted like actual dirt. Tires sinking down through its watery quality could easily high-center a car on its dirt-like quality.

There was only one answer: power, and lots of it. Of course that only stirred it all the more. *Fesh fesh* clogged air filters, blocked vision, and coated everything like glue. Windshield wipers could help a little, as long as no water was used. Any water instantly turned the fine dirt into an impenetrable mudpack.

To make matters even worse, it was almost impossible to see other vehicles that hadn't made it through the mess and were stuck in the trap. Not colliding with a downed motorcycle or a stuck car was a major road hazard.

In half-second gaps in the brown swirl, they both tried to assess what lay ahead of them.

Then the Citroën's nose would plow into the next dip, Zoe would pound on the accelerator, and another brownout cloud was thrown aloft.

Races had been won and lost in *fesh fesh*. It was only a miracle that no one had ever died in the stuff.

They were still in it deep when the Citroën jerked hard.

"What did we hit?" Zoe cried out.

Nothing that Luke had seen. Instinct had him glancing back to see if they'd run over someone, though they'd already be invisible in the dust cloud. What he saw in the rear window was the massive grill of one of the racing trucks. In fact it was *all* he could see out the rear window, with the truck's logo dead center like a stainless steel branding iron ready to stomp on them.

"Who do we know who drives a MAN SE?"

Zoe swerved around a motorcycle that Luke didn't see until it went by mere inches from his side window. The woman apparently had built-in radar.

"MAN SE? About a third of the field, why?"

"Guy's an asshole. He smacked us."

"You're kidding, right? The trucks are the only ones high enough to see clearly in this crap." She cut sharply right to avoid a mired car and bounced off the green wall of thick growth on Luke's side.

Another slam shook them.

"Well, at least I won't be getting stuck in this. If I do, he'll just shove me back into motion."

"Or run over the top of us."

"You're right," Zoe tried accelerating to the very limits of even semi-safe visibility. Then he clobbered them again.

"I guess we're not going fast enough for him."

"Well I'm getting sick of this. I can't risk a look in the back mirror. Tell me the moment before he's going to hit us again."

Luke twisted in the seat enough to see him. Nothing but brown cloud.

Then the window-filling black radiator emerged from the latest wall of *fesh fesh.*

"Ten meters."

"Five and coming hard."

"Hang on!"

Luke turned, braced himself against the seat, and grabbed the handles.

Along the *fesh fesh* route, officials were stationed in any of the wide spots to try and keep everyone safe.

Zoe steered way wide of the track and was on the verge of ramming one of the official trucks. She twisted them sideways at the last second, almost brushing steel down her entire length as she plunged back into the *fesh fesh,* throwing up the biggest cloud yet.

The MAN SE truck—whose driver must have only been focused on following them—wasn't nearly as maneuverable and it plowed into the official's parked Hilux Toyota pickup before slamming to a halt. Then the brownout closed in behind them. No way to see who it was.

"Do you think—" Zoe left the question open as she managed a jump out of a patch of *fesh fesh*.

"That Hathyaron drives a MAN SE truck? Yeah, I do." Then Luke had to chuckle even though it twisted in his throat.

"What?"

"Picture a MAN logo. What color is it?"

"Silver," Zoe gasped. "Oh, poor Bernie." He'd seen his death coming as the silver MAN logo on Hathyaron's front grill.

Their next landing plunged them back into another patch that exploded outward in billowing clouds.

# CHAPTER 35

It was another hundred kilometers before a MAN SE truck came near them again. They were out of the track country and hopefully clear of any more *fesh fesh* holes. If he never ate *fesh fesh* dust again in his life, it would be too soon.

Behind them, the Peruvian Andes drew a looming wall that extended along the entire eastern horizon. Someday he was going to have to come back to this country when he could move slowly enough to admire it.

They were deep in dune country. These weren't the monster dunes like the last time they'd hit them in Chili, but they weren't in nice linear rows either. Their directions could best be described as confused—like a confused sea that had no directional wave pattern after a hurricane. It was as if they'd been built by contrary and battling winds, duking it out on a colossal scale with fifty- and hundred-meter-high dunes. With no clear direction, it was anyone's guess how best to cross through this topography.

Apparently Zoe's guess was to run perpendicular to the dunes: racing up one face, jumping the crest, then flying down the other side. The MAN SE appeared as if by magic, racing along the valley between the dunes at right angles to their own track.

"Goddamn it," Zoe swore vehemently. "It's Goldfarb out of the Netherlands. I wouldn't have guessed him in a hundred years."

Luke agreed, except he'd met enough men who presented one face, then tried to stab you in the back while wearing another, that he didn't trust anyone. The SEAL operator who'd been fucking Marva in Luke's bed had been one of Luke's most eager and friendly companions in the bars.

"Take the bastard out."

"He's ten tons, we're less than three. Any suggestions?"

"If you can't figure it out, just get me close enough and I'll shoot the bastard."

"With what?"

Luke simply growled at her, even if she was right. All racers were subject to surprise inspections for illegal navigation equipment. They would freak if they found lethal weaponry aboard. Still, his palm itched for something more dangerous than his working knife.

They continued converging at right angles. They were definitely going to get within shouting distance.

"I can't think of anything to do except outdrive him and run away again."

Luke didn't know either, but then he saw the truck more clearly and relaxed.

"What?" Zoe must have noticed the change in him as easily as he noticed every single change in her. Again, encouraging.

"It's not him. His front end isn't all bunged up from ramming us."

Goldfarb waved as he raced past not far in front of them.

Luke only barely resisted giving him the finger in response. He was convinced that someone was indeed after Zoe now, and that was unforgivable even if it was part of the plan. Luke wanted a piece of whoever it was and he wanted it now. At the moment he hated Goldfarb simply because he wasn't Hathyaron.

# CHAPTER 36

The dunes continued to be mayhem. Zoe was passed by motorcycles going the other way, who would then circle and head back and race by her, assuming she knew what she was doing and they were wrong. It was a marginal bet at best.

She did feel sorry for them. The dunes between Nazca and the finish line at Lima were far too close to sea level. This was no high-altitude course. The sun was blazing hot, cooking the sands to sun surface temperatures. Every time they turned so that the sun shone in the windshield, it felt as if their air conditioner had broken. The guys on the bikes must feel like burnt toast.

Zoe really wished she hadn't thought of that analogy. The image of Bernie's face came back to her.

"Where is that bastard?" she finally snarled out. She wanted a piece of him. A big one.

"We'll get him," Luke said with all the stupid calm of his I'm-just-a-patiently-waiting-SEAL-super-warrior thing.

Fat chance, how could they find Hathyaron when she didn't even have a clue where they themselves were? The Road Book had unchar-acteristically provided a compass heading and nothing else on a thirty-kilometer run…too bad they couldn't drive in a straight line across this terrain. Going a kilometer southwest to skirt an uncrossable dune, then two klicks due north to find a pass over the next, when her true heading was supposed to be northwest…

She was just thankful that Luke was navigator. He gave each direction change with such easy confidence that she couldn't decide if he was making it all up or if SEALs had built-in little magnets in their heads—just like fish that used the earth's magnetic field to navigate. Maybe Navy SEALs had to be half-human and half-dolphin to be let in.

Though there'd been nothing fishy about his lovemaking. He'd been magnificent and she'd missed it every night. When he'd shattered her father's world, she'd been so furious. And as she sat by Dad's bedside holding his hand alone through that long, long night, the thing she'd wished the most was that Luke was beside her, holding *her* hand.

Her life was an utter mess.

She wasn't a field operative.

She wasn't a rally driver.

And she was no longer Luke's lover.

Who the hell was Zoe DeMille?

*The Soldier of Style.* That much at least she knew for certain. Except what had Luke said? *You aren't that fluff ball, Tweety Bird Soldier of Style. You're so much more than that.*

Zoe took a moment to glance at Luke while he was staring off into the distance doing his aligning with the Earth's magnetic field thing. He clearly didn't think much of *The Soldier of Style.* She'd spent so many hours over the years perfecting that persona that she didn't know who else Zoe DeMille might be.

Luke saw her as the opposite of how she saw herself: a woman capable of being a field operative, a rally driver whom he'd cheered on at every turn (not once in the two weeks had he pulled the I'm-the-guy-so-I-should-drive card), and…

She didn't know what else was in that *so much more* that he'd called her. Probably because she was no longer on speaking terms with him outside the bounds of the race. Shutting out the best lover—the best man—to ever enter her life because he'd done what, told the truth?

*Not exactly your best move, girl.*

Well, she'd never been one to let sleeping dogs lie. "Luke, I—"

That's when she almost died.

She'd been clawing along a dune's slip face, looking for the right spot to turn upslope, when a vast shadow blocked out the sun. If not for that shadow, she *would* have died.

Instinct had her yanking the wheel to turn downslope and stamping on the accelerator. With an ear-deafening roar, the Citroën leaped ahead. Maybe it was a sand avalanche. Or a—

Just as she pulled clear of the shadow, she glanced upward—and stared into the undercarriage of a massive racing truck. The long drive shafts to the front and rear axles seem to spin in slow motion. Each tread of the huge tires was going to be imprinted upon her mind's eye forever.

Then it thudded down into the sand close behind her like an elephant with dreams of being a pouncing lion. It had just jumped over the dune and nearly landed on top of her.

It was an accident. Just bad luck that had nearly killed her—or rather it was good luck that she'd survived.

Now running downslope, she could see the truck slam into the dune's flank once more after bouncing up from its landing, then come zooming toward her.

A MAN SE.

With a badly mangled front bumper. Maybe he'd hit a rock or maybe...

Zoe veered north.

"Hey, where are you going?"

The truck turned hard on her tail.

"Does the view behind us look familiar?" Zoe could hear the thinness of her voice. She wasn't the sort cut out for near-death experiences.

Luke twisted to look back between the seats. Out of the corner of her eye, she saw his smile and it looked truly evil.

"Who's number 507?"

She glanced back herself. All she could see was the dented metal of the bumper, the bent front grill with its shining silver MAN emblem, and a small white rectangle bearing the truck's Dakar Rally entry number—507.

Zoe sighed. "What is it with you and women?"

"What do you mean? Oh." At least Luke wasn't slow.

"Maybe she's trying to kill you for turning her down. Maybe I'm not the target at all."

"Or maybe she wants you out of the way so that she can have her way with me." Luke was actually teasing her and she couldn't help smiling at him.

Tammy Hall, with her long *naturally* blonde hair (that Zoe hated her a little for) and her killer body (which Zoe hated her *a lot* for), was definitely on the warpath. Not so much with being the sweet lady from Texas.

Zoe made an attempt to cut north, but Tammy sliced up onto the dune's face to block her. Zoe didn't necessarily want to get away, but she didn't want to get sandwiched somewhere either.

"Any bright ideas?"

"Yep!" was Luke's cheery reply. "Just keep us alive for the next five minutes or so."

"That's not helpful." And not terribly likely. Tammy was a masterful driver, currently running Number Two in the truck classification. If Zoe could get up on the dune's slip face, she'd have some advantage because she was more agile. But Tammy knew that and kept closing the door with her truck's tremendous power. Zoe should be able to outrun the truck, but Tammy must have some sort of illegal system hidden in her engine. She was accelerating like she was using nitrous oxide—a totally illegal option. To go along with whatever illegal tracking equipment had let her find them.

"Try," was Luke's only suggestion.

"You know, if you were any kind of a decent SEAL, you'd pull out an MP7 or a howitzer or something right now."

"Didn't think the inspectors would appreciate finding a submachine gun aboard. And howitzers are Army shit. I'm hoping for something a little more subtle."

With nature's vicious sense of perfect timing, Zoe plowed into soft sand. Not *fesh fesh*, but soft enough that Tammy had just gained a major advantage with her big fifty-inch wheels.

Tammy managed to clip the Citroën's rear corner and they spun wildly—almost tumbling had they caught an unseen hummock.

The recovery was whip-snap vicious. Why was there never a race official around when you needed one? That's when she realized they must be well off their original vector. Some routing that Luke understood and she didn't had taken them away from most of the field.

Was it a strategic racing move or did he know that Tammy couldn't resist hunting her down given the opportunity? Had the woman also installed illegal tracking equipment in her truck?

"Are you *trying* to get me killed?"

"Nope," was the extent of Luke's infuriatingly cheery reply.

Zoe shot over the top of a dune. It was a bad choice, leading to a harsh landing, but it bought her a few moments before Tammy's truck lurched over the crest as well. Annoyingly, she didn't roll, flip, or even get stuck for a moment. Instead the resilient suspension had popped the big truck out of the deep sand in a single bound and put Tammy back on Zoe's tail.

"Please tell me you didn't screw her."

"Never even considered it."

"Good!" At least that tiny thing had gone right with her sex life.

She cut south, hoping to get back in view of the media helicopters. Except there weren't any in the air. For twelve days they'd buzzed along the course like a pack of gigantic mosquitos and now when she needed one, they were nowhere to be found.

"Where are all the damn helos?"

"Grounded." Luke seemed sublimely calm. Too calm. What did he know that he wasn't telling her? With the amount the man *didn't* speak, that could be a very long list.

"Grounded? Why?"

"There are several hobby drones flying along the course at the moment."

Zoe knew that the small hobby drones could down a helo—turbine engines spinning at three thousand rpm didn't like it when they ingested the heavy lithium batteries inside hobby drones. So if someone had launched some small drones, all of the usual helos would have been told to clear out for safety until the perpetrator had been found.

As she slewed down a graveled slope at the lowest point between two dunes, with Tammy still hot on her tail, Zoe wondered how Luke could possibly know that. They weren't allowed a radio or any other messaging device except for the emergency satellite phone.

Unless of course he'd arranged for them to be launched beforehand.

But launched by whom? And why?

The answer to the second question was obvious once she thought about it. Sofia, far aloft, would have tracked the truck ever since it had beat on them in the *fesh fesh*. And when they ended up far off the course together, she'd have known the final confrontation was coming and signaled the release of the hobby drones.

Then the answer to the first question flew by close over her head. Even at the speed she was racing, the downdraft of the Black Hawk made the Citroën shudder.

And it wasn't any standard Black Hawk. It had the stealth configuration that only the 5E flew. She recognized the piloting from the hundreds of missions she'd watched over them—Rafe and Julian. Funny, wild, and fantastic pilots.

Suddenly Tammy had other things to worry about.

"If he shoots her, I'm going to get arrested for it," Zoe didn't like that at all. "And if they decide that it was a military operation, I'm going to end up in a National Directorate of Intelligence dungeon and

I'll never be seen again. I don't want to end up in a Peruvian jail, but I *really* don't want to end up in a dungeon."

"He's not that foolish."

Then what?

"Get some distance on her."

Easier said than done. Zoe decided to slow down, slow until Tammy was so close that all her rearview mirror showed was bent radiator grill.

Then she shoved in the clutch and dropped down a gear. Tammy's blow, while the Citroën was in neutral, shoved the car ahead whiplash hard.

Zoe responded by popping the clutch and hammering down on the gas. It wasn't much, but it was a gap.

And into that gap, Julian dropped a pair of gas cylinders. Knock-out gas.

It was brilliant. They were far off course from the other racers, there were no other helos in the air because of the drones that they'd launched from the Black Hawk, and they'd just sleepy bombed Tammy and her crew.

Except it didn't work at all.

Tammy blew through the cloud and kept right on coming. She must have guessed what was happening at the last moment and closed the outside air intake just as she would if driving through *fesh fesh*.

Luke grunted unhappily.

The valley between the dunes was narrowing rapidly.

In a desperate move, Julian eased down until his skids were beside the top of Tammy's truck. Zoe watched in the rearview as he tried to flip her onto her side, but she was too canny for that. Instead, she counter-steered sharply into the helo's skids at the last moment, catching him by surprise.

For five seconds, ten tons of elite military helicopter and ten tons of Dakar racing truck shoved against each other. But Julian's traction was only air and Tammy' had four big tires on the ground. With a sudden twist of the wheel, she almost flipped Julian onto his side. How he managed to recover without plunging a rotor blade into the side of a dune and crashing was one of the most impressive pieces of flying she'd ever seen.

As he moved up and back to recover and think of something new, Zoe focused ahead.

The dune to her left was the obvious escape route. The face was climbable to a low pass. She might even be able to outpace Tammy, at least to the crest.

To her right...

# CHAPTER 37

*Z*oe recognized the dune's shape and prayed she could pull off the maneuver a second time. This dune was a monster, a Mother of All Dunes that rose for hundreds of meters above them.

No time to ask Luke. No time to pray. No time to even think.

Zoe kept her foot down to the floor and cranked the wheel to the right. Five hundred horsepower responded with all the heart she'd come to expect from the Citroën.

Tammy was hot on her trail. Any respectable, legally configured truck would have petered out around the halfway mark. Tammy just kept climbing, so close to Zoe's tail that she could feel the blonde breathing down her neck.

The race to the top was going to be close. A sand slip threatened her advantage. Then some hard-pack gave it back.

Back at the Huckfest, by flying with all those overeager boys and men, she'd seen dozens of attack methods for an up-dune climb.

Some thought it was all about raw power.

Well, neither she nor Tammy had a real power advantage.

More advanced jumpers thought about the angle of their attack on the dune's slope, sometimes angling slightly to the left or right to use the edge of their tires like the edge of a water-skier's skis. They carved their way to more traction as they climbed.

The very best, who consistently achieved the best jumps after the long run-up ramp, made constant little adjustments. They trusted to their instinct and the instant-to-instant feel of the sand communicated through the steering wheel.

By each moment a patch of sand was giving way, she was already turning the other direction.

The tiniest flattening of slope was met with eased acceleration, which let her spin less and gain another shred of speed with improved traction.

Steeper? Hit it with raw power.

"Holy shit!" Luke muttered softly and she could see him brace himself against the handles. He didn't call her off. He didn't tell her she couldn't do it.

Luke understood what was about to happen. And he trusted her to do it.

This had better work. There were a lot of things she still wanted to say to the man beside her. Because whoever the hell Zoe DeMille was, she knew one thing about herself. She was totally in love with Luke Altman.

It wasn't just because he trusted her.

He knew her better than anyone—far better than she knew herself.

And still he believed in her. She didn't know how that was possible, but she wanted more of that like she wanted air to breathe.

Tammy was too far back. The truck was hitting its limits.

Zoe needed her to be too close to hesitate when they reached the dune crest.

She didn't ease off on the gas, instead she let a small sideslip bleed off a tiny bit of the Citroën's speed.

The gap closed.

The crest came nearer.

Five car lengths away.

"Luke, grab the handbrake. Pull when I tell you."

He reached out one of those big wonderful hands and wrapped it around the tall handle.

Two car lengths.

Tammy was positioned perfectly.

Zoe hit the crest but didn't let the car fly. Instead, she threw it into a sideways drift.

"Now!" She screamed it out as she fought the wheel while dropping a gear.

For just an instant, she was staring out her door's window straight into the truck's enormous bumper. Roll cage or not, the truck was going to shred her.

She looked up into Tammy's eyes.

Tammy had the big steering wheel clenched in her hands and was leaning forward to look down at her. Zoe offered her own best feral smile in response, then popped the clutch and jammed down on the gas.

Without needing to be told, Luke released the handbrake.

The Citroën hesitated for a long moment, spewing a twin rooster tail of sand out the back. Then it caught and jolted forward.

The MAN SE clipped the rear of the Citroën, knocking both rear wheels across the crest.

Zoe managed to keep one front tire hooked over the edge of the crest exactly as she had the first time. The instant she was clear, she stopped and both she and Luke turned to watch.

The MAN SE didn't pause at the crest. Even over the Citroën's engine, Zoe could hear the roar of the truck's engine. It never decelerated.

Just like that dune in Stage Two, the back was a carved bowl that was impossibly steep. The sand, in some form of hyper-stability, was close to vertical.

The truck leapt out into that void.

It was a humongous jump. This was the Mother of All Dunes. The truck continued its long arcing flight with its nose to the sky. The front wheels twisted one way. Impossible to fix now. The truck seemed to hang forever as it fell.

The record jump at Huckfest had been after she left for the Army. Mike "Hollywood" Higgins had jumped 169 feet with a hang time of well over a second. He'd done it in a highly-modified pickup truck engineered to be as light as possible.

Tammy blew that away in a lipstick-red ten-ton racing truck.

For six full seconds, Truck #507 fell fifty stories out of the sky.

It didn't crash on impact, it disintegrated.

The impact also destabilized the slip face. The dune avalanched over the wreckage. A thousand, a *million* tons of sand spilling over the shredded scrap metal.

"Zoe!" Luke screamed.

She saw what had alarmed him and didn't waste time responding. Zoe herself skipped right over alarmed and went straight to terrified.

She could feel the rear end of their car sagging downward.

Despite gunning the Citroën, she couldn't crawl back to the other side of the dune. Everything she and the car had weren't enough to escape the crumbling of the Mother Dune's crest from under her wheels.

But she was on top of the dune's collapse, not under it.

Giving in to the slip, she aimed downslope and fought for high ground. She really wished she'd surfed as a kid because some practice would really help right about now. Every moment of the gigantic sand slide, the surface shifted. To hesitate was to be buried forever—or at least until the winds rolled the dunes aside, which could be centuries.

Dodging from spot to spot on the back of the ongoing slip, she was sometimes on top and sometimes wheel-deep.

The slip couldn't have lasted more than another twenty seconds, but all she knew was that it was the longest drive of her life.

She came to in darkness, gripping the wheel with both hands. The silence broken only by her own desperate breath and the creaking of the car's metal.

The engine was dead.

And so were they. Buried under a million tons of sand. She'd almost rather have died like Tammy, in one great pyrrhic leap—the victory of the beautiful jump somehow worth the horrific cost. To die of suffocation beneath the sands of Peru didn't have quite the same panache to it.

"Now that," Luke spoke softly from beside her, "was *most* excellent."

Zoe turned to look at him by the faint glow of the dashboard lights.

"Are you nuts?"

"No, I'm absolutely serious. If we get out of this alive, I'm so adding a sand course to SEAL driver training. And what you just did? I hope that Julian or Sofia got video of it just to show what's really possible."

"You *are* nuts. I've killed both of us." She hadn't saved anything.

"Ain't dead yet."

He had a point, but she wouldn't be placing any bets. "Let's see. There's no way to open the doors. The moment we smash one of the windows, it would end us. The sand would pour in and bury us before we could climb out. This is sand, not even *fesh fesh*."

"Too bad this isn't Dune, the desert planet," Luke sounded…cheerful. When had he started doing that?

"You're being unusually happy, Luke. What's up with that? We might as well have been eaten by a sandworm."

"I'm always happy at the successful end of a mission."

"You've got a weird definition of success."

He cocked an ear to one side, "Maybe. Maybe not."

She listened too. Somewhere outside the car was a low muffled thud like a heavy heartbeat. No, like a Black Hawk helicopter.

Less than thirty seconds later, a clear *clank* sounded along the car's frame from the rear. And moments later they were hauled from the sand, dangling butt first from a Black Hawk helicopter's lifting cable.

In the whole world-ending sand avalanche, she'd managed to keep them near the surface.

The sunlight was a shock as thorough as being born anew. Like… huh! Like someone finally opening the garage doors wide enough to purge all the shadows. She liked the sound of that, the feel of that, a lot.

Luke just grinned at her as they dangled from their harnesses while the Black Hawk lowered them to the flat area at the bottom of the dune.

"You were right."

"I was?" Luke pretended to sound shocked.

"Most excellent."

And their shared laugh—only a little bit laced with hysteria— might well be the best sound she'd ever heard.

---

"GOT THE WHOLE THING ON VIDEO," Rafe bubbled as the four of them met on the sand.

Luke high-fived him.

"Seriously, girl," Julian agreed. "That's some wicked-cool moves you got there." He mimicked driving a car half like a racer and half like a bronc rider.

"You landed ass up, so we were able to snap on a cargo hook."

"Told you that you had a cute ass," Luke whispered in Zoe's ear and enjoyed seeing the bright blush.

"Whoa!" Rafe remarked. "When did that happen?"

"What happen?" Zoe asked but blushed harder.

Julian waved his index finger between them, "Seriously? Okay, totally getting the cutest couple of the year award."

"Better shut up, you two," Luke grinned at them. "Or next time Zoe may guide you straight into the side of a mountain from her RPA."

"Oh, I'd never do that," she said sweetly. "I'd send them right over an enemy's gun emplacement instead. Then no one could say it was my fault."

Rafe and Julian groaned.

The crew chiefs who'd been working in the back of the Black Hawk stepped out onto the sand with small remote control boxes. In moments, they were landing hobby drones on the sand and packing them into padded cases.

"Time's short," Julian checked his watch, then clicked on his radio. "Sofia? Did we get them?"

"Roger that. Drake and Nikita have the other four members of Truck #507's team in captivity. We told the officials they were needed for questioning over an illegal customs issue. They've handed them over to the CIA, who'll have them airborne back to the States within the next twenty minutes. And the team's leader has a Pakistani passport, as well as several others. We think he's American, but we don't know. All of the others have Pakistani stamps in their various passports, including the truck's three crew members."

"Thankfully not our problem. Thanks and out," he clicked off the radio.

"That's your cue," Rafe tossed him the satellite phone from the unearthed Citroën. "We're out of here."

Luke wrapped his arms around Zoe and turned his back to the sand kicked up by the helicopter's down-blast. In moments, it had slipped away along the valley and even the echoes were dying. Silence.

To hold Zoe for even that second was such a joy. But it was also a liberty he should never have assumed so he let her go before she could complain.

He turned his back on her so that she couldn't see how badly he wanted her and how badly he wished he could undo what he'd done.

Luke punched the speed dial on the phone. When the safety officer answered, Luke spoke.

"I'd like to report an accident."

And he hoped like he'd never hoped for anything in his life that Zoe would forgive him for the accident he'd made with her father.

# CHAPTER 39

He almost didn't recognize her; wouldn't have except that he'd memorized everything about Zoe DeMille during those long days they were apart. She couldn't hide her walk as she strolled past the massed members of *The Soldier of Style Brigade* without any of them noticing, but everything else was so changed it was hard to believe.

She'd erased the buoyant Tweety Bird—completely.

It also didn't hurt that the party at the Lima, Peru, finish line had been in full swing for hours and sobriety had gone south long before the final riders made it to the Dakar Rally's finish line. Christian was thrilled to take the accolades for the highest finish his car had ever achieved. They'd held on for fifth despite their long sidetrack and delay waiting for the race officials to arrive once they'd overcome their fear of the tiny hobbyist drones and dared fly their helos again.

It was doubtful that anyone would pay for the operation to unearth Truck #507 or the remains of its three-person crew—it would cost a fortune.

After the race, Zoe had simply disappeared.

Now she was back, but she was no longer *The Soldier of Style*.

Her blonde hair with the black part was now all the same jet black as her father's. It made her deeply blue eyes shine forth. She'd shed her yellow sunglasses as well, a pair of mirrored shades just like his were pushed up into her hair holding back the straight glorious fall. In fact, there wasn't a single thing about her that was yellow. Blue jeans, red tennies with pink shoelaces, a matching red Dakar t-shirt, and a lightweight black leather jacket that made her look terribly sleek and urban in the dusk of the cool Peruvian evening.

She walked up to him without comment and, more importantly, without any of the media noticing. She looked so different, like…she was finally herself.

Liesl, who'd been standing right next to him, was most of the way through introducing herself before she startled and reached for her camera. Then she hesitated for half a moment before lowering it again and offered a radiant smile.

"I want the last-ever interview with *The Soldier of Style*."

"Too late, she's already gone," Zoe declared her line in the sand. "But she just might have taped a few final thoughts on video for you to post as part of your wrap-up story." Zoe handed her a thumb drive. "When you're done, the crosslink will be her site's last-ever post."

Liesl bounced it on her palm a few times before pocketing it and turning to Drake and Nikita, "Let's go get drunk somewhere. You've never really been to Lima until you've gotten hammered—that is the right word, *ja?*—on Pisco Sours."

Drake had been talking to Ahmed and apparently missed Zoe's near-miraculous transformation. Christian was off with the other Legends. Nikita didn't even blink, pausing just long enough to give Zoe a hug as if nothing had changed.

"Where's your father?"

"I sent him home. The race is over and he was really terribly homesick. I don't know if he's ever left southern California before."

"Just remember, he came for you and he stayed for you." Nikita hugged her again and moved off with the others.

Now they were alone in the middle of a crowd that was surging up and down the main plaza.

Zoe simply stood and waited him out.

"I'm…so sorry," Luke finally dredged up the only apology he could think of for what he'd done to her father.

She reached out and tentatively touched a hand on his crossed arms. When she left it there, hardly trusting himself, he unfolded one of his arms so that he could rest his hand over hers. She didn't pull away.

"I believe you, Luke. And I'm sure that if I'd told you the truth about my father and his best friend, you'd never have betrayed that trust."

Too late to argue that one way or the other. He'd already done the damage so he kept his mouth shut.

"Maybe if you spoke more, asked me a question once in a while instead of swallowing it down so hard that it was choking you, I'd have told you the truth and we'd have avoided the whole mess. Though maybe not. It was locked away awfully deep."

He started to nod, then decided to speak instead, "Yeah, maybe."

"Wow! Three whole syllables, Luke. That was masterful."

Rather than speaking, he offered her a triumphant smile. And why not? He was feeling pretty damn triumphant. They'd survived The Dakar for a fifth place finish. And they'd taken out Hathyaron—who turned out to be a father/team manager and his daughter, Tammy the driver.

"Oh, that's why it's Hathyaron, the plural, not Hathyar," he finally got it.

"Weapons, not weapon," Zoe blinked in surprise. "We never thought to look for a family team—Dad-and-daughter Gunrunners Incorporated."

They shared a smile.

And there was Zoe, the real Zoe—shining in the look she'd been born with—right here with him.

"One last thing I have to tell you. You can never talk about this except with me or Nikita. You can never let *anyone* else know."

"The one question I've never asked," Luke knew it couldn't be anything else.

"...My mother," Zoe just said it flat, though he could see her eyes closing down and her struggle to not do that.

Her *mother? She* was the one other person who knew about the horrors of Zoe's past? Luke didn't know what to do with that. He'd never have guessed that in a hundred years. He reached for her, but Zoe raised a hand to stop him. She left it on the center of his chest, anchoring him in place—at a safe distance. No, so she could watch his face.

"I went to her first. I could see the shock, the horror, then she sort of shook herself, like a duck shaking off water."

"She didn't *believe you?*" Luke wasn't going to *not speak* to her, he was going to strangle her until she felt even half the pain her daughter had.

"I think that she *couldn't.* She knew what it would do to my father. If you think he's a gentle dreamer now, you should have met him twenty years ago. It absolutely would have destroyed him, as it almost destroyed him this time. If Mom is smart, she'll never admit a thing to him when he tells her about it. Because without her, I know my father would never survive."

Luke could only sigh. She was probably right. He'd ended up liking Brian DeMille, but her father was not a strong man used to facing life's harsh realities.

"Mom and I were never close, I was always a daddy's girl. Let's just say we've been even less close since then."

Without thinking, Luke finally pulled her against his chest this time and held on. Soon he could feel the hot tears through his t-shirt. She wasn't sobbing or shaking, she was crying as gently as her father had because she was absolutely Brian DeMille's daughter.

"*I'm sure you misinterpreted what happened. Bob would never do such a thing,*" Zoe managed in a dead voice that sounded nothing like her. "That's what she said to me. Told me to not exaggerate things all the time. I'd been a fanciful girl up until that point—perhaps *too* much like my father. But I didn't misinterpret a thing. I was only eleven when it started and I barely understood what was happening to me. He was...

Uncle Bob. Somehow convincing me that it was my fault he couldn't keep his hands off me. It went on until I was fourteen—the pain and the fear had become my new normal. Then one day I sort of woke up in mid-attack and went after him with a shop knife. After that I always wore a blade and I made sure he knew it. Don't mess with me in a knife fight, Luke. I've taken a lot of classes. From Spec Ops instructors too."

"You took control of your own life." Luke also made a mental note to heed her advice on the knife.

"I guess," she sniffled against his chest. "I abused myself, went full-on slut for…far too long. *The Soldier of Style* was my way out of that, though I didn't really understand that until very recently. I just knew that if I kept reinventing myself, I never had to look at my real self."

Luke knew she was strong. He'd learned that one the hard way. But did she know, really know that about herself as she was now?

He stepped her back enough to look at her. He combed his fingers through her lovely pure black hair, then brushed at the tears still trickling from those brilliant blue eyes.

"You are so goddamn beautiful, Zoe. You, not the mask you raised," he stroked her cheek. "And I'm not talking about your lovely face. Please tell me I get to keep looking at you for the rest of our lives."

She nodded once, like a puppet jerked on a string. Then, as his words sank in, she threw her arms around his waist and pulled herself tightly against him once more. This time the hot tears didn't worry him, he'd seen the bright flash of joy in her eyes.

The words that should have been a shock—*What idiot believes in long-term commitments?*—felt perfectly natural now that he'd said them.

The most classic Maine joke—*Cain't get thea from heal!*—oddly didn't apply at all. You could get there from here, as long as there included Zoe DeMille.

"Had an idea," he mumbled against her hair.

He could feel her hold her breath.

"Next year. The Dakar."

And her happy sobs turned into delighted giggles. Damn but he loved this woman.

"Though," Luke dragged it out enough to make her pause. "Unless you want to be mobbed by *The Soldier of Style Brigade* again, you might want to consider changing your name. At least your last one."

"I do that and you *will* be stuck with me for life."

"Works for me."

"Zoe Altman," she whispered as she snuggled more tightly into his arms. "I like the sound of that. We'll make one hell of a car team."

"Malles Motos."

She kept her arms tight about him, but leaned back enough to look up at him with those sparkling blues of hers. "But I don't ride motorcycles."

"They're the best. I'll teach you."

"Okay," she smiled at him so sweetly, he could feel himself melting. "Or maybe, if you're a good boy, I'll teach you how to really drive a rally car. Then, instead of competing against each other, we can race together. I bet I can talk Christian into being a team manager and financing us."

Luke had to admit that he liked that image, "Your dad as our mechanic."

Her little gasp of delight told him it was the perfect thing to say.

Zoe pulled him down into a kiss and he could feel her smile. He knew he'd just lost that coin toss—rally car it was—but he was still buying her a motorcycle as soon as they hit US soil.

"I guess we're gonna do it. I know by now that there's nothing you can't do once you set your heart on it."

"I like that, Luke," she whispered against his lips. "I've got my heart set on you—a lifetime's worth. And you're actually pretty good with words. Don't stop, okay?"

In answer he simply held her. He'd been right the very first time he'd met her: there was no other woman like Zoe DeMille. Which was good, because one of her was about all he could handle.

# CHRISTMAS AT STEEL BEACH
# (EXCERPT)

## THE NIGHT STALKERS AND THE NAVY #1

*U*.S. Navy Chief Steward Gail Miller held on for dear life as the small boat raced across the warm seas off West Africa.

The six Marines driving the high-speed small unit riverine boat appeared to think that scaring the daylights out of her was a good sport. It was like a Zodiac rubber dinghy's big brother. It was a dozen meters long with large machine guns mounted fore and aft. The massive twin diesels sent it jumping off every wave, even though the rollers in the Gulf of Guinea were less than a meter high today.

Gail wondered if they were making the ride extra rough just for her or were they always like this; she suspected the latter. Still she wanted to shout at them like Bones from *Star Trek*: *I'm a chef, not a soldier, dammit.* But being a good girl from South Carolina, she instead kept her mouth shut and stared at her fast-approaching new billet.

The USS *Peleliu* was an LHA, a Landing Helicopter Assault ship. She could deliver an entire Marine Expeditionary Unit with her helicopters and amphibious craft. Twenty-five hundred Navy and Marines personnel aboard and it would be her job to feed them. All the nerves she'd been feeling for the last five days about her new posting had finally subsided, buried beneath the tidal wave of wondering if she was going to survive to even reach the *Peleliu.*

At first, the ship started out as black blot on the ocean, silhouetted by the setting sun that was turning the sky from a golden orange over to more of a dark rose color.

Then the ship got bigger.

And bigger.

In a dozen years in the Navy she'd been aboard an aircraft carrier only once, and it lay twenty minutes behind her. She'd been there less than a half hour from when the E-2 Hawkeye had trapped on the deck. They'd shipped her to the *Peleliu* so fast she wanted to check herself and see if she was radioactive.

It didn't matter though; she was almost there. From down in the little riverine speed boat, her new ship looked huge. The second largest ships in the whole Navy, after the aircraft carriers, were the helicopter carriers.

Gail knew that the *Peleliu* was the last of her class, all of her sister ships already replaced by newer and better vessels, but even six months or a year aboard before her decommissioning would be a fantastic opportunity for a Chief Steward. Maybe that's why they'd assigned Gail to this ship, someone to fill in before the decommissioning.

Fine with her.

She was still unsure how she'd actually landed the assignment. She'd spent a half-dozen years working on the Perry Class frigates as a CS, a culinary specialist. Her first Chief Steward billet had been at SUBASE Bangor in Washington state feeding submariners while ashore until she thought she'd go mad. She missed the ship's galleys and the life aboard.

Then she'd applied for a transfer, never in her life expecting to land Chief Steward on an LHA. After the aircraft carriers, they were the premier of Navy messes. Chefs vied for years to get these slots and she'd somehow walked into this one.

*No, girl! You've cooked Navy food like a demon for over a decade to earn this posting.* Her brain's strong insistence that she'd earned this did little to convince her.

And she hadn't walked into this, she'd flown. It had taken three days: Seattle, New York, London, Madrid, and Dakar, each with at least six hours on the ground, but never enough to get a room and sleep. And then an eyeblink on the aircraft carrier.

It didn't matter. It was hers now for whatever reason and she couldn't wait.

The LHA really did look like an aircraft carrier. She knew it was shorter and narrower, but from down here on the waves, it loomed and towered. *One heck of an impressive place to land, girl.* She could feel the "new posting" nerves fighting back against the "near death" nerves of her method of transit over the waves.

The flattop upper deck didn't overhang as much as an aircraft carrier, but that was the only obvious difference. Like a carrier, the Flight Deck was ruled over by a multi-story communications tower superstructure and its gaggle of antennas above.

On the deck she could see at least a half-dozen helicopters and people working on them, probably putting them away for the end of the day. It seemed odd to Gail that they were operating so far from the carrier group. It had taken an hour even at the riverine's high speed to reach the *Peleliu* and she appeared to be out here alone; not another ship in sight.

In the fading sunset, the ship's lights were showing more and more as long rows of bright pinpricks. The flattop was at least five stories above the water.

The riverine boat circled past the bow and rocketed toward the stern. Gail had departed the aircraft carrier down a ladder on the outside of the hull amidships. But here they approached the stern.

That was the big difference with the LHAs; they had a massive Well Deck right inside the rear of the ship. She'd seen pictures, but when her orders came, they'd been for "Immediate departure." No time to read up on the *Peleliu.* So, she'd learn on the job.

A massive stern ramp was being lowered down even as they circled the boat. It was as if the entire cliff-like stern of the boat was opening like a giant mailbox, the door hinging down to make a steel beach in the water.

Also like a mailbox, it revealed a massive cavern inside. Fifteen meters wide, nearly as tall, and a football field deep; it penetrated into the ship at sea level. Landing craft could be driven right inside the ship's belly, loaded with vehicles from the internal garages or Marines from the barracks, and then floated back out.

The last of the fast equatorial sunset was fading from the sky as the riverine whipped around the stern at full-speed in a turn she was half sure would toss her overboard into the darkness, and roared up to the steel beach.

Inside the cavern of the Well Deck, dim red lights suggested shapes and activities she couldn't quite make out.

THE SUNSET WAS STILL FLOODING the Well Deck through the gap above the *Peleliu's* unopened stern ramp as U.S. Navy Chief Petty Officer Sly Stowell did his best to look calm. After nineteen years in, it was his job to radiate steadiness to his customers, the troops he was transporting. That wasn't a problem.

He was also supposed to actually *be* calm during mission preparations, but it never seemed to work that way. A thousand hours of drill still never prepared him for the adrenaline rush of a live op and tonight he'd been given the "go for operation." This section of the attack—presently loading up on his LCAC hovercraft deep inside the belly of the USS *Peleliu*—was all his.

"Get a Navy move-on, boys," he shouted to the Ranger platoon loading up, "'nuff of this lazy-ass Army lollygag."

A couple of the newbies flinched, but all the old hands just grinned at him and kept pluggin' along. They all wore camo gear and armored vests. Their packs were only large for this mission, not massive. It was supposed to be an in and out, but it was always better to be prepared.

Two of the old hands wore Santa hats, had their Kevlar brain buckets with the clipped on night-vision gear dangling off their rifles. It was December first and he liked the spirit of it, celebrating the season, though he managed not to smile at them. It was the sworn duty of every soldier to look down on every other, especially for the Navy to look down on everyone else. It was only what the ground pounders and sky jockeys deserved, after all.

---

*B*UY *now to keep reading at: www.buchmanbookworks.com*

# ABOUT THE AUTHOR

USA Today and Amazon #1 Bestseller M. L. "Matt" Buchman started writing on a flight south from Japan to ride his bicycle across the Australian Outback. Just part of a solo around-the-world trip that ultimately launched his writing career.

From the very beginning, his powerful female heroines insisted on putting character first, *then* a great adventure. He's since written over 60 action-adventure thrillers and military romantic suspense novels. And just for the fun of it: 100 short stories, and a fast-growing pile of read-by-author audiobooks.

Booklist says: "3X Top 10 of the Year." PW says: "Tom Clancy fans open to a strong female lead will clamor for more." His fans say: "I want more now...of everything." That his characters are even more insistent than his fans is a hoot.

As a 30-year project manager with a geophysics degree who has designed and built houses, flown and jumped out of planes, and solo-sailed a 50' ketch, he is awed by what is possible. More at: www. mlbuchman.com.

# Other works by M. L. Buchman: *(* - also in audio)*

## Thrillers

### Dead Chef
*One Chef!*
*Two Chef!*

### Miranda Chase
*Drone**
*Thunderbolt**
*Condor**
*Ghostrider**

## Romantic Suspense

### Delta Force
*Target Engaged**
*Heart Strike**
*Wild Justice**
*Midnight Trust**

### Firehawks
**MAIN FLIGHT**
*Pure Heat*
*Full Blaze*
*Hot Point**
*Flash of Fire**
*Wild Fire*

**SMOKEJUMPERS**
*Wildfire at Dawn**
*Wildfire at Larch Creek**
*Wildfire on the Skagit**

### The Night Stalkers
**MAIN FLIGHT**
*The Night Is Mine*
*I Own the Dawn*
*Wait Until Dark*
*Take Over at Midnight*
*Light Up the Night*
*Bring On the Dusk*
*By Break of Day*

**AND THE NAVY**
*Christmas at Steel Beach*
*Christmas at Peleliu Cove*
**WHITE HOUSE HOLIDAY**
*Daniel's Christmas**
*Frank's Independence Day**
*Peter's Christmas**
*Zachary's Christmas**
*Roy's Independence Day**
*Damien's Christmas**
5E
*Target of the Heart*
*Target Lock on Love*
*Target of Mine*
*Target of One's Own*

### Shadow Force: Psi
*At the Slightest Sound**
*At the Quietest Word**

### White House Protection Force
*Off the Leash**
*On Your Mark**
*In the Weeds**

## Contemporary Romance

### Eagle Cove
*Return to Eagle Cove*
*Recipe for Eagle Cove*
*Longing for Eagle Cove*
*Keepsake for Eagle Cove*

### Henderson's Ranch
*Nathan's Big Sky**
*Big Sky, Loyal Heart**
*Big Sky Dog Whisperer**

### Love Abroad
*Heart of the Cotswolds: England*
*Path of Love: Cinque Terre, Italy*

# Other works by M. L. Buchman:

## Contemporary Romance (cont)

**Where Dreams**
*Where Dreams are Born*
*Where Dreams Reside*
*Where Dreams Are of Christmas*
*Where Dreams Unfold*
*Where Dreams Are Written*

## Science Fiction / Fantasy

**Deities Anonymous**
*Cookbook from Hell: Reheated*
*Saviors 101*

**Single Titles**
*The Nara Reaction*
*Monk's Maze*
*the Me and Elsie Chronicles*

## Non-Fiction

**Strategies for Success**
*Managing Your Inner Artist/Writer*
*Estate Planning for Authors*
*Character Voice*


# Short Story Series by M. L. Buchman:

## Romantic Suspense

**Delta Force**
*Delta Force*

**Firehawks**
*The Firehawks Lookouts*
*The Firehawks Hotshots*
*The Firebirds*

**The Night Stalkers**
*The Night Stalkers*
*The Night Stalkers 5E*
*The Night Stalkers CSAR*
*The Night Stalkers Wedding Stories*

**US Coast Guard**
*US Coast Guard*

**White House Protection Force**
*White House Protection Force*

## Contemporary Romance

**Eagle Cove**
*Eagle Cove*

**Henderson's Ranch**
*Henderson's Ranch*

**Where Dreams**
*Where Dreams*

## Thrillers

**Dead Chef**
*Dead Chef*

## Science Fiction / Fantasy

**Deities Anonymous**
*Deities Anonymous*

**Other**
*The Future Night Stalkers*
*Single Titles*

SIGN UP FOR M. L. BUCHMAN'S
NEWSLETTER TODAY


*and receive:*
*Release News*
*Free Short Stories*
*an awesome collection*

*Do it today. Do it now.*
*www.mlbuchman.com/newsletter*